Collected Stories

FRANK O'CONNOR

Collected Stories

Introduction by Richard Ellmann

Vintage Books
A Division of Random House
New York

First Vintage Books Edition September 1982

Copyright 1931, 1936, 1937, 1944, 1945, 1946, 1947, 1948, 1949, 1950, 1951, 1952, 1953, 1954 © 1955, 1956, 1957, 1958, 1959, 1960, 1961, 1966 by Frank O'Connor

Copyright 1945, ©1955, 1957, 1958, 1966, 1967, 1969, 1981 by Harriet O'Donovan Sheehy, Executrix of the Estate of Frank O'Connor

Introduction Copyright © 1981 by Richard Ellmann

Most of the stories in this collection have been previously published in *The Common Chord*, *Apple Jelly*, *Domestic Relations*, *Guests of the Nation*, *More Stories*, *A Set of Variations*, *The Stories of Frank O'Connor*, and *Traveller's Samples* by Frank O'Connor.

The following stories were originally published in *The New Yorker:* "Achilles' Heel," "An Act of Charity," "The American Wife," "The Babes in the Woods," "The Cheapjack," "Christmas Morning," "The Corkerys," "Darcy in the Land of Youth," "The Drunkard," "Expectation of Life," "Fish for Friday," "A Great Man," "The Long Road to Ummera," "The Man of the House," "Masculine Protest," "The Mass Island," "News for the Church," "An Out-and-Out Free Gift," "The Pretender," "Requiem," "A Sense of Responsibility," "A Set of Variations on a Borrowed Theme," "The Study of History," "The Teacher's Mass," "Unapproved Route," and "The Weeping Children."

Library of Congress Cataloging in Publication Data
O'Connor, Frank, 1903-1966.
Collected stories.
Originally published: New York: Knopf, 1981.
I. Title.
PR6029.D58A15 1982 823'.912 82-40039
ISBN 0-394-71048-7 AACR2

Contents

Contents

Introduction
by Richard Ellmann

THESE wonderful stories of Frank O'Connor refresh and delight long after they are first read. They pass into our experience like incidents we have ourselves known or almost known. Generous in spirit, acute in perception, they sum up a provincial culture in terms that are less provincial, but never cosmopolitan. Detachment from his own country was not one of Frank O'Connor's aims. Nobody was more aware than he of the mules, crows, and foxes, who with dogs, horses, gazelles, and doves populated in human form his island home, and nobody was more unwilling to give up the local fauna. His stories preserve in ink like amber his perceptive, amused, and sometimes tender observations of the fabric of Irish customs, pieties, superstitions, loves, and hates. He wrote at the moment when that fabric was being slowly torn by modern conditions. "Crab apple jelly" was his own description of the sweet and tart mixture thus compounded. His best stories stir those facial muscles which, we are told, are the same for both laughing and weeping.

Frank O'Connor himself was a man of great affections that were just below the surface of expression, ready to emerge in the form of actions or literary insights. Not that the stories were spontaneous bursts. Except for a few such as "My Oedipus Complex" and "The Bridal Night," which almost wrote themselves, he sifted, shaped, revised, revised again. A story might be given fifty forms before he was satisfied with it, and then be given still another before it was republished.* The question of form was always dominant, because what he called the "glowing center of action" depended upon dense, accurate, and yet poetic presentment. It must not, he insisted, be described naturalistically

* O'Connor sometimes changed the title of a reworked story. Since, in this volume, the version used is the last one, some titles may be unfamiliar to certain readers. The stories themselves appear in the order in which they were first published in book form.

"as if it were a leg of mutton." Avant-garde methods of narration did not interest him either. He saw that his own talent required, like Yeats's poetry, the sense of an actual man, talking. That man, under whatever cover, was his own spirited, flashing self, bountiful and painstaking. However peculiar the things the characters did, they must appear incontestably real. The kernel of a story might be heard in a pub or on the street, but gathering or inventing the necessary detail, infusing the whole with a theme so powerful and simple that it could be written on a post card, and commanding the reader's assent as all that was fluid became solid, required stamina as well as enthusiasm. It was a stern regimen, Flaubert among the bogs.

Few writers from humble circumstances have begun quite so humbly as Frank O'Connor did. He was born in Cork, a city that prided itself on being unlike Dublin. Yeats would one day praise him for his sharp Corkman's eye. O'Connor himself would speak afterwards with affection of the city's "warm dim odorous feckless evasive southern quality," but in his youth he was more conscious of what he called in an early letter its "barbarous mediocrity." Neither view was possible for him in childhood, when hunger and squalor were what he could see of the city. His real name, Michael O'Donovan, he shared with his father, a soldier who had played the big drum in the band and, after discharge from the British army, worked sometimes as a navvy. Tall and handsome, the father looked to his bookish son like the young Maxim Gorky. Unfortunately he drank heavily in a more indigenous tradition.

The only child in this household regarded himself as a mother's boy, and it was Minnie O'Donovan who made conceivable his escape from his surroundings in all but memory. She was pretty and unusually polite, a grace as unexpected as it was pleasant. Perhaps it was the latter quality that made her, as he recorded, suspicious of emotional demonstrativeness; and it may have encouraged him to scrutinize such outbursts for their real worth. Mrs. O'Donovan went out each day to do housework and brought back small wages, some of which with luck she could save from being converted into her husband's pints of Guinness. Her reward for this maneuvering was his anger. He would brandish his razor at her while their small son risked injury in an attempt to defend her. No wonder the child had pseudo-epileptic fits.

No wonder, either, that when he needed to write under a pseudonym because he was a county librarian, he reverted to his mother's maiden name of O'Connor. There was a long period during which he would gladly have disclaimed the O'Donovan lineage, yet in later life he found himself less ready to spurn the bluff, foolish man who had begotten him. His first volume of autobiography, *An Only Child*, celebrated Minnie O'Donovan's "noble nature"; his second, though it could not present his other parent in so lyrical a light, indulged the dense mixture in himself by bearing the title *My Father's Son*.

Poverty and talent went together. Frank O'Connor later on would praise the way that Yeats, Lady Gregory, and Synge all wrote miracle plays in which people turned into what they imagined themselves to be. He did as much himself. That he might do so began to be signalled by the time he was six. He was already then a devoted reader, if only of success stories about English public schools. These were as remote as possible from his own primary and trades school, which he attended until he was fourteen. Yet bad literature, too, can foster ambition. O'Connor would deny later that Madame Bovary could have gone to pieces "as a result of reading the novels of Scott," and he remained smilingly grateful for the sense of another way of life which his early reading in trashy books had given him. There were also fateful moments in school such as the day when one of his teachers wrote on the blackboard some indecipherable words. They proved to be Irish. The teacher, a little man with a game leg, turned out to be a writer named Daniel Corkery, and this initial impulse from him helped to spur O'Connor to the brilliant translations of Irish poetry which he would make later.

It was his readings in English that had the most immediate influence. Here his mother helped him. Before her marriage, when she had worked as a live-in maid, she had come upon a copy of Shakespeare's works among the unread books in an employer's house. She read them right through. Her son took up her interest, and eventually would write a knowledgeable and shrewd book about *Shakespeare's Progress*. He learned from his mother also to love poetry: first the sung lyrics of Thomas Moore, then gradually the body of English poetry. In the twenties he was reading not only Donne but Hopkins. He was also desperate to read poetry in other languages, and learned French and German so he could keep the lines of Ronsard, Verlaine, Heine, and Goethe in his head.

But the art of fiction swayed him even more than that of verse. "To have grown up in an Irish provincial town in the first quarter of the twentieth century," he said later, "was to have known the nineteenth-century novel as a contemporary art form." Around him in real life he began to see the characters he knew in books by Turgenev, Tolstoy, Chekhov, Gogol, Babel, Balzac, Maupassant. He would say later of his youth that it had been not so much lived as hallucinated. He was "half in, half out of the dream" and saw everything "through the veil of literature." The writers whom he loved were all realists, and he always considered himself to be a nineteenth-century realist, too. Yet to share his life with their characters was a form of romance.

His reverie was only partially interrupted by the rush of Irish nationalism, in which he would take part. He was twelve years old when the Easter Rising occurred in 1916, and he had to watch from the sidelines the Black and Tan War in 1918 and 1919. But when the Civil War broke out, O'Connor, then eighteen, overrode his father's protests and joined the republican forces against the Free State. He knew from Tolstoy and Stendhal the vast confusion of war, and the indistinct battle lines, tactical confusion, and conflicting loyalties of the Irish troubles bore out what they had written. Unthinking obedience was not his way. When he was ordered to shoot unarmed Free State soldiers who were walking out with girl friends, he brought the matter to higher authority and got the order rescinded. After taking part in some skirmishes he was captured and put in a prisoner-of-war camp. Here too he showed his unwillingness to fit into any stereotype. When the republican prisoners of war throughout the country were ordered by their leaders to go on hunger strike, O'Connor was almost alone in bravely refusing to join in. It was his farewell to obsessional politics. Martyrdom on orders was not the course he had marked out for himself.

The hunger strike collapsed. Instead of vindication for common sense, O'Connor found he had achieved notoriety for standing out against the foolhardy majority. The experience told upon him. It did not make him any the less intransigent; the contrary rather, for he embraced many unpopular causes later. But when his mother saw him on his release, she could see that her child was now a man. A sentence in Gogol's story "The Overcoat" summed up O'Connor's state of mind, and he would borrow it later when writing about prisoners: "And anything that happened to me after I never felt the same about again." He now had the point of view from which he would write his first book, *Guests of the Nation*. In the title story, the "guests of the nation" are two British soldiers who have become close friends of their captors. But an order comes for their execution, because the opposite side has executed two men. With this illustration of the cruelty of war, and its absurdity, O'Connor was launched on his literary career.

The implied theme, that flexible people can suddenly become fixed, that the other side may be less the enemy than one's own incrustation, is the theme of many O'Connor's stories. Hearts or circumstances harden when they might be expected to soften. In "The Luceys" a father refuses to take his brother's hand, because of misplaced pride over his dead son. In "The Mad Lomasneys" a pert young woman who has lived by whim suddenly faces unalterable bleakness because a whim has gone wrong. And yet Frank O'Connor was an obstinate man himself, and could understand being dead set on something. So not every fixity is invalidated. In "The Masculine Principle" a suitor sticks to his intention of marrying his girl only when he has saved two hundred pounds. Years pass in the process, and he comes near losing her altogether. In the end, though, his stubbornness is respected and rewarded. In "The Long Road to Ummera" an old woman is determined to be buried nowhere but in the one place, and she has her way, the living being obliged at great inconvenience to obey her wishes. A later story tells how a priest's seemingly bizarre wish to be buried remotely on "The Mass Island" is carried out with reluctance, only to be validated when an enormous crowd of mourners gathers for the funeral.

If fixity is one pole in the stories, the opposite is accommodation. Ireland is a collusive country, with all sorts of secret understandings that can be invoked when needed. When a curate commits suicide, his priest, "an old pro," insists that the village doctor certify death from natural causes; when the doctor demurs, a threat of losing his medical practice brings him to heel. In "Peasants," however, a priest refuses to accommodate a group of peasants who beg him, and then try to bribe him, to leave the police out of a case where a young man has stolen club funds. They for their part are convinced that the priest's obduracy comes only from his having been born and raised in another village, "fifteen long miles away," and so not of their "country." The priest persists in his decision, the young man is tried and given a light sentence. On his release he is provided by his friends with enough money to set up a shop. What interests O'Connor is not the question of illegality or immorality, but the personal warmth that renders collusion inevitable and implies that most offenses are venial anyway and trivial beside communal bonds.

Beyond fixities and accommodations is O'Connor's portrait of Ireland with all its quirks and qualities. He did not have much to say about the ascendancy class which his friend Yeats half praised and half chastised, but he knew all the gradations in the middle and lower classes, such as the barrier between a farmer's son and a laborer's daughter. Though for long an unbeliever, he recognized the role religion played in people's lives. He regrets, in an early story, that a woman has become a nun, though he knows that there can be pleasure in having one's life settled, in fearing nothing and hoping for nothing. But in a later treatment of this theme, "The Shepherds," he likes the old priest who is trying to save a young woman of his parish from being "corrupted" by a French sea captain. The captain cannot understand the fuss over two people sleeping together.

As for women, though they occupy a subordinate place in the economy, O'Connor is on their side as they slice through male palaver, and they do not seem submerged or disparaged. He admires them when like himself they are unintimidated. The woman teacher in "The Bridal Night" lies beside her lunatic lover and calms him chastely to sleep in utter indifference to the contumely she may suffer for being in his bed. O'Connor sympathizes with women as they struggle with sexual desire in a country where men are "death on girls' pasts," and he often deals with the problems of hiding or recognizing illegitimate children. Legitimate or illegitimate, children fascinate him, and he delights in showing their upturned faces as they stare at adults whose behavior is so irrational in comparison with their own. Pervading these and other facets of the country is that extraordinary language, which dots his text with such expressions as "in the ease of the world," "while the life was in her," "giving him the hard word." The text tingles with these localisms.

Frank O'Connor in the course of his sixty years wrote in most of the possible literary forms: two novels, dramatizations, a biography of Michael Collins, a book of poetry, as well as his translations from Irish, some lively travel books, autobiography, and literary criticism. Some people thought him flamboyant in his views; he did not so regard himself. He thought he was stating conclusions that nobody in his right mind could miss. The strength of *The Mirror in the Roadway* and *The Lonely Voice*, which deal with the novel and the short story respectively, comes from this assumptive tone. He begins in close observation but then, in an almost visionary way, renders writers, objects, and themes malleable. Whatever writer he discusses, O'Connor will not release him until he has revealed the network of interconnecting passageways between the external and internal man or woman. If he is bold he is also subtle, as when he says of the mayor's garden in *The Red and the Black:* "Any real estate agent worth his salt could give us a clearer impression of the property of Monsieur de Renal than Stendhal."

The burden of his criticism is that fiction has not been faithful to Stendhal's definition of the novel as a mirror dawdling down a road. Instead it has insisted upon going behind the mirror, becoming self-absorbed and indifferent to that crowd which it had once brilliantly particularized. The switch occurred, O'Connor thought, in Henry James, and he depicted it in an enviable figure: "Somewhere in his work the change takes place between the two; somewhere the ship has been boarded by pirates, and when at last it comes into harbor, nobody could recognize in its rakish lines the respectable passenger ship that set sail from the other side of the water. The passengers would seem to have been murdered on the way, and there is nothing familiar about the dark foreign faces that peer at us over the edge." On the whole, he regretted this development. What he longed for was candor, not circumlocution, cards on the table rather than held close to the chest. For this reason and others, he could not approve of Joyce, feeling that when artistic method had become so dominating life was lost. He liked and practiced a more open confrontation.

Mrs. Yeats used to call him Michael Frank, combining his private and literary selves into one affectionate nickname. There was in fact no hyphen between the two, no impulsion to play artist or reluctance to be man. In him the struggle to express was always involved with a sense of exhilaration, whether he was writing or talking. His friends recognized it not only in his arrowing mind, but also in the great bow of his being, now reposeful now taut. For his readers there is the pleasure of catching Ireland as it was changing, and of enjoying and cherishing it, flyspecks and all. Nor is it so different from America; continents, after all, are only large islands.

Collected Stories

Guests of the Nation

AT DUSK the big Englishman Belcher would shift his long legs out of the ashes and ask, "Well, chums, what about it?" and Noble or me would say, "As you please, chum" (for we had picked up some of their curious expressions), and the little Englishman 'Awkins would light the lamp and produce the cards. Sometimes Jeremiah Donovan would come up of an evening and supervise the play, and grow excited over 'Awkins's cards (which he always played badly), and shout at him as if he was one of our own, "Ach, you divil you, why didn't you play the tray?" But, ordinarily, Jeremiah was a sober and contented poor devil like the big Englishman Belcher, and was looked up to at all only because he was a fair hand at documents, though slow enough at these, I vow. He wore a small cloth hat and big gaiters over his long pants, and seldom did I perceive his hands outside the pockets of that pants. He reddened when you talked to him, tilting from toe to heel and back and looking down all the while at his big farmer's feet. His uncommon broad accent was a great source of jest to me, I being from the town as you may recognize.

I couldn't at the time see the point of me and Noble being with Belcher and 'Awkins at all, for it was and is my fixed belief you could have planted that pair in any untended spot from this to Claregalway and they'd have stayed put and flourished like a native weed. I never seen in my short experience two men that took to the country as they did.

They were handed on to us by the Second Battalion to keep when the search for them became too hot, and Noble and myself, being young, took charge with a natural feeling of responsibility. But little 'Awkins made us look right fools when he displayed he knew the countryside as well as we did and something more. "You're the bloke they calls Bonaparte?" he said to me. "Well, Bonaparte, Mary Brigid Ho'Connell was arskin abaout you and said 'ow you'd a pair of socks belonging to 'er young brother." For it seemed, as they explained it, that the Second used to have little evenings of their own, and some of the girls of the neighborhood would turn in, and seeing they were such decent fellows, our lads couldn't well ignore the two Englishmen, but invited them in and were hail-fellow-well-met with them. 'Awkins told me he learned to dance "The Walls of Limerick" and "The Siege of Ennis" and "The Waves of Tory" in a night or two, though naturally he could not return the compliment, because our lads at that time did not dance foreign dances on principle.

So whatever privileges and favors Belcher and 'Awkins had with the Second they duly took with us, and after the first evening we gave up all pretense of keeping a close eye on their behavior. Not that they could have got far, for they had a notable accent and wore khaki tunics and overcoats with civilian pants and boots. But it's my belief they never had an idea of escaping and were quite contented with their lot.

Now, it was a treat to see how Belcher got off with the old woman of the house we were staying in. She was a great warrant to scold, and crotchety even with us, but before ever she had a chance of giving our guests, as I may call them, a lick of her tongue, Belcher had made her his friend for life. She was breaking sticks at the time, and Belcher, who hadn't been in the house for more than ten minutes, jumped up out of his seat and went across to her.

"Allow me, madam," he says, smiling his queer little smile; "please allow me," and takes the hatchet from her hand. She was struck too parlatic to speak, and ever after Belcher would be at her heels carrying a bucket, or basket, or load of turf, as the case might be. As Noble wittily remarked, he got into looking before she leapt, and hot water or any little thing she wanted Belcher would have it ready for her. For such a huge man (and though I am five foot ten myself I had to look up to him) he had an uncommon shortness—or should I say lack—of speech. It took us some time to get used to him walking in and out like a ghost, without a syllable out of him. Especially because 'Awkins talked enough for a platoon, it was strange to hear big Belcher with his toes in the ashes come out with a solitary "Excuse me, chum," or "That's right, chum." His one and only abiding passion was cards, and I will say for him he was a good card-player. He could have fleeced me and Noble many a time; only if we lost to him, 'Awkins lost to us, and 'Awkins played with the money Belcher gave him.

'Awkins lost to us because he talked too much, and I think now we lost to Belcher for the same reason. 'Awkins and Noble would spit at one another about religion into the early hours of the morning; the little Englishman as you could see worrying the soul out of young Noble (whose brother was a priest) with a string of questions that would puzzle a cardinal. And to make it worse, even in treating of these holy subjects, 'Awkins had a deplorable tongue; I never in all my career struck across a man who could mix such a variety of cursing and bad language into the simplest topic. Oh, a terrible man was little 'Awkins, and a fright to argue! He never did a stroke of work, and when he had no one else to talk to he fixed his claws into the old woman.

I am glad to say that in her he met his match, for one day when he tried to get her to complain profanely of the drought she gave him a great comedown by blaming the drought upon Jupiter Pluvius (a deity neither 'Awkins nor I had ever even heard of, though Noble said among the pagans he was held to have something to do with rain). And another day the same 'Awkins was swearing at the capitalists for starting the German war, when the old dame laid down her iron, puckered up her little crab's mouth and said, "Mr. 'Awkins, you can say what you please about the war, thinking to deceive me because I'm an ignorant old woman, but I know well what started the war. It was that Italian count that stole the heathen divinity out of the temple in Japan, for believe me, Mr. 'Awkins, nothing but sorrow and want follows them that disturbs the hidden powers!" Oh, a queer old dame, as you remark!

So one evening we had our tea together, and 'Awkins lit the lamp and we all sat in to cards. Jeremiah Donovan came in too, and sat down and watched us for a while. Though he was a shy man and didn't speak much, it was easy to see he had no great love for the two Englishmen, and I was surprised it hadn't struck me so clearly before. Well, like that in the story, a terrible dispute blew up late in the evening between 'Awkins and Noble, about capitalists and priests and love for your own country.

"The capitalists," says 'Awkins, with an angry gulp, "the capitalists pays the priests to tell you all abaout the next world, so's you won't notice what they do in this!"

"Nonsense, man," says Noble, losing his temper, "before ever a capitalist was thought of people believed in the next world."

'Awkins stood up as if he was preaching a sermon. "Oh, they did, did they?" he says with a sneer. "They believed all the things you believe, that's what you mean? And you believe that God created Hadam and Hadam created Shem and Shem created Jehoshophat? You believe all the silly hold fairy-tale abaout Heve and Heden and the happle? Well, listen to me, chum. If you're entitled to 'old to a silly belief like that, I'm entitled to 'old to my own silly belief—which is,

that the fust thing your God created was a bleedin' capitalist with
mirality and Rolls Royce complete. Am I right, chum?" he says then
to Belcher.

"You're right, chum," says Belcher, with his queer smile, and gets
up from the table to stretch his long legs into the fire and stroke his
mustache. So, seeing that Jeremiah Donovan was going, and there was
no knowing when the conversation about religion would be over, I
took my hat and went out with him. We strolled down towards the
village together, and then he suddenly stopped, and blushing and
mumbling, and shifting, as his way was, from toe to heel, he said I
ought to be behind keeping guard on the prisoners. And I, having it
put to me so suddenly, asked him what the hell he wanted a guard on
the prisoners at all for, and said that so far as Noble and me were concerned we had talked it over and would rather be out with a column.
"What use is that pair to us?" I asked him.

He looked at me for a spell and said, "I thought you knew we were
keeping them as hostages." "Hostages—?" says I, not quite understanding. "The enemy," he says in his heavy way, "have prisoners belong' to us, and now they talk of shooting them. If they shoot our prisoners we'll shoot theirs, and serve them right." "Shoot them?" said I,
the possibility just beginning to dawn on me. "Shoot them exactly,"
said he. "Now," said I, "wasn't it very unforeseen of you not to tell me
and Noble that?" "How so?" he asks. "Seeing that we were acting as
guards upon them, of course." "And hadn't you reason enough to
guess that much?" "We had not, Jeremiah Donovan, we had not. How
were we to know when the men were on our hands so long?" "And
what difference does it make? The enemy have our prisoners as long or
longer, haven't they?" "It makes a great difference," said I. "How so?"
said he sharply; but I couldn't tell him the difference it made, for I was
struck too silly to speak. "And when may we expect to be released
from this anyway?" said I. "You may expect it tonight," says he. "Or
tomorrow or the next day at latest. So if it's hanging round here that
worries you, you'll be free soon enough."

I cannot explain it even now, how sad I felt, but I went back to the
cottage, a miserable man. When I arrived the discussion was still on,
'Awkins holding forth to all and sundry that there was no next world
at all and Noble answering in his best canonical style that there was.
But I saw 'Awkins was after having the best of it. "Do you know what,
chum?" he was saying, with his saucy smile. "I think you're jest as big
a bleedin' hunbeliever as I am. You say you believe in the next world
and you know jest as much abaout the next world as I do, which is
sweet damn-all. What's 'Eaven? You dunno. Where's 'Eaven? You

dunno. Who's in 'Eaven? You dunno. You know sweet damn-all! I arsk you again, do they wear wings?"

"Very well then," says Noble, "they do; is that enough for you? They do wear wings." "Where do they get them then? Who makes them? 'Ave they a fact'ry for wings? 'Ave they a sort of store where you 'ands in your chit and tikes your bleedin' wings? Answer me that."

"Oh, you're an impossible man to argue with," says Noble. "Now listen to me— " And off the pair of them went again.

It was long after midnight when we locked up the Englishmen and went to bed ourselves. As I blew out the candle I told Noble what Jeremiah Donovan had told me. Noble took it very quietly. After we had been in bed about an hour he asked me did I think we ought to tell the Englishmen. I having thought of the same thing myself (among many others) said no, because it was more than likely the English wouldn't shoot our men, and anyhow it wasn't to be supposed the Brigade who were always up and down with the Second Battalion and knew the Englishmen well would be likely to want them bumped off. "I think so," says Noble. "It would be sort of cruelty to put the wind up them now." "It was very unforeseen of Jeremiah Donovan anyhow," says I, and by Noble's silence I realized he took my meaning.

So I lay there half the night, and thought and thought, and picturing myself and young Noble trying to prevent the Brigade from shooting 'Awkins and Belcher sent a cold sweat out through me. Because there were men on the Brigade you daren't let nor hinder without a gun in your hand, and at any rate, in those days disunion between brothers seemed to me an awful crime. I knew better after.

It was next morning we found it so hard to face Belcher and 'Awkins with a smile. We went about the house all day scarcely saying a word. Belcher didn't mind us much; he was stretched into the ashes as usual with his usual look of waiting in quietness for something unforeseen to happen, but little 'Awkins gave us a bad time with his audacious gibing and questioning. He was disgusted at Noble's not answering him back. "Why can't you tike your beating like a man, chum?" he says. "You with your Hadam and Heve! I'm a Communist—or an Anarchist. An Anarchist, that's what I am." And for hours after he went round the house, mumbling when the fit took him "Hadam and Heve! Hadam and Heve!"

I don't know clearly how we got over that day, but get over it we did, and a great relief it was when the tea things were cleared away and

Belcher said in his peaceable manner, "Well, chums, what about it?" So we all sat round the table and 'Awkins produced the cards, and at that moment I heard Jeremiah Donovan's footsteps up the path, and a dark presentiment crossed my mind. I rose quietly from the table and laid my hand on him before he reached the door. "What do you want?" I asked him. "I want those two soldier friends of yours," he says reddening. "Is that the way it is, Jeremiah Donovan?" I ask. "That's the way. There were four of our lads went west this morning, one of them a boy of sixteen." "That's bad, Jeremiah," says I.

At that moment Noble came out, and we walked down the path together talking in whispers. Feeney, the local intelligence officer, was standing by the gate. "What are you going to do about it?" I asked Jeremiah Donovan. "I want you and Noble to bring them out: you can tell them they're being shifted again; that'll be the quietest way." "Leave me out of that," says Noble suddenly. Jeremiah Donovan looked at him hard for a minute or two. "All right so," he said peaceably. "You and Feeney collect a few tools from the shed and dig a hole by the far end of the bog. Bonaparte and I'll be after you in about twenty minutes. But whatever else you do, don't let anyone see you with the tools. No one must know but the four of ourselves."

We saw Feeney and Noble go round to the houseen where the tools were kept, and sidled in. Everything if I can so express myself was tottering before my eyes, and I left Jeremiah Donovan to do the explaining as best he could, while I took a seat and said nothing. He told them they were to go back to the Second. 'Awkins let a mouthful of curses out of him at that, and it was plain that Belcher, though he said nothing, was duly perturbed. The old woman was for having them stay in spite of us, and she did not shut her mouth until Jeremiah Donovan lost his temper and said some nasty things to her. Within the house by this time it was pitch dark, but no one thought of lighting the lamp, and in the darkness the two Englishmen fetched their khaki topcoats and said good-bye to the woman of the house. "Just as a man mikes a 'ome of a bleedin' place," mumbles 'Awkins, shaking her by the hand, "some bastard at Headquarters thinks you're too cushy and shunts you off." Belcher shakes her hand very hearty. "A thousand thanks, madam," he says, "a thousand thanks for everything . . ." as though he'd made it all up.

We go round to the back of the house and down towards the fatal bog. Then Jeremiah Donovan comes out with what is in his mind. "There were four of our lads shot by your fellows this morning so now you're to be bumped off." "Cut that stuff out," says 'Awkins, flaring up. "It's bad enough to be mucked about such as we are without you plying at soldiers." "It's true," says Jeremiah Donovan, "I'm sorry, 'Awkins, but 'tis true," and comes out with the usual rigmarole about doing our duty and obeying our superiors. "Cut it out," says 'Awkins irritably. "Cut it out!"

Then, when Donovan sees he is not being believed he turns to me, "Ask Bonaparte here," he says. "I don't need to arsk Bonaparte. Me and Bonaparte are chums." "Isn't it true, Bonaparte?" says Jeremiah Donovan solemnly to me. "It is," I say sadly, "it is." 'Awkins stops. "Now, for Christ's sike. . . ." "I mean it, chum," I say. "You daon't saound as if you mean it. You knaow well you don't mean it." "Well, if he don't I do," says Jeremiah Donovan. "Why the 'ell sh'd you want to shoot me, Jeremiah Donovan?" "Why the hell should your people take out four prisoners and shoot them in cold blood upon a barrack square?" I perceive Jeremiah Donovan is trying to encourage himself with hot words.

Anyway, he took little 'Awkins by the arm and dragged him on, but it was impossible to make him understand that we were in earnest. From which you will perceive how difficult it was for me, as I kept feeling my Smith and Wesson and thinking what I would do if they happened to put up a fight or ran for it, and wishing in my heart they would. I knew if only they ran I would never fire on them. "Was Noble in this?" 'Awkins wanted to know, and we said yes. He laughed. But why should Noble want to shoot him? Why should we want to shoot him? What had he done to us? Weren't we chums (the word lingers painfully in my memory)? Weren't we? Didn't we understand him and didn't he understand us? Did either of us imagine for an instant that he'd shoot us for all the so-and-so brigadiers in the so-and-so British Army? By this time I began to perceive in the dusk the desolate edges of the bog that was to be their last earthly bed, and, so great a sadness overtook my mind, I could not answer him. We walked along the edge of it in the darkness, and every now and then 'Awkins would call a halt and begin again, just as if he was wound up, about us being chums, and I was in despair that nothing but the cold and open grave made ready for his presence would convince him that we meant it all. But all the same, if you can understand, I didn't want him to be bumped off.

AT LAST we saw the unsteady glint of a lantern in the distance and made towards it. Noble was carrying it, and Feeney stood somewhere in the darkness behind, and somehow the picture of the two of them so silent in the boglands was like the pain of death in my heart. Belcher, on recognizing Noble, said " 'Allo, chum" in his usual peaceable way, but 'Awkins flew at the poor boy immediately, and the dispute began all over again, only that Noble hadn't a word to say for himself, and stood there with the swaying lantern between his gaitered legs.

It was Jeremiah Donovan who did the answering. 'Awkins asked for the twentieth time (for it seemed to haunt his mind) if anybody thought he'd shoot Noble. "You would," says Jeremiah Donovan shortly. "I wouldn't, damn you!" "You would if you knew you'd be shot for not doing it." "I wouldn't, not if I was to be shot twenty times over; he's my chum. And Belcher wouldn't—isn't that right, Belcher?" "That's right, chum," says Belcher peaceably. "Damned if I would. Anyway, who says Noble'd be shot if I wasn't bumped off? What d'you think I'd do if I was in Noble's place and we were out in the middle of a blasted bog?" "What would you do?" "I'd go with him wherever he was going. I'd share my last bob with him and stick by 'im through thick and thin."

"We've had enough of this," says Jeremiah Donovan, cocking his revolver. "Is there any message you want to send before I fire?" "No, there isn't, but . . ." "Do you want to say your prayers?" 'Awkins came out with a cold-blooded remark that shocked even me and turned to Noble again. "Listen to me, Noble," he said. "You and me are chums. You won't come over to my side, so I'll come over to your side. Is that fair? Just you give me a rifle and I'll go with you wherever you want."

Nobody answered him.

"Do you understand?" he said. "I'm through with it all. I'm a deserter or anything else you like, but from this on I'm one of you. Does that prove to you that I mean what I say?" Noble raised his head, but as Donovan began to speak he lowered it again without answering. "For the last time have you any messages to send?" says Donovan in a cold and excited voice.

"Ah, shut up, you, Donovan; you don't understand me, but these fellows do. They're my chums; they stand by me and I stand by them. We're not the capitalist tools you seem to think us."

I alone of the crowd saw Donovan raise his Webley to the back of 'Awkins's neck, and as he did so I shut my eyes and tried to say a prayer. 'Awkins had begun to say something else when Donovan let fly, and, as I opened my eyes at the bang, I saw him stagger at the knees and lie out flat at Noble's feet, slowly, and as quiet as a child, with the lantern light falling sadly upon his lean legs and bright farmer's boots. We all stood very still for a while watching him settle out in the last agony.

Then Belcher quietly takes out a handkerchief, and begins to tie it about his own eyes (for in our excitement we had forgotten to offer the same to 'Awkins), and, seeing it is not big enough, turns and asks for a loan of mine. I give it to him and as he knots the two together he points with his foot at 'Awkins. " 'E's not quite dead," he says, "better give 'im another." Sure enough 'Awkins's left knee as we see it under the lantern is rising again. I bend down and put my gun to his ear; then, recollecting myself and the company of Belcher, I stand up again with a few hasty words. Belcher understands what is in my mind. "Give 'im 'is first," he says. "I don't mind. Poor bastard, we dunno what's 'ap-pening to 'im now." As by this time I am beyond all feeling I kneel down again and skilfully give 'Awkins the last shot so as to put him forever out of pain.

Belcher who is fumbling a bit awkwardly with the handkerchiefs comes out with a laugh when he hears the shot. It is the first time I have heard him laugh, and it sends a shiver down my spine, coming as it does so inappropriately upon the tragic death of his old friend. "Poor blighter," he says quietly, "and last night he was so curious abaout it all. It's very queer, chums, I always think. Naow, 'e knows as much abaout it as they'll ever let 'im know, and last night 'e was all in the dark."

Donovan helps him to tie the handkerchiefs about his eyes. "Thanks, chum," he says. Donovan asks him if there are any messages he would like to send. "Naow, chum," he says, "none for me. If any of you likes to write to 'Awkins's mother you'll find a letter from 'er in 'is pocket. But my missus left me eight years ago. Went away with an-other fellow and took the kid with her. I likes the feelin' of a 'ome (as you may 'ave noticed) but I couldn't start again after that."

We stand around like fools now that he can no longer see us. Dono-van looks at Noble and Noble shakes his head. Then Donovan raises his Webley again and just at that moment Belcher laughs his queer nervous laugh again. He must think we are talking of him; anyway, Donovan lowers his gun. " 'Scuse me, chums," says Belcher, "I feel I'm talking the 'ell of a lot . . . and so silly . . . abaout me being so 'andy abaout a 'ouse. But this thing come on me so sudden. You'll for-give me, I'm sure." "You don't want to say a prayer?" asks Jeremiah Donovan. "No, chum," he replies, "I don't think that'd 'elp. I'm ready if you want to get it over." "You understand," says Jeremiah Donovan, "it's not so much our doing. It's our duty, so to speak." Belcher's head is raised like a real blind man's, so that you can only see his nose and chin in the lamplight. "I never could make out what duty was myself," he said, "but I think you're all good lads, if that's what you mean. I'm not complaining." Noble, with a look of desperation, signals to Donovan, and in a flash Donovan raises his gun and fires. The big man goes over like a sack of meal, and this time there is no need of a second shot.

I don't remember much about the burying, but that it was worse than all the rest, because we had to carry the warm corpses a few yards before we sunk them in the windy bog. It was all mad lonely, with only a bit of lantern between ourselves and the pitch blackness, and birds hooting and screeching all round disturbed by the guns. Noble had to search 'Awkins first to get the letter from his mother. Then having smoothed all signs of the grave away, Noble and I collected our tools, said good-bye to the others, and went back along the desolate edge of the treacherous bog without a word. We put the tools in the houseen and went into the house. The kitchen was pitch black and cold, just as we left it, and the old woman was sitting over the hearth telling her beads. We walked past her into the room, and Noble struck a match to light the lamp. Just then she rose quietly and came to the doorway, being not at all so bold or crabbed as usual.

"What did ye do with them?" she says in a sort of whisper, and Noble took such a mortal start the match quenched in his trembling hand. "What's that?" he asks without turning round. "I heard ye," she said. "What did you hear?" asks Noble, but sure he wouldn't deceive a child the way he said it. "I heard ye. Do you think I wasn't listening to ye putting the things back in the houseen?" Noble struck another match and this time the lamp lit for him. "Was that what ye did with them?" she said, and Noble said nothing—after all what could he say?

So then, by God, she fell on her two knees by the door, and began telling her beads, and after a minute or two Noble went on his knees by the fireplace, so I pushed my way out past her, and stood at the door, watching the stars and listening to the damned shrieking of the birds. It is so strange what you feel at such moments, and not to be written afterwards. Noble says he felt he seen everything ten times as big, perceiving nothing around him but the little patch of black bog with the two Englishmen stiffening into it; but with me it was the other way, as though the patch of bog where the two Englishmen were was a thousand miles away from me, and even Noble mumbling just behind me and the old woman and the birds and the bloody stars were all far away, and I was somehow very small and very lonely. And anything that ever happened me after I never felt the same about again.

The Late Henry Conran

"I'VE ANOTHER little story for you," said the old man.

"I hope it's a good one," said I.

"The divil a better. And if you don't believe me you can go down to Courtenay's Road and see the truth of it with your own eyes. Now it isn't every wan will say that to you?"

"It is not then."

"And the reason I say it is, I know the people I'm talking about. I knew Henry in the old days—Henry Conran that is, otherwise known as 'Prosperity' Conran—and I'll say for him he had the biggest appetite for liquor of any man I ever met or heard of. You could honestly say Prosperity Conran would drink porter out of a sore heel. Six foot three he was, and he filled it all. He was quiet enough when he was sober, but when he was drunk—Almighty and Eternal, you never knew what divilment he'd be up to!

"I remember calling for him wan night to go to a comity meeting— he was a great supporter of John Redmond—and finding him mad drunk, in his shirt and drawers; he was trying to change out of his old working clothes. Well, with respects to you, he got sick on it, and what did he do before me own two eyes but strip off every stitch he had on him and start wiping up the floor with his Sunday clothes. Oh, every article he could find he shoved into it. And there he was idioty drunk in his pelt singing,

'Up the Mollies! Hurray!
We don't care about Quarry Lane,
All we want is our own Fair Lane.'

"Well, of course, poor Henry couldn't keep any job, and his own sweet Nellie wasn't much help to him. She was a nagging sort of woman, if you understand me, an unnatural sort of woman. She had six children to rear, and, instead of going quietly to work and softening Henry, she was always calling in the priest or the minister to him. And

Henry, to get his own back, would smash every bit of china she had. Not that he was a cross man by any manner of means, but he was a bit independent, and she could never see how it slighted him to call in strangers like that.

"Henry hung round idle for six months. Then he was offered a job to go round the town as a walking advertisement for somebody's ale. That cut him to the heart. As he said himself, 'Is it me, a comity man of the Ancient Order of Hibernians, a man dat shook hands with John Dillon, to disgrace meself like dat before the town? And you wouldn't mind but I couldn't as much as stomach the same hogwash meself!'

"So he had to go to America, and sorry I was to lose him, the decent man! Nellie told me after 'twould go through you to see him on the deck of the tender, blue all over and smothered with sobs. 'Nellie,' says he to her, 'Nellie, give the word and I'll trow me ticket in the water.' 'I will not,' says Nellie, 'for you were always a bad head to me.'

"Now that was a hard saying, and maybe it wasn't long before she regretted it. There she was with her six children, and wan room between the seven of them, and she trying to do a bit of laundry to keep the life in their bodies.

"Well, it would be a troublesome thing for me to relate all that happened them in the twenty-five long years between that day and this. But maybe you'd remember how her son, Aloysius, mixed himself up in the troubles? Maybe you would? Not that he ever did anything dangerous except act as clerk of the court, and be on all sorts of relief comities, and go here and go there on delegations and deputations. No shooting or jailing for Aloysius. 'Lave that,' says he, 'to the rank and file!' All he ever had his eye on was the main chance. And grander and grander he was getting in himself, my dear! First he had to buy out the house, then he had an electric bell put in, then he bought or hobbled a motor car, then he found tidy jobs for two of his sisters and one for his young brother. Pity to God the two big girls were married already or he'd have made a rare haul! But God help them, they were tied to two poor boozy sops that weren't half nor quarter the cut of their father! So Aloysius gave them the cold shoulder.

"Now Nellie wasn't liking this at all in her own mind. She often said to me, 'For all me grandeur, I'd be better off with poor Henry,' and so she would, for about that time Aloysius began to think of choosing a wife. Of course, the wife-to-be was a flashy piece from the country, and Nellie, who didn't like her at all, was forever crossing her and finding fault with her. Sure, you ought to remember the row she kicked up when the damsel appeared wan night in wan of them new fangled sleeping things with trousers. Nellie was so shocked she went to the priest and complained her, and then complained her to all the neighbors, and she shamed and disgraced Aloysius so much that for months he wouldn't speak to her. But begod, if she didn't make that girl wear a plain shift every other time she came to stay with them!

"After the scandal about the trousers nothing would content Aloysius but that they must live away from the locality, so they got another house, a bigger wan this time, and it was from the new house that Aloysius got married. Nellie, poor woman, couldn't read nor write, so she had nothing at all to do with the preparations, and what was her surprise when the neighbors read out the marriage announcement to her! 'Aloysius Gonzaga Conran, son of Ellen Conran, Courtenay's Road'—and divil the word about poor Henry! The whole town was laughing at it, but what annoyed Nellie most was not the slight on herself, but the slight on her man. So up with her to Aloysius, and 'this and that,' she says, 'I didn't pick you up from under a bush, so give your father the bit of credit that's due to him or I'll put in the note meself!' My dear, she was foaming! Aloysius was in a cleft stick, and they fought and fought, Aloysius calling his father down and Nellie praising him, and then the young wife drops the suggestion that they should put in 'the late Henry Conran.' So Nellie not having a word to say against that, next day there is another announcement—nothing about Nellie this time only plain 'son of the late Henry Conran.'

"Well, the town is roaring yet! Wan day the man have no father to speak of and the next day he have a dead father and no mother at all. And everybody knowing at the same time that Henry was in America, safe and sound, and wilder than ever he was at home.

"But that's not the end of it. I was in me bed the other night when a knock came to the door. My daughter-in-law opened it and I heard a strange voice asking for me. Blast me if I could place it! And all at once the stranger forces his way in apast her and stands in the bedroom door, with his head bent down and wan hand on the jamb. 'Up the Mollies!' says he in the top of his voice. 'Me ould flower, strike up the antem of Fair Lane! Do you remember the night we carried deat and destruction into Blackpool? Shout it, me hearty man—Up the Mollies!'

"But 'twas the height I recognized.

" ' 'Tis Prosperity Conran,' says I.

" 'Prosperity Conran it is,' says he.

" 'The same ould six foot three?' says I.

" 'Every inch of it!' says he, idioty drunk.

" 'And what in the name of God have you here?' says I.

" 'Me wife dat put a notice in the papers saying I was dead. Am

I dead, Larry Costello? Me lovely man, you knew me since I was tree—tell me if I'm dead. Feel me! Feel dat muscle of mine and tell me the trute, am I alive or dead?'

" 'You're not dead,' says I after I felt his arm.

" 'I'll murder her, dat's what I'll do! I'll smash every bone in her body. Get up now, Larry, and I'll show you the greatest bust-up dat was ever seen or heard of in dis city. Where's the All-for-Ireland Headquarters till I fling a brick at it?'

" 'The All-for-Irelands is no more,' says I.

He looked at me unsteadily for a minute.

" 'Joking me you are,' says he.

" 'Divil a joke,' says I.

" 'The All-for-Irelands gone?'

" 'All gone,' says I.

" 'And the Mollies?'

" 'All gone.'

" 'All gone?'

" 'All gone.'

" 'Dat you might be killed?'

" 'That I might be killed stone dead.'

" 'Merciful God! I must be an ould man then, huh?'

" ' 'Tisn't younger we're getting,' says I.

" 'An ould man,' says he, puzzled-like. 'Maybe I'm dead after all? Do you think I'm dead, Larry?'

" 'In a manner of speaking you are,' says I.

" 'Would a court say I was dead?'

" 'A clever lawyer might argue them into it,' says I.

" 'But not *dead*, Larry? Christ, he couldn't say I was *dead*?'

" 'Well, as good as dead, Henry.'

" 'I'll carry the case to the High Courts,' says he, getting excited. 'I'll prove I'm not dead. I'm an American citizen and I can't be dead.'

" 'Aisy! Aisy!' says I, seeing him take it so much to heart.

" 'I won't be aisy,' says he, flaring up. 'I've a summons out agin me wife for defaming me character, and I'll never go back to Chicago till I clear me name in the eyes of the world.'

" 'Henry,' says I, 'no wan ever said wan word against you. There isn't as much as a shadow of an aspersion on your character.'

" 'Do you mane,' says he, ' 'tis no aspersion on me character to say I'm dead? God damn you, man, would you like a rumor like dat to be going round about yourself?'

" 'I would not, Henry, I would not, but 'tis no crime to be dead. And anyway, as I said before, 'tis only a manner of speaking. A man might be stone dead, or he might be half dead, or dead to you and me, or, for the matter of that, he might be dead to God and the world as we've often been ourselves.'

" 'Dere's no manner of speaking in it at all,' says Henry, getting madder and madder. 'No bloody manner of speaking. I might be dead drunk as you say, but dat would be no excuse for calling me the late Henry Conran. . . . Dere's me charge sheet,' says he, sitting on the bed and pulling out a big blue paper. 'Ellen Conran, for defamation of character. Wan man on the boat wanted me to charge her with attempted bigamy, but the clerk wouldn't have it.'

" 'And did you come all the way from America to do this?' says I.

" 'Of course I did. How could I stay on in America wit a ting like dat hanging over me? Blast you, man, you don't seem to know the agony I went trough for weeks and weeks before I got on the boat!'

" 'And do Nellie know you're here?' says I.

" 'She do not, and I mane her not to know till the policeman serves his warrant on her.'

" 'Listen to me, Henry,' says I, getting out of bed, 'the sooner you have this out with Nellie the better for all.'

" 'Do you tink so?' says he a bit stupid-like.

" 'How long is it since you put your foot aboard the liner in Queenstown, Henry?'

" ' 'Tis twenty-five years and more,' says he.

" ' 'Tis a long time not to see your own lawful wife,' says I.

" ' 'Tis,' says he, ' 'tis, a long time,' and all at wance he began to cry, with his head in his two hands.

" 'I knew she was a hard woman, Larry, but blast me if I ever tought she'd do the like of dat on me! Me poor ould heart is broke! And the Mollies—did I hear you say the Mollies was gone?'

" 'The Mollies is gone,' says I.

" 'Anyting else but dat, Larry, anyting else but dat!'

" 'Come on away,' says I.

"So I brought him down the road by the hand just like a child. He never said wan word till I knocked at the door, and all at wance he got fractious again. I whispered into Nellie to open the door. When she seen the man with me she nearly went through the ground.

" 'Who is it?' says she.

" 'An old friend of yours,' says I.

" 'Is it Henry?' says she, whispering-like.

" 'It is Henry,' says I.

" 'It is not Henry!' bawls out me hero. 'Well you know your poor ould Henry is dead and buried without a soul in the world to shed a tear over his corpse.'

" 'Henry!' says she.

" 'No, blast you!' says he with a shriek, 'but Henry's ghost come to ha'ant you.'

" 'Come in, come in the pair of ye,' says I. 'Why the blazes don't ye kiss wan another like any Christian couple?"

"After a bit of trouble I dragged him inside.

" 'Ah, you hard-hearted woman!' says he moaning, with his two paws out before him like a departed spirit. 'Ah, you cruel, wicked woman! What did you do to your poor ould husband?'

" 'Help me to undress him, Nellie,' says I. 'Sit down there on the bed, Henry, and let me unlace your boots.'

"So I pushed him back on the bed, but, when I tried to get at his boots, he began to kick his feet up in the air, laughing like a kid.

" 'I'm dead, dead, dead, dead,' says he.

" 'Let me get at him, Larry,' says Nellie in her own determined way, so, begod, she lifted his leg that high he couldn't kick without falling over, and in two minits she had his boots and stockings off. Then I got off his coat, loosened his braces and held him back in the bed while she pulled his trousers down. At that he began to come to himself a bit.

" 'Show it to her! Show it to her!' says he, getting hot and making a dive for his clothes.

" 'Show what to her?' says I.

" 'Me charge sheet. Give it to me, Larry. There you are, you jade of hell! Seven and six-pence I paid for it to clear me character.'

" 'Get into bed, sobersides,' says I.

" 'I wo' not go into bed!'

" 'And there's an old nightshirt all ready,' says Nellie.

" 'I don't want no nightshirt. I'll take no charity from any wan of ye. I wants me character back, me character that ye took on me.'

" 'Take off his shirt, Larry,' says she.

"So I pulled the old stinking shirt up over his gray pate, and in a tick of the clock she had his nightshirt on.

" 'Now, Nellie,' says I, 'I'll be going. There's nothing more I can do for you.'

" 'Thanks, Larry, thanks,' says she. 'You're the best friend we ever had. There's nothing else you can do. He'll be asleep in a minit, don't I know him well?'

" 'Good-night, Henry,' says I.

" 'Good-night, Larry. Tomorrow we'll revive the Mollies.'

"Nellie went to see me to the door, and outside was the two ladies and the young gentleman in their nighties, listening.

" 'Who is it, Mother?' says they.

" 'Go back to bed the three of ye!' says Nellie. ' 'Tis only your father.'

" 'Jesus, Mary and Joseph!' says the three of them together.

"At that minit we heard Henry inside bawling his heart out.

" 'Nellie, Nellie, where are you, Nellie?'

" 'Go back and see what he wants,' says I, 'before I go.'

"So Nellie opened the door and looked in.

" 'What's wrong with you now?' says she.

" 'You're not going to leave me sleep alone, Nellie,' says he.

" 'You ought to be ashamed of yourself,' says she, 'talking like that and the children listening. . . . Look at him,' says she to me, 'look at him for the love of God!' The eyes were shining in her head with pure relief. So I peeped in, and there was Henry with every bit of clothes in the bed around him and his back to us all. 'Look at his ould gray pate!' says she.

" 'Still in all,' says Henry over his shoulder, 'you had no right to say I was dead!' "

The Bridal Night

IT WAS sunset, and the two great humps of rock made a twilight in the cove where the boats were lying high up the strand. There was one light only in a little whitewashed cottage. Around the headland came a boat and the heavy dipping of its oars was like a heron's flight. The old woman was sitting on the low stone wall outside her cottage.

" 'Tis a lonesome place," said I.

" 'Tis so," she agreed, "a lonesome place, but any place is lonesome without one you'd care for."

"Your own flock are gone from you, I suppose?" I asked.

"I never had but the one," she replied, "the one son only," and I knew because she did not add a prayer for his soul that he was still alive.

"Is it in America he is?" I asked. (It is to America all the boys of the locality go when they leave home.)

"No, then," she replied simply. "It is in the asylum in Cork he is on me these twelve years."

I had no fear of trespassing on her emotions. These lonesome people in the wild places, it is their nature to speak; they must cry out their sorrows like the wild birds.

"God help us!" I said. "Far enough!"

"Far enough," she sighed. "Too far for an old woman. There was a nice priest here one time brought me up in his car to see him. All the ways to this wild place he brought it, and he drove me into the city. It is a place I was never used to, but it eased my mind to see poor Denis well-cared-for and well-liked. It was a trouble to me before that, not knowing would they see what a good boy he was before his madness came on him. He knew me; he saluted me, but he said nothing until the superintendent came to tell me the tea was ready for me. Then poor Denis raised his head and says: 'Leave ye not forget the toast. She was ever a great one for her bit of toast.' It seemed to give him ease and he cried after. A good boy he was and is. It was like him after seven long years to think of his old mother and her little bit of toast."

"God help us," I said for her voice was like the birds', hurrying high, immensely high, in the colored light, out to sea to the last islands where their nests were.

"Blessed be His holy will," the old woman added, "there is no turning aside what is in store. It was a teacher that was here at the time. Miss Regan her name was. She was a fine big jolly girl from the town. Her father had a shop there. They said she had three hundred pounds to her own cheek the day she set foot in the school, and—'tis hard to believe but 'tis what they all said: I will not belie her—'twasn't banished she was at all, but she came here of her own choice, for the great liking she had for the sea and the mountains. Now, that is the story, and with my own eyes I saw her, day in day out, coming down the little pathway you came yourself from the road and sitting beyond there in a hollow you can hardly see, out of the wind. The neighbors could make nothing of it, and she being a stranger, and with only the book Irish, they left her alone. It never seemed to take a peg out of her, only sitting in that hole in the rocks, as happy as the day is long, reading her little book or writing her letters. Of an odd time she might bring one of the little scholars along with her to be picking posies.

"That was where my Denis saw her. He'd go up to her of an evening and sit on the grass beside her, and off and on he might take her out in the boat with him. And she'd say with that big laugh of hers: 'Denis is my beau.' Those now were her words and she meant no more harm by it than the child unborn, and I knew it and Denis knew it, and it was a little joke we had, the three of us. It was the same way she used to joke about her little hollow. 'Mrs. Sullivan,' she'd say, 'leave no one near it. It is my nest and my cell and my little prayer-house, and maybe I would be like the birds and catch the smell of the stranger and then fly away from ye all.' It did me good to hear her laugh, and whenever I saw Denis moping or idle I would say it to him myself: 'Denis, why wouldn't you go out and pay your attentions to Miss Regan and all saying you are her intended?' It was only a joke. I would say the same thing to her face, for Denis was such a quiet boy, no way rough or accustomed to the girls at all—and how would he in this lonesome place?

"I will not belie her; it was she saw first that poor Denis was after more than company, and it was not to this cove she came at all then but to the little cove beyond the headland, and 'tis hardly she would go there itself without a little scholar along with her. 'Ah,' I says, for I missed her company, 'isn't it the great stranger Miss Regan is becoming?' and Denis would put on his coat and go hunting in the dusk till he came to whatever spot she was. Little ease that was to him, poor boy, for he lost his tongue entirely, and lying on his belly before her, chewing an old bit of grass, is all he would do till she got up and left him. He could not help himself, poor boy. The madness was on him, even then, and it was only when I saw the plunder done that I knew there was no cure for him only to put her out of his mind entirely. For 'twas madness in him and he knew it, and that was what made him lose his tongue—he that was maybe without the price of an ounce of 'baccy—I will not deny it: often enough he had to do without it when the hens would not be laying, and often enough stirabout and praties was all we had for days. And there was she with money to her name in the bank! And that wasn't all, for he was a good boy; a quiet, good-natured boy, and another would take pity on him, knowing he would make her a fine steady husband, but she was not the sort, and well I knew it from the first day I laid eyes on her, that her hand would never rock the cradle. There was the madness out and out.

"So here was I, pulling and hauling, coaxing him to stop at home, and hiding whatever little thing was to be done till evening the way his hands would not be idle. But he had no heart in the work, only listening, always listening, or climbing the cnuceen to see would he catch a glimpse of her coming or going. And, oh, Mary, the heavy sigh he'd give when his bit of supper was over and I bolting the house for the night, and he with the long hours of darkness forninst him—my heart was broken thinking of it. It was the madness, you see. It was on him. He could hardly sleep or eat, and at night I would hear him, turning and groaning as loud as the sea on the rocks.

"It was then when the sleep was a fever to him that he took to walking in the night. I remember well the first night I heard him lift the latch. I put on my few things and went out after him. It was standing here I heard his feet on the stile. I went back and latched the door and hurried after him. What else could I do, and this place terrible after the fall of night with rocks and hills and water and streams, and he, poor soul, blinded with the dint of sleep. He travelled the road a piece, and then took to the hills, and I followed him with my legs all torn with briars and furze. It was over beyond by the new house that he gave up. He turned to me then the way a little child that is running away turns and clings to your knees; he turned to me and said: 'Mother, we'll go home now. It was the bad day for you ever you brought me into the world.' And as the day was breaking I got him back to bed and covered him up to sleep.

"I was hoping that in time he'd wear himself out, but it was worse he was getting. I was a strong woman then, a mayen-strong woman. I could cart a load of seaweed or dig a field with any man, but the night-walking broke me. I knelt one night before the Blessed Virgin and prayed whatever was to happen, it would happen while the light of life was in me, the way I would not be leaving him lonesome like that in a wild place.

"And it happened the way I prayed. Blessed be God, he woke that night or the next night on me and he roaring. I went in to him but I couldn't hold him. He had the strength of five men. So I went out and locked the door behind me. It was down the hill I faced in the starlight to the little house above the cove. The Donoghues came with me: I will not belie them; they were fine powerful men and good neighbors. The father and the two sons came with me and brought the rope from the boats. It was a hard struggle they had of it and a long time before they got him on the floor, and a longer time before they got the ropes on him. And when they had him tied they put him back into bed for me, and I covered him up, nice and decent, and put a hot stone to his feet to take the chill of the cold floor off him.

"Sean Donoghue spent the night sitting beside the fire with me, and in the morning he sent one of the boys off for the doctor. Then Denis called me in his own voice and I went into him. 'Mother,' says Denis, 'will you leave me this way against the time they come for me?' I hadn't the heart. God knows I hadn't. 'Don't do it, Peg,' says Sean. 'If 'twas a hard job trussing him before, it will be harder the next time, and I won't answer for it.'

" 'You're a kind neighbor, Sean,' says I, 'and I would never make little of you, but he is the only son I ever reared and I'd sooner he'd kill me now than shame him at the last.'

"So I loosened the ropes on him and he lay there very quiet all day

without breaking his fast. Coming on to evening he as̶
sup of tea and he drank it, and soon after the doctor and
came in the car. They said a few words to Denis but he ̶
answer and the doctor gave me the bit of writing. 'It will
before they come for him,' says he, 'and 'tisn't right for yo̶
in the house with the man.' But I said I would stop with h̶.̶.̶ ̶a̶nd Sean
Donoghue said the same.

"When darkness came on there was a little bit of a wind blew up
from the sea and Denis began to rave to himself, and it was her name
he was calling all the time. 'Winnie,' that was her name, and it was the
first time I heard it spoken. 'Who is that he is calling?' says Sean. 'It is
the schoolmistress,' says I, 'for though I do not recognize the name, I
know 'tis no one else he'd be asking for.' 'That is a bad sign,' says
Sean. 'He'll get worse as the night goes on and the wind rises. 'Twould
be better for me go down and get the boys to put the ropes on him
again while he's quiet.' And it was then something struck me, and I
said: 'Maybe if she came to him herself for a minute he would be quiet
after.' 'We can try it anyway,' says Sean, 'and if the girl has a kind
heart she will come.'

"It was Sean that went up for her. I would not have the courage to
ask her. Her little house is there on the edge of the hill; you can see it
as you go back the road with the bit of garden before it the new teacher
left grow wild. And it was a true word Sean said for 'twas worse Denis
was getting, shouting out against the wind for us to get Winnie for
him. Sean was a long time away or maybe I felt it long, and I thought
it might be the way she was afeared to come. There are many like that,
small blame to them. Then I heard her step that I knew so well on the
boreen beside the house and I ran to the door, meaning to say I was
sorry for the trouble we were giving her, but when I opened the door
Denis called out her name in a loud voice, and the crying fit came on
me, thinking how lighthearted we used to be together.

"I couldn't help it, and she pushed in apast me into the bedroom
with her face as white as that wall. The candle was lighting on the
dresser. He turned to her roaring with the mad look in his eyes, and
then went quiet all of a sudden, seeing her like that overright him with
her hair all tumbled in the wind. I was coming behind her. I heard it.
He put up his two poor hands and the red mark of the ropes on his
wrists and whispered to her: 'Winnie, asthore, isn't it the long time
you were away from me?'

" 'It is, Denis, it is indeed,' says she, 'but you know I couldn't help
it.'

" 'Don't leave me anymore now, Winnie,' says he, and then he said
no more, only the two eyes lighting out on her as she sat by the bed.

⅃d Sean Donoghue brought in the little stooleen for me, and there ⅄e were, the three of us, talking, and Denis paying us no attention, only staring at her.

"'Winnie,' says he, 'lie down here beside me.'

"'Oye,' says Sean, humoring him, 'don't you know the poor girl is played out after her day's work? She must go home to bed.'

"'No, no, no,' says Denis and the terrible mad light in his eyes. 'There is a high wind blowing and 'tis no night for one like her to be out. Leave her sleep here beside me. Leave her creep in under the clothes to me the way I'll keep her warm.'

"'Oh, oh, oh, oh,' says I, 'indeed and indeed, Miss Regan, 'tis I'm sorry for bringing you here. 'Tisn't my son is talking at all but the madness in him. I'll go now,' says I, 'and bring Sean's boys to put the ropes on him again.'

"'No, Mrs. Sullivan,' says she in a quiet voice. 'Don't do that at all. I'll stop here with him and he'll go fast asleep. Won't you, Denis?'

"'I will, I will,' says he, 'but come under the clothes to me. There does a terrible draught blow under that door.'

"'I will indeed, Denis,' says she, 'if you'll promise me to go to sleep.'

"'Oye, whisht, girl,' says I. ' 'Tis you that's mad. While you're here you're in my charge, and how would I answer to your father if you stopped in here by yourself?'

"'Never mind about me, Mrs. Sullivan,' she said. 'I'm not a bit in dread of Denis. I promise you there will no harm come to me. You and Mr. Donoghue can sit outside in the kitchen and I'll be all right here.'

"She had a worried look but there was something about her there was no mistaking. I wouldn't take it on myself to cross the girl. We went out to the kitchen, Sean and myself, and we heard every whisper that passed between them. She got into the bed beside him: I heard her. He was whispering into her ear the sort of foolish things boys do be saying at that age, and then we heard no more only the pair of them breathing. I went to the room door and looked in. He was lying with his arm about her and his head on her bosom, sleeping like a child, sleeping like he slept in his good days with no worry at all on his poor face. She did not look at me and I did not speak to her. My heart was too full. God help us, it was an old song of my father's that was going through my head: 'Lonely Rock is the one wife my children will know.'

"Later on, the candle went out and I did not light another. I wasn't a bit afraid for her then. The storm blew up and he slept through it all, breathing nice and even. When it was light I made a cup of tea for her and beckoned her from the room door. She loosened his hold and slipped out of bed. Then he stirred and opened his eyes.

" 'Winnie,' says he, 'where are you going?'

" 'I'm going to work, Denis,' says she. 'Don't you know I must be at school early?'

" 'But you'll come back to me tonight, Winnie?' says he.

" 'I will, Denis,' says she. 'I'll come back, never fear.'

"And he turned on his side and went fast asleep again.

"When she walked into the kitchen I went on my two knees before her and kissed her hands. I did so. There would no words come to me, and we sat there, the three of us, over our tea, and I declare for the time being I felt 'twas worth it all, all the troubles of his birth and rearing and all the lonesome years ahead.

"It was a great ease to us. Poor Denis never stirred, and when the police came he went along with them without commotion or handcuffs or anything that would shame him, and all the words he said to me was: 'Mother, tell Winnie I'll be expecting her.'

"And isn't it a strange and wonderful thing? From that day to the day she left us there did no one speak a bad word about what she did, and the people couldn't do enough for her. Isn't it a strange thing and the world as wicked as it is, that no one would say the bad word about her?"

Darkness had fallen over the Atlantic, blank gray to its farthest reaches.

The Grand Vizier's
Daughters

"THE PLOW?" said my uncle's voice from the front gate. "Do you mean to say you don't know the Plow? That's the Plow, man, up there. And over there, low down, above the lighthouse—d'ye see?—the ruffian with the red head, that's Orion. Just so! Irish, of course; an old Tipperary family, armed to the teeth."

I chuckled as his maudlin voice called it all up: the starlight over the sleeping town of which he was town clerk; the world's worst town clerk, but that's neither here nor there. For an hour or more I lay listening to himself and the maid gossiping in the kitchen, and their mumbling voices and the hissing of the range half lulled me to sleep. Then I heard him get up, and Nora began to whisper in protest till he grew crotchety. "Now, can't you—?" I heard him hiss. "I'm all right, girl. I won't say anything to her." I wondered which of the girls he wanted to talk to. He came upstairs quietly; I knew he wasn't coming to bed because he hadn't locked the doors. As I heard him try the handle of the girls' door I slipped out of bed and put on a dressing gown.

"Halloaaa," he said at last in a long, whimsical, insinuating drawl.

"Hallo," piped my cousin Josie in her high-pitched, timid voice.

"Is Mom asleep?" he asked.

"She is. . . . No, she isn't, though. You're after waking her."

"Oh, dear, dear!" he said.

"Is that you, Daddy?" said Monica, sleepy and cross, "what time is it?"

Curiosity was too much for me. I opened my bedroom door. He heard it, rushed out and clawed me in after him, beaming at me. I knew from the smell he must have been on the skite again. He was a tall, gaunt, melancholy-looking man. I worshipped him and he never saw it, the old idiot. Often when we met in town he went by without noticing me, lost in his own thoughts, his hands behind his back, his head bowed into the collar of his overcoat, while his lips moved as if he were talking to himself. If I stopped him he started out of his reverie with an animation and a wealth of gesture that was entirely fictitious, a laugh too loud, a glare of the deep-set fanatical eyes, a flush on the hollow temples and high cheekbones, while he leaned forward or sideways like a yacht in a gale in a long, raking, astonished line, clawing madly at his hat or at the flapping skirts of his coat. It wasn't wishing to me to break in on him.

"Come in, Willie," he said, laughing, "come in, boy! I was only just saying to Nora that I hardly ever get the chance of a talk with ye."

The candle on the dressing-table exaggerated the slashing line of his head with the high, bald, narrow cranium, the high cheekbones and sunken temples and eyes—the face of an El Greco saint. He swept the chair clean with a wave of his hand and held it out to me. Then he sat himself on the end of the bed and gave each of us a quizzical look, his mouth puckered up and his eyes in slits as if he was trying to keep in his laughter.

"And now what are we going to talk about?" he asked archly. "Here we are, the whole family. We have everything: the setting, the time, the company. What are we going to discuss?"

"Tell us a story, can't you?" said Josie. She had continued to gape at him with her big, scared brown eyes, the bedclothes drawn close under her chin, from modesty. I was sorry for her. She was always afraid of him when he had a drop taken. She was like that; a gentle, nunlike soul, not like Monica who went through town with a sailor stride, northeast, northwest, cracking jokes with everyone. On Sunday mornings poor Josie would come tapping at the Boss's door to tell him he'd be late for Mass, and then stand uncertainly in the hall with a flush on her cheeks and the same wide, uncomprehending stare in her great brown eyes. I liked Josie and I could have killed that little sugar, Hennessey, when he let her down.

"Story?" said the Boss with a laugh, drawing away from her in mock surprise. "Sure, my goodness, ye're too big for stories."

"Not for good ones," said Monica.

"What sort of story?" he asked, frowning and sucking in his cheeks till the whole hollow cage of his skull stood out.

"Well, for instance, what you and Owney Mac were up to tonight," Monica said saucily.

"Me and Owney—?" he exclaimed with a worried look. "No, no, Mon, 'pon my soul, I wasn't. I just happened to drop in for a minute." Then his face cleared; he smiled and winked. "Go away, you ruffian!" he said.

"A story?" he continued musingly with his head in the air. "I wonder now could I think of a little story that came into my head tonight. Let me think! What was it? About a young fellow, a rather simple young fellow, but nice. . . . I want you to remember that. He was nice. . . . Damn it, who was it told me or did I read it somewhere? Never mind, 'twill come back to me. . . . And a long time ago he came to live in a certain town. He had a job there; a good enough job for the town, but nothing much outside. Of course, he was hoping for promotion. We'll call him the Grand Vizier."

"It must have been in Turkey so," Monica cried, lifting herself on her elbow.

"Exactly!" my uncle exclaimed excitedly, punching his left palm with his fist. " 'Pon my word, Mon, you have it! Turkey! The very place. The name of the town will come back to me too in a minute. Not that 'twould mean anything to ye; a miserable place; a dirty old Eastern town with houses falling down at every step; mountains of dirt in the streets, and the unfortunate people living on top of one another, in filthy holes and corners, like savages—the way they live in Turkey.

And this young fellow—he was a bit foolish, I told you that—thought he'd be a great fellow and change it all."

"And marry the Sultan's daughter," chimed in Monica with her ringing laugh.

"What Sultan's daughter?" my uncle exclaimed testily. "I said nothing about a Sultan's daughter! Now, my goodness, can't you let me tell the story my own way? This young fellow was married already—sure, I told ye he was simple."

"Oh!" said Monica. She was disappointed.

"He was from Constantinople," my uncle said impatiently, articulating every syllable and emphasizing it with his fist while his forehead took on a certain resemblance to Crewe Junction. "And as well as that he was after travelling a good deal: Paris, Vienna, Rome; the whole blooming shoot! Oh, he was none of your stick-in-the-muds at all, none of your country yobs, but a jing-bang, up-to-the-minute, European-ized young Turk with plus-fours and horn-rimmed specs! He knew what he wanted; a fine, big, open town with wide streets and boulevards, big houses, libraries, schools and gardens; something he could show his butties from Paris."

My uncle paused and looked away into a corner of the room while the brows darkened over his deep fanatical eyes.

"But there was one class of people in this town," he went on gravely, "who didn't like what the Grand Vizier was up to. They were a very curious class of people. The like of them didn't exist outside Turkey. Muftis, they were called; men muftis and women muftis, and they lived in big houses like barracks all round the town. They never did anything for their living only go on pilgrimages to Mecca, and they were never happy only when they were spending millions building big, ugly old mosques or muezzins or whatever the devil they called them. A queer sort of life! Every evening up on top of their old chimney-stacks with their two arms out chanting 'La laha, il Allah.'

"So begor, the Grand Vizier had a look at his books and what did he notice, only that for ten years the muftis weren't paying a ha'penny in taxes. The poor people were paying it for them. And there and then he sat down and he sent them a—they have a word for it!"

"They have," said Monica, racking her brains.

"A fiat," said my uncle. "No, that's not it. A firman! I have it now. He sent them a firman, and what do you think the muftis said? They said the Grand Vizier was trying to make the poor people restless, taking their minds off chimney-stacks and giving them notions above their station."

"Ah, what ould guff you have!" Nora shouted from the kitchen.

"Trouble enough I'll have trying to root you out to work in the morning!"

"Well, one day," my uncle went on hastily, pretending not to hear, "one day while the Grand Vizier was sitting in state in his—his what you may call it—"

"Palace," whispered Josie.

"I forget the Turkish word but that's what it comes to—there was a knock at the door. The young Grand Vizier opens the door himself, and who does he see only the Grand Mufti; a big, fat, red-faced man with a high fez on him and an umbrella tucked under his arm. Like this!" And my uncle raised his nose superciliously and held his arm as though he were clutching an umbrella.

"I didn't know they had umbrellas in Turkey," said Monica suspiciously.

"Now, now, now, now," shouted my uncle in anguish, shaking his fist at her, "order please, order! Of course they had umbrellas. The umbrella was a sacred thing, like the fez. 'Tis distinctly mentioned in all the history books. Rolled up of course, under the arm, just as I say."

"Ah, this is a queer old story," Josie said restlessly, her great brown eyes fixed on him in alarm.

"But, God Almighty, when ye won't listen to me! How the blazes can I tell the story at all if ye keep on interrupting me? Now I'm after forgetting it all again. Where was I?"

"In the palace," Monica replied, a little subdued.

"I remember now." My uncle bowed his head and fingered his chin. " 'Twas when he opened the door and saw the Grand Mufti outside on the landing. There was a big stairs at each side."

"Like the Town Hall?" said Monica, who couldn't be repressed.

"Precisely! Only grander, of course, all gilt and fancy work. A little barbaric but very handsome, very handsome. Well, the Grand Vizier salaamed." My uncle raised his hands to his temples and bowed his head to his knees in an attitude of abject reverence. " 'Salaam, effendi,' he says, and he tried to take the umbrella and fez from the Grand Mufti. But the Grand Mufti gave a wicked little grunt and walked in past him with his fez on his pate.... Now, the Grand Vizier, as I explained to you, was a Constantinople man, and all Constantinople men have the divil's own temper. You wouldn't know you were after insulting one of them before you got a knife in your ribs; and in Constantinople to walk into another man's room with your fez on was as much as to say you thought he was no better than a Christian. But the Grand Vizier, being young and inexperienced, thought he'd better wait and see. So he salaamed again. 'Grand Mufti,' he says, 'what can the least of the servants of Allah do for you?' 'The least of the servants of Allah,' says the Grand Mufti, 'will have to stop preaching his subversive doctrines.' 'Most Excellent' "—my uncle joined his hands and bowed his head meekly—" 'utterance is obedience, as the Prophet says.' 'No more foreign notions!' says the Grand Mufti. 'No more infidel Christian ideas!' 'My Lord Steeplejack,' says the Grand Vizier, 'obedience is forgetfulness.' 'Well, remember it,' says the Grand Mufti, 'for one word more out of you about taxes, and so help me, Allah, off comes your head.'

"Now, I won't swear to the exact words," my uncle continued excitedly, clawing the air with his hands. "I heard the story so long ago, and Turkish is a very confusing language. But those were the sentiments—'off comes your head!' "

"Goodness!" cried Josie, so round-eyed with consternation that Monica and I both laughed outright at her. She stared from one to the other of us in confusion and blinked. My uncle smiled and paused to wipe his face in a large handkerchief.

"Well," he continued, "this, I needn't say, wasn't the sort of language the young Grand Vizier was accustomed to in Paris. He couldn't take his eyes off the—" He tapped his forehead.

"Fez," supplied Monica.

" 'Twas very high; a most remarkable headgear, only worn by the steeplejacks. 'Twas a terrible temptation, but what kept him back was that shocking passage in the Koran about what happens anyone that lays irreverent hands on a mufti's fez. Seven different damnations! But just at that moment the Grand Mufti thumped his umbrella on the floor and said, 'Rakaki skulati dinjji.' "

"What does that mean?" asked Josie with a frown.

" 'Nuff said,' " explained my uncle. "And then the Grand Vizier imagined what his pals in Paris would say if they saw him then, taking back-chat from a fat old mufti, and the Constantinople blood boiled in his veins. He opened the door behind him with his left hand and with his right he reached out and took hold of the fez—like this."

"And threw it out the door," cried Monica with her ringing laugh.

"Down the full length of the palace stairs and along the hall," said my uncle eagerly, leaning half across the bed towards her. "And two out-of-works that were keeping up the palace door, discussing tips for the two-thirty, nearly jumped out of their skins when it landed between them. Imagine it, at their very feet, the sacred fez of a mufti! But listen now! Listen to this! This is good! The next thing they saw shooting through the air on top of them was the Grand Mufti's umbrella. And then—then what do you think they saw?"

"The Grand Mufti himself?" gasped Josie.

"They saw the Grand Vizier dragging the Grand Mufti, body and bones, by the collar of the coat and the slack of the breeches across the landing. He was too heavy to throw, but the Grand Vizier laid him neatly on the top step and gave him one good push with his boot that sent him rolling down like a barrel. And then the Grand Vizier went in and slammed the door behind him, and even from the hall they could hear him laughing like a madman, to think he was the first Mussulman in history to get hold of a mufti by the slack of the breeches."

"And did they kill him then?" asked Josie eagerly.

"My goodness, can't you let me tell the story my own way?" my uncle said irritably. "They didn't kill him at all; 'twas out of fashion at the time, but the steeplejacks tipped the wink to the Caliph, and the Caliph had a few words with the Sultan, and the Sultan passed it on to all the provincial Emirs. That's the way things were done in Turkey then. They found it worked grand. Nothing crude, nothing bloodthirsty; nobody said a cross word; the thing was never mentioned again, and everyone was all salaams and smiles, but the Grand Vizier knew his goose was cooked."

My uncle brought out the last phrase with sudden savagery. He drew a deep breath through his nose, then rose and drew the curtains. I saw the sudden matchflare of the lighthouse spurting in the black water.

"Wisha, bad cess to you, you ould show, are you going to be there all night?" shouted Nora from the foot of the stairs.

"This minute, Nora," he replied with a laugh.

"And what happened him after?" asked Monica.

"Who?" he asked innocently. "Oh, the Grand Vizier? He took to drinking raki."

"Whiskey?"

"No raki. The same sort of thing but more powerful. It made him talk too much. He ended up as an old bore."

"Go on," said Monica quietly.

"But my goodness," he protested with his roguish laugh, "that's all there is. Nothing more. A simple story about a simple fellow. Ah, I didn't tell it right, though. I used to know it better—all the glamor of the East.... Well," he added briskly, "I'd better let ye get some sleep."

"That's not all of it," Monica said in the same quiet way.

"But, my goodness, girl," he shouted in exasperation, "when I tell you it is!"

He glared down at her, a tall, raking galoot of a man with his clenched fists held stiffly out.

"Ah, that's a queer old story," Josie said uneasily. "You used to have better stories than that."

"Tell us the rest of it," Monica said challengingly.

"I don't even know what you're talking about," he said in bewilderment. "What ails you? What more do you want?"

"The Grand Vizier had two daughters," she cried, kneeling up in the bed, her long bare arm stretched out accusingly.

"I never said he had two daughters," he snarled.

"But he had!"

"He hadn't."

"And I tell you he had."

"You're mixing it up, girl," he said savagely. "You're thinking of a different story altogether."

Then his head went up with a little jerk, he drew a deep breath through his nose and looked at the ceiling. His voice dropped to a whisper and faltered incredulously.

"One moment," he said as though he were speaking to himself. "My memory isn't what it was. Maybe you're right. Maybe he had a daughter. 'Pon my soul, Mon, I believe you are. One daughter at any rate. Now what did I hear about her?"

He sank back on the end of the bed and clutched his lean skull in his hands. When he spoke again it was in the same low, faltering voice as though recollecting something he'd heard many years before. I began to shiver all over violently. It was very queer.

"He had a daughter," he went on, "and she went to a school where the women muftis were teaching. But that must have been a long time after. She'd only have been a baby when all this occurred. Her father wouldn't tell her, of course. He wouldn't ask for pity. He'd be too proud. And she—'tis coming back to me!—she was attracted by a young fellow in the town, a shopkeeper's son. She was afraid to ask him to the house because she didn't want him to meet her disreputable old father—a respectable boy like that! The old Grand Vizier saw it all but he said nothing. He was too proud. Then the young fellow's father, the tool of the steeplejacks, the old bloodsucker, interfered; the boy took up with another girl, and the women muftis she was always in and out to told the Grand Vizier's daughter that 'twas only what she might expect on account of her father; a drunken, blasphemous old man, no better than a Christian. And the Grand Vizier's daughter . . ."—my uncle slowly raised his head, joined his hands and looked at the ceiling as though he were snatching the words out of the air—"the Grand Vizier's daughter mooned and cried for weeks on end . . . because she was . . . ashamed of her father."

"I'm not ashamed," Monica shouted angrily.

With eyes that seemed to see nothing, my uncle rose and moved towards the door like a man in a trance. For a moment I forgot that he was only an adorable, cranky, unreliable old gasbag of a man who had just been out boozing with Owney Mac in Riordan's disreputable pub on the quays. He looked like a king: a Richard or a Lear. He filled the room, the town, the very night with his presence. Suddenly he drew himself erect, head in air, and his voice rang like thunder through the house.

"God help us," he said bitterly, "she was ashamed of her father."

"They wouldn't say it to me," Monica shouted hysterically, the tears starting from her eyes. "I'd tear their eyes out, the smug old bitches!"

My uncle didn't reply but we heard his heavy tread down the stairs to the kitchen. Suddenly Josie sprang clean out of bed and rushed after him. Her great brown eyes were starting from her head with terror. Her face was like the face of a little child left alone in a strange place.

"Daddy, Daddy," she cried, "I'm not ashamed. Oh Daddy, I'll never do it again! Daddy, come back to me! Come back!"

Song Without Words

EVEN IF there were only two men left in the world and both of them saints they wouldn't be happy. One of them would be bound to try and improve the other. That is the nature of things.

I am not, of course, suggesting that either Brother Arnold or Brother Michael was a saint. In private life Brother Arnold was a postman, but as he had a great name as a cattle doctor they had put him in charge of the monastery cows. He had the sort of face you would expect to see advertising somebody's tobacco; a big, innocent, contented face with a pair of blue eyes that were always twinkling. According to the rule he was supposed to look sedate and go about in a composed and measured way, but he could not keep his eyes downcast for any length of time and wherever his eyes glanced they twinkled, and his hands slipped out of his long white sleeves and dropped some remark in sign language. Most of the monks were good at the deaf and dumb language; it was their way of getting round the rule of silence, and it was remarkable how much information they managed to pick up and pass on.

Now, one day it happened that Brother Arnold was looking for a bottle of castor oil and he remembered that he had lent it to Brother Michael, who was in charge of the stables. Brother Michael was a man he did not get on too well with; a dour, dull sort of man who kept to himself. He was a man of no great appearance, with a mournful wizened little face and a pair of weak red-rimmed eyes—for all the world the sort of man who, if you shaved off his beard, clapped a bowler hat on his head and a cigarette in his mouth, would need no other reference to get a job in a stable.

There was no sign of him about the stable yard, but this was only natural because he would not be wanted till the other monks returned from the fields, so Brother Arnold pushed in the stable door to look for the bottle himself. He did not see the bottle, but he saw something which made him wish he had not come. Brother Michael was hiding in one of the horse-boxes; standing against the partition with something hidden behind his back and wearing the look of a little boy who has been caught at the jam. Something told Brother Arnold that at that moment he was the most unwelcome man in the world. He grew red, waved his hand to indicate that he did not wish to be involved, and returned to his own quarters.

It came as a shock to him. It was plain enough that Brother Michael was up to some shady business, and Brother Arnold could not help wondering what it was. It was funny, he had noticed the same thing when he was in the world; it was always the quiet, sneaky fellows who were up to mischief. In chapel he looked at Brother Michael and got the impression that Brother Michael was looking at him, a furtive look to make sure he would not be noticed. Next day when they met in the yard he caught Brother Michael glancing at him and gave back a cold look and a nod.

The following day Brother Michael beckoned him to come over to the stables as though one of the horses was sick. Brother Arnold knew it wasn't that; he knew he was about to be given some sort of explanation and was curious to know what it would be. He was an inquisitive man; he knew it, and blamed himself a lot for it.

Brother Michael closed the door carefully after him and then leaned back against the jamb of the door with his legs crossed and his hands behind his back, a foxy pose. Then he nodded in the direction of the horse-box where Brother Arnold had almost caught him in the act, and raised his brows inquiringly. Brother Arnold nodded gravely. It was not an occasion he was likely to forget. Then Brother Michael put his hand up his sleeve and held out a folded newspaper. Brother Arnold shrugged his shoulders as though to say the matter had nothing to do with him, but the other man nodded and continued to press the news-paper on him.

He opened it without any great curiosity, thinking it might be some local paper Brother Michael smuggled in for the sake of the news from home and was now offering as the explanation of his own furtive behavior. He glanced at the name and then a great light broke on him. His whole face lit up as though an electric torch had been switched on behind, and finally he burst out laughing. He couldn't help himself. Brother Michael did not laugh but gave a dry little cackle which was as near as he ever got to laughing. The name of the paper was *The Irish Racing News*.

Now that the worst was over Brother Michael grew more relaxed. He pointed to a heading about the Curragh and then at himself. Brother Arnold shook his head, glancing at him expectantly as though he were hoping for another laugh. Brother Michael scratched his head for some indication of what he meant. He was a slow-witted man and had never been good at the sign talk. Then he picked up the sweeping brush and straddled it. He pulled up his skirts, stretched out his left hand holding the handle of the brush, and with his right began flog-ging the air behind him, a grim look on his leathery little face. Inquir-ingly he looked again and Brother Arnold nodded excitedly and put his thumbs up to show he understood. He saw now that the real reason Brother Michael had behaved so queerly was that he read racing papers on the sly and he did so because in private life he had been a jockey on the Curragh.

He was still laughing like mad, his blue eyes dancing, wishing only for an audience to tell it to, and then he suddenly remembered all the things he had thought about Brother Michael and bowed his head and beat his breast by way of asking pardon. Then he glanced at the paper again. A mischievous twinkle came into his eyes and he pointed the paper at himself. Brother Michael pointed back, a bit puzzled. Brother Arnold chuckled and stowed the paper up his sleeve. Then Brother Michael winked and gave the thumbs-up sign. In that slow cautious way of his he went down the stable and reached to the top of the wall where the roof sloped down on it. This, it seemed, was his hiding-hole. He took down several more papers and gave them to Brother Arnold.

For the rest of the day Brother Arnold was in the highest spirits. He winked and smiled at everyone till they all wondered what the joke was. He still pined for an audience. All that evening and long after he had retired to his cubicle he rubbed his hands and giggled with delight whenever he thought of it; it was like a window let into his loneliness; it gave him a warm, mellow feeling, as though his heart had expanded to embrace all humanity.

It was not until the following day that he had a chance of looking at the papers himself. He spread them on a rough desk under a feeble electric light bulb high in the roof. It was four years since he had seen a paper of any sort, and then it was only a scrap of local newspaper which one of the carters had brought wrapped about a bit of bread and butter. But Brother Arnold had palmed it, hidden it in his desk, and studied it as if it were a bit of a lost Greek play. He had never known until then the modern appetite for words—printed words, regardless of their meaning. This was merely a County Council wrangle about the appointment of seven warble-fly inspectors, but by the time he was done with it he knew it by heart.

So he did not just glance at the racing papers as a man would in the train to pass the time. He nearly ate them. Blessed words like fragments of tunes coming to him out of a past life; paddocks and point-to-points and two-year-olds, and again he was in the middle of a racecourse crowd on a spring day with silver streamers of light floating down the sky like heavenly bunting. He had only to close his eyes and he could see the refreshment tent again with the golden light leaking like spilt honey through the rents in the canvas, and the girl he had been in love with sitting on an upturned lemonade box. "Ah, Paddy," she had said, "sure there's bound to be racing in heaven!" She was fast, too fast for Brother Arnold, who was a steady-going fellow and had never got over the shock of discovering that all the time she had been running another man. But now all he could remember of her was her smile and the tone of her voice as she spoke the words which kept running through his head, and afterwards whenever his eyes met Brother Michael's he longed to give him a hearty slap on the back and say: "Michael, boy, there's bound to be racing in heaven." Then he grinned and Brother Michael, though he didn't hear the words or the tone of voice, without once losing his casual melancholy air, replied with a wall-faced flicker of the horny eyelid, a tick-tack man's signal, a real, expressionless, horsy look of complete understanding.

One day Brother Michael brought in a few papers. On one he pointed to the horses he had marked, on the other to the horses who had won. He showed no signs of his jubilation. He just winked, a leathery sort of wink, and Brother Arnold gaped as he saw the list of winners. It filled him with wonder and pride to think that when so many rich and clever people had lost, a simple little monk living hundreds of miles away could work it all out. The more he thought of it the more excited he grew. For one wild moment he felt it might be his duty to tell the Abbot, so that the monastery could have the full advantage of Brother Michael's intellect, but he realized that it wouldn't do. Even if Brother Michael could restore the whole abbey from top to bottom with his winnings, the ecclesiastical authorities would disapprove of it. But more than ever he felt the need of an audience.

He went to the door, reached up his long arm, and took down a loose stone from the wall above it. Brother Michael shook his head several times to indicate how impressed he was by Brother Arnold's ingenuity. Brother Arnold grinned. Then he took down a bottle and handed it to Brother Michael. The ex-jockey gave him a questioning look as though he were wondering if this wasn't cattle-medicine; his face did not change but he took out the cork and sniffed. Still his face did not change. All at once he went to the door, gave a quick glance up and a quick glance down and then raised the bottle to his lips. He reddened and coughed; it was good beer and he wasn't used to it. A shudder as of delight went through him and his little eyes grew moist as he watched Brother Arnold's throttle working on well-oiled hinges. The big man put the bottle back in its hiding-place and indicated by signs that Brother Michael could go there himself whenever he wanted and have a drink. Brother Michael shook his head doubtfully, but Brother Arnold nodded earnestly. His fingers moved like lightning while he explained how a farmer whose cow he had cured had it left in for him every week.

The two men were now fast friends. They no longer had any secrets from one another. Each knew the full extent of the other's little weakness and liked him the more for it. Though they couldn't speak to one another they sought out one another's company and whenever other things failed they merely smiled. Brother Arnold felt happier than he had felt for years. Brother Michael's successes made him want to try his hand, and whenever Brother Michael gave him a racing paper with his own selections marked, Brother Arnold gave it back with his, and they waited impatiently till the results turned up three or four days late. It was also a new lease of life to Brother Michael, for what comfort is it to a man if he has all the winners when not a soul in the world can ever know whether he has or not. He felt now that if only he could have a bob each way on a horse he would ask no more of life.

It was Brother Arnold, the more resourceful of the pair, who solved that difficulty. He made out dockets, each valued for so many Hail Marys, and the loser had to pay up in prayers for the other man's intention. It was an ingenious scheme and it worked admirably. At first Brother Arnold had a run of luck. But it wasn't for nothing that Brother Michael had had the experience; he was too tough to make a fool of himself even over a few Hail Marys, and everything he did was carefully planned. Brother Arnold began by imitating him, but the moment he struck it lucky he began to gamble wildly. Brother Michael had often seen it happen on the Curragh and remembered the fate of those it had happened to. Men he had known with big houses and cars were now cadging drinks in the streets of Dublin. It struck him that God had been very good to Brother Arnold in calling him to a monastic life where he could do no harm to himself or to his family.

And this, by the way, was quite uncalled for, because in the world Brother Arnold's only weakness had been for a bottle of stout and the only trouble he had ever caused his family was the discomfort of having to live with a man so good and gentle, but Brother Michael was rather given to a distrust of human nature, the sort of man who goes looking for a moral in everything even when there is no moral in it. He tried to make Brother Arnold take an interest in the scientific side of betting but the man seemed to treat it all as a great joke. A flighty sort of fellow! He bet more and more wildly with that foolish good-natured grin on his face, and after a while Brother Michael found himself being owed a deuce of a lot of prayers, which his literal mind insisted on translating into big houses and cars. He didn't like that either. It gave him scruples of conscience and finally turned him against betting altogether. He tried to get Brother Arnold to drop it, but as became an inventor, Brother Arnold only looked hurt and indignant, like a child who has been told to stop his play. Brother Michael had that weakness on his conscience too. It suggested that he was getting far too attached to Brother Arnold, as in fact he was. It would have been very difficult not to. There was something warm and friendly about the man which you couldn't help liking.

Then one day he went in to Brother Arnold and found him with a pack of cards in his hand. They were a very old pack which had more than served their time in some farmhouse, but Brother Arnold was looking at them in rapture. The very sight of them gave Brother Michael a turn. Brother Arnold made the gesture of dealing, half playfully, and the other shook his head sternly. Brother Arnold blushed and bit his lip but he persisted, seriously enough now. All the doubts Brother Michael had been having for weeks turned to conviction. This was the primrose path with a vengeance, one thing leading to another. Brother Arnold grinned and shuffled the deck; Brother Michael, biding his time, cut for deal and Brother Arnold won. He dealt two hands of five and showed the five of hearts as trump. He wanted to play twenty-five. Still waiting for a sign, Brother Michael looked at his own hand. His face grew grimmer. It was not the sort of sign he had expected but it was a sign all the same; four hearts in a bunch; the ace, jack, two other trumps, and the three of spades. An unbeatable hand. Was that luck? Was that coincidence or was it the Adversary himself, taking a hand and trying to draw him deeper in the mire?

He liked to find a moral in things, and the moral in this was plain, though it went to his heart to admit it. He was a lonesome, melancholy man and the horses had meant a lot to him in his bad spells. At times it had seemed as if they were the only thing that kept him sane. How could he face twenty, perhaps thirty, years more of life, never knowing what horses were running or what jockeys were up—Derby Day, Punchestown, Leopardstown, and the Curragh all going by while he knew no more of them than if he were already dead?

"O Lord," he thought bitterly, "a man gives up the whole world for You, his chance of a wife and kids, his home and his family, his friends and his job, and goes off to a bare mountain where he can't even tell his troubles to the man alongside him; and still he keeps something back, some little thing to remind him of what he gave up. With me 'twas the horses and with this man 'twas the sup of beer, and I dare say there are fellows inside who have a bit of a girl's hair hidden somewhere they can go and look at it now and again. I suppose we all have our little hiding-hole if the truth was known, but as small as it is, the whole world is in it, and bit by bit it grows on us again till the day You find us out."

Brother Arnold was waiting for him to play. He sighed and put his hand on the desk. Brother Arnold looked at it and at him. Brother Michael idly took away the spade and added the heart and still Brother Arnold couldn't see. Then Brother Michael shook his head and pointed to the floor. Brother Arnold bit his lip again as though he were on the point of crying, then threw down his own hand and walked to the other end of the cowhouse. Brother Michael left him so for a few moments. He could see the struggle going on in the man, could almost hear the Devil whisper in his ear that he (Brother Michael) was only an old woman—Brother Michael had heard that before; that life was long and a man might as well be dead and buried as not have some little innocent amusement—the sort of plausible whisper that put many a man on the gridiron. He knew, however hard it was now, that

Brother Arnold would be grateful to him in the other world. "Brother Michael," he would say, "I don't know what I'd ever have done without your example."

Then Brother Michael went up and touched him gently on the shoulder. He pointed to the bottle, the racing paper, and the cards. Brother Arnold fluttered his hands despairingly but he nodded. They gathered them up between them, the cards, the bottle, and the papers, hid them under their habits to avoid all occasion of scandal, and went off to confess their guilt to the Prior.

The Shepherds

FATHER WHELAN, the parish priest, called on his curate, Father Devine, one evening in autumn. Father Whelan was a tall, stout man with a broad chest, a head that didn't detach itself too clearly from the rest of his body, bushes of wild hair in his ears, and the rosy, innocent, good-natured face of a pious old countrywoman who made a living by selling eggs.

Devine was pale and worn-looking, with a gentle, dreamy face which had the soft gleam of an old piano keyboard, and he wore pince-nez perched on his unhappy, insignificant little nose. He and Whelan got on very well, considering—considering, that is to say, that Devine, who didn't know when he was well off, had fathered a dramatic society and an annual festival on Whelan, who had to put in an attendance at both; and that whenever the curate's name was mentioned, the parish priest, a charitable old man who never said an unkind word about anybody, tapped his forehead and said poor Devine's poor father was just the same. "A national teacher—sure, I knew him well, poor man!"

What Devine said about Whelan in that crucified drawl of his consisted mostly of the old man's words, with just the faintest inflection which isolated and underlined their fatuity. "I know some of the clergy are very opposed to books, but I like a book myself. I'm very fond of Zane Grey. Even poetry I like. Some of the poems you see on advertisements are very clever." And then Devine, who didn't often laugh, broke into a thin little cackle at the thought of Whelan representing the intellect and majesty of the Church. Devine was clever; he was lonely; he had a few good original water-colors and a bookcase full of works that were a constant source of wonder to Whelan. The old man stood in front of them now, his hat in his hands, lifting his warty old nose, while his eyes held a blank, hopeless, charitable look.

"Nothing there in your line, I'm afraid," said Devine with his maddeningly respectful, deprecating air, as if he put the parish priest's tastes on a level with his own.

" 'Tisn't that," said Whelan in a hollow faraway voice, "but I see you have a lot of foreign books. I suppose you know the languages well."

"Well enough to read," Devine said wearily, his handsome head on one side. "Why?"

"That foreign boat at the jetties," Whelan said without looking round. "What is it? French or German? There's terrible scandal about it."

"Is that so?" drawled Devine, his dark eyebrows going up his narrow, slanting forehead. "I didn't hear."

"Terrible," Whelan said mournfully, turning on him the full battery of his round, rosy old face and shining spectacles. "There's girls on it every night. I told Sullivan I'd go round tonight and give them the hunt. It occurred to me we might want someone to speak the language."

"I'm afraid my French would hardly rise to that," Devine said dryly, but he made no other objection, for, except for his old-womanly fits of virtue, Whelan was all right as parish priests go. Devine had had sad experience of how they could go. He put on his faded old coat and clamped his battered hat down over his pince-nez, and the two priests went down the Main Street to the post-office corner. It was deserted but for two out-of-works supporting either side of the door like ornaments, and a few others hanging hypnotized over the bridge while they studied the foaming waters of the weir. Devine had taken up carpentry himself in order to lure them into the technical classes, but it hadn't worked too well.

"The dear knows," he said thoughtfully, "you'd hardly wonder where those girls would go."

"Ah," said the parish priest, holding his head as though it were a flowerpot that might fall and break, "what do they want to go anywhere for? They're mad on pleasure. That girl Nora Fitzpatrick is one of them, and her mother at home dying."

"That might be her reason," said Devine, who visited the Fitzpatricks and knew what their home was like, with six children, and a mother dying of cancer.

"Ah, the girl's place is at home," said Whelan without rancor.

They went down past the technical school to the quays, these, too, deserted but for a coal boat and the big foreign grain boat, rising high and dark above the edge of the quay on a full tide. The town was historically reputed to have been a great place—well, about a hundred years ago—and had masses of gray stone warehouses, all staring with sightless eyes across the river. Two men who had been standing against the wall, looking up at the grain boat, came to join them. One was a tall, gaunt man with a long, sour, melancholy face which looked particularly hideous because it sported a youthful pink and white complexion and looked exactly like the face of an old hag, heavily made up. He wore a wig and carried a rolled-up umbrella behind his back. His name was Sullivan; he was the manager of a shop in town, and was forever in and out of the church. Devine hated him. The other, Joe Sheridan, was a small, fat, Jewish-looking man with dark skin and an excitable manner. Devine didn't dislike him so much. He was merely the inevitable local windbag, who got drunk on his own self-importance. As the four men met, Devine looked up and saw two young foreign faces, propped on their hands, peering at them over the edge of the boat.

"Well, boys?" asked Whelan.

"There's two aboard at present, father," Sullivan said in a shrill scolding voice. "Nora Fitzpatrick and Phillie O'Malley."

"Well, you'd better go aboard and tell them come off," Whelan said tranquilly.

"I wonder what our legal position is, father?" Sheridan asked, scowling. "I mean, have we any sort of *locus standi*?"

"Oh, in the event of your being stabbed, I think they could be tried," Devine replied with bland malice. "Of course, I don't know if your wife and children could claim compensation."

The malice was lost on Whelan, who laid one hairy paw on Devine's shoulder and the other on Sheridan's to calm the fears of both. He exuded a feeling of pious confidence. It was the eggs all over again. God would look after His hens.

"Never mind about the legal position," he said paternally. "I'll be answerable for that."

"That's good enough for me, father," Sheridan said, and, pulling his hat down over his eyes and joining his hands behind his back, he strode up the gangway, with the air of a detective in a bad American film, while Sullivan, clutching his umbrella against the small of his back, followed him, head in air. A lovely pair, Devine thought. They went up to the two sailors.

"Two girls," Sullivan said in his shrill, scolding voice. "We're looking for the two girls that came aboard a half an hour ago."

Neither of the sailors stirred. One of them turned his eyes lazily and looked Sullivan up and down.

"Not this boat," he said impudently. "The other one. There's always girls on that."

Then Sheridan, who had glanced downstairs through an open doorway, began to beckon.

"Phillie O'Malley!" he shouted in a raucous voice. "Father Whelan and Father Devine are out here. Come on! They want to talk to you."

"Tell her if she doesn't come I'll go and bring her," the parish priest called anxiously.

"He says if you don't he'll come and bring you," repeated Sheridan.

Nothing happened for a moment or two. Then a tall girl with a consumptive face emerged on deck with a handkerchief pressed to her eyes. Devine couldn't help feeling sick at the sight of her wretched finery, her cheap hat and bead necklace. He was angry and ashamed and a cold fury of sarcasm rose in him. The Good Shepherd indeed!

"Come on, lads," the parish priest said encouragingly. "What about the second one?"

Sheridan, flushed with triumph, was about to disappear down the companionway when one of the sailors gave him a heave which threw him to the edge of the ship. Then the sailor stood nonchalantly in the doorway, blocking the way. Whelan's face grew red with anger and he only waited for the girl to leave the gangway before going up himself. Devine paused to whisper a word to her.

"Get off home as quick as you can, Phillie," he said, "and don't upset yourself."

At the tenderness in his voice she took the handkerchief from her face and began to weep in earnest. Then Devine went up after the others. It was a ridiculous scene with the fat old priest, his head in the air, trembling with senile anger and astonishment.

"Get out of the way at once!" he said.

"Don't be a fool, man!" Devine said with quiet ferocity. "They're not accustomed to being spoken to like that. If you got a knife in your ribs, it would be your own fault. We want to talk to the captain." And then, bending forward with his eyebrows raised in a humble, deprecating manner, he asked: "I wonder if you'd be good enough to tell the captain we'd like to see him."

The sailor who was blocking their way looked at him for a moment and then nodded in the direction of the upper deck. Taking his parish priest's arm and telling Sullivan and Sheridan to stay behind, Devine went up the ship. When they had gone a little way the second sailor passed them out, knocked at a door, and said something Devine did not catch. Then, with a scowl, he held open the door for them. The captain was a middle-aged man with a heavily lined, sallow face, close-cropped black hair, and a black mustache. There was something Mediterranean about his air.

"Bonsoir, messieurs," he said in a loud, businesslike tone which did not conceal a certain nervousness.

"Bonsoir, monsieur le capitaine," Devine said with the same plaintive, ingratiating air as he bowed and raised his battered old hat. "Est-ce que nous vous dérangeons?"

"Mais, pas du tout; entrez, je vous prie," the captain said heartily, clearly relieved by Devine's amiability. "Vous parlez français alors?"

"Un peu, monsieur le capitaine," Devine said deprecatingly. "Vous savez, ici en Irlande on n'a pas souvent l'occasion."

"Ah, well," the captain said cheerfully, "I speak English too, so we will understand one another. Won't you sit down?"

"I wish my French were anything like as good as your English," Devine said as he sat.

"One travels a good deal," the captain replied with a flattered air. "You'll have a drink? Some brandy, eh?"

"I'd be delighted, of course," Devine said regretfully, "but I'm afraid we have a favor to ask you first."

"A favor?" the captain said enthusiastically. "Certainly, certainly. Anything you like. Have a cigar?"

"Never smoke them," Whelan said in a dull stubborn voice, looking first at the cigar-case and then looking away; and, to mask his rudeness, Devine, who never smoked cigars, took one and lit it.

"I'd better explain who we are," he said, sitting back, his head on one side, his long, delicate hands hanging over the arms of the chair. "This is Father Whelan, the parish priest. My name is Devine; I'm the curate."

"And mine," the captain said proudly, "is Platon Demarrais. I bet you never before heard of a fellow called Platon?"

"A relation of the philosopher, I presume," said Devine.

"The very man! And I have two brothers, Zenon and Plotin."

"What an intellectual family!"

"Pagans, of course," the captain explained complacently. "Greeks. My father was a schoolteacher. He called us that to annoy the priest. He was anticlerical."

"That's not confined to schoolteachers in France," Devine said dryly. "My father was a schoolteacher, but he never got round to calling me Aristotle. Which might be as well," he added with a chuckle. "At any rate, there's a girl called Fitzpatrick on the ship, with some sailor, I suppose. She's one of Father Whelan's parishioners, and we'd be very grateful to you if you'd have her put off."

"Speak for yourself, father," said Whelan, raising his stubborn old peasant head and quelling fraternization with a glance. "I wouldn't be grateful to any man for doing what 'tis only his duty to do."

"Then, perhaps you'd better explain your errand yourself, Father Whelan," Devine said with an abnegation not far removed from waspishness.

"I think so, father," Whelan said stubbornly. "That girl, Captain Whatever-your-name-is," he went on slowly, "has no business to be on your ship at all. It is no place for a young unmarried girl to be at this hour of night."

"I don't understand," the captain said uneasily, with a sideway glance at Devine. "Is she a relative of yours?"

"No, sir," Whelan said emphatically. "She's nothing whatever to me."

"Then I don't see what you want her for," said the captain.

"That's as I'd expect, sir," Whelan said stolidly, studying his nails.

"Oh, for Heaven's sake!" exclaimed Devine, exasperated by the old man's boorishness. "You see, captain," he said patiently, bending forward with his worried air, his head tilted back as though he feared his pince-nez might fall off, "this girl is one of Father Whelan's parishioners. She's not a very good girl—not that I mean there's much harm in her," he added hastily, catching a note of unction in his own tone which embarrassed him, "but she's a bit wild. It's Father Whelan's duty to keep her as far as he can from temptation. He is the shepherd, and she is one of his stray sheep," he added with a faint smile at his own eloquence.

The captain bent forward and touched him lightly on the knee.

"You're a funny race," he said with interest. "I've travelled the whole world and met with Englishmen everywhere, and I will never understand you. Never!"

"We're not English, man," Whelan said with the first trace of interest he had so far displayed. "Don't you know what country you're in? This is Ireland."

"Same thing," said the captain.

"It is not the same thing," said Whelan.

"Surely, captain," Devine protested gently with his head cocked, sizing up his man, "we admit some distinction?"

"Distinction?" the captain said. "Pooh!"

"At the Battle of the Boyne you fought for us," Devine said persuasively. "We fought for you at Fontenoy and Ramillies.

> "When on Ramillies bloody field
> The baffled French were forced to yield,
> The victor Saxon backward reeled
> Before the shock of Clare's Dragoons."

He recited the lines with the same apologetic smile he had worn when speaking of sheep and shepherds, as though to excuse his momentary lapse into literature, but the captain waved him aside impatiently.

"Your beard!" he said with a groan and a shrug. "I know all that. You call yourselves Irish, and the others call themselves Scotch, but you are all English. There is no difference. It is always the same; always women, always hypocrisy; always the plaster saint. Who is this girl? The curé's daughter?"

"The curé's daughter?" Devine exclaimed in surprise.

"Whose daughter?" asked Whelan with his mouth hanging.

"Yours, I gather," Devine said dryly.

"Well, well, well!" the old man said blushing. "What sort of upbringing do they have? Does he even know we can't get married?"

"I should say he takes it for granted," replied Devine over his shoulder, more dryly even than before. "Elle n'est pas sa fille," he added with amusement to the captain.

"C'est sûr?"

"C'est certain."

"Sa maîtresse alors?"

"Ni cela non plus," Devine replied evenly with only the faintest of smiles on the worn shell of his face.

"Ah, bon, bon, bon!" the captain exclaimed excitedly, springing from his seat and striding about the cabin, scowling and waving his arms. "Bon. C'est bon. Vous vous moquez de moi, monsieur le curé. Comprenez donc, c'est seulement par politesse que j'ai voulu faire croire que c'était sa fille. On voit bien que le vieux est jaloux. Est-ce que je n'ai pas vu les flics qui surveillent mon bateau toute la semaine? Mais croyez-moi, monsieur, je me fiche de lui et de ses agents."

"He seems to be very excited," Whelan said with distaste. "What is he saying?"

"I'm trying to persuade him that she isn't your mistress," Devine couldn't refrain from saying with quiet malice.

"My what?"

"Your mistress; the woman you live with. He says you're jealous and that you've had detectives watching his ship for a week."

The blush which had risen to the old man's face began to spread to his neck and ears, and when he spoke, his voice quavered with emotion.

"Well, well, well!" he said. "We'd better go home, Devine. 'Tis no good talking to that man. He's not right in the head."

"He probably thinks the same of us," Devine said as he rose. "Venez manger demain soir et je vous expliquerai tout," he added to the captain.

"Je vous remercie, monsieur," the captain replied with a shrug, "mais je n'ai pas besoin d'explications. Il n'y a rien d'inattendu, mais vous en faites toute une histoire." He clapped his hand jovially on Devine's shoulder and almost embraced him. "Naturellement je vous rends la fille, parce que vous la demandez, mais comprenez bien que je le fais à cause de vous, et non pas à cause de monsieur et de ses agents." He drew himself up to his full height and glared at the parish priest, who stood in a dumb stupor.

"Oh, quant à moi," Devine said with weary humor, "vous feriez mieux en l'emmenant où vous allez. Et moi-même aussi."

"Quoi?" shouted the captain in desperation, clutching his forehead. "Vous l'aimez aussi?"

"No, no, no, no," Devine said good-humoredly, patting him on the arm. "It's all too complicated. I wouldn't try to understand it if I were you."

"What's he saying now?" asked Whelan with sour suspicion.

"Oh, he seems to think she's my mistress as well," Devine replied pleasantly. "He thinks we're sharing her, so far as I can see."

"Come on, come on!" said Whelan despairingly, making for the gangway. "My goodness, even I never thought they were as bad as that. And we sending missions to the blacks!"

Meanwhile, the captain had rushed aft and shouted down the stairway. The second girl appeared, small, plump, and weeping too, and the captain, quite moved, slapped her encouragingly on the shoulder and said something in a gruff voice which Devine suspected must be in the nature of advice to choose younger lovers for the future. Then the captain went up bristling to Sullivan, who stood by the gangway, leaning on his folded umbrella, and with fluttering hands and imperious nods ordered him off the vessel.

"Allez-vous-en!" he said curtly. "Allez, allez, allez!"

Sullivan and Sheridan went first. Dusk had crept suddenly along the quays and lay heaped there the color of blown sand. Over the bright river mouth, shining under a bank of dark cloud, a star twinkled. "The star that bids the shepherd fold," Devine thought with sad humor. He felt hopeless and lost, as though he were returning to the prison-house of his youth. The parish priest preceded him down the gangway with his old woman's dull face sunk in his broad chest. At the foot he stopped and gazed back at the captain, who was scowling fiercely at him over the ship's side.

"Anyway," he said heavily, "thanks be to the Almighty God, your accursed race is withering off the face of the earth."

Devine, with a bitter smile, raised his battered old hat and pulled the skirts of his coat about him as he stepped on the gangway.

"Vous viendrez demain, monsieur le capitaine?" he asked in his most ingratiating tone.

"Avec plaisir. A demain, monsieur le berger," replied the captain with a knowing look.

The Long Road to Ummera

Stay for me there. I will not fail
To meet thee in that hollow vale.

ALWAYS in the evenings you saw her shuffle up the road to Miss O.'s for her little jug of porter, a shapeless lump of an old woman in a plaid shawl, faded to the color of snuff, that dragged her head down on to her bosom where she clutched its folds in one hand; a canvas apron and a pair of men's boots without laces. Her eyes were puffy and screwed up in tight little buds of flesh and her rosy old face that might have been carved out of a turnip was all crumpled with blindness. The old heart was failing her, and several times she would have to rest, put down the jug, lean against the wall, and lift the weight of the shawl off her head. People passed; she stared at them humbly; they saluted her; she turned her head and peered after them for minutes on end. The rhythm of life had slowed down in her till you could scarcely detect its faint and sluggish beat. Sometimes from some queer instinct of shyness she turned to the wall, took a snuffbox from her bosom, and shook out a pinch on the back of her swollen hand. When she sniffed it it smeared her nose and upper lip and spilled all over her old black blouse. She raised the hand to her eyes and looked at it closely and reproachfully, as though astonished that it no longer served her properly. Then she dusted herself, picked up the old jug again, scratched herself against her clothes, and shuffled along close by the wall, groaning aloud.

When she reached her own house, which was a little cottage in a terrace, she took off her boots, and herself and the old cobbler who lodged with her turned out a pot of potatoes on the table, stripping them with their fingers and dipping them in the little mound of salt while they took turn and turn about with the porter jug. He was a lively and philosophic old man called Johnny Thornton.

After their supper they sat in the firelight, talking about old times in the country and long-dead neighbors, ghosts, fairies, spells, and charms. It always depressed her son, finding them together like that when he called with her monthly allowance. He was a well-to-do businessman with a little grocery shop in the South Main Street and a little house in Sunday's Well, and nothing would have pleased him better than that his mother should share all the grandeur with him, the carpets and the china and the chiming clocks. He sat moodily between them, stroking his long jaw, and wondering why they talked so much about death in the old-fashioned way, as if it was something that made no difference at all.

"Wisha, what pleasure do ye get out of old talk like that?" he asked one night.

"Like what, Pat?" his mother asked with her timid smile.

"My goodness," he said, "ye're always at it. Corpses and graves and people that are dead and gone."

"Arrah, why wouldn't we?" she replied, looking down stiffly as she tried to button the open-necked blouse that revealed her old breast. "Isn't there more of us there than here?"

"Much difference 'twill make to you when you won't know them or see them!" he exclaimed.

"Oye, why wouldn't I know them?" she cried angrily. "Is it the Twomeys of Lackroe and the Driscolls of Ummera?"

"How sure you are we'll take you to Ummera!" he said mockingly.

"Och aye, Pat," she asked, shaking herself against her clothes with her humble stupid wondering smile, "and where else would you take me?"

"Isn't our own plot good enough for you?" he asked. "Your own son and your grandchildren?"

"Musha, indeed, is it in the town you want to bury me?" She shrugged herself and blinked into the fire, her face growing sour and obstinate. "I'll go back to Ummera, the place I came from."

"Back to the hunger and misery we came from," Pat said scornfully.

"Back to your father, boy."

"Ay, to be sure, where else? But my father or grandfather never did for you what I did. Often and often I scoured the streets of Cork for a few ha'pence for you."

"You did, amossa, you did, you did," she admitted, looking into the fire and shaking herself. "You were a good son to me."

"And often I did it and the belly falling out of me with hunger," Pat went on, full of self-pity.

" 'Tis true for you," she mumbled, " 'tis, 'tis, 'tis true. 'Twas often and often you had to go without it. What else could you do and the way we were left?"

"And now our grave isn't good enough for you," he complained. There was real bitterness in his tone. He was an insignificant little man and jealous of the power the dead had over her.

She looked at him with the same abject, half-imbecile smile, the wrinkled old eyes almost shut above the Mongolian cheekbones, while with a swollen old hand, like a pot-stick, it had so little life in it, she smoothed a few locks of yellow-white hair across her temples—a trick she had when troubled.

"Musha, take me back to Ummera, Pat," she whined. "Take me back to my own. I'd never rest among strangers. I'd be rising and drifting."

"Ah, foolishness, woman!" he said with an indignant look. "That sort of thing is gone out of fashion."

"I won't stop here for you," she shouted hoarsely in sudden, impotent fury, and she rose and grasped the mantelpiece for support.

"You won't be asked," he said shortly.

"I'll haunt you," she whispered tensely, holding on to the mantelpiece and bending down over him with a horrible grin.

"And that's only more of the foolishness," he said with a nod of contempt. "Haunts and fairies and spells."

She took one step towards him and stood, plastering down the two little locks of yellowing hair, the half-dead eyes twitching and blinking in the candlelight, and the swollen crumpled face with the cheeks like cracked enamel.

"Pat," she said, "the day we left Ummera you promised to bring me back. You were only a little gorsoon that time. The neighbors gathered round me and the last word I said to them and I going down the road was: 'Neighbors, my son Pat is after giving me his word and he'll bring me back to ye when my time comes.' ... That's as true as the Almighty God is over me this night. I have everything ready." She went to the shelf under the stairs and took out two parcels. She seemed to be speaking to herself as she opened them gloatingly, bending down her head in the feeble light of the candle. "There's the two brass candlesticks and the blessed candles alongside them. And there's my shroud aired regular on the line."

"Ah, you're mad, woman," he said angrily. "Forty miles! Forty miles into the heart of the mountains!"

She suddenly shuffled towards him on her bare feet, her hand raised clawing the air, her body like her face blind with age. Her harsh croaking old voice rose to a shout.

"I brought you from it, boy, and you must bring me back. If 'twas the last shilling you had and you and your children to go to the poorhouse after, you must bring me back to Ummera. And not by the short road either! Mind what I say now! The long road! The long road to Ummera round the lake, the way I brought you from it. I lay a heavy curse on you this night if you bring me the short road over the hill. And ye must stop by the ash tree at the foot of the boreen where ye can see my little house and say a prayer for all that were ever old in it and all that played on the floor. And then—Pat! Pat Driscoll! Are you listening? Are you listening to me, I say?"

She shook him by the shoulder, peering down into his long miserable face to see how was he taking it.

"I'm listening," he said with a shrug.

"Then"—her voice dropped to a whisper—"you must stand up overright the neighbors and say—remember now what I'm telling you!—'Neighbors, this is Abby, Batty Heige's daughter, that kept her promise to ye at the end of all.' "

She said it lovingly, smiling to herself, as if it were a bit of an old song, something she went over and over in the long night. All West Cork was in it: the bleak road over the moors to Ummera, the smooth gray pelts of the hills with the long spider's web of the fences ridging them, drawing the scarecrow fields awry, and the whitewashed cottages, poker-faced between their little scraps of holly bushes looking this way and that out of the wind.

"Well, I'll make a fair bargain with you," said Pat as he rose. Without seeming to listen she screwed up her eyes and studied his weak melancholy face. "This house is a great expense to me. Do what I'm always asking you. Live with me and I'll promise I'll take you back to Ummera."

"Oye, I will not," she replied sullenly, shrugging her shoulders helplessly, an old sack of a woman with all the life gone out of her.

"All right," said Pat. " 'Tis your own choice. That's my last word; take it or leave it. Live with me and Ummera for your grave, or stop here and a plot in the Botanics."

She watched him out the door with shoulders hunched about her ears. Then she shrugged herself, took out her snuffbox and took a pinch.

"Arrah, I wouldn't mind what he'd say," said Johnny. "A fellow like that would change his mind tomorrow."

"He might and he mightn't," she said heavily, and opened the back door to go out to the yard. It was a starry night and they could hear the noise of the city below them in the valley. She raised her eyes to the bright sky over the back wall and suddenly broke into a cry of loneliness and helplessness.

"Oh, oh, oh, 'tis far away from me Ummera is tonight above any other night, and I'll die and be buried here, far from all I ever knew and the long roads between us."

Of course old Johnny should have known damn well what she was up to the night she made her way down to the cross, creeping along beside the railings. By the blank wall opposite the lighted pub Dan Regan, the jarvey, was standing by his old box of a covered car with his pipe in his gob. He was the jarvey all the old neighbors went to. Abby beckoned to him and he followed her into the shadow of a gateway overhung with ivy. He listened gravely to what she had to say, sniffing and nodding, wiping his nose in his sleeve, or crossing the pavement to hawk his nose and spit in the channel, while his face with its drooping mustaches never relaxed its discreet and doleful expression.

Johnny should have known what that meant and why old Abby, who had always been so open-handed, sat before an empty grate sooner than light a fire, and came after him on Fridays for the rent, whether he had it or not, and even begrudged him the little drop of porter which had always been give and take between them. He knew himself it was a change before death and that it all went into the wallet in her bosom. At night in her attic she counted it by the light of her candle and when the coins dropped from her lifeless fingers he heard her roaring like an old cow as she crawled along the naked boards, sweeping them blindly with her palms. Then he heard the bed creak as she tossed about in it, and the rosary being taken from the bedhead, and the old voice rising and falling in prayer; and sometimes when a high wind blowing up the river roused him before dawn he could hear her muttering: a mutter and then a yawn; the scrape of a match as she peered at the alarm clock—the endless nights of the old—and then the mutter of prayer again.

But Johnny in some ways was very dense, and he guessed nothing till the night she called him and, going to the foot of the stairs with a candle in his hand, he saw her on the landing in her flour-bag shift, one hand clutching the jamb of the door while the other clawed wildly at her few straggly hairs.

"Johnny!" she screeched down at him, beside herself with excitement. "He was here."

"Who was there?" he snarled back, still cross with sleep.

"Michael Driscoll, Pat's father."

"Ah, you were dreaming, woman," he said in disgust. "Go back to your bed in God's holy name."

"I was not dreaming," she cried. "I was lying broad awake, saying my beads, when he come in the door, beckoning me. Go down to Dan Regan's for me, Johnny."

"I will not, indeed, go down to Dan Regan's for you. Do you know what hour of night it is?"

" 'Tis morning."

" 'Tis. Four o'clock! What a thing I'd do! . . . Is it the way you're feeling bad?" he added with more consideration as he mounted the stairs. "Do you want him to take you to hospital?"

"Oye, I'm going to no hospital," she replied sullenly, turning her back on him and thumping into the room again. She opened an old chest of drawers and began fumbling in it for her best clothes, her bonnet and cloak.

"Then what the blazes do you want Dan Regan for?" he snarled in exasperation.

"What matter to you what I want him for?" she retorted with senile suspicion. "I have a journey to go, never you mind where."

"Ach, you old oinseach, your mind is wandering," he cried. "There's a divil of a wind blowing up the river. The whole house is shaking. That's what you heard. Make your mind easy now and go back to bed."

"My mind is not wandering," she shouted. "Thanks be to the Almighty God I have my senses as good as you. My plans are made. I'm going back now where I came from. Back to Ummera."

"Back to where?" Johnny asked in stupefaction.

"Back to Ummera."

"You're madder than I thought. And do you think or imagine Dan Regan will drive you?"

"He will drive me then," she said, shrugging herself as she held an old petticoat to the light. "He's booked for it any hour of the day or night."

"Then Dan Regan is madder still."

"Leave me alone now," she muttered stubbornly, blinking and shrugging. "I'm going back to Ummera and that was why my old comrade came for me. All night and every night I have my beads wore out, praying the Almighty God and His Blessed Mother not to leave me die among strangers. And now I'll leave my old bones on a high hilltop in Ummera."

Johnny was easily persuaded. It promised to be a fine day's outing and a story that would delight a pub, so he made tea for her and after that went down to Dan Regan's little cottage, and before smoke showed from any chimney on the road they were away. Johnny was hopping about the car in his excitement, leaning out, shouting through the window of the car to Dan and identifying big estates that he hadn't seen for years. When they were well outside the town, himself and Dan went in for a drink, and while they were inside the old woman dozed. Dan Regan roused her to ask if she wouldn't take a drop of something and at first she didn't know who he was and then she asked where they were and peered out at the public-house and the old dog sprawled asleep in the sunlight before the door. But when next they halted she had fallen asleep again, her mouth hanging open and her breath coming in noisy gusts. Dan's face grew gloomier. He looked hard at her and spat. Then he took a few turns about the road, lit his pipe and put on the lid.

"I don't like her looks at all, Johnny," he said gravely. "I done wrong. I see that now. I done wrong."

After that, he halted every couple of miles to see how she was and Johnny, threatened with the loss of his treat, shook her and shouted at her. Each time Dan's face grew graver. He walked gloomily about the road, clearing his nose and spitting in the ditch. "God direct me!" he said solemnly. " 'Twon't be wishing to me. Her son is a powerful man. He'll break me yet. A man should never interfere between families. Blood is thicker than water. The Regans were always unlucky."

When they reached the first town he drove straight to the police barrack and told them the story in his own peculiar way.

"Ye can tell the judge I gave ye every assistance," he said in a reasonable brokenhearted tone. "I was always a friend of the law. I'll keep nothing back—a pound was the price agreed. I suppose if she dies 'twill be manslaughter. I never had hand, act or part in politics. Sergeant Daly at the Cross knows me well."

When Abby came to herself she was in a bed in the hospital. She began to fumble for her belongings and her shrieks brought a crowd of unfortunate old women about her.

"Whisht, whisht, whisht!" they said. "They're all in safe-keeping. You'll get them back."

"I want them now," she shouted, struggling to get out of bed while they held her down. "Leave me go, ye robbers of hell! Ye night-walking rogues, leave me go. Oh, murder, murder! Ye're killing me."

At last an old Irish-speaking priest came and comforted her. He left her quietly saying her beads, secure in the promise to see that she was buried in Ummera no matter what anyone said. As darkness fell, the beads dropped from her swollen hands and she began to mutter to herself in Irish. Sitting about the fire, the ragged old women whispered and groaned in sympathy. The Angelus rang out from a nearby church. Suddenly Abby's voice rose to a shout and she tried to lift herself on her elbow.

"Ah, Michael Driscoll, my friend, my kind comrade, you didn't forget me after all the long years. I'm a long time away from you but I'm coming at last. They tried to keep me away, to make me stop among foreigners in the town, but where would I be at all without you and all the old friends? Stay for me, my treasure! Stop and show me the way.... Neighbors," she shouted, pointing into the shadows, "that man there is my own husband, Michael Driscoll. Let ye see he won't leave me to find my way alone. Gather round me with yeer lanterns, neighbors, till I see who I have. I know ye all. 'Tis only the sight that's weak on me. Be easy now, my brightness, my own kind loving comrade. I'm coming. After all the long years I'm on the road to you at last...."

It was a spring day full of wandering sunlight when they brought her the long road to Ummera, the way she had come from it forty years before. The lake was like a dazzle of midges; the shafts of the sun revolving like a great millwheel poured their cascades of milky sunlight over the hills and the little whitewashed cottages and the little black mountain cattle among the scarecrow fields. The hearse stopped at the foot of the lane that led to the roofless cabin just as she had pictured it to herself in the long nights, and Pat, looking more melancholy than ever, turned to the waiting neighbors and said:

"Neighbors, this is Abby, Batty Heige's daughter, that kept her promise to ye at the end of all."

The Cheapjack

EVERYONE was sorry after Sam Higgins, the headmaster. Sam was a right good skin, one of the decentest men in Ireland, but too honest.

He was a small fat man with a round, rosy, good-natured face, a high bald brow, and specs. He wore a bowler hat and a stiff collar the hottest day God sent, because no matter how sociable he might be, he never entirely forgot his dignity. He lived with his sister, Delia, in a house by the station and suffered a good deal from nerves and dyspepsia. The doctors tried to make out that they were one and the same thing but they weren't; they worked on entirely different circuits. When it was the nerves were bad Sam went on a skite. The skite, of course, was good for the nerves but bad for the dyspepsia, and for months afterwards he'd be on a diet and doing walks in the country. The walks, on the other hand, were good for the dyspepsia but played hell with the nerves, so Sam had to try and take the harm out of them by dropping into Johnny Desmond's on the way home for a pint. Johnny had a sort of respect for him as an educated man, which Johnny wasn't, and a sort of contempt for him as a man who, for all his education, couldn't keep his mind to himself—an art Johnny was past master of.

One day they happened to be discussing the Delea case, which Johnny, a cautious, religious man, affected to find peculiar. There was nothing peculiar about it. Father Ring had landed another big fish; that was all. Old Jeremiah Delea had died and left everything to the Church, nothing to his wife and family. There was to be law about that, according to what Johnny had heard—ah, a sad business, a peculiar business! But Sam, who hated Father Ring with a hate you might describe as truly religious, rejoiced.

"Fifteen thousand, I hear," he said with an ingenuous smile.

"So I believe," said Johnny with a scowl. "A man that couldn't write his own name for you! Now what do you say to the education?"

"Oh, what I always said," replied Sam with his usual straightforwardness. " 'Tis nothing only a hindrance."

"Ah, I wouldn't go so far as that," said Johnny, who, though he tended to share this view, was too decent to criticize any man's job to his face, and anyway had a secret admiration for the polish which a good education can give. "If he might have held onto the wireless shares he'd be good for another five thousand. I suppose that's where the education comes in."

Having put in a good word for culture, Johnny now felt it was up to him to say something in the interests of religion. There was talk about Father Ring and Johnny didn't like it. He didn't think it was lucky. Years of observation of anticlericals in his pub had convinced Johnny that none of them ever got anywhere.

"Of course, old Jerry was always a very good-living man," he added doubtfully.

"He was," Sam said dryly. "Very fond of the Children of Mary."

"That so?" said Johnny, as if he didn't know what a Child of Mary would be.

"Young and old," Sam said enthusiastically. "They were the poor man's great hobbies."

That was Sam all out; too outspoken, too independent! No one like that ever got anywhere. Johnny went to the shop door and looked after him as he slouched up Main Street with his sailor's roll and his bowler hat and wondered to himself that an educated man wouldn't have more sense.

DELIA and Mrs. MacCann, the new teacher in the girl's school, were sitting on deck chairs in the garden when Sam got back. It did more than the pint to rouse his spirits after that lonesome rural promenade. Mrs. MacCann was small, gay and go-as-you-please. Sam thought her the pleasantest woman he had ever met and would have told her as much only that she was barely out of mourning for her first husband. He felt it was no time to approach any woman with proposals of marriage, which showed how little Sam knew of women.

"How're ye, Nancy?" he cried heartily, holding out a fat paw.

"Grand, Sam," she replied, sparkling with pleasure. "How's the body?"

"So-so," said Sam. He took off his coat and squatted to give the lawnmower a drop of oil. "As pleasant a bit of news as I heard this long time I'm after hearing today."

"What's that, Sam?" Delia asked in her high-pitched, fluting voice.

"Chrissie Delea that's going to law with Ring over the legacy."

"Ah, you're not serious, Sam?" cried Nancy.

"Oh, begod I am," growled Sam. "She has Canty the solicitor in

Asragh on to it. Now Ring will be having Sister Mary Milkmaid and the rest of them making novenas to soften Chrissie's hard heart. By God I tell you 'twill take more than novenas to do that."

"But will she get it, Sam?" asked Nancy.

"Why wouldn't she get it?"

"Anyone that got money out of a priest ought to have a statue put up to her."

"She'll get it all right," Sam said confidently. "After all the other scandals the bishop will never let it go to court. Sure, old Jerry was off his rocker years before he made that will. I'd give evidence myself that I saw him stopping little girls on their way from school to try and look up their clothes."

"Oh, God, Sam, the waste of it!" said Nancy with a chuckle. "Anyway, we'll have rare gas with a lawcase and a new teacher."

"A new what?" asked Sam, stopping dead in his mowing.

"Why? Didn't Ormond tell you he got the shift?" she asked in surprise.

"No, Nancy, he did not," Sam said gravely.

"But surely, Ormond would never keep a thing like that from you?"

"He wouldn't," said Sam, "and I'll swear he knows nothing about it. Where did you hear it?"

"Plain Jane told me." (She meant Miss Daly, the head.)

"And she got it from Ring, I suppose," Sam said broodingly. "And Ring was in Dublin for the last couple of days. Now we know what he was up for. You didn't hear who was coming in Ormond's place?"

"I didn't pay attention, Sam," Nancy said with a frown. "But she said he was from Kerry. Isn't that where Father Ring comes from?"

"Oh, a cousin of Ring's for a fortune!" Sam said dolefully, wiping his sweaty brow. He felt suddenly very depressed and very tired. Even the thought of Chrissie Delea's lawcase couldn't cheer him. He felt the threat of Ring now shadowing himself. A bad manager is difficult enough. A bad manager with a spy in the school can destroy a teacher.

He was right about the relationship with Ring. The new teacher arrived in a broken-down two-seater which he seemed to think rather highly of. His name was Carmody. He was tall and thin with a high, bumpy forehead, prominent cheekbones, and a dirty complexion. He held himself stiffly, obviously proud of his figure. He wore a tight-fitting cheap city suit with stripes, and Sam counted two fountain pens and a battery of colored pencils in his breast pocket. He had a little red diary sticking from the top pocket of his waistcoat, and while Sam was talking he made notes—a businesslike young fellow. Then he pushed the pencil behind his ear, stuck his thumbs in the armholes of his vest, and giggled at Sam. Giggled was the only way Sam could describe it. It was almost as though he found Sam funny. Within five minutes he was giving him advice on the way they did things in Kerry. Sam, his hands in his trouser pockets and wearing his most innocent air, looked him up and down and his tone grew dryer.

"You seem to get on very well with your class," he said later in the day.

"I make a point of it," Carmody explained pompously.

"Treat them as man to man, like?" Sam said, luring him on.

"That's the modern method, of course," said Carmody.

"That so?" Sam said dryly, and at the same moment he made a face. It was the first twinge of the dyspepsia.

He and Nancy usually had their lunch together in the open air, sitting on the low wall between the two schools. They were there a few minutes when Carmody came out. He stood on the steps and sunned himself, thrusting out his chest and drawing in deep gulps of what a Kerryman would call the ozone.

"Fine figure of a man, Sam," Nancy said, interpreting and puncturing his pose.

As though he had heard her and taken it in earnest Carmody came up to them with an air which he probably thought quizzical.

"That's a fine view you have," he said jocularly.

"You won't be long getting tired of it," Sam said coldly.

"I believe 'tis a quiet sort of place," said Carmody, unaware of any lack of warmth.

"It must be simply shocking after Kerry," Sam said, giving Nancy a nudge. "Were you ever in Kerry, Mrs. Mac?"

"Never, Mr. Higgins," said Nancy, joining in the sport. "But I believe 'tis wonderful."

"Wonderful," Sam agreed mournfully. "You'd wonder where the people got the brains till you saw the scenery."

Carmody, as became a modest man, overlooked the implication that the intellect of a Kerryman might be due to environment rather than heredity; he probably didn't expect better from a native.

"Tell me," he asked with great concern, "what *do* you do with yourselves?"

The impudence of this was too much even for Sam. He gaped at Carmody to see was he in earnest. Then he pointed to the town.

"See the bridge?"

"I do."

"See the abbey tower near it?"

"Yes."

"When we get tired of life we chuck ourselves off that."

"I was being serious," Carmody said icily.

"Oh, begor, so was I," said Sam. "That tower is pretty high."

"I believe you have some sort of dramatic society," Carmody went on to Nancy as though he couldn't be bothered carrying on conversation at Sam's level.

"We have," said Nancy brightly. "Do you act?"

"A certain amount," said Carmody. "Of course, in Kerry we go in more for the intellectual drama."

"Go on!" said Sam. "That'll be a shock to the dramatic society."

"It probably needs one," said Carmody.

"It does," said Sam blithely, getting down and looking at Carmody with his lower lip hanging and the sunlight dazzling on his spectacles. "The town needs a bit of attention too. You might notice 'tis on the downgrade. And then you can have the whole country to practice on. It often struck me it needed a bombshell to wake it up. Maybe you're the bombshell."

It wasn't often that Sam, who was a bit tongue-tied, made a speech as long as that. It should have shut anyone up, but Carmody only stuck his thumbs in his armholes, thrust out his chest, and giggled.

"But of course I'm a bombshell," he said with a sidelong glance at Nancy. You couldn't pierce Carmody's complacency so easily.

A WEEK or two later Sam dropped into Johnny Desmond's for his pint.

"Mrs. Mac and the new teacher seem to be getting very great," Johnny said by way of no harm.

"That so, Johnny?" Sam replied in the same tone.

"I just saw them going off for a spin together," added Johnny.

"Probably giving her a lift home," said Sam. "He does it every day. I hope she's insured."

"'Twasn't that at all," Johnny said, opening a bottle of boiled sweets and cramming a fistful into his mouth. "Out Bauravullen way they went. Have a couple of these, Mr. Higgins!"

"Thanks, Johnny, I won't," Sam said sourly, glancing out the door the way Johnny wouldn't notice how he was hit. There was damn little Johnny didn't notice, though. He went to the door and stood there, crunching sweets.

"Widows are the devil," he said reflectively. "Anything at all so long as 'tis in trousers. I suppose they can't help it."

"You seem to know a lot about them," said Sam.

"My own father died when I was only a boy," Johnny explained discreetly. "Clever chap, young Carmody," he added with his eyes on the ground.

"A human bombshell," said Sam with heavy irony.

"So I believe, so I believe," said Johnny, who didn't know what irony was but who was going as far as a man like himself could go towards indicating that there were things about Carmody he didn't approve of. "A pity he's so quarrelsome in drink," he said, looking back at Sam.

"Is he so?" said Sam.

"Himself and Donovan of the Exchange were at it here last night. I believe Father Ring is hoping he'll settle down. I dunno will he?"

"God forbid!" said Sam.

He went home but he couldn't read or rest. It was too cold for the garden, too hot for the room. He put on his hat again and went for a walk. At least, he explained it to himself as going for a walk, but it took him past Nancy's bungalow. There was no sign of life in that and Sam didn't know whether this was a good sign or a bad one. He dropped into Johnny's, expecting to find the Bombshell there, but there were only a couple of fellows from the County Council inside, and Sam had four drinks which was three more than was good for him. When he came out the moon was up. He returned the same way, and there, sure enough, was a light in Nancy's sitting-room window and the Bombshell's car standing outside.

For two days Sam didn't show his nose in the playground at lunchtime. When he looked out he saw Carmody leaning over the wall, talking to Nancy, and giggling.

On the afternoon of the third day, while Sam was in the garden, Nancy called and Delia opened the door.

"Oh, my!" Delia cried in her laughing, piping voice. "Such a stranger as you're becoming!"

"You'd never guess what I was up to?" Nancy asked.

"I believe you were motoring," replied Delia with a laugh.

"Ah, you can't do anything in this old town," Nancy said with a shrug of disgust. "Where the blazes is Sam? I didn't see him these ages."

"He's in the workshop," said Delia. "Will I call him in?"

"Time enough," Nancy said gaily, grabbing her by the arm. "Come on in till I talk to you."

"And how's your friend, Mr. Carmody?" asked Delia, trying to keep the hurt out of her voice.

"He's all right as long as you don't go out in a motor car with him," laughed Nancy, not noticing Delia's edginess. "Whoever gave him that car was no friend."

"I'm not in much danger of being asked, dear, am I?" Delia asked, half joking, half wincing. "And is he still homesick for Kerry? I dare say not."

"He'll settle down," said Nancy, blithely unconscious of the volcano of emotion under her feet. "A poor gom like that, brought up in the wilds, what more could you expect?"

"I dare say," said Delia. "He has every inducement."

Just then Sam came up the garden and in the back door without noticing Nancy's presence. He stood at the door, wiping his boots, his hat shading his eyes, and laughed in an embarrassed way. Even then, if only he could have welcomed her as he longed to do, things might have been all right, but no more than Delia was he able to conceal his feelings.

"Oh, hullo," he drawled idly. "How're you?"

"Grand, Sam," Nancy said, sitting up and flashing him an extra-special look. "Where were you the last couple of days?"

"Working," said Sam. "Or trying to. It's hard to do anything with people pinching your things. Did you take the quarter-inch chisel, Delia?"

"Is that a big chisel, Sam?" she asked innocently.

"No," he drawled. "Not much bigger that a quarter of an inch, if you know what that is."

"I think it might be on top of the press, Sam," she said guiltily.

"Why the hell women can't put things back where they find them!" he grunted as he got a chair. He pawed about on top of the press till he found the chisel. Then he held it up to the light and closed one eye. "Holy God!" he moaned. "Were you using it as a screwdriver or what?"

"I thought it was a screwdriver, Sam," she replied with a nervous laugh.

"You ought to use it on yourself," he said with feeling, and went out again.

Nancy frowned. Delia laughed again, even more nervously. She knew what the scene meant, but Nancy was still incredulous.

"He seems very busy," she said in a hurt tone.

"He's always pulling the house to pieces," Delia explained apologetically.

"There's nothing wrong with him?" Nancy asked suspiciously.

"No, dear," Delia said. "Only his digestion. That's always a trouble to him."

"I suppose it must be," said Nancy, growing pale. Only now was she beginning to realize that the Higginses wanted to have no more to do with her. Deeply offended, she began to collect her things.

"You're not going so soon, Nancy?"

"I'd better. I promised Nellie the afternoon off."

"Oh, dear, Sam will be so disappointed," sighed Delia.

"He'll get over it," said Nancy. "So long, Delia."

"Good-bye, dear," said Delia and, after shutting the door, began to cry. In a small town the end of a friendship has something of death about it. Delia had had hopes of something closer than friendship. Nancy had broken down her jealousy of other women; when she came to the house Sam was more cheerful and Delia found herself more cheerful too. She brought youth and gaiety into their lives.

Delia had a good long cry before Sam came in from the back. He said nothing about Nancy but went into the front room and took down a book. After a while Delia washed her eyes and went in. It was dark inside, and when she opened the door he started, always a bad sign.

"You wouldn't like to come for a little walk with me, dear?" Delia asked in a voice that went off into a squeak.

"No, Dee," he said without looking around. "I wouldn't be able."

"I'm sure a little drink in Johnny's would cheer you up," she persisted.

"No, Dee," he went on dully. "I couldn't stand his old guff."

"Then wouldn't you run up to town and see a doctor, Sam?"

"Ah, what good are doctors?"

"But it must be something, Sam," she said. She wished he'd say it and be done with it and let her try to comfort him as best she could: the two of them there, growing old, in a lonesome, unfriendly place.

"I know what it is myself," he said. "It's that cheapjack, Carmody. Twenty years I'm in that school and I was never laughed at to my face before. Now he's turning the boys against me."

"I think you only fancy that, dear," she said timidly. "I don't believe Mr. Carmody could ever turn anybody against you."

"There's where you're wrong, Dee," he replied, shaking his head, infallible even in despair. "That fellow was put there with a purpose. Ring chose his man well. They'll be having a new head one of these days."

SCHOOL had become a real torture to Sam. Carmody half-suspected his jealousy and played on it. He sent boys to the girls' school with notes and read the replies with a complacent smirk. Sam went about as though he was doped. He couldn't find things he had just left out of his hand, he forgot the names of the boys, and sometimes sat for a quarter of an hour at a time in a desk behind his class, rubbing his eyes and brow in a stupor.

He came to life only when he wrangled with Carmody. There was a window that Sam liked open and Carmody liked shut. That was enough to set the pair of them off. When Carmody sent a boy to shut the window Sam asked the boy who gave him permission. Then Carmody came up, stiff and blustering, and said no one was going to make him work with a draught down the back of his neck and Sam replied that a better man had worked there for ten years without noticing any draught at all. It was all as silly as that, and Sam knew it was silly, but that was how it took him, and no amount of good resolutions made it any better.

All through November he ate his lunch by the school fire, and when he looked out it was to see Carmody and Nancy eating theirs outside and Nancy putting up her hand to tidy her hair and breaking into a sudden laugh. Sam always felt the laugh was at him.

One day he came out, ringing the school bell, and Carmody, who had been sitting on the wall, jumped off with such an affectation of agility that the diary fell from his vest pocket. He was so occupied with Nancy that he didn't notice it, and Sam was so full of his own troubles that he went on down the playground and he didn't notice it either. He saw a bit of paper that someone's lunch had been wrapped in, picked it up and crumpled it into a ball. At the same time he noticed the diary, and, assuming that one of the boys had dropped it, picked it up and glanced through it. It puzzled him, for it did not seem like the notebook of a schoolboy. It was all about some girl that the writer was interested in. He couldn't help reading on till he came to a name that caused him to blush. Then he recognized the writing; it was Carmody's. When he turned the pages and saw how much of it there was, he put it in his pocket. Afterwards, he knew what he had done and saw it was wrong, but at the time he never even thought of an alternative. During the first lesson he sat at a desk and read on, his head in his hands.

Now, Carmody was a conceited young man who thought that everything about himself was of such importance that it had to be recorded for the benefit of posterity. Things Sam would have been ashamed even to think about himself he had all written down. Besides, Sam had led a sheltered life. He didn't know much of any woman but Delia. He had thought of Nancy as an angelic little creature whose life had been wrecked by her husband's death and who spent most of her time thinking of him. It was clear from the diary that this was not how she spent her time at all, but that, like any other bad, flighty, sensual girl, she let herself be made love to in motor cars by cheapjacks like

Carmody, who even on his own admission had no respect for her and only wanted to see how far a widow like that would go. "Anything at all so long as 'tis in trousers," as Johnny said. Johnny was right. Johnny knew the sort of woman she was. That was all Sam needed to make him hate Nancy as much as he already hated Carmody. She was another cheapjack.

Then he looked at the clock. Dictation came next. Without a moment's thought he went to the blackboard, wiped out the sums on it, and wrote in a neat, workmanlike hand: "The Diary of a Cheapjack." Even then he had no notion of what he was actually going to do, but as the boys settled themselves he took a deep breath and began to read.

"October twenty-first," he dictated in a dull voice. "I think I have bowled the widow over."

There was a shocked silence and some boy giggled.

"It's all right," Sam explained blandly, pointing to the blackboard. "I told you this fellow was only a cheapjack, one of those lads you see at the fair, selling imitation jewelry. You'll see it all in a minute."

And on he went again in a monotonous voice, one hand holding the diary, the other in his trouser pocket. He knew he was behaving oddly, even scandalously, but it gave him an enormous feeling of release, as though all the weeks of misery and humiliation were being paid for at last. It was everything he had ever thought of Carmody, only worse. Worse, for how could Sam have suspected that Carmody would admit the way he had first made love to Nancy, just to keep his hand in (his own very words!), or describe the way love came to him at last one evening up Bauravullen when the sun was setting behind the pine trees and he found he no longer despised Nancy.

The fellows began to titter. Sam raised his brows and looked at them with a wondering smile as if he did not quite know what they were laughing at. In a curious way he was beginning to enjoy it himself. He began to parody it in the style of a bad actor, waving one arm, throwing back his head and cooing out the syrupy pseudo-Byronic sentences. "And all for a widow!" he read, raising his voice and staring at Carmody. "A woman who went through it all before."

Carmody heard him and suddenly recognized the diary. He came up the classroom in a few strides and tore the book out of Sam's hand. Sam let it go with him and only gaped.

"Hi, young man," he asked amiably, "where are you going with that?"

"What are you doing with it?" Carmody asked in a terrible voice, equally a caricature of a bad actor's. He was still incredulous; he could not believe that Sam had actually been reading it aloud to his class.

"Oh, that's our piece for dictation," Sam said and glanced at the blackboard. "I'm calling it 'The Diary of a Cheapjack.' I think that about hits it off."

"You stole my diary!" hissed Carmody.

"Your diary?" Sam replied with assumed concern. "You're not serious?"

"You knew perfectly well it was mine," shouted Carmody beside himself with rage. "You saw my name and you know my writing."

"Oh, begod I didn't," Sam protested stolidly. "If anyone told me that thing was written by an educated man I'd call him a liar."

Then Carmody did the only thing he could do, the thing that Sam in his heart probably hoped for—he gave Sam a punch in the jaw. Sam staggered, righted himself and made for Carmody. They closed. The boys left their desks, shouting. One or two ran out of the school. In a few moments the rest had formed a cheering ring about the two struggling teachers. Sam was small and gripped his man low. Carmody punched him viciously and effectively about the head but Sam hung on, pulling Carmody right and left till he found it hard to keep his feet. At last Sam gave one great heave and sent Carmody flying. His head cracked off the iron leg of a desk. He lay still for some moments and then rose, clutching his head.

At the same moment Miss Daly and Nancy came in.

"Sam!" Nancy cried. "What's the matter?"

"Get out of my way," Carmody shouted, skipping round her. "Get out of my way till I kill him."

"Come on, you cheapjack!" drawled Sam. His head was down, his hands were hanging, and he was looking dully at Carmody over his spectacles. "Come on and I'll give you more of it."

"Mr. Higgins, Mr. Higgins!" screamed Miss Daly. "Is it mad ye are, the pair of ye?"

They came to their senses at that. Miss Daly took charge. She rang the bell and cleared the school. Sam turned away and began fumbling blindly with the lid of a chalk-box. Carmody began to dust himself. Then, with long backward glances, he and the two women went into the playground, where Sam heard them talking in loud, excited voices. He smiled vaguely, took off his glasses and wiped them carefully before he picked up his books, his hat, and his coat, and locked the school door behind him. He knew he was doing it for the last time and wasn't sorry. The three other teachers drew away and he went past them without a glance. He left the keys at the presbytery and told the housekeeper he'd write. Next morning he went away by an early train and never came back.

We were all sorry for him. Poor Sam! As decent a man as ever drew breath but too honest, too honest!

The Luceys

IT'S EXTRAORDINARY, the bitterness there can be in a town like ours between two people of the same family. More particularly between two people of the same family. I suppose living more or less in public as we do we are either killed or cured by it, and the same communal sense that will make a man be battered into a reconciliation he doesn't feel gives added importance to whatever quarrel he thinks must not be composed. God knows, most of the time you'd be more sorry for a man like that than anything else.

The Luceys were like that. There were two brothers, Tom and Ben, and there must have been a time when the likeness between them was greater than the difference, but that was long before most of us knew them. Tom was the elder; he came in for the drapery shop. Ben had to have a job made for him on the County Council. This was the first difference and it grew and grew. Both were men of intelligence and education but Tom took it more seriously. As Ben said with a grin, he could damn well afford to with the business behind him.

It was an old-fashioned shop which prided itself on only stocking the best, and though the prices were high and Tom in his irascible opinionated way refused to abate them—he said haggling was degrading!—a lot of farmers' wives would still go nowhere else. Ben listened to his brother's high notions with his eyes twinkling, rather as he read the books which came his way, with profound respect and the feeling that this would all be grand for some other place, but was entirely inapplicable to the affairs of the County Council. God alone would ever be able to disentangle these, and meanwhile the only course open to a prudent man was to keep his mind to himself. If Tom didn't like the way the County Council was run, neither did Ben, but that was the way things were, and it rather amused him to rub it in to his virtuous brother.

Tom and Ben were both married. Tom's boy, Peter, was the great friend of his cousin, Charlie—called "Charliss" by his Uncle Tom.

They were nice boys; Peter a fat, heavy, handsome lad who blushed whenever a stranger spoke to him, and Charlie with a broad face that never blushed at anything. The two families were always friendly; the mothers liked to get together over a glass of port wine and discuss the fundamental things that made the Lucey brothers not two inexplicable characters but two aspects of one inexplicable family character; the brothers enjoyed their regular chats about the way the world was going, for intelligent men are rare and each appreciated the other's shrewdness.

Only young Charlie was occasionally mystified by his Uncle Tom; he hated calling for Peter unless he was sure his uncle was out, for otherwise he might be sent into the front room to talk to him. The front room alone was enough to upset any high-spirited lad, with its thick carpet, mahogany sideboard, ornamental clock, and gilt mirror with cupids. The red curtains alone would depress you, and as well as these there was a glass-fronted mahogany bookcase the length of one wall, with books in sets, too big for anyone only a priest to read: *The History of Ireland, The History of the Popes, The Roman Empire, The Life of Johnson,* and *The Cabinet of Literature.* It gave Charlie the same sort of shivers as the priest's front room. His uncle suited it, a small, frail man, dressed in clerical black with a long pinched yellow face, tight lips, a narrow skull going bald up the brow, and a pair of tin specs.

All conversations with his uncle tended to stick in Charlie's mind for the simple but alarming reason that he never understood what the hell they were about, but one conversation in particular haunted him for years as showing the dangerous state of lunacy to which a man could be reduced by reading old books. Charlie was no fool, far from it; but low cunning and the most genuine benevolence were mixed in him in almost equal parts, producing a blend that was not without charm but gave no room for subtlety or irony.

"Good afternoon, Charliss," said his uncle after Charlie had tied what he called "the ould pup" to the leg of the hallstand. "How are you?"

"All right," Charlie said guardedly. (He hated being called Charliss, it made him sound such a sissy.)

"Take a seat, Charliss," said his uncle benevolently. "Peter will be down in a minute."

"I won't," said Charlie. "I'd be afraid of the ould pup."

"The expression, Charliss," said his uncle in that rasping little voice of his, "sounds like a contradiction in terms, but, not being familiar with dogs, I presume 'tis correct."

"Ah, 'tis," said Charlie, just to put the old man's mind at rest.

"And how is your father, Charliss?"

"His ould belly is bad again," said Charlie. "He'd be all right only the ould belly plays hell with him."

"I'm sorry to hear it," his uncle said gravely. "And tell me, Charliss," he added, cocking his head on one side like a bird, "what is he saying about me now?"

This was one of the dirtiest of his Uncle Tom's tricks, assuming that Charlie's father was saying things about him, which to give Ben his due, he usually was. But on the other hand, he was admitted to be one of the smartest men in town, so he was entitled to do so, while everyone without exception appeared to agree that his uncle had a slate loose. Charlie looked at him cautiously, low cunning struggling with benevolence in him, for his uncle though queer was open-handed, and you wouldn't want to offend him. Benevolence won.

"He's saying if you don't mind yourself you'll end up in the poorhouse," he said with some notion that if only his uncle knew the things people said about him he might mend his ways.

"Your father is right as always, Charliss," said his uncle, rising and standing on the hearth with his hands behind his back and his little legs well apart. "Your father is perfectly right. There are two main classes of people, Charliss—those who gravitate towards the poorhouse and those who gravitate towards the jail. . . . Do you know what 'gravitate' means, Charliss?"

"I do not," said Charlie without undue depression. It struck him as being an unlikely sort of word.

" 'Gravitate,' Charliss, means 'tend' or 'incline.' Don't tell me you don't know what they mean!"

"I don't," said Charlie.

"Well, do you know what this is?" his uncle asked smilingly as he held up a coin.

"I do," said Charlie, humoring him as he saw that the conversation was at last getting somewhere. "A tanner."

"I am not familiar with the expression, Charliss," his uncle said tartly and Charlie knew, whatever he'd said out of the way, his uncle was so irritated that he was liable to put the tanner back. "We'll call it sixpence. Your eyes, I notice, gravitate towards the sixpence" (Charlie was so shocked that his eyes instantly gravitated towards his uncle), "and in the same way, people gravitate, or turn naturally, towards the jail or poorhouse. Only a small number of either group reach their destination, though—which might be just as well for myself and your father," he added in a low impressive voice, swaying forward and tightening his lips. "Do you understand a word I'm saying, Charliss?" he added with a charming smile.

"I do not," said Charlie.

"Good man! Good man!" his uncle said approvingly. "I admire an honest and manly spirit in anybody. Don't forget your sixpence, Charliss."

And as he went off with Peter, Charlie scowled and muttered savagely under his breath: "Mod! Mod! Mod! The bleddy mon is mod!"

WHEN the boys grew up Peter trained for a solicitor while Charlie, one of a large family, followed his father into the County Council. He grew up a very handsome fellow with a square, solemn, dark-skinned face, a thick red lower lip, and a mass of curly black hair. He was reputed to be a great man with greyhounds and girls and about as dependable with one as with the other. His enemies called him "a crooked bloody bastard" and his father, a shrewd man, noted with alarm that Charlie thought him simpleminded.

The two boys continued the best of friends, though Peter, with an office in Asragh, moved in circles where Charlie felt himself lost; professional men whose status was calculated on their furniture and food and wine. Charlie thought that sort of entertainment a great pity. A man could have all the fun he wanted out of life without wasting his time on expensive and unsatisfactory meals and carrying on polite conversation while you dodged between bloody little tables that were always falling over, but Charlie, who was a modest lad, admired the way Peter never knocked anything over and never said: "Chrisht!" Wine, coffee cups, and talk about old books came as easy to him as talk about a dog or a horse.

Charlie was thunderstruck when the news came to him that Peter was in trouble. He heard it first from Mackesy the detective, whom he hailed outside the courthouse. (Charlie was like his father in that; he couldn't let a man go by without a greeting.)

"Hullo, Matt," he shouted gaily from the courthouse step. "Is it myself or my father you're after?"

"I'll let ye off for today," said Mackesy, making a garden seat of the crossbar of his bicycle. Then he lowered his voice so that it didn't travel further than Charlie. "I wouldn't mind having a word with a relative of yours, though."

"A what, Matt?" Charlie asked, skipping down the steps on the scent of news. (He was like his father in that, too.) "You don't mean one of the Luceys is after forgetting himself?"

"Then you didn't hear about Peter?"

"Peter! Peter in trouble! You're not serious, Matt?"

"There's a lot of his clients would be glad if I wasn't, Cha," Mackesy said grimly. "I thought you'd know about it as ye were such pals."

"But we are, man, we are," Charlie insisted. "Sure, wasn't I at the dogs with him—when was it?—last Thursday? I never noticed a bloody thing, though, now you mention it, he was lashing pound notes on that Cloonbullogue dog. I told him the Dalys could never train a dog."

Charlie left Mackesy, his mind in a whirl! He tore through the cashier's office. His father was sitting at his desk, signing paying-orders. He was wearing a gray tweed cap, a gray tweed suit, and a brown cardigan. He was a stocky, powerfully built man with a great expanse of chest, a plump, dark, hairy face, long quizzical eyes that tended to close in slits; hair in his nose, hair in his ears; hair on his high cheekbones that made them like small cabbage-patches.

He made no comment on Charlie's news, but stroked his chin and looked worried. Then Charlie shot out to see his uncle. Quill, the assistant, was serving in the shop and Charlie stumped in behind the counter to the fitting room. His uncle had been looking out the back, all crumpled up. When Charlie came in he pulled himself erect with fictitious jauntiness. With his old black coat and wrinkled yellow face he had begun to look like an old rabbi.

"What's this I hear about Peter?" began Charlie, who was never one to be ceremonious.

"Bad news travels fast, Charlie," said his uncle in his dry little voice, clamping his lips so tightly that the wrinkles ran up his cheeks from the corners of his mouth. He was so upset that he forgot even to say "Charliss."

"Have you any notion how much it is?" asked Charlie.

"I have not, Charlie," Tom said bitterly. "I need hardly say my son did not take me into his confidence about the extent of his robberies."

"And what are you going to do?"

"What can I do?" The lines of pain belied the harsh little staccato that broke up every sentence into disjointed phrases as if it were a political speech. "You saw yourself, Charliss, the way I reared that boy. You saw the education I gave him. I gave him the thing I was denied myself, Charliss. I gave him an honorable profession. And now for the first time in my life I am ashamed to show my face in my own shop. What can I do?"

"Ah, now, ah, now, Uncle Tom, we know all that," Charlie said truculently, "but that's not going to get us anywhere. What can we do now?"

"Is it true that Peter took money that was entrusted to him?" Tom asked oratorically.

"To be sure he did," replied Charlie without the thrill of horror which his uncle seemed to expect. "I do it myself every month, only I put it back."

"And is it true he ran away from his punishment instead of standing his ground like a man?" asked Tom, paying no attention to him.

"What the hell else would he do?" asked Charlie, who entirely failed to appreciate the spiritual beauty of atonement. "Begod, if I had two years' hard labor facing me you wouldn't see my heels for dust."

"I dare say you think I'm old-fashioned, Charliss," said his uncle, "but that's not the way I was reared, nor the way my son was reared."

"And that's where the ferryboat left ye," snorted Charlie. "Now that sort of thing may be all very well, Uncle Tom, but 'tis no use taking it to the fair. Peter made some mistake, the way we all make mistakes, but instead of coming to me or some other friend, he lost his nerve and started gambling. Chrisht, didn't I see it happen to better men? You don't know how much it is?"

"No, Charliss, I don't."

"Do you know where he is, even?"

"His mother knows."

"I'll talk to my old fellow. We might be able to do something. If the bloody fool might have told me on Thursday instead of backing that Cloonbullogue dog!"

Charlie returned to the office to find his father sitting at his desk with his hands joined and his pipe in his mouth, staring nervously at the door.

"Well?"

"We'll go over to Asragh and talk to Toolan of the Guards ourselves," said Charlie. "I want to find out how much he let himself in for. We might even get a look at the books."

"Can't his father do it?" Ben asked gloomily.

"Do you think he'd understand them?"

"Well, he was always fond of literature," Ben said shortly.

"God help him," said Charlie. "He has enough of it now."

" 'Tis all his own conceit," Ben said angrily, striding up and down the office with his hands in his trouser pockets. "He was always good at criticizing other people. Even when you got in here it was all influence. Of course, he'd never use influence. Now he wants us to use it."

"That's all very well," Charlie said reasonably, "but this is no time for raking up old scores."

"Who's raking up old scores?" his father shouted angrily.

"That's right," Charlie said approvingly. "Would you like me to open the door so that you can be heard all over the office?"

"No one is going to hear me at all," his father said in a more reasonable tone—Charlie had a way of puncturing him. "And I'm not raking up any old scores. I'm only saying now what I always said. The boy was ruined."

"He'll be ruined with a vengeance unless we do something quick," said Charlie. "Are you coming to Asragh with me?"

"I am not."

"Why?"

"Because I don't want to be mixed up in it at all. That's why. I never liked anything to do with money. I saw too much of it. I'm only speaking for your good. A man done out of his money is a mad dog. You won't get any thanks for it, and anything that goes wrong, you'll get the blame."

Nothing Charlie could say would move his father, and Charlie was shrewd enough to know that everything his father said was right. Tom wasn't to be trusted in the delicate negotiations that would be needed to get Peter out of the hole; the word here, the threat there; all the complicated machinery of family pressure. And alone he knew he was powerless. Despondently he went and told his uncle and Tom received the news with resignation, almost without understanding.

But a week later Ben came back to the office deeply disturbed. He closed the door carefully behind him and leaned across the desk to Charlie, his face drawn. For a moment he couldn't speak.

"What ails you?" Charlie asked with no great warmth.

"Your uncle passed me just now in the Main Street," whispered his father.

Charlie wasn't greatly put out. All of his life he had been made a party to the little jabs and asides of father and uncle, and he did not realize what it meant to a man like his father, friendly and popular, this public rebuke.

"That so?" he asked without surprise. "What did you do to him?"

"I thought you might know that," his father said, looking at him with a troubled air from under the peak of his cap.

"Unless 'twas something you said about Peter?" suggested Charlie.

"It might, it might," his father agreed doubtfully. "You didn't—ah—repeat anything I said to you?"

"What a bloody fool you think I am!" Charlie said indignantly. "And indeed I thought you had more sense. What did you say?"

"Oh, nothing. Nothing only what I said to you," replied his father and went to the window to look out. He leaned on the sill and then

tapped nervously on the frame. He was haunted by all the casual remarks he had made or might have made over a drink with an acquaintance—remarks that were no different from those he and Tom had been
passing about one another all their lives. "I shouldn't have said anything at all, of course, but I had no notion 'twould go back."

"I'm surprised at my uncle," said Charlie. "Usually he cares little
enough what anyone says of him."

But even Charlie, who had moments when he almost understood his
peppery little uncle, had no notion of the hopes he had raised and
which his more calculating father had dashed. Tom Lucey's mind was
in a rut, a rut of complacency, for the idealist too has his complacency
and can be aware of it. There are moments when he would be glad to
walk through any mud, but he no longer knows the way; he needs to
be led; he cannot degrade himself even when he is most ready to do so.
Tom was ready to beg favors from a thief. Peter had joined the Air
Force under an assumed name, and this was the bitterest blow of all to
him, the extinction of the name. He was something of an amateur ge-
nealogist, and had managed to convince himself, God knows how, that
his family was somehow related to the Gloucestershire Lucys. This
was already a sort of death.

The other death didn't take long in coming. Charlie, in the way he
had, got wind of it first, and, having sent his father to break the news to
Min, he went off himself to tell his uncle. It was a fine spring morning.
The shop was empty but for his uncle, standing with his back to the
counter studying the shelves.

"Good morning, Charliss," he crackled over his shoulder. "What's
the best news?"

"Bad, I'm afraid, Uncle Tom," Charlie replied, leaning across the
counter to him.

"Something about Peter, I dare say?" his uncle asked casually, but
Charlie noticed how, caught unawares, he had failed to say "my son,"
as he had taken to doing.

"Just so."

"Dead, I suppose?"

"Dead, Uncle Tom."

"I was expecting something of the sort," said his uncle. "May the
Almighty God have mercy on his soul! . . . Con!" he called at the back
of the shop while he changed his coat. "You'd better close up the shop.
You'll find the crepe on the top shelf and the mourning-cards in my
desk."

"Who is it, Mr. Lucey?" asked Con Quill. " 'Tisn't Peter?"

" 'Tis, Con, 'tis, I'm sorry to say," and Tom came out briskly with his umbrella over his arm. As they went down the street two people stopped them: the news was already round.

Charlie, who had to see about the arrangements for the funeral, left his uncle outside the house and so had no chance of averting the scene that took place inside. Not that he would have had much chance of doing so. His father had found Min in a state of collapse. Ben was the last man in the world to look after a woman, but he did manage to get her a pillow, put her legs on a chair and cover her with a rug, which was more than Charlie would have given him credit for. Min smelt of brandy. Then Ben strode up and down the darkened room with his hands in his pockets and his cap over his eyes, talking about the horrors of airplane travel. He knew he was no fit company for a woman of sensibility like Min, and he almost welcomed Tom's arrival.

"That's terrible news, Tom," he said.

"Oh, God help us!" cried Min. "They said he disgraced us but he didn't disgrace us long."

"I'd sooner 'twas one of my own, Tom," Ben said excitedly. "As God is listening to me I would. I'd still have a couple left, but he was all ye had."

He held out his hand to Tom. Tom looked at it, then at him, and then deliberately put his own hands behind his back.

"Aren't you going to shake hands with me, Tom?" Ben asked appealingly.

"No, Ben," Tom said grimly. "I am not."

"Oh, Tom Lucey!" moaned Min with her crucified smile. "Over your son's dead body!"

Ben looked at his brother in chagrin and dropped his hand. For a moment it looked as though he might strike him. He was a volatile, hot-tempered man.

"That wasn't what I expected from you, Tom," he said, making a mighty effort to control himself.

"Ben," said his brother, squaring his frail little shoulders, "you disrespected my son while he was alive. Now that he's dead I'd thank you to leave him alone."

"I disrespected him?" Ben exclaimed indignantly. "I did nothing of the sort. I said things I shouldn't have said. I was upset. You know the sort I am. You were upset yourself and I dare say you said things you regret."

"'Tisn't alike, Ben," Tom said in a rasping, opinionated tone. "I said them because I loved the boy. You said them because you hated him."

"I hated him?" Ben repeated incredulously. "Peter? Are you out of your mind?"

"You said he changed his name because it wasn't grand enough for him," Tom said, clutching the lapels of his coat and stepping from one foot to another. "Why did you say such a mean, mocking, cowardly thing about the boy when he was in trouble?"

"All right, all right," snapped Ben. "I admit I was wrong to say it. There were a lot of things you said about my family, but I'm not throwing them back at you."

"You said you wouldn't cross the road to help him," said Tom. Again he primmed up the corners of his mouth and lowered his head. "And why, Ben? I'll tell you why. Because you were jealous of him."

"I was jealous of him?" Ben repeated. It seemed to him that he was talking to a different man, discussing a different life, as though the whole of his nature was being turned inside out.

"You were jealous of him, Ben. You were jealous because he had the upbringing and education your own sons lacked. And I'm not saying that to disparage your sons. Far from it. But you begrudged my son his advantages."

"Never!" shouted Ben in a fury.

"And I was harsh with him," Tom said, taking another nervous step forward while his neat waspish little voice grew harder. "I was harsh with him and you were jealous of him, and when his hour of trouble came he had no one to turn to. Now, Ben, the least you can do is to spare us your commiserations."

"Oh, wisha, don't mind him, Ben," moaned Min. "Sure, everyone knows you never begrudged my poor child anything. The man isn't in his right mind."

"I know that, Min," Ben said, trying hard to keep his temper. "I know he's upset. Only for that he'd never say what he did say—or believe it."

"We'll see, Ben, we'll see," said Tom grimly.

THAT was how the row between the Luceys began, and it continued like that for years. Charlie married and had children of his own. He always remained friendly with his uncle and visited him regularly; sat in the stuffy front room with him and listened with frowning gravity to Tom's views, and no more than in his childhood understood what the old man was talking about. All he gathered was that none of the political parties had any principle and the country was in a bad way due to the inroads of the uneducated and ill-bred. Tom looked more and more like a rabbi. As is the way of men of character in provincial towns, he tended more and more to become a collection of mannerisms, a caricature of himself. His academic jokes on his simple customers became more elaborate; so elaborate, in fact, that in time he gave up trying to explain them and was content to be set down as merely queer. In a way it made things easier for Ben; he was able to treat the breach with Tom as another example of his brother's cantankerousness, and spoke of it with amusement and good nature.

Then he fell ill. Charlie's cares were redoubled. Ben was the world's worst patient. He was dying and didn't know it, wouldn't go to hospital, and broke the heart of his wife and daughter. He was awake at six, knocking peremptorily for his cup of tea; then waited impatiently for the paper and the post. "What the hell is keeping Mick Duggan? That fellow spends half his time gossiping along the road. Half past nine and no post!" After that the day was a blank to him until evening when a couple of County Council chaps dropped in to keep him company and tell him what was afoot in the court-house. There was nothing in the long low room, plastered with blue and green flowered wallpaper, but a bedside table, a press, and three or four holy pictures, and Ben's mind was not on these but on the world outside—feet passing and re-passing on errands which he would never be told about. It broke his heart. He couldn't believe he was as bad as people tried to make out; sometimes it was the doctor he blamed, sometimes the chemist who wasn't careful enough of the bottles and pills he made up—Ben could remember some shocking cases. He lay in bed doing involved calculations about his pension.

Charlie came every evening to sit with him. Though his father didn't say much about Tom, Charlie knew the row was always there in the back of his mind. It left Ben bewildered, a man without bitterness. And Charlie knew he came in for some of the blame. It was the illness all over again: someone must be slipping up somewhere; the right word hadn't been dropped in the right quarter or a wrong one had been dropped instead. Charlie, being so thick with Tom, must somehow be to blame. Ben did not understand the inevitable. One night it came out.

"You weren't at your uncle's?" Ben asked.

"I was," Charlie said with a nod. "I dropped in on the way up."

"He wasn't asking about me?" Ben asked, looking at him out of the corner of his eye.

"Oh, he was," Charlie said with a shocked air. "Give the man his due, he always does that. That's one reason I try to drop in every day. He likes to know."

But he knew this was not the question his father wanted answered. That question was: "Did you say the right words? Did you make me out the feeble figure you should have made me out, or did you say the wrong thing, letting him know I was better?" These things had to be managed. In Charlie's place Ben would have managed it splendidly.

"He didn't say anything about dropping up?" Ben asked with affected lightness.

"No," Charlie said with assumed thoughtfulness. "I don't remember."

"There's blackness for you!" his father said with sudden bitterness. It came as a shock to Charlie; it was the first time he had heard his father speak like that, from the heart, and he knew the end must be near.

"God knows," Charlie said, tapping one heel nervously, "he's a queer man. A queer bloody man!"

"Tell me, Charlie," his father insisted, "wouldn't you say it to him? 'Tisn't right and you know 'tisn't right."

" 'Tisn't," said Charlie, tearing at his hair, "but to tell you the God's truth I'd sooner not talk to him."

"Yes," his father added in disappointment. "I see it mightn't do for you."

Charlie realized that his father was thinking of the shop, which would now come to him. He got up and stood against the fireplace, a fat, handsome, moody man.

"That has nothing to do with it," he said. "If he gave me cause I'd throw his bloody old shop in his face in the morning. I don't want anything from him. 'Tis just that I don't seem to be able to talk to him. I'll send Paddy down tonight and let him ask him."

"Do, do," his father said with a knowing nod. "That's the very thing you'll do. And tell Julie to bring me up a drop of whiskey and a couple of glasses. You'll have a drop yourself?"

"I won't."

"You will, you will. Julie will bring it up."

Charlie went to his brother's house and asked him to call on Tom and tell him how near the end was. Paddy was a gentle, good-natured boy with something of Charlie's benevolence and none of his guile.

"I will to be sure," he said. "But why don't you tell him? Sure, he thinks the world of you."

"I'll tell you why, Paddy," Charlie whispered with his hand on his brother's sleeve. "Because if he refused me I might do him some injury."

"But you don't think he will?" Paddy asked in bewilderment.

"I don't think at all, Paddy," Charlie said broodingly. "I know."

He knew all right. When he called on his way home the next afternoon his mother and sister were waiting for him, hysterical with
excitement. Paddy had met with a cold refusal. Their hysteria was infectious. He understood now why he had caught people glancing at
him curiously in the street. It was being argued out in every pub,
what Charlie Lucey ought to do. People couldn't mind their own
bloody business. He rapped out an oath at the two women and took
the stairs three at a time. His father was lying with his back to the
window. The whiskey was still there as Charlie had seen it the previous evening. It tore at his heart more than the sight of his father's
despair.

"You're not feeling too good?" he said gruffly.

"I'm not, I'm not," Ben said, lifting the sheet from his face. "Paddy
didn't bring a reply to that message?" he added questioningly.

"Do you tell me so?" Charlie replied, trying to sound shocked.

"Paddy was always a bad man to send on a message," his father said
despondently, turning himself painfully in the bed, but still not looking at Charlie. "Of course, he hasn't the sense. Tell me, Charlie," he
added in a feeble voice, "weren't you there when I was talking about
Peter?"

"About Peter?" Charlie exclaimed in surprise.

"You were, you were," his father insisted, looking at the window.
"Sure, 'twas from you I heard it. You wanted to go to Asragh to look at
the books, and I told you if anything went wrong you'd get the blame.
Isn't that all I said?"

Charlie had to readjust his mind before he realized that his father
had been going over it all again in the long hours of loneliness and
pain, trying to see where he had gone wrong. It seemed to make him
even more remote. Charlie didn't remember what his father had said;
he doubted if his uncle remembered.

"I might have passed some joke about it," his father said, "but sure I
was always joking him and he was always joking me. What the hell
more was there in it?"

"Oh, a chance remark!" agreed Charlie.

"Now, the way I look at that," his father said, seeking his eyes for
the first time, "someone was out to make mischief. This town is full
of people like that. If you went and told him he'd believe you."

"I will, I will," Charlie said, sick with disgust. "I'll see him myself
today."

He left the house, cursing his uncle for a brutal egotist. He felt the
growing hysteria of the town concentrating on himself and knew that
at last it had got inside him. His sisters and brothers, the people in the

little shops along the street, expected him to bring his uncle to book, and failing that, to have done with him. This was the moment when people had to take their side once and for all. And he knew he was only too capable of taking sides.

Min opened the door to him, her red-rimmed eyes dirty with tears and the smell of brandy on her breath. She was near hysterics, too.

"What way is he, Charlie?" she wailed.

"Bad enough, Aunt Min," he said as he wiped his boots and went past her. "He won't last the night."

At the sound of his voice his uncle had opened the sitting-room door and now he came out and drew Charlie in by the hand. Min followed. His uncle didn't release his hand, and betrayed his nervousness only by the way his frail fingers played over Charlie's hand, like a woman's.

"I'm sorry to hear it, Charliss," he said.

"Sure, of course you are, Uncle Tom," said Charlie, and at the first words the feeling of hysteria within him dissolved and left only a feeling of immense understanding and pity. "You know what brought me?"

His uncle dropped his hand.

"I do, Charliss," he said and drew himself erect. They were neither of them men to beat about the bush.

"You'll come and see the last of him," Charlie said, not even marking the question.

"Charliss," Tom said with that queer tightening at the corners of his mouth, "I was never one to hedge or procrastinate. I will not come."

He almost hissed the final words. Min broke into a loud wail.

"Talk to him, Charlie, do! I'm sick and tired of it. We can never show our faces in the town again."

"And I need hardly say, Charliss," his uncle continued with an air of triumph that was almost evil, "that that doesn't trouble me."

"I know," Charlie said earnestly, still keeping his eyes on the withered old face with the narrow-winged, almost transparent nose. "And you know that I never interfered between ye. Whatever disagreements ye had, I never took my father's side against you. And 'twasn't for what I might get out of you."

In his excitement his uncle grinned, a grin that wasn't natural, and that combined in a strange way affection and arrogance, the arrogance of the idealist who doesn't realize how easily he can be fooled.

"I never thought it, boy," he said, raising his voice. "Not for an instant. Nor 'twasn't in you."

"And you know too you did this once before and you regretted it."

"Bitterly! Bitterly!"

"And you're going to make the same mistake with your brother that you made with your son?"

"I'm not forgetting that either, Charliss," said Tom. "It wasn't today nor yesterday I thought of it."

"And it isn't as if you didn't care for him," Charlie went on remorselessly. "It isn't as if you had no heart for him. You know he's lying up there waiting for you. He sent for you last night and you never came. He had the bottle of whiskey and the two glasses by the bed. All he wants is for you to say you forgive him.... Jesus Christ, man," he shouted with all the violence in him roused, "never mind what you're doing to him. Do you know what you're doing to yourself?"

"I know, Charliss," his uncle said in a cold, excited voice. "I know that too. And 'tisn't as you say that I have no heart for him. God knows it isn't that I don't forgive him. I forgave him long years ago for what he said about—one that was very dear to me. But I swore that day, Charliss, that never the longest day I lived would I take your father's hand in friendship, and if God was to strike me dead at this very moment for my presumption I'd say the same. You know me, Charliss," he added, gripping the lapels of his coat. "I never broke my word yet to God or man. I won't do it now."

"Oh, how can you say it?" cried Min. "Even the wild beasts have more nature."

"Some other time I'll ask you to forgive me," added Tom, ignoring her.

"You need never do that, Uncle Tom," Charlie said with great simplicity and humbleness. " 'Tis yourself you'll have to forgive."

At the door he stopped. He had a feeling that if he turned he would see Peter standing behind him. He knew his uncle's barren pride was all he could now offer to the shadow of his son, and that it was his dead cousin who stood between them. For a moment he felt like turning and appealing to Peter. But he was never much given to the supernatural. The real world was trouble enough for him, and he went slowly homeward, praying that he might see the blinds drawn before him.

Uprooted

SPRING had only come and already he was tired to death; tired of the city, tired of his job. He had come up from the country intending to do wonders, but he was as far as ever from that. He would be lucky if he could carry on, be at school each morning at half past nine and satisfy his half-witted principal.

He lodged in a small red-brick house in Rathmines that was kept by a middle-aged brother and sister who had been left a bit of money and thought they would end their days enjoyably in a city. They did not enjoy themselves, regretted their little farm in Kerry, and were glad of Ned Keating because he could talk to them about all the things they remembered and loved.

Keating was a slow, cumbrous young man with dark eyes and a dark cow's-lick that kept tumbling into them. He had a slight stammer and ran his hand through his long limp hair from pure nervousness. He had always been dreamy and serious. Sometimes on market days you saw him standing for an hour in Nolan's shop, turning the pages of a schoolbook. When he could not afford it he put it back with a sigh and went off to find his father in a pub, just raising his eyes to smile at Jack Nolan. After his elder brother Tom had gone for the church he and his father had constant rows. Nothing would do Ned now but to be a teacher. Hadn't he all he wanted now? his father asked. Hadn't he the place to himself? What did he want going teaching? But Ned was stubborn. With an obstinate, almost despairing determination he had fought his way through the training college into a city job. The city was what he had always wanted. And now the city had failed him. In the evenings you could still see him poking round the second-hand bookshops on the quays, but his eyes were already beginning to lose their eagerness.

It had all seemed so clear. But then he had not counted on his own temper. He was popular because of his gentleness, but how many concessions that involved! He was hesitating, good-natured, slow to see guile, slow to contradict. He felt he was constantly underestimating his own powers. He even felt he lacked spontaneity. He did not drink, smoked little, and saw dangers and losses everywhere. He blamed himself for avarice and cowardice. The story he liked best was about the country boy and the letter box. "Indeed, what a fool you think I am! Put me letther in a pump!"

He was in no danger of putting his letter in a pump or anywhere else for the matter of that. He had only one friend, a nurse in Vincent's Hospital, a wild, lighthearted, lightheaded girl. He was very fond of her and supposed that some day when he had money enough he would ask her to marry him; but not yet: and at the same time something that was both shyness and caution kept him from committing himself too far. Sometimes he planned excursions besides the usual weekly walk or visit to the pictures but somehow they seldom came to anything.

He no longer knew why he had come to the city, but it was not for the sake of the bed-sitting room in Rathmines, the oblong of dusty garden outside the window, the trams clanging up and down, the shelf full of second-hand books, or the occasional visit to the pictures. Half humorously, half despairingly, he would sometimes clutch his head in his hands and admit to himself that he had no notion of what he wanted. He would have liked to leave it all and go to Glasgow or New York as a laborer, not because he was romantic, but because he felt that only when he had to work with his hands for a living and was no longer sure of his bed would he find out what all his ideals and emotions meant and where he could fit them into the scheme of his life.

But no sooner did he set out for school next morning, striding slowly along the edge of the canal, watching the trees become green again and the tall claret-colored houses painted on the quiet surface of the water, than all his fancies took flight. Put his letter in a pump indeed! He would continue to be submissive and draw his salary and wonder how much he could save and when he would be able to buy a little house to bring his girl into; a nice thing to think of on a spring morning: a house of his own and a wife in the bed beside him. And his nature would continue to contract about him, every ideal, every generous impulse another mesh to draw his head down tighter to his knees till in ten years' time it would tie him hand and foot.

Том, who was a curate in Wicklow, wrote and suggested that they might go home together for the long weekend, and on Saturday morning they set out in Tom's old Ford. It was Easter weather, pearly and cold. They stopped at several pubs on the way and Tom ordered whiskeys. Ned was feeling expansive and joined him. He had never quite grown used to his brother, partly because of old days when he felt that Tom was getting the education he should have got, partly because his ordination seemed to have shut him off from the rest of the family, and now it was as though he were trying to surmount it by his boisterous manner and affected bonhomie. He was like a man shouting to his comrades across a great distance. He was different from Ned; lighter in color of hair and skin; fat-headed, fresh-complexioned, deep-voiced, and autocratic; an irascible, humorous, friendly man who was well-liked by those he worked for. Ned, who was shy and all tied up within himself, envied him his way with men in garages and barmaids in hotels.

It was nightfall when they reached home. Their father was in his shirtsleeves at the gate waiting to greet them, and immediately their mother rushed out as well. The lamp was standing in the window and threw its light as far as the whitewashed gateposts. Little Brigid, the girl from up the hill who helped their mother now she was growing old, stood in the doorway in half-silhouette. When her eyes caught theirs she bent her head in confusion.

Nothing was changed in the tall, bare, whitewashed kitchen. The harness hung in the same place on the wall, the rosary on the same nail in the fireplace, by the stool where their mother usually sat; table under the window, churn against the back door, stair without banisters mounting straight to the attic door that yawned in the wall—all seemed as unchanging as the sea outside. Their mother sat on the stool, her hands on her knees, a colored shawl tied tightly about her head, like a gipsy woman with her battered yellow face and loud voice. Their father, fresh-complexioned like Tom, stocky and broken-bottomed, gazed out the front door, leaning with one hand on the dresser in the pose of an orator while Brigid wet the tea.

"I said ye'd be late," their father proclaimed triumphantly, twisting his mustache. "Didn't I, woman? Didn't I say they'd be late?"

"He did, he did," their mother assured them. " 'Tis true for him."

"Ah, I knew ye'd be making halts. But damn it, if I wasn't put astray by Thade Lahy's car going east!"

"And was that Thade Lahy's car?" their mother asked in a shocked tone.

"I told ye 'twas Thade Lahy's," piped Brigid, plopping about in her long frieze gown and bare feet.

"Sure I should know it, woman," old Tomas said with chagrin. "He must have gone into town without us noticing him."

"Oye, and how did he do that?" asked their mother.

"Leave me alone now," Tomas said despairingly. "I couldn't tell you, I could not tell you."

"My goodness, I was sure that was the Master's car," their mother said wonderingly, pulling distractedly at the tassels of her shawl.

"I'd know the rattle of Thade Lahy's car anywhere," little Brigid said very proudly and quite unregarded.

It seemed to Ned that he was interrupting a conversation that had been going on since his last visit, and that the road outside and the sea beyond it, and every living thing that passed before them, formed a pantomime that was watched endlessly and passionately from the darkness of the little cottage.

"Wisha, I never asked if ye'd like a drop of something," their father said with sudden vexation.

"Is it whiskey?" boomed Tom.

"Why? Would you sooner whiskey?"

"Can't you pour it out first and ask us after?" growled Tom.

"The whiskey, is it?"

" 'Tis not. I didn't come all the ways to this place for what I can get better at home. You'd better have a bottle ready for me to take back."

"Coleen will have it. Damn it, wasn't it only last night I said to Coleen that you'd likely want a bottle? Some way it struck me you would. Oh, he'll have it, he'll have it."

"Didn't they catch that string of misery yet?" asked Tom with the cup to his lips.

"Ah, man alive, you'd want to be a greyhound to catch him. God Almighty, hadn't they fifty police after him last November, scouring the mountains from one end to the other and all they caught was a glimpse of the white of his ass. Ah, but the priest preached a terrible sermon against him—by name, Tom, by name!"

"Is old Murphy blowing about it still?" growled Tom.

"Oh, let me alone now!" Tomas threw his hands to heaven and strode to and fro in his excitement, his bucket-bottom wagging. Ned knew to his sorrow that his father could be prudent, silent, and calculating; he knew only too well the cock of the head, the narrowing of the eyes, but, like a child, the old man loved innocent excitement and revelled in scenes of the wildest passion, all about nothing. Like an old actor he turned everything to drama. "The like of it for abuse was never heard, never heard, never heard! How Coleen could ever raise his head again after it! And where the man got the words from! Tom, my treasure, my son, you'll never have the like."

"I'd spare my breath to cool my porridge," Tom replied scornfully. "I dare say you gave up your own still so?"

"I didn't, Tom, I didn't. The drop I make, 'twould harm no one. Only a drop for Christmas and Easter."

The lamp was in its own place on the rear wall, and made a circle of brightness on the fresh lime wash. Their mother was leaning over the fire with joined hands, lost in thought. The front door was open and night thickening outside, the colored night of the west; and as they ate, their father walked to and fro in long ungainly strides, pausing each time at the door to give a glance up and down the road and at the fire to hoist his broken bottom to warm. Ned heard steps come up the road from the west. His father heard them too. He returned to the door and glued his hand to the jamb. Ned covered his eyes with his hands and felt that everything was as it had always been. He could hear the noise of the strand as a background to the voices.

"God be with you, Tomas," the voice said.

"God and Mary be with you, Teig." (In Irish they were speaking.) "What way are you?"

"Well, honor and praise be to God. 'Tis a fine night."

" 'Tis, 'tis, 'tis so indeed. A grand night, praise be to God."

"Musha, who is it?" their mother asked, looking round.

" 'Tis young Teig," their father replied, looking after him.

"Shemus's young Teig?"

" 'Tis, 'tis, 'tis."

"But where would Shemus's young Teig be going at this hour of night? 'Tisn't to the shop?"

"No, woman, no, no, no. Up to the uncle's I suppose."

"Is it Ned Willie's?"

"He's sleeping at Ned Willie's," Brigid chimed in in her high-pitched voice, timid but triumphant. " 'Tis since the young teacher came to them."

There was no more to be said. Everything was explained and Ned smiled. The only unfamiliar voice, little Brigid's, seemed the most familiar of all.

Tom said first Mass next morning and the household, all but Brigid, went. They drove, and Tomas in high glee sat in front with Tom, waving his hand and shouting greetings at all they met. He was like a boy, so intense was his pleasure. The chapel was perched high above the road. Outside the morning was gray and beyond the windy edge of the cliff was the sea. The wind blew straight in, setting cloaks and petticoats flying.

After dinner as the two boys were returning from a series of visits to the neighbors' houses their father rushed down the road to meet them, shaking them passionately by the hand and asking were they well. When they were seated in the kitchen he opened up the subject of his excitement.

"Well," he said, "I arranged a grand little outing for ye tomorrow, thanks be to God," and to identify further the source of his inspiration he searched at the back of his neck for the peak of his cap and raised it solemnly.

"Musha, what outing are you talking about?" their mother asked angrily.

"I arranged for us to go over the bay to your brother's."

"And can't you leave the poor boys alone?" she bawled. "Haven't they only the one day? Isn't it for the rest they came?"

"Even so, even so, even so," Tomas said with mounting passion. "Aren't their own cousins to lay eyes on them?"

"I was in Carriganassa for a week last summer," said Tom.

"Yes, but I wasn't, and Ned wasn't. 'Tis only decent."

" 'Tisn't decency is worrying you at all but drink," growled Tom.

"Oh!" gasped his father, fishing for the peak of his cap to swear with, "that I might be struck dead!"

"Be quiet, you old heathen!" crowed his wife. "That's the truth, Tom my pulse. Plenty of drink is what he wants where he won't be under my eye. Leave ye stop at home."

"I can't stop at home, woman," shouted Tomas. "Why do you be always picking at me? I must go whether they come or not. I must go, I must go, and that's all there is about it."

"Why must you?" asked his wife.

"Because I warned Red Pat and Dempsey," he stormed. "And the woman from the island is coming as well to see a daughter of hers that's married there. And what's more, I borrowed Cassidy's boat and he lent it at great inconvenience, and 'twould be very bad manners for me to throw his kindness back in his face. I must go."

"Oh, we may as well all go," said Tom.

It blew hard all night and Tomas, all anxiety, was out at break of day to watch the whitecaps on the water. While the boys were at breakfast he came in and, leaning his arms on the table with hands joined as though in prayer, he announced in a caressing voice that it was a beautiful day, thank God, a pet day with a moist gentle little bit of a breezheen that would only blow them over. His voice would have put a child to sleep, but his wife continued to nag and scold, and he stumped out again in a fury and sat on the wall with his back to the house and his legs crossed, chewing his pipe. He was dressed in his best clothes, a respectable blue tailcoat and pale frieze trousers with only one patch on the seat. He had turned his cap almost right way round so that the peak covered his right ear.

He was all over the boat like a boy. Dempsey, a haggard, pock-marked, melancholy man with a soprano voice of astounding penetration, took the tiller and Red Patrick the sail. Tomas clambered into the bows and stood there with one knee up, leaning forward like a figure-head. He knew the bay like a book. The island woman was perched on the ballast with her rosary in her hands and her shawl over her eyes to shut out the sight of the waves. The cumbrous old boat took the sail lightly enough and Ned leaned back on his elbows against the side, rejoicing in it all.

"She's laughing," his father said delightedly when her bows ran white.

"Whose boat is that, Dempsey?" he asked, screwing up his eyes as another brown sail tilted ahead of them.

" 'Tis the island boat," shrieked Dempsey.

" 'Tis not, Dempsey. 'Tis not indeed, my love. That's not the island boat."

"Whose boat is it then?"

"It must be some boat from Carriganassa, Dempsey."

" 'Tis the island boat I tell you."

"Ah, why will you be contradicting me, Dempsey, my treasure? 'Tis not the island boat. The island boat has a dark brown sail; 'tis only a month since 'twas tarred, and that's an old tarred sail, and what proves it out and out, Dempsey, the island-boat sail has a patch in the corner."

He was leaning well over the bows, watching the rocks that fled beneath them, a dark purple. He rested his elbow on his raised knee and looked back at them, his brown face sprinkled with spray and lit from below by the accumulated flickerings of the water. His flesh seemed to dissolve, to become transparent, while his blue eyes shone with extraordinary brilliance. Ned half-closed his eyes and watched sea and sky slowly mount and sink behind the red-brown, sun-filled sail and the poised and eager figure.

"Tom!" shouted his father, and the battered old face peered at them from under the arch of the sail, with which it was almost one in tone, the silvery light filling it with warmth.

"Well?" Tom's voice was an inexpressive boom.

"You were right last night, Tom, my boy. My treasure, my son, you were right. 'Twas for the drink I came."

"Ah, do you tell me so?" Tom asked ironically.

" 'Twas, 'twas, 'twas," the old man said regretfully. " 'Twas for the drink. 'Twas so, my darling. They were always decent people, your mother's people, and 'tis her knowing how decent they are makes her so suspicious. She's a good woman, a fine woman, your poor mother, may the Almighty God bless her and keep her and watch over her."

"Aaa-men," Tom chanted irreverently as his father shook his old cap piously towards the sky.

"But Tom! Are you listening, Tom?"

"Well, what is it now?"

"I had another reason."

"Had you indeed?" Tom's tone was not encouraging.

"I had, I had, God's truth, I had. God blast the lie I'm telling you, Tom, I had."

" 'Twas boasting out of the pair of ye," shrieked Dempsey from the stern, the wind whipping the shrill notes from his lips and scattering them wildly like scraps of paper.

" 'Twas so, Dempsey, 'twas so. You're right, Dempsey. You're always right. The blessing of God on you, Dempsey, for you always had the true word." Tomas's laughing leprechaun countenance gleamed under the bellying, tilting, chocolate-colored sail and his powerful voice beat Dempsey's down. "And would you blame me?"

"The O'Donnells hadn't the beating of them in their own hand," screamed Dempsey.

"Thanks be to God for all His goodness and mercy," shouted Tomas, again waving his cap in a gesture of recognition towards the spot where he felt the Almighty might be listening, "they have not. They have not so, Dempsey. And they have a good hand. The O'Donnells are a good family and an old family and a kind family, but they never had the like of my two sons."

"And they were stiff enough with you when you came for the daughter," shrieked Dempsey.

"They were, Dempsey, they were. They were stiff. They were so. You wouldn't blame them, Dempsey. They were an old family and I was nothing only a landless man." With a fierce gesture the old man pulled his cap still further over his ear, spat, gave his mustache a tug and leaned at a still more precarious angle over the bow, his blue eyes dancing with triumph. "But I had the gumption, Dempsey. I had the gumption, my love."

The islands slipped past; the gulf of water narrowed and grew calmer, and white cottages could be seen scattered under the tall ungainly church. It was a wild and rugged coast, the tide was full, and they had to pull in as best they could among the rocks. Red Patrick leaped lightly ashore to draw in the boat. The others stepped after him into several inches of water and Red Patrick, himself precariously poised, held them from slipping. Rather shamefastly, Ned and Tom took off their shoes.

"Don't do that!" shrieked their father. "We'll carry ye up. Mother of God, yeer poor feet!"

"Will you shut your old gob?" Tom said angrily.

They halted for a moment at the stile outside Caheragh's. Old Caheragh had a red beard and a broad, smiling face. Then they went on to O'Donnell's who had two houses, modern and old, separated by a yard. In one lived Uncle Maurice and his family and in the other Maurice's married son, Sean. Ned and Tom remained with Sean and his wife. Tom and he were old friends. When he spoke he rarely looked at Tom, merely giving him a sidelong glance that just reached to his chin and then dropped his eyes with a peculiar timid smile. " 'Twas," Ned heard him say, and then: "He did," and after that: "Hardly." Shuvaun was tall, nervous, and matronly. She clung to their hands with an excess of eagerness as though she couldn't bear to let them go, uttering ejaculations of tenderness, delight, astonishment, pity, and admiration. Her speech was full of diminutives: "childeen," "handeen," "boateen." Three young children scrambled about the floor with a preoccupation scarcely broken by the strangers. Shuvaun picked her way through them, filling the kettle and cutting the bread, and then, as though afraid of neglecting Tom, she clutched his hand again. Her feverish concentration gave an impression that its very intensity bewildered her and made it impossible for her to understand one word they said. In three days' time it would all begin to drop into place in her mind and then she would begin quoting them.

Young Niall O'Donnell came in with his girl; one of the Deignans from up the hill. She was plump and pert; she had been in service in town. Niall was a well-built boy with a soft, wild-eyed, sensuous face and a deep mellow voice of great power. While they were having a cup of tea in the parlor where the three or four family photos were skyed, Ned saw the two of them again through the back window. They were standing on the high ground behind the house with the spring sky behind them and the light in their faces. Niall was asking her something but she, more interested in the sitting-room window, only shook her head.

"Ye only just missed yeer father," said their Uncle Maurice when they went across to the other house for dinner. Maurice was a tight-lipped little man with a high bald forehead and a snappy voice. "He went off to Owney Pat's only this minute."

"The devil!" said Tom. "I knew he was out to dodge me. Did you give him whiskey?"

"What the hell else could I give him?" snapped Maurice. "Do you think 'twas tea the old coot was looking for?"

Tom took the place of honor at the table. He was the favorite. Through the doorway into the bedroom could be seen a big canopy bed and on the whiteness of a raised pillow a skeleton face in a halo of smoke-blue hair surmounted with what looked suspiciously like a mauve tea-cosy. Sometimes the white head would begin to stir and everyone fell silent while Niall, the old man's pet, translated the scarcely audible whisper. Sometimes Niall would go in with his stiff ungainly swagger and repeat one of Tom's jokes in his drawling, powerful bass. The hens stepped daintily about their feet, poking officious heads between them, and rushing out the door with a wild flutter and shriek when one of the girls hooshed them. Something timeless, patriarchal, and restful about it made Ned notice everything. It was as though he had never seen his mother's house before.

"Tell me," Tom boomed with mock concern, leaning over confidentially to his uncle and looking under his brows at young Niall, "speaking as a clergyman and for the good of the family and so on, is that son of yours coorting Delia Deignan?"

"Why? Was the young blackguard along with her again?" snapped Maurice in amusement.

"Of course I might be mistaken," Tom said doubtfully.

"You wouldn't know a Deignan, to be sure," Sean said dryly.

"Isn't any of them married yet?" asked Tom.

"No, by damn, no," said Maurice. "Isn't it a wonder?"

"Because," Tom went on in the same solemn voice, "I want someone to look after this young brother of mine. Dublin is a wild sort of place and full of temptations. Ye wouldn't know a decent little girl I could ask?"

"Cait! Cait!" they all shouted, Niall's deep voice loudest of all.

"Now all the same, Delia looks a smart little piece," said Tom.

"No, Cait! Cait! Delia isn't the same since she went to town. She has notions of herself. Leave him marry Cait!"

Niall rose gleefully and shambled in to the old man. With a gamesome eye on the company Tom whispered:

"Is she a quiet sort of girl? I wouldn't like Ned to get anyone rough."

"She is, she is," they said, "a grand girl!"

Sean rose quietly and went to the door with his head bowed.

"God knows, if anyone knows he should know and all the times he manhandled her."

Tom sat bolt upright with mock indignation while the table rocked. Niall shouted the joke into his grandfather's ear. The mauve tea-cosy shook; it was the only indication of the old man's amusement.

THE DEIGNANS' house was on top of a hill high over the road and commanded a view of the countryside for miles. The two brothers with Sean and the O'Donnell girls reached it by a long winding boreen that threaded its way uncertainly through little gray rocky fields and walls of unmortared stone which rose against the sky along the edges of the hill like lacework. On their way they met another procession coming down the hill. It was headed by their father and the island woman, arm in arm, and behind came two locals with Dempsey and Red Patrick. All the party except the island woman were well advanced in liquor. That was plain when their father rushed forward to shake them all by the hand and ask them how they were. He said that divil such honorable and kindly people as the people of Carriganassa were to be found in the whole world, and of these there was no one a patch on the O'Donnells; kings and sons of kings as you could see from one look at them. He had only one more call to pay and promised to be at Caheragh's within a quarter of an hour.

They looked over the Deignans' half-door. The kitchen was empty. The girls began to titter. They knew the Deignans must have watched them coming from Maurice's door. The kitchen was a beautiful room; woodwork and furniture, homemade and shapely, were painted a bright red-brown and the painted dresser shone with pretty ware. They entered and looked about them. Nothing was to be heard but the tick of the cheap alarm clock on the dresser. One of the girls began to giggle hysterically. Sean raised his voice.

"Are ye in or are ye out, bad cess to ye!"

For a moment there was no reply. Then a quick step sounded in the attic and a girl descended the stairs at a run, drawing a black knitted shawl tighter about her shoulders. She was perhaps twenty-eight or thirty, with a narrow face, sharp like a ferret's, and blue nervous eyes. She entered the kitchen awkwardly sideways, giving the customary greetings but without looking at anyone.

"A hundred welcomes. . . . How are ye? . . . 'Tis a fine day."

The O'Donnell girls giggled again. Nora Deignan looked at them in astonishment, biting nervously at the tassel of her shawl. She had tiny sharp white teeth.

"What is it, aru?" she asked.

"Musha, will you stop your old cimeens," boomed Tom, "and tell

us where's Cait from you? You don't think 'twas to see your ugly puss
that we came up here?"

"Cait!" Nora called in a low voice.

"What is it?" another voice replied from upstairs.

"Damn well you know what it is," bellowed Tom, "and you crosseyed expecting us since morning. Will you come down out of that or
will I go up and fetch you?"

There was the same hasty step and a second girl descended the
stairs. It was only later that Ned was able to realize how beautiful she
was. She had the same narrow pointed face as her sister, the same
slight features sharpened by a sort of animal instinct, the same blue
eyes with their startled brightness; but all seemed to have been differently composed, and her complexion had a transparency as though
her whole nature were shining through it. "Child of Light, thy limbs
are burning through the veil which seems to hide them," Ned found
himself murmuring. She came on them in the same hostile way,
blushing furiously. Tom's eyes rested on her; soft, bleary, emotional
eyes incredibly unlike her own.

"Have you nothing to say to me, Cait?" he boomed, and Ned
thought his very voice was soft and clouded.

"Oh, a hundred welcomes." Her blue eyes rested for a moment on
him with what seemed a fierce candor and penetration and went past
him to the open door. Outside a soft rain was beginning to fall; heavy
clouds crushed down the gray landscape, which grew clearer as it
merged into one common plane; the little gray bumpy fields with the
walls of gray unmortared stone that drifted hither and over across
them like blown sand, the whitewashed farmhouses lost to the sun
sinking back into the brown-gray hillsides.

"Nothing else, my child?" he growled, pursing his lips.

"How are you?"

"The politeness is suffocating you. Where's Delia?"

"Here I am," said Delia from the doorway immediately behind him.
In her furtive way she had slunk round the house. Her bland impertinence raised a laugh.

"The reason we called," said Tom, clearing his throat, "is this young
brother of mine that's looking for a wife."

Everyone laughed again. Ned knew the oftener a joke was repeated
the better they liked it, but for him this particular joke was beginning
to wear thin.

"Leave him take me," said Delia with an arch look at Ned who
smiled and gazed at the floor.

"Be quiet, you slut!" said Tom. "There are your two sisters before
you."

"Even so, I want to go to Dublin. . . . Would you treat me to lemonade, mister?" she asked Ned with her impudent smile. "This is a rotten hole. I'd go to America if they left me."

"America won't be complete without you," said Tom. "Now, don't let me hurry ye, ladies, but my old fellow will be waiting for us in Johnny Kit's."

"We'll go along with you," said Nora, and the three girls took down three black shawls from inside the door. Some tension seemed to have gone out of the air. They laughed and joked between themselves.

"Ye'll get wet," said Sean to the two brothers.

"Cait will make room for me under her shawl," said Tom.

"Indeed I will not," she cried, starting back with a laugh.

"Very shy you're getting," said Sean with a good-natured grin.

" 'Tisn't that at all but she'd sooner the young man," said Delia.

"What's strange is wonderful," said Nora.

Biting her lip with her tiny front teeth, Cait looked angrily at her sisters and Sean, and then began to laugh. She glanced at Ned and smilingly held out her shawl in invitation, though at the same moment angry blushes chased one another across her forehead like squalls across the surface of a lake. The rain was a mild, persistent drizzle and a strong wind was blowing. Everything had darkened and grown lonely and, with his head in the blinding folds of the shawl, which reeked of turf-smoke, Ned felt as if he had dropped out of Time's pocket.

They waited in Caheragh's kitchen. The bearded old man sat in one chimney corner and a little barelegged boy in the other. The dim blue light poured down the wide chimney on their heads in a shower with the delicacy of light on old china, picking out surfaces one rarely saw; and between them the fire burned a bright orange in the great whitewashed hearth with the black, swinging bars and pothook. Outside the rain fell softly, almost soundlessly, beyond the half-door. Delia, her black shawl trailing from her shoulders, leaned over it, acting the part of watcher as in a Greek play. Their father's fifteen minutes had strung themselves out to an hour and two little barefooted boys had already been sent to hunt him down.

"Where are they now, Delia?" one of the O'Donnells would ask.

"Crossing the fields from Patsy Kit's."

"He wasn't there so."

"He wouldn't be," the old man said. "They'll likely go on to Ned Kit's now."

"That's where they're making for," said Delia. "Up the hill at the far side of the fort."

"They'll find him there," the old man said confidently.

Ned felt as though he were still blanketed by the folds of the turf-reeking shawl. Something seemed to have descended on him that filled him with passion and loneliness. He could scarcely take his eyes off Cait. She and Nora sat on the form against the back wall, a composition in black and white, the black shawl drawn tight under the chin, the cowl of it breaking the curve of her dark hair, her shadow on the gleaming wall behind. She did not speak except to answer some question of Tom's about her brother, but sometimes Ned caught her looking at him with naked eyes. Then she smiled swiftly and secretly and turned her eyes again to the door, sinking back into pensiveness. Pensiveness or vacancy? he wondered. While he gazed at her face with the animal instinctiveness of its overdelicate features it seemed like a mirror in which he saw again the falling rain, the rocks and hills and angry sea.

The first announced by Delia was Red Patrick. After him came the island woman. Each had last seen his father in a different place. Ned chuckled at a sudden vision of his father, eager and impassioned and aflame with drink, stumping with his broken bottom across endless fields through pouring rain with a growing procession behind him. Dempsey was the last to come. He doubted if Tomas would be in a condition to take the boat at all.

"What matter, aru?" said Delia across her shoulder. "We can find room for the young man."

"And where would we put him?" gaped Nora.

"He can have Cait's bed," Delia said innocently.

"Oye, and where would Cait sleep?" Nora asked and then skitted and covered her face with her shawl. Delia scoffed. The men laughed and Cait, biting her lip furiously, looked at the floor. Again Ned caught her eyes on him and again she laughed and turned away.

Tomas burst in unexpected on them all like a sea wind that scattered them before him. He wrung Tom's hand and asked him how he was. He did the same to Ned. Ned replied gravely that he was very well.

"In God's holy name," cried his father, waving his arms like a windmill, "what are ye all waiting for?"

The tide had fallen. Tomas grabbed an oar and pushed the boat on to a rock. Then he raised the sail and collapsed under it and had to be extricated from its drenching folds, glauming and swearing at Cassidy's old boat. A little group stood on a naked rock against a gray background of drifting rain. For a long time Ned continued to wave back to the black shawl that was lifted to him. An extraordinary feeling of exultation and loss enveloped him. Huddled up in his overcoat he sat with Dempsey in the stern, not speaking.

"It was a grand day," his father declared, swinging himself to and fro, tugging at his Viking mustache, dragging the peak of his cap farther over his ear. His gestures betrayed a certain lack of rhythmical cohesion; they began and ended abruptly. "Dempsey, my darling, wasn't it a grand day?"

" 'Twas a grand day for you," shrieked Dempsey as if his throat would burst.

" 'Twas, my treasure, 'twas a beautiful day. I got an honorable reception and my sons got an honorable reception."

By this time he was flat on his belly, one leg completely over the edge of the boat. He reached back a clammy hand to his sons.

" 'Twas the best day I ever had," he said. "I got porter and I got whiskey and I got poteen. I did so, Tom, my calf. Ned, my brightness, I went to seven houses and in every house I got seven drinks and with every drink I got seven welcomes. And your mother's people are a hand of trumps. It was no slight they put on me at all even if I was nothing but a landless man. No slight, Tom. No slight at all."

Darkness had fallen, the rain had cleared, the stars came out of a pitch-black sky under which the little tossing, nosing boat seemed lost beyond measure. In all the waste of water nothing could be heard but the splash of the boat's sides and their father's voice raised in tipsy song.

> "The evening was fair and the sunlight was yellow,
> I halted, beholding a maiden bright
> Coming to me by the edge of the mountain,
> Her cheeks had a berry-bright rosy light."

NED was the first to wake. He struck a match and lit the candle. It was time for them to be stirring. It was just after dawn, and at half past nine he must be in his old place in the schoolroom before the rows of pinched little city faces. He lit a cigarette and closed his eyes. The lurch of the boat was still in his blood, the face of Cait Deignan in his mind, and as if from far away he heard a line of the wild love-song his father had been singing: "And we'll drive the geese at the fall of night."

He heard his brother mumble something and nudged him. Tom looked big and fat and vulnerable with his fair head rolled sideways and his heavy mouth dribbling on to the sleeve of his pajamas. Ned slipped quietly out of bed, put on his trousers, and went to the window. He drew the curtains and let in the thin cold daylight. The bay was just visible and perfectly still. Tom began to mumble again in a frightened voice and Ned shook him. He started out of his sleep with a cry of fear, grabbing at the bedclothes. He looked first at Ned, then at the candle and drowsily rubbed his eyes.

"Did you hear it too?" he asked.

"Did I hear what?" asked Ned with a smile.

"In the room," said Tom.

"There was nothing in the room," replied Ned. "You were ramaishing so I woke you up."

"Was I? What was I saying?"

"You were telling no secrets," said Ned with a quiet laugh.

"Hell!" Tom said in disgust and stretched out his arm for a cigarette. He lit it at the candle flame, his drowsy red face puckered and distraught. "I slept rotten."

"Oye!" Ned said quietly, raising his eyebrows. It wasn't often Tom spoke in that tone. He sat on the edge of the bed, joined his hands and leaned forward, looking at Tom with wide gentle eyes.

"Is there anything wrong?" he asked.

"Plenty."

"You're not in trouble?" Ned asked without raising his voice.

"Not that sort of trouble. The trouble is in myself."

Ned gave him a look of intense sympathy and understanding. The soft emotional brown eyes were searching him for a judgment. Ned had never felt less like judging him.

"Ay," he said gently and vaguely, his eyes wandering to the other side of the room while his voice took on its accustomed stammer, "the trouble is always in ourselves. If we were contented in ourselves the other things wouldn't matter. I suppose we must only leave it to time. Time settles everything."

"Time will settle nothing for me," Tom said despairingly. "You have something to look forward to. I have nothing. It's the loneliness of my job that kills you. Even to talk about it would be a relief but there's no one you can talk to. People come to you with their troubles but there's no one you can go to with your own."

Again the challenging glare in the brown eyes and Ned realized with infinite compassion that for years Tom had been living in the same state of suspicion and fear, a man being hunted down by his own nature; and that for years to come he would continue to live in this way, and perhaps never be caught again as he was now.

"A pity you came down here," stammered Ned flatly. "A pity we went to Carriganassa. 'Twould be better for both of us if we went somewhere else."

"Why don't you marry her, Ned?" Tom asked earnestly.

"Who?" asked Ned.

"Cait."

"Yesterday," said Ned with the shy smile he wore when he confessed something, "I nearly wished I could."

"But you can, man," Tom said eagerly, sitting upon his elbow. Like all men with frustration in their hearts he was full of schemes for others. "You could marry her and get a school down here. That's what I'd do if I was in your place."

"No," Ned said gravely. "We made our choice a long time ago. We can't go back on it now."

Then with his hands in his trouser pockets and his head bowed he went out to the kitchen. His mother, the colored shawl about her head, was blowing the fire. The bedroom door was open and he could see his father in shirtsleeves kneeling beside the bed, his face raised reverently towards a holy picture, his braces hanging down behind. He unbolted the half-door, went through the garden and out on to the road. There was a magical light on everything. A boy on a horse rose suddenly against the sky, a startling picture. Through the apple-green light over Carriganassa ran long streaks of crimson, so still they might have been enamelled. Magic, magic, magic! He saw it as in a children's picture-book with all its colors intolerably bright; something he had outgrown and could never return to, while the world he aspired to was as remote and intangible as it had seemed even in the despair of youth.

It seemed as if only now for the first time was he leaving home; for the first time and forever saying good-bye to it all.

The Mad Lomasneys

NED LOWRY and Rita Lomasney had, one might say, been lovers from childhood. The first time they had met was when he was fourteen and she a year or two younger. It was on the North Mall on a Saturday afternoon, and she was sitting on a bench under the trees; a tall, bony string of a girl with a long, obstinate jaw. Ned was a studious young fellow in a blue and white college cap, thin, pale, and spectacled. As he passed he looked at her owlishly and she gave him back an impudent stare. This upset him—he had no experience of girls—so he blushed and raised his cap. At that she seemed to relent.

"Hello," she said experimentally.

"Good afternoon," he replied with a pale smile.

"Where are you off to?" she asked.

"Oh, just up the dike for a walk."

"Sit down," she said in a sharp voice, laying her hand on the bench beside her, and he did as he was told. It was a lovely summer evening, and the white quay walls and tall, crazy, claret-colored tenements under a blue and white sky were reflected in the lazy water, which wrinkled only at the edges and seemed like a painted carpet.

"It's very pleasant here," he said complacently

"Is it?" she asked with a truculence that startled him. "I don't see anything very pleasant about it."

"Oh, it's very nice and quiet," he said in mild surprise as he raised his fair eyebrows and looked up and down the Mall at the old Georgian houses and the nursemaids sitting under the trees. "My name is Lowry," he added politely.

"Oh, are ye the ones that have the jeweler's shop on the Parade?" she asked.

"That's right," replied Ned with modest pride.

"We have a clock we got from ye," she said. " 'Tisn't much good of an old clock either," she added with quiet malice.

"You should bring it back to the shop," he said in considerable concern. "It probably needs overhauling."

"I'm going down the river in a boat with a couple of chaps," she said, going off at a tangent. "Will you come?"

"Couldn't," he said with a smile.

"Why not?"

"I'm only left go up the dike for a walk," he said complacently. "On Saturdays I go to Confession at St. Peter and Paul's, then I go up the dike and back the Western Road. Sometimes you see very good cricket matches. Do you like cricket?"

"A lot of old sissies pucking a ball!" she said shortly. "I do not."

"I like it," he said firmly. "I go up there every Saturday. Of course, I'm not supposed to talk to anyone," he added with mild amusement at his own audacity.

"Why not?"

"My mother doesn't want me to."

"Why doesn't she?"

"She comes of an awfully good family," he answered mildly, and but for his gentle smile she might have thought he was deliberately insulting her. "You see," he went on gravely in his thin, pleasant voice, ticking things off on his fingers and then glancing at each finger individually as he ticked it off—a tidy sort of boy—"there are three main branches of the Hourigan family: the Neddy Neds, the Neddy Jerrys, and the Neddy Thomases. The Neddy Neds are the Hayfield Hourigans. They are the oldest branch. My mother is a Hayfield Hourigan, and she'd have been a rich woman only for her father backing a bill for a Neddy Jerry. He defaulted and ran away to Australia," he concluded with a contemptuous sniff.

"Cripes!" said the girl. "And had she to pay?"

"She had. But, of course," he went on with as close as he ever seemed likely to get to a burst of real enthusiasm, "my grandfather was a well-behaved man. When he was eating his dinner the boys from the National School in Bantry used to be brought up to watch him, he had such beautiful table manners. Once he caught my uncle eating cabbage with a knife and he struck him with a poker. They had to put four stitches in him after," he added with a joyous chuckle.

"Cripes!" the girl said again. "What did he do that for?"

"To teach him manners," Ned said earnestly.

"He must have been dotty."

"Oh, I wouldn't say so," Ned exclaimed in mild surprise. Everything this girl said came as a shock to him. "But that's why my mother won't let me mix with other children. On the other hand, we read a good deal. Are you fond of reading, Miss—I didn't catch the name."

"You weren't told it," she said, showing her claws. "But if you want to know, it's Rita Lomasney."

"Do you read much, Miss Lomasney?"

"I couldn't be bothered."

"I read all sorts of books," he said enthusiastically. "And as well as that, I'm learning the violin from Miss Maude on the Parade. Of course, it's very difficult, because it's all classical music."

"What's classical music?" she asked with sudden interest.

"*Maritana* is classical music," he replied eagerly. He was a bit of a puzzle to Rita. She had never before met anyone with such a passion for handing out instruction. "Were you at *Maritana* in the opera house, Miss Lomasney?"

"I was never there at all," she said curtly.

"And *Alice Where Art Thou* is classical music," he added. "It's harder than plain music. You see," he went on, composing signs in the air, "it has signs on it like this, and when you see the signs, you know it's after turning into a different tune, though it has the same name. Irish music is all the same tune and that's why my mother won't let us learn it."

"Were you ever at the opera in Paris?" she asked suddenly.

"No," said Ned. "I was never in Paris. Why?"

"That's where you should go," she said with airy enthusiasm. "You couldn't hear any operas here. The staircase alone is bigger than the whole opera house here."

It seemed as if they were in for a really informative conversation when two fellows came down Wyse's Hill. Rita got up to meet them. Lowry looked up at them and then rose too, lifting his cap politely.

"Well, good afternoon," he said cheerfully. "I enjoyed the talk. I hope we meet again."

"Some other Saturday," said Rita.

"Oh, good evening, old man," one of the two fellows said in an affected drawl, pretending to raise a top hat. "Do come and see us soon again."

"Shut up, Foster!" Rita said sharply. "I'll give you a puck in the gob."

"Oh, by the way," Ned said, coming back to hand her a number of the *Gem* which he took from his coat pocket, "you might like to look at this. It's not bad."

"Thanks, I'd love to," she said insincerely, and he smiled and touched his cap again. Then with a polite and almost deferential air he went up to Foster. "Did you say something?" he asked.

Foster looked as astonished as if a kitten had suddenly got on its hind legs and challenged him to fight.

"I did not," he said, and backed away.

"I'm glad," Ned said, almost purring. "I was afraid you might be looking for trouble."

It came as a surprise to Rita as well. Whatever opinion she might have formed of Ned Lowry, fighting was about the last thing she would have associated him with.

THE LOMASNEYS lived in a house on Sunday's Well, a small house with a long, sloping garden and a fine view of the river and city. Harry Lomasney, the builder, was a small man who wore gray tweed suits and soft collars several sizes too big for him. He had a ravaged brick-red face with keen blue eyes, and a sandy, straggling mustache with one side going up and the other down, and his workmen said you could tell his humor by the side he pulled. He was nicknamed "Hasty

Harry." "Great God!" he fumed when his wife was having her first baby. "Nine months over a little job like that! I'd do it in three weeks if I could only get started." His wife was tall and matronly and very pious, but her piety never got much in her way. A woman who had survived Hasty would have survived anything. Their eldest daughter, Kitty, was loud-voiced and gay and had been expelled from school for writing indecent letters to a boy. She had copied the letters out of a French novel but she failed to tell the nuns that. Nellie was placider and took more after her mother; besides, she didn't read French novels.

Rita was the exception among the girls. There seemed to be no softness in her. She never had a favorite saint or a favorite nun; she said it was soppy. For the same reason she never had flirtations. Her friendship with Ned Lowry was the closest she ever got to that, and though Ned came regularly to the house, and the pair of them went to the pictures together, her sisters would have found it hard to say whether she cared any more for him than she did for any of her girl acquaintances. There was something in her they didn't understand, something tongue-tied, twisted, and unhappy. She had a curious raw, almost timid smile as though she felt people desired no better sport than hurting her. At home she was reserved, watchful, almost mocking. She could listen for hours to her mother and sisters without once opening her mouth, and then suddenly mystify them by dropping a well-aimed jaw-breaker—about classical music, for instance—before relapsing into a sulky silence; as though she had merely drawn back the veil for a moment on depths in herself which she would not permit them to explore.

After taking her degree, she got a job in a convent school in a provincial town in the west of Ireland. She and Ned corresponded and he even went to see her there. He reported at home that she seemed quite happy.

But this didn't last. A few months later the Lomasney family were at supper one evening when they heard a car stop, the gate squeaked, and steps came up the long path to the front door. Then came the sound of a bell and a cheerful voice from the hall.

"Hullo, Paschal, I suppose ye weren't expecting me?"

" 'Tis never Rita!" said her mother, meaning that it was but that it shouldn't be.

"As true as God, that one is after getting into trouble," Kitty said prophetically.

The door opened and Rita slouched in, a long, stringy girl with a dark, glowing face. She kissed her father and mother lightly.

"Hullo," she said. "How's tricks?"

"What happened you?" her mother asked, rising.

"Nothing," replied Rita, an octave up the scale. "I just got the sack."

"The sack?" said her father, beginning to pull the wrong side of his mustache. "What did you get the sack for?"

"Give me a chance to get something to eat first, can't you?" Rita said laughingly. She took off her hat and smiled at herself in the mirror over the mantelpiece. It was a curious smile as though she were amused by the spectacle of what she saw. Then she smoothed back her thick black hair. "I told Paschal to bring in whatever was going. I'm on the train since ten. The heating was off as usual. I'm frizzled."

"A wonder you wouldn't send us a wire," said Mrs. Lomasney as Rita sat down and grabbed some bread and butter.

"Hadn't the tin," replied Rita.

"Can't you tell us what happened?" Kitty asked brightly.

"I told you. You'll hear more in due course. Reverend Mother is bound to write and tell ye how I lost my character."

"But what did you do, child?" her mother asked placidly. Her mother had been through all this before, with Hasty and Kitty, and she knew God was very good and nothing much ever happened.

"Fellow that wanted to marry me," said Rita. "He was in his last year at college, and his mother didn't like me, so she got Reverend Mother to give me the push."

"And what has it to do with Reverend Mother?" Nellie asked indignantly. "What business is it of hers?"

"That's what I say," said Rita.

But Kitty looked suspiciously at her. Rita wasn't natural; there was something wild about her, and this was her first real love affair. Kitty just couldn't believe that Rita had gone about it the same as anyone else.

"Still, I must say you worked pretty fast," she said.

"You'd have to in that place," said Rita. "There was only one possible man in the whole village and he was the bank clerk. We called him 'The One.' I wasn't there a week when the nuns ticked me off for riding on the pillion of his motorbike."

"And did you?" asked Kitty.

"I never got the chance, girl. They did it to every teacher on principle to give her the idea that she was well watched. I only met Tony Donoghue a fortnight ago—home after a breakdown."

"Well, well, well!" her mother exclaimed without rancor. "No wonder his poor mother was upset. A boy that's not left college yet! Couldn't ye wait till he was qualified anyway?"

"Not very well," said Rita. "He's going to be a priest."

Kitty sat back with a superior grin. Of course, Rita could do nothing like anyone else. If it wasn't a priest it would have been a Negro, and Rita would have made theatre of it in precisely the same deliberate way.

"A what?" asked her father, springing to his feet.

"All right, don't blame me!" Rita said hastily. "It wasn't my fault. He told me he didn't want to be a priest. It was his mother was driving him into it. That's why he had the breakdown."

"Let me out of this," said her father, "before I—"

"Go on!" Rita said with tender mockery (she was very fond of her father). "Before you what?"

"Before I wish I was a priest myself," he snarled. "I wouldn't be saddled with a family like I am."

He stumped out of the room, and the girls laughed. The idea of their father as a priest appealed to them almost as much as the idea of him as a mother. Hasty had a knack of stating his grievances in such a way that they inevitably produced laughter. But Mrs. Lomasney did not laugh.

"Reverend Mother was perfectly right," she said severely. "As if it wasn't hard enough on the poor boys without girls like you throwing temptation in their way. I think you behaved very badly, Rita."

"All right, if you say so," Rita said shortly with a boyish shrug of her shoulders, and refused to answer any more questions.

After her supper she went to bed, and her mother and sisters sat on in the front room discussing the scandal. Someone rang and Nellie opened the door.

"Hullo, Ned," she said. "I suppose you came up to congratulate us on the good news?"

"Hullo," Ned said, smiling with his mouth primly shut. With a sort of automatic movement he took off his coat and hat and hung them on the rack. Then he emptied the pockets with the same thoroughness. He hadn't changed much. He was thin and pale, spectacled and clever, with the same precise and tranquil manner, "like an old Persian cat," as Nellie said. He read too many books. In the last year or two something seemed to have happened him. He didn't go to Mass any longer. Not going to Mass struck all the Lomasneys as too damn clever. "What good news?" he added, having avoided any unnecessary precipitation.

"You didn't know who was here?"

"No," he replied, raising his brows mildly.

"Rita!"

"Oh!" The same tone. It was part of his cleverness not to be surprised at anything.

"She's after getting the sack for trying to run off with a priest," said Nellie.

If Nellie thought that would shake him she was mistaken. He merely tossed his head with a silent chuckle and went in, adjusting his pince-nez. For a fellow who was supposed to be in love with her since they were kids, he behaved in a very peculiar manner. He put his hands in his trouser pockets and stood on the hearth with his legs well apart.

"Isn't it awful, Ned?" Mrs. Lomasney asked in her deep voice.

"Is it?" Ned purred, smiling.

"With a priest?" cried Nellie.

"Now, he wasn't a priest, Nellie," said Mrs. Lomasney reprovingly. " 'Tis bad enough as it is without making it any worse."

"Suppose you tell me what happened," suggested Ned.

"But we don't know, Ned," cried Mrs. Lomasney. "You know what that one is like in one of her sulky fits. Maybe she'll tell you. She's up in bed."

"I'll try," said Ned.

Still with his hands in his pockets, he rolled after Mrs. Lomasney up the thickly carpeted stairs to Rita's little bedroom on top of the house. She left him on the landing and he paused for a moment to look out over the river and the lighted city behind it. Rita, wearing a pink dressing-jacket, was lying with one arm under her head. By the bed was a table with a packet of cigarettes she had been using as an ashtray. He smiled and shook his head reprovingly at her.

"Hullo, Ned," she cried, reaching him a bare arm. "Give us a kiss. I'm quite kissable now."

He didn't need to be told that. He was astonished at the change in her. Her whole bony, boyish face seemed to have gone mawkish and soft and to be lit up from inside. He sat on an armchair by the bed, carefully pulling up the bottoms of his trousers, then put his hands in his trouser pockets again and sat back with crossed legs and shoulders slightly hunched.

"I suppose they're all in a floosther downstairs?" Rita asked with amusement.

"They seem a little excited," said Ned with bowed head cocked a little sideways, looking like a wise old bird.

"Wait till they hear the details and they'll have something to be excited about," said Rita grimly.

"Why?" he asked mildly. "Are there details?"

"Masses of them," said Rita. "Honest to God, Ned, I used to laugh at the glamor girls in the convent. I never knew you could get like that about a fellow. It's like something busting inside you. Cripes, I'm as soppy as a kid!"

"And what's the fellow like?" Ned asked curiously.

"Tony Donoghue? His mother had a shop in the Main Street. He's decent enough, I suppose. I don't know. He kissed me one night coming home. I was furious. I cut the blooming socks off him. Next evening he came round to apologize. I never got up or asked him to sit down or anything. I suppose I was still mad with him. He said he never slept a wink. 'Didn't you?' said I. 'It didn't trouble me much.' Bloody lies, of course. 'I did it because I was fond of you,' says he. 'Is that what you told the last one too?' said I. Then he got into a wax too. Said I was calling him a liar. 'And aren't you?' said I. Then I waited for him to hit me, but, begor, he didn't, and I ended up sitting on his knee. Talk about the Babes in the Wood! First time he ever had a girl on his knee, he said, and you know how much of it I did."

They heard a step on the stairs and Mrs. Lomasney smiled benevolently at them both round the door.

"I suppose 'tis tea Ned is having?" she asked in her deep voice.

"No, I'm having the tea," said Rita. "Ned says he'd sooner a drop of the hard tack."

"Oh, isn't that a great change, Ned?" cried Mrs. Lomasney.

"'Tis the shock," Rita explained lightly, throwing him a cigarette. "He didn't think I was that sort of girl."

"He mustn't know much about girls," said Mrs. Lomasney.

"He's learning now," said Rita.

When Paschal brought up the tray, Rita poured out tea for Ned and whiskey for herself. He made no comment. Things like that were a commonplace in the Lomasney household.

"Anyway," she went on, "he told his old one he wanted to chuck the Church and marry me. There was ructions, of course. The people in the shop at the other side of the street had a son a priest. She wanted to be as good as them. So away with her up to Reverend Mother, and Reverend Mother sends for me. Did I want to destroy the young man's life and he on the threshold of a great calling? I told her 'twas they wanted to destroy him. I asked her what sort of priest Tony would make. Oh, 'twas a marvellous sacrifice, and after it he'd be twice the man. Honest to God, Ned, the way that woman went on, you'd think she was talking about doctoring an old tomcat. I told her that was all she knew about Tony, and she said they knew him since he was an altar boy in the convent. 'Did he ever tell you how he used to slough the convent orchard and sell the apples in town?' says I. So then she dropped the Holy Willie stuff and told me his ma was after getting into debt to put him in for the priesthood, and if he chucked it, he'd never be able to get a job at home to pay it back. Three hundred quid! Wouldn't they kill you with style?"

"And what did you do then?" asked Ned with amusement.

"I went to see his mother."

"You didn't!"

"I did. I thought I might work it with the personal touch."

"You don't seem to have been very successful."

"I'd as soon try the personal touch on a traction engine, Ned. That woman was too tough for me altogether. I told her I wanted to marry Tony. 'I'm sorry,' she said; 'you can't.' 'What's to stop me?' said I. 'He's gone too far,' says she. 'If he was gone farther it wouldn't worry me,' says I. I told her then what Reverend Mother said about her being three hundred pounds in debt and offered to pay it back to her if she let him marry me."

"And had you the three hundred?" Ned asked in surprise.

"Ah, where would I get three hundred?" she replied ruefully. "And she knew it too, the old jade! She didn't believe a word I said. After that I saw Tony. He was crying; said he didn't want to break his mother's heart. As true as God, Ned, that woman had as much heart as a traction engine."

"Well, you seem to have done it in style," Ned said approvingly as he put away his teacup.

"That wasn't the half of it. When I heard the difficulties his mother was making, I offered to live with him instead."

"Live with him?" asked Ned. Even he was startled.

"Well, go away on holidays with him. Lots of girls do it. I know they do. And, God Almighty, isn't it only natural?"

"And what did he say to that?" asked Ned curiously.

"He was scared stiff."

"He would be," said Ned, wrinkling up his nose and giving his superior little sniff as he took out a packet of cigarettes.

"Oh, it's all very well for you," Rita cried, bridling up. "You may think you're a great fellow, all because you read Tolstoy and don't go to Mass, but you'd be just as scared if a girl offered to go to bed with you."

"Try me," Ned said sedately as he lit her cigarette for her, but somehow the notion of suggesting such a thing to Ned only made her laugh.

He stayed till quite late, and when he went downstairs the girls and Mrs. Lomasney fell on him and dragged him into the sitting room.

"Well, doctor," said Mrs. Lomasney, "how's the patient?"

"Oh, I think the patient is coming round nicely," said Ned.

"But would you ever believe it, Ned?" she cried. "A girl that wouldn't look at the side of the road a fellow was at, unless 'twas to go robbing orchards with him. You'll have another drop of whiskey?"

"I won't."

"And is that all you're going to tell us?" asked Mrs. Lomasney.

"Oh, you'll hear it all from herself."

"We won't."

"I dare say not," he said with a hearty chuckle, and went for his coat.

"Wisha, Ned," said Mrs. Lomasney, "what'll your mother say when she hears it?"

" 'All *quite* mad,' " said Ned, sticking his nose in the air and giving an exaggerated version of what Mrs. Lomasney called "his Hayfield sniff."

"The dear knows, I think she's right," she said with resignation, helping him with his coat. "I hope your mother doesn't notice the smell of whiskey from your breath," she added dryly, just to show him that she couldn't be taken in, and then stood at the door, looking up and down, as she waited for him to wave from the gate.

"Ah," she sighed as she closed the door behind her, "with the help of God it might be all for the best."

"If you think he's going to marry her, I can tell you now he's not," said Kitty. "I'd like to see myself trying it on Bill O'Donnell. He'd have my sacred life. That fellow only enjoys it."

"Ah, God is good," her mother said cheerfully, kicking a mat into place. "Some men might like that."

INSIDE a week Kitty and Nellie were sick to death of the sight of Rita round the house. She was bad enough at the best of times, but now she just brooded and mooned and snapped the head off you. In the afternoons she strolled down the dike and into Ned's little shop, where she sat on the counter, swinging her legs and smoking, while Ned leaned against the side of the window, tinkering at the insides of a watch with some delicate instrument. Nothing seemed to rattle him. When he had finished work, he changed his coat and they went out to tea. He sat at the back of the teashop in a corner, pulled up the legs of his trousers, and took out a packet of cigarettes and a box of matches, which he placed on the table before them with a look that almost commanded them to stay there and not get lost. His face was pale and clear and bright, like an evening sky when the last light has drained from it.

"Anything wrong?" he asked one evening when she was moodier than usual.

"Just fed up," she said, thrusting out her jaw.

"What is it?" he asked gently. "Still fretting?"

"Ah, no. I can get over that. It's Kitty and Nellie. They're bitches, Ned; proper bitches. And all because I don't wear my heart on my sleeve. If one of them got a knock from a fellow she'd take two aspirins and go to bed with the other one. They'd have a lovely talk—can't you imagine? 'And was it then he said he loved you?' I can't do that sort of stuff. And it's all because they're not sincere, Ned. They couldn't be sincere."

"Remember, they have a long start on you," Ned said smiling.

"Is that it?" she asked without interest. "They think I'm batty. Do you?"

"I've no doubt that Mrs. Donoghue, if that's her name, thought something of the sort," replied Ned with a tightlipped smile.

"And wasn't she right?" asked Rita with sudden candor. "Suppose she'd agreed to take the three hundred quid, wouldn't I be in a nice pickle? I wake in a sweat whenever I think of it. I'm just a blooming chancer, Ned. Where would I get three hundred quid?"

"Oh, I dare say someone would have lent it to you," he said with a shrug.

"They would like fun. Would you?"

"Probably," he said gravely after a moment's thought.

"Are you serious?" she whispered earnestly.

"Quite."

"Cripes," she gasped, "you must be very fond of me."

"It looks like it," said Ned, and this time he laughed with real heartiness, a boy's laugh of sheer delight at the mystification he was causing her. It was characteristic of Rita that she should count their friendship of years as nothing, but his offer of three hundred pounds in cash as significant.

"Would you marry me?" she asked frowningly. "I'm not proposing to you, only asking," she added hastily.

"Certainly," he said, spreading out his hands. "Whenever you like."

"Honest to God?"

"Cut my throat."

"And why didn't you ask me before I went down to that kip? I'd have married you then like a shot. Was it the way you weren't keen on me then?"

"No," he replied matter-of-factly, drawing himself together like an old clock preparing to strike. "I think I've been keen on you as long as I know you."

"It's easily seen you're a Neddy Ned," she said with amusement. "I go after mine with a scalping knife."

"I stalk mine," said Ned.

"Cripes, Ned," she said with real regret, "I wish you'd told me sooner. I couldn't marry you now."

"No?"

"No. It wouldn't be fair to you."

"Isn't that my look-out?"

"It's my look-out now." She glanced around the restaurant to make sure no one was listening and then went on in a dry voice, leaning one elbow on the table. "I suppose you'll think this is all cod, but it's not. Honest to God, I think you're the finest bloody man I ever met—even though you do think you're an atheist or something," she added maliciously with a characteristic Lomasney flourish in the cause of Faith and Fatherland. "There's no one in the world I have more respect for. I think I'd nearly cut my throat if I did something you really disapproved of—I don't mean telling lies or going on a skite," she added hastily, to prevent misunderstandings. "They're only gas. Something that really shocked you is what I mean. I think if I was tempted to do anything like that I'd ask myself: 'What would that fellow Lowry think of me now?' "

"Well," Ned said in an extraordinary quiet voice, squelching the butt of his cigarette on his plate, "that sounds to me like a very good beginning."

"It is not, Ned," she said sadly, shaking her head. "That's why I say it's my look-out. You couldn't understand it unless it happened to yourself; unless you fell in love with a girl the way I fell in love with Tony. Tony is a scut, and a cowardly scut, but I was cracked about him. If he came in here now and said: 'Come on, girl, we're going to Killarney for the weekend,' I'd go out and buy a nightdress and toothbrush and be off with him. And I wouldn't give a damn what you or anybody thought. I might chuck myself in the lake afterwards, but I'd go. Christ, Ned," she exclaimed, flushing and looking as though she might burst into tears, "he couldn't come into a room but I went all mushy inside. That's what the real thing is like."

"Well," Ned said sedately, apparently not in the least put out—in fact, looking rather pleased with himself, Rita thought—"I'm in no hurry. In case you get tired of scalping them, the offer will still be open."

"Thanks, Ned," she said absent-mindedly, as though she weren't listening.

While he paid the bill, she stood in the porch, doing her face in the big mirror that flanked it, and paying no attention to the crowds, coming homeward through streets where the shop windows were already lit. As he emerged from the shop she turned on him suddenly.

"About that matter, Ned," she said, "will you ask me again, or do I have to ask you?"

Ned just refrained from laughing outright. "As you like," he replied with quiet amusement. "Suppose I repeat the proposal every six months."

"That would be the hell of a long time to wait if I changed my mind," she said with a thoughtful scowl. "All right," she said, taking his arm. "I know you well enough to ask you. If you don't want me by that time, you can always say so. I won't mind."

NED's proposal came as a considerable comfort to Rita. It bolstered up her self-esteem, which was always in danger of collapse. She might be ugly and uneducated and a bit of a chancer, but the best man in Cork—the best in Ireland, she sometimes thought—wanted to marry her, even after she had been let down by another man. That was a queer one for her enemies! So while her sisters made fun of her, Rita considered the situation, waiting for the best possible moment to let them know she had been proposed to and could marry before either of them if it suited her. Since her childhood Rita had never given anything away without extracting the last ounce of theatrical effect from it. She would tell her sisters, but not before she could make them sick with the news.

That was a pity, for it left Rita unaware that Ned, whom she respected, was far from being the only one who liked her. For instance, there was Justin Sullivan, the lawyer, who had once been by way of being engaged to Nellie. He hadn't become engaged to her, because she was as slippery as an eel, and her fancy finally lit on a solicitor called Fahy whom Justin despised with his whole heart and soul as a lightheaded, butterfly sort of man. But Justin continued to visit the house as a friend of the girls. There happened to be no other house that suited him half as well, and besides he knew that sooner or later Nellie would make a mess of her life with Fahy, and his services would be required.

Justin, in other words, was a sticker. He was a good deal older than Rita, a tall, burly man with a broad face, a brow that was rising from baldness as well as brains, and a slow, watchful ironic air. Like many lawyers, he tended to conduct conversation as though the person he was speaking to were a hostile witness who had either to be coaxed into an admission of perjury or bullied into one of mental deficiency. When Justin began, Fahy simply clutched his head and retired to sit on the stairs. "Can't anyone shut that fellow up?" he would moan with a martyred air. Nobody could. The girls shot their little darts at him, but he only brushed them aside. Ned Lowry was the only one who could even stand up to him, and when the pair of them argued about religion, the room became a desert. Justin, of course, was a pillar of orthodoxy. "Imagine for a moment," he would declaim in a throaty rounded voice that turned easily to pomposity, "that I am Pope." "Easiest thing in the world, Justin," Kitty assured him. He drank whiskey like water, and the more he drank, the more massive and logical and orthodoxly Catholic he became.

At the same time, under his truculent air he was exceedingly gentle, patient, and understanding, and disliked the ragging of Rita by her sisters.

"Tell me, Nellie," he asked one night in his lazy, amiable way, "do you talk like that to Rita because you like it, or because you think it's good for her?"

"How soft you have it!" Nellie cried. "We have to live with her. You haven't."

"That may be my misfortune, Nellie," said Justin with a broad smile.

"Is that a proposal, Justin?" asked Kitty shrewdly.

"Scarcely, Kitty," said Justin. "You're not what I might call a good jury."

"Better be careful or you'll have her dropping in on your mother, Justin," Kitty said maliciously.

"Thanks, Kitty," Rita said with a flash of cold fury.

"I hope my mother would have sufficient sense to realize it was an honor, Kitty," Justin said severely.

When he rose to go, Rita accompanied him to the hall.

"Thanks for the moral support, Justin," she said in a low voice, and then threw her overcoat over her shoulders to go as far as the gate with him. When he opened the door they both stood and gazed about them. It was a moonlit night; the garden, patterned in black and silver, sloped to the quiet roadway, where the gas lamps burned with a dim green light, and in the farther walls gateways shaded by black trees led to flights of steps or to steep-sloping avenues which led to moonlit houses on the river's edge.

"God, isn't it lovely?" Rita said in a hushed voice.

"Oh, by the way, Rita," he said, slipping his arm through hers, "that was a proposal."

"Janey Mack, they're falling," she said, giving his arm a squeeze.

"What are falling?"

"Proposals."

"Why? Had you others?"

"I had one anyway."

"And did you accept it?"

"No," Rita said doubtfully. "Not quite. At least, I don't think I did."

"You might consider this one," Justin said with unusual humility. "You know, of course, that I was very fond of Nellie. At one time I was very fond of her indeed. You don't mind that, I hope. It's all over and done with now, and there are no regrets on either side."

"No, Justin, of course I don't mind. If I felt like marrying you I wouldn't give it a second thought. But I was very much in love with Tony too, and that's not all over and done with yet."

"I know that, Rita," he said gently. "I know exactly what you feel. We've all been through it." If he had left it at that everything might have been all right, but Justin was a lawyer, which meant that he liked to keep things absolutely shipshape. "But that won't last forever. In a month or two you'll be over it, and then you'll wonder what you saw in that fellow."

"I don't think so, Justin," she said with a crooked little smile, not altogether displeased to be able to enlighten him on the utter hopelessness of her position. "I think it will take a great deal longer than that."

"Well, say six months, even," Justin went on, prepared to yield a point to the defense. "All I ask is that in one month or six, whenever you've got over your regrets for this—this amiable young man" (momentarily his voice took on its familiar ironic ring), "you'll give me a thought. I'm old enough not to make any more mistakes. I know I'm fond of you, and I feel pretty sure I could make a success of my end of it."

"What you really mean," said Rita, keeping her temper with the greatest difficulty, "is that I wasn't in love with Tony at all. Isn't that it?"

"Not quite," Justin said judiciously. Even if he'd had a serenade as well as the moonlight and the girl, it couldn't have kept him from correcting what he considered to be a false deduction. "I've no doubt you were very much attracted by this—this clerical Adonis; this Mr. Whatever-his-name-is, or that at any rate you thought you were, which in practice comes to the same thing, but I also know that that sort of thing, though it's painful enough while it lasts, doesn't last very long."

"You mean yours didn't, Justin," Rita said tartly.

"I mean mine or anybody else's," Justin said pompously. "Because love—the only sort of thing you can really call love—is something that comes with experience. You're probably too young yet to know what the real thing is."

As Rita had only recently told Ned that he didn't yet know what the real thing was, she found this rather hard to stomach.

"How old would you say you'd have to be?" she asked viciously. "Thirty-five?"

"You'll know soon enough—when it hits you," said Justin.

"Honest to God, Justin," she said, withdrawing her arm and looking at him with suppressed fury, "I think you're the thickest man I ever met."

"Good night, my dear," said Justin with perfect good humor, and he raised his cap and took the few steps to the gate at a run.

Rita stood gazing after him with folded arms. At the age of eighteen to be told that there is anything you don't know about love is like a knife in your heart.

KITTY and Nellie grew so tired of her moodiness that they persuaded her mother that the best way of distracting her mind was to find her another job. A new environment was also supposed to be good for her complaint, so Mrs. Lomasney wrote to her sister who was a nun in England, and the sister found her work in a convent there. Rita let on to pay no attention, though she let Ned see something of her resentment.

"But why England?" he asked wonderingly.

"Why not?" replied Rita challengingly.

"Wouldn't any place nearer do you?"

"I suppose I wouldn't be far enough away from them."

"But why not make up your own mind?"

"I'll probably do that too," she said with a short laugh. "I'd like to see what's in theirs first though."

On Friday she was to leave for England, and on Wednesday the girls gave a farewell party. This, too, Rita affected to take no great interest in. Wednesday was the half-holiday, and it rained steadily all day. The girls' friends all turned up. Most were men: Bill O'Donnell of the bank, who was engaged to Kitty; Fahy, the solicitor, who was Justin's successful rival for Nellie; Justin himself, who simply could not be kept out of the house by anything short of an injunction; Ned Lowry, and a few others. Hasty soon retired with his wife to the dining room to read the evening paper. He said all his daughters' young men looked exactly alike and he never knew which of them he was talking to.

Bill O'Donnell was acting as barman. He was a big man, bigger even than Justin, with a battered boxer's face and a Negro smile, which seemed to well up from depths of good humor with life rather than from any immediate contact with others. He carried on loud conversations with everyone he poured out drink for, and his voice overrode every intervening tête-à-tête, and challenged even the piano, on which Nellie was vamping music-hall songs.

"Who's this one for, Rita?" he asked. "A bottle of Bass for Paddy. Ah, the stout man! Remember the New Year's Day in Bandon, Paddy? Remember how you had to carry me up to the bank in evening dress and jack me up between the two wings of the desk? Kitty, did I ever tell you about that night in Bandon?"

"Once a week for the past five years, Bill," said Kitty philosophically.

"Nellie," said Rita, "I think it's time for Bill to sing his song. 'Let Me like a Soldier Fall,' Bill!"

"My one little song!" Bill said with a roar of laughter. "My one and only song, but I sing it grand. Don't I, Nellie? Don't I sing it fine?"

"Fine!" agreed Nellie, looking up at his big, beaming moonface shining at her over the piano. "As the man said to my mother, 'Finest bloody soprano I ever heard.'"

"He did not, Nellie," Bill said sadly. "You're making that up. . . . Silence please!" he shouted joyously, clapping his hands. "Ladies and gentlemen, I must apologize. I ought to sing something like Tosti's 'Good-bye,' but the fact is, ladies and gentlemen, that I don't know Tosti's 'Good-bye.'"

"Recite it, Bill," said Justin amiably.

"I don't know the words of it either, Justin," said Bill. "In fact, I'm not sure if there's any such song, but if there is, I ought to sing it."

"Why, Bill?" Rita asked innocently. She was wearing a long black dress that threw up the unusual brightness of her dark, bony face. She looked happier than she had looked for months. All the evening it was as though she were laughing to herself.

"Because 'twould be only right, Rita," said Bill with great melancholy, putting his arm about her and drawing her closer to him. "You know I'm very fond of you, don't you, Rita?"

"And I'm mad about you, Bill," said Rita candidly.

"I know that, Rita," he said mournfully, pulling at his collar as though to give himself air. "I only wish you weren't going, Rita. This place isn't the same without you. Kitty won't mind my saying that," he added with a nervous glance at Kitty, who was flirting with Justin on the sofa.

"Are you going to sing your blooming old song or not?" Nellie asked impatiently, running her fingers over the keys.

"I'm going to sing now in one minute, Nellie," Bill said ecstatically, stroking Rita fondly under the chin. "I only want Rita to know the way we'll miss her."

"Damn it, Bill," Rita said, snuggling up to him with her dark head on his chest, "if you go on like that I won't go at all. Tell me, would you really prefer me not to go?"

"I would prefer you not to go, Rita," he replied, stroking her cheeks and eyes. "You're too good for the fellows over there."

"Oh, go on doing that," she said hastily, as he dropped his hand. "It's gorgeous, and you're making Kitty mad jealous."

"Kitty isn't jealous," Bill said fondly. "Kitty is a lovely girl and you're a lovely girl. I hate to see you go, Rita."

"That settles it, Bill," she said, pulling herself free of him with a determined air. "I simply couldn't cause you all that suffering. As you put it that way, I won't go."

"Won't you, just?" said Kitty with a grin.

"Now, don't worry your head about it anymore, Bill," said Rita briskly. "It's all off."

Justin, who had been quietly consuming large whiskeys, looked round lazily.

"Perhaps I ought to have mentioned," he boomed, "that the young lady has just done me the honor of proposing to me and I've accepted her."

Ned Lowry, who had been enjoying the scene between Bill and Rita, looked at him for a moment in surprise.

"Bravo! Bravo!" cried Bill, clapping his hands with childish delight. "A marriage has been arranged and all the rest of it—what? I must give you a kiss, Rita. Justin, you don't mind if I give Rita a kiss?"

"Not at all, not at all," replied Justin with a lordly wave of his hand. "Anything that's mine is yours, old man."

"You're not serious, Justin, are you?" Kitty asked incredulously.

"Oh, I'm serious all right," said Justin. "I'm not quite certain whether your sister is. Are you, Rita?"

"What?" Rita asked as though she hadn't heard.

"Serious," repeated Justin.

"Why?" asked Rita. "Trying to give me the push already?"

"We're much obliged for the information," Nellie said ironically as she rose from the piano. "Now, maybe you'd oblige us further and tell us does Father know."

"Hardly," said Rita coolly. "It was only settled this evening."

"Well, maybe 'twill do with some more settling by the time Father is done with you," Nellie said furiously. "The impudence of you! How dare you! Go in at once and tell him."

"Keep your hair on, girl," Rita advised with cool malice and then went jauntily out of the room. Kitty and Nellie began to squabble viciously with Justin. They were convinced that the whole scene had been arranged by Rita to make them look ridiculous, and in this they weren't very far out. Justin sat back and began to enjoy the sport. Then Ned Lowry struck a match and lit another cigarette, and something about the slow, careful way in which he did it drew everyone's attention. Just because he was not the sort to make a fuss, people realized from his strained look that his mind was very far away. The squabble stopped as quickly as it had begun and a feeling of awkwardness ensued. Ned was too old a friend of the family for the girls not to feel that way about him.

Rita returned, laughing.

"Well?" asked Nellie.

"Consent refused," growled Rita, bowing her head and pulling the wrong side of an imaginary mustache.

"What did I say?" exclaimed Nellie, but without rancor.

"You don't think it makes any difference?" Rita asked dryly.

"I wouldn't be too sure of that," said Nellie. "What else did he say?"

"Oh, he hadn't a notion who I was talking about," Rita said lightly. " 'Justin who?' " she mimicked. " 'How the hell do you think I can remember all the young scuts ye bring to the house?' "

"Was he mad?" asked Kitty with amusement.

"Hopping."

"He didn't call us scuts?" asked Bill in a wounded tone.

"Oh, begor, that was the very word he used, Bill," said Rita.

"Did you tell him he was very fond of me the day I gave him the tip for Golden Boy at the Park Races?" asked Justin.

"I did," said Rita. "I said you were the stout block of a fellow with the brown hair that he said had the fine intelligence, and he said he never gave a damn about intelligence. He wanted me to marry the thin fellow with the specs. 'Only bloody gentleman that comes to the house.' "

"Is it Ned?" cried Nellie.

"Who else?" said Rita. "I asked him why he didn't tell me that before and he nearly ate the head off me. 'Jesus Christ, girl, don't I feed ye and clothe ye? Isn't that enough without having to coort for ye as well? Next thing, ye'll be asking me to have a few babies for ye.' Anyway, Ned," she added with a crooked, almost malicious smile, "you can always say you were Pa's favorite."

Once more the attention was directed to Ned. He put his cigarette down with care and sprang up with a broad smile, holding out his hand.

"I wish you all the luck in the world, Justin," he said.

"I know that well, Ned," boomed Justin, catching Ned's hand in his own two. "And I'd feel the same if it was you."

"And you too, Miss Lomasney," Ned said gaily.

"Thanks, Mr. Lowry," she replied with the same crooked smile.

JUSTIN and Rita got married, and Ned, like all the Hayfield Hourigans, behaved in a decorous and sensible manner. He didn't take to drink or break the crockery or do any of the things people are expected to do under the circumstances. He gave them a very expensive clock as a wedding present, went once or twice to visit them and permitted Justin to try and convert him, and took Rita to the pictures when Justin was away from home. At the same time he began to walk out with an assistant in Halpin's; a gentle, humorous girl with a great mass of jet-black hair, a snub nose, and a long, pointed melancholy face. You saw them everywhere together.

He also went regularly to Sunday's Well to see the old couple and Nellie, who wasn't yet married. One evening when he called, Mr. and Mrs. Lomasney were at the chapel, but Rita was there, Justin being again away. It was months since she and Ned had met; she was having a baby and very near her time; and it made her self-conscious and rude. She said it made her feel like a yacht that had been turned into a cargo boat. Three or four times she said things to Ned which would have maddened anyone else, but he took them in his usual way, without resentment.

"And how's little Miss Bitch?" she asked insolently.

"Little Miss who?" he asked mildly.

"Miss—how the hell can I remember the names of all your dolls? The Spanish-looking one who sells the knickers at Halpin's."

"Oh, she's very well, thanks," Ned said primly.

"What you might call a prudent marriage," Rita went on, all on edge.

"How's that, Rita?"

"You'll have the ring and the trousseau at cost price."

"How interested you are in her!" Nellie said suspiciously.

"I don't give a damn about her," Rita with a shrug. "Would Señorita What's-her-name ever let you stand godfather to my footballer, Ned?"

"Why not?" Ned asked mildly. "I'd be delighted, of course."

"You have the devil's own neck to ask him after the way you treated him," said Nellie. Nellie was interested; she knew Rita and knew that she was in one of her emotional states, and was determined on finding out what it meant. Ordinarily Rita, who also knew her sister, would have delighted in thwarting her, but now it was as though she wanted an audience.

"How did I treat him?" she asked with amusement.

"Codding him along like that for years, and then marrying a man that was twice your age."

"Well, how did he expect me to know?"

Ned rose and took out a packet of cigarettes. Like Nellie he knew that Rita had deliberately staged the scene and was on the point of telling him something. She was leaning very far back in her chair and laughed up at him while she took a cigarette and waited for him to light it.

"Come on, Rita," he said encouragingly. "As you've said so much you might as well tell us the rest."

"What else is there to tell?"

"What you had against me."

"Who said I had anything against you? Didn't I distinctly tell you when you asked me to marry you that I didn't love you? Maybe you thought I didn't mean it."

He paused for a moment and then raised his brows.

"I did," he said quietly.

She laughed.

"The conceit of that fellow!" she said to Nellie, and then with a change of tone: "I had nothing against you, Ned. This was the one I had the needle in. Herself and Kitty were forcing me into it."

"Well, the impudence of you!" cried Nellie.

"Isn't it true for me?" Rita said sharply. "Weren't you both trying to get me out of the house?"

"We weren't," Nellie replied hotly, "and anyway that has nothing to do with it. It was no reason why you couldn't have married Ned if you wanted to."

"I didn't want to. I didn't want to marry anyone."

"And what changed your mind?"

"Nothing changed my mind. I didn't care about anyone, only Tony, but I didn't want to go to that damn place, and I had no alternative. I had to marry one of you, so I made up my mind that I'd marry the first of you that called."

"You must have been mad," Nellie said indignantly.

"I felt it. I sat at the window the whole afternoon, looking at the rain. Remember that day, Ned?"

He nodded.

"The rain had a lot to do with it. I think I half hoped you'd come first. Justin came instead—an old aunt of his was sick and he came for supper. I saw him at the gate and he waved to me with his old brolly. I ran downstairs to open the door for him. 'Justin,' I said, grabbing him by the coat, 'if you still want to marry me, I'm ready.' He gave me a dirty look—you know Justin! 'Young woman,' he said, 'there's a time and place for everything.' And away with him up to the lavatory. Talk about romantic engagements! Damn the old kiss did I get off him, even!"

"I declare to God!" said Nellie in stupefaction.

"I know," Rita cried, laughing again over her own irresponsibility. "Cripes, when I knew what I was after doing I nearly dropped dead."

"Oh, so you came to your senses?" Nellie asked ironically.

"What do you think? That's the trouble with Justin; he's always right. That fellow knew I wouldn't be married a week before I didn't give a snap of my fingers for Tony. And me thinking my life was over and that was that or the river! God, the idiots we make of ourselves over men!"

"And I suppose 'twas then you found out you'd married the wrong man?" Nellie asked.

"Who said I married the wrong man?" Rita asked hotly.

"I thought that was what you were telling us," Nellie said innocently.

"You get things all wrong, Nellie," Rita replied shortly. "You jump to conclusions too much. If I did marry the wrong man I wouldn't be likely to tell you—or Ned Lowry either."

She looked mockingly at Ned, but her look belied her. It was plain enough now why she wanted Nellie as an audience. It kept her from admitting more than she had to admit, from saying things which, once said, might make her own life impossible. Ned rose and flicked his cigarette ash into the fire. Then he stood with his back to it, his hands behind his back, his feet spread out on the hearth.

"You mean if I'd come earlier you'd have married me?" he asked quietly.

"If you'd come earlier, I'd probably be asking Justin to stand godfather to your brat," said Rita. "And how do you know but Justin would be walking out the señorita, Ned?"

"Then maybe you wouldn't be quite so interested whether he was or not," said Nellie, but she didn't say it maliciously. It was now only too plain what Rita meant, and Nellie was sorry for her.

Ned turned and lashed his cigarette savagely into the fire. Rita looked up at him mockingly.

"Go on!" she taunted him. "Say it, blast you!"

"I couldn't," he said bitterly.

A month later he married the señorita.

News for the Church

WHEN Father Cassidy drew back the shutter of the confessional he was a little surprised at the appearance of the girl at the other side of the grille. It was dark in the box but he could see she was young, of medium height and build, with a face that was full of animation and charm. What struck him most was the long pale slightly freckled cheeks, pinned high up behind the gray-blue eyes, giving them a curiously Oriental slant.

She wasn't a girl from the town, for he knew most of these by sight and many of them by something more, being notoriously an easygoing confessor. The other priests said that one of these days he'd give up hearing confessions altogether on the ground that there was no such thing as sin and that even if there was it didn't matter. This was part and parcel of his exceedingly angular character, for though he was kind enough to individual sinners, his mind was full of obscure abstract hatreds. He hated England; he hated the Irish government, and he particularly hated the middle classes, though so far as anyone knew none of them had ever done him the least bit of harm. He was a heavy-built man, slow-moving and slow-thinking with no neck and a Punchinello chin, a sour wine-colored face, pouting crimson lips, and small blue hot-tempered eyes.

"Well, my child," he grunted in a slow and mournful voice that sounded for all the world as if he had pebbles in his mouth, "how long is it since your last confession?"

"A week, father," she replied in a clear firm voice. It surprised him a little, for though she didn't look like one of the tough shots, neither did she look like the sort of girl who goes to Confession every week. But with women you could never tell. They were all contrary, saints and sinners.

"And what sins did you commit since then?" he asked encouragingly.

"I told lies, father."

"Anything else?"

"I used bad language, father."

"I'm surprised at you," he said with mock seriousness. "An educated girl with the whole of the English language at your disposal! What sort of bad language?"

"I used the Holy Name, father."

"Ach," he said with a frown, "you ought to know better than that. There's no great harm in damning and blasting but blasphemy is a different thing. To tell you the truth," he added, being a man of great natural honesty, "there isn't much harm in using the Holy Name either. Most of the time there's no intentional blasphemy but at the same time it coarsens the character. It's all the little temptations we don't indulge in that give us true refinement. Anything else?"

"I was tight, father."

"Hm," he grunted. This was rather more the sort of girl he had imagined her to be; plenty of devilment but no real badness. He liked her bold and candid manner. There was no hedging or false modesty about her as about most of his women penitents. "When you say you were 'tight' do you mean you were just merry or what?"

"Well, I mean I passed out," she replied candidly with a shrug.

"I don't call that 'tight,' you know," he said sternly. "I call that beastly drunk. Are you often tight?"

"I'm a teacher in a convent school so I don't get much chance," she replied ruefully.

"In a convent school?" he echoed with new interest. Convent schools and nuns were another of his phobias; he said they were turning the women of the country into imbeciles. "Are you on holidays now?"

"Yes. I'm on my way home."

"You don't live here then?"

"No, down the country."

"And is it the convent that drives you to drink?" he asked with an air of unshakable gravity.

"Well," she replied archly, "you know what nuns are."

"I do," he agreed in a mournful voice while he smiled at her through the grille. "Do you drink with your parents' knowledge?" he added anxiously.

"Oh, yes. Mummy is dead but Daddy doesn't mind. He lets us take a drink with him."

"Does he do that on principle or because he's afraid of you?" the priest asked dryly.

"Ah, I suppose a little of both," she answered gaily, responding to his queer dry humor. It wasn't often that women did, and he began to like this one a lot.

"Is your mother long dead?" he asked sympathetically.

"Seven years," she replied, and he realized that she couldn't have been much more than a child at the time and had grown up without a mother's advice and care. Having worshipped his own mother, he was always sorry for people like that.

"Mind you," he said paternally, his hands joined on his fat belly, "I don't want you to think there's any harm in a drop of drink. I take it myself. But I wouldn't make a habit of it if I were you. You see, it's all very well for old jossers like me that have the worst of their temptations behind them, but yours are all ahead and drink is a thing that grows on you. You need never be afraid of going wrong if you remember that your mother may be watching you from Heaven."

"Thanks, father," she said, and he saw at once that his gruff appeal had touched some deep and genuine spring of feeling in her. "I'll cut it out altogether."

"You know, I think I would," he said gravely, letting his eyes rest on her for a moment. "You're an intelligent girl. You can get all the excitement you want out of life without that. What else?"

"I had bad thoughts, father."

"Ach," he said regretfully, "we all have them. Did you indulge them?"

"Yes, father."

"Have you a boy?"

"Not a regular: just a couple of fellows hanging round."

"Ah, that's worse than none at all," he said crossly. "You ought to have a boy of your own. I know there's old cranks that will tell you different, but sure, that's plain foolishness. Those things are only fancies, and the best cure for them is something real. Anything else?"

There was a moment's hesitation before she replied but it was enough to prepare him for what was coming.

"I had carnal intercourse with a man, father," she said quietly and deliberately.

"You what?" he cried, turning on her incredulously. "You had carnal intercourse with a man? At your age?"

"I know," she said with a look of distress. "It's awful."

"It is awful," he replied slowly and solemnly. "And how often did it take place?"

"Once, father—I mean twice, but on the same occasion."

"Was it a married man?" he asked, frowning.

"No, father, single. At least I think he was single," she added with sudden doubt.

"You had carnal intercourse with a man," he said accusingly, "and you don't know if he was married or single!"

"I assumed he was single," she said with real distress. "He was the last time I met him but, of course, that was five years ago."

"Five years ago? But you must have been only a child then."

"That's all, of course," she admitted. "He was courting my sister, Kate, but she wouldn't have him. She was running round with her present husband at the time and she only kept him on a string for amusement. I knew that and I hated her because he was always so nice to me. He was the only one that came to the house who treated me like a grown-up. But I was only fourteen, and I suppose he thought I was too young for him."

"And were you?" Father Cassidy asked ironically. For some reason he had the idea that this young lady had no proper idea of the enormity of her sin and he didn't like it.

"I suppose so," she replied modestly. "But I used to feel awful, being sent up to bed and leaving him downstairs with Kate when I knew she didn't care for him. And then when I met him again the whole thing came back. I sort of went all soft inside. It's never the same with another fellow as it is with the first fellow you fall for. It's exactly as if he had some sort of hold over you."

"If you were fourteen at the time," said Father Cassidy, setting aside the obvious invitation to discuss the power of first love, "you're only nineteen now."

"That's all."

"And do you know," he went on broodingly, "that unless you can break yourself of this terrible vice once for all it'll go on like that till you're fifty?"

"I suppose so," she said doubtfully, but he saw that she didn't suppose anything of the kind.

"You suppose so!" he snorted angrily. "I'm telling you so. And what's more," he went on, speaking with all the earnestness at his command, "it won't be just one man but dozens of men, and it won't be decent men but whatever low-class pups you can find who'll take advantage of you—the same horrible, mortal sin, week in week out till you're an old woman."

"Ah, still, I don't know," she said eagerly, hunching her shoulders ingratiatingly, "I think people do it as much from curiosity as anything else."

"Curiosity?" he repeated in bewilderment.

"Ah, you know what I mean," she said with a touch of impatience. "People make such a mystery of it!"

"And what do you think they should do?" he asked ironically. "Publish it in the papers?"

"Well, God knows, 'twould be better than the way some of them go on," she said in a rush. "Take my sister, Kate, for instance. I admit she's a couple of years older than me and she brought me up and all the rest of it, but in spite of that we were always good friends. She showed me her love letters and I showed her mine. I mean, we discussed things as equals, but ever since that girl got married you'd hardly recognize her. She talks to no one only other married women, and they get in a huddle in a corner and whisper, whisper, whisper, and the moment you come into the room they begin to talk about the weather, exactly as if you were a blooming kid! I mean you can't help feeling 'tis something extraordinary."

"Don't you try and tell me anything about immorality," said Father Cassidy angrily. "I know all about it already. It may begin as curiosity but it ends as debauchery. There's no vice you could think of that gets a grip on you quicker and degrades you worse, and don't you make any mistake about it, young woman! Did this man say anything about marrying you?"

"I don't think so," she replied thoughtfully, "but of course that doesn't mean anything. He's an airy, lighthearted sort of fellow and it mightn't occur to him."

"I never supposed it would," said Father Cassidy grimly. "Is he in a position to marry?"

"I suppose he must be since he wanted to marry Kate," she replied with fading interest.

"And is your father the sort of man that can be trusted to talk to him?"

"Daddy?" she exclaimed aghast. "But I don't want Daddy brought into it."

"What you want, young woman," said Father Cassidy with sudden exasperation, "is beside the point. Are you prepared to talk to this man yourself?"

"I suppose so," she said with a wondering smile. "But about what?"

"About what?" repeated the priest angrily. "About the little matter he so conveniently overlooked, of course."

"You mean ask him to marry me?" she cried incredulously. "But I don't want to marry him."

Father Cassidy paused for a moment and looked at her anxiously through the grille. It was growing dark inside the church, and for one horrible moment he had the feeling that somebody was playing an elaborate and most tasteless joke on him.

"Do you mind telling me," he inquired politely, "am I mad or are you?"

"But I mean it, father," she said eagerly. "It's all over and done with now. It's something I used to dream about, and it was grand, but you can't do a thing like that a second time."

"You can't what?" he asked sternly.

"I mean, I suppose you can, really," she said, waving her piously joined hands at him as if she were handcuffed, "but you can't get back the magic of it. Terry is lighthearted and good-natured, but I couldn't live with him. He's completely irresponsible."

"And what do you think you are?" cried Father Cassidy, at the end of his patience. "Have you thought of all the dangers you're running, girl? If you have a child who'll give you work? If you have to leave this country to earn a living what's going to become of you? I tell you it's your bounden duty to marry this man if he can be got to marry you—which, let me tell you," he added with a toss of his great head, "I very much doubt."

"To tell you the truth I doubt it myself," she replied with a shrug that fully expressed her feelings about Terry and nearly drove Father Cassidy insane. He looked at her for a moment or two and then an incredible idea began to dawn on his bothered old brain. He sighed and covered his face with his hand.

"Tell me," he asked in a faraway voice, "when did this take place?"

"Last night, father," she said gently, almost as if she were glad to see him come to his senses again.

"My God," he thought despairingly, "I was right!"

"In town, was it?" he went on.

"Yes, father. We met on the train coming down."

"And where is he now?"

"He went home this morning, father."

"Why didn't you do the same?"

"I don't know, father," she replied doubtfully as though the question had now only struck herself for the first time.

"Why didn't you go home this morning?" he repeated angrily. "What were you doing round town all day?"

"I suppose I was walking," she replied uncertainly.

"And of course you didn't tell anyone?"

"I hadn't anyone to tell," she said plaintively. "Anyway," she added with a shrug, "it's not the sort of thing you can tell people."

"No, of course," said Father Cassidy. "Only a priest," he added grimly to himself. He saw now how he had been taken in. This little trollop, wandering about town in a daze of bliss, had to tell someone her secret, and he, a good-natured old fool of sixty, had allowed her to use him as a confidant. A philosopher of sixty letting Eve, aged nineteen, tell him all about the apple! He could never live it down.

Then the fighting blood of the Cassidys began to warm in him. Oh, couldn't he, though? He had never tasted the apple himself, but he knew a few things about apples in general and that apple in particular that little Miss Eve wouldn't learn in a whole lifetime of apple-eating. Theory might have its drawbacks but there were times when it was better than practice. "All right, my lass," he thought grimly, "we'll see which of us knows most!"

In a casual tone he began to ask her questions. They were rather intimate questions, such as a doctor or priest may ask, and, feeling broadminded and worldly wise in her new experience, she answered courageously and straightforwardly, trying to suppress all signs of her embarrassment. It emerged only once or twice, in a brief pause before she replied. He stole a furtive look at her to see how she was taking it, and once more he couldn't withhold his admiration. But she couldn't keep it up. First she grew uncomfortable and then alarmed, frowning and shaking herself in her clothes as if something were biting her. He grew graver and more personal. She didn't see his purpose; she only saw that he was stripping off veil after veil of romance, leaving her with nothing but a cold, sordid, cynical adventure like a bit of greasy meat on a plate.

"And what did he do next?" he asked.

"Ah," she said in disgust, "I didn't notice."

"You didn't notice!" he repeated ironically.

"But does it make any difference?" she burst out despairingly, trying to pull the few shreds of illusion she had left more tightly about her.

"I presume you thought so when you came to confess it," he replied sternly.

"But you're making it sound so beastly!" she wailed.

"And wasn't it?" he whispered, bending closer, lips pursed and brows raised. He had her now, he knew.

"Ah, it wasn't, father," she said earnestly. "Honest to God it wasn't. At least at the time I didn't think it was."

"No," he said grimly, "you thought it was a nice little story to run and tell your sister. You won't be in such a hurry to tell her now. Say an Act of Contrition."

She said it.

"And for your penance say three Our Fathers and three Hail Marys."

He knew that was hitting below the belt, but he couldn't resist the parting shot of a penance such as he might have given a child. He knew it would rankle in that fanciful little head of hers when all his other warnings were forgotten. Then he drew the shutter and didn't open the farther one. There was a noisy woman behind, groaning in an excess of contrition. The mere volume of sound told him it was drink. He felt he needed a breath of fresh air.

He went down the aisle creakily on his heavy policeman's-feet and in the dusk walked up and down the path before the presbytery, head bowed, hands behind his back. He saw the girl come out and descend the steps under the massive fluted columns of the portico, a tiny, limp, dejected figure. As she reached the pavement she pulled herself together with a jaunty twitch of her shoulders and then collapsed again. The city lights went on and made globes of colored light in the mist. As he returned to the church he suddenly began to chuckle, a fat good-natured chuckle, and as he passed the statue of St. Anne, patron of marriageable girls, he almost found himself giving her a wink.

Judas

"SURE you won't be late, Jerry?" said the mother and I going out.

"Am I ever late?" said I, and I laughed.

That was all we said, Michael John, but it stuck in my mind. As I was going down the road I was thinking it was months since I'd taken her to the pictures. Of course, you might think that funny, but after the father's death we were thrown together a lot. And I knew she hated being alone in the house after dark.

At the same time I had my own troubles. You see, Michael John, being an only child I never knocked round the way other fellows did. All the fellows in the office went out with girls, or at any rate they let on they did. They said "Who was the old doll I saw you with last night, Jerry? You'd better mind yourself, or you'll be getting into trouble." To hear them you'd imagine there was no sport in the world, only girls, and that they'd always be getting you into trouble. Paddy Kinnane, for instance, talked like that, and he never saw the way it upset me. I think he thought it was a great compliment. It wasn't until years after that I began to suspect that Paddy's acquaintance with girls was about of one kind with my own.

Then I met Kitty Doherty. Kitty was a hospital nurse, and all the chaps in the office said a fellow should never go with hospital nurses. Ordinary girls were bad enough, but nurses were a fright—they knew too much. I knew when I met Kitty that that was a lie. She was a well-educated superior girl; she lived up the river in a posh locality, and her mother was on all sorts of councils and committees. Kitty was small and wiry; a good-looking girl, always in good humor, and when she talked, she hopped from one thing to another like a robin on a frosty morning.

I used to meet her in the evening up the river road, as if I was walking there by accident and very surprised to see her. "Fancy meeting you!" I'd say, or "Well, well, isn't this a great surprise!" Mind you, it usually was, for, no matter how much I was expecting her, I was never prepared for the shock of her presence. Then we'd stand talking for half an hour and I'd see her home. Several times she asked me in, but I was too nervous. I knew I'd lose my head, break the china, use some dirty word, and then go home and cut my throat. Of course, I never asked her to come to the pictures or anything of the sort. She was above that. My only hope was that if I waited long enough I might be able to save her from drowning or the white slavers or something else dramatic, which would show in a modest and dignified way how I felt about her. At the same time I had a bad conscience because I knew I should stay at home more with the mother, but the very thought that I might be missing an opportunity of fishing Kitty out of the river would spoil a whole evening on me.

That night in particular I was nearly distracted. It was three weeks since I'd seen Kitty. I was sure that, at the very least, she was dying and asking for me, and that no one knew my address. A week before, I had felt I simply couldn't bear it any longer, so I had made an excuse and gone down to the post office. I rang up the hospital and asked for Kitty. I fully expected them to say in gloomy tones that Kitty had died half an hour before, and got the shock of my life when the girl at the other end asked my name. I lost my head. "I'm afraid I'm a stranger to Miss Doherty," I said with an embarrassed laugh, "but I have a message for her from a friend."

Then I grew completely panic-stricken. What could a girl like Kitty make of a damned, deliberate lie like that? What else was it but a trap laid by an old and cunning hand? I held the receiver out and looked at it as if it was someone whose neck I was going to wring. "Moynihan," I said to it, "you're mad. An asylum, Moynihan, is the only place for you."

I heard Kitty's voice not in my ear at all, but in the telephone booth as though she were standing before me, and nearly dropped the receiver in terror. Then I raised it and asked in what I thought of as a French accent: "Who is dat speaking, please?" "This is Kitty Doherty," she replied impatiently. "Who are you?"

That was exactly what I was wondering myself. "I am Monsieur Bertrand," I went on cautiously. "I am afraid I have the wrong number. I am so sorry." Then I put down the receiver carefully and thought how nice it would be if only I had a penknife handy to cut my throat with. It's funny, but from the moment I met Kitty I was always coveting sharp things like razors and penknives.

After that an awful idea dawned on me. Of course, I should have thought of it before, but, as you can see, I wasn't exactly knowledgeable where girls were concerned. I began to see that I wasn't meeting Kitty for the very good reason that Kitty didn't want to meet me. What her reason was, I could only imagine, but imagination was my strong point. I examined my conscience to see what I might have said to her. I remembered every remark I had made. The reason was only too clear. Every single remark I had made was either brutal, indecent or disgusting. I had talked of Paddy Kinnane as a fellow who "went with dolls." What could a pure-minded girl think of a chap who naturally used such a phrase except—what unfortunately was quite true—that he had a mind like a cesspit.

But this evening I felt more confident. It was a lovely summer evening with views of hillsides and fields between the gaps in the houses, and it raised my spirits. Perhaps I was wrong; perhaps she hadn't noticed or understood my filthy conversation, perhaps we might meet and walk home together. I walked the full length of the river road and back, and then started to walk it again. The crowds were thinning out as fellows and girls slipped off up the lanes or down to the riverbank, courting. As the streets went out like lamps about me, my hopes sank lower and lower. I saw clearly that she was avoiding me; that she knew I was not the quiet, good-natured fellow I let on to be but a volcano of brutality and lust. "Lust, lust, lust!" I hissed to myself, clenching my fists. I could have forgiven myself anything but the lust.

Then I glanced up and saw her on a tram. I instantly forgot about the lust and smiled and waved my cap to her, but she was looking ahead and didn't see me. I raced after the car, intending to jump onto it, to sit in one of the back seats on top where she would not see me, and then say in astonishment as she got off "Fancy meeting you here!" But as if the driver knew what was in my mind, he put on speed, and the old tram went tossing and screeching down the one straight bit of road in the town, and I stood panting in the roadway, smiling as though missing a tram were the best joke in the world, and wishing all the time that I had a penknife and the courage to use it. My position was hopeless!

Then I must have gone a bit mad—really mad, I mean—for I started to race the tram. There were still lots of people out walking, and they stared after me in an incredulous way, so I lifted my fists to my chest in the attitude of a professional runner and dropped into what I fondly hoped would look like a comfortable stride and delude them into the belief that I was in training for a big race. By the time I was finished, I *was* a runner, and full of indignation against the people who still continued to stare at me.

Between my running and the tram's halts I just managed to keep it in view as far as the other side of town. When I saw Kitty get off and go up a hilly street, I collapsed and was only just able to drag myself after her. When she went into a house on a terrace, I sat on the high curb with my head between my knees until the panting stopped. At any rate I felt safe. I could afford to rest, could walk up and down before the house until she came out, and accost her with an innocent smile and say "Fancy meeting you!"

But my luck was dead out that night. As I was walking up and down, close enough to the house to keep it in view but not close enough to be observed from the windows, I saw a tall man strolling up at the opposite side of the road and my heart sank. It was Paddy Kinnane.

"Hallo, Jerry," he chuckled with that knowing grin he put on whenever he wanted to compliment you on being discovered in a compromising situation. "What are you doing here?"

"Just waiting for a chap I had a date with, Paddy," I said, trying to sound casual.

"Looks more as if you were waiting for an old doll, to me," Paddy said flatteringly. "Still waters run deep. When are you supposed to be meeting him?"

Cripes, I didn't even know what the time was!

"Half eight," I said at random.

"Half eight?" said Paddy. " 'Tis nearly nine now."

"Ah, he's a most unpunctual fellow," I said. "He's always the same. He'll turn up all right."

"I may as well wait with you," said Paddy, leaning against the wall and taking out a packet of cigarettes. "You might find yourself stuck by the end of the evening. There's people in this town that have no consideration for anyone."

That was Paddy all out: a heart of gold; no trouble too much for him if he could do you a good turn—I'd have loved to strangle him.

"Ah, to hell with him!" I said impatiently. "I won't bother waiting. It only struck me this minute that I have another appointment up the Western Road. You'll excuse me now, Paddy. I'll tell you all about it another time."

And away I went hell-for-leather to the tram. I mounted it and went on to the other terminus, near Kitty's house. There, at least, Paddy Kinnane could not get at me. I sat on the river wall in the dusk. The moon was rising, and every quarter of an hour a tram came grunting and squeaking over the old bridge and went black-out while the conductor switched his trolley. Each time I got off the wall and stood on the curb in the moonlight, searching for Kitty among the passengers. Then a policeman came along, and, as he seemed to be watching me, I slunk slowly off up the hill and stood against a wall in shadow. There was a high wall at the other side of the road as well, and behind it the roof of a house was cut out of the sky in moonlight. Every now and then a tram came in and people passed, and the snatches of conversation I caught were like the warmth from an open door to the heart of a homeless man. It was quite clear now that my position was hopeless. If Kitty had walked or been driven she could have reached home from the opposite direction. She could be at home in bed by now. The last tram came and went, and still there was no Kitty, and still I hung on despairingly. While one glimmer of a chance remained I could not go home.

Then I heard a woman's step. I couldn't even pretend to myself that it might be Kitty until she suddenly shuffled past me with that hasty little walk of hers. I started and called her name. She glanced quickly over her shoulder and, seeing a man emerge from the shadow, took fright and ran. I ran too, but she put on speed and began to outdistance me. At that I despaired. I stood on the pavement and shouted after her at the top of my voice.

"Kitty! Kitty, for God's sake wait!"

She ran a few steps further and then halted incredulously. She looked back, and then turned and slowly retraced her steps.

"Jerry Moynihan!" she whispered in astonishment. "What are you doing here?"

I was summoning strength to tell her that I had happened to be taking a stoll in that direction and was astonished to see her when I realized the improbability of it and began to cry instead. Then I laughed.

It was hysteria, I suppose. But Kitty had had a bad fright and, now she was getting over it, she was as cross as two sticks.

"What's wrong with you, I say?" she snapped. "Are you out of your mind or what?"

"But I didn't see you for weeks," I burst out.

"I know," she replied. "I wasn't out. What about it?"

"I thought it might be something I said to you," I said desperately.

"What did you say?" she asked in bewilderment, but I couldn't repeat the hideous things I had already said. Perhaps, after all, she hadn't noticed them!

"How do I know?"

"Oh, it's not that," she said impatiently. "It's just Mother."

"Why?" I asked almost joyously. "Is there something wrong with her?"

"Ah, no, but she made such a fuss about it. I felt it wasn't worth it."

"A fuss? What did she make a fuss about?"

"About you, of course," Kitty said in exasperation.

"But what did I do?" I asked, clutching my head. This was worse than anything I had ever imagined. This was terrible!

"You didn't do anything, but people were talking about us. And you wouldn't come in and be introduced like anyone else. I know she's a bit of a fool, and her head is stuffed with old nonsense about her family. I could never see that they were different to anyone else, and anyway she married a commercial traveller herself, so she has nothing to talk about. Still, you needn't be so superior."

I felt cold shivers run through me. I had thought of Kitty as a secret between God, herself, and me and assumed that she only knew the half of it. Now it seemed I didn't even know the half. People were talking about us! I was superior! What next?

"But what has she against me?" I asked despairingly.

"She thinks we're doing a tangle, of course," snapped Kitty as if she was astonished at my stupidity, "and I suppose she imagines you're not grand enough for a great-great-grandniece of Daniel O'Connell. I told her you were above that sort of thing, but she wouldn't believe me. She said I was a deep, callous, crafty little intriguer and I hadn't a drop of Daniel O'Connell's blood in my veins." Kitty giggled at the thought of herself as an intriguer, and no wonder.

"That's all she knows," I said despairingly.

"I know," Kitty agreed. "She has no sense. And anyway she has no reason to think I'm telling lies. Cissy and I always had fellows, and we spooned with them all over the shop under her very nose, so I don't see why she thinks I'm trying to conceal anything."

At this I began to laugh like an idiot. This was worse than appalling.

This was a nightmare. Kitty, whom I had thought so angelic, talking in cold blood about "spooning" with fellows all over the house. Even the bad women in the books I had read didn't talk about love-making in that cold-blooded way. Madame Bovary herself had at least the decency to pretend that she didn't like it. It was another door opening on the outside world, but Kitty thought I was laughing at her and started to apologize.

"Of course, I had no sense at the time," she said. "You were the first fellow I met that treated me properly. The others only wanted to fool around, and now, because I don't like it, Mother thinks I'm into something ghastly. I told her I liked you better than any fellow I knew, but that I'd grown out of all that sort of thing."

"And what did she say to that?" I asked fiercely. I was beginning to see that imagination wasn't enough; that all round me there was an objective reality that was a thousand times more nightmarish than any fantasy of my own. I couldn't hear enough about it, though at the same time it turned my stomach.

"Ah, I told you she was silly," Kitty said in embarrassment.

"Go on!" I shouted. "I want to know."

"Well," said Kitty with a demure grin, "she said you were a deep, designing guttersnipe who knew exactly how to get round feather-pated little idiots like me. . . . You see, it's quite hopeless. The woman is common. She doesn't understand."

"Oh, God!" I said almost in tears. "I only wish she was right."

"Why do you wish she was right?" Kitty asked with real curiosity.

"Because then I'd have some chance of you," I said.

"Oh!" said Kitty, as if this was news to her. "To tell you the truth," she added after a moment, "I thought you were a bit keen at first, but then I wasn't sure. When you didn't kiss me or anything, I mean."

"God," I said bitterly, "when I think what I've been through in the past few weeks!"

"I know," said Kitty, biting her lip. "I was a bit fed up too."

Then we said nothing for a few moments.

"You're sure you mean it?" she said suspiciously.

"But I tell you I was on the point of committing suicide," I said angrily.

"What good would that be?" she asked with another shrug, and this time she looked at me and laughed outright—the little jade!

I insisted on telling her about my prospects. She didn't want to hear about my prospects; she wanted me to kiss her, but that seemed to me a very sissy sort of occupation, so I told her just the same, in the intervals. It was as if a stone had been lifted off my heart, and I went home in the moonlight, singing. Then I heard the clock strike, and the singing stopped. I remembered the mother's "Sure you won't be late?" and my own "Am I ever late?" This was desperation too, but of a different sort.

The door was ajar and the kitchen in darkness. I saw her sitting before the fire by herself, and just as I was about to throw my arms around her, I smelt Kitty's perfume and was afraid to go near her. God help us, as though that would have told her anything!

"Hullo Mum," I said with a nervous laugh, rubbing my hands. "You're all in darkness."

"You'll have a cup of tea?" she said.

"I might as well."

"What time is it?" she said, lighting the gas. "You're very late."

"I met a fellow from the office," I said, but at the same time I was stung by the complaint in her tone.

"You frightened me," she said with a little whimper. "I didn't know what happened you. What kept you at all?"

"Oh, what do you think?" I said, goaded by my own sense of guilt. "Drinking and blackguarding as usual."

I could have bitten my tongue off as I said it; it sounded so cruel, as if some stranger had said it instead of me. She turned to me with a frightened stare as if she were seeing the stranger too, and somehow I couldn't bear it.

"God Almighty!" I said. "A fellow can have no life in his own house."

I went hastily upstairs, lit the candle, undressed, and got into bed. A chap could be a drunkard and blackguard and not be made to suffer what I was being made to suffer for being out late one single night. This, I felt, was what you got for being a good son.

"Jerry," she called from the foot of the stairs, "will I bring you up your cup?"

"I don't want it now, thanks," I said.

I heard her sigh and turn away. Then she locked the doors, front and back. She didn't wash up, and I knew that my cup of tea was standing on the table with a saucer on top in case I changed my mind. She came slowly upstairs and her walk was that of an old woman. I blew out the candle before she reached the landing, in case she came in to ask if I wanted anything else, and the moonlight came in the attic window and brought me memories of Kitty. But every time I tried to imagine her face as she grinned up at me, waiting for me to kiss her, it was the mother's face that came up instead, with that look like a child's when you strike him for the first time—as if he suddenly saw the stranger in you. I remembered all our life together from the night my father died; our early Mass on Sunday; our visits to the pictures, and our plans for the future, and Christ! Michael John, it was as if I was inside her mind while she sat by the fire waiting for the blow to fall. And now it had fallen, and I was a stranger to her, and nothing I could ever do would make us the same to one another again. There was something like a cannon-ball stuck in my chest, and I lay awake till the cocks started crowing. Then I could bear it no longer. I went out on the landing and listened.

"Are you awake, Mother?" I asked in a whisper.

"What is it, Jerry?" she replied in alarm, and I knew that she hadn't slept any more than I had.

"I only came to say I was sorry," I said, opening the door of her room, and then as I saw her sitting up in bed under the Sacred Heart lamp, the cannon-ball burst inside me and I began to cry like a kid.

"Oh, child, child, child!" she exclaimed, "what are you crying for at all, my little boy?" She spread out her arms to me. I went to her and she hugged me and rocked me as she did when I was only a nipper. "Oh, oh, oh," she was saying to herself in a whisper, "my storeen bawn, my little man!"—all the names she hadn't called me in years. That was all we said. I couldn't bring myself to tell her what I had done, nor could she confess to me that she was jealous: all she could do was to try and comfort me for the way I'd hurt her, to make up to me for the nature she had given me. "My storeen bawn!" she said. "My little man!"

The Babes in the Wood

WHENEVER Mrs. Early made Terry put on his best trousers and gansey he knew his aunt must be coming. She didn't come half often enough to suit Terry, but when she did it was great gas. Terry's mother was dead and he lived with Mrs. Early and her son, Billy. Mrs. Early was a rough, deaf, scolding old woman, doubled up with rheumatics, who'd give you a clout as quick as she'd look at you, but Billy was good gas too.

This particular Sunday morning Billy was scraping his chin frantically and cursing the bloody old razor while the bell was ringing up
the valley for Mass, when Terry's aunt arrived. She come into the dark
little cottage eagerly, her big rosy face toasted with sunshine and her
hand out in greeting.

"Hello, Billy," she cried in a loud, laughing voice, "late for Mass
again?"

"Let me alone, Miss Conners," stuttered Billy, turning his lathered
face to her from the mirror. "I think my mother shaves on the sly."

"And how's Mrs. Early?" cried Terry's aunt, kissing the old woman
and then fumbling at the strap of her knapsack in her excitable way.
Everything about his aunt was excitable and high-powered; the words
tumbled out of her so fast that sometimes she became incoherent.

"Look, I brought you a couple of things—no, they're fags for Billy"
("God bless you, Miss Conners," from Billy) "—this is for you, and
here are a few things for the dinner."

"And what did you bring me, Auntie?" Terry asked.

"Oh, Terry," she cried in consternation, "I forgot about you."

"You didn't."

"I did, Terry," she said tragically. "I swear I did. Or did I? The bird
told me something. What was it he said?"

"What sort of bird was it?" asked Terry. "A thrush?"

"A big gray fellow?"

"That's the old thrush all right. He sings in our back yard."

"And what was that he told me to bring you?"

"A boat!" shouted Terry.

It was a boat.

After dinner the pair of them went up the wood for a walk. His aunt
had a long, swinging stride that made her hard to keep up with, but she
was great gas and Terry wished she'd come to see him oftener. When
she did he tried his hardest to be grown-up. All the morning he had
been reminding himself: "Terry, remember you're not a baby any
longer. You're nine now, you know." He wasn't nine, of course; he was
still only five and fat, but nine, the age of his girl friend Florrie, was
the one he liked pretending to be. When you were nine you understood everything. There were still things Terry did not understand.

When they reached the top of the hill his aunt threw herself on her
back with her knees in the air and her hands under her head. She liked
to toast herself like that. She liked walking; her legs were always bare;
she usually wore a tweed skirt and a pullover. Today she wore black
glasses, and when Terry looked through them he saw everything dark;
the wooded hills at the other side of the valley and the buses and cars
crawling between the rocks at their feet, and, still farther down, the

railway track and the river. She promised him a pair for himself next time she came, a small pair to fit him, and he could scarcely bear the thought of having to wait so long for them.

"When will you come again, Auntie?" he asked. "Next Sunday?"

"I might," she said and rolled on her belly, propped her head on her hands, and sucked a straw as she laughed at him. "Why? Do you like it when I come?"

"I love it."

"Would you like to come and live with me altogether, Terry?"

"Oh, Jay, I would."

"Are you sure now?" she said, half-ragging him. "You're sure you wouldn't be lonely after Mrs. Early or Billy or Florrie?"

"I wouldn't, Auntie, honest," he said tensely. "When will you bring me?"

"I don't know yet," she said. "It might be sooner than you think."

"Where would you bring me? Up to town?"

"If I tell you where," she whispered, bending closer, "will you swear a terrible oath not to tell anybody?"

"I will."

"Not even Florrie?"

"Not even Florrie."

"That you might be killed stone dead?" she added in a blood-curdling tone.

"That I might be killed stone dead!"

"Well, there's a nice man over from England who wants to marry me and bring me back with him. Of course, I said I couldn't come without you and he said he'd bring you as well. . . . Wouldn't that be gorgeous?" she ended, clapping her hands.

" 'Twould," said Terry, clapping his hands in imitation. "Where's England?"

"Oh, a long way off," she said, pointing up the valley. "Beyond where the railway ends. We'd have to get a big boat to take us there."

"Chrisht!" said Terry, repeating what Billy said whenever something occurred too great for his imagination to grasp, a fairly common event. He was afraid his aunt, like Mrs. Early, would give him a wallop for it, but she only laughed. "What sort of a place is England, Auntie?" he went on.

"Oh, a grand place," said his aunt in her loud, enthusiastic way. "The three of us would live in a big house of our own with lights that went off and on, and hot water in the taps, and every morning I'd take you to school on your bike."

"Would I have a bike of my own?" Terry asked incredulously.

"You would, Terry, a two-wheeled one. And on a fine day like this we'd sit in the park—you know, a place like the garden of the big house where Billy works, with trees and flowers and a pond in the middle to sail boats in."

"And would we have a park of our own, too?"

"Not our own; there'd be other people as well; boys and girls you could play with. And you could be sailing your boat and I'd be reading a book, and then we'd go back home to tea and I'd bath you and tell you a story in bed. Wouldn't it be massive, Terry?"

"What sort of story would you tell me?" he asked cautiously. "Tell us one now."

So she took off her black spectacles and, hugging her knees, told him the story of the Three Bears and was so carried away that she acted it, growling and wailing and creeping on all fours with her hair over her eyes till Terry screamed with fright and pleasure. She was really great gas.

NEXT DAY Florrie came to the cottage for him. Florrie lived in the village so she had to come a mile through the woods to see him, but she delighted in seeing him and Mrs. Early encouraged her. "Your young lady" she called her and Florrie blushed with pleasure. Florrie lived with Miss Clancy in the Post Office and was very nicely behaved; everyone admitted that. She was tall and thin, with jet-black hair, a long ivory face, and a hook nose.

"Terry!" bawled Mrs. Early. "Your young lady is here for you," and Terry came rushing from the back of the cottage with his new boat.

"Where did you get that, Terry?" Florrie asked, opening her eyes wide at the sight of it.

"My auntie," said Terry. "Isn't it grand?"

"I suppose 'tis all right," said Florrie, showing her teeth in a smile which indicated that she thought him a bit of a baby for making so much of a toy boat.

Now, that was one great weakness in Florrie, and Terry regretted it because he really was fond of her. She was gentle, she was generous, she always took his part; she told creepy stories so well that she even frightened herself and was scared of going back through the woods alone, but she was jealous. Whenever she had anything, even if it was only a raggy doll, she made it out to be one of the seven wonders of the world, but let anyone else have a thing, no matter how valuable, and she pretended it didn't even interest her. It was the same now.

"Will you come up to the big house for a pennorth of goosegogs?" she asked.

"We'll go down the river with this one first," insisted Terry, who knew he could always override her wishes when he chose.

"But these are grand goosegogs," she said eagerly, and again you'd think no one in the world but herself could even have a gooseberry. "They're that size. Miss Clancy gave me the penny."

"We'll go down the river first," Terry said cantankerously. "Ah, boy, wait till you see this one sail—ssss!"

She gave in as she always did when Terry showed himself head-strong, and grumbled as she always did when she had given in. She said it would be too late; that Jerry, the under-gardener, who was their friend, would be gone and that Mr. Scott, the head gardener, would only give them a handful, and not even ripe ones. She was terrible like that, an awful old worrier.

When they reached the riverbank they tied up their clothes and went in. The river was deep enough, and under the trees it ran beautifully clear over a complete pavement of small, brown, smoothly rounded stones. The current was swift, and the little sailing-boat was tossed on its side and spun dizzily round and round before it stuck in the bank. Florrie tired of this sport sooner than Terry did. She sat on the bank with her hands under her bottom, trailing her toes in the river, and looked at the boat with growing disillusionment.

"God knows, 'tisn't much of a thing to lose a pennorth of goosegogs over," she said bitterly.

"What's wrong with it?" Terry asked indignantly. " 'Tis a fine boat."

"A wonder it wouldn't sail properly so," she said with an accusing, schoolmarmish air.

"How could it when the water is too fast for it?" shouted Terry.

"That's a good one," she retorted in pretended grown-up amusement. " 'Tis the first time we ever heard of water being too fast for a boat." That was another very aggravating thing about her—her calm assumption that only what she knew was knowledge. " 'Tis only a cheap old boat."

" 'Tisn't a cheap old boat," Terry cried indignantly. "My aunt gave it to me."

"She never gives anyone anything only cheap old things," Florrie replied with the coolness that always maddened other children. "She gets them cost price in the shop where she works. Everyone knows that."

"Because you're jealous," he cried, throwing at her the taunt the village children threw whenever she enraged them with her supercilious airs.

"That's a good one too," she said in a quiet voice, while her long thin face maintained its air of amusement. "I suppose you'll tell us now what we're jealous of?"

"Because Auntie brings me things and no one ever brings you anything."

"She's mad about you," Florrie said ironically.

"She is mad about me."

"A wonder she wouldn't bring you to live with her so."

"She's going to," said Terry, forgetting his promise in his rage and triumph.

"She is, I hear!" Florrie said mockingly. "Who told you that?"

"She did; Auntie."

"Don't mind her at all, little boy," Florrie said severely. "She lives with her mother, and her mother wouldn't let you live with her."

"Well, she's not going to live with her anymore," Terry said, knowing he had the better of her at last. "She's going to get married."

"Who is she going to get married to?" Florrie asked casually, but Terry could see she was impressed.

"A man in England, and I'm going to live with them. So there!"

"In England?" Florrie repeated, and Terry saw he had really knocked the stuffing out of her this time. Florrie had no one to bring her to England, and the jealousy was driving her mad. "And I suppose you're going?" she asked bitterly.

"I am going," Terry said, wild with excitement to see her overthrown; the grand lady who for all her airs had no one to bring her to England with them. "And I'm getting a bike of my own. So now!"

"Is that what she told you?" Florrie asked with a hatred and contempt that made him more furious still.

"She's going to, she's going to," he shouted furiously.

"Ah, she's only codding you, little boy," Florrie said contemptuously, splashing her long legs in the water while she continued to fix him with the same dark, evil, round-eyed look, exactly like a witch in a storybook. "Why did she send you down here at all so?"

"She didn't send me," Terry said, stooping to fling a handful of water in her face.

"But sure, I thought everyone knew that," she said idly, merely averting her face slightly to avoid the splashes. "She lets on to be your aunt but we all know she's your mother."

"She isn't," shrieked Terry. "My mother is dead."

"Ah, that's only what they always tell you," Florrie replied quietly. "That's what they told me too, but I knew it was lies. Your mother isn't dead at all, little boy. She got into trouble with a man and her mother made her send you down here to get rid of you. The whole village knows that."

"God will kill you stone dead for a dirty liar, Florrie Clancy," he said and then threw himself on her and began to pummel her with his little fat fists. But he hadn't the strength, and she merely pushed him off lightly and got up on the grassy bank, flushed and triumphant, pretending to smooth down the front of her dress.

"Don't be codding yourself that you're going to England at all, little boy," she said reprovingly. "Sure, who'd want you? Jesus knows I'm sorry for you," she added with mock pity, "and I'd like to do what I could for you, but you have no sense."

Then she went off in the direction of the wood, turning once or twice to give him her strange stare. He glared after her and danced and shrieked with hysterical rage. He had no idea what she meant, but he felt that she had got the better of him after all. "A big, bloody brute of nine," he said, and then began to run through the woods to the cottage, sobbing. He knew that God would kill her for the lies she had told, but if God didn't, Mrs. Early would. Mrs. Early was pegging up clothes on the line and peered down at him sourly.

"What ails you now didn't ail you before?" she asked.

"Florrie Clancy was telling lies," he shrieked, his fat face black with fury. "Big bloody brute!"

"Botheration to you and Florrie Clancy!" said Mrs. Early. "Look at the cut of you! Come here till I wipe your nose."

"She said my aunt wasn't my aunt at all," he cried.

"She what?" Mrs. Early asked incredulously.

"She said she was my mother—Auntie that gave me the boat," he said through his tears.

"Aha," Mrs. Early said grimly, "let me catch her round here again and I'll toast her backside for her, and that's what she wants, the little vagabond! Whatever your mother might do, she was a decent woman, but the dear knows who that one is or where she came from."

ALL THE SAME it was a bad business for Terry. A very bad business! It is all very well having fights, but not when you're only five and live a mile away from the village, and there is nowhere for you to go but across the footbridge to the little railway station and the main road where you wouldn't see another kid once in a week. He'd have been very glad to make it up with Florrie, but she knew she had done wrong and that Mrs. Early was only lying in wait for her to ask her what she meant.

And to make it worse, his aunt didn't come for months. When she did, she came unexpectedly and Terry had to change his clothes in a hurry because there was a car waiting for them at the station. The car made up to Terry for the disappointment (he had never been in a car before), and to crown it, they were going to the seaside, and his aunt had brought him a brand-new bucket and spade.

They crossed the river by the little wooden bridge and there in the yard of the station was a posh gray car and a tall man beside it whom Terry hadn't seen before. He was a posh-looking fellow too, with a gray hat and a nice manner, but Terry didn't pay him much attention at first. He was too interested in the car.

"This is Mr. Walker, Terry," his aunt said in her loud way. "Shake hands with him nicely."

"How're ye, mister?" said Terry.

"But this fellow is a blooming boxer," Mr. Walker cried, letting on to be frightened of him. "Do you box, young Samson?" he asked.

"I do not," said Terry, scrambling into the back of the car and climbing up on the seat. "Hey, mister, will we go through the village?" he added.

"What do you want to go through the village for?" asked Mr. Walker.

"He wants to show off," said his aunt with a chuckle. "Don't you, Terry?"

"I do," said Terry.

"Sound judge!" said Mr. Walker, and they drove along the main road and up through the village street just as Mass was ending, and Terry, hurling himself from side to side, shouted to all the people he knew. First they gaped, then they laughed, finally they waved back. Terry kept shouting messages but they were lost in the noise and rush of the car. "Billy! Billy!" he screamed when he saw Billy Early outside the church. "This is my aunt's car. We're going for a spin. I have a bucket and spade." Florrie was standing outside the Post Office with her hands behind her back. Full of magnanimity and self-importance, Terry gave her a special shout and his aunt leaned out and waved, but though Florrie looked up she let on not to recognize them. That was Florrie all out, jealous even of the car!

Terry had not seen the sea before, and it looked so queer that he decided it was probably England. It was a nice place enough but a bit on the draughty side. There were whitewashed houses all along the beach. His aunt undressed him and made him put on bright blue bathing-drawers, but when he felt the wind he shivered and sobbed and clasped himself despairingly under the armpits.

"Ah, wisha, don't be such a baby!" his aunt said crossly.

She and Mr. Walker undressed too and led him by the hand to the edge of the water. His terror and misery subsided and he sat in a shallow place, letting the bright waves crumple on his shiny little belly. They were so like lemonade that he kept on tasting them, but they tasted salt. He decided that if this was England it was all right, though he would have preferred it with a park and a bicycle. There were other children making sand-castles and he decided to do the same, but after a while, to his great annoyance, Mr. Walker came to help him. Terry couldn't see why, with all that sand, he wouldn't go and make castles of his own.

"Now we want a gate, don't we?" Mr. Walker asked officiously.

"All right, all right, all right," said Terry in disgust. "Now, you go and play over there."

"Wouldn't you like to have a daddy like me, Terry?" Mr. Walker asked suddenly.

"I don't know," replied Terry. "I'll ask Auntie. That's the gate now."

"I think you'd like it where I live," said Mr. Walker. "We've much nicer places there."

"Have you?" asked Terry with interest. "What sort of places?"

"Oh, you know—roundabouts and swings and things like that."

"And parks?" asked Terry.

"Yes, parks."

"Will we go there now?" asked Terry eagerly.

"Well, we couldn't go there today; not without a boat. It's in England, you see; right at the other side of all that water."

"Are you the man that's going to marry Auntie?" Terry asked, so flabbergasted that he lost his balance and fell.

"Now, who told you I was going to marry Auntie?" asked Mr. Walker, who seemed astonished too.

"She did," said Terry.

"Did she, by Jove?" Mr. Walker exclaimed with a laugh. "Well, I think it might be a very good thing for all of us, yourself included. What else did she tell you?"

"That you'd buy me a bike," said Terry promptly. "Will you?"

"Sure thing," Mr. Walker said gravely. "First thing we'll get you when you come to live with me. Is that a bargain?"

"That's a bargain," said Terry.

"Shake," said Mr. Walker, holding out his hand.

"Shake," replied Terry, spitting on his own.

He was content with the idea of Mr. Walker as a father. He could see he'd make a good one. He had the right principles.

They had their tea on the strand and then got back late to the sta-

tion. The little lamps were lit on the platform. At the other side of the
valley the high hills were masked in dark trees and no light showed the
position of the Earlys' cottage. Terry was tired; he didn't want to leave
the car, and began to whine.

"Hurry up now, Terry," his aunt said briskly as she lifted him out.
"Say night-night to Mr. Walker."

Terry stood in front of Mr. Walker, who had got out before him, and
then bowed his head.

"Aren't you going to say good-night, old man?" Mr. Walker asked in
surprise.

Terry looked up at the reproach in his voice and then threw himself
blindly about his knees and buried his face in his trousers. Mr. Walker
laughed and patted Terry's shoulder. His voice was quite different
when he spoke again.

"Cheer up, Terry," he said. "We'll have good times yet."

"Come along now, Terry," his aunt said in a brisk official voice that
terrified him.

"What's wrong, old man?" Mr. Walker asked.

"I want to stay with you," Terry whispered, beginning to sob. "I
don't want to stay here. I want to go back to England with you."

"Want to come back to England with me, do you?" Mr. Walker repeated. "Well, I'm not going back tonight, Terry, but if you ask Auntie nicely we might manage it another day."

"It's no use stuffing up the child with ideas like that," she said
sharply.

"You seem to have done that pretty well already," Mr. Walker said
quietly. "So you see, Terry, we can't manage it tonight. We must leave
it for another day. Run along with Auntie now."

"No, no, no," Terry shrieked, trying to evade his aunt's arms. "She
only wants to get rid of me."

"Now, who told you that wicked nonsense, Terry?" Mr. Walker
said severely.

"It's true, it's true," said Terry. "She's not my auntie. She's my
mother."

Even as he said it he knew it was dreadful. It was what Florrie
Clancy said, and she hated his auntie. He knew it even more from the
silence that fell on the other two. His aunt looked down at him and her
look frightened him.

"Terry," she said with a change of tone, "you're to come with me at
once and no more of this nonsense."

"Let him to me," Mr. Walker said shortly. "I'll find the place."

She did so and at once Terry stopped kicking and whining and nosed his way into Mr. Walker's shoulder. He knew the Englishman was for him. Besides he was very tired. He was half asleep already. When he heard Mr. Walker's step on the planks of the wooden bridge he looked up and saw the dark hillside, hooded with pines, and the river like lead in the last light. He woke again in the little dark bedroom which he shared with Billy. He was sitting on Mr. Walker's knee and Mr. Walker was taking off his shoes.

"My bucket," he sighed.

"Oh, by gum, lad," Mr. Walker said, "I'd nearly forgotten your bucket."

EVERY Sunday after, wet or fine, Terry found his way across the footbridge and the railway station to the main road. There was a pub there, and men came from up from the valley and sat on the wall outside, waiting for the coast to be clear to slip in for a drink. In case there might be any danger of having to leave them behind, Terry brought his bucket and spade as well. You never knew when you'd need things like those. He sat at the foot of the wall near the men, where he could see the buses and cars coming from both directions. Sometimes a gray car like Mr. Walker's appeared from round the corner and he waddled up the road towards it, but the driver's face was always a disappointment. In the evenings when the first buses were coming back he returned to the cottage and Mrs. Early scolded him for moping and whining. He blamed himself a lot because all the trouble began when he broke his word to his aunt.

One Sunday, Florrie came up the main road from the village. She went past him slowly, waiting for him to speak to her, but he wouldn't. It was all her fault, really. Then she stopped and turned to speak to him. It was clear that she knew he'd be there and had come to see him and make it up.

"Is it anyone you're waiting for, Terry?" she asked.

"Never mind," Terry replied rudely.

"Because if you're waiting for your aunt, she's not coming," Florrie went on gently.

Another time Terry wouldn't have entered into conversation, but now he felt so mystified that he would have spoken to anyone who could tell him what was keeping his aunt and Mr. Walker. It was terrible to be only five, because nobody ever told you anything.

"How do you know?" he asked.

"Miss Clancy said it," replied Florrie confidently. "Miss Clancy knows everything. She hears it all in the Post Office. And the man with the gray car isn't coming either. He went back to England."

Terry began to snivel softly. He had been afraid that Mr. Walker wasn't really in earnest. Florrie drew closer to him and then sat on the grass bank beside him. She plucked a stalk and began to shred it in her lap.

"Why wouldn't you be said by me?" she asked reproachfully. "You know I was always your girl and I wouldn't tell you a lie."

"But why did Mr. Walker go back to England?" he asked.

"Because your aunt wouldn't go with him."

"She said she would."

"Her mother wouldn't let her. He was married already. If she went with him he'd have brought you as well. You're lucky he didn't."

"Why?"

"Because he was a Protestant," Florrie said primly. "Protestants have no proper religion like us."

Terry did his best to grasp how having a proper religion made up to a fellow for the loss of a house with lights that went off and on, a park and a bicycle, but he realized he was too young. At five it was still too deep for him.

"But why doesn't Auntie come down like she always did?"

"Because she married another fellow and he wouldn't like it."

"Why wouldn't he like it?"

"Because it wouldn't be right," Florrie replied almost pityingly. "Don't you see the English fellow have no proper religion, so he wouldn't mind, but the fellow she married owns the shop she works in, and Miss Clancy says 'tis surprising he married her at all, and he wouldn't like her to be coming here to see you. She'll be having proper children now, you see."

"Aren't we proper children?"

"Ah, no, we're not," Florrie said despondently.

"What's wrong with us?"

That was a question that Florrie had often asked herself, but she was too proud to show a small boy like Terry that she hadn't discovered the answer.

"Everything," she sighed.

"Florrie Clancy," shouted one of the men outside the pub, "what are you doing to that kid?"

"I'm doing nothing to him," she replied in a scandalized tone, starting as though from a dream. "He shouldn't be here by himself at all. He'll get run over.... Come on home with me now, Terry," she added, taking his hand.

"She said she'd bring me to England and give me a bike of my own," Terry wailed as they crossed the tracks.

"She was only codding," Florrie said confidently. Her tone changed gradually; it was becoming fuller, more scornful. "She'll forget all about you when she has other kids. Miss Clancy says they're all the same. She says there isn't one of them worth bothering your head about, that they never think of anyone only themselves. She says my father has pots of money. If you were in with me I might marry you when you're a bit more grown-up."

She led him up the short cut through the woods. The trees were turning all colors. Then she sat on the grass and sedately smoothed her frock about her knees.

"What are you crying for?" she asked reproachfully. "It was all your fault. I was always your girl. Even Mrs. Early said it. I always took your part when the others were against you. I wanted you not to be said by that old one and her promises, but you cared more for her and her old toys than you did for me. I told you what she was, but you wouldn't believe me, and now, look at you! If you'll swear to be always in with me I'll be your girl again. Will you?"

"I will," said Terry.

She put her arms about him and he fell asleep, but she remained solemnly holding him, looking at him with detached and curious eyes. He was hers at last. There were no more rivals. She fell asleep too and did not notice the evening train go up the valley. It was all lit up. The evenings were drawing in.

The Frying-Pan

FATHER FOGARTY'S only real friends in Kilmulpeter were the Whittons. Whitton was the teacher there. He had been to the seminary and college with Fogarty, and, like him, intended to be a priest, but when the time came for him to take the vow of celibacy, he had contracted scruples of conscience and married the principal one. Fogarty, who had known her too, had to admit that she wasn't without justification, and now, in this lonely place where chance had thrown them together again, she formed the real center of what little social life he had. With Tom Whitton he had a quiet friendship compounded of exchanges of opinion about books or wireless talks. He had the impression that

Whitton didn't really like him and considered him a man who would have been better out of the Church. When they went to the races together, Fogarty felt that Whitton disapproved of having to put on bets for him and thought that preists should not bet at all. Like other outsiders, he knew perfectly what priests should be, without the necessity for having to be that way himself. He was sometimes savage in the things he said about the parish priest, old Father Whelan. On the other hand, he had a pleasant sense of humor and Fogarty enjoyed retailing his cracks against the cloth. Men as intelligent as Whitton were rare in country schools, and soon, too, he would grow stupid and wild for lack of educated society.

One evening Father Fogarty invited them to dinner to see some films he had taken at the races. Films were his latest hobby. Before this it had been fishing and shooting. Like all bachelors, he had a mania for adding to his possessions, and his lumber-room was piled high with every possible sort of junk from chest-developers to field-glasses, and his library cluttered with works on everything from Irish history to Freudian psychology. He passed from craze to craze, each the key to the universe.

He sprang up at the knock, and found Una at the door, all in furs, her shoulders about her ears, her big, bony, masculine face blue with cold but screwed up in an amiable monkey-grin. Tom, a handsome man, was tall and self-conscious. He had graying hair, brown eyes, a prominent jaw, and was quiet-spoken in a way that concealed passion. He and Una disagreed a lot about the way the children should be brought up. He thought she spoiled them.

"Come in, let ye, come in!" cried Fogarty hospitably, showing the way into his warm study with its roaring turf fire, deep leather chairs, and the Raphael print above the mantelpiece; a real bachelor's room. "God above!" he exclaimed, holding Una's hand a moment longer than was necessary. "You're perished! What'll you have to drink, Una?"

"Whi-hi-hi—" stammered Una excitedly, her eyes beginning to pop. "I can't say the bloody word."

"Call it malt, girl," said the priest.

"That's enough! That's enough!" she cried laughingly, snatching the glass from him. "You'll send me home on my ear, and then I'll hear about it from this fellow."

"Whiskey, Tom?"

"Whiskey, Jerry," Whitton said quietly with a quick conciliatory glance. He kept his head very stiff and used his eyes a lot instead.

Meanwhile Una, unabashably inquisitive, was making the tour of the room with the glass in her hand, to see if there was anything new in it. There usually was.

"Is this new, father?" she asked, halting before a pleasant eighteenth-century print.

"Ten bob," the priest said promptly. "Wasn't it a bargain?"

"I couldn't say. What is it?"

"The old courthouse in town."

"Go on!" said Una.

Whitton came and studied the print closely. "That place is gone these fifty years and I never saw a picture of it," he said. "This is a bargain all right."

"I'd say so," Fogarty said with quiet pride.

"And what's the sheet for?" Una asked, poking at a tablecloth pinned between the windows.

"That's not a sheet, woman!" Fogarty exclaimed. "For God's sake, don't be displaying your ignorance!"

"Oh, I know," she cried girlishly. "For the pictures! I'd forgotten about them. That's grand!"

Then Bella, a coarse, good-looking country girl, announced dinner, and the curate, with a self-conscious, boyish swagger, led them into the dining room and opened the door of the sideboard. The dining room was even more ponderous than the sitting room. Everything in it was large, heavy, and dark.

"And now, what'll ye drink?" he asked over his shoulder, studying his array of bottles. "There's some damn good Burgundy—'pon my soul, 'tis great!"

"How much did it cost?" Whitton asked with poker-faced humor. "The only way I have of identifying wines is by the price."

"Eight bob a bottle," Fogarty replied at once.

"That's a very good price," said Whitton with a nod. "We'll have some of that."

"You can take a couple of bottles home with you," said the curate, who, in the warmth of his heart, was always wanting to give his treasures away. "The last two dozen he had—wasn't I lucky?"

"You have the appetite of a canon on the income of a curate," Whitton said in the same tone of grave humor, but Fogarty caught the scarcely perceptible note of criticism in it. He did not allow this to upset him.

"Please God, we won't always be curates," he said sunnily.

"Bella looks after you well," said Una when the meal was nearly over. The compliment was deserved so far as it went, though it was a man's meal rather than a woman's.

"Doesn't she, though?" Fogarty exclaimed with pleasure. "Isn't she damn good for a country girl?"

"How does she get on with Stasia?" asked Una—Stasia was Father Whelan's old housekeeper, and an affliction to the community.

"They don't talk. Stasia says she's an immoral woman."

"And is she?" Una asked hopefully.

"If she isn't, she's wasting her own time and my whiskey," said Fogarty. "She entertains Paddy Coakley in the kitchen every Saturday night. I told her I wouldn't keep her unless she got a boy. And wasn't I right? One Stasia is enough for any parish. Father Whelan tells me I'm going too far."

"And did you tell him to mind his own business?" Whitton asked with a penetrating look.

"I did, to be sure," said Fogarty, who had done nothing of the sort.

"Ignorant, interfering old fool!" Whitton said quietly, the ferocity of his sentiments belied by the mildness of his manner.

"That's only because you'd like to do the interfering yourself," said Una good-humoredly. She frequently had to act as peacemaker between the parish priest and her husband.

"And a robber," Tom Whitton added to the curate, ignoring her. "He's been collecting for new seats for the church for the last ten years. I'd like to know where that's going."

"He had a collection for repairing my roof," said the curate, "and 'tis leaking still. He must be worth twenty thousand."

"Now, that's not fair, father," Una said flatly. "You know yourself there's no harm in Father Whelan. It's just that he's certain he's going to die in the workhouse. It's like Bella and her boy. He has nothing more serious to worry about, and he worries about that."

Fogarty knew there was a certain amount of truth in what Una said, and that the old man's miserliness was more symbolic than real, and at the same time he felt in her words criticism of a different kind from her husband's. Though Una wasn't aware of it she was implying that the priest's office made him an object of pity rather than blame. She was sorry for old Whelan, and, by implication, for him.

"Still, Tom is right, Una," he said with sudden earnestness. "It's not a question of what harm Father Whelan intends, but what harm he does. Scandal is scandal, whether you give it deliberately or through absent-mindedness."

Tom grunted, to show his approval, but he said no more on the subject, as though he refused to enter into an argument with his wife about subjects she knew nothing of. They returned to the study for coffee, and Fogarty produced the film projector. At once the censoriousness of Tom Whitton's manner dropped away, and he behaved like a pleasant and intelligent boy of seventeen. Una, sitting by the fire with her legs crossed, watched them with amusement. Whenever they came to the priest's house, the same sort of thing happened. Once it had been a microscope, and the pair of them had amused themselves with it for hours. Now they were kidding themselves that their real interest in the cinema was educational. She knew that within a month the cinema, like the microscope, would be lying in the lumber-room with the rest of the junk.

Fogarty switched off the light and showed some films he had taken at the last race meeting. They were very patchy, mostly out of focus, and had to be interpreted by a running commentary, which was always a shot or two behind.

"I suppose ye wouldn't know who that is?" he said as the film showed Una, eating a sandwich and talking excitedly and demonstratively to a couple of wild-looking country boys.

"It looks like someone from the Country Club," her husband said dryly.

"But wasn't it good?" Fogarty asked innocently as he switched on the lights again. "Now, wasn't it very interesting?" He was exactly like a small boy who had performed a conjuring trick.

"Marvellous, father," Una said with a sly and affectionate grin.

He blushed and turned to pour them out more whiskey. He saw that she had noticed the pictures of herself. At the same time, he saw she was pleased. When he had driven them home, she held his hand and said they had had the best evening for years—a piece of flattery so gross and uncalled-for that it made her husband more tongue-tied than ever.

"Thursday, Jerry?" he said with a quick glance.

"Thursday, Tom," said the priest.

The room looked terribly desolate after her; the crumpled cushions, the glasses, the screen and the film projector, everything had become frighteningly inert, while outside his window the desolate countryside had taken on even more of its supernatural animation: bogs, hills, and field, full of ghosts and shadows. He sat by the fire, wondering what his own life might have been like with a girl like that, all furs and scent and laughter, and two bawling, irrepressible brats upstairs. When he tiptoed up to his bedroom he remembered that there would never be children there to wake, and it seemed to him that with all the things he bought to fill his home, he was merely trying desperately to stuff the yawning holes in his own big, empty heart.

On Thursday, when he went to their house, Ita and Brendan, though already in bed, were refusing to sleep till he said good-night to them. While he was taking off his coat the two of them rushed to the banisters and screamed: "We want Father Fogey." When he went upstairs they were sitting bolt upright in their cots, a little fat, fair-haired rowdy boy and a solemn baby girl.

"Father," Brendan began at once, "will I be your altar boy when I grow up?"

"You will to be sure, son" replied Fogarty.

"Ladies first! Ladies first!" the baby shrieked in a frenzy of rage. "Father, will I be your altar boy?"

"Go on!" Brendan said scornfully. "Little girls can't be altar boys, sure they can't, father?"

"I can," shrieked Ita, who in her excitement exactly resembled her mother. "Can't I, father?"

"We might be able to get a dispensation for you," said the curate. "In a pair of trousers, you'd do fine."

He was in a wistful frame of mind when he came downstairs again. Children would always be a worse temptation to him than women. Children were the devil! The house was gay and spotless. They had no fine mahogany suite like his, but Una managed to make the few colored odds and ends they had seem deliberate. There wasn't a cigarette end in the ashtrays; the cushions had not been sat on. Tom, standing before the fireplace (not to disturb the cushions, thought Fogarty), looked as if someone had held his head under the tap, and was very self-consciously wearing a new brown tie. With his graying hair plastered flat, he looked schoolboyish, sulky, and resentful, as though he were meditating ways of restoring his authority over a mutinous household. The thought crossed Fogarty's mind that he and Una had probably quarrelled about the tie. It went altogether too well with his suit.

"We want Father Fogey!" the children began to chant monotonously from the bedroom.

"Shut up!" shouted Tom.

"We want Father Fogey," the chant went on, but with a groan in it somewhere.

"Well, you're not going to get him. Go to sleep!"

The chant stopped. This was clearly serious.

"You don't mind if I drop down to a meeting tonight, Jerry?" Tom asked in his quiet, anxious way. "I won't be more than half an hour."

"Not at all, Tom," said Fogarty heartily. "Sure, I'll drive you."

"No, thanks," Whitton said with a smile of gratitude. "It won't take me ten minutes to get there."

It was clear that a lot of trouble had gone to the making of supper, but out of sheer perversity Tom let on not to recognize any of the dishes. When they had drunk their coffee, he rose and glanced at his watch.

"I won't be long," he said.

"Tom, you're not going to that meeting?" Una asked appealingly.

"I tell you I have to," he replied with unnecessary emphasis.

"I met Mick Mahoney this afternoon, and he said they didn't need you."

"Mick Mahoney knows nothing about it."

"I told him to tell the others you wouldn't be coming, that Father Fogarty would be here," she went on desperately, fighting for the success of her evening.

"Then you had no business to do it," her husband retorted angrily, and even Fogarty saw that she had gone the worst way about it, by speaking to members of his committee behind his back. He began to feel uncomfortable. "If they come to some damn fool decision while I'm away, it'll be my responsibility."

"If you're late, you'd better knock," she sang out gaily to cover up his bad manners. "Will we go into the sitting room, father?" she asked overeagerly. "I'll be with you in two minutes. There are fags on the mantelpiece, and you know where to find the whi-hi-hi—blast that word!"

Fogarty lit a cigarette and sat down. He felt exceedingly uncomfortable. Whitton was an uncouth and irritable bastard, and always had been so. He heard Una upstairs, and then someone turned on the tap in the bathroom. "Bloody brute!" he thought indignantly. There had been no need for him to insult her before a guest. Why the hell couldn't he have finished his quarrelling while they were alone? The tap stopped and he waited, listening, but Una didn't come. He was a warm-hearted man and could not bear the thought of her alone and miserable upstairs. He went softly up the stairs and stood on the landing. "Una!" he called softly, afraid of waking the children. There was a light in the bedroom; the door was ajar and he pushed it in. She was sitting at the end of the bed and grinned at him dolefully.

"Sorry for the whine, father," she said, making a brave attempt to smile. And then, with the street-urchin's humor which he found so attractive: "Can I have a loan of your shoulder, please?"

"What the blazes ails Tom?" he asked, sitting beside her.

"He—he's jealous," she stammered, and began to weep again with her head on his chest. He put his arm about her and patted her awkwardly.

"Jealous?" he asked incredulously, turning over in his mind the half-dozen men whom Una could meet at the best of times. "Who the blazes is he jealous of?"

"You!"

"Me?" Fogarty exclaimed indignantly, and grew red, thinking of how he had given himself away with his pictures. "He must be mad! I never gave him any cause for jealousy."

"Oh, I know he's completely unreasonable," she stammered. "He always was."

"But you didn't say anything to him, did you?" Fogarty asked anxiously.

"About what?" she asked in surprise, looking up at him and blinking back her tears.

"About me?" Fogarty mumbled in embarrassment.

"Oh, he doesn't know about that," Una replied frantically. "I never mentioned that to him at all. Besides, he doesn't care that much about me."

And Fogarty realized that in the simplest way in the world he had been brought to admit to a married woman that he loved her and she to imply that she felt the same about him, without a word being said on either side. Obviously, these things happened more innocently than he had ever thought possible. He became more embarrassed than ever.

"But what is he jealous of so?" he added truculently.

"He's jealous of you because you're a priest. Surely, you saw that?"

"I certainly didn't. It never crossed my mind."

Yet at the same time he wondered if this might not be the reason for the censoriousness he sometimes felt in Whitton against his harmless bets and his bottles of wine.

"But he's hardly ever out of your house, and he's always borrowing your books, and talking theology and church history to you. He has shelves of them here—look!" And she pointed at a plain wooden bookcase, filled with solid-looking works. "In my b-b-bedroom! That's why he really hates Father Whelan. Don't you see, Jerry," she said, calling him for the first time by his Christian name, "you have all the things he wants."

"I have?" repeated Fogarty in astonishment. "What things?"

"Oh, how do I know?" she replied with a shrug, relegating these to the same position as Whelan's bank-balance and his own gadgets, as things that meant nothing to her. "Respect and responsibility and freedom from the worries of a family, I suppose."

"He's welcome to them," Fogarty said with wry humor. "What's that the advertisements say?—owner having no further use for same."

"Oh, I know," she said with another shrug, and he saw that from the beginning she had realized how he felt about her and been sorry for him. He was sure that there was some contradiction here which he should be able to express to himself, between her almost inordinate piety and her lighthearted acceptance of his adoration for her—something that was exclusively feminine, but which he could not isolate with her there beside him, willing him to make love to her, offering herself to his kiss.

"It's a change to be kissed by someone who cares for you," she said after a moment.

"Ah, now, Una, that's not true," he protested gravely, the priest in him getting the upper hand of the lover who had still a considerable amount to learn. "You only fancy that."

"I don't, Jerry," she replied with conviction. "It's always been the same, from the first month of our marriage—always! I was a fool to marry him at all."

"Even so," Fogarty said manfully, doing his duty by his friend with a sort of schoolboy gravity, "you know he's still fond of you. That's only his way."

"It isn't, Jerry," she went on obstinately. "He wanted to be a priest and I stopped him."

"But you didn't."

"That's how he looks at it. I tempted him."

"And damn glad he was to fall!"

"But he did fall, Jerry, and that's what he can never forgive. In his heart he despises me and despises himself for not being able to do without me."

"But why should he despise himself? That's what I don't understand."

"Because I'm only a woman, and he wants to be independent of me and every other woman as well. He has to teach to keep a home for me, and he doesn't want to teach. He wants to say Mass and hear confessions, and be God Almighty for seven days of the week."

Fogarty couldn't grasp it, but he realized that there was something in what she said, and that Whitton was really a lonely, frustrated man who felt he was forever excluded from the only things which interested him.

"I don't understand it," he said angrily. "It doesn't sound natural to me."

"It doesn't sound natural to you because you have it, Jerry," she said. "I used to think Tom wasn't normal, either, but now I'm beginning to think there are more spoiled priests in the world than ever went into seminaries. You see, Jerry," she went on in a rush, growing very red, "I'm a constant reproach to him. He thinks he's a terrible blackguard because he wants to make love to me once a month. . . . I can talk like this to you because you're a priest."

"You can, to be sure," said Fogarty with more conviction than he felt.

"And even when he does make love to me," she went on, too full of her grievance even to notice the anguish she caused him, "he manages to make me feel that I'm doing all the love-making."

"And why shouldn't you?" asked Fogarty gallantly, concealing the way his heart turned over in him.

"Because it's a sin!" she cried tempestuously.

"Who said it's a sin?"

"He makes it a sin. He's like a bear with a sore head for days after. Don't you see, Jerry," she cried, springing excitedly to her feet and shaking her head at him, "it's never anything but adultery with him, and he goes away and curses himself because he hasn't the strength to resist it."

"Adultery?" repeated Fogarty, the familiar word knocking at his conscience as if it were Tom Whitton himself at the door.

"Whatever you call it," Una rushed on. "It's always adultery, adultery, adultery, and I'm always a bad woman, and he always wants to show God that it wasn't him but me, and I'm sick and tired of it. I want a man to make me feel like a respectable married woman for once in my life. You see, I feel quite respectable with you, although I know I shouldn't." She looked in the mirror of the dressing-table and her face fell. "Oh, Lord!" she sighed. "I don't look it. . . . I'll be down in two minutes now, Jerry," she said eagerly, thrusting out her lips to him, her old, brilliant, excitable self.

"You're grand," he muttered.

As she went into the bathroom, she turned in another excess of emotion and threw her arms about him. As he kissed her, she pressed herself close to him till his head swam. There was a mawkish, girlish grin on her face. "Darling!" she said in an agony of passion, and it was as if their loneliness enveloped them like a cloud.

As he went downstairs, he was very thoughtful. He heard Tom's key in the lock and looked at himself in the mirror over the fireplace. He heard Tom's step in the hall, and it sounded in his ears as it had never sounded before, like that of a man carrying a burden too great for him. He realized that he had never before seen Whitton as he really was, a man at war with his animal nature, longing for some high, solitary existence of the intellect and imagination. And he knew that the three of them, Tom, Una, and himself, would die as they had lived, their desires unsatisfied.

The Miracle

VANITY, according to the Bishop, was the Canon's great weakness, and there might be some truth in that. He was a tall, good-looking man, with a big chin, and a manner of deceptive humility. He deplored the fact that so many of the young priests came of poor homes where good manners weren't taught, and looked back regretfully to the old days when, according to him, every Irish priest read his Virgil. He went in a lot for being an authority on food and wine, and ground and brewed his own coffee. He refused to live in the ramshackle old presbytery which had served generations of priests, and had built for himself a residence that was second only to the Bishop's palace and that was furnished with considerably more taste and expense. His first innovation in the parish had been to alter the dues which, all over the Christian world, are paid at Christmas and Easter and have them paid four times a year instead. He said that this was because poor people couldn't afford large sums twice a year, and that it was easier for them to pay their dues like that; but in fact it was because he thought the dues that had been fixed were far too low to correspond in any way with the dignity of his office. When he was building his house he had them collected five times during the year, and, as well as that, threw in a few raffles and public subscriptions. He disliked getting into debt. And there he ate his delicate meals with the right wines, brewed coffee and drank green chartreuse, and occasionally dipped into ecclesiastical history. He liked to read about days when the clergy were really well off.

It was distasteful to the Canon the way the lower classes were creeping into the Church and gaining high office in it, but it was a real heartbreak that its functions and privileges were being usurped by new men and methods, and that miracles were now being performed out of bottles and syringes. He thought that a very undignified way of performing miracles himself, and it was a real bewilderment of spirit to him when some new drug was invented to make the medicine men more indispensable than they were at present. He would have liked surgeons to remain tradesmen and barbers as they were in the good old days, and, though he would have been astonished to hear it himself, was as jealous as a prima donna at the interference of Bobby Healy, the doctor, with his flock. He would have liked to be able to do it all himself, and sometimes thought regretfully that it was a peculiar dispensation of Providence that when the Church was most menaced, it couldn't draw upon some of its old grace and perform occasional miracles. The Canon knew he would have performed a miracle with a real air. He had the figure for it.

There was certainly some truth in the Bishop's criticism. The Canon hated competition, he liked young Dr. Devaney, who affected to believe that medicine was all hocus-pocus (which was what the Canon believed himself), and took a grave view of Bobby Healy, which caused Bobby's practice to go down quite a bit. When the Canon visited a dying man he took care to ask: "Who have you?" If he was told "Dr. Devaney," he said: "A good young man," but if it was "Dr. Healy" he merely nodded and looked grave, and everyone understood that Bobby had killed the unfortunate patient as usual. Whenever the two men met, the Canon was courteous and condescending, Bobby was respectful and obliging, and nobody could ever have told from the doctor's face whether or not he knew what was going on. But there was very little which Bobby didn't know. There is a certain sort of guile that goes deeper than any cleric's: the peasant's guile. Dr. Healy had that.

But there was one person in his parish whom the Canon disliked even more than he disliked the doctor. That was a man called Bill Enright. Nominally, Bill was a farmer and breeder of greyhounds; really, he was the last of a family of bandits who had terrorized the countryside for generations. He was a tall, gaunt man with fair hair and a tiny, gold mustache; perfectly rosy skin, like a baby's, and a pair of bright blue eyes which seemed to expand into a wide unwinking, animal glare. His cheekbones were so high that they gave the impression of cutting his skin. They also gave his eyes an Oriental slant, and, with its low, sharp-sloping forehead, his whole face seemed to point outward to the sharp tip of his nose and then retreat again in a pair of high teeth, very sharp and very white, a drooping lower lip, and a small, weak, feminine chin.

Now, Bill, as he would be the first to tell you, was not a bad man. He was a traditionalist who did as his father and grandfather had done before him. He had gone to Mass and the Sacraments and even paid his dues four times a year, which was not traditional, and been prepared to treat the Canon as a bandit of similar dignity to himself. But the Canon had merely been incensed at the offer of parity with Bill and set out to demonstrate that the last of the Enrights was a common ruffian who should be sent to jail. Bill was notoriously living in sin with his housekeeper, Nellie Mahony from Doonamon, and the Canon ordered her to leave the house. When he failed in this he went to her brothers and demanded that they should drag her home, but her brothers had had too much experience of the Enrights to try such a risky experiment with them, and Nellie remained on, while Bill, declaring loudly that there was nothing in religion, ceased going to Mass. People agreed that it wasn't altogether Bill's fault, and that the Canon could not brook another authority than his own—a hasty man!

To Bobby Healy, on the other hand, Bill Enright was bound by the strongest tie that could bind an Enright, for the doctor had once cured a greyhound for him, the mother of King Kong. Four or five times a year he was summoned to treat Bill for an overdose of whiskey; Bill owed him as much money as it was fitting to owe to a friend, and all Bill's friends knew that when they were in trouble themselves, it would be better for them to avoid further trouble by having Dr. Healy as well. Whatever the Canon might think, Bill was a man it paid to stand in well with.

One spring day Bobby got one of his usual summonses to the presence. Bill lived in a fine Georgian house a mile outside the town. It had once belonged to the Rowes, but Bill had got them out of it by the simple expedient of making their lives a hell for them. The avenue was overgrown, and the house with its fine Ionic portico looked dirty and dilapidated. Two dogs got up and barked at him in a neighborly way. They hated it when Bill was sick, and they knew Bobby had the knack of putting him on his feet again.

Nellie Mahony opened the door. She was a small, fat country girl with a rosy complexion and a mass of jet-black hair that shone almost as brilliantly as her eyes. The doctor, who was sometimes seized with these fits of amiable idiocy, took her by the waist, and she gave a shriek of laughter that broke off suddenly.

"Wisha, Dr. Healy," she said complainingly, "oughtn't you to be ashamed, and the state we're in!"

"How's that, Nellie?" he asked anxiously. "Isn't it the usual thing?"

"The usual thing?" she shrieked. She had a trick of snatching up and repeating someone's final words in a brilliant tone, a full octave higher, like a fiddle repeating a phrase from the double-bass. Then with dramatic abruptness she let her voice drop to a whisper and dabbed her eyes with her apron. "He's dying, doctor," she said.

"For God's sake!" whispered the doctor. Life had rubbed down his principles considerably, and the fact that Bill was suspected of a share in at least one murder didn't prejudice him in the least. "What happened him? I saw him in town on Monday and he never looked better."

"Never looked better?" echoed the fiddles, while Nellie's beautiful black eyes filled with a tragic emotion that was not far removed from joy. "And then didn't he go out on the Tuesday morning on me, in the pouring rain, with three men and two dogs, and not come back till the Friday night, with the result" (this was a boss phrase of Nellie's, always followed by a dramatic pause and a change of key) "that he caught a chill up through him and never left the bed since."

"What are you saying to Bobby Healy?" screeched a man's voice from upstairs. It was nearly as high-pitched as Nellie's, but with a wild nervous tremolo in it.

"What am I saying to Bobby Healy?" she echoed mechanically. "I'm saying nothing at all to him."

"Well, don't be keeping him down there, after I waiting all day for him."

"There's nothing wrong with his lungs anyway," the doctor said professionally as he went up the stairs. They were bare and damp. It was a lifelong grievance of Bill Enright's that the Rowes had been mean enough to take the furniture to England with them.

He was sitting up in an iron bed, and the gray afternoon light and the white pillows threw up the brilliance of his coloring, already heightened with a touch of fever.

"What was she telling you?" he asked in his high-pitched voice—the sort of keen and unsentimental voice you'd attribute in fantasy to some cunning and swift-footed beast of prey, like a fox.

"What was I telling him?" Nellie echoed boldly, feeling the doctor's authority behind her. "I was telling him you went out with three men and two dogs and never came back to me till Friday night."

"Ah, Bill," said the doctor reproachfully, "how often did I tell you to stick to women and cats? What ails you?"

"I'm bloody bad, doctor," whinnied Bill.

"You look it," said Bobby candidly. "That's all right, Nellie," he added by way of dismissal.

"And make a lot of noise downstairs," said Bill after her.

Bobby gave his patient a thorough examination. So far as he could see there was nothing wrong with him but a chill, though he realized from the way Bill's mad blue eyes followed him that the man was in a panic. He wondered whether, as he sometimes did, he shouldn't put

him in a worse one. It was unprofessional, but it was the only treatment that ever worked, and with most of his men patients he was
compelled to choose a moment, before it was too late and hadn't yet
passed from fiction to fact, when the threat of heart-disease or cirrhosis
might reduce their drinking to some reasonable proportion. Then the
inspiration came to him like Heaven opening to poor sinners, and he
sat for several moments in silence, working it out. Threats would be
lost on Bill Enright. What Bill needed was a miracle, and miracles
aren't things to be lightly undertaken. Properly performed, a miracle
might do as much good to the doctor as to Bill.

"Well, Bobby?" asked Bill, on edge with nerves.

"How long is it since you were at Confession, Bill?" the doctor
asked gravely.

Bill's rosy face turned the color of wax, and the doctor, a kindly
man, felt almost ashamed of himself.

"Is that the way it is, doctor?" Bill asked in a shrill, expressionless
voice.

"I put it too strongly, Bill," said the doctor, already relenting.
"Maybe I should have a second opinion."

"Your opinion is good enough for me, Bobby," said Bill wildly,
pouring coals of fire on Bobby as he sat up in bed and pulled the
clothes about him. "Take a fag and light one for me. What the hell difference does it make? I lived my life and bred the best greyhound
bitches in Europe."

"And I hope you'll live to breed a good many more," said the doctor.
"Will I go for the Canon?"

"The Half-Gent?" snorted Bill indignantly. "You will not."

"He has an unfortunate manner," sighed the doctor. "But I could
bring you someone else."

"Ah, what the hell do I want with any of them?" asked Bill. "Aren't
they all the same? Money! Money! That's all that's a trouble to them."

"Ah, I wouldn't say that, Bill," the doctor said thoughtfully as he
paced the room, his wrinkled old face as gray as his homespun suit. "I
hope you won't think me intruding," he added anxiously. "I'm talking
as a friend."

"I know you mean it well, Bobby."

"But you see, Bill," the doctor went on, screwing up his left cheek as
though it hurt him, "the feeling I have is that you need a different sort
of priest altogether. Of course, I'm not saying a word against the
Canon, but, after all, he's only a secular. You never had a chat with a
Jesuit, I suppose?"

The doctor asked it with an innocent air, as if he didn't know that the one thing a secular priest dreads after Old Nick himself is a Jesuit, and that a Jesuit was particularly hateful to the Canon, who considered that as much intellect and authority as could ever be needed by his flock was centered in himself.

"Never," said Bill.

"They're a very cultured order," said the doctor.

"What the hell do I want with a Jesuit?" Bill cried in protest. "A drop of drink and a bit of skirt—what harm is there in that?"

"Oh, none in the world, man," agreed Bobby cunningly. " 'Tisn't as if you were ever a bad-living man."

"I wasn't," said Bill with unexpected self-pity. "I was a good friend to anyone I liked."

"And you know the Canon would take it as a personal compliment if anything happened you—I'm speaking as a friend."

"You are, Bobby," said Bill, his voice hardening under the injustice of it. "You're speaking as a Christian. Anything to thwart a fellow like that! I could leave the Jesuits a few pounds for Masses, Bobby," he added with growing enthusiasm. "That's what would really break Lanigan's heart. Money is all he cares about."

"Ah, I wouldn't say that, Bill," Bobby said with a trace of alarm. His was a delicate undertaking, and Bill was altogether too apt a pupil for his taste.

"No," said Bill with conviction, "but that's what you mean. All right, Bobby. You're right as usual. Bring whoever you like and I'll let him talk. Talk never broke anyone's bones, Bobby."

The doctor went downstairs and found Nellie waiting for him with an anxious air.

"I'm running over to Aharna for a priest, Nellie," he whispered. "You might get things ready while I'm away."

"And is that the way it is?" she asked, growing pale.

"Ah, we'll hope for the best," he said, again feeling ashamed.

In a very thoughtful frame of mind he drove off to Aharna, where an ancient Bishop called McGinty, whose name was remembered in clerical circles only with sorrow, had permitted the Jesuits to establish a house. There he had a friend called Father Finnegan, a stocky, middle-aged man with a tight mouth and little clumps of white hair in his ears. It is not to be supposed that Bobby told him all that was in his mind, or that Father Finnegan thought he did, but there is very little a Jesuit doesn't know, and Father Finnegan knew that this was an occasion.

As they drove up the avenue, Nellie rushed out to meet them.

"What is it, Nellie?" the doctor asked anxiously. He couldn't help dreading that at the last moment Bill would play a trick on him and die of shock.

"He's gone mad, doctor,"she replied reproachfully, as though she hadn't thought a professional man would do a thing like that to her.

"When did he go mad?" Bobby asked doubtfully.

"When he seen me putting up the altar. Now he's after barricading the door and says he'll shoot the first one that tries to get in."

"That's quite all right, my dear young lady," said Father Finnegan soothingly. "Sick people often go on like that."

"Has he a gun, Nellie?" Bobby asked cautiously.

"Did you ever know him without one?" retorted Nellie.

The doctor, who was of a rather timid disposition, admired his friend's coolness as they mounted the stair. While Bobby knocked, Father Finnegan stood beside the door, his hands behind his back and his head bowed in meditation.

"Who's there?" Bill cried shrilly.

" 'Tis only me, Bill," the doctor replied soothingly. "Can I come in?"

"I'm too sick," shouted Bill. "I'm not seeing anyone."

"One moment, doctor," Father Finnegan said calmly, putting his shoulder to the door. The barricade gave way and they went in. One glance was enough to show Bobby that Bill had had time to get panic-stricken. He hadn't a gun, but this was the only thing that was lacking to remind Bobby of Two-Gun Joe's last stand. He was sitting well up, supported on his elbows, his head craned forward, his bright blue eyes flashing unseeingly from the priest to Bobby and from Bobby to the improvised altar. Bobby was sadly afraid that Bill was going to disappoint him. You might as well have tried to convert something in the zoo.

"I'm Father Finnegan, Mr. Enright," the Jesuit said, going up to him with his hand stretched out.

"I didn't send for you," snapped Bill.

"I appreciate that, Mr. Enright," said the priest. "But any friend of Dr. Healy is a friend of mine. Won't you shake hands?"

"I don't mind," whinnied Bill, letting him partake slightly of a limp paw but without looking at him. "But I warn you I'm not a religious sort of bloke. I never went in for that at all. Anyone that thinks I'm not a hard nut to crack is in for a surprise."

"If I went in for cracking nuts, I'd say the same," said Father Finnegan gamely. "You look well able to protect yourself."

Bill gave a harsh snort indicative of how much could be said on the score if the occasion were more propitious; his eyes continued to wander unseeingly like a mirror in a child's hand, but Bobby felt the priest had struck the right note. He closed the door softly behind him and went down to the drawing room. The six windows opened on three landscapes. The lowing of distant cows pleased his ear. Then he swore and threw open the door to the hall. Nellie was sitting comfortably on the stairs with her ear cocked. He beckoned her down.

"What is it, doctor?" she asked in surprise.

"Get us a light. And don't forget the priest will want his supper."

"You don't think I was listening?" she said indignantly.

"No," Bobby said dryly. "You looked as if you were joining in the devotions."

"Joining in the devotions?" she cried. "I'm up since six, waiting hand and foot on him, with the result that I dropped down in a dead weakness on the stairs. Would you believe that now?"

"I would not," said Bobby.

"You would not?" she repeated incredulously. "Jesus!" she added after a moment. "I'll bring you the lamp," she said in a defeated tone.

Nearly an hour passed before there was any sound upstairs. Then Father Finnegan came down, rubbing his hands briskly and complaining of the cold. Bobby found the lamp lit in the bedroom and the patient lying with one arm under his head.

"How are you feeling now, Bill?" the doctor asked.

"Fine, Bobby," said Bill. "I'm feeling fine. You were right about the priest, Bobby. I was a fool to bother my head about the Canon. He's not educated at all, Bobby, not compared with that man."

"I thought you'd like him," said Bobby.

"I like a fellow to know his job, Bobby," said Bill in the tone of one expert appraising another. "There's nothing like the bit of education. I wish I met him sooner." The wild blue eyes came to rest hauntingly on the doctor's face. "I feel the better of it already, Bobby. What sign would that be?"

"I dare say 'tis the excitement," said Bobby, giving nothing away. "I'll have another look at you."

"What's that she's frying, Bobby? Sausages and bacon?"

"It smells like it."

"There's nothing I'm so fond of," Bill said wistfully. "Would it make me worse, Bobby? My stomach feels as if it was sand-papered."

"I don't suppose so. But tea is all you can have with it."

"Hah!" crowed Bill. " 'Tis all I'm ever going to have if I live to be as old as Methuselah. But I'm not complaining, Bobby. I'm a man of my word. Oh, God, yes."

"Go on!" said Bobby. "Did you take the pledge?"

"Christ, Bobby," said the patient, giving a wild heave in the bed, "I took the whole bloody ship, masts, and anchor. . . . God forgive me for swearing!" he added piously. "He made me promise to marry the Screech," he said with a look which challenged the doctor to laugh if he dared.

"Ah, well, you might do worse, Bill," said the doctor.

"How sure he is I'll have him!" bawled Nellie cheerfully, showing her moony face at the door.

"You see the way it is, Bobby," said Bill without rancor. "That's what I have to put up with."

"Excuse me a minute, Nellie," said the doctor. "I'm having a look at Bill. . . . You had a trying day of it," he added, sitting on the bed and taking Bill's wrist. Then he took his temperature, and flashed the torch into his eyes and down his throat while Bill looked at him with a hypnotized glare.

"Begor, Bill, I wouldn't say but you're right," the doctor said approvingly. "I'd almost say you were a shade better."

"But that's what I'm saying, man!" cried Bill, beginning to do physical exercises for him. "Look at that, Bobby! I couldn't do that before. I call it a blooming miracle."

"When you've seen as much as I have, you won't have so much belief in miracles," said the doctor. "Take a couple of these tablets anyway, and I'll have another look at you in the morning."

It was almost too easy. The most up-to-date treatments were wasted on Bobby's patients. What they all secretly desired was to be rubbed with three pebbles from a Holy Well. Sometimes it left him depressed.

"Well, on the whole, Dr. Healy," Father Finnegan said as they drove off, "that was a very satisfactory evening."

"It was," Bobby said guardedly. He had no intention of telling his friend how satisfactory it was from his point of view.

"People do make extraordinary rallies after the Sacraments," went on Father Finnegan, and Bobby saw it wasn't even necessary to tell him. Educated men can understand one another without embarrassing admissions. His own conscience was quite easy. A little religion wouldn't do Bill the least bit of harm. The Jesuit's conscience, he felt, wasn't troubling him either. Even without a miracle Bill's conversion would have opened up the Canon's parish to the order. With a miracle, they'd have every old woman, male and female, for miles around, calling them in.

"They do," Bobby said wonderingly. "I often noticed it."

"And I'm afraid, Dr. Healy, that the Canon won't like it," added the Jesuit.

"He won't," said the doctor as though the idea had only just occurred to himself. "I'm afraid he won't like it at all."

He was an honest man who gave credit where credit was due, and he knew it wasn't only the money—a couple of hundred a year at the least— that would upset the Canon. It was the thought that under his own very nose a miracle had been worked on one of his own parishioners by one of the hated Jesuits. Clerics are almost as cruel as small boys. The Canon wouldn't be allowed to forget the Jesuit miracle the longest day he lived.

But for the future he'd let Bobby alone.

Don Juan's Temptation

AGAINST the Gussie Leonards of the world, we poor whores have no defenses. Sons of bitches to a man, we can't like them, we can't even believe them, and still we must listen to them because deep down in every man jack of us there is the feeling that our own experience of life is insufficient. Humanly we understand our wives and girls and daughters; we put up with their tantrums and consider what we imagine are their wishes, but then the moment comes and we realize that that fat sleeky rascal understands them at a level where we can never even meet them, as if they put off their ordinary humanity as they put off their clothes, and went wandering through the world invisible except to the men like Gussie whose eyes are trained only to see them that way. The only consolation we have is that they too have their temptations—or so at least they say. The sons of bitches! Even that much you can't believe from them.

Anyhow, Gussie met this girl at a party in the Green and picked her out at once. She was young, tall, dark, good-looking, but it wasn't so much her looks that appealed to Gussie as the naturalness with which she moved among all those wooden dolls in night-dresses. She was a country town girl who had never learned to dress up and pose, and however she moved or whatever she said it always seemed to be natural and right.

They left together and she took Gussie's arm with a boyish camara-
derie that delighted him. It was a lovely night with the moon nearly at
the full. Gussie's flat was in a Georgian house on the street which ran
through the Green; she had a room in Pembroke Road, and as they
passed the house Gussie halted and asked her in. She gave a slight
start, but Gussie, having a few drinks in, didn't notice that until later.

"For what?" she asked gaily.

"Oh, for the night if you like," Gussie replied in the same tone and
felt like biting off his tongue when he heard it. It sounded so awkward,
like a schoolboy the first time he goes with a girl.

"No, thanks," she said shortly. "I have a room of my own."

"Oh, please, Helen, please!" he moaned, taking her hand and
squeezing it in the way of an old friend of the family. "You're not taking offense at my harmless little joke. Now you'll have to come up and
have a drink, just to show there's no ill feeling."

"Some other night," she said, "when it's not so late."

He let it go at that because he knew that anything further he said
would only frighten her more. He knew perfectly well what had happened. The Sheehans, mischief-makers and busybodies, had warned
her against him, and he had walked straight into the trap. She still held
onto his arm, but that was only not to make a fuss. Inside she was as
hurt as anything. Hurt and surprised. In spite of the Sheehans' warnings she had taken him at his face value, not believing him to be that
sort at all. Or rather, as Gussie, whose eyes were differently focused
from ours, phrased it to himself, knowing damn well he was that sort
but hoping that he would reveal it gradually so that she wouldn't be
compelled to take notice.

She stopped at the canal bridge and leaned over to look at the view.
It was beautiful there in the moonlight with the still water, the trees,
the banked houses with odd windows caught in the snowy light, but
Gussie knew it was not the moonlight she was thinking of. She was
getting over her fright and now it was her pride that was hurt.

"Tell us," she said, letting on to be very lighthearted and interested
in the subject, as it were, only from the psychological standpoint, "do
you ask all the girls you meet the same thing?"

"But my goodness, didn't I tell you it was only a joke?" Gussie
asked reproachfully.

She rested her head on her arms and looked back at him over her
shoulder, the cloche hat shading her face to the chin. It was a natural,
beautiful pose but Gussie knew she wasn't aware of it.

"Now you're not being honest," she said.

"Are you?" Gussie asked with a faint smile.

"Am I what?" she replied with a start.

"Can't you admit that you were warned against me?" he said.

"As a matter of fact I was," she replied candidly, "but I didn't pay much attention. I take people as I find them."

"Now you're talking sensibly," said Gussie and thought in a fatherly way: "The girl is nice. She's a bit shocked but she'll have to learn sooner or later and it would be better for her to learn from someone who knows." The awkwardness of Irish husbands was a theme song of Gussie's. The things their wives told you were almost incredible.

"You probably wouldn't believe me if I told you how few women interest me enough for that," he said.

"But the ones you do ask," she went on, sticking to her point, though pretending to be quite detached as though she really were only looking for information, "do they come?"

"Some," he said, smiling at her innocence. "Sometimes you meet a difficult girl who makes a hullabaloo and won't even come and get a drink with you afterwards."

"Married women or girls?" she asked in the tone of an official filling up a form, but the quaver in her voice gave her away.

"Both," said Gussie. If he had been perfectly honest he would have had to admit that at that time there was only one of the former and not exactly a queue of the latter but he had decided, purely in Helen's own interest, that since she needed to have her mind broadened there was no use doing it by halves. It was better to get it over and be done with it, like having a tooth out. "Why?"

"Oh, nothing," she said casually, "but I'm not surprised you have such a poor opinion of women if you can pick them up as easily as that."

This view of the matter came as a real surprise to Gussie, who would never have described his conduct in that way.

"But my dear young lady," he said offering her a cigarette, "whoever said I have a poor opinion of women? What would I be doing with women if I had? On the contrary, I have a very high opinion of women, and the more I see of them the more I like them."

"Have you?" she said, stooping low over the match-flame so that he shouldn't see her face. He guessed that it was very flushed. "It must be a poor opinion of me so."

"What an extraordinary idea!" said Gussie, still genuinely trying to fathom it. "How can you make out that wanting to see more of you means I have a poor opinion of you. Even if I do want to make love to you. As a matter of fact, if it's any news to you, I do."

"You want it rather easy, don't you?" she asked with a trace of resentment.

"Why?" he asked blandly. "Do you think it should be made difficult?"

"I thought it was the usual thing to ask a girl to go to the pictures with you first," she said with a brassy air that wouldn't have taken in a child.

"I wouldn't know," murmured Gussie in amusement. "Anyway, I suppose I thought you weren't the usual sort of girl."

"But if you get it as easy as that, how do you know if it's the real thing or not?" she asked.

"How do you know anything is the real thing?" he retorted. "As you say yourself, you have to take things as you find them."

"Taking them as you find them doesn't mean swallowing them whole," she said. "It would be rather late in the day to change your mind about a thing like that."

"But what difference does it make?" he asked wonderingly. "It happens every day of the week. You do it yourself with boys you go out walking with. You spoon with them till you find they bore you and then you drop them. There's no difference. You don't suddenly change your character. People don't say when they meet you in the street: 'How different that girl is looking! You can see she has a man.' Of course, if you attach so much importance to the physical side of it—"

"I do," she said quickly. By this time Gussie noticed to his surprise that she was almost laughing. She had got over her fright and hurt and felt that in argument she was more than a match for him. "Isn't it awful?" she added brightly. "But I'm very queer like that."

"Oh, there's nothing queer about it," Gussie said, determined on keeping control of the situation and not letting her away with anything. "It's just ordinary schoolgirl romanticism."

"Is that all?" she asked lightly, and though she pretended not to care he saw she was stung. "You have an answer for everything, haven't you?"

"If you call that everything, my dear child," he replied paternally patting her on the shoulder. "I call it growing pains. I don't know, with that romantic nature of yours, whether you've noticed that there's a nasty wind coming up the canal."

"No," she said archly, "I hadn't," and then turned to face him, resting her elbow on the coping of the bridge. "Anyhow, I like it. Go on with what you were saying. Being romantic is thinking you ought to stick to someone you're fond of, isn't that it?"

Gussie was amused again. The girl was so transparent. It was clear now that she was in love with some young fellow who couldn't afford to marry her and that they were scarifying one another in the usual adolescent rough-and-tumble without knowing what ailed them.

"No, my dear, it isn't," said Gussie. "Being romantic is thinking you're very fond of someone you really don't give a damn about, and imagining on that account that you're never going to care for anyone else. It goes with your age. Come on now, or you'll be catching something worse."

"You don't mean you were ever like that?" she asked, taking his arm again as they went on down Pembroke Road. Even her tone revealed her mingled fascination and loathing. It didn't worry Gussie. He was used to it.

"Oh," he said sentimentally, "we all go through it."

There were a lot of contradictions in Gussie. Despising youth and its illusions, he could scarcely ever think of his own youth without self-pity. He had been lonely enough; sometimes he felt no one had ever been so lonely. He had woken up from a nice, well-ordered, intelligible world to find eternity stretching all round him and no one, priest or scientist, who could explain it to him. And with that awakening had gone the longing for companionship and love which he had not known how to satisfy, and often he had walked for hours, looking up at the stars and thinking that if only he could meet an understanding girl it would all explain itself naturally. The picture of Gussie's youth seemed to amuse Helen.

"Go on!" she said gaily, her face turned to his, screwed up with mischief. "I could have sworn you must have been born like that. How did you get sense so young?"

"Quite naturally," Gussie said with a grave priestly air. "I saw I was only making trouble for myself, as you're doing now, and as there seemed to be quite enough trouble in the world without that, I gave it up."

"And lived happy ever after?" she said mockingly. "And the women you knock round with? Aren't they romantic either?"

"Not since they were your age," he said mockingly.

"You needn't rub it in about the age," she said without taking umbrage. "It'll cure itself soon enough. Tell us more about your girls—the married ones, for instance."

"That's easy," he said. "There's only one at the moment."

"And her husband? Does he know?"

"I never asked him," Gussie said slyly. "But I dare say he finds it more convenient not to."

"Obliging sort of chap," she said. "I could do with a man like that myself."

Gussie stopped dead. As I say there were contradictions in Gussie, and for some reason her scorn of Francie's husband filled him with indignation. It was so uncalled-for, so unjust!

"Now you are talking like a schoolgirl," he said reproachfully.

"Am I?" she asked doubtfully, noticing the change in him. "How?"

"What business have you talking in that tone about a man you never met?" Gussie went on, growing quite heated. "He isn't a thief or a blackguard. He's a decent, good-natured man. It's not his fault if after seventeen or eighteen years of living together his wife and himself can't bear the living sight of one another. That's a thing that happens everybody. He only does what he thinks is the best thing for his family. You think, I suppose, that he should take out a gun to defend his wife's honor?"

"I wasn't thinking of her honor," she protested quietly.

"His own then?" Gussie cried mockingly. "At the expense of his wife and children? He's to drag her name in the mud all because some silly schoolgirl might think his position undignified. Ah, for goodness' sake, child, have sense! His wife would have something to say to that. Besides, don't you see that at his age it would be a very serious thing if she was to leave him?"

"More serious than letting her go to your flat—how often did you say?"

"Now you're talking like a little cat," he snapped, and went on. He really was furious. "But as a matter of fact it would," he went on in a more reasonable tone. "Where she goes in the evenings is nobody's business. Whether the meals are ready is another matter. They have two daughters at school— one nearly the one age with yourself."

"I wonder if he lets them out at night," she said dryly. "And what sort of woman is their mother?"

"You wouldn't believe me if I told you," said Gussie, "but she's a great sort; a woman who'd give you her heart out."

"I wonder what she'd say if she heard you asking another girl to spend the night," she added in the same casual tone. Gussie was beginning to conceive a considerable respect for her tongue.

"Ah," he said without conviction, "I don't suppose she has many illusions left," but the girl had scored and she knew it. The trouble with Francie was that she had far too many illusions left, even about Gussie. And the greatest illusion of all was that if only she had married a man whose intelligence she respected as she respected his, she could have been faithful to him.

"She can't have," said Helen, "but I still have a few."

"Oh, you!" Gussie said with a jolly laugh which had got him out of many tight corners. "You're walking with them."

"They must be in the family," she said. "Daddy died five years ago and Mum still thinks he was the one really great man that walked the world."

"I dare say," Gussie said wearily. "And they were probably often sick to death of one another."

"They were," she agreed. "They used to fight like mad and not talk for a week, and then Dad would go on the booze and Mum would take it out of me. Cripes, I used to go up to him with my bottom so sore I could hardly sit down and there he'd be sprawled in his big chair with his arms hanging down, looking into the grate as if 'twas the end of the world, and he'd just beckon me to come on his knee. We'd stop like that for hours without opening our gobs, just thinking what a bitch of hell Mum was. . . . But the thing is, young man, they stuck it out, and when 'tis her turn to go, she won't regret it because she's certain the Boss will be waiting for her. She goes to Mass every morning but that's only not to give God any excuse for making distinctions. Do you think he will?"

"Who will?" said Gussie. In a curious way the story had gripped him. A woman could bawl her heart out on Gussie, and he'd only think her a nuisance, but he was exceedingly vulnerable to indirect sentiment.

"The Boss," she explained. "Meet her, I mean?"

"Well," Gussie said feebly, "there's nothing like optimism." At the same time he knew he was not being altogether truthful, because orthodoxy was one of Gussie's strongest lines.

"I know," the girl said quickly. "That's the lousy part of it. But I suppose she's lucky even to be able to kid herself about it. Death doesn't frighten her the way it frightens me. . . . But that's what I mean by love, Mr. L.," she added lightheartedly.

"I hope you get it, Miss C.," replied Gussie in the same tone.

"I don't suppose I'm likely to," she said with resignation. "There doesn't seem to be much of it round. I suppose it's the shortage of optimists."

When they reached her flat, she leaned against the railings with her legs crossed and her hands behind her back—again a boyish attitude which attracted Gussie.

"Well, good night, Miss Romantic," he said ceremoniously, taking her hand and kissing it.

"Good night, Don Juan," she replied to Gussie's infinite delight. Nobody had ever called Gussie that before.

"When do I see you again?"

"Are you sure you want to see me?" she asked with light mockery. "An old-fashioned girl like me!"

"I still have hopes of converting you," said Gussie.

"That's marvellous," she said. "I love being converted. I was nearly converted by a parson once. Give us a ring-up some time."

"I will to be sure," said Gussie, and it was not until he reached the canal bridge that he realized he had really meant: "What a fool you think I am!" He felt sore all over. "The trouble with me is that I'm getting things too easy," he thought. He felt exactly like a man with a thousand a year whom somebody wanted to push back into the thirty-shilling-a-week class. Thirty shillings a week was all right when you had never been accustomed to anything else, but to Gussie it meant only one thing—destitution. He knew exactly what he would be letting himself in for if he took the girl on her own terms; the same thing that same poor devil of a boy was enduring with her now; park benches and canal banks with a sixty-mile-an-hour gale blowing round the corner, and finally she would be detained at the office—by a good-looking chap in uniform. "What a fool I am!" he thought mockingly.

But even to find himself summing up the odds like this was a new experience for Gussie. He was attracted by the girl; he couldn't deny that. Instead of crossing the bridge he turned up the moonlit walk by the canal. This was another new thing and he commented ironically on it to himself. "Now this, Gussie," he said, "is what you'll be letting yourself in for if you're not careful." He suddenly realized what it was that attracted him. It was her resemblance to Joan, a girl who had crossed for a moment his lonely boyhood. He had haunted the roads at night, trying to catch even a glimpse of her as she passed. She was a tall, thin, reedy girl, and, though Gussie did not know it, already far gone with the disease which killed her. On the night before she left for the sanatorium he had met her coming from town, and as they came up the hill she had suddenly slipped her hand into his. So she too, it seemed, had been lonely. He had been too shy to look for more; he hadn't even wished to ask for more. Perfectly happy, he had held her hand the whole way home and neither had spoken a word. It had been something complete and perfect, for in six months' time she was dead. He still dreamt of her sometimes. Once he dreamt that she came into the room where he was sitting with Francie, and sat on the other side of him and spoke to Francie in French, but Francie was too indignant to reply.

And now, here he was fifteen years later feeling the same sort of thing about another girl who merely reminded him of her, and though he knew Helen was talking rubbish he understood perfectly what she wanted; what Joan had wanted that night before she went to the sana-torium; something bigger than life that would last beyond death. He felt himself a brute for trying to deprive her of her illusions. Perhaps people couldn't do without illusions. Walking by the canal in the moonlight, Gussie felt he would give anything to be able to feel like that about a woman again. Even a sixty-mile-an-hour gale would not have put him off.

Then, as he came back up the street from the opposite direction, he noticed how the moonlight fell on the doctors' houses at the other side. His was in darkness. He put his key in the lock and then started, feeling frightened and weak. There was a figure by the door, leaning back against the railings, her hands by her side, her face very white. She stood there as though hoping he would pass without noticing her. "It's Joan" was his first thought, and then: "She's coming back," and finally, with a growing feeling of incredulity: "So it does last." He looked again and saw who it really was.

"My goodness, Helen," he said almost petulantly, "what are you doing here?"

"Well," she said in a low voice, doing her best to smile, "you see I was converted after all."

He led her silently up the stairs with a growing feeling of relief, but it wasn't until they were in his own flat that he really knew how overjoyed he was. It was all over now, but he felt he had been through a really terrible temptation, the temptation of a lifetime. Only that people might interpret it wrongly, and he was really a most decorous man, he would have said his guardian angel had been looking after him.

Sons of bitches! That's what they are, to a man.

First Confession

ALL THE TROUBLE began when my grandfather died and my grandmother—my father's mother—came to live with us. Relations in the one house are a strain at the best of times, but, to make matters worse, my grandmother was a real old country woman and quite unsuited to the life in town. She had a fat, wrinkled old face, and, to Mother's great indignation, went round the house in bare feet—the boots had her crippled, she said. For dinner she had a jug of porter and a pot of potatoes with—sometimes—a bit of salt fish, and she poured out the pota-toes on the table and ate them slowly, with great relish, using her fin-gers by way of a fork.

Now, girls are supposed to be fastidious, but I was the one who suf-fered most from this. Nora, my sister, just sucked up to the old woman for the penny she got every Friday out of the old-age pension, a thing I could not do. I was too honest, that was my trouble; and when I was playing with Bill Connell, the sergeant-major's son, and saw my grandmother steering up the path with the jug of porter sticking out from beneath her shawl I was mortified. I made excuses not to let him come into the house, because I could never be sure what she would be up to when we went in.

When Mother was at work and my grandmother made the dinner I wouldn't touch it. Nora once tried to make me, but I hid under the table from her and took the bread-knife with me for protection. Nora let on to be very indignant (she wasn't, of course, but she knew Mother saw through her, so she sided with Gran) and came after me. I lashed out at her with the bread-knife, and after that she left me alone. I stayed there till Mother came in from work and made my dinner, but when Father came in later Nora said in a shocked voice: "Oh, Dadda, do you know what Jackie did at dinnertime?" Then, of course, it all came out; Father gave me a flaking; Mother interfered, and for days after that he didn't speak to me and Mother barely spoke to Nora. And all because of that old woman! God knows, I was heart-scalded.

Then, to crown my misfortunes, I had to make my first confession and Communion. It was an old woman called Ryan who prepared us for these. She was about the one age with Gran; she was well-to-do, lived in a big house on Montenotte, wore a black cloak and bonnet, and came every day to school at three o'clock when we should have been going home, and talked to us of Hell. She may have mentioned the other place as well, but that could only have been by accident, for Hell had the first place in her heart.

She lit a candle, took out a new half-crown, and offered it to the first boy who would hold one finger—only one finger!—in the flame for five minutes by the school clock. Being always very ambitious I was tempted to volunteer, but I thought it might look greedy. Then she asked were we afraid of holding one finger—only one finger!—in a lit-tle candle flame for five minutes and not afraid of burning all over in roasting hot furnaces for all eternity. "All eternity! Just think of that! A whole lifetime goes by and it's nothing, not even a drop in the ocean of your sufferings." The woman was really interesting about Hell, but my attention was all fixed on the half-crown. At the end of the lesson she put it back in her purse. It was a great disappointment; a religious woman like that, you wouldn't think she'd bother about a thing like a half-crown.

Another day she said she knew a priest who woke one night to find a fellow he didn't recognize leaning over the end of his bed. The priest was a bit frightened—naturally enough—but he asked the fellow what he wanted, and the fellow said in a deep, husky voice that he wanted to go to Confession. The priest said it was an awkward time and wouldn't it do in the morning, but the fellow said that last time he went to Confession, there was one sin he kept back, being ashamed to mention it, and now it was always on his mind. Then the priest knew it was a bad case, because the fellow was after making a bad confession and committing a mortal sin. He got up to dress, and just then the cock crew in the yard outside, and—lo and behold!—when the priest looked round there was no sign of the fellow, only a smell of burning timber, and when the priest looked at his bed didn't he see the print of two hands burned in it? That was because the fellow had made a bad confession. This story made a shocking impression on me.

But the worst of all was when she showed us how to examine our conscience. Did we take the name of the Lord, our God, in vain? Did we honor our father and our mother? (I asked her did this include grandmothers and she said it did.) Did we love our neighbor as ourselves? Did we covet our neighbor's goods? (I thought of the way I felt about the penny that Nora got every Friday.) I decided that, between one thing and another, I must have broken the whole ten commandments, all on account of that old woman, and so far as I could see, so long as she remained in the house I had no hope of ever doing anything else.

I was scared to death of Confession. The day the whole class went I let on to have a toothache, hoping my absence wouldn't be noticed; but at three o'clock, just as I was feeling safe, along comes a chap with a message from Mrs. Ryan that I was to go to Confession myself on Saturday and be at the chapel for Communion with the rest. To make it worse, Mother couldn't come with me and sent Nora instead.

Now, that girl had ways of tormenting me that Mother never knew of. She held my hand as we went down the hill, smiling sadly and saying how sorry she was for me, as if she were bringing me to the hospital for an operation.

"Oh, God help us!" she moaned. "Isn't it a terrible pity you weren't a good boy? Oh, Jackie, my heart bleeds for you! How will you ever think of all your sins? Don't forget you have to tell him about the time you kicked Gran on the shin."

"Lemme go!" I said, trying to drag myself free of her. "I don't want to go to Confession at all."

"But sure, you'll have to go to Confession, Jackie," she replied in the same regretful tone. "Sure, if you didn't, the parish priest would be up to the house, looking for you. 'Tisn't, God knows, that I'm not sorry for you. Do you remember the time you tried to kill me with the bread-knife under the table? And the language you used to me? I don't know what he'll do with you at all, Jackie. He might have to send you up to the Bishop."

I remember thinking bitterly that she didn't know the half of what I had to tell—if I told it. I knew I couldn't tell it, and understood perfectly why the fellow in Mrs. Ryan's story made a bad confession; it seemed to me a great shame that people wouldn't stop criticizing him. I remember that steep hill down to the church, and the sunlit hillsides beyond the valley of the river, which I saw in the gaps between the houses like Adam's last glimpse of Paradise.

Then, when she had manoeuvred me down the long flight of steps to the chapel yard, Nora suddenly changed her tone. She became the raging malicious devil she really was.

"There you are!" she said with a yelp of triumph, hurling me through the church door. "And I hope he'll give you the penitential psalms, you dirty little caffler."

I knew then I was lost, given up to eternal justice. The door with the colored-glass panels swung shut behind me, the sunlight went out and gave place to deep shadow, and the wind whistled outside so that the silence within seemed to crackle like ice under my feet. Nora sat in front of me by the confession box. There were a couple of old women ahead of her, and then a miserable-looking poor devil came and wedged me in at the other side, so that I couldn't escape even if I had the courage. He joined his hands and rolled his eyes in the direction of the roof, muttering aspirations in an anguished tone, and I wondered had he a grandmother too. Only a grandmother could account for a fellow behaving in that heartbroken way, but he was better off than I, for he at least could go and confess his sins; while I would make a bad confession and then die in the night and be continually coming back and burning people's furniture.

Nora's turn came, and I heard the sound of something slamming, and then her voice as if butter wouldn't melt in her mouth, and then another slam, and out she came. God, the hypocrisy of women! Her eyes were lowered, her head was bowed, and her hands were joined very low down on her stomach, and she walked up the aisle to the side altar looking like a saint. You never saw such an exhibition of devotion;

and I remembered the devilish malice with which she had tormented me all the way from our door, and wondered were all religious people like that, really. It was my turn now. With the fear of damnation in my soul I went in, and the confessional door closed of itself behind me.

It was pitch-dark and I couldn't see priest or anything else. Then I really began to be frightened. In the darkness it was a matter between God and me, and He had all the odds. He knew what my intentions were before I even started; I had no chance. All I had ever been told about Confession got mixed up in my mind, and I knelt to one wall and said: "Bless me, father, for I have sinned; this is my first confession." I waited for a few minutes, but nothing happened, so I tried it on the other wall. Nothing happened there either. He had me spotted all right.

It must have been then that I noticed the shelf at about one height with my head. It was really a place for grown-up people to rest their elbows, but in my distracted state I thought it was probably the place you were supposed to kneel. Of course, it was on the high side and not very deep, but I was always good at climbing and managed to get up all right. Staying up was the trouble. There was room only for my knees, and nothing you could get a grip on but a sort of wooden molding a bit above it. I held on to the molding and repeated the words a little louder, and this time something happened all right. A slide was slammed back; a little light entered the box, and a man's voice said: "Who's there?"

" 'Tis me, father," I said for fear he mightn't see me and go away again. I couldn't see him at all. The place the voice came from was under the molding, about level with my knees, so I took a good grip of the molding and swung myself down till I saw the astonished face of a young priest looking up at me. He had to put his head on one side to see me, and I had to put mine on one side to see him, so we were more or less talking to one another upside-down. It struck me as a queer way of hearing confessions, but I didn't feel it my place to criticize.

"Bless me, father, for I have sinned; this is my first confession," I rattled off all in one breath, and swung myself down the least shade more to make it easier for him.

"What are you doing up there?" he shouted in an angry voice, and the strain the politeness was putting on my hold of the molding, and the shock of being addressed in such an uncivil tone, were too much for me. I lost my grip, tumbled, and hit the door an unmerciful wallop before I found myself flat on my back in the middle of the aisle. The people who had been waiting stood up with their mouths open. The priest opened the door of the middle box and came out, pushing his biretta back from his forehead; he looked something terrible. Then Nora came scampering down the aisle.

"Oh, you dirty little caffler!" she said. "I might have known you'd do it. I might have known you'd disgrace me. I can't leave you out of my sight for one minute."

Before I could even get to my feet to defend myself she bent down and gave me a clip across the ear. This reminded me that I was so stunned I had even forgotten to cry, so that people might think I wasn't hurt at all, when in fact I was probably maimed for life. I gave a roar out of me.

"What's all this about?" the priest hissed, getting angrier than ever and pushing Nora off me. "How dare you hit the child like that, you little vixen?"

"But I can't do my penance with him, father," Nora cried, cocking an outraged eye up at him.

"Well, go and do it, or I'll give you some more to do," he said, giving me a hand up. "Was it coming to Confession you were, my poor man?" he asked me.

" 'Twas, father," said I with a sob.

"Oh," he said respectfully, "a big hefty fellow like you must have terrible sins. Is this your first?"

" 'Tis, father," said I.

"Worse and worse," he said gloomily. "The crimes of a lifetime. I don't know will I get rid of you at all today. You'd better wait now till I'm finished with these old ones. You can see by the looks of them they haven't much to tell."

"I will, father," I said with something approaching joy.

The relief of it was really enormous. Nora stuck out her tongue at me from behind his back, but I couldn't even be bothered retorting. I knew from the very moment that man opened his mouth that he was intelligent above the ordinary. When I had time to think, I saw how right I was. It only stood to reason that a fellow confessing after seven years would have more to tell than people that went every week. The crimes of a lifetime, exactly as he said. It was only what he expected, and the rest was the cackle of old women and girls with their talk of Hell, the Bishop, and the penitential psalms. That was all they knew. I started to make my examination of conscience, and barring the one bad business of my grandmother it didn't seem so bad.

The next time, the priest steered me into the confession box himself and left the shutter back the way I could see him get in and sit down at the further side of the grille from me.

"Well, now," he said, "what do they call you?"

"Jackie, father," said I.

"And what's a-trouble to you, Jackie?"

"Father," I said, feeling I might as well get it over while I had him in good humor, "I had it all arranged to kill my grandmother."

He seemed a bit shaken by that, all right, because he said nothing for quite a while.

"My goodness," he said at last, "that'd be a shocking thing to do. What put that into your head?"

"Father," I said, feeling very sorry for myself, "she's an awful woman."

"Is she?" he asked. "What way is she awful?"

"She takes porter, father," I said, knowing well from the way Mother talked of it that this was a mortal sin, and hoping it would make the priest take a more favorable view of my case.

"Oh, my!" he said, and I could see he was impressed.

"And snuff, father," said I.

"That's a bad case, sure enough, Jackie," he said.

"And she goes round in her bare feet, father," I went on in a rush of self-pity, "and she knows I don't like her, and she gives pennies to Nora and none to me, and my da sides with her and flakes me, and one night I was so heart-scalded I made up my mind I'd have to kill her."

"And what would you do with the body?" he asked with great interest.

"I was thinking I could chop that up and carry it away in a barrow I have," I said.

"Begor, Jackie," he said, "do you know you're a terrible child?"

"I know, father," I said, for I was just thinking the same thing myself. "I tried to kill Nora too with a bread-knife under the table, only I missed her."

"Is that the little girl that was beating you just now?" he asked.

"'Tis, father."

"Someone will go for her with a bread-knife one day, and he won't miss her," he said rather cryptically. "You must have great courage. Between ourselves, there's a lot of people I'd like to do the same to but I'd never have the nerve. Hanging is an awful death."

"Is it, father?" I asked with the deepest interest—I was always very keen on hanging. "Did you ever see a fellow hanged?"

"Dozens of them," he said solemnly. "And they all died roaring."

"Jay!" I said.

"Oh, a horrible death!" he said with great satisfaction. "Lots of the fellows I saw killed their grandmothers too, but they all said 'twas never worth it."

He had me there for a full ten minutes talking, and then walked out the chapel yard with me. I was genuinely sorry to part with him, because he was the most entertaining character I'd ever met in the religious line. Outside, after the shadow of the church, the sunlight was like the roaring of waves on a beach; it dazzled me; and when the frozen silence melted and I heard the screech of trams on the road my heart soared. I knew now I wouldn't die in the night and come back, leaving marks on my mother's furniture. It would be a great worry to her, and the poor soul had enough.

Nora was sitting on the railing, waiting for me, and she put on a very sour puss when she saw the priest with me. She was mad jealous because a priest had never come out of the church with her.

"Well," she asked coldly, after he left me, "what did he give you?"

"Three Hail Marys," I said.

"Three Hail Marys," she repeated incredulously. "You mustn't have told him anything."

"I told him everything," I said confidently.

"About Gran and all?"

"About Gran and all."

(All she wanted was to be able to go home and say I'd made a bad confession.)

"Did you tell him you went for me with the bread-knife?" she asked with a frown.

"I did to be sure."

"And he only gave you three Hail Marys?"

"That's all."

She slowly got down from the railing with a baffled air. Clearly, this was beyond her. As we mounted the steps back to the main road she looked at me suspiciously.

"What are you sucking?" she asked.

"Bullseyes."

"Was it the priest gave them to you?"

" 'Twas."

"Lord God," she wailed bitterly, "some people have all the luck! 'Tis no advantage to anybody trying to be good. I might just as well be a sinner like you."

The Man of the House

As a kid I was as good as gold so long as I could concentrate. Concentration, that was always my weakness, in school and everywhere else. Once I was diverted from whatever I was doing, I was lost.

It was like that when the mother got ill. I remember it well; how I waked that morning and heard the strange cough in the kitchen below. From that very moment I knew something was wrong. I dressed and went down. She was sitting in a little wickerwork chair before the fire, holding her side. She had made an attempt to light the fire but it had gone against her.

"What's wrong, Mum?" I asked.

"The sticks were wet and the fire started me coughing," she said, trying to smile, though I could see she was doubled up with pain.

"I'll light the fire and you go back to bed," I said.

"Ah, how can I, child?" she said. "Sure, I have to go to work."

"You couldn't work like that," I said. "Go on up to bed and I'll bring up your breakfast."

It's funny about women, the way they'll take orders from anything in trousers, even if 'tis only ten.

"If you could make a cup of tea for yourself, I'd be all right in an hour or so," she said, and shuffled feebly upstairs. I went with her, supporting her arm, and when she reached the bed she collapsed. I knew then she must be feeling bad. I got more sticks—she was so economical that she never used enough—and I soon had the fire roaring and the kettle on. I made her toast as well; I was always a great believer in buttered toast.

I thought she looked at the cup of tea rather doubtfully.

"Is that all right?" I asked.

"You wouldn't have a sup of boiling water left?" she asked.

" 'Tis too strong," I agreed, with a trace of disappointment I tried to keep out of my voice. "I'll pour half it away. I can never remember about tea."

"I hope you won't be late for school," she said anxiously.

"I'm not going to school," I said. "I'll get you your tea now and do the messages afterwards."

She didn't say a word about my not going to school. It was just as I said; orders were all she wanted. I washed up the breakfast things, then I washed myself and went up to her with the shopping basket, a piece of paper, and a lead pencil.

"I'll do the messages if you'll write them down," I said. "I suppose I'll go to Mrs. Slattery first?"

"Tell her I'll be in tomorrow without fail."

"Write down Mrs. Slattery," I said firmly. "Would I get the doctor?"

"Indeed, you'll do nothing of the kind," Mother said anxiously. "He'd only want to send me to hospital. They're all alike. You could ask the chemist to give you a good strong cough bottle."

"Write it down," I said, remembering my own weakness. "If I haven't it written down I might forget it. And put 'strong' in big letters. What will I get for the dinner? Eggs?"

That was really only a bit of swank, because eggs were the one thing I could cook, but the mother told me to get sausages as well in case she was able to get up.

It was a lovely sunny morning. I called first on Mrs. Slattery, whom my mother worked for, to tell her she wouldn't be in. Mrs. Slattery was a woman I didn't like much. She had a big broad face that needed big broad features, but all she had was narrow eyes and a thin pointed nose that seemed to be all lost in the breadth of her face.

"She said she'll try to get in tomorrow, but I don't know will I let her get up," I said.

"I wouldn't if she wasn't well, Gus," she said, and she gave me a penny.

I went away feeling very elevated. I had always known a fellow could have his troubles, but if he faced them manfully, he could get advantages out of them as well. There was the school, for instance. I stood opposite it for a full ten minutes, staring. The schoolhouse and the sloping yard were like a picture, except for the chorus of poor sufferers through the open windows, and a glimpse of Danny Delaney's bald pate as he did sentry-go before the front door with his cane wriggling like a tail behind his back. It was nice too to be chatting to the fellows in the shops and telling them about the mother's cough. I made it out a bit worse to make a good story of it, but I had a secret hope that when I got home she'd be up so that we could have sausages for dinner. I hated boiled eggs, and anyway I was already beginning to feel the strain of my responsibilities.

But when I got home it was to find Minnie Ryan with her. Minnie was a middle-aged woman, gossipy and pious, but very knowledge-able.

"How are you feeling now, Mum?" I asked.

"I'm miles better," she said with a smile.

"She won't be able to get up today, though," Minnie said firmly.

"I'll pour you out your cough bottle so, and make you a cup of tea," I said, concealing my disappointment.

"Wisha, I'll do that for you, child," said Minnie, getting up.

"Ah, you needn't mind, Miss Ryan," I said without fuss. "I can manage all right."

"Isn't he great?" I heard her say in a low wondering voice as I went downstairs.

"Minnie," whispered my mother, "he's the best anyone ever reared."

"Why, then, there aren't many like him," Minnie said gloomily. "The most of the children that's going now are more like savages than Christians."

In the afternoon my mother wanted me to go out and play, but I wouldn't go far. I remembered my own weakness. I knew if once I went a certain distance I should drift towards the Glen, with the bar-rack drill-field perched on a cliff above it; the rifle range below, and below that again the mill-pond and mill-stream running through a wooded gorge—the Rockies, Himalayas, or Highlands according to your mood. Concentration; that was what I had to practice. One slip and I should be among those children that Minnie Ryan disapproved of, who were more like savages than Christians.

Evening came; the street-lamps were lit and the paper-boy went crying up the road. I bought a paper, lit the lamp in the kitchen and the candle in the bedroom, and read out the police-court news to my mother. I knew it was the piece she liked best, all about people being picked up drunk out of the channels. I wasn't very quick about it be-cause I was only at words of one syllable, but she didn't seem to mind.

Later Minnie Ryan came again, and as she left I went to the door with her. She looked grave.

"If she isn't better in the morning I think I'd get a doctor to her, Gus," she said.

"Why?" I asked in alarm. "Would you say she's worse?"

"Ah, no," she said, giving her old shawl a tug, "only I'd be fright-ened of the old pneumonia."

"But wouldn't he send her to hospital, Miss Ryan?"

"Ah, he might and he mightn't. Anyway, he could give her a good bottle. But even if he did, God between us and all harm, wouldn't it be better than neglecting it? . . . If you had a drop of whiskey, you could give it to her hot with a squeeze of lemon."

"I'll get it," I said at once.

Mother didn't want the whiskey; she said it cost too much; but I knew it would cost less than hospital and all the rest of it, so I wouldn't be put off.

I had never been in a public-house before and the crowd inside frightened me.

"Hullo, my old flower," said one tall man, grinning at me diabolically. "It must be ten years since I saw you last. One minute now—wasn't it in South Africa?"

My pal, Bob Connell, boasted to me once how he asked a drunk man for a half-crown and the man gave it to him. I was always trying to work up courage to do the same, but even then I hadn't the nerve.

"It was not," I said. "I want a half glass of whiskey for my mother."

"Oh, the thundering ruffian!" said the man, clapping his hands. "Pretending 'tis for his mother, and he the most notorious boozer in Capetown."

"I am not," I said on the verge of tears. "And 'tis for my mother. She's sick."

"Leave the child alone, Johnny," the barmaid said. "Don't you hear him say his mother is sick?"

Mother fell asleep after drinking the hot whiskey, but I couldn't rest. I was wondering how the man in the public-house could have thought I was in South Africa, and blaming myself a lot for not asking him for the half-crown. A half-crown would come in very handy if the mother was really sick. When I did fall asleep I was wakened again by her coughing, and when I went in, she was rambling in her speech. It frightened me more than anything that she didn't recognize me.

When next morning, in spite of the whiskey, she was no better, the disappointment was really terrible. After I had given her her breakfast I went to see Minnie Ryan.

"I'd get the doctor at once," she said. "I'll go and stop with her while you're out."

To get a doctor I had first to go to the house of an undertaker who was a Poor Law guardian to get a ticket to show we couldn't pay, and afterwards to the dispensary. Then I had to rush back, get the house ready, and prepare a basin of water, soap, and a towel for the doctor to wash his hands.

He didn't come till after dinner. He was a fat, slow-moving, loud-voiced man with a gray mustache and, like all the drunks of the medical profession, supposed to be "the cleverest man in Cork if only he'd mind himself." From the way he looked he hadn't been minding himself much that morning.

"How are you going to get this now?" he growled, sitting on the edge of the bed with his prescription pad on his knee. "The only place open is the North Dispensary."

"I'll go, doctor," I said at once.

" 'Tis a long way," he said doubtfully. "Would you know where it is?"

"I'll find it," I said confidently.

"Isn't he a great help to you?" he said to the mother.

"The best in the world, doctor," she sighed with a long look at me. "A daughter couldn't be better to me."

"That's right," he told me. "Look after your mother while you can. She'll be the best for you in the long run. . . . We don't mind them when we have them," he added to Mother, "and then we spend the rest of our lives regretting them."

I didn't think myself he could be a very good doctor, because, after all my trouble, he never washed his hands, but I was prepared to overlook that since he said nothing about the hospital.

The road to the dispensary led uphill through a thickly populated poor locality as far as the barrack, which was perched on the hilltop, and then it descended between high walls till it suddenly almost disappeared over the edge of the hill in a stony pathway flanked on the right-hand side by red-brick Corporation houses and on the other by a wide common with an astounding view of the city. It was more like the back-cloth of a theatre than a real town. The pathway dropped away to the bank of a stream where a brewery stood; and from this, far beneath you, the opposite hillside, a murmuring honeycomb of factory chimneys and houses, whose noises came to you, dissociated and ghostlike, rose steeply, steeply to the gently rounded hilltop with a limestone spire, and a purple sandstone tower rising out of it and piercing the clouds. It was so wide and bewildering a view that it was never all lit up at the same time; sunlight wandered across it as across a prairie, picking out a line of roofs with a brightness like snow or delving into the depth of some dark street and outlining in shadow the figures of climbing carts and straining horses. I felt exalted, a voyager, a heroic figure. I made up my mind to spend the penny Mrs. Slattery had given me on a candle to the Blessed Virgin in the cathedral on the hilltop for my mother's speedy recovery. I felt sure I'd get more value in a great church like that so close to Heaven.

The dispensary was a sordid hallway with a bench to one side and a window like a railway ticket office at the end of it. There was a little girl with a green plaid shawl about her shoulders sitting on the bench. She gave me a quick look and I saw that her eyes were green too. For years after, whenever a girl gave me a hasty look like that, I hid. I knew what it meant, but at the time I was still innocent. I knocked at the window and a seedy, angry-looking man opened it. Without waiting to hear what I had to say he grabbed bottle and prescription and banged the shutter down again without a word. I waited a minute and then lifted my hand to knock a second time.

"You'll have to wait, little boy," the girl said quickly.

"Why will I have to wait?" I asked.

"He have to make it up," she explained. "He might be half an hour. You might as well sit down."

As she obviously knew her way round, I did what she told me.

"Where are you from?" she went on, dropping the shawl, which she held in front of her mouth the way I had seen old women do it whenever they spoke. "I live in Blarney Lane."

"I live by the barrack," I said.

"And who's the bottle for?" she asked.

"My mother."

"What's wrong with her?"

"She have a bad cough."

"She might have consumption," the little girl said cheerfully. "That's what my sister that died last year had. My other sister have to have tonics. That's what I'm waiting for. 'Tis a queer old world. Is it nice up where ye live?"

I told her about the Glen, and she told me about the river out to Carrigrohane. It seemed to be a nicer place altogether than ours, the way she described it. She was a pleasant talkative little girl and I never noticed the time passing. Suddenly the shutter went up and a bottle was banged on the counter.

"Dooley!" said the man, and the window was shut again.

"That's me," said the little girl. "My name is Nora Dooley. Yours won't be ready for a long time yet. Is it a red or a black one?"

"I don't know," said I. "I never got a bottle before."

"Black ones is better," she said. "Red is more for hacking coughs. Still, I wouldn't mind a red one now."

"I have better than that," I said. "I have a lob for sweets."

I had decided that, after all, it wouldn't be necessary for me to light a candle. In a queer way the little girl restored my confidence. I knew I was exaggerating things and that Mother would be all right in a day or two.

The bottle, when I got it, was black. The little girl and I sat on the steps of the infirmary and ate the sweets I'd bought. At the end of the lane was the limestone spire of Shandon; all along it young trees overhung the high, hot walls, and the sun, when it came out in hot, golden blasts behind us, threw our linked shadows onto the road.

"Give us a taste of your bottle, little boy," she said.

"Can't you have a taste of your own?" I replied suspiciously.

"Ah, you couldn't drink mine," she said. "Tonics is all awful. Try!"

I did, and I spat it out hastily. It was awful. But after that I couldn't do less than let her taste mine. She took a long drink out of it, which alarmed me.

"That's beautiful," she said. "That's like my sister that died last year used to have. I love cough bottles."

I tried it myself and saw she was right in a way. It was very sweet and sticky, like treacle.

"Give us another," she said.

"I will not," I said in alarm. "What am I going to do with it now?"

"All you have to do is put water in it, out of a pump. No one will know."

Somehow, I couldn't refuse her. Mother was far away, and I was swept from anchorage into an unfamiliar world of spires, towers, trees, steps, and little girls who liked cough bottles. I worshipped that girl. We both took another drink and I began to panic. I saw that even if you put water in it, you couldn't conceal the fact that it wasn't the same, and began to snivel.

"It's all gone," I said. "What am I going to do?"

"Finish it and say the cork fell out," she said, as though it were the most natural thing in the world, and, God forgive me, I believed her. We finished it, and then, as I put away the empty bottle, I remembered my mother sick and the Blessed Virgin slighted, and my heart sank. I had sacrificed both to a girl and she didn't even care for me. It was my cough bottle she had been after all the time from the first moment I appeared in the dispensary. I saw her guile and began to weep.

"What ails you?" she asked in surprise.

"My mother is sick, and you're after drinking her medicine, and now if she dies, 'twill be my fault," I said.

"Ah, don't be an old cry-baby!" she said contemptuously. "No one ever died of a cough. You need only say the cork fell out—'tis a thing might happen to anyone."

"And I promised the Blessed Virgin a candle, and spent it on sweets for you," I cried, and ran away up the road like a madman, holding the empty bottle. Now I had only one hope—a miracle. I went into the cathedral to the shrine of the Blessed Virgin and, having told her of my fall, promised a candle with the next penny I got if only she would make Mother better by the time I got home. I looked at her face carefully in the candlelight and thought it didn't seem too cross. Then I went miserably home. All the light had gone out of the day, and the echoing hillside had become a vast, alien, cruel world. Besides, I felt terribly sick. It even struck me that I might die myself. In one way that would be a great ease to me.

When I reached home, the silence of the kitchen and the sight of the empty grate showed me at once that my prayers had not been heard. Mother was still sick in bed. I began to howl.

"What is it all, child?" she cried anxiously from upstairs.

"I lost the medicine," I bellowed from the foot of the stairs, and then dashed blindly up and buried my face in the bedclothes.

"Ah, wisha, wisha, if that's all that's a-trouble to you, you poor misfortunate child!" she cried in relief, running her hand through my hair. "I was afraid you were lost. Is anything the matter?" she added anxiously. "You feel hot."

"I drank the medicine," I bawled, and buried my face again.

"And if you did itself, what harm?" she murmured soothingly. "You poor child, going all that way by yourself, without a proper dinner or anything, why wouldn't you? Take off your clothes now, and lie down here till you're better."

She rose, put on her slippers and an overcoat, and unlaced my shoes while I sat on the bed. Even before she was finished I was asleep. I didn't hear her dress herself or go out, but some time later I felt a cool hand on my forehead, and saw Minnie Ryan peering down at me.

"Ah, 'tis nothing, woman," she said lightly. "He'll sleep that off by morning. Well, aren't they the devil! God knows, you'd never be up to them. And indeed and indeed, Mrs. Sullivan, 'tis you should be in bed."

I knew all that. I knew it was her judgment on me; I was one of those who were more like savages than Christians; I was no good as a nurse, no good to anybody. I accepted it all. But when Mother came up with her evening paper and sat reading by my bed, I knew the miracle had happened. She'd been cured all right.

The Drunkard

IT WAS a terrible blow to Father when Mr. Dooley on the terrace died. Mr. Dooley was a commercial traveller with two sons in the Dominicans and a car of his own, so socially he was miles ahead of us, but he had no false pride. Mr. Dooley was an intellectual, and, like all intellectuals the thing he loved best was conversation, and in his own limited way Father was a well-read man and could appreciate an intelligent talker. Mr. Dooley was remarkably intelligent. Between business acquaintances and clerical contacts, there was very little he didn't know about what went on in town, and evening after evening he crossed the road to our gate to explain to Father the news behind the news. He had a low, palavering voice and a knowing smile, and Father would listen in astonishment, giving him a conversational lead now and again, and then stump triumphantly in to Mother with his face aglow and ask: "Do you know what Mr. Dooley is after telling me?" Ever since, when somebody has given me some bit of information off the record I have found myself on the point of asking: "Was it Mr. Dooley told you that?"

Till I actually saw him laid out in his brown shroud with the rosary beads entwined between his waxy fingers I did not take the report of his death seriously. Even then I felt there must be a catch and that some summer evening Mr. Dooley must reappear at our gate to give us the lowdown on the next world. But Father was very upset, partly because Mr. Dooley was about one age with himself, a thing that always gives a distinctly personal turn to another man's demise; partly because now he would have no one to tell him what dirty work was behind the latest scene at the Corporation. You could count on your fingers the number of men in Blarney Lane who read the papers as Mr. Dooley did, and none of these would have overlooked the fact that Father was only a laboring man. Even Sullivan, the carpenter, a mere nobody, thought he was a cut above Father. It was certainly a solemn event.

"Half past two to the Curragh," Father said meditatively, putting down the paper.

"But you're not thinking of going to the funeral?" Mother asked in alarm.

" 'Twould be expected," Father said, scenting opposition. "I wouldn't give it to say to them."

"I think," said Mother with suppressed emotion, "it will be as much as anyone will expect if you go to the chapel with him."

("Going to the chapel," of course, was one thing, because the body was removed after work, but going to a funeral meant the loss of a half-day's pay.)

"The people hardly know us," she added.

"God between us and all harm," Father replied with dignity, "we'd be glad if it was our own turn."

To give Father his due, he was always ready to lose a half day for the sake of an old neighbor. It wasn't so much that he liked funerals as that he was a conscientious man who did as he would be done by; and nothing could have consoled him so much for the prospect of his own death as the assurance of a worthy funeral. And, to give Mother her due, it wasn't the half-day's pay she begrudged, badly as we could afford it.

Drink, you see, was Father's great weakness. He could keep steady for months, even for years, at a stretch, and while he did he was as good as gold. He was first up in the morning and brought the mother a cup of tea in bed, stayed at home in the evenings and read the paper; saved money and bought himself a new blue serge suit and bowler hat. He laughed at the folly of men who, week in week out, left their hard-earned money with the publicans; and sometimes, to pass an idle hour, he took pencil and paper and calculated precisely how much he saved each week through being a teetotaller. Being a natural optimist he sometimes continued this calculation through the whole span of his prospective existence and the total was breathtaking. He would die worth hundreds.

If I had only known it, this was a bad sign; a sign he was becoming stuffed up with spiritual pride and imagining himself better than his neighbors. Sooner or later, the spiritual pride grew till it called for some form of celebration. Then he took a drink—not whiskey, of course; nothing like that—just a glass of some harmless drink like lager beer. That was the end of Father. By the time he had taken the first he already realized that he had made a fool of himself, took a second to forget it and a third to forget that he couldn't forget, and at last came home reeling drunk. From this on it was "The Drunkard's Progress," as in the moral prints. Next day he stayed in from work with a sick head while Mother went off to make his excuses at the works, and inside a fortnight he was poor and savage and despondent again. Once he began he drank steadily through everything down to the kitchen clock. Mother and I knew all the phases and dreaded all the dangers. Funerals were one.

"I have to go to Dunphy's to do a half-day's work," said Mother in distress. "Who's to look after Larry?"

"I'll look after Larry," Father said graciously. "The little walk will do him good."

There was no more to be said, though we all knew I didn't need anyone to look after me, and that I could quite well have stayed at home and looked after Sonny, but I was being attached to the party to act as a brake on Father. As a brake I had never achieved anything, but Mother still had great faith in me.

Next day, when I got home from school, Father was there before me and made a cup of tea for both of us. He was very good at tea, but too heavy in the hand for anything else; the way he cut bread was shocking. Afterwards, we went down the hill to the church, Father wearing his best blue serge and a bowler cocked to one side of his head with the least suggestion of the masher. To his great joy he discovered Peter Crowley among the mourners. Peter was another danger signal, as I knew well from certain experiences after Mass on Sunday morning; a mean man, as Mother said, who only went to funerals for the free drinks he could get at them. It turned out that he hadn't even known Mr. Dooley! But Father had a sort of contemptuous regard for him as one of the foolish people who wasted their good money in public-houses when they could be saving it. Very little of his own money Peter Crowley wasted!

It was an excellent funeral from Father's point of view. He had it all well studied before we set off after the hearse in the afternoon sunlight.

"Five carriages!" he exclaimed. "Five carriages and sixteen covered cars! There's one alderman, two councillors and 'tis unknown how many priests. I didn't see a funeral like this from the road since Willie Mack, the publican, died."

"Ah, he was well liked," said Crowley in his husky voice.

"My goodness, don't I know that?" snapped Father. "Wasn't the man my best friend? Two nights before he died—only two nights—he was over telling me the goings-on about the housing contract. Them fellows in the Corporation are night and day robbers. But even I never imagined he was as well connected as that."

Father was stepping out like a boy, pleased with everything: the

other mourners, and the fine houses along Sunday's Well. I knew the
danger signals were there in full force: a sunny day, a fine funeral, and
a distinguished company of clerics and public men were bringing out
all the natural vanity and flightiness of Father's character. It was with
something like genuine pleasure that he saw his old friend lowered into
the grave; with the sense of having performed a duty and the pleasant
awareness that however much he would miss poor Mr. Dooley in the
long summer evenings, it was he and not poor Mr. Dooley who would
do the missing.

"We'll be making tracks before they break up," he whispered to
Crowley as the gravediggers tossed in the first shovelfuls of clay, and
away he went, hopping like a goat from grassy hump to hump. The
drivers, who were probably in the same state as himself, though without months of abstinence to put an edge on it, looked up hopefully.

"Are they nearly finished, Mick?" bawled one.

"All over now bar the last prayers," trumpeted Father in the tone of
one who brings news of great rejoicing.

The carriages passed us in a lather of dust several hundred yards
from the public-house, and Father, whose feet gave him trouble in hot
weather, quickened his pace, looking nervously over his shoulder for
any sign of the main body of mourners crossing the hill. In a crowd
like that a man might be kept waiting.

When we did reach the pub the carriages were drawn up outside,
and solemn men in black ties were cautiously bringing out consolation
to mysterious females whose hands reached out modestly from behind
the drawn blinds of the coaches. Inside the pub there were only the
drivers and a couple of shawly women. I felt if I was to act as a brake at
all, this was the time, so I pulled Father by the coattails.

"Dadda, can't we go home now?" I asked.

"Two minutes now," he said, beaming affectionately. "Just a bottle
of lemonade and we'll go home."

This was a bribe, and I knew it, but I was always a child of weak
character. Father ordered lemonade and two pints. I was thirsty and
swallowed my drink at once. But that wasn't Father's way. He had
long months of abstinence behind him and an eternity of pleasure before. He took out his pipe, blew through it, filled it, and then lit it with
loud pops, his eyes bulging above it. After that he deliberately turned
his back on the pint, leaned one elbow on the counter in the attitude of
a man who did not know there was a pint behind him, and deliberately
brushed the tobacco from his palms. He had settled down for the evening. He was steadily working through all the important funerals he
had ever attended. The carriages departed and the minor mourners
drifted in till the pub was half full.

"Dadda," I said, pulling his coat again, "can't we go home now?"

"Ah, your mother won't be in for a long time yet," he said benevolently enough. "Run out in the road and play, can't you?"

It struck me as very cool, the way grown-ups assumed that you could play all by yourself on a strange road. I began to get bored as I had so often been bored before. I knew Father was quite capable of lingering there till nightfall. I knew I might have to bring him home, blind drunk, down Blarney Lane, with all the old women at their doors, saying: "Mick Delaney is on it again." I knew that my mother would be half crazy with anxiety; that next day Father wouldn't go out to work; and before the end of the week she would be running down to the pawn with the clock under her shawl. I could never get over the lonesomeness of the kitchen without a clock.

I was still thirsty. I found if I stood on tiptoe I could just reach Father's glass, and the idea occurred to me that it would be interesting to know what the contents were like. He had his back to it and wouldn't notice. I took down the glass and sipped cautiously. It was a terrible disappointment. I was astonished that he could even drink such stuff. It looked as if he had never tried lemonade.

I should have advised him about lemonade but he was holding forth himself in great style. I heard him say that bands were a great addition to a funeral. He put his arms in the position of someone holding a rifle in reverse and hummed a few bars of Chopin's Funeral March. Crowley nodded reverently. I took a longer drink and began to see that porter might have its advantages. I felt pleasantly elevated and philosophic. Father hummed a few bars of the Dead March in *Saul*. It was a nice pub and a very fine funeral, and I felt sure that poor Mr. Dooley in Heaven must be highly gratified. At the same time I thought they might have given him a band. As Father said, bands were a great addition.

But the wonderful thing about porter was the way it made you stand aside, or rather float aloft like a cherub rolling on a cloud, and watch yourself with your legs crossed, leaning against a bar counter, not worrying about trifles but thinking deep, serious, grown-up thoughts about life and death. Looking at yourself like that, you couldn't help thinking after a while how funny you looked, and suddenly you got embarrassed and wanted to giggle. But by the time I had finished the pint, that phase too had passed; I found it hard to put back the glass, the counter seemed to have grown so high. Melancholia was supervening again.

"Well," Father said reverently, reaching behind him for his drink, "God rest the poor man's soul, wherever he is!" He stopped, looked first at the glass, and then at the people round him. "Hello," he said in a fairly good-humored tone, as if he were prepared to consider it a joke, even if it was in bad taste, "who was at this?"

There was silence for a moment while the publican and the old women looked first at Father and then at his glass.

"There was no one at it, my good man," one of the women said with an offended air. "Is it robbers you think we are?"

"Ah, there's no one here would do a thing like that, Mick," said the publican in a shocked tone.

Well, someone did it," said Father, his smile beginning to wear off.

"If they did, they were them that were nearer it," said the woman darkly, giving me a dirty look; and at the same moment the truth began to dawn on Father. I suppose I must have looked a bit starry-eyed. He bent and shook me.

"Are you all right, Larry?" he asked in alarm.

Peter Crowley looked down at me and grinned.

"Could you beat that?" he exclaimed in a husky voice.

I could, and without difficulty. I started to get sick. Father jumped back in holy terror that I might spoil his good suit, and hastily opened the back door.

"Run! run! run!" he shouted.

I saw the sunlit wall outside with the ivy overhanging it, and ran. The intention was good but the peformance was exaggerated, because I lurched right into the wall, hurting it badly, as it seemed to me. Being always very polite, I said "Pardon" before the second bout came on me. Father, still concerned for his suit, came up behind and cautiously held me while I got sick.

"That's a good boy!" he said encouragingly. "You'll be grand when you get that up."

Begor, I was not grand! Grand was the last thing I was. I gave one unmerciful wail out of me as he steered me back to the pub and put me sitting on the bench near the shawlies. They drew themselves up with an offended air, still sore at the suggestion that they had drunk his pint.

"God help us!" moaned one, looking pityingly at me, "isn't it the likes of them would be fathers?"

"Mick," said the publican in alarm, spraying sawdust on my tracks, "that child isn't supposed to be in here at all. You'd better take him home quick in case a bobby would see him."

"Merciful God!" whimpered Father, raising his eyes to Heaven and clapping his hands silently as he only did when distraught, "what misfortune was on me? Or what will his mother say? . . . If women might stop at home and look after their children themselves!" he added in a snarl for the benefit of the shawlies. "Are them carriages all gone, Bill?"

"The carriages are finished long ago, Mick," replied the publican.

"I'll take him home," Father said despairingly. . . . "I'll never bring you out again," he threatened me. "Here," he added, giving me a clean handkerchief from his breast pocket, "put that over your eye."

The blood on the handkerchief was the first indication I got that I was cut, and instantly my temple began to throb and I set up another howl.

"Whisht, whisht, whisht!" Father said testily, steering me out the door. "One'd think you were killed. That's nothing. We'll wash it when we get home."

"Steady now, old scout!" Crowley said, taking the other side of me. "You'll be all right in a minute."

I never met two men who knew less about the effects of drink. The first breath of fresh air and the warmth of the sun made me groggier than ever and I pitched and rolled between wind and tide till Father started to whimper again.

"God Almighty, and the whole road out! What misfortune was on me didn't stop at my work! Can't you walk straight?"

I couldn't. I saw plain enough that, coaxed by the sunlight, every woman old and young in Blarney Lane was leaning over her half-door or sitting on her doorstep. They all stopped gabbling to gape at the strange spectacle of two sober, middle-aged men bringing home a drunken small boy with a cut over his eye. Father, torn between the shamefast desire to get me home as quick as he could, and the neighborly need to explain that it wasn't his fault, finally halted outside Mrs. Roche's. There was a gang of old women outside a door at the opposite side of the road. I didn't like the look of them from the first. They seemed altogether too interested in me. I leaned against the wall of Mrs. Roche's cottage with my hands in my trouser pockets, thinking mournfully of poor Mr. Dooley in his cold grave on the Curragh, who would never walk down the road again, and, with great feeling, I began to sing a favorite song of Father's.

> "Though lost to Mononia and cold in the grave
>   He returns to Kincora no more."

"Wisha, the poor child!" Mrs. Roche said. "Haven't he a lovely voice, God bless him!"

That was what I thought myself, so I was the more surprised when Father said "Whisht!" and raised a threatening finger at me. He didn't seem to realize the appropriateness of the song, so I sang louder than ever.

"Whisht, I tell you!" he snapped, and then tried to work up a smile for Mrs. Roche's benefit. "We're nearly home now. I'll carry you the rest of the way."

But, drunk and all as I was, I knew better than to be carried home ignominiously like that.

"Now," I said severely, "can't you leave me alone? I can walk all right. 'Tis only my head. All I want is a rest."

"But you can rest at home in bed," he said viciously, trying to pick me up, and I knew by the flush on his face that he was very vexed.

"Ah, Jasus," I said crossly, "what do I want to go home for? Why the hell can't you leave me alone?"

For some reason the gang of old women at the other side of the road thought this very funny. They nearly split their sides over it. A gassy fury began to expand in me at the thought that a fellow couldn't have a drop taken without the whole neighborhood coming out to make game of him.

"Who are ye laughing at?" I shouted, clenching my fists at them. "I'll make ye laugh at the other side of yeer faces if ye don't let me pass."

They seemed to think this funnier still; I had never seen such ill-mannered people.

"Go away, ye bloody bitches!" I said.

"Whisht, whisht, whisht, I tell you!" snarled Father, abandoning all pretense of amusement and dragging me along behind him by the hand. I was maddened by the women's shrieks of laughter. I was maddened by Father's bullying. I tried to dig in my heels but he was too powerful for me, and I could only see the women by looking back over my shoulder.

"Take care or I'll come back and show ye!" I shouted. "I'll teach ye to let decent people pass. Fitter for ye to stop at home and wash yeer dirty faces."

" 'Twill be all over the road," whimpered Father. "Never again, never again, not if I lived to be a thousand!"

To this day I don't know whether he was forswearing me or the drink. By way of a song suitable to my heroic mood I bawled "The Boys of Wexford," as he dragged me in home. Crowley, knowing he was not safe, made off and Father undressed me and put me to bed. I couldn't sleep because of the whirling in my head. It was very unpleasant, and I got sick again. Father came in with a wet cloth and mopped up after me. I lay in a fever, listening to him chopping sticks to start a fire. After that I heard him lay the table.

Suddenly the front door banged open and Mother stormed in with Sonny in her arms, not her usual gentle, timid self, but a wild, raging woman. It was clear that she had heard it all from the neighbors.

"Mick Delaney," she cried hysterically, "what did you do to my son?"

"Whisht, woman, whisht, whisht!" he hissed, dancing from one foot to the other. "Do you want the whole road to hear?"

"Ah," she said with a horrifying laugh, "the road knows all about it by this time. The road knows the way you filled your unfortunate innocent child with drink to make sport for you and that other rotten, filthy brute."

"But I gave him no drink," he shouted, aghast at the horrifying interpretation the neighbors had chosen to give his misfortune. "He took it while my back was turned. What the hell do you think I am?"

"Ah," she replied bitterly, "everyone knows what you are now. God forgive you, wasting our hard-earned few ha'pence on drink, and bringing up your child to be a drunken corner-boy like yourself."

Then she swept into the bedroom and threw herself on her knees by the bed. She moaned when she saw the gash over my eye. In the kitchen Sonny set up a loud bawl on his own, and a moment later Father appeared in the bedroom door with his cap over his eyes, wearing an expression of the most intense self-pity.

"That's a nice way to talk to me after all I went through," he whined. "That's a nice accusation, that I was drinking. Not one drop of drink crossed my lips the whole day. How could it when he drank it all? I'm the one that ought to be pitied, with my day ruined on me, and I after being made a show for the whole road."

But next morning, when he got up and went out quietly to work with his dinner-basket, Mother threw herself on me in the bed and kissed me. It seemed it was all my doing, and I was being given a holiday till my eye got better.

"My brave little man!" she said with her eyes shining. "It was God did it you were there. You were his guardian angel."

Christmas Morning

I NEVER really liked my brother, Sonny. From the time he was a baby he was always the mother's pet and always chasing her to tell her what mischief I was up to. Mind you, I was usually up to something. Until I was nine or ten I was never much good at school, and I really believe it was to spite me that he was so smart at his books. He seemed to know by instinct that this was what Mother had set her heart on, and you might almost say he spelt himself into her favor.

"Mummy," he'd say, "will I call Larry in to his t-e-a?" or: "Mummy, the k-e-t-e-l is boiling," and, of course, when he was wrong she'd correct him, and next time he'd have it right and there would be no standing him. "Mummy," he'd say, "aren't I a good speller?" Cripes, we could all be good spellers if we went on like that!

Mind you, it wasn't that I was stupid. Far from it. I was just restless and not able to fix my mind for long on any one thing. I'd do the lessons for the year before, or the lessons for the year after: what I couldn't stand were the lessons we were supposed to be doing at the time. In the evenings I used to go out and play with the Doherty gang. Not, again, that I was rough, but I liked the excitement, and for the life of me I couldn't see what attracted Mother about education.

"Can't you do your lessons first and play after?" she'd say, getting white with indignation. "You ought to be ashamed of yourself that your baby brother can read better than you."

She didn't seem to understand that I wasn't, because there didn't seem to me to be anything particularly praiseworthy about reading, and it struck me as an occupation better suited to a sissy kid like Sonny.

"The dear knows what will become of you," she'd say. "If only you'd stick to your books you might be something good like a clerk or an engineer."

"I'll be a clerk, Mummy," Sonny would say smugly.

"Who wants to be an old clerk?" I'd say, just to annoy him. "I'm going to be a soldier."

"The dear knows, I'm afraid that's all you'll ever be fit for," she would add with a sigh.

I couldn't help feeling at times that she wasn't all there. As if there was anything better a fellow could be!

Coming on to Christmas, with the days getting shorter and the shopping crowds bigger, I began to think of all the things I might get from Santa Claus. The Dohertys said there was no Santa Claus, only what your father and mother gave you, but the Dohertys were a rough class of children you wouldn't expect Santa to come to anyway. I was rooting round for whatever information I could pick up about him, but there didn't seem to be much. I was no hand with a pen, but if a letter would do any good I was ready to chance writing to him. I had plenty of initiative and was always writing off for free samples and prospectuses.

"Ah, I don't know will he come at all this year," Mother said with a worried air. "He has enough to do looking after steady boys who mind their lessons without bothering about the rest."

"He only comes to good spellers, Mummy," said Sonny. "Isn't that right?"

"He comes to any little boy who does his best, whether he's a good speller or not," Mother said firmly.

Well, I did my best. God knows I did! It wasn't my fault if, four days before the holidays, Flogger Dawley gave us sums we couldn't do, and Peter Doherty and myself had to go on the lang. It wasn't for love of it, for, take it from me, December is no month for mitching, and we spent most of our time sheltering from the rain in a store on the quays. The only mistake we made was imagining we could keep it up till the holidays without being spotted. That showed real lack of fore-sight.

Of course, Flogger Dawley noticed and sent home word to know what was keeping me. When I came in on the third day the mother gave me a look I'll never forget, and said: "Your dinner is there." She was too full to talk. When I tried to explain to her about Flogger Daw-ley and the sums she brushed it aside and said: "You have no word." I saw then it wasn't the langing she minded but the lies, though I still didn't see how you could lang without lying. She didn't speak to me for days. And even then I couldn't make out what she saw in education, or why she wouldn't let me grow up naturally like any-one else.

To make things worse, it stuffed Sonny up more than ever. He had the air of one saying: "I don't know what they'd do without me in this blooming house." He stood at the front door, leaning against the jamb with his hands in his trouser pockets, trying to make himself look like

Father, and shouted to the other kids so that he could be heard all over the road.

"Larry isn't left go out. He went on the lang with Peter Doherty and me mother isn't talking to him."

And at night, when we were in bed, he kept it up.

"Santa Claus won't bring you anything this year, aha!"

"Of course he will," I said.

"How do you know?"

"Why wouldn't he?"

"Because you went on the lang with Doherty. I wouldn't play with them Doherty fellows."

"You wouldn't be left."

"I wouldn't play with them. They're no class. They had the bobbies up at the house."

"And how would Santa know I was on the lang with Peter Doherty?" I growled, losing patience with the little prig.

"Of course he'd know. Mummy would tell him."

"And how could Mummy tell him and he up at the North Pole? Poor Ireland, she's rearing them yet! 'Tis easy seen you're only an old baby."

"I'm not a baby, and I can spell better than you, and Santa won't bring you anything."

"We'll see whether he will or not," I said sarcastically, doing the old man on him.

But, to tell the God's truth, the old man was only bluff. You could never tell what powers these superhuman chaps would have of knowing what you were up to. And I had a bad conscience about the langing because I'd never before seen the mother like that.

That was the night I decided that the only sensible thing to do was to see Santa myself and explain to him. Being a man, he'd probably understand. In those days I was a good-looking kid and had a way with me when I liked. I had only to smile nicely at one old gent on the North Mall to get a penny from him, and I felt if only I could get Santa by himself I could do the same with him and maybe get something worth while from him. I wanted a model railway: I was sick of Ludo and Snakes-and-Ladders.

I started to practice lying awake, counting five hundred and then a thousand, and trying to hear first eleven, then midnight, from Shandon. I felt sure Santa would be round by midnight, seeing that he'd be coming from the north, and would have the whole of the South Side to do afterwards. In some ways I was very farsighted. The only trouble was the things I was farsighted about.

I was so wrapped up in my own calculations that I had little attention to spare for Mother's difficulties. Sonny and I used to go to town
with her, and while she was shopping we stood outside a toyshop in
the North Main Street, arguing about what we'd like for Christmas.

On Christmas Eve when Father came home from work and gave her
the housekeeping money, she stood looking at it doubtfully while her
face grew white.

"Well?" he snapped, getting angry. "What's wrong with that?"

"What's wrong with it?" she muttered. "On Christmas Eve!"

"Well," he asked truculently, sticking his hands in his trouser
pockets as though to guard what was left, "do you think I get more because it's Christmas?"

"Lord God," she muttered distractedly. "And not a bit of cake in the
house, nor a candle, nor anything!"

"All right," he shouted, beginning to stamp. "How much will the
candle be?"

"Ah, for pity's sake," she cried, "will you give me the money and
not argue like that before the children? Do you think I'll leave them
with nothing on the one day of the year?"

"Bad luck to you and your children!" he snarled. "Am I to be slav-
ing from one year's end to another for you to be throwing it away on
toys? Here," he added, tossing two half-crowns on the table, "that's all
you're going to get, so make the most of it."

"I suppose the publicans will get the rest," she said bitterly.

Later she went into town, but did not bring us with her, and returned with a lot of parcels, including the Christmas candle. We
waited for Father to come home to his tea, but he didn't, so we had our
own tea and a slice of Christmas cake each, and then Mother put
Sonny on a chair with the holy-water stoup to sprinkle the candle, and
when he lit it she said: "The light of Heaven to our souls." I could see
she was upset because Father wasn't in—it should be the oldest and
youngest. When we hung up our stockings at bedtime he was still out.

Then began the hardest couple of hours I ever put in. I was mad
with sleep but afraid of losing the model railway, so I lay for a while,
making up things to say to Santa when he came. They varied in tone
from frivolous to grave, for some old gents like kids to be modest and
well-spoken, while others prefer them with spirit. When I had re-
hearsed them all I tried to wake Sonny to keep me company, but that
kid slept like the dead.

Eleven struck from Shandon, and soon after I heard the latch, but it
was only Father coming home.

"Hello, little girl," he said, letting on to be surprised at finding

Mother waiting up for him, and then broke into a self-conscious giggle. "What have you up so late?"

"Do you want your supper?" she asked shortly.

"Ah, no, no," he replied. "I had a bit of pig's cheek at Daneen's on my way up." (Daneen was my uncle.) "I'm very fond of a bit of pig's cheek. . . . My goodness, is it that late?" he exclaimed, letting on to be astonished. "If I knew that I'd have gone to the North Chapel for midnight Mass. I'd like to hear the *Adeste* again. That's a hymn I'm very fond of—a most touching hymn."

Then he began to hum it falsetto.

> "Adeste fideles
>   Solus domus dagus."

Father was very fond of Latin hymns, particularly when he had a drop in, but as he had no notion of the words he made them up as he went along, and this always drove Mother mad.

"Ah, you disgust me!" she said in a scalded voice, and closed the room door behind her. Father laughed as if he thought it a great joke; and he struck a match to light his pipe and for a while puffed at it noisily. The light under the door dimmed and went out but he continued to sing emotionally.

> "Dixie medearo
>   Tutum tonum tantum
>   Venite adoremus."

He had it all wrong but the effect was the same on me. To save my life I couldn't keep awake.

Coming on to dawn, I woke with the feeling that something dreadful had happened. The whole house was quiet, and the little bedroom that looked out on the foot and a half of back yard was pitch-dark. It was only when I glanced at the window that I saw how all the silver had drained out of the sky. I jumped out of bed to feel my stocking, well knowing that the worst had happened. Santa had come while I was asleep, and gone away with an entirely false impression of me, because all he had left me was some sort of book, folded up, a pen and pencil, and a tuppenny bag of sweets. Not even Snakes-and-Ladders! For a while I was too stunned even to think. A fellow who was able to drive over rooftops and climb down chimneys without getting stuck—God, wouldn't you think he'd know better?

Then I began to wonder what that foxy boy, Sonny, had. I went to his side of the bed and felt his stocking. For all his spelling and sucking-up he hadn't done so much better, because, apart from a bag of sweets like mine, all Santa had left him was a popgun, one that fired a cork on a piece of string and which you could get in any huxter's shop for sixpence.

All the same, the fact remained that it was a gun, and a gun was better than a book any day of the week. The Dohertys had a gang, and the gang fought the Strawberry Lane kids who tried to play football on our road. That gun would be very useful to me in many ways, while it would be lost on Sonny who wouldn't be let play with the gang, even if he wanted to.

Then I got the inspiration, as it seemed to me, direct from Heaven. Suppose I took the gun and gave Sonny the book! Sonny would never be any good in the gang: he was fond of spelling, and a studious child like him could learn a lot of spellings from a book like mine. As he hadn't seen Santa any more than I had, what he hadn't seen wouldn't grieve him. I was doing no harm to anyone; in fact, if Sonny only knew, I was doing him a good turn which he might have cause to thank me for later. That was one thing I was always keen on; doing good turns. Perhaps this was Santa's intention the whole time and he had merely become confused between us. It was a mistake that might happen to anyone. So I put the book, the pencil, and the pen into Sonny's stocking and the popgun in my own and returned to bed and slept again. As I say, in those days I had plenty of initiative.

It was Sonny who woke me, shaking me to tell me that Santa had come and left me a gun. I let on to be surprised and rather disappointed in the gun, and to divert his mind from it made him show me his picture book, and cracked it up to the skies.

As I knew, that kid was prepared to believe anything, and nothing would do him then but to take the presents in to show Father and Mother. This was a bad moment for me. After the way she had behaved about the langing, I distrusted Mother, though I had the consolation of believing that the only person who could contradict me was now somewhere up by the North Pole. That gave me a certain confidence, so Sonny and I burst in with our presents, shouting: "Look what Santa Claus brought!"

Father and Mother woke, and Mother smiled, but only for an instant. As she looked at me her face changed. I knew that look; I knew it only too well. It was the same she had worn the day I came home from langing, when she said I had no word.

"Larry," she said in a low voice, "where did you get the gun?"

"Santa left it in my stocking, Mummy," I said, trying to put on an injured air, though it baffled me how she guessed that he hadn't. "He did, honest."

"You stole it from that poor child's stocking while he was asleep," she said, her voice quivering with indignation. "Larry, Larry, how could you be so mean?"

"Now, now, now," Father said deprecatingly, " 'tis Christmas morning."

"Ah," she said with real passion, "it's easy it comes to you. Do you think I want my son to grow up a liar and a thief?"

"Ah, what thief, woman?" he said testily. "Have sense, can't you?" He was as cross if you interrupted him in his benevolent moods as if they were of the other sort, and this one was probably exacerbated by a feeling of guilt for his behavior of the night before. "Here, Larry," he said, reaching out for the money on the bedside table, "here's sixpence for you and one for Sonny. Mind you don't lose it now!"

But I looked at Mother and saw what was in her eyes. I burst out crying, threw the popgun on the floor, and ran bawling out of the house before anyone on the road was awake. I rushed up the lane behind the house and threw myself on the wet grass.

I understood it all, and it was almost more than I could bear; that there was no Santa Claus, as the Dohertys said, only Mother trying to scrape together a few coppers from the housekeeping; that Father was mean and common and a drunkard, and that she had been relying on me to raise her out of the misery of the life she was leading. And I knew that the look in her eyes was the fear that, like my father, I should turn out to be mean and common and a drunkard.

My First Protestant

IT WAS when I was doing a line with Maire Daly that I first came to know Winifred Jackson. She was my first Protestant. There were a number in our locality, but they kept to themselves. The Jacksons were no exception. The father was a bank manager, a tall, thin, weary-looking man, and the mother a chubby, pious woman who had a lot to do with religious bazaars. I met her once with Winifred and liked her. They had one son, Ernest, a medical student who was forever trying to get engaged to some trollop who had caught his fancy for the moment—a spoiled pup if ever there was one.

But Winifred caused her parents far more concern than he did. They probably felt she had to be taken seriously. She and Maire were both learning the piano from old Streichl, and they became great friends. The Dalys' was a grand house in those days. The father was a builder; a tall, thin, sardonic man who, after long and bitter experience, had come to the conclusion that the whole town was in a conspiracy against him, and that his family—all but his wife, whom he regarded as a friendly neutral—was allied with the town. His wife was a handsome woman, whose relations with the enemy were far closer than her husband ever suspected. As for the traitors—Joe, Maire, Brenda, and Peter, the baby—they had voices like trumpets from shouting one another down and exceedingly dirty tongues to use when the vocal cords gave out.

Joe was the eldest; a lad with a great head for whiskey and an even better one for books if only he had taken them seriously, but it was a convention of the Daly family to take nothing seriously but money and advancement. Like a lot of other conventions this one didn't bear much relation to the fundamental facts. The only exception to the convention was Peter, who later became a Jesuit, and Peter had something in common with a submarine. He was a handsome lad with an enormous brow and bright blue eyes; he sometimes saluted you with a curt nod, but more often cut you dead, being submerged. For weeks he sat in his room, reading with ferocity, and then suddenly one night decided to come up for air and a little light conversation, and argued like a mad dog until two in the morning. That, the Dalys said flatly, was what reading did for you.

Yet it was a wonderfully pleasant house on a Sunday evening when the children and their friends were in, and old Daly concluded an armistice with us for the evening. There was always lashings of stuff; the Dalys, for all their shrewdness, could do nothing in a small and niggardly way. If you borrowed a cigarette from one of them, you were quite liable to be given a box of a hundred, and attempting to repay it might well be regarded as a deadly insult. Brenda, the younger girl, slouched round with sandwiches and gibes; Joe sang "Even Bravest Heart May Swell" with an adoring leer at "Loving smile of sister kind"; while Maire, who played his accompaniment, muttered furiously: "Of all the bloody nonsense! A puck in the gob was all that we ever got."

"Really," Winifred said with a sigh as I saw her home one night, "they are an extraordinary family."

I didn't take this as criticism. Having been brought up in a fairly quiet home myself, I sometimes felt the same bewilderment.

"Isn't that why you like them?" I asked.

"Is it, do you think?" she said with surprise. "I dare say you're right. I wish Daddy thought the same."

"What does he object to?" I asked.

"Oh, nothing in particular," she replied with a shrug. "Just that they're the wrong persuasion. Haven't I nice girls of my own class to mix with? Don't I realize that everything said in that house is reported in Confession? . . . Is it, by the way?" she added eagerly.

"Not everything."

"I hardly thought so," she added dryly. "Anyhow, they can confess everything I say to them."

"You're not afraid of being converted?" I asked.

"Oh, they're welcome to try," she said indifferently. "Really, people are absurd about religion."

I didn't say that some such ambition was not far from Mrs. Daly's mind. I had seen for myself that she liked Winifred and thought she was good company for Maire, and it was only natural that a woman so big-hearted should feel it a pity that such a delightful girl dug with the wrong foot. It probably wasn't necessary to say it to Winifred. There was little about the Dalys which she wasn't shrewd enough to observe for herself. That was part of their charm.

On the whole her parents did well to worry. What had begun as a friendship between herself and Maire continued as a love affair between herself and Joe. It came to a head during the summer holidays when the Dalys took a house by the sea in Crosshaven and Winifred stayed with them. I went down for occasional weekends, and found it just like Cork, and even more so. By some mysterious mental process of his own, Mr. Daly had worked out that, as part of a general conspiracy, the property-owners of Crosshaven charged high rents and then encouraged you to dissipate the benefits of your seaside holiday by depriving you of your sleep, and insisted on everybody's being in bed at eleven o'clock of a summer night, so, with the connivance of the neutral power, we all slipped out again when he was asleep, for a dance in some neighbor's house, a moonlight swim or row, or a walk along the cliffs. I was surprised at the change in Winifred. When first I had seen her, she was prim and demure, and, when anyone ragged her out of this, inclined to be truculent and awkward. Now she had grown to accept the ragging that was part of the Dalys' life, and evolved a droll and impudent expression which gave people the impression that it was she who was making fun of them. Naturally, this was far more effective.

"She's coming on," I said to Maire one evening when we were lying on the cliffs.

"She's getting more natural," admitted Maire. "At first she'd disgrace you. It wasn't bad enough wanting to pay for her own tea, but when she tried to give me the penny for the bus I thought I'd die with shame. God, Dan, do you know I was so flabbergasted I took it from her."

The picture of Maire taking the penny made me laugh outright, for she too had all the Daly lavishness, and there was nothing flashy about it; it was just that the story of their lives was written like that, in large capital letters.

"It's all very well for you," said Maire, who didn't know what I was laughing at, "but that family of hers must be as mean as hell."

"Not mean," I said. "Just prudent."

"Prudent! Pshaw!"

"Where is she now?"

"Spooning with Joe, I suppose. They're doing a terrible line. She'd be grand for him. She wouldn't stand for any of his nonsense."

"Is that the sort Joe is?" I asked, closing my eyes to enjoy the sun.

"He's as big a bully as Father," said Maire, busily tickling my nose with a blade of grass. "God, the way Mother ruins that fellow!—she expects us to let him walk on us. Aren't Protestants great, Dan?"

"We'll see when her family hears she's walking out with Joe," I said.

"Oh, I believe they're kicking up hell about that already," she said, throwing away one blade and picking up another to chew, a most restless woman. I looked round and she was sitting with one leg under her, staring away towards the sea. "They think he was put on to her by the Pope."

"And wasn't he?"

"Is it Mother?" laughed Maire. "God help us, you wouldn't blame her. Two birds with one stone—a wife for Joe and a soul for God."

I watched Winifred's romance with sympathy, perhaps with a reminiscence of Romeo and Juliet in my mind, perhaps already with a feeling of revolt against the cliques and factions of a provincial town. But for a time it almost appeared to mean more to me than my own relationship with Maire.

One autumn evening when I was coming home from the office I saw Winifred emerge from a house on Summerhill. She saw me too and waved, before she came charging after me with her long legs flying. She always remained leggy even in middle age; a tall, thin girl with a long, eager face, blue eyes, and fair hair. When she caught up on me she took my arm. That was the sort of thing I liked in her; the way she ran, the way she grabbed your arm; her capacity for quick, spontaneous moments of intimacy without any element of calculation in them.

"How's Joe?" I asked. "I haven't seen him this past week."

"No more have I," she replied lightly.

"How's that?" I asked gravely. "I thought you'd be giving us a night by this time."

"Ah, I don't think it'll ever come to that, Dan," she replied in the same tone, but without any regret that I could see.

"You're not going to disappoint us?" I asked, and I fancy there must have been more feeling in my voice than in hers.

"Well, we've discussed it, of course," she said in a businesslike tone, "but it seems impossible. He can't marry me unless I become a Catholic."

"Can't he?" I asked in surprise.

"Well, I suppose he couldn't be stopped, but you know how it would affect his business."

"I dare say it would," I said, and mind you, it was the first time the idea of that had crossed my mind—I must have been even more sentimental than I know, even now. "But you could get a dispensation."

"Yes, if I agreed to have the children brought up as Catholics."

"And wouldn't you?"

"Really, Dan, how could I?" she asked wearily. "It's all that the parents threatened me with from the beginning. I suppose it was wrong of me really to start anything with Joe, but I couldn't walk out on them now."

"It's your life, not theirs," I pointed out.

"Even so, Dan, I have to consider their feelings, just as Joe has to consider his mother's. She wouldn't like to see her grandchildren brought up as Protestants, and they feel just the same. You may think their opinions are wrong, but it would hurt them just as much as if they were right."

"I think the sooner people with opinions like those get hurt, the better," I said with a queer feeling of disappointment.

"Oh, I know," she retorted, flaring up at me like a real little termagant. "You're just like Joe. You're the normal person. I'm the freak; consequently, you expect me to make all the sacrifices."

We were passing the Cross at the time, and I stopped dead and looked at her. Up to this I had never, I thought, felt so intensely about anything.

"If that's the sort you think I am, you're very much mistaken," I said. "If you were my girl I wouldn't let God, man, or devil come between us."

Her face suddenly cleared and she gave my arm a little squeeze.

"You know, Dan, I almost wish I was," she said in a tone that restored all our intimacy.

Anyone who didn't know her would have taken it for an invitation, but even then, emotional as I felt, I knew it was nothing of the sort. I had a great admiration for her; I knew she'd make an excellent wife for Joe, and I couldn't help feeling that there was something wrong about letting religion come between them.

The following evening I went for a walk with Joe up the Western Road and we had it out.

"I had a talk with Winnie last night," I said. "I hope you won't think me interfering if I mention it to you."

"I know anything you said would be kindly meant, Dan," he replied reasonably.

That was one nice thing about Joe. However much of a bully he might be, you didn't have to skirmish for position with him. It had something to do with the capital letters that the Dalys used as if by nature. They had no time for trifles.

"I think she's very fond of you, Joe," I said.

"I think the same, Dan," he agreed warmly, "and 'tisn't all on one side. I needn't tell you that."

"You couldn't come to some agreement with her about religion?" I asked.

"I'd like to know what agreement we could come to," he said. "I can talk to you about it because you know what it means. You know what would happen the business if I defied everybody and married her in a register office."

"But you want her to do it instead, Joe," I said.

"'Tisn't alike, Dan," he said in his monumental way. "And you know 'tisn't alike. This is a Catholic country. Her people haven't the power they had. It might mean ruin to me, but it would mean nothing to her."

"That only makes it worse," I said. "You want her to give up a religion that may mean something to her for one that doesn't mean anything to you, only what harm it can do you."

"I never said it meant nothing to me," he said without taking offense. "But you've shifted your ground, Dan. That's a different proposition entirely. We were talking about my responsibility to provide for a family."

"Very well then," I said, seeing what I thought a way out of it. "Tell her that! Tell her what you've told me; that you'll marry her your way and take the responsibility for what happens, or marry her her way and let her take the responsibility."

"Aren't you forgetting that it would still be my responsibility, Dan?" he asked, laying a friendly hand on my shoulder.

"And because it is, she won't take it," I said warmly.

"Ah, well, Dan," he said, "she mightn't be as intelligent as you about it, and then I'd have to face the consequences."

"That's not the sort of girl she is at all," I said.

"Dan," he said whimsically, "I'm beginning to think you're the one that should marry her."

"I'm beginning to think the same," I said huffily.

We didn't discuss the subject again, but I'd still take my oath that if he had done what I suggested she'd have pitched her family to blazes and married him. All a girl like that wanted was proof that he cared enough for her to take a risk, to do the big thing, and that was what Joe wouldn't do. Capital letters aren't enough where love is concerned. I don't blame him now, but at that age when you feel that a friend should be everything I felt disillusioned in him.

Winifred wasted no tears over him, and in a few months she was walking out in a practical way with a schoolteacher of her own persuasion. She still called at the Dalys', but things weren't the same between them. Mrs. Daly was disappointed in her. It seemed strange to her that an intelligent girl like Winifred couldn't see the error of Protestantism, and from the moment she knew there was to be no spectacular public conversion, she gave it up as a bad job. She told me she had never approved of mixed marriages, and for once she got me really angry.

"All marriages are mixed marriages, Mrs. Daly," I said stiffly. "They're all right when the mixture is all right."

And then I began to notice that between Maire and myself the mixture had ceased to be all right. It was partly the feeling that the house was not the same without Winifred there. These things happen to people and to families; some light in them goes out, and afterwards they are never the same again. Maire said the change was in me; that I was becoming conceited and argumentative; and she dropped me.

I was sore about that for months. It wasn't Maire I missed so much as the family. My own home life had been quiet, too quiet, and I had loved the capital letters, the gaiety and bad tempers. I had now drifted into another spell of loneliness, but loneliness with a new and disturbing feeling of alienation, and Cork is a bad place for one who feels like that. It was as though I could talk to nobody. One Sunday, instead of going to Mass, I walked down the quays and along the river. It was charming there, and I sat on a bench under the trees and watched the reflection of the big painted houses and the cliffs above them at the opposite side of the river, and wondered why I hadn't thought of doing this before. I made a vow that for the future I'd bring a book. A long, leisurely book.

I had been doing that for months when one day I noticed a man who turned up each Sunday about the same time as myself. I knew him. He was a teacher from the South Side, with a big red face and a wild mop of hair. We chatted, and the following Sunday when we met again he said in an offhand way:

"You seem to be very fond of ships, Mr. Hogan?"

"Mr. Reilly," I said, "those that go down to the sea in ships are to me the greatest wonder of the Lord."

"Oh, is that so?" he said without surprise. "I just wondered when I saw you here so much."

That morning I was feeling a bit depressed, and I didn't care much who knew my reason for being there.

"It happens to be the most convenient spot to the church where my family think I am at the moment," I said with a touch of bitterness.

"I fancied that from the book you have under your arm," he said. "I wouldn't let too many people see that book if I was you. They might misunderstand you." Then as he noticed another man we had both seen before come towards us, he added with amusement: "I wonder would he, by any chance, be one of us too?"

As a matter of fact, he was. It was remarkable, after we all got to know one another, the number of educated men who found their way down the Marina Walk on Sunday mornings. Reilly called us "the Atheists' Club" but that was only swank, because there was only one atheist. Reilly and myself were agnostics, and the rest were anticlericals or young fellows with scruples. All this revealed itself gradually in our Sunday-morning arguments. It was also revealed to me that I was not the only young man in town who was lonely and unhappy.

After Winifred married I visited her a few times, and her husband and I got on well together. He was a plump, jolly, good-humored man, fond of his game of golf and his glass of whiskey, and he and she seemed to hit it off excellently. They had two sons. Joe Daly never gave her any cause to regret him, because, though his business prospered, he proved a handful for the girl who married him. Drink was his trouble and he bore it with great dignity. At one time half the police in Cork seemed to be exclusively occupied in preventing him from being charged with drunkenness, and, except for one small fine for being on unlicensed premises after hours—a young policeman was to blame and he was transferred immediately—he never was charged.

But, of course, we all drifted apart. Ten years later when I heard that Winifred's husband was dead, I went to the funeral for the sake of old times, but I knew nobody there and slipped away again before it reached the cemetery.

A couple of months later I strolled back from the Atheists' Club one Sunday morning as Mass was ending to pick up two orthodox acquaintances who I knew would attend it. It was a sunny day. The church, as usual, was crammed, and I stood on the pavement watching the crowds pour down the steps. Suddenly I glimpsed Winifred passing under the portico at right angles in the direction of the back entrance. She had the two children with her. It was the sight of these that convinced me I wasn't imagining it all. I made a dash through the crowd to reach her, and when she saw me her face lit up. She caught my hands—it was one of those instinctive gestures that at once brought back old times to me.

"Dan!" she cried in astonishment. "What on earth brings you here?"

"Young woman," I said, "I'm the one that should ask that question."

"Oh, that's a long story," she said with a laugh. "If you're coming back my way I might tell you. . . . Run along, Willie!" she called to the elder boy, and he and his brother went ahead of us up the steps.

"So you took the high jump!" I said.

"Ah, there's nothing to keep me back now," she said with a shrug. "Daddy and Mummy are dead, and you know how much Ernest cares."

"Well, you still seem quite cheerful," I said. "Almost as cheerful as a roaring agnostic like me."

"Ah, but look at you!" she said mockingly, taking my hand again quite without self-consciousness. "A bachelor, with nothing in the world to worry you! Why on earth wouldn't you be cheerful?"

I nearly told her why but thought better of it. It was complicated enough as it was. But for the first time I understood how her life had gone awry. A woman always tries to give her children whatever it is she feels she has missed in life. Sometimes you don't even know what it is till you see what she is trying to give them. Perhaps she doesn't know herself. With some it's money, with others it's education; with others still, it is love. And the kids never value it, of course. They have never really known the loss of it.

And there, as we sat over our drinks in the front room of her little house, two old cronies, I thought how strange it was that the same thing should have blown us in opposite directions. A man and woman in search of something are always blown apart, but it's the same wind that blows them.

Legal Aid

DELIA CARTY came of a very respectable family. It was going as maid to the O'Gradys of Pouladuff that ruined her. That whole family was slightly touched. The old man, a national teacher, was hardly ever at home, and the daughters weren't much better. When they weren't away visiting, they had people visiting them, and it was nothing to Delia to come in late at night and find one of them plastered round some young fellow on the sofa.

That sort of thing isn't good for any young girl. Like mistress like maid; inside six months she was smoking, and within a year she was carrying on with one Tom Flynn, a farmer's son. Her father, a respectable, hard-working man, knew nothing about it, for he would have realized that she was no match for one of the Flynns, and even if Tom's father, Ned, had known, he would never have thought it possible that any laborer's daughter could imagine herself a match for Tom.

Not, God knows, that Tom was any great catch. He was a big uncouth galoot who was certain that love-making, like drink, was one of the simple pleasures his father tried to deprive him of, out of spite. He used to call at the house while the O'Gradys were away, and there would be Delia in one of Eileen O'Grady's frocks and with Eileen O'Grady's lipstick and powder on, dong the lady over the tea things in the parlor. Throwing a glance over his shoulder in case anyone might spot him, Tom would heave himself onto the sofa with his boots over the end.

"Begod, I love sofas," he would say with simple pleasure.

"Put a cushion behind you," Delia would say.

"Oh, begod," Tom would say, making himself comfortable, "if ever I have a house of my own 'tis unknown what sofas and cushions I'll have. Them teachers must get great money. What the hell do they go away at all for?"

Delia loved making the tea and handing it out like a real lady, but you couldn't catch Tom out like that.

"Ah, what do I want tay for?" he would say with a doubtful glance at the cup. "Haven't you any whiskey? Ould O'Grady must have gallons of it. . . . Leave it there on the table. Why the hell don't they have proper mugs with handles a man could get a grip on? Is that taypot silver? Pity I'm not a teacher!"

It was only natural for Delia to show him the bedrooms and the dressing-tables with the three mirrors, the way you could see yourself from all sides, but Tom, his hands under his head, threw himself with incredulous delight on the low double bed and cried: "Springs! Begod, 'tis like a car!"

What the springs gave rise to was entirely the O'Gradys' fault since no one but themselves would have left a house in a lonesome part to a girl of nineteen to mind. The only surprising thing was that it lasted two years without Delia showing any signs of it. It probably took Tom that time to find the right way.

But when he did he got into a terrible state. It was hardly in him to believe that a harmless poor devil like himself whom no one ever bothered his head about could achieve such unprecedented results on one girl, but when he understood it he knew only too well what the result of it would be. His father would first beat hell out of him and then throw him out and leave the farm to his nephews. There being no hope of conciliating his father, Tom turned his attention to God, who, though supposed to share Ned Flynn's views about fellows and girls, had some nature in Him. Tom stopped seeing Delia, to persuade God that he was reforming and to show that anyway it wasn't his fault. Left alone he could be a decent, good-living young fellow, but the Carty girl was a forward, deceitful hussy who had led him on instead of putting him off the way any well-bred girl would do. Between lipstick, sofas, and tay in the parlor, Tom put it up to God that it was a great wonder she hadn't got him into worse trouble.

Delia had to tell her mother, and Mrs. Carty went to Father Corcoran to see could he induce Tom to marry her. Father Corcoran was a tall, testy old man who, even at the age of sixty-five, couldn't make out for the life of him what young fellows saw in girls, but if he didn't know much about lovers he knew a lot about farmers.

"Wisha, Mrs. Carty," he said crankily, "how could I get him to marry her? Wouldn't you have a bit of sense? Some little financial arrangement, maybe, so that she could leave the parish and not be a cause of scandal—I might be able to do that."

He interviewed Ned Flynn, who by this time had got Tom's version of the story and knew financial arrangements were going to be the order of the day unless he could put a stop to them. Ned was a man of over six foot with a bald brow and a smooth unlined face as though he

never had a care except his general concern for the welfare of humanity which made him look so abnormally thoughtful. Even Tom's conduct hadn't brought a wrinkle to his brow.

"I don't know, father," he said, stroking his bald brow with a
dieaway air, "I don't know what you could do at all."

"Wisha, Mr. Flynn," said the priest who, when it came to the pinch,
had more nature than twenty Flynns, "wouldn't you do the handsome
thing and let him marry her before it goes any farther?"

"I don't see how much farther it could go, father," said Ned.

"It could become a scandal."

"I'm afraid 'tis that already, father."

"And after all," said Father Corcoran, forcing himself to put in a
good word for one of the unfortunate sex whose very existence was a
mystery to him, "is she any worse than the rest of the girls that are
going? Bad is the best of them, from what I see, and Delia is a great
deal better than most."

"That's not my information at all, father," said Ned, looking like
"The Heart Bowed Down."

"That's a very serious statement, Mr. Flynn," said Father Corcoran,
giving him a challenging look.

"It can be proved, father," said Ned gloomily. "Of course I'm not
denying the boy was foolish, but the cleverest can be caught."

"You astonish me, Mr. Flynn," said Father Corcoran who was beginning to realize that he wasn't even going to get a subscription. "Of
course I can't contradict you, but 'twill cause a terrible scandal."

"I'm as sorry for that as you are, father," said Ned, "but I have my
son's future to think of."

Then, of course, the fun began. Foolish to the last, the O'Gradys
wanted to keep Delia on till it was pointed out to them that Mr.
O'Grady would be bound to get the blame. After this, her father had
to be told. Dick Carty knew exactly what became a devoted father, and
he beat Delia till he had to be hauled off her by the neighbors. He was
a man who loved to sit in his garden reading his paper; now he felt he
owed it to himself not to be seen enjoying himself, so instead he sat
over the fire and brooded. The more he brooded the angrier he became. But seeing that, with the best will in the world, he could not
beat Delia every time he got angry, he turned his attention to the
Flynns. Ned Flynn, that contemptible bosthoon, had slighted one of
the Cartys in a parish where they had lived for hundreds of years with
unblemished reputations; the Flynns, as everyone knew, being mere
upstarts and outsiders without a date on their gravestones before
1850—nobodies!

He brought Delia to see Jackie Canty, the solicitor in town. Jackie was a little jenny-ass of a man with thin lips, a pointed nose, and a pince-nez that wouldn't stop in place, and he listened with grave enjoyment to the story of Delia's misconduct. "And what happened then, please?" he asked in his shrill singsong, looking at the floor and trying hard not to burst out into a giggle of delight. "The devils!" he thought. "The devils!" It was as close as Jackie was ever likely to get to the facts of life, an opportunity not to be missed.

"Anything in writing?" he sang, looking at her over the pince-nez. "Any letters? Any documents?"

"Only a couple of notes I burned," said Delia, who thought him a very queer man, and no wonder.

"Pity!" Jackie said with an admiring smile. "A smart man! Oh, a very smart man!"

"Ah, 'tisn't that at all," said Delia uncomfortably, "only he had no occasion for writing."

"Ah, Miss Carty," cried Jackie in great indignation, looking at her challengingly through the specs while his voice took on a steely ring, "a gentleman in love always finds plenty of occasion for writing. He's a smart man; your father might succeed in an action for seduction, but if 'tis defended 'twill be a dirty case."

"Mr. Canty," said her father solemnly, "I don't mind how dirty it is so long as I get justice." He stood up, a powerful man of six feet, and held up his clenched fist. "Justice is what I want," he said dramatically. "That's the sort I am. I keep myself to myself and mind my own business, but give me a cut, and I'll fight in a bag, tied up."

"Don't forget that Ned Flynn has the money, Dick," wailed Jackie.

"Mr. Canty," said Dick with a dignity verging on pathos, "you know me?"

"I do, Dick, I do."

"I'm living in this neighborhood, man and boy, fifty years, and I owe nobody a ha'penny. If it took me ten years, breaking stones by the road, I'd pay it back, every penny."

"I know, Dick, I know," moaned Jackie. "But there's other things as well. There's your daughter's reputation. Do you know what they'll do? They'll go into court and swear someone else was the father."

"Tom could never say that," Delia cried despairingly. "The tongue would rot in his mouth."

Jackie had no patience at all with this chit of a girl, telling him his business. He sat back with a weary air, his arm over the back of his chair.

"That statement has no foundation," he said icily. "There is no record of any such things happening a witness. If there was, the inhabitants of Ireland would have considerably less to say for themselves.

You would be surprised the things respectable people will say in the witness box. Rot in their mouths indeed! Ah, dear me, no. With documents, of course, it would be different, but it is only our word against theirs. Can it be proved that you weren't knocking round with any other man at this time, Miss Carty?"

"Indeed, I was doing nothing of the sort," Delia said indignantly. "I swear to God I wasn't, Mr. Canty. I hardly spoke to a fellow the whole time, only when Tom and myself might have a row and I'd go out with Timmy Martin."

"Timmy Martin!" Canty cried dramatically, pointing an accusing finger at her. "There is their man!"

"But Tom did the same with Betty Daly," cried Delia on the point of tears, "and he only did it to spite me. I swear there was nothing else in it, Mr. Canty, nor he never accused me of it."

"Mark my words," chanted Jackie with a mournful smile, "he'll make up for lost time now."

In this he showed considerably more foresight than Delia gave him credit for. After the baby was born and the action begun, Tom and his father went to town to see their solicitor, Peter Humphreys. Peter, who knew all he wanted to know about the facts of life, liked the case much less than Jackie. A crosseyed, full-blooded man who had made his money when law was about land, not love, he thought it a terrible comedown. Besides, he didn't think it nice to be listening to such things.

"And so, according to you, Timmy Martin is the father?" he asked Tom.

"Oh, I'm not swearing he is," said Tom earnestly, giving himself a heave in his chair and crossing his legs. "How the hell could I? All I am saying is that I wasn't the only one, and what's more she boasted about it. Boasted about it, begod!" he added with a look of astonishment at such female depravity.

"Before witnesses?" asked Peter, his eyes doing a double cross with hopelessness.

"As to that," replied Tom with great solemnity, looking over his shoulder for an open window he could spit through, "I couldn't swear."

"But you understood her to mean Timmy Martin?"

"I'm not accusing Timmy Martin at all," said Tom in great alarm, seeing how the processes of law were tending to involve him in a row with the Martins, who were a turbulent family with ways of getting their own back unknown to any law. "Timmy Martin is one man she used to be round with. It might be Timmy Martin or it might be someone else, or what's more," he added with the look of a man who has had a sudden revelation, "it might be more than one." He looked from Peter to his father and back again to see what effect the revelation was having, but like other revelations it didn't seem to be going down too well. "Begod," he said, giving himself another heave, "it might be any God's number. . . . But, as to that," he added cautiously, "I wouldn't like to swear."

"Nor indeed, Tom," said his solicitor with a great effort at politeness, "no one would advise you. You'll want a good counsel."

"Begod, I suppose I will," said Tom with astonished resignation before the idea that there might be people in the world bad enough to doubt his word.

There was great excitement in the village when it became known that the Flynns were having the Roarer Cooper as counsel. Even as a first-class variety turn Cooper could always command attention, and everyone knew that the rights and wrongs of the case would be relegated to their proper position while the little matter of Eileen O'Grady's best frock received the attention it deserved.

On the day of the hearing the court was crowded. Tom and his father were sitting at the back with Peter Humphreys, waiting for Cooper, while Delia and her father were talking to Jackie Canty and their own counsel, Ivers. He was a well-built young man with a high brow, black hair, and half-closed, red-tinged sleepy eyes. He talked in a bland drawl.

"You're not worrying, are you?" he asked Delia kindly. "Don't be a bit afraid. . . . I suppose there's no chance of them settling, Jackie?"

"Musha, what chance would there be?" Canty asked scoldingly. "Don't you know yourself what sort they are?"

"I'll have a word with Cooper myself," said Ivers. "Dan isn't as bad as he looks." He went to talk to a coarse-looking man in wig and gown who had just come in. To say he wasn't as bad as he looked was no great compliment. He had a face that was almost a square, with a big jaw and blue eyes in wicked little slits that made deep dents across his cheekbones.

"What about settling this case of ours, Dan?" Ivers asked gently.

Cooper didn't even return his look; apparently he was not responsive to charm.

"Did you ever know me to settle when I could fight?" he growled.

"Not when you could fight your match," Ivers said, without taking offense. "You don't consider that poor girl your match?"

"We'll soon see what sort of girl she is," replied Cooper complacently as his eyes fell on the Flynns. "Tell me," he whispered, "what did she see in my client?"

"What you saw yourself when you were her age, I suppose," said Ivers. "You don't mean there wasn't a girl in a tobacconist's shop that you thought came down from Heaven with the purpose of consoling you?"

"She had nothing in writing," Cooper replied gravely. "And, unlike your client, I never saw double."

"You don't believe that yarn, do you?"

"That's one of the things I'm going to inquire into."

"I can save you the trouble. She was too fond of him."

"Hah!" snorted Cooper as though this were a good joke. "And I suppose that's why she wants the cash."

"The girl doesn't care if she never got a penny. Don't you know yourself what's behind it? A respectable father. Two respectable fathers! The trouble about marriage in this country, Dan Cooper, is that the fathers always insist on doing the coorting."

"Hah!" grunted Cooper, rather more uncertain of himself. "Show me this paragon of the female sex, Ivers."

"There in the brown hat beside Canty," said Ivers without looking round. "Come on, you old devil, and stop trying to pretend you're Buffalo Bill. It's enough going through what she had to go through. I don't want her to go through any more."

"And why in God's name do you come to me?" Cooper asked in sudden indignation. "What the hell do you take me for? A Society for Protecting Fallen Women? Why didn't the priest make him marry her?"

"When the Catholic Church can make a farmer marry a laborer's daughter the Kingdom of God will be at hand," said Ivers. "I'm surprised at you, Dan Cooper, not knowing better at your age."

"And what are the neighbors doing here if she has nothing to hide?"

"Who said she had nothing to hide?" Ivers asked lightly, throwing in his hand. "Haven't you daughters of your own? You know she played the fine lady in the O'Gradys' frocks. If 'tis any information to you she wore their jewelry as well."

"Ivers, you're a young man of great plausibility," said Cooper, "but you can spare your charm on me. I have my client's interests to consider. Did she sleep with the other fellow?"

"She did not."

"Do you believe that?"

"As I believe in my own mother."

"The faith that moves mountains," Cooper said despondently. "How much are ye asking?"

"Two hundred and fifty," replied Ivers, shaky for the first time.

"Merciful God Almighty!" moaned Cooper, turning his eyes to the ceiling. "As if any responsible Irish court would put that price on a girl's virtue. Still, it might be as well. I'll see what I can do."

He moved ponderously across the court and with two big arms outstretched like wings shepherded out the Flynns.

"Two hundred and fifty pounds?" gasped Ned, going white. "Where in God's name would I get that money?"

"My dear Mr. Flynn," Cooper said with coarse amiability, "that's only half the yearly allowance his Lordship makes the young lady that obliges him, and she's not a patch on that girl in court. After a lifetime of experience I can assure you that for two years' fornication with a fine girl like that you won't pay a penny less than five hundred."

Peter Humphreys's eyes almost grew straight with the shock of such reckless slander on a blameless judge. He didn't know what had come over the Roarer. But that wasn't the worst. When the settlement was announced and the Flynns were leaving he went up to them again.

"You can believe me when I say you did the right thing, Mr. Flynn," he said. "I never like cases involving good-looking girls. Gentlemen of his Lordship's age are terribly susceptible. But tell me, why wouldn't your son marry her now as he's about it?"

"Marry her?" echoed Ned, who hadn't yet got over the shock of having to pay two hundred and fifty pounds and costs for a little matter he could have compounded for with Father Corcoran for fifty. "A thing like that!"

"With two hundred and fifty pounds, man?" snarled Cooper. " 'Tisn't every day you'll pick up a daughter-in-law with that. . . . What do you say to the girl yourself?" he asked Tom.

"Oh, begod, the girl is all right," said Tom.

Tom looked different. It was partly relief that he wouldn't have to perjure himself, partly astonishment at seeing his father so swiftly overthrown. His face said: "The world is wide."

"Ah, Mr. Flynn, Mr. Flynn," whispered Cooper scornfully, "sure you're not such a fool as to let all that good money out of the family?"

Leaving Ned gasping, he went on to where Dick Carty, aglow with pride and malice, was receiving congratulations. There were no congratulations for Delia who was standing near him. She felt a big paw on her arm and looked up to see the Roarer.

"Are you still fond of that boy?" he whispered.

"I have reason to be, haven't I?" she retorted bitterly.

"You have," he replied with no great sympathy. "The best. I got you that money so that you could marry him if you wanted to. Do you want to?"

Her eyes filled with tears as she thought of the poor broken china of an idol that was being offered her now.

"Once a fool, always a fool," she said sullenly.

"You're no fool at all, girl," he said, giving her arm an encouraging squeeze. "You might make a man of him yet. I don't know what the law in this country is coming to. Get him away to hell out of this till I find Michael Ivers and get him to talk to your father."

The two lawyers made the match themselves at Johnny Desmond's pub, and Johnny said it was like nothing in the world so much as a mission, with the Roarer roaring and threatening hellfire on all concerned, and Michael Ivers piping away about the joys of Heaven. Johnny said it was the most instructive evening he ever had. Ivers was always recognized as a weak man so the marriage did him no great harm, but of course it was a terrible comedown for a true Roarer, and Cooper's reputation has never been the same since then.

The Masculine Principle

MYLES REILLY was a building contractor in a small way of business that would never be any larger owing to the difficulty he found in doing sums. For a man of expansive nature sums are hell; they narrow and degrade the mind. And Myles was expansive, a heavy, shambling man, always verging on tears or laughter, with a face like a sunset, and something almost physically boneless about his make-up. A harassed man too, for all his fat, because he was full of contradictory impulses. He was a first-rate worker, but there was no job, however fascinating, which he wouldn't leave for the sake of a chat, and no conversation, however delightful, which did not conceal a secret sense of guilt. "God, I promised Gaffney I'd be out of that place by Saturday, Joe. I know I ought to be going; I declare to my God I ought, but I love an intelligent talk. That's the thing I miss most, Joe—someone intelligent to talk to."

But even if he was no good at sums he was great at daughters. He had three of these, all stunners, but he never recognized his real talent and continued to lament the son he wanted. This was very short-sighted of him because there wasn't a schoolboy in town who didn't raise his cap to Myles in hopes of impressing his spotty visage on him, so that one day he might say to his daughters "Who's that charming fellow from St. Joseph's Terrace—best-mannered boy in the town. Why don't we ever have him round here?" There was nó recorded instance of his saying anything of the sort, which might have been as well, because if the boys' mothers didn't actually imply that the girls were fast, they made no bones about saying they were flighty. Mothers, unfortunately, are like that.

They were three grand girls. Brigid, the eldest, was tall and bossy like a reverend mother; Joan, the youngest, was small and ingratiating, but Evelyn was a bit of a problem. She seemed to have given up early any hope of competing with her sisters and resigned herself to being the next best thing to a missing son. She slouched, she swore, she drank, she talked with the local accent which her sisters had discarded; and her matey air inspired fierce passions in cripples, out-of-works, and middle-aged widowers, who wrote her formal proposals beginning: "Dearest Miss Reilly, since the death of my dear wife R. I. P. five years ago I gave up all hopes of meeting another lady that would mean the same to me till I had the good fortune to meet your charming self. I have seven children; the eldest is eighteen and will soon be leaving home and the other six are no trouble."

Then Jim Piper came on the scene. Nobody actually remembered inviting him, nobody pressed him to come again, but he came and hung on. It was said that he wasn't very happy at home. He was a motor mechanic by trade. His mother kept a huxter shop, and in her spare time was something of a collector, mostly of shillings and six-penny bits. This was supposed to be why Jim was so glad to get out of the house. But, as Father Ring was the first to discover, Jim had a tough streak too.

Father Ring was also a collector. Whatever pretty girls he had banished from his conscious mind came back to him in dreams, disguised as pound notes, except the plainer, coarser types who took the form of ten-shilling notes. Mrs. Piper was shocked by this, and when Father Ring came for his dues, she fought him with all the guile and passion of a fellow collector. When Jim was out of his time Father Ring decided that it would be much more satisfactory to deal with him; a nice, easygoing boy with nothing of the envy and spite of his mother.

Jim agreed at once to pay the dues himself. He took out his wallet and produced a ten-shilling note. Now, ten shillings was a lot of money to a working man, and at least four times what his mother had ever paid, but the sight of it sent a fastidious shudder through Father Ring. As I say, he associated it with the coarser type of female.

"Jim," he said roguishly, "I think you could make that a pound."

"I'm afraid I couldn't, father," Jim replied respectfully, trying to look Father Ring in the eye, a thing that was never easy.

"Of course, Jim," Father Ring said in a tone of grief, " 'tis all one to me what you pay; I won't touch a penny of it; but at the same time, I'd only be getting into trouble taking it from you. 'Twouldn't be wishing to me."

"I dare say not, father," said Jim. Though he grew red he behaved with perfect respect. "I won't press you."

So Father Ring went off in the lofty mood of a man who has defended a principle at a great sacrifice to himself, but that very night he began to brood and he continued to brood till that sickly looking voluptuary of a ten-shilling note took on all the radiance and charm of a virgin of seventeen. Back he went to Jim for it.

"Don't say a word to anybody," he whispered confidentially. "I'll put that through."

"At Christmas you will, father," Jim said with a faint smile, apparently quite unaware of the favor Father Ring thought he was doing him. "The Easter dues were offered and refused."

Father Ring flushed and almost struck him. He was a passionate man; the lovers' quarrel over, the reconciliation complete, the consummation at hand, he saw her go off to spend the night with another man—his beautiful, beautiful ten-shilling note!

"I beg your pardon," he snapped. "I thought I was talking to a Christian."

It was more than a man should be asked to bear. He had been too hasty, too hasty! A delicate, high-spirited creature like her! Father Ring went off to brood again, and the more he brooded, the dafter his schemes became. He thought of having a special collection for the presbytery roof but he felt the Bishop would probably only send down the diocesan architect. Bishops, like everything else, were not what they used to be; there was no gravity in them, and excommunication was practically unknown. A fortnight later he was back to Jim.

"Jim, boy," he whispered, "I'll be wanting you for a concert at the end of the month."

Now, Jim wasn't really much of a singer; only a man in the throes of passion would have considered him a singer at all, but such was his contrariness that he became convinced that Father Ring was only out to get his money, by hook or crook.

"All right, father," he said smoothly. "What's the fee?"

"Fee?" gasped Father Ring. "What fee?"

"The fee for singing, father."

And not one note would Jim sing without being paid for it! It was the nearest thing to actual free-thinking Father Ring had ever encountered, the reflection among the laity of the bishops' cowardice, and he felt that at last he understood the sort of man Voltaire must have been. A fee!

Myles Reilly loved telling that story, not because he was against the Church but because he was expansive by temperament and felt himself jailed by the mean-spiritedness of life about him. "God, I love a man!" he muttered and turned to his pint. "A man, not a pincushion," he added, drinking and looking fiercely away. He liked Jim because he was what he would have wished a son of his own to be. When Evelyn and Jim became engaged he was deeply moved. "You picked the best of the bunch," he muttered to Jim with tears in his eyes. "God, I'm not criticizing any of them because I love them all, but Evvie is out on her own. She may have a bit of a temper, but what good is anyone without it?"

He said the same things about Jim to the girls, but they, being romantic, didn't pay much heed to him, even Evelyn herself. He had no patience with the sort of fellows they knocked round with; counter-jumpers and bank clerks with flannel bags and sports coats; tennis players, tea-party gents carrying round plates of sandwiches—"Will you have some of this or some of that, please?" God Almighty, how could anyone put up with it? When Jim started bringing Evelyn ten shillings a week out of his wages to put in her Post Office account towards the wedding, Myles drew the lesson for them. There was the good, steady tradesman—the man, the *man*—not like the sports coats and flannel bags who'd have been more likely to touch them for the ten bob. When Evelyn had two hundred saved he'd build a house for them himself. It would be like no house they ever saw; modern, if you wished, and with every labor-saving device, but it would be a house, a *house*, not a bloody concrete box. The girls listened to him with amusement; they always enjoyed their father's temperamental grumblings and moanings without ever taking them seriously.

"You don't know what you're letting yourself in for," Evelyn said dryly to Jim. "You may be engaged to me but you're going to marry my da. Greatest mistake anyone could make, getting too thick with their in-laws."

In fact, Jim was more popular with father than with daughters. They, of course, were not haunted by the image of a son they could not have. Evelyn liked Jim well enough, and given a chance, she might even have loved him, but the sense of inferiority towards her sisters

left her peculiarly vulnerable to their criticisms. They didn't understand what she could see in Jim, a poor fish of a fellow who only came
to their house because he wasn't happy at home. The ten shillings a
week put the finishing touches to him. How any girl of feeling could
go with a man who saved ten shillings a week towards his wedding was
beyond them. Evelyn defended him as best she could, but secretly she
felt they were right, and that as usual she had got the second best out
of life, a decent poor slob of a mechanic whom her sisters would turn
up their noses at.

Then, at Christmas, she went out to do the shopping with the
week's housekeeping in her purse, ran into a crowd of fellows home
from Dublin for the holidays, and started to drink with them. She kept
saying she had all the money in the house and must really go off and do
the shopping, but all the Reillys had a remarkable capacity for reminding themselves of what they should be doing without doing it,
and what began as a protest ended up as a turn. The fellows said she
was a great card. When she came home half tight with only half the
shopping done Brigid smacked her face.

Evelyn knew she ought to kill Brigid, but she didn't do that either.
Instead she went to her room and wept. Jim came up later to go to
midnight Mass with her. He was a bit lit up too but drink only gave
Jim words without warmth. It roused his sense of abstract justice, and
instead of soothing Evelyn as he should have done he set out to prove
to her how unreasonable she was.

"My goodness," he said with a feeble oratorical gesture, "what do
you expect? Here's poor Brigid trying to get things ready for
Christmas and you drinking yourself stupid down in Johnny Desmond's with Casserley and Doyle and Maurice the Slug. Sure, of
course, she was mad."

"That's right," Evelyn said, beginning to flame. "It's all my fault as
usual."

"There's nothing usual about it," Jim went on with futile reasonableness, "only you don't know what a good sister you have. The girl
was a mother to you. A mother! I only wish I had a mother like her."

"You have time still," said Evelyn, beside herself.

"I wouldn't be good enough for her," said Jim with sickly servility.

"If you're not good enough for her you're not good enough for me."

"I never said I was. Are you going to make it up and come to Mass?"

"Go to hell!" snapped Evelyn.

All through the holidays she brooded over him and over her own
weak character and rotten luck, and the day after the holidays, in the
mood of disillusionment that follows Christmas, while still feeling that
no one in the world gave a damn for her, she took out Jim's savings and

caught the boat for London. The Reillys had friends there; a disorderly family called Ronan who had once lived on the terrace and had to get out of it in a hurry.

This was a scandal, if you like! The only one who really had a tolerant word to say for Evelyn was Joan, who said that, though, of course, it was wrong of Evelyn to have stolen the money, running away was the only decent way out of an impossible marriage. But then, Joan, as well as disliking Jim, loved romance and excitement. In Brigid the romantic was subdued a little by the mother; she knew it would be her responsibility to get Joan off her father's hands and that it had all been made ten times more difficult by the reports that were now going round that the Reilly girls were really what the schoolboys' mothers had always proclaimed them to be.

As for Myles, he was brokenhearted, or as near brokenhearted as his temperament permitted him to be. "The one decent boy that ever came to the house," he said with his face in his hands, "and he had to be robbed, and robbed by a daughter of mine. God, Bridgie, isn't it cruel?" After that he began to cry quietly to himself. "I loved that boy: I loved him as if he was my own son. I could have spent my last days happily with him. And the little house I was going to build for him and all—everything gone!" Then he beat the wall with his fists and cried: "God, if only I could lay my hands on her I'd strangle her! Evelyn, Evelyn, you were the last I thought would shame me."

Jim took it as you'd expect a fellow like that to take it. The person he seemed most concerned about was Myles. When he took Myles out for a drink, the old boy sat with the tears in his eyes and then spread out his big paws like claws and silently closed them round the spot where he imagined his daughter's neck to be.

"That's what I'd like to do to her, Jim," he said.

"Ah, you're not still chewing over that!" Jim said reproachfully.

Myles closed his eyes and shook his head.

"What the hell else can I do?" he asked, almost sobbing. "It's not the money, Jim; it's not the money, boy. I'll pay that back."

"You'll do nothing of the sort," Jim said quietly. "That's a matter between Evelyn and me. It has nothing to do with you."

"No, no, it's my responsibility, my responsibility entirely, Jim," cried Myles in agony, swaying to and fro. He was indignant at the very suggestion that he wasn't responsible; if he'd had it he would have paid it ten times over sooner than carry the burden of it on his mind. But Jim knew his capacity for discussing what was the right thing to do without doing it, and indeed, without any prospect of doing it. Within a few weeks it had boiled down to the skilled assistance Jim would receive in any house he built for the girl who replaced Evelyn. But Jim showed no signs of even wanting to replace her. For months he was drinking more than he should have been.

THEN, when all the commotion had died away, when Jim ceased to go to the Reillys' and there was no longer even a question of the ninety pounds being paid back, Evelyn came home. There was no nonsense about her slinking in the back door in the early hours of the morning. She wore a grand new tailormade with a hat like a hoop and arrived at the house in a car. Brigid watched her pay off the driver, and her face looked old and grim.

"I suppose that was the last of the money?" she asked bitterly.

"What money?" Evelyn asked, on the defensive at once.

"Why? Did you rob some other man as well?" Brigid asked. "What money, indeed?"

"That's gone long ago," Evelyn said haughtily. "I'm paying it back. I suppose I can get a job, can't I?"

"I suppose so," said Brigid. "If Jim Piper will give you a character."

Myles got up and stumped upstairs to his room. He was very agitated. He told Brigid that he'd kill Evelyn with his own two hands, and became still more agitated when Brigid told him sharply that it would be better if he used a stick. He told Brigid that he didn't like being spoken to in that way. He didn't either. The truth was that Myles was in a very difficult position. Ever since Evelyn's fall Brigid had developed a high moral tone which was far too like her mother's to be wholesome. Unlike her mother's it could not be short-circuited by blandishments or embraces or even softened by tears. The girl wanted him to keep regular hours; she wanted him, suffering as he was from cruel responsibilities, to deny himself the consolation of a family chat after his day's work. There was a hard streak in Brigid; she never realized the strain he was living under.

For all her faults, no one could say that of Evelyn. She might be weak and a thief and deserve strangling, but she always knew the proper tone to adopt to a father a bit the worse for drink who knew he had done wrong and didn't want to be reminded of it. He knew he had sworn that she should never set foot in the house again, but damn it, she was his daughter, and—though it was something he wouldn't like to say—he was glad to see her home.

Joan too was glad, and she showed it. She was doing a tearing line with a bank clerk, a gorgeous fellow of violent passions, and Brigid, regardless of the way she had behaved herself with Ben Hennessy, chaperoned her like mad. Brigid herself had contracted a regular, a draper called Considine, and drapers being exceedingly respectable, she was taking no more chances. The Reillys were to be respectable if it killed them. Again and again with her cutting tongue she made it plain that Evelyn wasn't wanted. Joan thought it disgusting.

Besides, Evelyn's descriptions of life in London were a revelation to her. It seemed that in disgust with herself and life she had begun a sordid and idiotic love affair, and used it merely to lacerate herself further. It was only when she realized that the man she was associating with despised her almost as much as she despised herself that she broke it off and came home. Joan put this down to her sister's unfortunate character and her inability to get the best out of life. In Evelyn's position she would have acted quite differently. She wouldn't have permitted any man to despise her; she would certainly not have despised herself, and under no circumstances would she have come home. It worked so much on Joan's imagination that she even thought of going away, just to show Evelyn how it should be done.

But there was still one thing Evelyn had to reckon with. She had to face Jim. This is one of the tests which the small town imposes, which cannot be avoided and cannot really be worked out in advance. One evening late when she was coming home from a friend's she ran into Jim. There was no getting out of it. He was taken aback though he tried not to show it. He raised his cap and stopped. Evelyn stopped too. When it came to the test she found she couldn't walk past him; she was a girl of weak character.

"Hullo, Evelyn," he said in a tone of surprise.

"Hullo," she replied chokingly.

"Back for a holiday?" he asked—as if he didn't know!

"No, for good."

"Homesick?" he added, still trying to make talk.

"Ah, for God's sake," she cried with sudden violence. "If you want to talk, come away where we won't have the whole town looking at us."

She led the way, walking fast and silently, full of suppressed anger and humiliation. Jim loped along beside her, his hands in the pockets of his trench coat. She turned up Lovers' Lane, a place they had used in their courting days. It was a long, dark, winding boreen with high walls, between two estates. Then she turned on him, at bay.

It is extraordinary what women can do in self-defense. She shouted at him. She said it was all his fault for being such a doormat; that no one with a spark of manliness in him could have let her be treated as she was at home, and that he knew she was heart-scalded and hadn't the spirit to stand up for her. She all but implied that it was he who had pinched her savings. He didn't try to interrupt her.

"Well," he said lamely when she had talked herself out, "it's no use crying over spilt milk."

"Oh, if it was only milk!" she said and began to cry. "Ronan's is no better than a kip. I never meant to take your money. I meant to get a job and send it back to you, but they kept cadging and cadging until every penny was gone."

"I suppose we can be thankful it was no worse," he said, and then held out his hand. "Anyway, are we quits now?"

She threw her arms about him and squeezed him fiercely. She was weeping hysterically and he patted her back gently, talking to her in a low, soothing voice. She did not tell him about the fellow in London. She wanted to forget it, for it made her ashamed every time she thought of it. Besides, she couldn't see that it was any business of Jim's.

After that night they continued to meet, but in a peculiar way, unknown to their families. Both were self-conscious about it. Evelyn would not invite Jim to the house and he was too proud to invite himself. The truth was that she felt Jim was behaving with his usual lack of manliness. He should have cut her dead when they met, or failing that, should have got drunk and beaten her up, all the more because she had behaved so badly in London. The fact that she hadn't told him of what took place in London only made his conduct more indefensible, and she suffered almost as much on his account as if the fault had been her own. They met after dark in out-of-the-way places, and it was weeks before word got round that they were walking out again. Joan was bitterly disappointed; she had thought better of Evelyn. Brigid, seeing a grand chance of washing out the scandal of the stolen money, changed her tune and demanded that Jim should see her sister at the house, but Evelyn refused sulkily. By this time her main anxiety was to keep Jim and Joan apart so that the London scandal mightn't leak out: not that she thought Joan would wish to betray her but because for some reason she was enormously proud of Evelyn's conduct and would be bound to boast of it. That was the worst of a romantic sister.

"If you're going to marry Jim Piper it's only right," said Brigid.

"Jim Piper didn't say he wanted to marry me," said Evelyn.

"Then what are ye walking out for?" cried Brigid.

"What do people usually walk out for?" Evelyn asked scornfully.

It was months before Brigid realized why Evelyn was so stubborn about not inviting Jim to the house, and by that time it was too late. Joan knew but Joan wouldn't tell. Evelyn told Jim one summer eve-

ning at the edge of a wood. She did it with an air of boyish toughness
and braggadocio, smoking a cigarette. Jim was aghast.

"Are you sure, Evvie?" he asked mildly.

"Certain," said Evelyn. "Joan looked it up in the library."

Jim gave a bitter, embarrassed laugh and lay back with his hands
under his head.

"That's a bit of a shock all right," he said. "What are we going to do
about it?"

"I suppose I'll only have to go back to Ronan's," Evelyn said lightly.
"They won't mind. What would shock them would sweat a black."

"I suppose so," Jim said ruefully. "We can't afford to rush into anything now."

"No one is trying to rush you into anything," she said hotly. "Get
that out of your head."

She was silent for a moment; then she got up quickly, brushed her
skirt and crossed the fence into the lane. Jim came after her with a
hangdog air. As he jumped down she turned and faced him, all ablaze.

"Don't attempt to follow me!" she cried.

"Why not?" he asked in surprise.

"Why not?" she repeated mockingly. "As if you didn't know! Oh,
you codded me nicely! You wanted to get your own back for the
money and you did, if that's any satisfaction to you."

"It's no satisfaction at all to me," Jim said, raising his voice. There
was a queer, unhappy doggedness about his air. He put his hands in
his trouser pockets and stood with his legs wide. His voice lacked reso-
nance. "And I wasn't trying to get my own back for anything, though
I had plenty of cause."

"You had; you and your old money; I wish I never saw it."

"It's not the money."

"Then what is it?"

He didn't reply. He had no need to. Under his accusing eyes she
reddened again. It had never crossed her mind that he might know.

"I suppose Joan was chattering," she said bitterly.

"Nobody was chattering at all," he said scornfully. "I knew all
about it from the first night I saw you. You couldn't conceal it."

"I wasn't trying to conceal it," she blazed. "I have nothing to hide
from you."

"I'm not throwing it up to you," he protested. "I'll marry you just
the same when I can."

"Marry me?" she spat. "I wouldn't marry you if you were the last
living thing left in the world—you worm!"

Then she strode off down the lane, humiliated to the very depth of her being. If she had gone away without saying anything to him she could have kept her pride, but she knew that in her desperation she had as good as asked him to marry her and, what was worse, asked him under false pretenses. This was not what she had intended when she shut up about the London affair; then her only idea had been to protect her own wounded sensibilities, but now she realized that if ever the story got round, she would appear no better than any other little tart, pretending to be innocent so as to kid a man into marrying her. Nothing she could now do would alter that interpretation. She went home in such a fury of rage and misery that she blurted it out in a few sentences to Brigid.

"You'd better get some money for me somewhere. I'm going to have a kid, and I'll have to go to London to have it."

"You're going to—?" began Brigid, growing pale.

"Have a kid, I said," shouted Evelyn savagely.

"Is it Jim Piper?"

"Never mind!"

"He'll have to marry you."

"He won't. I asked him and he told me to go to hell."

"We'll soon see about that."

"You won't. I did the same thing with another fellow in London and he found out."

"You—so that's what you were up to in London."

"That's what I was up to," sneered Evelyn. "Anyway, I wouldn't marry that fellow now if he came to me on his knees."

Then she went to bed and Joan, for once a little awed, brought her up tea. Myles first wept and then went out and got drunk. He said if it was anyone else he'd go out at once and kill him with his own two hands, but a fellow who had had his savings stolen on him! That was the real tragedy of being poor, that it destroyed a man's self-respect and made it impossible for him to wipe out his humiliations in blood. *Blood*, that was what he wanted. But Brigid didn't want anyone's blood. She wanted to marry Considine, the draper, and though Considine was broadminded enough as drapers go, she didn't want to give him anything more to be broadminded about. She stormed out to interview Jim's mother.

With all her responsibilities, Brigid was still something of a child. Standing with one hand on the table and the other on her hip, Mrs. Piper dominated the scene from the first moment. She asked in the most ingenuous way in the world how such a thing could happen in a well-conducted house, and when Brigid assured her that it hadn't happened there Mrs. Piper said wasn't it lucky that Evelyn didn't get pneumonia as well. Brigid had as much chance against her as an innocent naked savage against a machine-gun post.

While they were arguing Jim came in and hung up his cap.

"You know what I came about, Jim," Brigid said challengingly.

"If I don't I can guess, Brigid," he replied with a tight smile.

"The girl has no mother."

"She has something as good, Brigid," Jim replied simply, and Brigid suddenly realized that his respect for her was something he did not put off and on as it suited him. It gave her new dignity and confidence.

"You'll marry her for my sake, Jim?" she asked.

"I'll marry her the minute I'm able, Brigid," he said stubbornly, putting his hands in his trouser pockets, a trick he had to give him the feeling of stability. "I may be able to marry her in a year's time, but I can't do it now."

"A year's time will be too late, Jim," Brigid cried. "A girl in her position can afford to do without a house but she can't do without a husband."

"And start off in furnished rooms with a kid?" Jim replied scornfully. "I saw too many do that, and I never saw one that came to any good."

Brigid looked at him doubtfully. She didn't believe him; she felt he was holding out on her only because of his bitterness about Evelyn's betrayal. It caused her to make a false move.

"I know she behaved like a bitch about that fellow in London," she said. "I only heard it today for the first time. But surely seeing the state she's in, you're big enough to forgive her."

The look on Jim's face convinced her that she was right. His expression showed pain, humiliation, and bewilderment, but his voice remained firm.

"If I didn't forgive her I wouldn't be in the fix I'm in now," he said.

"What's that?" his mother cried. "What's that about a fellow in London? So that's what she was up to, the vagabond! And now she's trying to put the blame on my innocent boy!"

"She's not trying to put the blame on anybody," Jim said with the first sign of real anger he had shown. "I'm responsible, and I'm not denying it, but I can't marry her now. She'll have to go to London."

"But we haven't the money to send her to London," Brigid cried in exasperation. "Don't you know well the way we're situated?"

"I'll pay my share," Jim said. "And I'll pay for the kid, but I won't do any more."

"Leave her pay for it out of what she stole!" hissed his mother. "Oh, my, that many a fine family was reared on less!"

"I'm going straight up to Father Ring," Brigid said desperately.

"You can spare yourself the trouble," said Jim flatly. "Ring isn't going to make me marry Evelyn, nor anyone else either."

This was strong language from a young fellow of Jim's age, but it was no more than Father Ring himself expected.

"Brigid," he said, squeezing the girl's arm sympathetically, "I'll do what I can but I wouldn't have much hope. To tell you the truth I never expected better. The best thing I can do is to see Lane."

So off he went to interview Jim's employer, Mick Lane, at his own home.

"You could warn him he'd get the sack if he didn't marry her," he suggested.

"Oh, begod, father, I could not," replied Lane in alarm. "I wouldn't mind anyone else, but Jim is the sort of fellow would walk out the door on me if he thought I was threatening him, and I'd be a hell of a long time getting as good a man. I might talk to him myself in a friendly way."

"Mick," said Father Ring in a disappointment, "you'd only be wasting your time. Is it a fellow that wouldn't sing at a parish concert without a fee? It might be the best thing for the poor girl in the long run."

NEXT TIME Evelyn came back from London without any finery; the baby was put out to nurse up the country and not referred to again. It caused a lot of talk. There were plenty to say that Jim was in the wrong, that, even allowing that the girl was damaged goods, a fellow might swallow his pride. Better men had had to do it. But Jim in his quiet, stubborn way went on as though he didn't even know there was talk.

Ultimately, it did the Reillys no great harm, because Joan became engaged to the gorgeous passionate fellow at the bank and Brigid married Considine. Evelyn set her teeth and stuck it out. She went twice to see Owen, her baby, but gave it up when she realized that you can't retain a child's affection by visiting him two or three times a year.

For months she didn't see Jim. Then one evening when she went for a walk in the country, she came on him about a mile out of town, studying the wreck of a car which he was trying to make something of. It was one of those occasions when anyone is at a disadvantage; when it depends on the weather or your digestion—or, going further back, what sort your parents were—what you do. Evelyn was her father's daughter and, having no true feminine pride to direct her, she naturally did the wrong thing.

"Hello," she said.

"Oh, hello, Evelyn," Jim said, raising his cap. "How are you getting on?"

"All right," she replied curtly, with the sinking of the heart she would have felt anyhow, knowing that the decision of a lifetime had been taken, and that, as usual, it was the wrong one.

"Can I give you a lift?"

"I wasn't going anywhere in particular," she said, realizing the enormous effort of will it would take to restore the situation to what it had been a moment before.

That night, crazy with rage, she wrote him a blistering letter, asking how he had dared to speak to her and warning him that if he did it again she would slap his face. Then, remembering the lonesome evening she would spend if she posted it, she put it in her bag and went off to meet him. While they were sitting on a gate up a country lane she realized that now she would never send the letter, and the thought of it in her bag irritated her. It was as though she saw the two women in her fighting for mastery. She took it out and tore it up.

"What's that?" asked Jim.

"A letter to you."

"Can't I see it?"

"You'd hate it."

That extraordinary man threw back his head and laughed like a kid. There was no doubt about it, he was a worm, but at any rate he was her worm; he didn't divide his attentions, and even if she didn't think much of him, there was no one else she thought more of. She couldn't merely sit at home, waiting for someone who'd overlook her past. Fellows in Ireland were death on girls' pasts.

But now the sense of guilt was ingrained: when she met Jim in town she merely saluted him, and if she had anyone with her she tried to avoid doing even that. It was funny, but she felt if she stopped to speak to him she would suddenly be overcome by the popular feeling and tear his eyes out. It was again that feeling that she was really two women and didn't know which of them she wanted to be.

As a result it was months before people knew they were walking out again. This time there was a thundering row and the Reillys were the most scandalized of all. Even Joan deserted her. It was all very well for Brigid, who had her draper where he couldn't escape, but Joan's bank clerk was still a toss-up and everyone knew the unmannerly way the banks had of prying into their officials' business.

"Honest to God," Joan said contemptuously, "you haven't a spark of pride or decency."

"Well, neither has he, so we're well matched," Evelyn said despondently.

"God knows, 'tis a pity to spoil two houses with ye."

"It's all very well for you, Joan," said Evelyn, "but I have the kid's future to think of."

This wasn't true; it was a long time since Evelyn had thought of Owen's future because it was only too plain that he had none, but it was the best excuse she could think of.

"You'd hate him to be an only child," snapped Joan.

"I'm not such a fool," said Evelyn, deeply hurt.

"Fool is the word," retorted Joan.

Her father ignored her presence in the house. The latest scandal was the final touch. He was disappointed in Evelyn but he was far more disappointed in Jim, who had once shown signs of character. Up to this he had felt it was only daughters who threatened a man's peace of mind; now he began to think a son might be as bad.

When Joan married it made things easier for him, though not for Evelyn. It is always a lonesome thing for a girl when the last of her sisters has gone and the prams have begun to come back. It was worse on her because she had never pushed her own pram, and the babies she fussed over were getting something her own would never get. It fixed and confirmed her feeling of inferiority to Brigid and Joan, almost as though she had done it deliberately. She sometimes wondered whether she hadn't.

But it gradually dawned on her father that if God had tried to reward him for a well-spent life with a secure old age, He couldn't well have planned anything more satisfactory than a more or less unmarriageable daughter who could never take a high moral line. If he came in drunk every night of the week and cut her down on the housekeeping, her sins would still outnumber his. A man like Myles in such an unassailable position of moral superiority could not help being kind. "God's truth," he muttered to his cronies, "I can't blame the girl. I'm as bad myself. It's a thing you can't talk about, but since the missis died I had my own temptations." Sometimes when he saw her getting ready to go out and see Jim Piper he patted her on the shoulder, mumbled a few words of encouragement, and went out with his eyes wet. Myles was like that, a man of no character!

ONE EVENING while he and Evelyn were having their tea the latch was lifted and Jim Piper himself walked in. It was his first visit since the faraway night when he had called to console Myles for his daughter's crime.

"God save all here," he said and beamed at them with unusual magnanimity.

Myles looked up, drew a deep breath through his nose and looked away. It was all damn well condoning his daughter's misbehavior, but he refused to condone Jim's. Even Evelyn was embarrassed and cross. It wasn't like Jim.

"Hello," she replied with no great warmth. "What do you want?"

"Oh, just a few words with you," Jim replied cheerfully, placing a chair for himself in the middle of the kitchen. "Nothing important. Don't interrupt yourself. Finish your supper. If you have a paper I could look at it."

"There you are," she said, mystified, but no newspaper was capable of halting Jim's unusual flow of garrulity.

"Good evening, Mr. Reilly," he said to her father, and then as Myles ignored him he threw back his head and laughed. "I don't know what's coming over Irish hospitality," he added with a touch of indignation. "You pass the time of day to a man and he won't even answer. Begod," he added with growing scorn, "they won't even ask you to sit down. Go on with their tea overright you, and not ask have you a mouth on you! 'What do you want?' " he echoed Evelyn.

She realized in a flash what was the matter with him. He was drunk. She had never seen him so bad before, and he was not the type which gets drunk gracefully. He was too angular for that. He threw his limbs about in a dislocated way like a rag doll. All the same it put her at her ease. She was always more comfortable with men like that.

"Far from tea you were today, wherever you were," she said, fetching a cup and saucer. "Do you want tea?"

"Oh, no," said Jim bitterly with another dislocated motion of his arm. "I'm only making conversation. I didn't have a bit to eat since morning and then I'm asked if I want tea!"

"You'd better have something to eat so," she said. "Will you have sausages?"

"Isn't it about time you asked me?" Jim asked with grave reproach, looking at her owlishly.

It was only with the greatest difficulty that she kept from laughing outright. But her father, who had recognized Jim's condition from the start, had the toper's sensitiveness. He drew a deep breath through his nose, banged his fist on the table, and exploded in a "Christ! In my own house!" Then he got up, went upstairs and slammed the bedroom door behind him. No doubt he was resisting the temptation to kill Jim with his own hands. Jim laughed. Apparently he had no notion of his peril.

"Call him back," he said, tossing his head.

"Why?"

"I want to ask him to my wedding."

"Go on!" she said with amusement. "Are you getting married?"

"I can't stand this bloody bachelor life," Jim said pathetically.

"So I noticed," she said. "Who's the doll?"

"One moment, please!" he said severely. "We're coming to that. First, I have a crow to pluck with you."

"Go on!" she said, her smile fading. People always seemed to have crows to pluck with Evelyn, and she was getting tired of it.

"You said you wouldn't marry me if I was the last living thing in the world," he said, wagging his finger sternly at her. "I'm not a man to bear malice but I'm entitled to remind you of what you said. As well as that, you said I was a worm. I'm not complaining about that either. All I'm doing is asking are you prepared—prepared to withdraw those statements?" he finished up successfully.

"You never know," she said, her lip beginning to quiver. "You might ask me again some time you're sober."

"You think I don't know what I'm saying?" he asked triumphantly as he rose to his feet—but he rose unsteadily.

"Do you?" she asked.

"I banked the last of two hundred quid today," said Jim in the same tone. "Two hundred quid and five for Ring, and if that's not enough for the old bastard I'll soon find someone that will be glad of it. I drank the rest. You can go down the country now, tomorrow if you like, and bring Ownie back, and tell the whole bloody town to kiss your ass. Now, do I know what I'm saying?" he shouted with the laughter bubbling up through his words.

It was a great pity he couldn't remain steady. But Evelyn no longer noticed that. She only noticed the laughter and triumph and realized how much of Jim's life she had wasted along with her own. She gave a low cry and ran upstairs after her father. Jim looked after her dazedly and collapsed with another dislocated gesture. It was useless trying to carry on a discussion with an unstable family like the Reillys who kept running up and down stairs the whole time.

It was her father's turn now. He stumped heavily down the stairs, gripping the banisters with both hands as though he were about to spring, and then stood at the foot. This time it was clear that Jim's hour had come. He didn't mind. He knew he was going to be sick anyway.

"What's wrong with that girl?" Myles asked in a shaking voice.

"I don't know," Jim said despondently, tossing the limp wet hair back from his forehead. "Waiting, I suppose."

"Waiting?" Myles asked. "Waiting for what?"

"This," shouted Jim, waving his arm wildly and letting it collapse by his side. "The money is there now. Two hundred quid, and five for the priest. You start work on that house at eight tomorrow morning. See?"

Myles took a few moments to digest this. Even for a man of expansive nature, from murder to marriage is a bit of a leap. He stroked his chin and looked at Jim, lying there with his head hanging and one arm dead by his side. He chuckled. Such a story! Christ, such a story!

"And not a drop of drink in the house!" he exclaimed. "Evelyn!" he called up the stairs.

There was no reply.

"Evelyn!" he repeated peremptorily, as though he were a man accustomed to instant obedience. "We'll let her alone for a while," he mumbled, scratching his head. "I suppose it came as a bit of shock to her. She's a good girl, Jim, a fine girl. You're making no mistake. Take it from me." But even in that state, Jim, he realized, was not the sort to need encouragement, and he beamed and rubbed his hands. For more than anything else in the world Myles loved a man, a *man*. He stood looking fondly down on his semiconscious son-in-law.

"You thundering ruffian!" he chuckled, shaking his head. "Oh, God, if only I might have done it thirty years ago I'd be a made man today."

The Sentry

FATHER MACENERNEY was finding it hard to keep Sister Margaret quiet. The woman was lonesome, but he was lonesome himself. He liked his little parish outside the big military camp near Salisbury; he liked the country and the people, and he liked his little garden (even if it was raided twice a week by the soldiers), but he suffered from the lack of friends. Apart from his housekeeper and a couple of private soldiers in the camp, the only Irish people he had to talk to were the three nuns in the convent, and that was why he went there so frequently for his supper and to say his office in the convent garden.

But even here his peace was being threatened by Sister Margaret's obstreperousness. The trouble was, of course, that before the war fathers, mothers, sisters, and brothers, as well as innumerable aunts and cousins, had looked into the convent or spent a few days at the inn, and, every week, long, juicy letters had arrived from home, telling the nuns by what political intrigue Paddy Dunphy had had himself appointed warble-fly inspector for the Benlicky area, but now it was years since anyone from Ireland had called and the letters from home were censored at both sides of the channel by inquisitive girls with a taste for scandal until a sort of creeping paralysis had descended on every form of intimacy. Sister Margaret was the worst hit, because a girl from her own town was in the Dublin censorship, and, according to Sister Margaret, she was a scandalmonger of the most objectionable kind. He had a job keeping her contented.

"Oh, Father Michael," she sighed one evening as they were walking round the garden, "I'm afraid I made a great mistake. A terrible mistake! I don't know how it is, but the English seem to me to have no nature."

"Ah, now, I wouldn't say that," protested Father Michael in his deep, sombre voice. "They have their little ways, and we have ours, and if we both knew more about one another we'd like one another better."

Then, to illustrate what he meant, he told her the story of old Father Dan Murphy, a Tipperary priest who had spent his life on the mission, and the Bishop. The Bishop was a decent, honorable little man, but quite unable to understand the ways of his Irish priests. One evening old Father Dan had called on Father Michael to tell him he would have to go home. The old man was terribly shaken. He had just received a letter from the Bishop, a terrible letter, a letter so bad that he couldn't even show it. It wasn't so much what the Bishop had said as the way he put it! And when Father Michael had pressed him the old man had whispered that the Bishop had begun his letter: "Dear Murphy."

"Oh!" cried Sister Margaret, clapping her hand to her mouth. "He didn't, Father Michael?"

So, seeing that she didn't understand the situation any more than Father Dan had done, Father Michael explained that this was how an Englishman would address anyone except a particular friend. It was a convention; nothing more.

"Oh, I wouldn't say that at all," Sister Margaret exclaimed indignantly. " 'Dear Murphy'? Oh, I'm surprised at you, Father Michael! What way is that to write to a priest? How can they expect people to have respect for religion when they show no respect for it themselves?

Oh, that's the English all out! Listen, I have it every day of my life from them. I don't know how anyone can stand them."

Sister Margaret was his best friend in the community; he knew the other nuns relied on him to handle her, and it was a genuine worry to him to see her getting into this unreasonable state.

"Oh, come! Come!" he said reproachfully. "How well Sister Teresa and Sister Bonaventura get on with them!"

"I suppose I shouldn't say it," she replied in a low, brooding voice, "but, God forgive me, I can't help it. I'm afraid Sister Teresa and Sister Bonaventura are not *genuine.*"

"Now, you're not being fair," he said gravely.

"Oh, now, it's no good you talking," she cried, waving her hand petulantly. "They're not genuine, and you know they're not genuine. They're lickspittles. They give in to the English nuns in everything. Oh, they have no independence! You wouldn't believe it."

"We all have to give in to things for the sake of charity," he said.

"I don't call that charity at all, father," she replied obstinately. "I call that moral cowardice. Why should the English have it all their own way? Even in religion they go on as if they owned the earth. They tell me I'm disloyal and a pro-German, and I say to them: 'What did you ever do to make me anything else?' Then they pretend that we were savages, and they came over and civilized us! Did you ever in all your life hear such impudence? People that couldn't even keep their religion when they had it, and now they have to send for us to teach it to them again."

"Well, of course, that's all true enough," he said, "but we must remember what they're going through."

"And what did we have to go through?" she asked shortly. "Oh, now, father, it's all very well to be talking, but I don't see why we should have to make all the sacrifices. Why don't they think of all the terrible things they did to us? And all because we were true to our religion when they weren't! I'm after sending home for an Irish history, father, and, mark my words, the next time one of them begins picking at me, I'll give her her answer. The impudence!"

Suddenly Father Michael stopped and frowned.

"What is it, father?" she asked anxiously.

"I just got a queer feeling," he muttered. "I was wondering was there someone at my onions."

The sudden sensation was quite genuine, though it might have happened in a normal way, for his onions were the greatest anxiety of Father Michael's life. He could grow them when the convent gardener failed, but, unlike the convent gardener, he grew them where they were a constant temptation to the soldiers at the other side of his wall.

"They only wait till they get me out of their sight," he said, and then got on one knee and laid his ear to the earth. As a country boy he knew what a conductor of sound the earth is.

"I was right," he shouted triumphantly as he sprang to his feet and made for his bicycle. "If I catch them at it they'll leave me alone for the future. I'll give you a ring, sister."

A moment later, doubled over the handlebars, he was pedalling down the hill towards his house. As he passed the camp gate he noticed that there was no sentry on duty, and it didn't take him long to see why. With a whoop of rage he threw his bicycle down by the gate and rushed across the garden. The sentry, a small man with fair hair, blue eyes, and a worried expression, dropped the handful of onions he was holding. His rifle was standing beside the wall.

"Aha!" shouted Father Michael. "So you're the man I was waiting for! You're the fellow that was stealing my onions!" He caught the sentry by the arm and twisted it viciously behind his back. "Now you can come up to the camp with me and explain yourself."

"I'm going, I'm going," the sentry cried in alarm, trying to wrench himself free.

"Oh, yes, you're going all right," Father Michael said grimly, urging him forward with his knee.

"Here!" the sentry cried in alarm. "You let me go! I haven't done anything, have I?"

"You haven't done anything?" echoed the priest, giving his wrist another spin. "You weren't stealing my onions!"

"Don't twist my wrist!" screamed the sentry, swinging round on him. "Try to behave like a civilized human being. I didn't take your onions. I don't even know what you're talking about."

"You dirty little English liar!" shouted Father Michael, beside himself with rage. He dropped the man's wrist and pointed at the onions. "Hadn't you them there, in your hand, when I came in? Didn't I see them with you, God blast you!"

"Oh, those things?" exclaimed the sentry, as though he had suddenly seen a great light. "Some kids dropped them and I picked them up."

"You picked them up," echoed Father Michael savagely, drawing back his fist and making the sentry duck. "You didn't even know they were onions!"

"I didn't have much time to look, did I?" the sentry asked hysterically. "I seen some kids in your bleeding garden, pulling the bleeding things. I told them get out and they defied me. Then I chased them and they dropped these. What do you mean, twisting my bleeding wrist like that? I was only trying to do you a good turn. I've a good mind to give you in charge."

The impudence of the fellow was too much for the priest, who couldn't have thought up a yarn like that to save his life. He never had liked liars.

"You what?" he shouted incredulously, tearing off his coat. "You'd give me in charge? I'd take ten little sprats like you and break you across my knee. Bloody little English thief! Take off your tunic!"

"I can't," the sentry said in alarm.

"Why not?"

"I'm on duty."

"On duty! You're afraid."

"I'm not afraid."

"Then take off your tunic and fight like a man." He gave the sentry a punch that sent him staggering against the wall. "Now will you fight, you dirty little English coward?"

"You know I can't fight you," panted the sentry, putting up his hands to protect himself. "If I wasn't on duty I'd soon show you whether I'm a coward or not. You're the coward, not me, you Irish bully! You know I'm on duty. You know I'm not allowed to protect myself. You're mighty cocky, just because you're in a privileged position, you mean, bullying bastard!"

Something in the sentry's tone halted the priest. He was almost hysterical. Father Michael couldn't hit him in that state.

"Get out of this so, God blast you!" he said furiously.

The sentry gave him a murderous look, then took up his rifle and walked back up the road to the camp gate. Father Michael stood and stared after him. He was furious. He wanted a fight, and if only the sentry had hit back he would certainly have smashed him up. All the MacEnerneys were like that. His father was the quietest man in County Clare, but if you gave him occasion he'd fight in a bag, tied up.

He went in but found himself too upset to settle down. He sat in his big chair and found himself trembling all over with frustrated violence. "I'm too soft," he thought despairingly. "Too soft. It was my one opportunity and I didn't take advantage of it. Now they'll all know that they can do what they like with me. I might as well give up trying to garden. I might as well go back to Ireland. This is no country for anyone." At last he went to the telephone and rang up Sister Margaret. Her voice, when she answered, was trembling with eagerness.

"Oh, father," she cried, "did you catch them?"

"Yes," he replied in an expressionless voice. "One of the sentries."

"And what did you do?"

"Gave him a clout," he replied in the same tone.

"Oh," she cried, "if 'twas me I'd have killed him!"

"I would, only he wouldn't fight," Father Michael said gloomily. "If I'm shot from behind a hedge one of these days, you'll know who did it."

"Oh, isn't that the English all out?" she said in disgust. "They have so much old talk about their bravery, and then when anyone stands up to them, they won't fight."

"That's right," he said, meaning it was wrong. He realized that for once he and Sister Margaret were thinking alike, and that the woman wasn't normal. Suddenly his conduct appeared to him in its true light. He had behaved disgracefully. After all his talk of charity, he had insulted another man about his nationality, had hit him when he couldn't hit back, and, only for that, might have done him a serious injury—all for a handful of onions worth about sixpence! There was nice behavior for a priest! There was a good example for non-Catholics! He wondered what the Bishop would say to that.

He sat back again in his chair, plunged in dejection. His atrocious temper had betrayed him again. One of these days it would land him in really serious trouble, he knew. And there were no amends he could make. He couldn't even go up to the camp, find the man, and apologize. He faithfully promised himself to do so if ever he saw him again. That eased his mind a little, and after saying Mass next morning he didn't feel quite so bad. The run across the downs in the early morning always gave him pleasure, the little red-brick village below in the hollow with the white spire rising out of black trees which resembled a stagnant pool, and the pale chalk-green of the hills with the barrows of old Celts showing on their polished surface. They, poor devils, had had trouble with the English too! He was nearly in good humor again when Elsie, the maid, told him that an officer from the camp wished to see him. His guilty conscience started up again like an aching tooth. What the hell was it now?

The officer was a tall, good-looking young man about his own age. He had a long, dark face with an obstinate jaw that stuck out like some advertisement for a shaving-soap, and a pleasant, jerky, conciliatory manner.

"Good morning, padre," he said in a harsh voice. "My name is Howe. I called about your garden. I believe our chaps have been giving you some trouble."

By this time Father Michael would cheerfully have made him a present of the garden.

"Ah," he said with a smile, "wasn't it my own fault for putting temptation in their way?"

"Well, it's very nice of you to take it like that," Howe said in a tone of mild surprise, "but the C.O. is rather indignant. He suggested barbed wire."

"Electrified?" Father Michael asked ironically.

"No," Howe said. "Ordinary barbed wire. Pretty effective, you know."

"Useless," Father Michael said promptly. "Don't worry any more about it. You'll have a drop of Irish? And ice in it. Go on, you will!"

"A bit early for me, I'm afraid," Howe said, glancing at his watch.

"Coffee, so," said the priest authoritatively. "No one leaves this house without some nourishment."

He shouted to Elsie for coffee and handed Howe a cigarette. Howe knocked it briskly on the chair and lit it.

"Now," he said in a businesslike tone, "this chap you caught last night—how much damage had he done?"

The question threw Father Michael more than ever on his guard. He wondered how the captain knew.

"Which chap was this?" he asked noncommittally.

"The chap you beat up."

"That I beat up?" echoed Father Michael wonderingly. "Who said I beat him up?"

"He did," Howe replied laconically. "He expected you to report him, so he decided to give himself up. You seem to have scared him pretty badly," he added with a laugh.

However much Father Michael might have scared the sentry, the sentry had now scared him worse. It seemed the thing was anything but over, and if he wasn't careful, he might soon find himself involved as a witness against the sentry. It was like the English to expect people to report them! They took everything literally, even to a fit of bad temper.

"But why did he expect me to report him?" he asked in bewilderment. "When do you say this happened? Last night?"

"So I'm informed," Howe said shortly. "Do you do it regularly? . . . I mean Collins, the man you caught stealing onions last evening," he went on, raising his voice as though he thought Father Michael might be slightly deaf, or stupid, or both.

"Oh, was that his name?" the priest asked watchfully. "Of course, I couldn't be sure he stole them. There were onions stolen all right, but that's a different thing."

"But I understand you caught him at it," Howe said with a frown.

"Oh, no," replied Father Michael gravely. "I didn't actually catch him at anything. I admit I charged him with it, but he denied it at once. At once!" he repeated earnestly as though this were an important point in the sentry's favor. "It seems, according to what he told me, that he saw some children in my garden and chased them away, and, as they were running, they dropped the onions I found. Those could be kids from the village, of course."

"First I've heard of anybody from the village," Howe said in astonishment. "Did you see any kids around, padre?"

"No," Father Michael admitted with some hesitation. "I didn't, but that wouldn't mean they weren't there."

"I'll have to ask him about that," said Howe. "It's a point in his favor. Afraid it won't make much difference though. Naturally, what we're really concerned with is that he deserted his post. He could be shot for that, of course."

"Deserted his post?" repeated Father Michael in consternation. This was worse than anything he had ever imagined. The wretched man might lose his life and for no reason but his own evil temper. He felt he was being well punished for it. "How did he desert his post?" he faltered.

"Well, you caught him in your garden," Howe replied brusquely. "You see, padre, in that time the whole camp could have been surprised and taken."

In his distress, Father Michael nearly asked him not to talk nonsense. As if a military camp in the heart of England was going to be surprised while the sentry nipped into the next garden for a few onions! But that was the English all out. They had to reduce everything to the most literal terms.

"Oh, hold on now!" he said, raising a commanding hand. "I think there must be a mistake. I never said I caught him in the garden."

"No," Howe snapped irritably. "He said that. Didn't you?"

"No," said Father Michael stubbornly, feeling that casuistry was no longer any use. "I did not. Are you quite sure that man is right in his head?"

Fortunately, at this moment Elsie appeared with the coffee and Father Michael was able to watch her and the coffee pot instead of Howe, who, he knew, was studying him closely. If he looked as he felt, he thought, he should be worth studying.

"Thanks," Howe said, sitting back with his coffee cup in his hand, and then went on remorselessly: "Am I to understand that you beat this chap up across the garden wall?"

"Listen, my friend," Father Michael said desperately, "I tell you that fellow is never right in the head. He must be a hopeless neurotic. They get like that, you know. He'd never talk that way if he had an experience of being beaten up. I give you my word of honor it's the wildest exaggeration. I don't often raise my fist to a man, but when I do I leave evidence of it."

"I believe that," Howe said with a cheeky grin.

"I admit I did threaten to knock this fellow's head off," continued Father Michael, "but that was only when I thought he'd taken my onions." In his excitement he drew closer to Howe till he was standing over him, a big, bulky figure of a man, and suddenly he felt the tears in his eyes. "Between ourselves," he said emotionally, "I behaved badly. I don't mind admitting that to you. He threatened to give me a charge."

"The little bastard!" said Howe incredulously.

"And he'd have been justified," the priest said earnestly. "I had no right whatever to accuse him without a scrap of evidence. I behaved shockingly."

"I shouldn't let it worry me too much," Howe said cheerfully.

"I can't help it," said Father Michael brokenly. "I'm sorry to say the language I used was shocking. As a matter of fact, I'd made up my mind to apologize to the man."

He stopped and returned to his chair. He was surprised to notice that he was almost weeping.

"This is one of the strangest cases I've ever dealt with," Howe said. "I wonder if we're not talking at cross purposes. This fellow you mean was tall and dark with a small mustache, isn't that right?"

For one moment Father Michael felt a rush of relief at the thought that after all it might be merely a case of mistaken identity. To mix it up a bit more was the first thought that came to his mind. He didn't see the trap until it was too late.

"That's right," he said.

"Listen, padre," Howe said, leaning forward in his chair while his long jaw suddenly shot up like a rat-trap, "why are you telling me all these lies?"

"Lies?" shouted Father Michael flushing.

"Lies, of course," said Howe without rancor. "Damned lies, transparent lies! You've been trying to fool me for the last ten minutes, and you very nearly succeeded."

"Ah, how could I remember?" Father Michael said wearily. "I don't attach all that importance to a few onions."

"I'd like to know what importance you attach to the rigmarole you've just told me," snorted Howe. "I presume you're trying to shield Collins, but I'm blessed if I see why."

Father Michael didn't reply. If Howe had been Irish, he wouldn't have asked such a silly question, and as he wasn't Irish, he wouldn't understand the answer. The MacEnerneys had all been like that. Father Michael's father, the most truthful, God-fearing man in County Clare, had been threatened with a prosecution for perjury committed in the interest of a neighbor.

"Anyway," Howe said sarcastically, "what really happened was that you came home, found your garden robbed, said 'Good-night' to the sentry, and asked him who did it. He said it was some kids from the village. Then you probably had a talk about the beautiful, beautiful moonlight. Now that's done, what about coming up to the mess some night for dinner?"

"I'd love it," Father Michael said boyishly. "I'm destroyed here for someone to talk to."

"Come on Thursday. And don't expect too much in the way of grub. Our mess is a form of psychological conditioning for modern warfare. But we'll give you lots of onions. Hope you don't recognize them."

And he went off, laughing his harsh but merry laugh. Father Michael laughed too, but he didn't laugh long. It struck him that the English had very peculiar ideas of humor. The interview with Howe had been anything but a joke. He had accused the sentry of lying, but his own attempts at concealing the truth had been even more unsuccessful than Collins's. It did not look well from a priest. He rang up the convent and asked for Sister Margaret. She was his principal confidante.

"Remember the sentry last night?" he asked expressionlessly.

"Yes, father," she said nervously. "What about him?"

"He's after being arrested."

"Oh!" she said, and then, after a long pause: "For what, father?"

"Stealing my onions and being absent from duty. I had an officer here, making inquiries. It seems he might be shot."

"Oh!" she gasped. "Isn't that awful?"

" 'Tis bad."

"Oh!" she cried. "Isn't that the English all out? The rich can do what they like, but a poor man can be shot for stealing a few onions! I suppose it never crossed their minds that he might be hungry. What did you say?"

"Nothing."

"You did right. I'd have told them a pack of lies."

"I did," said Father Michael.

"Oh!" she cried. "I don't believe for an instant that 'tis a sin, father. I don't care what anybody says. I'm sure 'tis an act of charity."

"That's what I thought too," he said, "but it didn't go down too well. I liked the officer, though. I'll be seeing him again and I might be able to get round him. The English are very good like that, when they know you."

"I'll start a novena at once," she said firmly.

The Lady of the Sagas

IT IS a terrible thing to have the name of a saga heroine and have no saga hero. Deirdre Costello, the new teacher at the convent, was a slight girl with reddish-brown hair pulled back from her ears and a long face with clear gray eyes. Having a name like that, she naturally thought of herself in terms of the sagas and imagined Connacht raided and Ulster burned for her.

But whatever our town may have been like in saga times, it is no great shakes today. It seemed to Deirdre to be more like an island; a small island where you couldn't walk a few hundred yards in any direction without glimpsing the sea, only that the sea was some watery view of pearly mountains and neglected fields with a red and blue cart upended beside a stack of turf. The islanders, except when they took a boat (which they kept on referring to as a car) and visited some mother island ten or fifteen miles away, were morose and self-centered, and spent their leisure hours not in cattle-raiding and love-making but in drinking and playing cards.

Tommy Dodd was the only man she met who even looked as though he had the makings of a saga hero in him. Tommy was the town's smartest solicitor, a tall, handsome man with a heroic build, a long pale face, dark hair, and an obstinate jaw. He was built more for defense than attack; a brusque man, rude and loud-voiced when it suited him, polite and stiff when it didn't. He was a high official in a Catholic secret society, the members of which wore colored cowls and robes in the manner of the Ku Klux Klan, talked in an elaborate jargon with titles like "Worthy Warden," and had a complicated system of grips and signs. He was almost obtrusively pious, and went to Mass each morning before breakfast. His room was filled with mechanical gadgets which were supposed to develop different parts of him, and he was quite obtrusively pernickety about food, insisting on all sorts of unusual things like bran, nuts, and nettles. He became quite violent if Joan, the landlady's daughter, crossed him in this fad.

"Take that away, Joan," he would say in a dead voice whenever she happened to bring him the wrong thing.

"Oh, Law!" Joan would exclaim with a laugh. "Aren't you eating that now?"

"I never eat it. Are there any oranges left?"

"Oranges, oye!" Joan would mutter. "A wonder you don't turn into a monkey!"

"If you knew anything about the general health of monkeys, you wouldn't talk about them in that ignorant way," said Tommy. "I don't know how you eat that stuff at all, Deirdre," he would go on anxiously. "You should see what that does to your insides. I couldn't touch it at all. 'Twould kill me."

As hard as Deirdre tried, this solicitude about what she ate was as close as she could get to a lover's attention from Tommy. He seemed more interested in her bowels than any other part of her. It was the same when they went driving. Tommy had a fine but blunted intelligence, so that he never seemed to know what would interest her. It took her quite a while to get him talking about his job ("Ah, what is it only old rubbish? You wouldn't care about things like that"), but when he did, he was fascinating. He knew who everyone was and what everybody was worth.

"How do you get all the information?" she asked. "I suppose the bank manager is in the Ku Klux Klan as well?"

"Is it Con Doody?" exclaimed Tommy, giving nothing away. "Ah, Con is too smart for that."

"He'd want to be."

"Begor, he would. And even then he's not as smart as the last man. Delaney used to have a phone on his desk, and if you asked him for an overdraft, he'd ring up head office in Dublin and recommend you. Oh, one of his most valued customers! And you wouldn't know the phone wasn't connected."

"But why would he do that?" she asked in bewilderment.

"Because after hearing all he said about you, you'd blame the bank and not him at all. Oh, begor, Delaney was a first-rate man."

"And did he charge for the calls?" Deirdre asked coldly.

"How would I know?" exclaimed Tommy in astonishment. "Why?"

"Is there anyone in this town that isn't an exploiter?" she asked with burning indignation.

"An exploiter?" echoed Tommy in bewilderment. "How do you make that out?"

"But you're all exploiters, man," cried Deirdre. "Doctors, priests, bank managers, and solicitors; you're out only for what you can get. Don't you ever want to give people anything?"

"I'm sure I'm as charitable as the next," Tommy said in a hurt tone. "Last year I must have given a good slice of my income in charity."

"Ah, who's talking about charity?" she cried impatiently. "You don't even know what I mean. Ye all have the minds of robbers, even you. This isn't a town at all. It's a camp of highway robbers."

"Begor, I wish it was," Tommy said blandly, stepping on the accelerator. "You'd get nice pickings."

For a man of such piety his morality struck Deirdre as deplorable. His sentiment was just as bad, and she sometimes wondered if she'd ever get down to the saga hero in him. He was far from being an uneducated man, and he had a lot of books of his own—serious works on history and philosophy which he read right through. The lighter types of literature he borrowed from her, and she made him read Joyce, George Moore, and Hemingway, in the hope that they might fan the spark of passion in him; but if they did, he managed to conceal it well. Instead he embarked on long and obscure arguments about St. Thomas Aquinas, Communism, the sanctity of marriage, and even anatomy. He called this "picking her brains." When he had got all he wanted, he said he had "got great value out of her." He talked as though she were another sort of chest-developer.

"But you wouldn't call that girl's conduct natural, would you?" he asked one night when he was discussing some novel she'd given him. "You don't imagine Joan here would let a fellow behave like that with her?"

"And who said Joan was natural?" asked Deirdre.

"Begod, I don't know," he said with a laugh. "Maybe she isn't. But to come back to the girl in the story. Now, she knew the man was living with somebody else already. Wouldn't that show her he wasn't reliable?"

"She mightn't want someone reliable," suggested Deirdre. "Anyway, lots of women would like it."

"Would you say that, Deirdre?" he asked in surprise, sticking his thumbs in the armholes in his vest. "Why would they like it?"

"Well, at least they'd know where they were with him," said Deirdre with a laugh.

"Excuse my being personal," he went on, "but as I'm picking your brains, I'd like to know what you think of it yourself. Would you like it?"

"That would depend on the man, Tommy," she replied. "Damn it, the girl was in love with him." Then seeing from the blank expression on Tommy's handsome face that he didn't even know what she was getting at, she beat the sofa cushion in exasperation. "Love, Tommy, love!" she cried. "Don't tell me you never heard of it."

"Oh, begor, I heard of it all right," said Tommy, who was very difficult to shake when he was on the defensive. "I was through it all before you were out of long clothes. I'm past it now though."

"Why? How old are you?"

"Thirty-five," he said with finality.

"But, my God, that's only the prime of life!"

"You feel the years beginning to tell on you all the same," said Tommy gravely. "What I'd like now is to settle down."

"Settle down?" Deirdre repeated in disappointment (as if anybody ever heard of a saga hero settling down!). "What do you want to settle down for?"

"I want a home of my own, of course," said Tommy. "You don't think I'm going to go on living in lodgings for the rest of my life, where I can't get a bit of decent food or anything?"

"And have you a girl?"

"I have not. Not yet."

"Ah, Tommy, you're putting the cart before the horse," she said mockingly. "You should get the girl first."

"I believe 'tis customary," said Tommy without permitting himself to get ruffled.

"But, Tommy," she burst out, "you don't want to make a home for a girl till there's nothing else left for you to do with her. She'd hate it. Surely you understand that?" But it struck her that he didn't; not entirely, at any rate; and if she wanted to reach down to the passion in him, she would have to begin in a key without sharps or flats. "Anyway," she added, "you'll find plenty to jump at you."

"I dare say," replied Tommy complacently. "I mightn't want to jump at them though."

"Now, who is there you couldn't get if you wanted to?" she asked cajolingly. "A fine, upstanding man like yourself!"

"Can't you guess?" he asked, causing her to groan within. This wasn't even C major; it was more like puff-puffs.

"Do I know her?"

"What would you say to the doctor?" asked Tommy.

"Dr. O'Brien?" said Deirdre with a sinking of the heart. She knew now she wasn't in for courting, but confidences, and if there was one thing more than another that destroyed her self-respect, it was confidences. It was revealed to her at that precise moment that the nuns and herself would have to part company. It was bad enough in the mornings, having to hitch down her dress behind to cover her chest without having to endure fellows talking to her about the charms of other women. "I suppose she has bags of tin?" she added.

"Fifteen thousand," replied Tommy complacently.

"You'd overlook a lot for that," said Deirdre.

"Begor, you would," said Tommy thoughtfully. "But isn't she very good-looking, Deirdre? I'd say she had great distinction."

"Another five thousand would make her a beauty," said Deirdre. "Honest to God, I used to think I knew what Irish towns were like, but I was only fooling myself. They're nothing but calculation and greed and cunning."

"Oh, come, Deirdre!" said Tommy gravely. "Aren't you taking things to the fair?"

"No," groaned Deirdre. "That's where ye take them."

SHE WAS so disgusted that next day she told it all to Joan. It wasn't that she particularly cared for Joan, who, in her opinion, was the sort of Irishwoman who make Irishmen what they are, but she had no one else to discuss it with. Joan was a big, platter-faced Child of Mary who scouted round men like some member of a primitive tribe observing the behavior of the first pale-faces.

"Mother of our Divine Redeemer!" she cried dramatically. "The box of chocolates!"

"What box of chocolates?"

"He have them for days hidden inside a clean shirt. Maybe he thought we wouldn't find them! Would you ever be equal to men? And what did he want telling you about her for?"

"I suppose he wanted someone to talk to," said Deirdre.

"He did, I hear!" retorted Joan ironically. "I suppose he thought you might put in a good word for him."

"But how could I when I don't even know the girl?"

"Maybe you might know someone that do," Joan suggested shrewdly. "Or maybe your father might have influence."

"Ah, it's not that at all," Deirdre said impatiently. "The man is soft on her, and he wants someone to talk to. Sure, 'tis only human nature."

"The divil a much nature that fellow have unless it suited his book," said Joan derisively. "He wouldn't tell you the time of day unless he wanted to borrow a match from you."

This all-pervading cynicism about love didn't agree with Deirdre at all. The country had obviously gone to hell since saga times. She wrote to a friend in Dublin, asking her to find her a job; after that she felt considerably better.

A few nights later Tommy invited her to the pictures. Afterwards, as they came down Main Street in the moonlight, he looked so imposing with his great build and long, handsome Viking head that she took his arm. She stopped him at the bridge. The abbey tower soared over its cluster of ragged gables with its fantastic battlements like cockades in the moonlight, and the water, tumbling over the weir, was so hatched with shadow that it seemed still, like seaweed left after the tide. There was a great sense of space and joy and contemplativeness inside her, as if a bit of the night had gone astray and nested in her.

"God, Tommy, isn't it lovely?" she whispered.

"Tell me," he asked, as though he were picking her brains again, "what do you see particularly beautiful about that?"

"Ah, stop your old catechism and try and feel something, man!" she said impatiently.

"I don't know why you say that," Tommy said in a hurt tone as he rested on the parapet of the bridge. "As a matter of fact, I feel things very deeply. As a kid, I was so unhappy at home that I had a row with my father and ran away to sea."

"Did you?" she asked in surprise. "How long were you at sea?"

"A fortnight," said Tommy.

"You didn't stop long enough, Tommy," she said as she sat up on the bridge. "Tommy," she added coaxingly, "did you ever go to bed with a girl?"

He flashed her a quick look of mistrust.

"Why?" he asked suspiciously. "Did someone tell you?"

"Nobody told me anything. I only asked. Did you?"

"Oh, begor, I did," said Tommy with a nod of his head.

"I never did anything like that," she said regretfully. "At least, I did, once, but the fellow said he respected me too much."

"Begor, I hope so," Tommy said in some alarm. "You're too young to be going in for that sort of thing, Deirdre."

"Ah, I don't know," Deirdre said, shaking her head regretfully. "People think they have time enough, and then, before they know where they are, their lives are wasted and they have nothing to show for them. For God's sake, look at the people of this town, Tommy! You'd think it was something they could put in the bank. Was this some girl you picked up?"

"No," replied Tommy, getting more and more guarded. "A girl in a house I was lodging in in Dublin."

"Was she nice?"

"I thought so anyway," said Tommy gallantly.

"But were you in love with her?"

"Oh, begor, I was in love with her all right," he said with a laugh.

"Ah, but I mean really, madly, hopelessly in love," persisted Deirdre, exasperated by his temperate tone.

"I was mad enough."

"And why didn't you marry her?"

"I wasn't in a position to marry her. My family wasn't well off and I couldn't afford it."

"Ah," Deirdre said angrily, as much to the night as to Tommy, "I have no patience with that sort of talk. Ye wouldn't starve."

"I wouldn't be too sure of that."

"And if ye did, what matter?"

"What matter if we starved?" he asked incredulously.

"What matter if ye lived? God, if I loved a man, I'd marry him on tuppence ha'penny. You're all terrified out of your wits of life, as if it was going to bite you."

"Now, that's exactly what it would do," said Tommy.

"Ah, what signifies a bite or two?" Deirdre asked laughingly, throwing off her irritation. "Anyway," she added reasonably, "you could marry her now."

"Is it Elsie?" said Tommy in surprise. "She's probably married herself by now."

"Well, can't you go and see, man?" said Deirdre. "Even if she is, she won't eat you. Anyway, wouldn't she be better for you than your old doctor and her fifteen thousand? God Almighty, Tommy, that's not life!"

"That's the question, of course," Tommy said sternly. "What is life?"

"I don't know, but I'm going to try and find out."

"I read a good many books, and I can't say I ever learned much about it," said Tommy. "How would you find out?"

"By living it."

"That was tried."

"It's a novelty round these parts. I'm hoping to go to a job in Dublin after Christmas. Did I tell you?"

"You did not," Tommy said in consternation. "What do you want going to Dublin for? Aren't you all right here?"

"My views are too large for a place this size," Deirdre replied with a laugh.

And after Tommy had drunk his cocoa in the sitting room, Deirdre went to drink tea with Joan in the kitchen. The two girls had the room to themselves.

"Well," asked Joan, "had you a great clatther with Mr. Dodd?"

"Oh, great!" said Deirdre, thinking how disappointed Joan would be if she knew how little clatthering they did.

"Maybe ye might make a match of it yet?" Joan said hopefully.

"I wouldn't say so," said Deirdre. "I fancy Tommy doesn't care much about me, except to be talking to."

"That fellow never cared about anyone," said Joan. "Only himself and his monkey nuts."

But Deirdre couldn't feel critical of him just then. She felt that the memory of his abortive romance would be linked in her mind with the bit of the night that had gone astray and nested in her; that she'd always have a soft spot in her heart for the town and its people because of that glimpse into their frustrated and lonely lives.

"Ah, Tommy is romantic enough when he gets the chance," she said. "You never heard about the girl he was living with in Dublin?"

"Living with in Dublin?" Joan said incredulously. "Tommy Dodd? You're not serious! Who was it?"

"Some girl he was in digs with. A university student, I suppose."

"And he was living with her?"

"Oh, not openly, of course," Deirdre said with regret. She could have wished Tommy some experience less furtive, but she knew it was impossible.

"Jesus!" Joan exclaimed. "I'd never trust a man again."

A WEEK passed and one wet afternoon Deirdre came in from school and Joan gave her dinner in the parlor. It was cold there and there was no fire. In the street she saw a father and son coming together at the other side of the road, each of them sucking a ripe tomato. They scarcely looked human.

"Mr. Dodd didn't say when he was going to give the doctor the chocolates?" asked Joan, turning as she reached the door.

"He never mentioned them," said Deirdre. "Why? Are they there still?"

"The divil a stir out of them," said Joan. "He's laying his traps well, but he might get a poacher's welcome."

"How's that?"

"I heard the doctor was saying she'd fling them in his face if he as much as opened his mouth to her," Joan said in blood-curdling tones.

"But how does she know about them?" Deirdre asked in alarm.

"I suppose he told someone," said Joan with a guilty air. "You don't think you were the only one he talked to about her, do you?"

That was precisely what Deirdre did think, and it gave her a nasty shock to know that his words had been passed on. She had only just begun to realize that in a town like ours, every remark starts a long and successful career as a public event.

"She needn't be so cocksure," she grumbled with her mouth full. "He's a better man than she's likely to get, even with her fifteen thousand."

"Is it fifteen thousand she have?" Joan asked in an awe-stricken whisper, and Deirdre realized that she'd done it again. To live in a town like ours you have to enunciate every word with an eye to its ultimate effect, which is probably why so many people find it easier to leave the town.

"If she had fifty Tommy Dodd would be too good for her," she said crossly.

"Too good for her?" gasped Joan. "And he with a fancy-woman in Dublin?"

"But she knows nothing about that," said Deirdre, now thoroughly alarmed.

"Doesn't she, indeed?" Joan said pityingly. "'Tisn't because I wouldn't know it that others wouldn't. Let me tell you, Deirdre," she went on, wagging a warning finger, "between the Post Office and the bobbies, there's very little that isn't known in this town. How well I could meet a woman this morning that could tell me where Celia Johnson's baby is after being put out to nurse, and I'll engage Celia Johnson thinks that no one knows she had a baby at all. He'd better mind himself. There's plenty of influential people were put out of business for less."

Deirdre finished her dinner in complete depression. Tommy was certainly going to be ruined, and it would be all her fault. She could never realize that others wouldn't look at things as she did; and that what for her had been the one interesting thing about Tommy, the one spot of brilliant color in the gray bogland of his life, might be murder to others. Worse than murder, in fact, because there was at least one notorious murderer on the town council, and people fell over themselves trying to conciliate him. But love, of course, was different. There was no money in love. And the worse of it was that any time now Tommy might find out from the doctor how she had betrayed what he probably regarded as his most intimate confidences. The only thing she could think of, in her desperation, was to try and keep him away from the doctor.

That evening, when he came into the parlor, she encouraged him to talk in his usual way about the townspeople. Poor man, he didn't know the sort of things the townspeople were saying about him now!

"You didn't propose to the doctor yet, Tommy?" she asked, taking the bull by the horns.

"The who?" Tommy asked with a start.

"The doctor."

"No," Tommy said without undue depression. "I'm in no great hurry."

"Sure, of course you're not," Deirdre agreed with a real relief. "You'd want to think a lot before you did a thing like that?"

"Why did you ask?" he inquired.

"I was only wondering was she the right sort for you."

"Is that so?" he asked. "Now, what makes you think she isn't, Deirdre?"

"I suppose it's just that I'm getting to know you better," said Deirdre. "Sometimes, you get very false impressions of people. It just struck me that you'd probably want someone more domesticated."

"You might be right," he conceded, and in the same breath: "Do you like chocolates?"

She could hardly believe in her own good fortune. It would be a real achievement to get the knife out of the child's hands before he did himself any damage.

"Love them," she said with a smile.

"I have some in my room," said Tommy, and went out with great strides and took the stairs three at a time. When he returned he handed her the box of chocolates as though it were a gun.

"Go on with what you were saying," he said.

"I don't know should I," she said thoughtfully, struggling with the box, though in fact nothing but an earthquake would have stopped her. "But, you know, Tommy, I have a sort of feeling that you're not half as calculating as you think."

"Who said I thought anything of the kind?" Tommy retorted indignantly.

"You do, Tommy," she said flatly. "You think you're the smartest crook in this town, and you're not. You have a much finer nature than you realize. If you married a woman like that, you'd want to cut your throat inside six months."

"I'd be more likely to cut hers," said Tommy with a chuckle.

"You wouldn't, Tommy," Deirdre said gravely. "You see, in your heart and soul, you're really an idealist. You can't help it. You ought to have married that girl in Dublin—Elsie What's-her-name."

"Begor, I ought not," said Tommy with grave enjoyment.

"You ought, Tommy," said Deirdre with finality. "Whatever you may think now, the girl had courage. You don't want to admit it, because you know you treated her badly."

"Oh, indeed, I did nothing of the sort," Tommy said with conviction.

"Ah, Tommy," Deirdre cried impatiently, "why do you be always denying the better part of your nature? You know yourself you treated her badly, whatever disagreement you may have had with her. You don't want to do the decent, manly thing even when you know you ought to. That girl might have had a child."

"There was no danger."

"There's always danger. Anyway, you ought to meet her again; even to talk to her. I think you'd find you looked at the whole thing differently now. I can't help feeling, Tommy, that Elsie was the only real thing in your whole life; that all the rest of it, your life here, and your plotting and planning with the Ku Klux Klan, doesn't mean any more to you than dreaming. Do you understand me, Tommy? She was the *only* real thing."

"Begor, I hope not," he said with a laugh, striking his knee.

"Why not?"

"Because there's no such woman," he said with a guffaw.

"But you told me yourself, Tommy."

"Ah, surely you can understand a joke?"

"That's a queer sort of joke," grumbled Deirdre, so shaken by this fresh revelation that she couldn't even be certain of her own original impression of his sincerity.

"What's queer about it? 'Twould be damn queer if there was any truth in it, if I went round doing that sort of thing, making an idiot of myself. 'Tis all very well in storybooks, Deirdre, but it won't do, girl, it won't do."

" 'Twould be no joke for you if someone went and repeated it," Deirdre said shortly, still incensed at the suggestion that she had mistaken a joke for a confession.

"No one would believe them, girl," said Tommy, but his face lost some of its glow.

"I wouldn't be too sure of that," Deirdre said stiffly. "Plenty of influential people were put out of business for less."

She hardly knew that she was quoting Joan, but Tommy recognized his master's voice. He might know little about love-making but he knew a lot about small towns and their inhabitants.

"Anyway, I didn't say it to anyone only you," he said humbly. "Will you marry me, Deirdre?"

"Ah, will I what?" she snapped at this fresh shock.

"Marry me? You know I never gave a damn for another girl only you. I'm telling you no lies. Ask anyone you like."

"But didn't you tell me yourself in this very room only a couple of weeks ago that 'twas the doctor you wanted to marry?" she cried angrily.

"Ah, for God's sake!" exclaimed Tommy. "You don't mean you took that seriously too. I couldn't be bothered with the old doctor. She hasn't a brain in her head. You were the only one I ever met that I respected enough to ask."

"But, Tommy," she cried almost in tears, "you said you wanted to marry her for the fifteen thousand."

Tommy looked at her in real surprise and consternation.

"And you took that seriously?" he exclaimed. "Do you know, Deirdre, I'm surprised at you. I declare to God I thought better of you. I'd have thought a woman of your discernment would know that I wasn't the sort to marry for money. If I wanted to do that I could have done it years ago. Anyway, she hasn't fifteen thousand."

"Tommy," Deirdre said desperately, "you don't mean that was all lies too."

"I don't know why you call it lies," Tommy said indignantly. "We have to say something. It seems to me there are a lot of misunderstandings. Anyway, will you marry me now?"

"I will not," snapped Deirdre ungraciously.

"Why not?" he shouted with real anger.

"Because you're too young."

"Too young? I'm fifteen years older than you."

"You're old enough to have sense," she retorted, picking up her handbag and strutting to the door. She felt hopelessly undignified. "Oh, God, for the age of the sagas!" she thought, and reaching the door, she broke down. "Ah, Tommy, what did you want to spoil it all for?" she wailed. "A fortnight ago I'd have jumped at you, but how the blazes could I marry you now? It's too ridiculous. Too ridiculous!"

Darcy in the
Land of Youth

ONE OF the few things Mick Darcy remembered of what the monks in the North Monastery had taught him was the story of Oisin, an old chap who fell in love with a fairy queen called Niamh and went to live with her in the Land of Youth. Then, one day when he was a bit homesick, he got leave from her to come back and have a look at Ireland, only she warned him he wasn't to get off his horse. When he got back, he found his pals all dead and the whole country under the rule of St. Patrick, and, seeing a poor laborer trying to lift a heavy stone that was too big for him but that would have been nothing at all to fellows of his own generation, Oisin bent down to give him a hand. While he was doing it, the saddle-girth broke and Oisin was thrown to the ground, an old, tired, spiritless man with nothing better to do than get converted and be thinking of how much better things used to be in his day. Mick had never thought much of it as a story. It had always struck him that Oisin was a bit of a mug, not to know when he was well off.

But the old legends all have powerful morals though you never realize it till one of them gives you a wallop over the head. During the war, when he was out of a job, Mick went to England as a clerk in a war factory, and the first few weeks he spent there were the most miserable of his life. He found the English as queer as they were always supposed to be; people with a great welcome for themselves and very little for anyone else.

Then there were the air-raids, which the English pretended not to notice. In the middle of the night Mick would be awakened by the wail of a siren, and the thump of faraway guns like all the windowpanes of Heaven rattling: the thud of artillery, getting louder, accompanied a faint buzz like a cat's purring that seemed to rise out of a corner of the room and mount the walls to the ceiling, where it hung, breathing in steady spurts, exactly like a cat. Pretending not to notice things like that struck Mick as too much of a good thing. He would rise and dress himself and sit lonesome by the gas fire, wondering what on earth had induced him to leave his little home in Cork, his girl, Ina, and his pal, Chris—his world.

The daytime was no better. The works were a couple of miles outside the town, and he shared an office with a woman called Penrose and a Jew called Isaacs. Penrose called him "Mr. Darcy," and when he asked her to call him "Mick" she wouldn't. The men all called him "Darcy," which sounded like an insult. Isaacs was the only one who called him "Mick," but it soon became plain that he only wanted to convert Mick from being what he called "a fellow traveller," whatever the hell that was.

"I'm after travelling too much," Mick said bitterly.

He wasn't a discontented man, but he could not like England or the English. On his afternoons off, he took long, lonesome country walks, but there was no proper country either, only red-brick farms and cottages with crumpled oak frames and high red-tiled roofs; big, smooth, sick-looking fields divided by low, neat hedges which made them look as though they all called one another by their surnames; handsome-looking pubs that were never open when you wanted them, with painted signs and nonsensical names like "The Star and Garter" or "The Shoulder of Mutton." Then he would go back to his lodgings and write long, cynical, mournful letters home to Chris and Ina, and all at once he and Chris would be strolling down the hill to Cork city in the evening light, and every old house and bush stood out in his imagination as if spotlit, and everyone who passed hailed them and called him Mick. It was so vivid that when his old landlady came in to draw the black-out, his heart would suddenly turn over.

But one day in the office he got chatting with a girl called Janet who had something to do with personnel. She was a tall, thin, fair-haired girl with a quick-witted laughing air. She listened to him with her head forward and her eyebrows raised. There was nothing in the least alarming about Janet, and she didn't seem to want to convert him to anything, unless it was books, which she seemed to be very well up in, so he asked her politely to have supper with him, and she agreed eagerly and even called him Mick without being asked. She seemed to know as if by instinct that this was what he wanted.

It was a great ease to him; he now had someone to argue with, and he was no longer scared of the country or the people. Besides, he had begun to master his job, and that always gave him a feeling of self-confidence. He had a quiet conviction of his own importance and hated servility of any sort. One day a group of them, including Janet, had broken off work for a chat when the boss's brisk step was heard, and they all scattered—even Janet hastily said: "Good-bye." But Mick just gazed out the window, his hands still in his pockets, and when the boss came in, brisk and lantern-jawed, Mick looked at him over his shoulder and gave him a greeting. The boss only grinned. "Settling in, Darcy?" he asked. "Just getting the hang of things," Darcy replied modestly. Next day the boss sent for him, but it was only to ask his advice about a scheme of office organization. Mick gave his opinions in a forthright way. That was another of his little weaknesses; he liked to hear himself talk. Judging by the way the boss questioned him, he had no great objection.

But country and people still continued to give him shocks. One evening, for instance, he had supper in the flat which Janet shared with a girl called Fanny, who was an analyst in one of the factories. Fanny was a good-looking, dark-haired girl with a tendency to moodiness. She asked how Mick was getting on with Mrs. Penrose.

"Oh," Mick said with a laugh, sitting back with his hands in his trouser pockets, "she still calls me Mister Darcy."

"I suppose that's only because she expects to be calling you something else before long," said Fanny.

"Oh, no, Fanny," said Janet. "You wouldn't know Penrose now. She's a changed woman. With her husband in Egypt, Peter posted to Yorkshire, and no one to play with but George, she's started to complain of people who can't appreciate the simple things of life. Any day now she'll start talking about primroses."

"Penrose?" Mick exclaimed with gentle incredulity, throwing himself back farther in his chair. "I never thought she was that sort. Are you sure, Janet? I'd have thought she was an iceberg."

"An iceberg?" Janet said gleefully, rubbing her hands. "Oh, boy! A blooming fireship!"

"You're not serious?" murmured Mick, looking doubtfully at the two girls and wondering what fresh abyss might remain beneath the smooth surface of English convention.

Going home that night through the pitch-dark streets, he no longer felt a complete stranger. He had made friends with two of the nicest girls a man could wish for—fine broad-minded girls you could talk to as you'd talk to a man. He had to step in the roadway to make room for a couple of other girls, flicking their torches on and off before them; schoolgirls, to judge by their voices. "Of course, he's married," one of them said as they passed, and then went off into a rippling scale of laughter that sounded almost unearthly in the sinister silence and darkness.

A bit too broad-minded, thought Mick, coming to himself. Freedom was all very well, but you could easily have too much of that too.

BUT the shock about Penrose was nothing to the shocks that came on top of it. In the spring evenings Janet and he cycled off into the near-by villages and towns for their drinks. Sometimes Fanny came too, but she didn't seem very keen on it. It was as though she felt herself in the way, but at the same time she saw them go off with such a reproachful air that she made Janet feel bad.

One Sunday evening they went to church together. It seemed to surprise Janet that Mick insisted on going to Mass every Sunday morning, and she wanted him to see what a Protestant service was like. Her own religion was a bit mixed. Her father had been a Baptist lay preacher; her mother a Methodist; but Janet herself had fallen in love with a parson at the age of eleven and become Church for a while till she joined the Socialist Party and decided that Church was too conservative. Most of the time she did not seem to Mick to have any religion at all, for she said that you were just buried and rotted and that was all anyone knew. That seemed the general view. There were any amount of religions, but nobody seemed to believe anything.

It was against Mick's principles, but Janet was so eager that he went. It was in a little town ten miles from where they lived, with a brown Italian fountain in the market-place and the old houses edging out the gray church with its balustraded parapet and its blue clock-face shining in the sun. Inside there was a young sailor playing the organ while another turned over for him. The parson rang the bell himself. Only three women, one of whom was the organist, turned up.

The service, to Mick's mind, was an awful sell. The parson turned his back on them and read prayers at the east window; the organist played a hymn, which the three people in church took up, and then the parson read more prayers. There was no religion in it that Mick could see, but Janet joined in the hymns and seemed to get all worked up.

"Pity about Fanny," she said when they were drinking their beer in the inn yard later. "We could be very comfortable in the flat only for her. Haven't you a friend who'd take her off our hands?"

"Only in Ireland," said Mick.

"Perhaps he'd come," said Janet. "Tell him you've a nice girl for him. She really is nice, Mick."

"Oh, I know," said Mick in surprise. "But hasn't she a fellow already?"

"Getting a fellow for Fanny is the great problem of my life," Janet said ruefully. "I'll never be afraid of a jealous husband after her. The sight of her johns with the seat up is enough to depress her for a week."

"I wonder if she'd have him," Mick said thoughtfully, thinking how very nice it would be to have a friend as well as a girl. Janet was excellent company, and a good woman to learn from, but there were times when Mick would have been glad of someone from home with whom he could sit in judgment on the country of his exile.

"If he's anything like you, she'd jump at him," said Janet.

"Oh, there's no resemblance," chuckled Mick, who had never before been buttered up like this and loved it. "Chris is a holy terror."

"A terror is about what Fanny needs," Janet said grimly.

It was only as the weeks went on that he realized that she wasn't exaggerating. Fanny always received him politely, but he had the feeling that one of these days she wouldn't receive him at all. She didn't intend to be rude, but she watched his plate as Janet filled it, and he saw she begrudged him even the food he ate. Janet did her best to shake her out of it by bringing her with them.

"Oh, come on, Fanny!" she said one evening with a weary air. "I only want to show Mick the Plough in Alton."

"Well, who'd know it better?" Fanny asked sepulchrally.

"There's no need to be difficult," Janet replied with a flash of temper.

"Well, it's not my fault if I'm inhibited, is it?" Fanny asked with a cowed air.

"I didn't say you were inhibited," Janet replied in a ringing tone. "I said you were difficult."

"Same thing from your point of view, isn't it?" Fanny asked. "Oh, I suppose I was born that way. You'd better let me alone."

All the way out, Janet was silent and Mick saw she was in a flaming temper, though he failed to understand what it was all about. It was distressing about Fanny, no doubt, but things were pleasanter without her. The evening was fine and the sun in wreath and veil, with the fields a bright blue-green. The narrow road wound between bulging walls of flint, laced with brick, and rows of old cottages with flower-beds in front that leaned this way and that as if they were taking life easy. It wasn't like Ireland, but still it wasn't bad. He was getting used to it as he was to being called Darcy. At the same time the people sometimes left him as mystified as ever. He didn't know what Fanny meant about being inhibited, or why she seemed to think it wrong. She spoke of it as if it was some sort of infectious disease.

"We'll have to get Chris for Fanny all right," he said. "It's extraordinary, though. An exceptional girl like that, you'd think she'd have fellows falling over her."

"I don't think Fanny will ever get a man," Janet replied in the shrill, scolding voice she used when upset. "I've thrown dozens of them in her way, but she won't even make an effort. I believe she's one of those quite attractive women who go through life without ever knowing what it's about. She's just a raging mass of inhibitions."

There it was again—prohibitions, exhibitions, inhibitions! He wished to God Janet would use simple words. He knew what exhibitions were from one old man in the factory who went to jail because of them. You would assume that inhibitions meant the opposite, but if so, what were the girls grousing about?

"Couldn't we do something about them?" he asked helpfully, not wishing to display his ignorance.

"Yes, darling," she replied with a mocking air. "You can take her away to Hell and give her a good roll in the hay."

Mick was so staggered that he didn't reply. Even then it took a long time for Janet's words to sink in. By this time he was used to English dirty jokes, but he knew that this was something different. No doubt Janet was joking about the roll in the hay—though he wasn't altogether sure that she was joking about that either and didn't half hope that he might take her at her word—but she was not joking about Fanny. She really meant that all that was wrong with Fanny was that she was still a virgin, and that this was a complaint she did not suffer from herself.

The smugness horrified him as much as the savagery with which it was uttered. Put in a certain way, it might be understandable, and even forgivable. Girls of Janet's kind were known at home as "damaged goods," but he had never permitted the expression to pass. He had a strong sense of justice and always tended to take the side of the underdog. Some girls had not the same strength of character as others; some were subjected to greater temptation than others; he had never met any, but he was quite sure that if he had he would have risen to the occasion. But to have a girl like that stand up and treat her own weakness as strength and another girl's strength as weakness was altogether too much for him to take. It was like asking him to stand on his head.

Having got rid of her spite, Janet began to brighten. "This is wonderful," she sighed with tranquil pleasure as they floated downhill towards Alton and the Plough, a pleasant little inn, standing at the bridge, half-timbered above and stone below, with a big yard to one side where a dozen cars were parked, and at the other a long garden with rustic seats overlooking the river. Mick didn't feel it was so very wonderful. He felt as lonely as he had done in his first weeks there. While Janet sat outside, he went to the bar for beer and stood there for a few minutes unnoticed. There was a little crowd at the bar; a bald fat man in an overcoat, with a pipe, a good-looking young man with a fancy waistcoat, and a local with a face like a turnip. The landlord, a man of about fifty, had a long, haggard face with horn-rimmed glasses, and his wife, apparently twenty years younger, was a good-looking young woman with bangs and a Lancashire accent. They were discussing a death in the village.

"I'm not against religion," the local spluttered excitedly. "I'm chapel myself, but I never tried to force me views on people. All them months poor Harry was paralyzed, his wife and daughter never so much as wet his lips. That idn't right, is it? That idn't religion?"

"No, Bill," the landlord said, shaking his head. "Going too far, I call that."

"Everyone is entitled to his views, but them weren't old Harry's views, were they?"

"No, Bill," sighed the landlord's wife, "they weren't."

"I'm for freedom," Bill said, tapping his chest. "The night before he died, I come in here and got a quart of old and mild, didn't I, Joe?"

"Mild, wadn't it, Bill?" the publican asked anxiously, resetting his glasses.

"No, Joe, old and mild was always Harry's drink."

"That's right, Joe," the landlady expostulated. "Don't you remember?"

"Funny," said her husband. "I could have swore it was mild."

"And I said to Millie and Sue, 'All right,' I said. 'You got other things to do. I'll sit up with old Harry.' Then I took out the bottle. His poor eyes lit up. Couldn't move, couldn't speak, but I shall never forget the way he looked at that bottle. I had to hold his mouth open"—Bill threw back his head and pulled one side of his mouth awry in illustration—"and let it trickle down. No. If that's religion give me beer!"

"Wonder where old Harry is now?" the fat man said, removing his pipe reverently. "It's a mystery, Joe, i'nt it?"

"Shocking," the landlord said, shaking his head.

"We don't know, do we, Charles?" the landlady said sadly.

"Nobody knows," Bill bawled scornfully as he took up his pint again. "How could they? Parson pretends to know, but he don't know any more than you and me. Shove you in the ground and let the worms get you—that's all anybody knows."

It depressed Mick even more, for he felt that in some way Janet's views and those of the people in the pub were of the same kind and only the same sort of conduct could be expected from them. Neither had any proper religion and so they could not know right from wrong.

"Isn't it lovely here?" Janet sang out when he brought the drinks.

"Oh, grand," said Mick without much enthusiasm.

"We must come and spend a few days here some time. It's wonderful in the early morning. . . . You don't think I was too bitchy about Fanny, do you, Mick?"

"Oh, it's not that," he said, seeing that she had noticed his depression. "I wasn't thinking of Fanny particularly. It's the whole set-up here that seems so queer to me."

"Does it?" she asked with interest.

"Well, naturally—fellows and girls from the works going off on weekends together, as if they were going to a dance."

He looked at her with mild concern as though he hoped she might enlighten him about a matter of general interest. But she didn't respond.

"Having seen the works, can you wonder?" she asked, and took a long drink of her beer.

"But when they get tired of one another, they go off with someone else," he protested. "Or back to the fellow they started with. Like Hilda in the packing shed. She's knocking round with Dorman, and when her husband comes back she'll drop him. At least, she says she will."

"Isn't that how it usually ends?" she asked politely, raising her brows and speaking in a superior tone that left him with nothing to say. This time she really succeeded in scandalizing him.

"Oh, come, come, Janet!" he said scornfully. "You can't take that line with me. You're not going to pretend there's nothing more than that in it?"

"Well, I suppose, like everything else, it's just what you make of it," she replied with a sophisticated shrug.

"But that's not making anything at all of it," he said, beginning to grow heated. "If it's no more than a roll in the hay, as you call it, there's nothing in it for anybody."

"And what do you think it should be?" she asked with a politeness that seemed to be the equivalent of his heat. He realized that he was not keeping to the level of a general discussion. He could distinctly hear how common his accent had become, but excitement and a deep-seated feeling of injury carried him away.

"But look here, Janet," he protested, sitting back stubbornly with his hands in his trouser pockets, "learning to live with somebody isn't a thing you can pick up in a weekend. It's a blooming job for life. You wouldn't take up a job somewhere in the middle, expecting to like it, and intending to drop it in a few months' time if you didn't, would you?"

"Oh, Mick," she groaned in mock distress, "don't tell me you have inhibitions too!"

"Oh, you can call them what you like," retorted Mick, growing commoner as he was dragged down from the heights of abstract discussion to the expression of his own wounded feelings. "I saw the fellows who have no inhibitions, as you call them, and they didn't seem to me to have very much else either. If that's all you want from a man, you won't have far to go."

By this time Janet had realized that she was dealing with feelings rather than with general ideas and was puzzled. After a moment's thought she began to seek for a point of reconciliation.

"But after all, Mick, you've had affairs yourself, haven't you?" she asked reasonably.

Now, of all questions, this was the one Mick dreaded most, because, owing to a lack of suitable opportunities, for which he was in no way to blame, he had not. For the matter of that, so far as he knew, nobody of his acquaintance had either. He knew that in the matter of experience, at least, Janet was his superior, and, coming from a country where men's superiority—affairs or no affairs—was unchallenged, he hesitated to admit that, so far as experience went, Fanny and he were in the one boat. He was not untruthful, and he had plenty of moral courage. There was no difficulty in imagining himself settling deeper down onto his bench and saying firmly and quietly: "No, Janet, I have not," but he did not say it.

"Well, naturally, I'm not an angel," he said in as modest a tone as he could command and with a shrug intended to suggest that it meant nothing in particular to him.

"Of course not, Mick," Janet replied with all the enthusiasm of a liberal mind discovering common ground with an opponent. "But then there's no argument."

"No argument, maybe," he said coldly, "but there are distinctions to be made."

"What distinctions?"

"Between playing the fool and making love," he replied with a weary air as though he could barely be bothered explaining such matters to a girl as inexperienced as she. From imaginary distinctions he went on to out-and-out prevarication. "If I went out with Penrose, for instance, that would be one thing. Going out with you is something entirely different."

"But why?" she asked as though this struck her as a doubtful compliment.

"Well, I don't like Penrose," he said mildly, hoping that he sounded more convincing than he felt. "I'm not even vaguely interested in Penrose. I am interested in you. See the difference?"

"Not altogether," Janet replied in her clear, unsentimental way. "You don't mean that if two people are in love with one another, they should have affairs with somebody else, do you?"

"Of course I don't," snorted Mick, disgusted by this horrid example of English literal-mindedness. "I don't see what they want having affairs at all for."

"Oh, so that's what it is!" she said with a nod.

"That's what it is," Mick said feebly, realizing the cat was out of the bag at last. "Love is a serious business. It's a matter of responsibilities. If I make a friend, I don't begin by thinking what use I can make of him. If I meet a girl I like, I'm not going to begin calculating how cheap I can get her. I don't want anything cheap," he added with passion. "I'm not going to rush into anything till I know the girl well enough to try and make a decent job of it. Is that plain?"

"Remarkably plain," Janet replied icily. "You mean you're not that sort of man. Let me buy you a drink."

"No, thanks."

"Then I think we'd better be getting back," she said, rising and looking like the wrath of God.

Mick, crushed and humiliated, followed her at a slouch, his hands still in his trouser pockets. It wasn't good enough. At home a girl would have gone on with the argument till one of them fell unconscious, and in argument Mick had real staying power, so he felt she was taking an unfair advantage. Of course, he saw that she had some reason. However you looked at it, she had more or less told him that she expected him to be her lover, and he had more or less told her to go to hell, and he had a suspicion that this was an entirely new experience for Janet. She might well feel mortified.

But the worst of it was that, thinking it over, he realized that even then he had not been quite honest. He had not told her he already had a girl at home. He believed all he had said, but he did not believe it quite so strongly as all that; not so as not to make exceptions. Given time, he might quite easily have made an exception of Janet. She was the sort of girl people made an exception of. It was the shock that had made him express himself so violently; the shock of realizing that a girl he cared for had lived with other men. He had reacted that way almost in protest against them.

But the real shock had been the discovery that he minded so much what she was.

THEY never resumed the discussion openly, on the same terms, and it seemed as though Janet had forgiven him, but only just. The argument was always there beneath the surface, ready to break out again. It flared up whenever she mentioned Fanny—"I suppose one day she'll meet an Irishman, and they can discuss one another's inhibitions." Or when she mentioned other men she had known, like Bill, with whom she had spent a holiday in Dorset, or an American called Tom with whom she had gone to the Plough in Alton, she seemed to be contrasting the joyous past with the dreary present, and she became cold and insolent.

Mick gave as good as he got. He had a dirty tongue, and he had considerable more ammunition than she. The canteen was always full of gossip about who was living with whom, or who had stopped living with whom, or whose wife or husband had returned and found him or her living with someone else, and he passed it on with a quizzical air. The first time she said "Good!" in a ringing voice. After that, she contented herself with a shrug, and Mick suggested ingenuously that perhaps it took all those religions to deal with so much fornication. "One religion would be more than enough for Ireland," she retorted, and Mick grinned and admitted himself beaten.

But, all the same, he could not help feeling that it wasn't nice. He remembered what Fanny had said about nobody's knowing the Plough better, and Janet about how nice it was in the early morning. Really, really, it wasn't nice! It seemed to show a complete lack of sensibility in her to think of bringing him to a place where she had stayed with somebody else, and made him suspicious of every other place she brought him. He had never been able to share her enthusiasm for old villages of red-brick cottages, all colored like geraniums, grouped about a gray church tower, but he lost even the desire to share it when he found himself wondering what connection it had with Bill or Tom.

At the same time, he could not do without her. They met every evening after work, went off together on Saturday afternoons, and she even came to Mass with him on Sunday mornings. Nor was there any feeling that she was critical of it. She followed the service with great devotion. As a result, before he returned home on his first leave, everything seemed to have changed between them. She no longer criticized Fanny's virginity and ceased altogether to refer to Bill and Tom. Indeed, from her conversation it would have been hard to detect that she had ever known such men, much less been intimate with them. Mick wondered whether it wasn't possible for a woman to be immoral and yet remain innocent at heart and decided regretfully that it wasn't likely. But no wife or sweetheart could have shown more devotion than she in the last week before his return, and when they went to the station and walked arm-in-arm to the end of the long, drafty platform to say good-bye, she was stiff with unspoken misery. She seemed to feel it was her duty to show no sign of emotion.

"You will come back, Mick, won't you?" she asked in a clear voice.

"Why?" Mick asked banteringly. "Do you think you can keep off Americans for a fortnight?"

That she spat out a word that showed only too clearly her intimacy with Americans and others. It startled Mick. The English had strong ideas about when you could joke and when you couldn't, and she seemed to think this was no time for joking. To his surprise, he found she was trembling all over.

At any other time he would have argued with her, but already in spirit he was half-way home. There, beyond the end of the line, was Cork, and with it home and meat and butter and nights of tranquil sleep. When he leaned out of the window to wave good-bye, she was standing like a statue, looking curiously desolate. Her image faded quickly, for the train was crowded with Irish servicemen and women, clerks and laborers, who gradually sorted themselves out into north and south, country and town, and within five minutes, Mick, in a fug of steam heat and tobacco smoke, was playing cards with a group of men from the South Side who were calling him by his Christian name. Janet was already farther away than any train could leave her.

It was the following evening when he reached home. He had told no one of his coming and arrived in an atmosphere of sensation. He went upstairs to his own little whitewashed room with the picture of the Sacred Heart over his bed and lost himself in the study of his shelf of books. Then he shaved and, without waiting for more than a cup of tea, set off down the road to Ina's. Ina was the youngest of a large family, and his arrival there created a sensation too. Elsie, the eldest, a fat, jolly girl, just home from work, shouted with laughter at him.

"He smelt the sausages."

"You can keep your old sausages," Mick said scornfully. "I'm taking Ina out to supper."

"You're what?" shouted Elsie. "You have high notions like the goats in Kerry."

"But I have to make my little brothers' supper, honey," Ina said laughingly as she smoothed his hair. She was a slight, dark, radiant girl with a fund of energy.

"Tell them make it themselves," Mick said scornfully.

"Tell them, you!" cried Elsie. "Someone ought to have told them years ago, the caubogues! They're thirty, and they have no more intention of marrying than flying. Have you e'er an old job for us over there? I'm damned for the want of a man."

Ina rushed upstairs to change. Her two brothers came in, expressed astonishment at Mick's appearance, satisfaction at his promotion, incredulity at his view that the English weren't beaten, and began hammering together on the table with their knives and forks.

"Supper up! Supper up!" shouted the elder, casting his eyes on the ceiling. "We can't wait all night. Where the hell is Ina?"

"Coming out to dinner with me," replied Mick with a sniff, feeling that for the first time in his life he was uttering a curtain line.

They called for Chris, an undersized lad with a pale face like a fist and a voice like melted butter. He expressed pleasure at seeing them, but gave no other signs of it. It was part of Chris's line never to be impressed by anything. In a drawling voice he commented on priests, women, and politicians, and there was little left of any of them when he had done. He had always regarded Mick as a bit of a softy because of his fondness for Ina. For himself, he would never keep a girl for more than a month because it gave them ideas.

"What do you want going to town for supper for?" he drawled incredulously, as though this were only another indication that Mick was a bit soft in the head. "Can't ye have it at home?"

"You didn't change much anyway," said Mick with a snort of delight. "Hurry up!"

He insisted on their walking so as not to miss the view of the city he had been dreaming of for months; the shadowy perspective of winding road between flowering trees, and the spires, river, and bridges far below in evening light. His heart was overflowing. Several times they were stopped by neighbors who wanted to know how things were in the outside world. Because of the censorship, their ideas were very vague.

"Oh, all right," Mick replied modestly.

"Ye're having it bad."

"A bit noisy at times, but you get used to it," he said lightly.

"I dare say, I dare say."

There was pity rather than belief in their voices, but Mick didn't mind. It was good to be back where people cared whether you were having it bad or not. But in his heart Mick felt you didn't get used to it, that you never could, and that all of it, even Janet, was slightly unreal. He had a suspicion that he would not return. He had had enough of it.

Next morning, while he was lying in bed in his little attic, he received a letter from Janet. It must have been written while he was still on the train. She said that trying to face things without him was like trying to get used to an amputated limb; she kept on making movements before realizing that it wasn't there. He dropped the letter at that point without trying to finish it. He couldn't help feeling that it sounded unreal too.

Mick revisited all his old haunts. "You should see Fair Hill," his father said with enthusiasm. " 'Tis unknown the size that place is growing." He went to Fair Hill, to the Lough, to Glanmire, seeing them with new eyes and wishing he had someone like Janet to show them off to. But he began to realize that without a job, without money, it would not be very easy to stay on. His parents encouraged him to stay, but he felt he must spend another six months abroad and earn a little more money. Instead, he started to coax Chris into coming back with him. He knew now that his position in the factory would ensure a welcome for anyone he brought in. Besides, he grew tired of Ina's brothers telling him how the Germans would win the war, and one evening was surprised to hear himself reply in Chris's cynical drawl: "They will and what else?" Ina's brothers were surprised as well. They hadn't expected Mick to turn his coat in that way.

"You get the feeling that people here never talk of anything only religion and politics," he said one evening to Chris as they went for their walk up the Western Road.

"Ah, how bad it is!" Chris said mockingly. "Damn glad you were to get back to it. You can get a night's sleep here anyway."

"You can," Mick said in the same tone. "There's no one to stop you."

Chris looked at him in surprise, uncertain whether or not Mick meant what he seemed to mean. Mick was developing out of his knowledge entirely.

"Go on!" he said with a cautious grin. "Are they as good-natured as that?"

"Better come and see," Mick said sedately. "I have the very girl for you."

"You don't say so!" Chris exclaimed with the smile of a child who has ceased to believe in Santa Claus but likes to hear about it just the same.

"Fine-looking girl with a good job and a flat of her own," Mick went on with a smile. "What more do you want?"

Chris suddenly beamed.

"I wouldn't let Ina hear me talking like that if I was you," he said. "Some of them quiet-looking girls are a terrible hand with a hatchet."

At that moment it struck Mick with cruel force how little Ina had to reproach him with. They were passing the college, and pairs of clerks and servant girls were strolling by, whistling and calling to one another. There was hardly another man in Ireland who would have behaved as he had done. He remembered Janet at the station with her desolate air, and her letter, which he had not answered. Perhaps, after all, she meant it. Suddenly everything seemed to turn upside down in him. He was back in the bar in Alton, listening to the little crowd discussing the dead customer, and carrying out the drinks to Janet on the rustic seat. It was no longer this that seemed unreal, but the Western Road and the clerks and the servant girls. They were like a dream from which he had wakened so suddenly that he had not even realized that he was awake. And he had waked up beside a girl like Janet and had not even realized that she was real.

He was so filled with consternation that he almost told Chris about her. But he knew that Chris would no more understand him than he had understood himself. Chris would talk sagaciously about "damaged goods" as if there were only one way in which a woman could be damaged. He knew that no one would understand, for already he was thinking in a different language. Suddenly he remembered the story of Oisin that the monks had told him, and it began to have meaning for him. He wondered wildly if he would ever get back or if, like Oisin in the story, he would suddenly collapse and spend the rest of his days walking up and down the Western Road with people as old and feeble as himself, and never see Niamh or the Land of Youth. You never knew what powerful morals the old legends had till they came home to you. On the other hand, their heroes hadn't the advantages of the telephone.

"I have to go back to town, Chris," he said, turning in his tracks. "I've just remembered I have a telephone call to put through."

"Good enough," Chris said knowingly. "I suppose you might as well tell her I'm coming too."

WHEN Chris and himself got in, the alert was still on and the station was in pitch-darkness. Outside, against the clear summer sky, shadowy figures moved with pools of light at their feet, and searchlights flickered like lightning over the battlements of the castle. For Chris, it had all the novelty it had once had for Mick, and he groaned. Mick gripped his arm and steered him confidently.

"This is nothing," he said cheerfully. "Probably only a scouting plane. Wait till they start dropping a few wagons of high explosive and you'll be able to talk."

It was sheer delight to Mick to hear himself speak in that light-hearted way of high explosives. He seemed to have become forceful and cool all at once. It had something to do with Chris's being there, as though it gave occupation to all his protective instincts. But there was something else as well. It was almost as though he were arriving home.

There was no raid, so he brought Chris round to meet the girls, and Chris groaned again at the channel of star-shaped traffic signals that twinkled between the black cliffs of houses whose bases opened mysteriously to reveal pale stencilled signs or caverns of smoky light.

Janet opened the door, gave one hasty, incredulous glance at Chris, and then hurled herself at Mick's neck. Chris opened his eyes with a start—he later admitted to Mick that he had never before seen a doll so quick off the mark. But Mick was beyond caring for appearances. While Chris and Fanny were in the throes of starting a conversation, he followed Janet into the kitchen, where she was recklessly tossing a week's rations into the pan. She was hot and excited and used two dirty words in quick succession, but he didn't mind these either. He leaned against the kitchen wall with his hands in his trouser pockets and smiled at her.

"I'm afraid you'll find I've left my principles behind me this time," he said with amusement.

"Oh, good!" she said—not as enthusiastically as he might have expected, but he put that down to the confusion caused by his unexpected arrival.

"What do you think of Chris?"

"A bit quiet, isn't he?" she asked doubtfully.

"Scared," replied Mick with a sniff of amusement. "He'll soon get over that. Should we go off somewhere for the weekend?"

"Next weekend?" she asked aghast.

"Or the one after. I don't mind."

"You're in a hurry, aren't you?"

"So would you be if you'd spent a fortnight in Cork."

"All of us?"

"The more the merrier. Let's go somewhere really good," he went on enthusiastically. "Take the bikes and make a proper tour of it. I'd like Chris to see a bit of the country."

It certainly made a difference, having Chris there. And a fortnight later the four of them set off on bicycles out of town. It was a perfect day of early summer. Landscape and houses gradually changed; old brick and flint giving place to houses of small yellow tile, tinted with golden moss, and walls of narrow tilelike stone with deep bands of mortar that made them seem as though woven. Out of the woven pull-overs rose gables with coifs of tile, like nuns' heads. It all came over Mick in a rush; the presence of his friend and of his girl and a country that he had learned to understand. While they sat on a bench outside a country public-house, he brought out the beer and smiled with quiet pride.

"Good?" he asked Chris with a slight lift of his brows.

"The beer isn't up to much, if that's what you mean," replied Chris, who still specialized in not being impressed.

In the late evening they reached their destination, having cycled through miles of suburb with gardens in flower, and dismounted in the cobbled yard of an inn where Queen Elizabeth was supposed to have stayed and Shakespeare's company performed; the walls of the nar-row, twisting stairs were dark with old prints, and the windows deep embrasures that overlooked the yard. The dining room had great oak beams and supports. At either end there was an oak dresser full of window-ware, with silver sauceboats hanging from the shelves and brass pitchers on top.

"You'd want to mind your head in this hole," Chris said with an ag-grieved air.

"But this place is four hundred years old, man," protested Mick.

"Begor, in that time you'd think they'd make enough to rebuild it," said Chris.

He was still acting in character, but Mick was just the least bit dis-appointed in him. He hit it off with Fanny, who had been thrown into such a panic that she was prepared to hit it off with anyone, but he seemed to have lost a lot of his dash. Mick wasn't quite sure yet but that he would take fright before Fanny. He would certainly do so if he knew what a blessed innocent she was. Whenever Mick looked at her, her dark, sullen face broke into a wistful smile that made him think of a Christian martyr's first glimpse of the lion. No doubt he would lead her to paradise, but the way was messy and uncomfortable.

After supper Janet showed them the town and finally led them to a very nice old pub which was on no street at all but was approached by a system of alleyways. The little barroom was full, and Janet and he were crowded into the yard, where they sat on a bench in the starlight. Beyond the clutter of old tiled roofs a square battlemented tower rose against the sky. Mick was perfectly happy.

"You're certain Fanny will be all right with Chris?" Janet asked anxiously.

"Oh, certain," replied Mick with a slight feeling of alarm lest his troops had opened negotiations behind his back. "Why? Did she say anything?"

"No," said Janet in a bustle of motherly solicitude, "but she's in a flat spin. I've told her everything, but she's afraid she'll get it mixed up, and if anyone could that girl will. He does understand, doesn't he?"

"Oh, perfectly," said Mick with a confidence he did not feel, but his troops were already sufficiently out of hand. If Janet started to give orders they would undoubtedly cut and run.

When they returned to the hotel and the boys retired to their room, the troops were even more depressed.

"A fellow doesn't know how well off he is," said Chris mournfully.

He said it by way of a joke, but Mick knew it was something more. Chris was even more out of his element than he had been. All his life he had practiced not being impressed by anything, but in this new country there was far too much not to be impressed about.

"Why?" Mick asked from his own bed. "Would you sooner be up the Western Road?"

"Don't talk to me about the Western Road!" groaned Chris. "I think I'll never see it."

He didn't sound in the least dashing, and Mick only hoped he wouldn't break down and beg Fanny to let him off. It would be a sad end to the picture he had built up of Chris as the romantic Irishman.

Then the handle of their door turned softly and Janet tiptoed in in her bathing-wrap, her usual competent self, as though arriving in men's bedrooms at that hour of night was second nature to her. "Ready Chris?" she whispered. Chris was a lad of great principle and Mick couldn't help admiring his manliness. With a face like death on him he went out, and Janet closed the door cautiously behind him. Mick listened to make sure he didn't hide in the toilet. Then Janet switched off the light, drew back the black-out, and, shivering slightly, opened the window on the darkened inn yard. They could hear the Klaxons from the street, while the stuffy room filled with the smells and rustlings of a summer night.

IN THE middle of the night Mick woke up and wondered where he was. When he recollected, it was with a feeling of profound satisfaction. It was as if he had laid down a heavy burden he had been carrying all his life, and in the laying down had realized that the burden was quite unnecessary. For the pleasantest part of it was that there was nothing particular about the whole business and that it left him the same man he had always been.

With a clearness of sight which seemed to be part of it, he realized that all the charm of the old town had only been a put-up job of Janet's because she had been here already with someone else. He should have known it when she took them to the pub. That, too, was her reason for suggesting this pleasant old inn. She had stayed there with someone else. It was probably the American and possibly the same bed. Women had no interest in scenery or architecture unless they had been made love to in them. And, Mick thought with amusement, that showed very good sense on their part. If he ever returned with another woman, he would also bring her here, because he had been happy here. Happiness, that was the secret the English had and the Irish lacked.

It was only then that he realized that what had wakened him was Janet's weeping. She was crying quietly beside him. At first it filled him with alarm. In his innocence he might quite easily have made a mess of it without even knowing. It was monstrous, keeping men in ignorance up to his age. He listened till he could bear it no longer.

"What is it, Jan?" he asked in concern.

"Oh, nothing," she replied, dabbing her nose viciously with her handkerchief. "Go to sleep."

"But how can I and you like that?" he asked plaintively. "Was it anything I did?"

"No, of course not, Mick."

"Because I'm sorry if it was."

"Oh, it's not that, it's not that," she replied, shaking her head miserably. "I'm just a fool, that's all."

The wretchedness of her tone made him forget his own doubts and think of her worries. Being a man of the world was all right, but Mick would always be more at home with other people's troubles. He put his arm about her and she sighed and threw a bare leg over him. It embarrassed him for a moment, but then he remembered that now he was a man of the world.

"Tell me," he whispered gently.

"Oh, it's what you said that night at the Plough," she sobbed.

"The Plough?" he echoed in surprise.

"The Plough at Alton."

Mick found it impossible to remember what he had said at the Plough, but he was used to the peculiar way women remembered things which some man had said and forgotten, and which he would have been glad if they had forgotten too.

"Remind me of it," he said.

"Oh, when you said love was a matter of responsibilities."

"Oh, yes, yes," he said. "I remember now." But he didn't. What he remembered mostly was that she had told him about the other men, and he had argued with her. "But you shouldn't take that too seriously, Jan."

"Oh, what else could I do but take it seriously?" she asked fiercely. "I was mad with you, but I knew you were right. I knew that was the way I'd always felt myself, only I blinded myself. Just as you said; taking up love like a casual job you could drop whenever you pleased. I'm well paid for my own bloody folly."

She began to sob again. Mick found it very difficult to readjust his mind to the new situation. One arm about her and the other supporting his head, he looked out the window and thought about it.

"Oh, of course, that's perfectly true, Janet," he agreed, "but, on the other hand, you can take it to the fair. You have to consider the other side of the question. Take people who're brought up to look at the physical facts of love as inhuman and disgusting. Think of the damage they do to themselves by living like that in superstitions. It would be better for them to believe in fairies or ghosts if they must believe in some sort of nonsense."

"Yes, but if I had a daughter, I'd prefer to bring her up like that than in the way I was brought up, Mick. At least she wouldn't fool with serious things, and that's what I've done. I made fun of Fanny because she didn't sleep around like the rest of us, but if Fanny falls for Chris, the joke will be on me."

Mick was silent again for a while. The conversation was headed in a direction he had not foreseen, and he could not yet see the end of it.

"You don't mean you didn't want to come?" he asked in astonishment.

"Oh, it's not that," she cried, beating her forehead with her fist. "Don't you see that I wanted to prove to myself that I could be a decent girl for you, and that I wasn't just one of the factory janes who'll sleep with anything? I wanted to give you something worth while, and I have nothing to give you."

"Oh, I wouldn't say that," Mick said in embarrassment. He was feeling terribly uncomfortable. Life was like that. At one moment you were on top of the world, and the next you were on the point of tears. At the same time it was hard to sacrifice his new-found freedom from inhibitions, all in a moment, as you might say. Here he had lain, rejoicing at being at last a man of the world, and now he was being asked to sacrifice it all and be an ordinary decent fellow again. That was the worst of dealing with the English, for the Irish, who had to be serious whether they liked it or not, only wanted to be frivolous, while the one thing in the world that the English seemed to demand was the chance of showing themselves serious. But the man of the world was too new a development in Mick to stand up to a crisis.

"Because you don't have to do it unless you like," he added gently. "We could always be married."

That threw her into positive convulsions, because if she agreed to this, she would never have the opportunity of showing him what she was really like, and it took him a long time to persuade her that he had never really thought her anything but a serious-minded girl—at least, for most of the time. Then she gave a deep sigh and fell asleep in the most awkward manner on his chest. Outside, the dawn was painting the old roofs and walls in the stiff artless colors of a child's paint-box. He felt a little lonely. He would have liked to remain a man of the world for just a little longer, to have had just one more such awakening to assure him that he had got rid of his inhibitions, but clearly it was not to be. He fell asleep soon after, and was only wakened by Chris, who seemed to have got over his ordeal well.

Chris was furious when Mick told him, and Mick himself realized that as a man of the world he had been a complete washout. Besides, Chris felt that now Fanny would expect him to marry her as well. She had already given indications of it.

Later, he became more reconciled to the idea, and when last heard of was looking for a house. Which seems to show that marriage comes more natural to us.

My Oedipus Complex

FATHER was in the army all through the war—the first war, I mean—so, up to the age of five, I never saw much of him, and what I saw did not worry me. Sometimes I woke and there was a big figure in khaki peering down at me in the candlelight. Sometimes in the early morning I heard the slamming of the front door and the clatter of nailed boots down the cobbles of the lane. These were Father's entrances and exits. Like Santa Claus he came and went mysteriously.

In fact, I rather liked his visits, though it was an uncomfortable squeeze between Mother and him when I got into the big bed in the early morning. He smoked, which gave him a pleasant musty smell, and shaved, an operation of astounding interest. Each time he left a trail of souvenirs—model tanks and Gurkha knives with handles made of bullet cases, and German helmets and cap badges and button-sticks, and all sorts of military equipment—carefully stowed away in a long box on top of the wardrobe, in case they ever came in handy. There was a bit of the magpie about Father; he expected everything to come in handy. When his back was turned, Mother let me get a chair and rummage through his treasures. She didn't seem to think so highly of them as he did.

The war was the most peaceful period of my life. The window of my attic faced southeast. My mother had curtained it, but that had small effect. I always woke with the first light and, with all the responsibilities of the previous day melted, feeling myself rather like the sun, ready to illumine and rejoice. Life never seemed so simple and clear and full of possibilities as then. I put my feet out from under the clothes—I called them Mrs. Left and Mrs. Right—and invented dramatic situations for them in which they discussed the problems of the day. At least Mrs. Right did; she was very demonstrative, but I hadn't the same control of Mrs. Left, so she mostly contented herself with nodding agreement.

They discussed what Mother and I should do during the day, what Santa Claus should give a fellow for Christmas, and what steps should be taken to brighten the home. There was that little matter of the baby, for instance. Mother and I could never agree about that. Ours was the only house in the terrace without a new baby, and Mother said we couldn't afford one till Father came back from the war because they cost seventeen and six. That showed how simple she was. The Geneys up the road had a baby, and everyone knew they couldn't afford seventeen and six. It was probably a cheap baby, and Mother wanted something really good, but I felt she was too exclusive. The Geneys' baby would have done us fine.

Having settled my plans for the day, I got up, put a chair under the attic window, and lifted the frame high enough to stick out my head. The window overlooked the front gardens of the terrace behind ours, and beyond these it looked over a deep valley to the tall, red-brick houses terraced up the opposite hillside, which were all still in shadow, while those at our side of the valley were all lit up, though with long strange shadows that made them seem unfamiliar; rigid and painted.

After that I went into Mother's room and climbed into the big bed. She woke and I began to tell her of my schemes. By this time, though I never seem to have noticed it, I was petrified in my nightshirt, and I thawed as I talked until, the last frost melted, I fell asleep beside her and woke again only when I heard her below in the kitchen, making the breakfast.

After breakfast we went into town; heard Mass at St. Augustine's and said a prayer for Father, and did the shopping. If the afternoon was fine we either went for a walk in the country or a visit to Mother's great friend in the convent, Mother St. Dominic. Mother had them all praying for Father, and every night, going to bed, I asked God to send him back safe from the war to us. Little, indeed, did I know what I was praying for!

One morning, I got into the big bed, and there, sure enough, was Father in his usual Santa Claus manner, but later, instead of uniform, he put on his best blue suit, and Mother was as pleased as anything. I saw nothing to be pleased about, because, out of uniform, Father was altogether less interesting, but she only beamed, and explained that our prayers had been answered, and off we went to Mass to thank God for having brought Father safely home.

The irony of it! That very day when he came in to dinner he took off his boots and put on his slippers, donned the dirty old cap he wore about the house to save him from colds, crossed his legs, and began to talk gravely to Mother, who looked anxious. Naturally, I disliked her looking anxious, because it destroyed her good looks, so I interrupted him.

"Just a moment, Larry!" she said gently.

This was only what she said when we had boring visitors, so I attached no importance to it and went on talking.

"Do be quiet, Larry!" she said impatiently. "Don't you hear me talking to Daddy?"

This was the first time I had heard those ominous words, "talking to Daddy," and I couldn't help feeling that if this was how God answered prayers, he couldn't listen to them very attentively.

"Why are you talking to Daddy?" I asked with as great a show of indifference as I could muster.

"Because Daddy and I have business to discuss. Now, don't interrupt again!"

In the afternoon, at Mother's request, Father took me for a walk. This time we went into town instead of out the country, and I thought at first, in my usual optimistic way, that it might be an improvement.

It was nothing of the sort. Father and I had quite different notions of a walk in town. He had no proper interest in trams, ships, and horses, and the only thing that seemed to divert him was talking to fellows as old as himself. When I wanted to stop he simply went on, dragging me behind him by the hand; when he wanted to stop I had no alternative but to do the same. I noticed that it seemed to be a sign that he wanted to stop for a long time whenever he leaned against a wall. The second time I saw him do it I got wild. He seemed to be settling himself for- ever. I pulled him by the coat and trousers, but, unlike Mother who, if you were too persistent, got into a wax and said: "Larry, if you don't behave yourself, I'll give you a good slap," Father had an extraordi- nary capacity for amiable inattention. I sized him up and wondered would I cry, but he seemed to be too remote to be annoyed even by that. Really, it was like going for a walk with a mountain! He either ignored the wrenching and pummelling entirely, or else glanced down with a grin of amusement from his peak. I had never met anyone so absorbed in himself as he seemed.

At teatime, "talking to Daddy" began again, complicated this time by the fact that he had an evening paper, and every few minutes he put it down and told Mother something new out of it. I felt this was foul play. Man for man, I was prepared to compete with him any time for Mother's attention, but when he had it all made up for him by other people it left me no chance. Several times I tried to change the subject without success.

"You must be quiet while Daddy is reading, Larry," Mother said impatiently.

It was clear that she either genuinely liked talking to Father better than talking to me, or else that he had some terrible hold on her which made her afraid to admit the truth.

"Mummy," I said that night when she was tucking me up, "do you think if I prayed hard God would send Daddy back to the war?"

She seemed to think about that for a moment.

"No, dear," she said with a smile. "I don't think he would."

"Why wouldn't he, Mummy?"

"Because there isn't a war any longer, dear."

"But, Mummy, couldn't God make another war, if He liked?"

"He wouldn't like to, dear. It's not God who makes wars, but bad people."

"Oh!" I said.

I was disappointed about that. I began to think that God wasn't quite what he was cracked up to be.

Next morning I woke at my usual hour, feeling like a bottle of champagne. I put out my feet and invented a long conversation in which Mrs. Right talked of the trouble she had with her own father till she put him in the Home. I didn't quite know what the Home was but it sounded the right place for Father. Then I got my chair and stuck my head out of the attic window. Dawn was just breaking, with a guilty air that made me feel I had caught it in the act. My head bursting with stories and schemes, I stumbled in next door, and in the half-darkness scrambled into the big bed. There was no room at Mother's side so I had to get between her and Father. For the time being I had forgotten about him, and for several minutes I sat bolt upright, racking my brains to know what I could do with him. He was taking up more than his fair share of the bed, and I couldn't get comfortable, so I gave him several kicks that made him grunt and stretch. He made room all right, though. Mother waked and felt for me. I settled back comfortably in the warmth of the bed with my thumb in my mouth.

"Mummy!" I hummed, loudly and contentedly.

"Sssh! dear," she whispered. "Don't wake Daddy!"

This was a new development, which threatened to be even more serious than "talking to Daddy." Life without my early-morning conferences was unthinkable.

"Why?" I asked severely.

"Because poor Daddy is tired."

This seemed to me a quite inadequate reason, and I was sickened by the sentimentality of her "poor Daddy." I never liked that sort of gush; it always struck me as insincere.

"Oh!" I said lightly. Then in my most winning tone: "Do you know where I want to go with you today, Mummy?"

"No, dear," she sighed.

"I want to go down the Glen and fish for thornybacks with my new net, and then I want to go out to the Fox and Hounds, and—"

"Don't-wake-Daddy!" she hissed angrily, clapping her hand across my mouth.

But it was too late. He was awake, or nearly so. He grunted and reached for the matches. Then he stared incredulously at his watch.

"Like a cup of tea, dear?" asked Mother in a meek, hushed voice I had never heard her use before. It sounded almost as though she were afraid.

"Tea?" he exclaimed indignantly. "Do you know what the time is?"

"And after that I want to go up the Rathcooney Road," I said loudly, afraid I'd forget something in all those interruptions.

"Go to sleep at once, Larry!" she said sharply.

I began to snivel. I couldn't concentrate, the way that pair went on, and smothering my early-morning schemes was like burying a family from the cradle.

Father said nothing, but lit his pipe and sucked it, looking out into the shadows without minding Mother or me. I knew he was mad. Every time I made a remark Mother hushed me irritably. I was mortified. I felt it wasn't fair; there was even something sinister in it. Every time I had pointed out to her the waste of making two beds when we could both sleep in one, she had told me it was healthier like that, and now here was this man, this stranger, sleeping with her without the least regard for her health!

He got up early and made tea, but though he brought Mother a cup he brought none for me.

"Mummy," I shouted, "I want a cup of tea, too."

"Yes, dear," she said patiently. "You can drink from Mummy's saucer."

That settled it. Either Father or I would have to leave the house. I didn't want to drink from Mother's saucer; I wanted to be treated as an equal in my own home, so, just to spite her, I drank it all and left none for her. She took that quietly, too.

But that night when she was putting me to bed she said gently:

"Larry, I want you to promise me something."

"What is it?" I asked.

"Not to come in and disturb poor Daddy in the morning. Promise?"

"Poor Daddy" again! I was becoming suspicious of everything involving that quite impossible man.

"Why?" I asked.

"Because poor Daddy is worried and tired and he doesn't sleep well."

"Why doesn't he, Mummy?"

"Well, you know, don't you, that while he was at the war Mummy got the pennies from the Post Office?"

"From Miss MacCarthy?"

"That's right. But now, you see, Miss MacCarthy hasn't any more pennies, so Daddy must go out and find us some. You know what would happen if he couldn't?"

"No," I said, "tell us."

"Well, I think we might have to go out and beg for them like the poor old woman on Fridays. We wouldn't like that, would we?"

"No," I agreed. "We wouldn't."

"So you'll promise not to come in and wake him?"

"Promise."

Mind you, I meant that. I knew pennies were a serious matter, and I was all against having to go out and beg like the old woman on Fridays. Mother laid out all my toys in a complete ring round the bed so that, whatever way I got out, I was bound to fall over one of them.

When I woke I remembered my promise all right. I got up and sat on the floor and played—for hours, it seemed to me. Then I got my chair and looked out the attic window for more hours. I wished it was time for Father to wake; I wished someone would make me a cup of tea. I didn't feel in the least like the sun; instead, I was bored and so very, very cold! I simply longed for the warmth and depth of the big featherbed.

At last I could stand it no longer. I went into the next room. As there was still no room at Mother's side I climbed over her and she woke with a start.

"Larry," she whispered, gripping my arm very tightly, "what did you promise?"

"But I did, Mummy," I wailed, caught in the very act. "I was quiet for ever so long."

"Oh, dear, and you're perished!" she said sadly, feeling me all over. "Now, if I let you stay will you promise not to talk?"

"But I want to talk, Mummy," I wailed.

"That has nothing to do with it," she said with a firmness that was new to me. "Daddy wants to sleep. Now, do you understand that?"

I understood it only too well. I wanted to talk, he wanted to sleep—whose house was it, anyway?

"Mummy," I said with equal firmness, "I think it would be healthier for Daddy to sleep in his own bed."

That seemed to stagger her, because she said nothing for a while.

"Now, once for all," she went on, "you're to be perfectly quiet or go back to your own bed. Which is it to be?"

The injustice of it got me down. I had convicted her out of her own mouth of inconsistency and unreasonableness, and she hadn't even attempted to reply. Full of spite, I gave Father a kick, which she didn't notice but which made him grunt and open his eyes in alarm.

"What time is it?" he asked in a panic-stricken voice, not looking at Mother but at the door, as if he saw someone there.

"It's early yet," she replied soothingly. "It's only the child. Go to sleep again. . . . Now, Larry," she added, getting out of bed, "you've wakened Daddy and you must go back."

This time, for all her quiet air, I knew she meant it, and knew that my principal rights and privileges were as good as lost unless I asserted them at once. As she lifted me, I gave a screech, enough to wake the dead, not to mind Father. He groaned.

"That damn child! Doesn't he ever sleep?"

"It's only a habit, dear," she said quietly, though I could see she was vexed.

"Well, it's time he got out of it," shouted Father, beginning to heave in the bed. He suddenly gathered all the bedclothes about him, turned to the wall, and then looked back over his shoulder with nothing showing only two small, spiteful, dark eyes. The man looked very wicked.

To open the bedroom door, Mother had to let me down, and I broke free and dashed for the farthest corner, screeching. Father sat bolt upright in bed.

"Shut up, you little puppy!" he said in a choking voice.

I was so astonished that I stopped screeching. Never, never had anyone spoken to me in that tone before. I looked at him incredulously and saw his face convulsed with rage. It was only then that I fully realized how God had codded me, listening to my prayers for the safe return of this monster.

"Shut up, you!" I bawled, beside myself.

"What's that you said?" shouted Father, making a wild leap out of the bed.

"Mick, Mick!" cried Mother. "Don't you see the child isn't used to you?"

"I see he's better fed than taught," snarled Father, waving his arms wildly. "He wants his bottom smacked."

All his previous shouting was as nothing to these obscene words referring to my person. They really made my blood boil.

"Smack your own!" I screamed hysterically. "Smack your own! Shut up! Shut up!"

At this he lost his patience and let fly at me. He did it with the lack of conviction you'd expect of a man under Mother's horrified eyes, and it ended up as a mere tap, but the sheer indignity of being struck at all by a stranger, a total stranger who had cajoled his way back from the war into our big bed as a result of my innocent intercession, made me completely dotty. I shrieked and shrieked, and danced in my bare feet, and Father, looking awkward and hairy in nothing but a short gray army shirt, glared down at me like a mountain out for murder. I think it must have been then that I realized he was jealous too. And there stood Mother in her nightdress, looking as if her heart was broken between us. I hoped she felt as she looked. It seemed to me that she deserved it all.

From that morning out my life was a hell. Father and I were enemies, open and avowed. We conducted a series of skirmishes against one another, he trying to steal my time with Mother and I his. When she was sitting on my bed, telling me a story, he took to looking for some pair of old boots which he alleged he had left behind him at the beginning of the war. While he talked to Mother I played loudly with my toys to show my total lack of concern. He created a terrible scene one evening when he came in from work and found me at his box, playing with his regimental badges, Gurkha knives and button-sticks. Mother got up and took the box from me.

"You mustn't play with Daddy's toys unless he lets you, Larry," she said severely. "Daddy doesn't play with yours."

For some reason Father looked at her as if she had struck him and then turned away with a scowl.

"Those are not toys," he growled, taking down the box again to see had I lifted anything. "Some of those curios are very rare and valuable."

But as time went on I saw more and more how he managed to alienate Mother and me. What made it worse was that I couldn't grasp his method or see what attraction he had for Mother. In every possible way he was less winning than I. He had a common accent and made noises at his tea. I thought for a while that it might be the newspapers she was interested in, so I made up bits of news of my own to read to her. Then I thought it might be the smoking, which I personally thought attractive, and took his pipes and went round the house dribbling into them till he caught me. I even made noises at my tea, but Mother only told me I was disgusting. It all seemed to hinge round that unhealthy habit of sleeping together, so I made a point of dropping into their bedroom and nosing round, talking to myself, so that they wouldn't know I was watching them, but they were never up to anything that I could see. In the end it beat me. It seemed to depend on being grown-up and giving people rings, and I realized I'd have to wait.

But at the same time I wanted him to see that I was only waiting, not giving up the fight. One evening when he was being particularly obnoxious, chattering away well above my head, I let him have it.

"Mummy," I said, "do you know what I'm going to do when I grow up?"

"No, dear," she replied. "What?"

"I'm going to marry you," I said quietly.

Father gave a great guffaw out of him, but he didn't take me in. I knew it must only be pretense. And Mother, in spite of everything, was pleased. I felt she was probably relieved to know that one day Father's hold on her would be broken.

"Won't that be nice?" she said with a smile.

"It'll be very nice," I said confidently. "Because we're going to have lots and lots of babies."

"That's right, dear," she said placidly. "I think we'll have one soon, and then you'll have plenty of company."

I was no end pleased about that because it showed that in spite of the way she gave in to Father she still considered my wishes. Besides, it would put the Geneys in their place.

It didn't turn out like that, though. To begin with, she was very pre-occupied—I supposed about where she would get the seventeen and six—and though Father took to staying out late in the evenings it did me no particular good. She stopped taking me for walks, became as touchy as blazes, and smacked me for nothing at all. Sometimes I wished I'd never mentioned the confounded baby—I seemed to have a genius for bringing calamity on myself.

And calamity it was! Sonny arrived in the most appalling hulla-baloo—even that much he couldn't do without a fuss—and from the first moment I disliked him. He was a difficult child—so far as I was concerned he was always difficult—and demanded far too much atten-tion. Mother was simply silly about him, and couldn't see when he was only showing off. As company he was worse than useless. He slept all day, and I had to go round the house on tiptoe to avoid waking him. It wasn't any longer a question of not waking Father. The slogan now was "Don't-wake-Sonny!" I couldn't understand why the child wouldn't sleep at the proper time, so whenever Mother's back was turned I woke him. Sometimes to keep him awake I pinched him as well. Mother caught me at it one day and gave me a most unmerciful flaking.

One evening, when Father was coming in from work, I was playing trains in the front garden. I let on not to notice him; instead, I pre-tended to be talking to myself, and said in a loud voice: "If another bloody baby comes into this house, I'm going out."

Father stopped dead and looked at me over his shoulder.

"What's that you said?" he asked sternly.

"I was only talking to myself," I replied, trying to conceal my panic. "It's private."

He turned and went in without a word. Mind you, I intended it as a solemn warning, but its effect was quite different. Father started being quite nice to me. I could understand that, of course. Mother was quite sickening about Sonny. Even at mealtimes she'd get up and gawk at him in the cradle with an idiotic smile, and tell Father to do the same. He was always polite about it, but he looked so puzzled you could see he didn't know what she was talking about. He complained of the way Sonny cried at night, but she only got cross and said that Sonny never cried except when there was something up with him—which was a flaming lie, because Sonny never had anything up with him, and only cried for attention. It was really painful to see how simpleminded she was. Father wasn't attractive, but he had a fine intelligence. He saw through Sonny, and now he knew that I saw through him as well.

One night I woke with a start. There was someone beside me in the bed. For one wild moment I felt sure it must be Mother, having come to her senses and left Father for good, but then I heard Sonny in convulsions in the next room, and Mother saying: "There! There! There!" and I knew it wasn't she. It was Father. He was lying beside me, wide awake, breathing hard and apparently as mad as hell.

After a while it came to me what he was mad about. It was his turn now. After turning me out of the big bed, he had been turned out himself. Mother had no consideration now for anyone but that poisonous pup, Sonny. I couldn't help feeling sorry for Father. I had been through it all myself, and even at that age I was magnanimous. I began to stroke him down and say: "There! There!" He wasn't exactly responsive.

"Aren't you asleep either?" he snarled.

"Ah, come on and put your arm around us, can't you?" I said, and he did, in a sort of way. Gingerly, I suppose, is how you'd describe it. He was very bony but better than nothing.

At Christmas he went out of his way to buy me a really nice model railway.

The Pretender

SUSIE and I should have known well that Denis Corby's coming "to play with us" would mean nothing only trouble. We didn't want anyone new to play with; we had plenty, and they were all good class. But Mother was like that; giddy, open-handed and ready to listen to any tall tale. That wouldn't have been so bad if only she confined her charity to her own things, but she gave away ours as well. You couldn't turn your back in that house but she had something pinched on you, a gansey, an overcoat, or a pair of shoes, and as for the beggars that used to come to the door—! As Susie often said, we had no life.

But we were still mugs enough to swallow the yarn about the lovely lonesome little boy she'd found to play with us up on the hill. Cripes, you never in all your life got such a suck-in! Eleven o'clock one Saturday morning this fellow comes to the door, about the one age with myself only bigger, with a round red face and big green goggle-eyes. I saw at the first glance that he was no class. In fact I took him at first for a messenger boy.

"What do you want?" I asked.

"Me mudder said I was to come and play with you," he said with a scowl, and you could see he liked it about as much as I did.

"Is your name Corby?" I asked in astonishment.

"What's that?" he asked and then he said: "Yes." I didn't honestly know whether he was deaf or an idiot or both.

"Mummy!" I shouted. "Look who's here"—wondering at the same time if she could have seen him before she asked him to the house.

But she'd seen him all right, because her face lit up and she told him to come in. He took off his cap and, after taking two steps and hearing the clatter he made in the hall with his hobnailed boots, he did the rest of it on tiptoe.

I could have cried. The fellow didn't know a single game, and when we went out playing with the Horgans and the Wrights I simply didn't know how to explain this apparition that hung on to us like some sort of poor relation.

When we sat down to dinner he put his elbows on the table and looked at us, ignoring his plate.

"Don't you like your dinner, Denis?" asked Mother—she never asked us if we liked our dinner.

"What's that?" he said, goggling at her. I was beginning to notice that he said "What's that?" only to give himself time to think up an answer. " 'Tis all right."

"Oh, you ought to eat up," said Father. "A big hefty fellow like you!"

"What does your mummy usually give you?" asked Mother.

"Soup," he said.

"Would you sooner I gave you a spoon so?"

"I would."

"What do you like for your dinner and I'll get it for you?"

"Jelly."

Now, if that had been me, not saying "please" or "thank you," I'd soon have got the back of my father's hand, but it seemed as if he could say what he liked and only eat what suited him. He took only a few mouthfuls of potatoes and gravy.

After dinner we went up to our bedroom so that we could show him our toys. He seemed as frightened of them as he was of a knife and fork.

"Haven't you any toys of your own?" I asked.

"No," he said.

"Where do you live?" asked Susie.

"The Buildings."

"Is that a nice place?"

" 'Tis all right." Everything was "all right" with him.

Now, I knew the Buildings because I passed it every day on the way to school and I knew it was not all right. It was far from it. It was a low-class sort of place where the kids went barefoot and the women sat all day on the doorsteps, talking.

"Haven't you any brothers and sisters?" Susie went on.

"No. Only me mudder. . . . And me Auntie Nellie," he added after a moment.

"Who's your Auntie Nellie?"

"My auntie. She lives down the country. She comes up of an odd time."

"And where's your daddy?" asked Susie.

"What's that?" he said, and again I could have sworn he was think-ing up an answer. There was a longer pause than usual. "I tink me daddy is dead," he added.

"How do you mean you think he's dead?" asked Susie. "Don't you know?"

"Me mudder said he was dead," he said doubtfully.

"Well, your mother ought to know," said Susie. "But if your daddy is dead where do ye get the money?"

"From my Auntie Nellie."

"It's because your daddy is dead that you have no toys," Susie said in her usual God-Almighty way. " 'Tis always better if your mummy dies first."

"It is not better, Susie Murphy," I said, horrified at the cold-blooded way that girl always talked about Mummy. "God will kill you stone dead for saying that. You're only saying it because you always suck up to Daddy."

"I do not always suck up to Daddy, Michael Murphy," she replied coldly. "And it's true. Everyone knows it. If Mummy died Daddy could still keep us, but if Daddy died, Mummy wouldn't have any-thing."

But though I always stuck up for Mummy against Susie, I had to admit that her latest acquisition wasn't up to much.

"Ah, that woman would sicken you," Susie said when we were in bed that night. "Bringing in old beggars and tramps and giving them their dinner in our kitchen, the way you couldn't have a soul in to play, and then giving away our best clothes. You couldn't have a blooming thing in this house."

Every Saturday after that Denis Corby came and tiptoed in the hall in his hobnailed boots and spooned at his dinner. As he said, the only thing he liked was jelly. He stayed on till our bedtime and listened to Mother reading us a story. He liked stories but he couldn't read himself, even comics, so Mother started teaching him and said he was very smart. A fellow who couldn't read at the age of seven, I didn't see how he could be smart. She never said I was smart.

But in other ways he was smart enough, too smart for me. Apparently a low-class boy and a complete outsider could do things I wasn't let do, like playing round the parlor, and if you asked any questions or passed any remarks, you only got into trouble. The old game of wardrobe-raiding had begun again, and I was supposed to admire the way Denis looked in my winter coat, though in secret I shed bitter tears over that coat, which was the only thing I had that went with my yellow tie. And the longer it went on, the deeper the mystery became.

One day Susie was showing off in her usual way about having been born in Dublin. She was very silly about that, because to listen to her you'd think no one had ever been born in Dublin only herself.

"Ah, shut up!" I said. "We all know you were born in Dublin and what about it?"

"Well, you weren't," she said, skipping round, "and Denis wasn't."

"How do you know he wasn't?" I asked. "Where were you born, Denis?"

"What's that?" he asked and gaped. Then, after a moment, he said: "In England."

"Where did you say?" Susie asked, scowling.

"In England."

"How do you know?"

"Me mudder told me."

I was delighted at the turn things had taken. You never in all your life saw anyone so put out as Susie at the idea that a common boy from the Buildings could be born in a place she wasn't born in. What made it worse was that Mummy had worked in England, and it seemed to Susie like a shocking oversight not to have had her in a place she could really brag about. She was leaping.

"When was your mummy in England?" she asked.

"She wasn't in England."

"Then how could you be born there, you big, silly fool?" she stormed.

"My Auntie Nellie was there," he said sulkily.

"You couldn't be born in England just because your Auntie Nellie was there," she said vindictively.

"Why couldn't I?" he asked, getting cross.

That stumped Susie properly. It stumped me as well. Seeing that we both thought Mother had bought us from the nurse, there didn't seem to be any good reason why an aunt couldn't have bought us as well. We argued about that for hours afterwards. Susie maintained with her usual Mrs. Know-all air that if an aunt bought a baby she stopped being his aunt and became his mummy but I wasn't sure of that at all. She said she'd ask Mummy, and I warned her she'd only get her head chewed off, but she said she didn't mind.

She didn't either. That kid was madly inquisitive, and she had ways of getting information out of people that really made me ashamed. One trick of hers was to repeat whatever she'd been told with a supercilious air and then wait for results. That's what she did about Denis Corby.

"Mummy," she said next day, "do you know what that silly kid, Denis, said?"

"No, dear."

"He said he was born in England and his mother was never in England at all," said Susie and went off into an affected laugh.

"The dear knows ye might find something better to talk about," Mother said in disgust. "A lot of difference it makes to the poor child where he was born."

"What did I tell you?" I said to her afterwards. "I told you you'd only put Mummy in a wax. I tell you there's a mystery about that fellow and Mummy knows what it is. I wish he never came here at all."

The Saturday following we were all given pennies and Denis and I were sent off for a walk. I thought it very cool of Mother, knowing quite well that Denis wasn't class enough for the fellows I mixed with, but it was one of those things she didn't seem to understand and I could never explain to her. I had the feeling that it would only make her mad.

It was a nice sunny afternoon, and we stayed at the cross, collecting cigarette pictures from fellows getting off the trams. We hadn't been there long when Bastable and another fellow came down the hill, two proper toffs—I mean they weren't even at my school but went to the Grammar School.

"Hullo, Bastable," I said, "where are ye off to?" and I went a few steps with them.

"We have a boat down the river," he said. "Will you come?"

I slouched along after them, between two minds. I badly wanted to go down the river, and it was jolly decent of Bastable to have asked me, but I was tied to Denis, who wasn't class enough to bring with me even if he was asked.

"I'm with this fellow," I said with a sigh, and Bastable looked back at Denis, who was sitting on the high wall over the church, and realized at the first glance that he wouldn't do.

"Ah, boy, you don't know what you're missing," he said.

I knew that only too well. I looked up and there was Denis, goggling down at us, close enough to remind me of the miserable sort of afternoon I'd have to spend with him if I stayed, but far enough away not to be on my conscience too much.

"Denis," I shouted, "I'm going down a bit of the way with these chaps. You can wait for me if you like."

Then I began to run and the others ran with me. I felt rather ashamed, but at the time I really did intend not to stay long with them. Of course, once I got to the river I forgot all my good resolutions—you know the way it is with boats—and it wasn't until I was coming back up the avenue in the dusk and noticed the gas lamps lit that I realized how late it was and my heart sank. I was really soft-hearted and I felt full of pity for poor old Denis waiting there for me all the time. When I reached the cross and found he wasn't there it only made it worse, because it must have meant he'd given me up and gone home. I was very upset about it, particularly about what I was going to say to the mother.

When I reached home I found the front door open and the kitchen in darkness. I went in quietly and to my astonishment I saw Mother and Denis sitting together over the fire. I just can't describe the extraordinary impression they made on me. They looked so snug, sitting there together in the firelight, that they made me feel like an outsider. I came in conscience-stricken and intending to bluff, and instead I suddenly found myself wanting to cry, I didn't know for what reason.

"Hullo," Denis said, giving me a grin. "Where did you go?"

"Ah, just down the river with Bastable," I said, hanging up my cap and trying to sound casual. "Where did you get to?"

"I came back," he said still grinning.

"And indeed, Michael, you should be thoroughly ashamed of yourself, leaving Denis like that," Mother said sharply.

"But really, Mummy, I didn't," I said weakly. "I only just went down a bit of the way with them, that's all."

I found it difficult enough to get even that much out without blubbing. Denis Corby had turned the tables on me with a vengeance. It was I who was jealous, and it took me weeks to see why. Then I suddenly tumbled to the fact that though he was quite ready to play with Susie and me it wasn't for that he came to the house. It was Mother, not us, he was interested in. He even arranged things so that he didn't have to come with us and could stay behind with her. Even when she didn't want him in the house he was content to sit on the wall outside just to have her to himself if she came to the door or wanted someone to run a message for her. It was only then that my suspicions turned to panic. After that I was afraid of leaving him behind me because of what he might do or say when my back was turned. And of course he knew I knew what was in his mind, and dared me.

One day I had to go on a message to the cross and I asked him to come. He wouldn't; he said he wanted to stay and play with Susie, and she, flattered at what she thought were his attentions, took his part.

"Go on now, Michael Murphy!" she said in her bossy way. "You were sent on the message and you can go by yourself. Denis is stopping here with me."

"It's not you he wants to stop with, you little fool!" I said, losing my patience with her. "It's Mummy."

"It is not," he said, and I saw from the way he reddened that he knew I had him caught.

"It is," I said truculently. "You're always doing it. You'd better let her alone. She's not your mother."

"She's my aunt," he said sullenly.

"That's a lie," I shouted, beside myself with rage. "She's not your aunt."

"She told me to call her that," he said.

"That has nothing to do with it," I said. "She's my mummy, not yours."

He suddenly gave me a queer look.

"How do you know?" he asked in a low voice.

For a moment I was too stunned to speak. It had never struck me before that if his Aunt Nellie could be his mother, Mummy, whom he called Aunt Kate, could be his mother as well. In fact, anyone could be a fellow's mother if only he knew. My only chance was to brazen it out.

"She couldn't be," I said. "Your mother lives up the Buildings."

"She's not me mudder," he said in the same low voice.

"Oh, there's a thing to say!" I cried, though the stupefaction was put on.

"How could she be me mudder?" he went on. "She was never in England."

The mystery was so close I felt I could solve it in a few words if only I knew which. Of course it was possible that Mother, having worked in England, could be his real mother while his own mother couldn't, and this was what had been between them both from the start. The shock of it was almost more than I could bear. I could keep my end up at all only by pretending to be scandalized.

"Oh," I cried, "I'll tell her what you said."

"You can if you like," he replied sullenly.

And of course he knew I couldn't. Whatever strange hold he had over her, you simply daren't ask her a reasonable question about him.

Susie was watching the pair of us curiously. She felt there was something wrong but didn't know what. I tried to enlighten her that night in bed: how it all fitted in, his mother who couldn't be his mother because she'd never been to England, his Aunt Nellie who could but probably wasn't because he saw so little of her, and Mummy who had not only been to England but saw him every week, made a pet of him, and wouldn't let you say a word against him. Susie agreed that this was quite probable, but she was as heartless as usual about it.

"She can be his mummy if she likes," she said with a shrug. "I don't care."

"That's only because you're Daddy's pet," I said.

"It is not, Michael Murphy, but it doesn't make any difference what she is so long as he only comes every Saturday."

"You wait," I whispered threateningly. "You'll see if his mother dies he'll come and live here. Then you'll be sorry."

Susie couldn't see the seriousness of it because she was never Mummy's pet as I was, and didn't see how Denis Corby was gradually replacing us both in Mother's affection, or how day after day she mentioned him only to praise him or compare him with us. I got heart-scalded hearing how good he was. I couldn't be good in that sly, insinuating way, just trying to get inside other people. I tried, but it was no use, and after a while I lost heart and never seemed to be out of mischief. I didn't know what was wrong with me, but I was always breaking, losing, pinching. Mother didn't know either and only got more impatient with me.

"I don't know under God what's come over you," she said angrily. "Every week that passes you're becoming more and more of a savage."

As if I could be anything else, knowing what I knew! It was Denis, Denis, Denis the whole time. Denis was sick and had to be taken to a doctor and the doctor said he was worrying about something. Nothing was said about the way I was worrying, seeing him turn me into a stranger in my own house. By this time I was really desperate.

It came to a head one day when Mother asked me to go on a message. I broke down and said I didn't want to. Mother in her fury couldn't see that it was only because I'd be leaving Denis behind me.

"All right, all right," she snapped. "I'll send Denis. I'm fed up with you."

But this was worse. This was the end of everything, the final proof that I had been replaced.

"No, no, Mummy, I'll go, I'll go," I said, and I took the money and went out sobbing. Denis Corby was sitting on the wall and Susie and two other little girls were playing pickie on the garden path. Susie looked at me in surprise, her left leg still lifted.

"What ails you?" she asked.

"I have to go on a message," I said, bawling like a kid.

"Well, that's nothing to cry about."

"I have to go by myself," I wailed, though I knew well it was a silly complaint, a baby's complaint, and one I'd never have made in my right mind. Susie saw that too, and she was torn between the desire to go on with her game and to come with me to find out what was wrong.

"Can't Denis go with you?" she asked, tossing the hair from her eyes.

"He wouldn't come," I sobbed.

"You never asked me," he said in a loud, surly voice.

"Go on!" I said, blind with misery and rage. "You never come anywhere with me. You're only waiting to go in to my mother."

"I am not," he shouted.

"You are, Denis Corby," Susie said suddenly in a shrill, scolding voice, and I realized that she had at last seen the truth for herself and come down on my side. "You're always doing it. You don't come here to play with us at all."

"I do."

"You don't, you don't," I hissed, losing all control of myself and going up to him with my fists clenched. "You Indian witch!"

It was the most deadly insult I could think of, and it roused him. He got off the wall and faced Susie and me, his hands hanging, his face like a lantern.

"I'm not an Indian witch," he said with smoldering anger.

"You are an Indian witch, you are an Indian witch," I said and gave him the coward's blow, straight in the face. He didn't try to hit back though he was twice my size, a proper little sissy.

"God help us!" one of the little girls bawled. "You ought to be ashamed of yourself, hitting the little boy like that, Michael Murphy."

"Then he ought to let our mummy alone," Susie screeched. Now that she saw the others turn against me she was dancing with rage, a real little virago. "He's always trying to make out that she's his mummy, and she isn't."

"I never said she was my mummy," he said, sulky and frightened.

"You did say it," I said, and I hit him again, in the chest this time. "You're trying to make out that I'm your brother and I'm not."

"And I'm not your sister either," Susie screeched defiantly, doing a war-dance about him. "I'm Michael Murphy's sister, and I'm not your sister, and if you say I am again I'll tell my daddy on you."

"Michael, Michael Murphy! Susie! What are you doing to the little boy?" shouted a wrathful voice, and when I looked up there was an officious neighbor, clapping her hands from the gate at us. There were others out as well. We had been all shouting so loudly that we had gathered an audience. Suddenly Susie and I got two clouts that sent us flying.

"What in God's holy name is the meaning of this?" cried Mother, taking Denis by the hand. "How dare you strike that child, you dirty little corner-boy?"

Then she turned and swept in with Denis, leaving the rest of us flabbergasted.

"Now we'll all be killed," Susie snivelled, between pain and fright. "She'll murder us. And 'twas all your fault, Michael Murphy."

But by then I didn't care what happened. Denis Corby had won at last and even before the neighbors was treated as Mother's pet. In an excited tone Susie began telling the other girls about Denis and all his different mothers and all the troubles they had brought on us.

He was inside a long time, a very long time it seemed to me. Then he came out by himself and it was only afterwards I remembered that he did it on tiptoe. Mother looked like murder all that day. The following Saturday Denis didn't come at all and the Saturday after Mother sent Susie and me up to the Buildings for him.

By that time I didn't really mind and I bore him no grudge for what had happened. Mother had explained to us that she wasn't really his mother, and that, in fact, he hadn't any proper mother. This was what she had told him when she brought him in, and it seems it was a nasty shock to him. You could understand that, of course. If a fellow really did think someone was his mother and then found she wasn't it would be quite a shock. I was full of compassion for him really. The whole week I'd been angelic—even Mummy admitted that.

When we went in he was sitting at the fire with his mother—the one he thought at first was his mother. She made a fuss of Susie and me and said what lovely children we were. I didn't like her very much myself. I thought her too sweet to be wholesome.

"Go on back with them now, Dinny boy," she said, pawing him on the knee. "Sure you haven't a soul to play with in this old hole."

But he wouldn't come, and nothing we said could make him. He treated us like enemies, almost. Really I suppose he felt a bit of a fool. His mother was a wrinkled old woman; the house was only a laborer's cottage without even an upstairs room; you could see they were no class, and as I said to Susie on the way home, the fellow had a cool cheek to imagine we were his brother and sister.

Freedom

When I was interned during the war with the British I dreamed endlessly of escape. As internment camps go, ours was pretty good. We had a theatre, games, and classes, and some of the classes were first-rate.

It was divided into two areas, North Camp and South, and the layout of the huts was sufficiently varied to give you a feeling of change when you went for a stroll around the wires. The tall wooden watchtowers, protected from the weather by canvas sheets, which commanded the barbed wire at intervals had a sort of ragged functional beauty of their own. You could do a five-mile walk there before breakfast and not feel bored.

But I ached to get away. It is almost impossible to describe how I ached. In the evenings I walked round the camp and always stopped at least once on a little hillock in the North Camp which had the best view of the flat green landscape of Kildare that stretched all round us for miles. It was brilliantly green, and the wide crowded skies had all the incredible atmospheric effects of flat country, with veil after veil of mist or rain even on the finest days, and I thought of the tinker families drifting or resting in the shadow of the hedges while summer lasted. God, I used to think, if only I could escape I'd never stop, summer or winter, but just go on and on, making my fire under a hedge and sleeping in a barn or under an upturned cart. Night and day I'd go on, maybe for years, maybe till I died. If only I could escape!

But there isn't any escape. I saw that even in the camp itself. I became friendly with two prisoners, Matt Deignan and Mick Stewart, both from Cork. They were nice lads; Mick sombre, reserved, and a bit lazy; Matt noisy, emotional, and energetic. They messed together and Matt came in for most of the work. That wasn't all he came in for. When Mick was in one of his violent moods and had to have someone to wrestle with, Matt was the victim. Mick wrestled with him, ground his arms behind his back, made him yelp with pain and plead for mercy. Sometimes he reduced Matt to tears, and for hours Matt wouldn't speak to him. It never went farther than that though. Matt was Caliban to Mick's Prospero and had to obey. He would come to me, a graceless gawk with a moony face, and moan to me about Mick's cruelty and insolence, but this was only because he knew Mick liked me, and he hoped to squelch Mick out of my mouth. If anyone else dared to say a word against Mick he mocked at them. They were jealous!

Matt had a job in the Quartermaster's store, the Quartermaster, one Clancy, being some sort of eminent, distant cousin of whom Matt was enormously proud. Mick and he both dossed in J Hut in the North Camp. Now J was always a rather tony hut, quite different from Q, where I hung out, which was nothing but a municipal slaughterhouse. The tone of J was kept up by about a dozen senior officers and politicians, businessmen and the like. The hut leader, Jim Brennan, a tough little Dublin mason whom I admired, though not class himself, liked class: he liked businessmen and fellows who wore silk pajamas and university students who could tell him all about God, V.D., and the next world. It broadened a man's mind a lot. These got off lightly; either they had doctor's certificates to prove they couldn't do fatigues or they had nominal jobs, which meant they didn't have to do them. You couldn't blame Jim; it was his hut, and he kept it like a battleship, and to get into it at all was considered a bit of luck. Nor did the other men in the hut object; they might be only poor country lads, but, like Jim, they enjoyed mixing with fellows of a different class and listening to arguments about religion over the stove at night. It might be the only opportunity most of them would ever have of hearing anything except about drains and diseases of cattle, and they were storing it up. It was a thoroughly happy hut, and it rather surprised me that two attempts at tunnelling had begun from it; if it wasn't that the occupants wanted to show off their intelligence, you wouldn't know what they wanted to escape for.

But Mick Stewart rather resented the undemocratic tone of the hut and was careful to keep the camp aristocracy at a distance. When someone like Jack Costello, the draper, addressed Mick with what he thought undue familiarity, Mick pretended not to hear. Costello was surprised and Brennan was seriously displeased. He thought it disrespectful. He never noticed Mick except to give him an order. A couple of times he made him go over a job twice, partly to see it was properly done, partly to put Mick in his place.

Now, Mick was one of those blokes who never know they have a place. One day he just struck. While the others continued scrubbing he threw himself on his bed with his hands under his head and told the hut leader to do it himself. He did it with an icy calm which anyone who knew Mick would have known meant danger.

"You mean you call that clean?" Brennan asked, standing at the end of Mick's bed with his hands in his trouser pockets and his old cap over one eye.

"It's not a matter of opinion," Mick said in his rather high-pitched, piping voice.

"Oh, isn't it?" asked Brennan and then called over Jack Costello. "Jack," he continued mildly, "is that what you'd call clean?"

"Ah, come on, Stewart, come on!" Costello said in his best "Arise, Ye Sons of Erin" manner. "Don't be a blooming passenger!"

"I didn't know I asked your advice, Costello," Mick said frostily, "but as you seem to be looking for a job as a deckhand, fire ahead!"

"I certainly will," Costello said gamely. "Just to show I'm not too proud to be a deckhand."

"No, you won't, Jack," Brennan said heavily. "There's going to be no passengers on this boat. Are you going to obey orders, Stewart?"

"If you mean am I going to do every job twice, I'm not," replied Mick with a glare.

"Good enough," Brennan said moodily as he turned away. "We'll see about that."

Now, I should perhaps have explained that the camp duplicated the whole British organization. Each morning we stood to attention at the foot of our beds to be counted, but one of our own officers always accompanied the counting party and ostensibly it was for him and not for the British officer that we paraded. It was the same with everything else; we recognized only our own officers. The Quartermaster drew the stores from the British and we received them from him and signed for them to him. The mail was sorted and delivered by our own post-office staff. We had our cooks, our doctors, our teachers and actors—even our police. Because, if one of our fellows was caught pinching another man's stuff, we had our own police to arrest him and our own military court to try him. In this way, we of the rank and file never came into contact at all with our jailers.

That morning two of the camp police, wearing tricolor armlets, came to march Mick down to the hut where his case was to be tried. One of them was a great galumphing lout called Kenefick, a bit of a simpleton, who cracked heavy jokes with Mick because he felt so self-conscious with his armlet. The case was heard in the camp office. When I passed I saw Matt Deignan outside, looking nervous and lonely. I stopped to talk with him and Brennan passed in, sulky and stubborn, without as much as a glance at either of us. Matt burst into a long invective against him, and I tried to shut him up, because in spite of his boorishness I respected Brennan.

"Ah, well," I said, "you can't put all the blame on Brennan. You know quite well that Mick is headstrong too."

"Headstrong?" yelped Matt, ready to eat me. "And wouldn't he want to be with a dirty lout like that?"

"Brennan is no lout," I said. "He's a fine soldier."

"He is," Matt said bitterly. "He'd want to walk on you."

"That's what soldiers are for," I said, but Matt wasn't in a mood for facetiousness.

The court seemed to be a long time sitting, and it struck me that it might have been indiscreet enough to start an argument with Mick. This would have been a long operation. But at last he came out, a bit red but quite pleased with himself, and I decided that if there had been an argument he had got the better of it. We set off for a brisk walk round the camp. Mick would talk of everything except the case. Mick all out! He knew poor Matt was broken down with anxiety and was determined on toughening him.

"Well," I said at last, "what's the verdict?"

"Oh, that business!" he said contemptuously. "Just what you'd expect."

"And what's the sentence? Death or a five-year dip?"

"A week's fatigues."

"That's not so bad," I said.

"Not so bad?" cried Matt, almost in tears. "And for what? Pure spite because Mick wouldn't kowtow to them. 'Tis all that fellow Costello, Mick boy," he went on with a tragic air. "I never liked him. He's the fellow that's poisoning them against you."

"He's welcome," Mick said frostily, deprecating all this vulgar emotionalism of Matt's. "I'm not doing extra fatigues for them."

"And you're right, Mick," exclaimed Matt, halting. "You're right. I'd see them in hell first."

"You don't mean you're going to refuse to obey the staff?" I asked doubtfully.

"What else can I do?" Mick asked in a shrill complaining voice.

"Don't you realize what will happen if I let Brennan get away with this? He'll make my life a misery."

"Starting a row with the camp command isn't going to make it exactly a honeymoon," I said.

It didn't, but even I was astonished at the feeling roused by Mick's rebellion. Men who knew that he and I were friendly attacked him to me. No one said a word in his favor. And it wasn't that they were worried by the thing that worried me—that right or wrong, the camp command was the only elected authority in the camp—oh, no. Mick was disloyal to the cause, disloyal to the camp; worst of all, he was putting on airs. You would think that men who were rebels themselves and suffering for their views would have some sympathy for him.

"But the man is only sticking out for what he thinks are his rights," I protested.

"Rights?" one man echoed wonderingly. "What rights has he? Haven't we all to work?"

After a while I gave up arguing. It left me with the feeling that liberty wasn't quite such a clear-cut issue as I had believed it. Clancy, the Quartermaster, though himself one of the staff, was the most reasonable man on the other side. No doubt he felt he had to be because Mick was his cousin's friend. He was a gallant little man, small, fiery, and conscientious, and never really himself till he began to blaspheme. This wasn't yet a subject for blasphemy so he wasn't quite himself. He grasped me firmly by the shoulder, stared at me closely with his bright blue eyes and then looked away into an infinite distance.

"Jack," he said in a low voice, "between friends, tell that boy, Stewart, to have sense. The Commandant is very vexed. He's a severe man. I wouldn't like to be in Stewart's shoes if he crosses him again."

"I suppose ye'd never use your brains and send Stewart and Matt to Q Hut?" I asked. "It's only the way Mick and Brennan don't get on, and two human beings would improve Q Hut enormously."

"Done!" he exclaimed, holding out his hand in a magnificent gesture. "The minute he has his fatigues done. I'll tell the Commandant."

I put that solution up to Mick and he turned it down in the most reasonable way in the world. That was one thing I was learning: your true rebel is nothing if not reasonable; it is only his premises that are dotty. Mick explained patiently that he couldn't agree to a compromise which would still leave him with a stain on his character because if ever we resurrected the army again and the army got down to keeping records it would count as a black mark against him.

"You mean for a pension?" I said, turning nasty, but Mick didn't realize that. He only thought it was rather crude of me to be so materialistic about a matter of principle. I was beginning to wonder if my own premises were quite sound.

Next morning I went over to J Hut to see how things were panning out. They looked pretty bad to me. It was a large, light, airy hut like a theatre with a low wooden partition down the middle and the beds ranged at either side of the partition and along the walls. It was unusually full for that hour of the morning, and there was a peculiar feeling you only get from a mob which is just on the point of getting out of hand. Mick was lying on his own bed, and Matt sitting on the edge of his, talking to him. No one seemed interested in them. The rest were sitting round the stove or fooling with macramé bags, waiting to see what happened. Three beds down from Mick was a handsome young Wexford fellow called Howard, also lying on his bed and ostensibly talking to his buddy. He saw me come in and raised his voice.

"The trouble is," he was saying, "people who won't pull their weight would be better at the other side of the wire."

"Are you referring to me, Howard?" Mick asked harshly.

Howard sat up and turned a beaming adolescent face on him.

"As a matter of fact I am, Stewart," he said.

"We were on the right side before ever ye were heard of, Howard," bawled Matt. "What the hell did ye ever do in Wexford beyond shooting a couple of misfortunate policemen?"

I started talking feverishly to avert the row, but fortunately just then Kenefick and another policeman of the right sort came in. This time they showed no embarrassment and there was nothing in the least matey about their attitude. It gave their tricolor armlets a certain significance. As we followed them out the whole hut began to hiss. Matt turned as though something had struck him but I pushed him out. It was all much worse than I expected.

Again Matt and I had to wait outside the office while the trial went on, but this time I wasn't feeling quite so lighthearted, and as for Matt, I could see it was the most tragic moment of his life. Never before had he thought of himself as a traitor, an enemy of society, but that was what they were trying to make of him.

This time when Mick emerged he had the two policemen with him. He tried to maintain a defiant air, but even he looked depressed.

"What happened, Mick?" bawled Matt, hurling himself on him like a distracted mother of nine.

"You're not supposed to talk to the prisoner," said Kenefick.

"Ah, shut up you, Kenefick!" I snapped. "What's the result, Mick?"

"Oh, I believe I'm going to jail," said Mick, laughing without amusement.

"Going where?" I asked incredulously.

"So I'm told," he replied with a shrug.

"But what jail?"

"Damned if I know," he said, and suddenly began to laugh with genuine amusement.

"You'll know soon enough," growled Kenefick, who seemed to resent the laughter as a slight on his office.

"Cripes, Kenefick," I said, "you missed your vocation."

It really was extraordinary, how everything in that camp became a sort of crazy duplicate of something in the outside world. Nothing but an armlet had turned a good-natured halfwit like Kenefick into a real policeman, exactly like the ones who had terrified me as a kid when I'd been playing football on the road. I had noticed it before; how the post-office clerks became sulky and uncommunicative; how the fellows who played girls in the Sunday-evening shows made scenes and threw up their parts exactly like film stars, and some of the teachers started sending them notes. But now the whole crazy pattern seemed to be falling into place. At any moment I expected to find myself skulking away from Kenefick.

We moved in a group between the huts to the rather unpleasant corner of the camp behind the cookhouse. Then I suddenly saw what Kenefick meant. There was a little hut you wouldn't notice, a small storeroom which might have been a timekeeper's hut in a factory only that its one small window had bars. The pattern was complete at last; as well as store, school, theatre, church, post office, and police court we now had a real jail of our own. Inside it had bedboards, a three-biscuit mattress, and blankets. They had thought of everything down to the bucket. It amused me so much that I scarcely felt any emotion at saying good-bye to Mick. But Matt was beside himself with rage.

"Where are you off to?" I asked as he tore away across the camp.

"I'm going to hand in my resignation to Clancy," he hissed.

"But what good will that do? It'll only mean you'll have to do fatigues instead and Brennan will get his knife in you too."

"And isn't that what I want?" he cried. "You don't think I'm going to stop outside in freedom and leave poor Mick in there alone?"

I was on the point of asking him his definition of freedom, but I realized in time that he wasn't in a state to discuss the question philosophically, so I thought I had better accompany him. Clancy received us in a fatherly way; his conscience was obviously at him about having sent Mick to jail.

"Now don't do anything in a hurry, boy," he said kindly. "I spoke to the Commandant about it. It seems he admires Stewart a lot, but he has to do it for the sake of discipline."

"Is that what you call discipline?" Matt asked bitterly. "You can tell the Commandant from me that I'm resigning from the army as well. I wouldn't be mixed up with tyrants like ye."

"Tyrants?" spluttered Clancy, getting red. "Who are you calling tyrants?"

"And what the hell else are ye?" cried Matt. "The English were gentlemen to ye."

"Clear out!" cried Clancy. "Clear out or I'll kick the ass off you, you ungrateful little pup!"

"Tyrant!" hissed Matt, turning purple.

"You young cur!" said Clancy. "Wait till I tell your father about you!"

That evening I stood for a long time outside the prison window with Matt, talking to Mick. Mick had to raise himself on the bucket; he held onto the bars with both hands; he had the appearance of a real prisoner. The camp too looked like a place where people were free; in the dusk it looked big and complex and citified. Twenty yards away the prisoners on their evening strolls went round and round, and among them were the camp command, the Commandant, the Adjutant, and Clancy, not even giving a look in our direction. I had the greatest difficulty in keeping Matt from taking a fistful of stones and going round breaking windows to get himself arrested. I knew that wouldn't help. His other idea was that the three of us should resign from the army and conclude a separate peace with the British. That, as I pointed out, would be even worse. The great thing was to put the staff in the wrong by showing ourselves more loyal than they. I proposed to prepare a full statement of the position to be smuggled out to our friends at Brigade Headquarters outside. This idea rather appealed to Mick who, as I say, was very reasonable about most things.

I spent the evening after lock-up and a good part of the following morning on it. In the afternoon I went over to J with it. Brennan was distributing the mail and there were a couple of letters for Matt.

"Isn't there anything for Stewart?" he asked in disappointment.

"Stewart's letters will be sent to the staff hut," growled Brennan.

"You mean you're not going to give the man his letters?" shouted Matt.

"I mean I don't know whether he's entitled to them or not," said Brennan. "That's a matter for the Commandant."

Matt had begun a violent argument before I led him away. In the temper of the hut he could have been lynched. I wondered more than ever at the conservatism of revolutionaries.

"Come to the staff hut and we'll inquire ourselves," I said. "Brennan is probably only doing this out of pique."

I should have gone alone, of course. The Adjutant was there with Clancy. He was a farmer's son from the Midlands, beef to the heels like a Mullingar heifer.

"Brennan says Mick Stewart isn't entitled to letters," Matt squeaked to Clancy. "Is that right?"

"Why wouldn't it be?" Clancy asked, jumping up and giving one truculent tug to his mustache, another to his waistcoat. Obviously he didn't know whether it was or not. With the new jail only just started, precedents were few.

"Whenever the English want to score off us they stop our letters and parcels," I said. "Surely to God ye could think up something more original."

"Do you know who you're speaking to?" the Adjutant asked.

"No," replied Matt before I could intervene. "Nor don't want to. Ye know what ye can do with the letters."

Mick, on the other hand, took the news coolly. He had apparently been thinking matters over during the night and planned his own campaign.

"I'm on hunger strike now," he said with a bitter smile.

The moment he spoke I knew he had found the answer. It was what we politicals always did when the British tried to make ordinary convicts of us. And it put the staff in an impossible position. Steadily more and more they had allowed themselves to become more tyrannical than the British themselves, and Mick's hunger strike showed it up clearly. If Mick were to die on hunger strike—and I knew him well enough to know that he would, rather than give in—no one would ever take the staff seriously again as suffering Irish patriots. And even if they wished to let him die, they might find it difficult, because without our even having to approach the British directly we involved them as well. As our legal jailers they would hate to see Mick die on anyone else's hands. The British are very jealous of privileges like that.

At the same time I was too fond of Mick to want things to reach such a pass, and I decided to make a final appeal to Clancy. I also decided to do it alone, for I knew Matt was beyond reasonable discussion.

When I went into him at the store, Clancy lowered his head and pulled his mustache at me.

"You know about Mick Stewart?" I began.

"I know everything about him from the moment he was got," shouted Clancy, putting his hand up to stop me. "If you didn't hear of that incident remind me to tell you some time."

This was a most unpromising beginning. The details of Mick's conception seemed to me beside the point.

"What are you going to do about it?" I asked.

"What do you think we're going to do about it?" he retorted, taking three steps back from me. "What do you think we are? Soldiers or old women? Let the bugger starve!"

"That's grand," I said, knowing I had him where I wanted him. "And what happens when we go on hunger strike and the British say: 'Let the buggers starve'?"

"That has nothing at all to do with it."

"Go on!" I said. "By the way, I suppose ye considered forcible feeding?"

Then he said something very nasty, quite uncalled-for, which didn't worry me in the least because it was the way he always talked when he was his natural self, and I got on very well with Clancy's natural self.

"By the way," I said, "don't be too sure the British will let ye starve him. You seem to forget that you're still prisoners yourselves, and Stewart is their prisoner as much as yours. The English mightn't like the persecution of unfortunate Irish prisoners by people like you."

Clancy repeated the uncalled-for remark, and I was suddenly filled with real pity for him. All that decent little man's life he had been suffering for Ireland, sacrificing his time and money and his little business, sleeping on the sofa and giving up his bed, selling raffle tickets, cycling miles in the dark to collect someone's subscription, and here was a young puppy taking the bread and water from his mouth.

That evening Matt and I stayed with Mick till the last whistle. You couldn't shift Matt from the window. He was on the verge of a breakdown. He had no one to coddle or be bullied by. Caliban without Prospero is a miserable spectacle.

But Clancy must have had a sleepless night. Next morning I found that Mick had already had a visit from the Adjutant. The proposal now was that Mick and Matt should come to my hut, and Mick could do his week's fatigues there—a mere formality so far as Q was concerned because anyone in that hut would do them for a sixpenny bit or five cigarettes. But no, Mick wouldn't agree to that either. He could accept nothing less than unconditional release, and even I felt that this was asking a lot of the staff.

But I was wrong. The staff had already given it up as a bad job. That afternoon we were summoned to the dining hall "to make arrangements about our immediate release" as the signaller told us—his idea of a joke. It looked like a company meeting. The staff sat round a table on the stage, Clancy wearing a collar and tie to show the importance of the occasion. The Commandant told us that the camp was faced with an unprecedented crisis. Clancy nodded three times, rapidly.

They were the elected representatives of the men, and one man was deliberately defying them. Clancy crossed his legs, folded his arms tightly and looked searchingly through the audience as if looking for the criminal. They had no choice only to come back for fresh instructions.

It was a nice little meeting. Jack Costello, speaking from the hall, did a touching little piece about the hunger strike as the last weapon of free men against tyrants, told us that it should never be brought into disrepute, and said that if the man in question were released his loyal comrades would no doubt show what they thought of his conduct. Matt tried to put in a few words but was at once shouted down by his loyal comrades. Oh, a grand little meeting! Then I got up. I didn't quite know what to say because I didn't quite know what I thought. I had intended to say that within every conception of liberty there was the skeleton of a tyranny; that there were as many conceptions of liberty as there were human beings, and that the sort of liberty one man needed was not that which another might need. But somehow when I looked round me, I couldn't believe it. Instead, I said that there was no crisis, and that the staff were making mountains of principle out of molehills of friction. I wasn't permitted to get far. The Adjutant interrupted to say that what Mick was sentenced for couldn't be discussed by the meeting. Apparently it couldn't be discussed at all except by a Court of Appeal which couldn't be set up until the Republic proclaimed in 1916 was re-established, or some such nonsense. Listening to the Adjutant always gave me the impression of having taken a powerful sleeping-pill; after a while your hold on reality began to weaken and queer dissociated sentences began to run through your mind. I went out, deciding it was better to walk it off. Matt and I met outside the jail and waited till Kenefick came to release the prisoner. He did it in complete silence. Apparently orders were that we were to be sent to Coventry.

That suited me fine. The three of us were now together in Q and I knew from old experience that anyone in Q would sell his old mother for a packet of cigarettes. But all the same I was puzzled and depressed. Puzzled because I couldn't clarify what I had really meant to say when I got up to speak at the meeting, because I couldn't define what I really meant by liberty; depressed because if there was no liberty which I could define then equally there was no escape. I remained awake for hours that night thinking of it. Beyond the restless searchlights which stole in through every window and swept the hut till it was bright as day I could feel the wide fields of Ireland all round me, but even the wide fields of Ireland were not wide enough. Choice was an illusion. Seeing that a man can never really get out of jail, the great thing is to ensure that he gets into the biggest possible one with the largest possible range of modern amenities.

Peasants

WHEN Michael John Cronin stole the funds of the Carricknabreena Hurling, Football and Temperance Association, commonly called the Club, everyone said: "Devil's cure to him!" " 'Tis the price of him!" "Kind father for him!" "What did I tell you?" and the rest of the things people say when an acquaintance has got what is coming to him.

And not only Michael John but the whole Cronin family, seed, breed, and generation, came in for it; there wasn't one of them for twenty miles round or a hundred years back but his deeds and sayings were remembered and examined by the light of this fresh scandal. Michael John's father (the heavens be his bed!) was a drunkard who beat his wife, and his father before him a land-grabber. Then there was an uncle or grand-uncle who had been a policeman and taken a hand in the bloody work at Mitchelstown long ago, and an unmarried sister of the same whose good name it would by all accounts have needed a regiment of husbands to restore. It was a grand shaking-up the Cronins got altogether, and anyone who had a grudge in for them, even if it was no more than a thirty-third cousin, had rare sport, dropping a friendly word about it and saying how sorry he was for the poor mother till he had the blood lighting in the Cronin eyes.

There was only one thing for them to do with Michael John; that was to send him to America and let the thing blow over, and that, no doubt, is what they would have done but for a certain unpleasant and extraordinary incident.

Father Crowley, the parish priest, was chairman of the committee. He was a remarkable man, even in appearance; tall, powerfully built, but very stooped, with shrewd, loveless eyes that rarely softened to anyone except two or three old people. He was a strange man, well on in years, noted for his strong political views, which never happened to coincide with those of any party, and as obstinate as the devil himself. Now what should Father Crowley do but try to force the committee to prosecute Michael John?

The committee were all religious men who up to this had never as much as dared to question the judgments of a man of God: yes, faith, and if the priest had been a bully, which to give him his due he wasn't, he might have danced a jig on their backs and they wouldn't have complained. But a man has principles, and the like of this had never been heard of in the parish before. What? Put the police on a boy and he in trouble?

One by one the committee spoke up and said so. "But he did wrong," said Father Crowley, thumping the table. "He did wrong and he should be punished."

"Maybe so, father," said Con Norton, the vice-chairman, who acted as spokesman. "Maybe you're right, but you wouldn't say his poor mother should be punished too and she a widow-woman?"

"True for you!" chorused the others.

"Serves his mother right!" said the priest shortly. "There's none of you but knows better than I do the way that young man was brought up. He's a rogue and his mother is a fool. Why didn't she beat Christian principles into him when she had him on her knee?"

"That might be, too," Norton agreed mildly. "I wouldn't say but you're right, but is that any reason his Uncle Peter should be punished?"

"Or his Uncle Dan?" asked another.

"Or his Uncle James?" asked a third.

"Or his cousins, the Dwyers, that keep the little shop in Lissnacarriga, as decent a living family as there is in County Cork?" asked a fourth.

"No, father," said Norton, "the argument is against you."

"Is it indeed?" exclaimed the priest, growing cross. "Is it so? What the devil has it to do with his Uncle Dan or his Uncle James? What are ye talking about? What punishment is it to them, will ye tell me that? Ye'll be telling me next 'tis a punishment to me and I a child of Adam like himself."

"Wisha now, father," asked Norton incredulously, "do you mean 'tis no punishment to them having one of their own blood made a public show? Is it mad you think we are? Maybe 'tis a thing you'd like done to yourself?"

"There was none of my family ever a thief," replied Father Crowley shortly.

"Begor, we don't know whether there was or not," snapped a little man called Daly, a hot-tempered character from the hills.

"Easy, now! Easy, Phil!" said Norton warningly.

"What do you mean by that?" asked Father Crowley, rising and grabbing his hat and stick.

"What I mean," said Daly, blazing up, "is that I won't sit here and listen to insinuations about my native place from any foreigner. There are as many rogues and thieves and vagabonds and liars in Cullough as ever there were in Carricknabreena—ay, begod, and more, and bigger! That's what I mean."

"No, no, no, no," Norton said soothingly. "That's not what he means at all, father. We don't want any bad blood between Cullough and Carricknabreena. What he means is that the Crowleys may be a fine substantial family in their own country, but that's fifteen long miles away, and this isn't their country, and the Cronins are neighbors of ours since the dawn of history and time, and 'twould be a very queer thing if at this hour we handed one of them over to the police. . . . And now, listen to me, father," he went on, forgetting his role of pacificator and hitting the table as hard as the rest, "if a cow of mine got sick in the morning, 'tisn't a Cremin or a Crowley I'd be asking for help, and damn the bit of use 'twould be to me if I did. And everyone knows I'm no enemy of the Church but a respectable farmer that pays his dues and goes to his duties regularly."

"True for you! True for you!" agreed the committee.

"I don't give a snap of my finger what you are," retorted the priest. "And now listen to me, Con Norton. I bear young Cronin no grudge, which is more than some of you can say, but I know my duty and I'll do it in spite of the lot of you."

He stood at the door and looked back. They were gazing blankly at one another, not knowing what to say to such an impossible man. He shook his fist at them.

"Ye all know me," he said. "Ye know that all my life I'm fighting the long-tailed families. Now, with the help of God, I'll shorten the tail of one of them."

Father Crowley's threat frightened them. They knew he was an obstinate man and had spent his time attacking what he called the "corruption" of councils and committees, which was all very well as long as it happened outside your own parish. They dared not oppose him openly because he knew too much about all of them and, in public at least, had a lacerating tongue. The solution they favored was a tactful one. They formed themselves into a Michael John Cronin Fund Committee and canvassed the parishioners for subscriptions to pay off what Michael John had stolen. Regretfully they decided that Father Crowley would hardly countenance a football match for the purpose.

Then with the defaulting treasurer, who wore a suitably contrite air, they marched up to the presbytery. Father Crowley was at his dinner but he told the houskeeper to show them in. He looked up in astonishment as his dining room filled with the seven committeemen, pushing before them the cowed Michael John.

"Who the blazes are ye?" he asked, glaring at them over the lamp.

"We're the Club Committee, father," replied Norton.

"Oh, are ye?"

"And this is the treasurer—the ex-treasurer, I should say."

"I won't pretend I'm glad to see him," said Father Crowley grimly.

"He came to say he's sorry, father," went on Norton. "He is sorry, and that's as true as God, and I'll tell you no lie. . . ." Norton made two steps forward and in a dramatic silence laid a heap of notes and silver on the table.

"What's that?" asked Father Crowley.

"The money, father. 'Tis all paid back now and there's nothing more between us. Any little crossness there was, we'll say no more about it, in the name of God."

The priest looked at the money and then at Norton.

"Con," he said, "you'd better keep the soft word for the judge. Maybe he'll think more of it than I do."

"The judge, father?"

"Ay, Con, the judge."

There was a long silence. The committee stood with open mouths, unable to believe it.

"And is that what you're doing to us, father?" asked Norton in a trembling voice. "After all the years, and all we done for you, is it you're going to show us up before the whole country as a lot of robbers?"

"Ay, ye idiots, I'm not showing ye up."

"You are then, father, and you're showing up every man, woman, and child in the parish," said Norton. "And mark my words, 'twon't be forgotten for you."

The following Sunday Father Crowley spoke of the matter from the altar. He spoke for a full half-hour without a trace of emotion on his grim old face, but his sermon was one long, venomous denunciation of the "long-tailed families" who, according to him, were the ruination of the country and made a mockery of truth, justice, and charity. He was, as his congregation agreed, a shockingly obstinate old man who never knew when he was in the wrong.

After Mass he was visited in his sacristy by the committee. He gave Norton a terrible look from under his shaggy eyebrows, which made that respectable farmer flinch.

"Father," Norton said appealingly, "we only want one word with you. One word and then we'll go. You're a hard character, and you said some bitter things to us this morning; things we never deserved from you. But we're quiet, peaceable poor men and we don't want to cross you."

Father Crowley made a sound like a snort.

"We came to make a bargain with you, father," said Norton, beginning to smile.

"A bargain?"

"We'll say no more about the whole business if you'll do one little thing—just one little thing—to oblige us."

"The bargain!" the priest said impatiently. "What's the bargain?"

"We'll leave the matter drop for good and all if you'll give the boy a character."

"Yes, father," cried the committee in chorus. "Give him a character! Give him a character!"

"Give him a what?" cried the priest.

"Give him a character, father, for the love of God," said Norton emotionally. "If you speak up for him, the judge will leave him off and there'll be no stain on the parish."

"Is it out of your minds you are, you half-witted angashores?" asked Father Crowley, his face suffused with blood, his head trembling. "Here am I all these years preaching to ye about decency and justice and truth and ye no more understand me than that wall there. Is it the way ye want me to perjure myself? Is it the way ye want me to tell a damned lie with the name of Almighty God on my lips? Answer me, is it?"

"Ah, what perjure!" Norton replied wearily. "Sure, can't you say a few words for the boy? No one is asking you to say much. What harm will it do you to tell the judge he's an honest, good-living, upright lad, and that he took the money without meaning any harm?"

"My God!" muttered the priest, running his hands distractedly through his gray hair. "There's no talking to ye, no talking to ye, ye lot of sheep."

When he was gone the committeemen turned and looked at one another in bewilderment.

"That man is a terrible trial," said one.

"He's a tyrant," said Daly vindictively.

"He is, indeed," sighed Norton, scratching his head. "But in God's holy name, boys, before we do anything, we'll give him one more chance."

That evening when he was at his tea the committeemen called again.

This time they looked very spruce, businesslike, and independent. Father Crowley glared at them.

"Are ye back?" he asked bitterly. "I was thinking ye would be. I declare to my goodness, I'm sick of ye and yeer old committee."

"Oh, we're not the committee, father," said Norton stiffly.

"Ye're not?"

"We're not."

"All I can say is, ye look mighty like it. And, if I'm not being impertinent, who the deuce are ye?"

"We're a deputation, father."

"Oh, a deputation! Fancy that, now. And a deputation from what?"

"A deputation from the parish, father. Now, maybe you'll listen to us."

"Oh, go on! I'm listening, I'm listening."

"Well, now, 'tis like this, father," said Norton, dropping his airs and graces and leaning against the table. " 'Tis about that little business this morning. Now, father, maybe you don't understand us and we don't understand you. There's a lot of misunderstanding in the world today, father. But we're quiet simple poor men that want to do the best we can for everybody, and a few words or a few pounds wouldn't stand in our way. Now, do you follow me?"

"I declare," said Father Crowley, resting his elbows on the table, "I don't know whether I do or not."

"Well, 'tis like this, father. We don't want any blame on the parish or on the Cronins, and you're the one man that can save us. Now all we ask of you is to give the boy a character—"

"Yes, father," interrupted the chorus, "give him a character! Give him a character!"

"Give him a character, father, and you won't be troubled by him again. Don't say no to me now till you hear what I have to say. We won't ask you to go next, nigh or near the court. You have pen and ink beside you and one couple of lines is all you need write. When 'tis over you can hand Michael John his ticket to America and tell him not to show his face in Carricknabreena again. There's the price of his ticket, father," he added, clapping a bundle of notes on the table. "The Cronins themselves made it up, and we have his mother's word and his own word that he'll clear out the minute 'tis all over."

"He can go to pot!" retorted the priest. "What is it to me where he goes?"

"Now, father, can't you be patient?" Norton asked reproachfully. "Can't you let me finish what I'm saying? We know 'tis no advantage to you, and that's the very thing we came to talk about. Now, supposing—just supposing for the sake of argument—that you do what we say, there's a few of us here, and between us, we'd raise whatever little contribution to the parish fund you'd think would be reasonable to cover the expense and trouble to yourself. Now do you follow me?"

"Con Norton," said Father Crowley, rising and holding the edge of the table, "I follow you. This morning it was perjury, and now 'tis bribery, and the Lord knows what 'twill be next. I see I've been wasting my breath. . . . And I see too," he added savagely, leaning across the table towards them, "a pedigree bull would be more use to ye than a priest."

"What do you mean by that, father?" asked Norton in a low voice.

"What I say."

"And that's a saying that will be remembered for you the longest day you live," hissed Norton, leaning towards him till they were glaring at one another over the table.

"A bull," gasped Father Crowley. "Not a priest."

" 'Twill be remembered."

"Will it? Then remember this too. I'm an old man now. I'm forty years a priest, and I'm not a priest for the money or power or glory of it, like others I know. I gave the best that was in me—maybe 'twasn't much but 'twas more than many a better man would give, and at the end of my days . . ." lowering his voice to a whisper he searched them with his terrible eyes, ". . . at the end of my days, if I did a wrong thing, or a bad thing, or an unjust thing, there isn't man or woman in this parish that would brave me to my face and call me a villain. And isn't that a poor story for an old man that tried to be a good priest?" His voice changed again and he raised his head defiantly. "Now get out before I kick you out!"

And true to his word and character not one word did he say in Michael John's favor the day of the trial, no more than if he was black. Three months Michael John got and by all accounts he got off light.

He was a changed man when he came out of jail, downcast and dark in himself. Everyone was sorry for him, and people who had never spoken to him before spoke to him then. To all of them he said modestly: "I'm very grateful to you, friend, for overlooking my misfortune." As he wouldn't go to America, the committee made another whip-round and between what they had collected before and what the Cronins had made up to send him to America, he found himself with enough to open a small shop. Then he got a job in the County Council, and an agency for some shipping company, till at last he was able to buy a public-house.

As for Father Crowley, till he was shifted twelve months later, he never did a day's good in the parish. The dues went down and the presents went down, and people with money to spend on Masses took it fifty miles away sooner than leave it to him. They said it broke his heart.

He has left unpleasant memories behind him. Only for him, people say, Michael John would be in America now. Only for him he would never have married a girl with money, or had it to lend to poor people in the hard times, or ever sucked the blood of Christians. For, as an old man said to me of him: "A robber he is and was, and a grabber like his grandfather before him, and an enemy of the people like his uncle, the policeman; and though some say he'll dip his hand where he dipped it before, for myself I have no hope unless the mercy of God would send us another Moses or Brian Boru to cast him down and hammer him in the dust."

The Majesty of the Law

OLD DAN BRIDE was breaking brosna for the fire when he heard a step on the path. He paused, a bundle of saplings on his knee.

Dan had looked after his mother while the life was in her, and after her death no other woman had crossed his threshold. Signs on it, his house had that look. Almost everything in it he had made with his own hands in his own way. The seats of the chairs were only slices of log, rough and round and thick as the saw had left them, and with the rings still plainly visible through the grime and polish that coarse trouser-bottoms had in the course of long years imparted. Into these Dan had rammed stout knotted ash-boughs that served alike for legs and back. The deal table, bought in a shop, was an inheritance from his mother and a great pride and joy to him though it rocked whenever he touched it. On the wall, unglazed and fly-spotted, hung in mysterious isolation a Marcus Stone print, and beside the door was a calendar with a picture of a racehorse. Over the door hung a gun, old but good, and in excellent condition, and before the fire was stretched an old setter who raised his head expectantly whenever Dan rose or even stirred.

He raised it now as the steps came nearer and when Dan, laying down the bundle of saplings, cleaned his hands thoughtfully on the seat of his trousers, he gave a loud bark, but this expressed no more than a desire to show off his own watchfulness. He was half human and knew people thought he was old and past his prime.

A man's shadow fell across the oblong of dusty light thrown over the half-door before Dan looked round.

"Are you alone, Dan?" asked an apologetic voice.

"Oh, come in, come in, sergeant, come in and welcome," exclaimed the old man, hurrying on rather uncertain feet to the door which the tall policeman opened and pushed in. He stood there, half in sunlight, half in shadow, and seeing him so, you would have realized how dark the interior of the house really was. One side of his red face was turned so as to catch the light, and behind it an ash tree raised its boughs of airy green against the sky. Green fields, broken here and there by clumps of red-brown rock, flowed downhill, and beyond them, stretched all across the horizon, was the sea, flooded and almost transparent with light. The sergeant's face was fat and fresh, the old man's face, emerging from the twilight of the kitchen, had the color of wind and sun, while the features had been so shaped by the struggle with time and the elements that they might as easily have been found impressed upon the surface of a rock.

"Begor, Dan," said the sergeant, " 'tis younger you're getting."

"Middling I am, sergeant, middling," agreed the old man in a voice which seemed to accept the remark as a compliment of which politeness would not allow him to take too much advantage. "No complaints."

"Begor, 'tis as well because no one would believe them. And the old dog doesn't look a day older."

The dog gave a low growl as though to show the sergeant that he would remember this unmannerly reference to his age, but indeed he growled every time he was mentioned, under the impression that people had nothing but ill to say of him.

"And how's yourself, sergeant?"

"Well, now, like the most of us, Dan, neither too good nor too bad. We have our own little worries, but, thanks be to God, we have our compensations."

"And the wife and family?"

"Good, praise be to God, good. They were away from me for a month, the lot of them, at the mother-in-law's place in Clare."

"In Clare, do you tell me?"

"In Clare. I had a fine quiet time."

The old man looked about him and then retired to the bedroom, from which he returned a moment later with an old shirt. With this he solemnly wiped the seat and back of the log-chair nearest the fire.

"Sit down now, sergeant. You must be tired after the journey. 'Tis a long old road. How did you come?"

"Teigue Leary gave me the lift. Wisha now, Dan, don't be putting yourself out. I won't be stopping. I promised them I'd be back inside an hour."

"What hurry is on you?" asked Dan. "Look, your foot was only on the path when I made up the fire."

"Arrah, Dan, you're not making tea for me?"

"I am not making it for you, indeed; I'm making it for myself, and I'll take it very bad of you if you won't have a cup."

"Dan, Dan, that I mightn't stir, but 'tisn't an hour since I had it at the barracks!"

"Ah, whisht, now, whisht! Whisht, will you! I have something here to give you an appetite."

The old man swung the heavy kettle onto the chain over the open fire, and the dog sat up, shaking his ears with an expression of the deepest interest. The policeman unbuttoned his tunic, opened his belt, took a pipe and a plug of tobacco from his breast pocket, and crossing his legs in an easy posture, began to cut the tobacco slowly and carefully with his pocket knife. The old man went to the dresser and took down two handsomely decorated cups, the only cups he had, which, though chipped and handleless, were used at all only on very rare occasions; for himself he preferred his tea from a basin. Happening to glance into them, he noticed that they bore signs of disuse and had collected a lot of the fine white turf-dust that always circulated in the little smoky cottage. Again he thought of the shirt, and, rolling up his sleeves with a stately gesture, he wiped them inside and out till they shone. Then he bent and opened the cupboard. Inside was a quart bottle of pale liquid, obviously untouched. He removed the cork and smelt the contents, pausing for a moment in the act as though to recollect where exactly he had noticed that particular smoky smell before. Then, reassured, he stood up and poured out with a liberal hand.

"Try that now, sergeant," he said with quiet pride.

The sergeant, concealing whatever qualms he might have felt at the idea of drinking illegal whiskey, looked carefully into the cup, sniffed, and glanced up at old Dan.

"It looks good," he commented.

"It should be good," replied Dan with no mock modesty.

"It tastes good too," said the sergeant.

"Ah, sha," said Dan, not wishing to praise his own hospitality in his own house, " 'tis of no great excellence."

"You'd be a good judge, I'd say," said the sergeant without irony.

"Ever since things became what they are," said Dan, carefully guarding himself against a too-direct reference to the peculiarities of the law administered by his guest, "liquor isn't what it used to be."

"I've heard that remark made before now, Dan," said the sergeant thoughtfully. "I've heard it said by men of wide experience that it used to be better in the old days."

"Liquor," said the old man, "is a thing that takes time. There was never a good job done in a hurry."

" 'Tis an art in itself."

"Just so."

"And an art takes time."

"And knowledge," added Dan with emphasis. "Every art has its secrets, and the secrets of distilling are being lost the way the old songs were lost. When I was a boy there wasn't a man in the barony but had a hundred songs in his head, but with people running here, there and everywhere, the songs were lost. . . . Ever since things became what they are," he repeated on the same guarded note, "there's so much running about the secrets are lost."

"There must have been a power of them."

"There was. Ask any man today that makes whiskey do he know how to make it out of heather."

"And was it made of heather?" asked the policeman.

"It was."

"You never drank it yourself?"

"I didn't, but I knew old men that did, and they told me that no whiskey that's made nowadays could compare with it."

"Musha, Dan, I think sometimes 'twas a great mistake of the law to set its hand against it."

Dan shook his head. His eyes answered for him, but it was not in nature for a man to criticize the occupation of a guest in his own home.

"Maybe so, maybe not," he said noncommittally.

"But sure, what else have the poor people?"

"Them that makes the laws have their own good reasons."

"All the same, Dan, all the same, 'tis a hard law."

The sergeant would not be outdone in generosity. Politeness required him not to yield to the old man's defense of his superiors and their mysterious ways.

"It is the secrets I'd be sorry for," said Dan, summing up. "Men die and men are born, and where one man drained another will plow, but a secret lost is lost forever."

"True," said the sergeant mournfully. "Lost forever."

Dan took his cup, rinsed it in a bucket of clear water by the door and cleaned it again with the shirt. Then he placed it carefully at the sergeant's elbow. From the dresser he took a jug of milk and a blue bag containing sugar; this he followed up with a slab of country butter and—a sure sign that he had been expecting a visitor—a round cake of homemade bread, fresh and uncut. The kettle sang and spat and the dog, shaking his ears, barked at it angrily.

"Go away, you brute!" growled Dan, kicking him out of his way.

He made the tea and filled the two cups. The sergeant cut himself a large slice of bread and buttered it thickly.

"It is just like medicines," said the old man, resuming his theme with the imperturbability of age. "Every secret there was is lost. And leave no one tell me that a doctor is as good a man as one that had the secrets of old times."

"How could he be?" asked the sergeant with his mouth full.

"The proof of that was seen when there were doctors and wise people there together."

"It wasn't to the doctors the people went, I'll engage?"

"It was not. And why?" With a sweeping gesture the old man took in the whole world outside his cabin. "Out there on the hillsides is the sure cure for every disease. Because it is written"—he tapped the table with his thumb—"it is written by the poets 'wherever you find the disease you will find the cure.' But people walk up the hills and down the hills and all they see is flowers. Flowers! As if God Almighty—honor and praise to Him!—had nothing better to do with His time than be making old flowers!"

"Things no doctor could cure the wise people cured," agreed the sergeant.

"Ah, musha, 'tis I know it," said Dan bitterly. "I know it, not in my mind but in my own four bones."

"Have you the rheumatics at you still?" the sergeant asked in a shocked tone.

"I have. Ah, if you were alive, Kitty O'Hara, or you, Nora Malley of the Glen, 'tisn't I'd be dreading the mountain wind or the sea wind; 'tisn't I'd be creeping down with my misfortunate red ticket for the blue and pink and yellow dribble-drabble of their ignorant dispensary."

"Why then indeed," said the sergeant, "I'll get you a bottle for that."

"Ah, there's no bottle ever made will cure it."

"That's where you're wrong, Dan. Don't talk now till you try it. It cured my own uncle when he was that bad he was shouting for the carpenter to cut the two legs off him with a handsaw."

"I'd give fifty pounds to get rid of it," said Dan magniloquently. "I would and five hundred."

The sergeant finished his tea in a gulp, blessed himself and struck a match which he then allowed to go out as he answered some question of the old man. He did the same with a second and third, as though titillating his appetite with delay. Finally he succeeded in getting his pipe alight and the two men pulled round their chairs, placed their toes side by side in the ashes, and in deep puffs, lively bursts of conversation, and long, long silences, enjoyed their smoke.

"I hope I'm not keeping you?" said the sergeant, as though struck by the length of his visit.

"Ah, what would you keep me from?"

"Tell me if I am. The last thing I'd like to do is waste another man's time."

"Begor, you wouldn't waste my time if you stopped all night."

"I like a little chat myself," confessed the policeman.

And again they became lost in conversation. The light grew thick and colored and, wheeling about the kitchen before it disappeared, became tinged with gold; the kitchen itself sank into cool grayness with cold light on the cups and basins and plates of the dresser. From the ash tree a thrush began to sing. The open hearth gathered brightness till its light was a warm, even splash of crimson in the twilight.

Twilight was also descending outside when the sergeant rose to go. He fastened his belt and tunic and carefully brushed his clothes. Then he put on his cap, tilted a little to side and back.

"Well, that was a great talk," he said.

" 'Tis a pleasure," said Dan, "a real pleasure."

"And I won't forget the bottle for you."

"Heavy handling from God to you!"

"Good-bye now, Dan."

"Good-bye, sergeant, and good luck."

Dan didn't offer to accompany the sergeant beyond the door. He sat in his old place by the fire, took out his pipe once more, blew through it thoughtfully, and just as he leaned forward for a twig to kindle it, heard the steps returning. It was the sergeant. He put his head a little way over the half-door.

"Oh, Dan!" he called softly.

"Ay, sergeant?" replied Dan, looking round, but with one hand still reaching for the twig. He couldn't see the sergeant's face, only hear his voice.

"I suppose you're not thinking of paying that little fine, Dan?"

There was a brief silence. Dan pulled out the lighted twig, rose slowly and shambled towards the door, stuffing it down in the almost empty bowl of the pipe. He leaned over the half-door while the sergeant with hands in the pockets of his trousers gazed rather in the direction of the laneway, yet taking in a considerable portion of the sea line.

"The way it is with me, sergeant," replied Dan unemotionally, "I am not."

"I was thinking that, Dan; I was thinking you wouldn't."

There was a long silence during which the voice of the thrush grew shriller and merrier. The sunken sun lit up rafts of purple cloud moored high above the wind.

"In a way," said the sergeant, "that was what brought me."

"I was just thinking so, sergeant, it only struck me and you going out the door."

"If 'twas only the money, Dan, I'm sure there's many would be glad to oblige you."

"I know that, sergeant. No, 'tisn't the money so much as giving that fellow the satisfaction of paying. Because he angered me, sergeant."

The sergeant made no comment on this and another long silence ensued.

"They gave me the warrant," the sergeant said at last, in a tone which dissociated him from all connection with such an unneighborly document.

"Did they so?" exclaimed Dan, as if he was shocked by the thoughtlessness of the authorities.

"So whenever 'twould be convenient for you—"

"Well, now you mention it," said Dan, by way of throwing out a suggestion for debate, "I could go with you now."

"Ah, sha, what do you want going at this hour for?" protested the sergeant with a wave of his hand, dismissing the notion as the tone required.

"Or I could go tomorrow," added Dan, warming to the issue.

"Would it be suitable for you now?" asked the sergeant, scaling up his voice accordingly.

"But, as a matter of fact," said the old man emphatically, "the day that would be most convenient to me would be Friday after dinner, because I have some messages to do in town, and I wouldn't have the journey for nothing."

"Friday will do grand," said the sergeant with relief that this delicate matter was now practically disposed of. "If it doesn't they can damn well wait. You could walk in there yourself when it suits you and tell them I sent you."

"I'd rather have yourself there, sergeant, if it would be no inconvenience. As it is, I'd feel a bit shy."

"Why then, you needn't feel shy at all. There's a man from my own parish there, a warder; one Whelan. Ask for him; I'll tell him you're coming, and I'll guarantee when he knows you're a friend of mine he'll make you as comfortable as if you were at home."

"I'd like that fine," Dan said with profound satisfaction. "I'd like to be with friends, sergeant."

"You will be, never fear. Good-bye again now, Dan. I'll have to hurry."

"Wait now, wait till I see you to the road."

Together the two men strolled down the laneway while Dan explained how it was that he, a respectable old man, had had the grave misfortune to open the head of another old man in such a way as to require his removal to hospital, and why it was that he couldn't give the old man in question the satisfaction of paying in cash for an injury brought about through the victim's own unmannerly method of argument.

"You see, sergeant," Dan said, looking at another little cottage up the hill, "the way it is, he's there now, and he's looking at us as sure as there's a glimmer of sight in his weak, wandering, watery eyes, and nothing would give him more gratification than for me to pay. But I'll punish him. I'll lie on bare boards for him. I'll suffer for him, sergeant, so that neither he nor any of his children after him will be able to raise their heads for the shame of it."

On the following Friday he made ready his donkey and butt and set out. On his way he collected a number of neighbors who wished to bid him farewell. At the top of the hill he stopped to send them back. An old man, sitting in the sunlight, hastily made his way indoors, and a moment later the door of his cottage was quietly closed.

Having shaken all his friends by the hand, Dan lashed the old donkey, shouted: "Hup there!" and set out alone along the road to prison.

Eternal Triangle

REVOLUTIONS? I never had any interest in them. A man in my position have to mind his job and not bother about what other people are doing. Besides, I never could see what good they did anybody, and I see more of that kind of thing than most people. A watchman have to be out at all hours in all kinds of weather. He have to keep his eyes open. All I ever seen out of things like that was the damage. And who pays for the damage? You and me and people like us, so that one set of jackeens can get in instead of another set of jackeens. What is it to me who's in or out? All I know is that I have to pay for the damage they do.

I remember well the first one I saw. It was a holiday, and when I turned up to the depot, I was told there was a tram after breaking down in town, and I was to go in and keep an eye on it. A lot of the staff was at the races, and it might be a couple of hours before they could get a breakdown gang. So I took my lunch and away with me into town. It was a nice spring day and I thought I might as well walk.

Mind you, I noticed nothing strange, only that the streets were a bit empty, but it struck me that a lot of people were away for the day. Then, all at once, just as I got to town, I noticed a handful of them Volunteer boys in the street. Some of them had green uniforms with slouch hats; more of them had nothing only belts and bandoliers. All of them had guns of one sort or another. I paid no attention. Seeing that it was a holiday, I thought they might be on some sort of manoeuvre. They were a crowd I never had anything to do with. As I say, I'm a man that minds his own business.

Suddenly, one of them raises his gun and halts me.

"Halt!" says he. "Where are you bound for, mate?"

"Just down here, to keep an eye on a tram," I said, taking it in good parts.

"A tram?" says he. "That's the very thing we want for a barricade. Could you drive it?"

"Ah, is it to have the union after me?" says I.

"Ah, to hell with the union," says a second fellow. "If you'll drive it we'll rig it up as an armored train."

Now, I did not like the tone them fellows took. They were making too free altogether, and it struck me as peculiar that there wouldn't be a bobby there to send them about their business. I went on a couple of hundred yards, and what did I see only a second party. These fellows were wearing khaki, and I recognized them as cadets from the college. They were standing on the steps of the big hotel overlooking the tram, and the young fellow that was supposed to be their officer was very excited.

"That tram is in the direct line of fire," he says. "It's not a safe place."

"Ah, well," I said, "in my job there's a lot of things aren't safe. I hope if anything happens me you'll put in a good word for me with the tramway company."

Mind you, I was still not taking them seriously. I didn't know what I was after walking into. And the first thing I did was to go over the tram to see was there anything missing. The world is full of light-fingered people, and a thing like that, if you only left it for five minutes, you wouldn't know what would be gone. I was shocked when I seen the upstairs. The glass was all broken and the upholstery ripped.

Then the shooting began, and I had to lie on the floor, but after a while it eased off, and I sat up and ate my lunch and read the daily paper. There was no one around, because whenever anyone showed himself at the end of the road, there was a bang and he ran for his life. Coming on to dusk, I began to worry a bit about whether I was going to be relieved at all that day. I knew Danny Delea, the foreman, was a conscientious sort of man, and if he couldn't get a relief, he'd send me word what to do, but no one came, and I was beginning to get a bit hungry. I don't mind admitting that a couple of times I got up to go home. I didn't like sitting there with the darkness coming on, not knowing was I going to be relieved that night or the next week. But each time I sat down again. That is the sort I am. I knew the light-fingered gentry, and I knew that, firing or no firing, they were on the look-out and I wouldn't be out of that tram before one of them would be along to see what could he pick up. I would not give it to say to the rest of the men that I would leave a valuable thing like a tram.

Then, all at once, the firing got hot again, and when I looked out, what did I see in the dusk only a girl coming from behind the railings in the park and running this way and that in an aimless sort of way. She looked as if she was out of her mind with fright, and I could see the fright was more a danger to her than anything else. Mind, I had no wish for her company! I saw what she was, and they are a sort of woman I would never have much to do with. They are always trying to make friends with watchmen, because we are out at all hours. At the same time, I saw if I didn't do something quick, she'd be killed under my eyes, so I stood on the platform and shouted to her to come in. She was a woman I didn't know by sight; a woman of about thirty-five. Cummins her name was. The family was from Waterford. She was a good-looking piece too, considering. I made her lie on the floor to get out of the shooting, but she was nearly hysterical, lifting her head to look at me and lowering it not to see what was going on.

"But who in hell is it, mister?" she says. "God Almighty, I only came out for a bit of sugar for me tea, and look at the capers I'm after walking into! . . . Sacred Heart of Jesus, they're off again. . . . You'd think I was something at a fair, the way they were banging their bloody bullets all round me. Who is it at all?"

"It's the cadets in the hotel here, shooting at the other fellows beyond the park," I said.

"But why don't someone send for the police? Damn soon them fellows would be along if it was only me talking to a fellow!"

" 'Twould take a lot of police to stop this," says I.

"But what are they shooting for, mister?" says she. "Is it for Ireland?"

"Ireland?" says I. "A fat lot Ireland have to hope for from little whipper-snappers like them."

"Still and all," says she, "if 'twas for Ireland, you wouldn't mind so much."

And I declare to God but she had a tear in her eye. That is the kind of women they are. They'll steal the false teeth from a corpse, but let them lay eyes on a green flag or a child in his First Communion suit, and you'd think patriotism and religion were the only two things ever in their minds.

"That sort of blackguarding isn't going to do any good to Ireland or anyone else," says I. "What I want to know is who is going to pay for the damage? Not them. They never did an honest day's work in their lives, most of them. We're going to pay for it, the way we always do."

"I'd pay them every bloody penny I have in the world this minute if only they'd shut up and go away," she says. "For God's sake, will you listen to them!"

Things were getting hotter again. What was after happening was that some of the Volunteer fellows were after crossing the park behind the shrubbery and were firing up at the hotel. They might as well be firing at the moon. The cadets were after knocking out every pane of glass and barricading the windows. One of the Volunteers jumped from a branch of a tree over the railings and ran across the road to the tram. He was an insignificant little article with a saucy air. You could tell by his accent he wasn't from Dublin. I took him to be from somewhere in the North. I didn't like him much. I never did like them Northerners anyway.

"What are ye doing here?" he says in surprise when he seen us lying on the floor.

"I'm the watchman," says I, cutting him short.

"Begor, a watchman ought to be able to watch himself better than that," he says, and without as much as "By your leave" he up with the rifle butt and knocked out every pane of glass in the side of the tram. It went to my heart to see it go. Any other time I'd have taken him and wrung his neck, but, you see, I was lying on the floor and couldn't get up to him with the firing. I pretended not to mind, but I looked at the glass and then I looked at him.

"And who," I said, "is going to pay for that?"

"Och, Mick MacQuaid to be sure," says he.

"Ah, the gentleman is right," says the woman. "Only for him we might all be kilt."

The way she about-faced and started to soft-solder that fellow got on my nerves. It is always the same with that sort of woman. They are people you can't trust.

"And what the hell is it to anyone whether you're killed or not?" I said. "No one asked you to stop. This is the tramway company's property, and if you don't like it you can leave it. You have no claim."

"We'll see whose property this is when it's all over," says the man, and he began shooting up at the windows of the hotel.

"Hey, mister," says the woman, "is that the English you're shooting at?"

"Who else do you think 'twould be?" says he.

"Ah, I was only saying when you came in that I'd never mind if 'twas against the English. I suppose 'twill be in the history books, mister, like Robert Emmet?"

"Robert Emmet!" I said. "I'd like to know where you and the likes of you would be only for the English."

"Well, do you know," she says, as innocent as you please, " 'tis a funny thing about me, but I never cared much for the English soldiers. Of course, mind you, you'd meet nice fellows everywhere, but you'd never know where you were with the English. They haven't the same nature as our own somehow."

Then someone blew a whistle in the park, and your man dropped his rifle and looked out to see how he was going to get back.

"You're going to get your nose shot off if you go out in that, mister," says the woman. "If you'll take my advice, you'll wait till 'tis dark."

"I'm after getting into a tight corner all right," says he.

"Oh, you'll never cross that street alive, mister," she says as if she was delighted with it. "The best thing you could do now would be to wait till after dark and come round to my little place for a cup of tea. You'd be safe there anyway."

"Och, to hell with it," says he. "I have only to take a chance," and he crept down the steps and made for the railings. They spotted him, because they all began to blaze together. The woman got on her hands and knees to look after him.

"Aha, he's away!" says she, clapping her hands like a child. "Good man you are, me bold fellow. . . . I wouldn't wish for a pound that anything would happen that young man," says she to me.

"The shooting on both sides is remarkably wide," says I. "That fellow should have more sense."

"Ah, we won't know till we're dead who have the sense and who haven't," says she. "Some people might get a proper suck-in. God, wouldn't I laugh."

"Some people are going to get a suck-in long before that," says I. "The impudence of that fellow, talking about the tramway company. He thinks they're going to hand it over to him. Whoever is in, he's not going to see much of it."

"Ah, what matter?" she said. " 'Tis only youth. Youth is lovely, I always think. And 'tis awful to think of young fellows being kilt, whoever they are. Like in France. God, 'twould go to your heart. And what is it all for? Ireland! Holy Moses, what did Ireland ever do for us? Bread and dripping and a kick in the ass is all we ever got out of it. You're right about the English, though. You'd meet some very genuine English chaps. Very sincere, in their own way."

"Oh, they have their good points," says I. "I never saw much to criticize in them, only they're given too much liberty."

"Ah, what harm did a bit of liberty ever do anyone, though?" says she.

"Now, it does do harm," says I. "Too much liberty is bad. People ought to mind themselves. Look at me! I'm on this job the best part of my life, and I have more opportunities than most, but thanks be to God, I can say I never took twopenceworth belonging to my employers nor never had anything to do with a woman outside my own door."

"And a hell of a lot of thanks you'll get for it in the heel of the hunt," says she. "Five bob a week pension and the old woman stealing it out of your pocket while you're asleep. Don't I know all about it? Oh, God, I wish I was back in me own little room. I'd give all the countries that ever was this minute for a cup of tea with sugar in it. I'd never mind the rations only for the bit of sugar. Hi, mister, would you ever see me home to the doss? I wouldn't be afraid if I had you with me."

"But I have to mind this tram," says I.

"You have what?" says she, cocking her head. "Who do you think is going to run away with it?"

"Now, you'd be surprised," says I.

"Surprised?" says she. "I'd be enchanted."

"Well," I said, "the way I look at it, I'm paid to look after it, and this is my place till I'm relieved."

"But how the hell could you be relieved with this merry-go-round?"

"That is a matter for my employers to decide," says I.

"God," says she, "I may be bad but you're looney," and then she looked at me and she giggled. She started giggling, and she went on giggling, just as if she couldn't stop. That is what I say about them women. There is a sort of childishness in them all, just as if they couldn't be serious about anything. That is what has them the way they are.

So the night came on, and the stars came out, and the shooting only got louder. We were sitting there in the tram, saying nothing, when all at once I looked out and saw the red light over the houses.

"That's a fire," says I.

"If it is, 'tis a mighty big fire," says she.

And then we saw another one to the left of it, and another and another till the whole sky seemed to be lit up, and the smoke pouring away out to sea as if it was the whole sky was moving.

"That's the whole city on fire," says I.

"And 'tis getting mighty close to us," says she. "God send they don't burn this place as well. 'Tis bad enough to be starved and frozen without being roasted alive as well."

I was too mesmerized to speak. I knew what 'twas worth. Millions of pounds' worth of property burning, and no one to pour a drop of water on it. That is what revolutions are like. People talk about poverty, and then it all goes up in smoke—enough to keep thousands comfortable.

Then, all at once, the shooting got nearer, and when I looked out I saw a man coming up the road. The first impression I got of him was that he was badly wounded, for he was staggering from one side of the road to the other with his hands in the air. "I surrender, I surrender," he was shouting, and the more he shouted, the harder they fired. He staggered out into the middle of the road again, stood there for a minute, and then went down like a sack of meal.

"Oh, the poor misfortunate man!" says the woman, putting her hands to her face. "Did you ever see such barbarity? Killing him like that in cold blood?"

But he wasn't killed yet, for he began to bawl all over again, and when he got tired of holding up his hands, he stuck his feet in the air instead.

"Cruel, bloody, barbarous brutes!" says the woman. "They ought to be ashamed of themselves. He told them he surrendered, and they won't let him." And without another word, away with her off down the street to him, bawling: "Here, mister, come on in here and you'll be safe."

A wonder we weren't all killed with her. He got up and started running towards the tram with his hands still in the air. When she grabbed him and pushed him up on the platform, he still had them there. I seen then by his appearance that he wasn't wounded but drunk. He was a thin-looking scrawny man with a cloth cap.

"I surrender," he bawls. *"Kamerad."*

"Hi, mister," says the woman, "would you for the love of the suffering God stop surrendering and lie down."

"But they won't let me lie down," says he. "That's all I want is to lie down, but every time I do they makes a cockshot of me. What in hell is it?"

"Oh, this is the Rising, mister," she says.

"The what?" says he.

"The Rising," says she. "Like they said in the papers there would be."

"Who's rising?" says he, grabbing his head. "What paper said that? I want to know is this the D.T.'s I have or isn't it?"

"Oh, 'tisn't the D.T.'s at all, mister," she says, delighted to be able to spread the good news. "This is all real, what you see. 'Tis the Irish rising. Our own boys, don't you know? Like in Robert Emmet's time. The Irish are on that side and the English are on this. 'Twas the English was firing at you, the low scuts!"

"Bugger them!" he says. "They're after giving me a splitting head. There's no justice in this bloody world." Then he sat on the inside step of the tram and put his head between his knees. "Like an engine," he says. "Have you e'er a drop of water?"

"Ah, where would we get it, man?" says the woman, brightening up when she seen him take the half pint of whiskey out of his hip pocket. 'Tis a mystery to me still it wasn't broken. "Is that whiskey you have, mister?"

"No water?" says he, and then he began to shudder all over and put his hand over his face. "Where am I?" says he.

"Where should you be?" says she.

"How the hell do I know and the trams not running?" says he. "Tell me, am I alive or dead?"

"Well, you're alive for the time being," says the woman. "How long we're all going to be that way is another matter entirely."

"Well, are you alive, ma'am?" says he. "You'll excuse me being personal?"

"Oh, no offense, mister," says she. "I'm still in the queue."

"And do you see what I see?" says he.

"What's that, mister?"

"All them fires."

"Oh," says she, "don't let a little thing like that worry you, mister. That's not Hell, if that's what you're afraid of. That's only the city burning."

"The what burning?" says he.

"The city burning," says she. "That's it, there."

"There's more than the bloody city burning," says he. "Haven't you e'er a drop of water at all?"

"Ah, we can spare it," she says. "I think it must be the Almighty God sent you, mister. I declare to you, with all the goings-on, I hadn't a mouthful to eat the whole day, not as much as a cup of tea."

So she took a swig of the bottle and passed it to me. It is stuff I would never much care for, the whiskey, but having nothing to eat, I was feeling in the want of something.

"Who's that fellow in there?" says he, noticing me for the first time.

"That's only the watchman," says she.

"Is he Irish or English?" says the drunk.

"Ah, what the hell would he be only Irish?"

"Because if he's English, he's getting none of my whiskey," says the drunk, beginning to throw his arms about. "I'd cut the throat of any bloody Englishman."

Oh, pure, unadulterated patriotism! Leave it to a boozer.

"Now, don't be attracting attention, like a good man," she says. "We all have our principles but we don't want to be overheard. We're in trouble enough, God knows."

"I'm not afraid of anyone," says he, staggering to his feet. "I'm not afraid to tell the truth. A bloody Englishman that would shoot a misfortunate man and he on the ground, I despise him. I despise the English."

Then there was a couple of bangs, and he threw up his hands and down with him like a scarecrow in a high wind.

"I declare to me God," says the woman with an ugly glance at the hotel, "them fellows in there are wound up. Are you hit, mister?" says she, giving him a shake. "Oh, begod, I'm afraid his number's up."

"Open his collar and give us a look at him," says I. By this time I was sick of the pair of them.

"God help us, and not a priest nor doctor to be had," says she. "Could you say the prayers for the dying?"

"How would I know the prayers for the dying?" says I.

"Say an act of contrition so," says she.

Well, I began, but I was so upset that I started the Creed instead.

"That's not the act of contrition," says she.

"Say it yourself as you're so smart," says I, and she began, but before she was finished, the drunk shook his fist in the air and said: "I'll cut the living lights out of any Englishman," and then he began to snore.

"Some people have the gift," says she.

Gift was no word for it. We sat there the whole night, shivering and not able to get more than a snooze, and that fellow never stirred, only for the roar of the snoring. He never woke at all until it was coming on to dawn, and then he put his head in his hands again and began complaining of the headache.

"Bad whiskey is the ruination of the world," says he.

"Everyone's trouble is their own," says the woman.

And at that moment a lot of cadets came out of the hotel and over to the tram.

"Will you look at them?" says the woman. "Didn't I tell you they were wound up?"

"You'll have to get out of this now," says the officer, swinging his gun.

"And where are we going to go?" says she.

"The city is all yours," says he.

"And so is the Bank of Ireland," says she. "If I was only in my own little room this minute, you could have the rest of the city—with my compliments. Where are you off to?" she asked the drunk.

"I'll have to get the Phibsboro tram," says he.

"You could order two while you're about it," she says. "The best thing the pair of ye can do is come along to my little place and wait till this jigmareel is over."

"I have to stop here," says I.

"You can't," says the officer.

"But I must stop till I'm relieved, man," says I, getting angry with him.

"You're relieved," he says. "I'm relieving you."

And, of course, I had to do what he said. All the same, before I went, I gave him a piece of my mind.

"There's no need for this sort of thing at all," I says. "There's nothing to be gained by destroying valuable property. If people would only do what they were told and mind their own business, there would be no need for any of this blackguarding."

The woman wanted me to come into her room for a cup of tea, but I wouldn't. I was too disgusted. Away with me across the bridge, and the fellows that were guarding it never halted me or anything, and I never stopped till I got home to my own place. Then I went to bed, and I didn't get up for a week, till the whole thing was over. They had prisoners going in by droves, and I never as much as looked out at them. I was never so disgusted with anything in my life.

Masculine Protest

FOR MONTHS things had been getting worse between Mother and me. At the time I was twelve, and we were living in Boharna, a small town twenty miles from the city—Father, Mother, Martha, and I. Father worked in the County Council and we didn't see much of him. I suppose that threw me more on Mother, but I could be perfectly happy sitting with her all day if only she let me. She didn't, though. She was always inventing excuses to get rid of me, even giving me money to go to the pictures, which she knew Father didn't like because I wasn't very bright at school and he thought the pictures were bad for me.

I blamed a lot of it on Martha at first. Martha was sly, and she was always trying to get inside me with Mother. She was always saving, whereas I always found money burned a hole in my pocket, and it was only to spite her that I kept a savings bank at all. As well as that, she told Mother about all the scrapes I got into. They weren't what you'd really call scrapes. It was just that we had a gang in our neighborhood, which was the classy one of the town, and we were always having battles with the slummy kids from the other side of town who wanted to play in our neighborhood. I was the Chief Gang Leader, and it was my job to keep them from expanding beyond their own frontiers.

Martha let on not to understand why I should be Chief Gang Leader. She let on not to know why we didn't want the slum kids overrunning our locality. Though she knew better than to tell Mother when I made Viking raids on the housekeeping money, she was always at me in a low, bloodcurdling voice, following me round like a witch. "You'll be caught yet, Denis Halligan. You'll be caught. The police will be after you. You took three shillings out of Mummy's purse. God sees you!" Sometimes she drove me so wild that I went mad and twisted her arm or pulled her hair, and she went off screeching, and I got a licking.

I had managed to kid myself into the belief that one day Mother would understand; one day she would wake up and see that the affection of Dad and Martha was insincere; that the two of them had long ago ganged up against her, and that I, the black sheep, was the one who really loved her.

This revelation was due to take place in rather unusual circumstances. We were all to be stranded in some dangerous desert, and Mother, with her ankle broken, would tell us to leave her to her fate, the way they did in storybooks. Dad and Martha, of course, would leave her, with only a pretense of concern, but I, in my casual way, would simply fold my hands about my knees and ask listlessly: "What use is life to me without you?" Nothing more; I was against any false drama, any raising of the voice. I had never been one for high-flown expressions like Martha: just the lift of the shoulder, the way I pulled a grass-blade to chew (it needn't be a desert), and Mother would realize at last that though I wasn't demonstrative—just a plain, rough, willing chap—I really had a heart of gold.

The trouble about Mother was that she had a genius for subjecting hearts of gold to intolerable strain. It wasn't that she was actively unkind, for she thought far too much of the impression she wanted to make to be anything like that. It was just that she didn't care a damn. She was always away from home. She visited friends in Galway, Dublin, Birr, and Athlone, and all we ever got to see of her was the flurry between one foray and the next, while she was packing and unpacking.

Things came to a head when she told me she wouldn't be at home for my birthday. At the same time, always conscientious, she had arranged a very nice treat for Martha and me. But the treat wasn't the same thing that I had been planning, when I proposed to bring a couple of fellows along and show Mother off to them, and I began to bawl. The trouble was that the moment I did, I seemed to have no reasons on my side. It was always like that with Mother; she invariably had all the reasons on her side, and made you feel contrary and a pig, but that was worse instead of better. You felt then that she was taking advantage of you. I sobbed and stamped and asked why she hadn't done that to Martha and why she was doing it to me. She looked at me coldly and said I was a pretty picture and that I had no manliness. Of course, I saw she was in the right about that too, and that there was no excuse for a fellow of my age complaining against not being treated like his younger sister, and that only made me madder still.

"Go on!" I screamed. "Who's trying to stop you? All you want is people to admire you."

I knew when I had said it that it was awful, and expected her to give me a clout, but she only drew herself up, looking twice as dignified and beautiful.

"That is a contemptible remark, Denis," she said in a biting tone. "It's one I wouldn't have expected even from you."

The way she said it made me feel like the scum of the earth. And then she went off for the evening in a car with the Clarkes, leaving Martha and me alone. Martha looked at me, half in pity, half in amusement. She was never really disappointed in Mother, because she expected less of her. Martha was born sly.

"What did I tell you?" she said, though she hadn't told me anything.

"Go on!" I said in a thick voice. "You sucker!" Then I went upstairs and bawled and used all the dirty words I knew. I knew now it was all over between Mother and me; that no circumstances would ever occur which would show how much I loved her, because after what had happened I could not live in the same house with her again. For quite a while I thought about suicide, but I put that on one side, because the only way I could contemplate committing suicide was by shooting, and my air pistol was not strong enough for that. I took out my post-office book. I had four pounds fifteen in the bank. As I've said, it was purely out of spite against Martha, but that made no difference now. It was enough to keep me for a month or so till I found some corner where people wanted me; a plain rough-spoken chap who only needed a little affection. I was afraid of nothing in the way of work. I was strong and energetic. At the worst, I could always make for Dublin, where my grandfather and Auntie May lived. I knew they would be glad to help me, because they thought that Dad had married the wrong woman and never pretended to like Mother. When Mother had told me this I was furious, but now I saw that they were probably cleverer than I was. It would give me great satisfaction to reach their door and tell Auntie May in my plain straightforward way: "You were right and I was wrong." For the last time I looked round my bedroom and burst into fresh tears. There is something heartrending about leaving for the last time a place where you have spent so much of your life. Then, trying to steady myself, I grabbed a little holy picture from the mantelpiece and a favorite storybook from the bookshelf and ran downstairs. Martha heard me taking out my bike and came to see. It had a dynamo lamp and a three-speed gear; a smashing bike!

"Where are you off to?" she asked.

"Never mind!" I said as I cycled off.

I had no particular feelings about seeing Martha for the last time.

Then I had my first shock, because as I cycled into Main Street I saw that all the shops were shuttered for the weekly half-holiday and I knew the Post Office would be shut too and I could not draw out my savings. It was the first time I felt what people so often feel in after life, that Fate has made a plaything of you. Why should I have had my final quarrel with Mother on the one day in the week when I could not get away from her? If that wasn't Fate, what was? And I knew my own weakness of character better than anyone. I knew that if I put it off until next day, the sight of Mother would be sufficient to set me servilely seeking for pardon. Even setting off across Ireland without a penny would be better than that.

Then I had what I thought was an inspiration. The city was only twenty miles away, and the General Post Office was bound to be open. I had calculated my time to and from school at twelve miles an hour; even allowing for the distance, it wouldn't take me more than two hours. As well as that, I had been to the city for the Christmas shopping, so I knew the look of it. I could get my money and stay in a hotel or have tea and then set off for Dublin. I liked that idea. Cycling all the way up through Ireland in the dark, through sleeping towns and villages; seeing the dawn break over Dublin as I cycled down the slopes of the Dublin mountains; arriving at Auntie May's door in the Shelbourne Road when she was lighting the fire—that would be smashing. I could imagine how she would greet me—"Child of grace, where did you come from?" "Ah, just cycled." My natural modesty always came out in those daydreams of mind, for I never, under any circumstances, made a fuss. Absolutely smashing!

All the same, it was no joke, a trip like that. I cycled slowly and undecidedly out the familiar main road where we walked on Sunday, past the little suburban houses. It was queer how hard it was to break away from places and people and things you knew. I thought of letting it go and of doing the best I could to patch it up with Mother. I thought of the gang and at that a real lump rose in my throat. Tomorrow night, when my absence was noticed, there would be a new Chief Gang Leader; somebody like Eddie Humphreys who would be so prim and cautious that he would be afraid to engage the enemy which threatened us on every side. In that moment of weakness I nearly turned back. At the same moment it brought me renewed decision, for I knew that I had not been chosen Chief Gang Leader because I was a little sissy like Eddie Humphreys but because I was afraid of nothing.

At one moment my feet had nearly stopped pedalling; at the next I was pedalling for all I was worth. It was as sudden as that, like the moment when you find yourself out of your depth and two inclinations struggle in you—to swim like hell back to the shallows or strike out boldly for the other side. Up to that I had thought mainly of what was behind me; now I thought only of what was ahead of me, and it was frightening enough. I was aware of great distances, of big cloud masses on the horizon, of the fragility of my tires compared with the rough surface of the road, and I thought only of the two-hour journey ahead of me. The romantic picture of myself cycling across Ireland in the dark disappeared. I should be quite content to get the first stage over me.

For the last ten miles I wasn't even tempted to look at the scenery. I was doubled over the handlebars. Things just happened; the road bent away under me; wide green rivers rose up and slipped away again under me, castles soared from the roadside with great arches blocked out in masses of shadow.

Then at last the little rocky fields closed behind me like a book, and the blessed electric-light poles escorted me up the last hill, and I floated proudly down between comfortable villas with long gardens till I reached the bridge. The city was stretched out on the other side of the river, shining in the evening light, and my heart rose at the thought that I had at least shown Mother whether or not I had manliness. I dismounted from my bicycle and pushed it along the Main Street, looking at the shops. They were far more interesting than the shops at home, and the people looked better too.

I found the Post Office in a side street and went up to the counter with my savings-bank book.

"I want to draw out my money," I said.

The clerk looked at the clock.

"You can't do that, sonny," he said. "The savings-bank counter is shut."

"When will it open again?" I asked.

"Not till tomorrow. Any time after nine."

"But can't I get it now?"

"No. The clerk is gone home now."

I slouched out of the Post Office with despair in my heart. I took my bicycle and pushed it wearily back to the Main Street. The crowds were still going by, but now it looked long and wide and lonesome, for I had no money and I didn't know a soul. Without a meal and a rest, I could not even set out for Dublin, if I had the heart, which I knew I hadn't. Nor could I even return home, for it was already late and I was dropping with weariness. One side of the Main Street was in shadow; the shadow seemed to spread with extraordinary rapidity, and you felt that the city was being quenched as with snuffers.

It was only then that I thought of Father. It was funny that I had not thought of him before, even when thinking of Grandfather and Auntie May. I had thought of these as allies against Mother, but I hadn't even considered him as an ally. Now as I thought of him, everything about him seemed different. It wasn't only the hunger and panic. It was something new for me. It was almost love. With fresh energy I pushed my bicycle back to the Post Office, left it outside the door where I could see it, and went up to the clerk I had already spoken to.

"Could I make a telephone call?" I asked.

"You could to be sure," he said. "Have you the money?"

"No, sir."

"Well, you can't make a call without the money. Where is it to?"

"Boharna," I said.

At once his face took on a severe expression.

"That's one and threepence," he said.

"And I can't ring unless I have the money?"

"Begor, you can't. I couldn't ring myself without that."

I went out and took my bicycle again. This time I could see no way out. I dawdled along the street, leaving my bicycle by the curb and gazing in shop windows. In one I found a mirror in which I could see myself full-length. I looked old and heartbroken. It was just like a picture of a child without a home, and I blinked away my tears.

Then, as I approached a public-house, I saw a barman in shirt-sleeves standing by the door. I remembered that I had seen him already on my way down and that he had looked at me. He nodded and smiled and I stopped. I was glad of anyone making a friendly gesture in that strange place.

"Are you waiting for someone?" he asked.

"No," I said. "I wanted to make a phone call."

"You're not from these parts?"

"No," I said. "I'm from Boharna."

"Are you, begor?" he said. "Was it on the bus you came?"

"No," I replied modestly. "I biked it."

"Biked it?"

"Yes."

"That's a hell of a distance," he said.

"It is long," I agreed.

"What did you come all that way for?" he asked in surprise.

"Ah, I was running away from home," I said despondently.

"You were what?" he asked in astonishment. "You're not serious."

"But I am," I said, very close to tears. "I did my best, but then I couldn't stick it any longer and I cleared out." I turned my head away because this time I was really crying.

"Oh, begor, I know what 'tis like," he said in a friendlier tone. "I did it myself."

"Did you?" I asked eagerly, forgetting my grief. This, I felt, was the very man I wanted to meet.

"Ah, indeed I did. I did it three times what's more. By that time they were getting fed up with me. Anyway, they say practice makes perfect. Tell me, is it your old fellow?"

"No," I said with a sigh. "My mother."

"Ah, do you tell me so? That's worse again. 'Tis bad enough to have the old man at you, but 'tis the devil entirely when the mother is against you. What are you going to do now?"

"I don't know," I said. "I wanted to get to Dublin, but the savings bank is shut, and all my money is in it."

"That's tough luck. Sure, you can't get anywhere without money. I'm afraid you'll have to go back and put up with it for another while."

"But I can't," I said. " 'Tis twenty miles."

" 'Tis all of that, begor. You couldn't go on the bus?"

"I can't. I haven't the money. That's what I asked them in the Post Office, to let me ring up Daddy, but they wouldn't."

"Where's your daddy?" he asked, and when I told him: "Ah, we'll try and get him for you anyway. Come on in."

There was a phone in the corner, and he rang up and asked for Daddy. Then he gave me a big smile and handed me the receiver. I heard Daddy's voice and I nearly wept with delight.

"Hullo, son," he said in astonishment. "Where on earth are you?"

"In the city, Daddy," I said modestly—even then I couldn't bring myself to make a lot of it, the way another fellow would.

"The city?" he repeated incredulously. "What took you there?"

"I ran away from home, Dad," I said, trying to make it sound as casual as possible.

"Oh!" he exclaimed and there was a moment's pause. I was afraid he was going to get angry, but his tone remained the same. "Had a row?"

"Yes, Dad."

"And how did you get there?"

"On the bike."

"All the way? But you must be dead."

"Just a bit tired," I said modestly.

"Tell me, did you even get a meal?"

"No, Dad. The savings bank was shut."

"Ah, blazes!" he said softly. "Of course, it's the half-day. And what are you going to do now?"

"I don't know, Dad. I thought you might tell me."

"Well, what about coming home?" he said, beginning to laugh.

"I don't mind, Dad. Whatever you say."

"Hold on now till I see what the buses are like. . . . Hullo! You can get one in forty minutes' time—seven ten. Tell the conductor I'll be meeting you and I'll pay your fare. Will that be all right?"

"That's grand, Dad," I said, feeling that the world was almost right again.

When I finished, the barman was waiting for me with his coat on. He had got another man to look after the bar for him.

"Now, you'd better come and have a cup of tea with me before your bus goes," he said. "The old bike will be safe outside."

He took me to a café, and I ate cake after cake and drank tea and he told me about how he'd run away himself. You could see he was a real hard case, worse even than I was. The first time, he'd pinched a bicycle and cycled all the way to Dublin, sleeping in barns and deserted cottages. The police had brought him home and his father had belted hell out of him. They caught him again the second time, but the third time he'd joined the army and not returned home for years.

He put me and my bicycle on the bus and paid my fare. He made me promise to tell Dad that he'd done it and that Dad owed me the money. He said in this world you had to stand up for your rights. He was a rough chap, but you could see he had a good heart. It struck me that maybe only rough chaps had hearts as good as that.

Dad was waiting for me at the bus stop, and he looked at me and laughed.

"Well, the gouger!" he said. "Who ever would think that the son of a good-living, upright man like me would turn into a common tramp."

All the same I could see he was pleased, and as he pushed my bike down the street he made me tell him all about my experiences. He laughed over the barman and promised to give me the fare. Then, seeing him so friendly, I asked the question that had been on my mind the whole way back on the bus.

"Mummy back yet, Dad?"

"No, son," he said. "Not yet. She probably won't be in till late."

What I was really asking him, of course, was "Does she know?" and now I was torn by the desire to ask him not to tell her, but it choked me. It would have seemed too much like trying to gang up against her. But he seemed to know what I was thinking, for he added with a sort of careful casualness that he had sent Martha to the pictures. I guessed that that was to get her out of the way so that she couldn't bring the story to Mother, and when we had supper together and washed up afterwards, I knew I was right.

Mother came in before we went to bed, and Father talked to her just as though nothing had happened. He was a little bit more forthcoming than usual, but that was the only indication he gave, and I was fascinated, watching him create an understanding between us. It was an understanding in more ways than one, because it dawned on me gradually that, like myself and the barman, Dad too had once run away from home, and for some reason—perhaps because the bank was shut or because he was hungry, tired, and lonely—he had come back. People mostly came back, but their protest remained to distinguish them from all the others who had never run away. It was the real sign of their manhood.

I never ran away after that. I never felt I needed to.

The Sorcerer's Apprentice

THEIR FRIENDS said that whenever Jimmy Foley named the day, Una MacDermott slipped a disk. They had been keeping company for five years, and at least half a dozen times they had been on the point of marriage, only to be put off by another row. Jimmy blamed this on Una, who was an only child, and whose father, according to him, simply ruined her. Una blamed it on Jimmy's mother, and declared loudly that Irish mothers were a menace to their sons. Their friends thought it a pity, because they got so much pleasure discussing which of them was in the wrong that you felt they would never be short of subjects to talk about.

Una was a warmhearted, excitable, talkative girl with a great flow of gossip. Jimmy was more reserved; a handsome man who dressed according to his looks, serious and rather pompous, though with great skittishness when he chose to relax. He was the center of a small planetary system of flappers, and these, Una said, were part of the trouble. Not that she was jealous, but they did spoil him, and after a trying day at the office he arrived at her house with a dying air; too dispirited to talk, and thought she had nothing better to do than to prop his head and feed him chocolates.

That was bad enough, but even when she fed him chocolates, he still didn't seem prepared to let her have views of her own. She didn't want much in the way of views, for she was an intensely pious girl, always in and out of churches; but she did like to gossip, and even this Jimmy denied her out of respect for what he called "facts." The "facts," of course, were the facts as admitted by Jimmy's newspaper, which was exceedingly orthodox. Anything more was scandal. She had only to tell some story against a minister for him to knit his brows and ask: "Where did you hear that, if I may ask?" On occasion, he even rang up the city editor in Dublin to confirm the story. The city editor, of course, never confirmed it.

After three rows in one week, Una decided again that they were entirely unsuited to one another and took a train to Dublin to stay with her friends the Sheehys, who had a flat on the South Side. Joan Sheehy was Una's oldest friend. When Una stayed with them, she got into Una's bed, and they lay awake half the night, discussing every problem of love and marriage in the most concrete terms. Joan had been a nurse, so she knew all the terms. Sometimes her husband got bored or cold, sleeping alone, and staggered in to them half asleep with a pillow in his hand, but talk about love always bored him, and in a few minutes he was usually snoring while they went on with their discussion in excited whispers.

But for a full year Una had been getting less and less sympathy from Joan, who had begun to suspect that the delay in the marriage was being caused by Una rather than by Jimmy, and that she had no intention of marrying at all. Una swore she had, but Joan didn't believe her.

"Ah, for goodness' sake, girl," she said, "it's about time you stopped making excuses and settled down. You're thirty, and if you go on like this much longer, you won't have any alternative."

"But I haven't an alternative now, Joanie," Una said earnestly. "Honestly, how can I marry a man that I fight with every week?"

"Well, it's good training for fighting with him every day," said Joan. "And I'm tired of the way you grouse about your men. It doesn't matter who they are—you're bound to find something wrong with them. There was Ned Buckley," she went on, ticking them off on her fingers.

"He was the best of the bunch, but he had no religion. Doyle, the fellow with the shop on the Grand Parade, had too much. He was at Mass every morning, so he got on your nerves. Michael Healy had a lovely voice, but he drank. Now for the last five years we're hearing about Jimmy. I suppose there's something wrong with every man if you go at him with a microscope. You're turning into a proper old maid, Una, that's what's happening you."

This was precisely what alarmed Una herself whenever she thought of it, and, to disprove the charge, she set out to flirt violently with the Sheehys' friend Denis O'Brien. Charm came natural to Una, but when she wanted to be charming, she could knock a man out in the first round. And Denis didn't look as though he had many defenses. He was forty-five, an age when every man becomes fair game for flattery. He was separated from his wife. As well as that, he was poor and plain. He had a plump, bright, beaming face, with a small dark mustache, a high, bald forehead, and a quiet voice with insinuating manners. He was lonely; he did not get much in the way of solid meals, so he came a good deal to the Sheehys, who were very fond of him. He was clearly delighted with Una, encouraged her to rattle on in her usual excitable, forthright way—the way that irritated Jimmy so much—and then poked good-natured fun at her. When he had gone, Joan warned Una that Denis wasn't quite so defenseless as he appeared.

This was quite sufficient to rouse Una's interest in him. When, two evenings later, he called in the Sheehys' absence, she invited him in and deliberately encouraged him to make love to her. He needed little in the way of encouragement. When they fell to discussing love, he took the line which always irritated her when people introduced it: that of treating love as a sort of natural expression of the personality. You couldn't be yourself while you repressed this tendency. She listened to him with grave disapproval. When she told him of her difficulties with Jimmy, he irritated her further by taking Jimmy's side and giving her precisely the same line as Joan had already given her—she even suspected that he might be a mouthpiece for Joan.

"Well, you see, Una," he said in that insinuating, sermonizing way of his, "you have to take a chance. There's no such thing in marriage as absolute security. You can be friends with a man for twenty years and think you know all about him, but when you marry him, you find out things about him you never even guessed. It's a gamble, however you do it. Sooner or later you'll have to take a chance, and you should take it before you get too set in your ways."

"Haven't you ever regretted taking a chance, Denis?" she asked mockingly.

"Well, no, dear," he said after a moment's hesitation. "I can't say I have. It's no use trying to be wise before the event, you know, not in matters like that."

"It's no use throwing your judgment out the window either," she retorted.

"No," he agreed quietly, "I wouldn't ask you to do that. But you've used your judgment, so far as it takes you, and now it won't take you any farther. It's only when you find you've let opportunity slip that you really start to throw your judgment out of the window. Think of all the women you know who made fools of themselves in their thirties."

"And the men who made fools of themselves in their forties," she said maliciously, but he only slapped his knee in delight and said: "Doesn't Jimmy ever knock you about, Una?"

She repeated this conversation to Joan, omitting the love-making, but Joan didn't seem to be flattered at Denis's giving the same advice as herself. She didn't like the way Una carried her personal problems to anyone who would listen; she felt it was almost a way of ridding herself of them and of the urge to get married.

"You mean you were talking to *Denis* about Jimmy?" she asked incredulously.

"Oh, just generally," Una replied with a blush.

"God help your husband if you go round talking of him like that after you're married," Joan added dryly.

Next evening Una went to the pictures with Denis and they returned to his flat for coffee. She felt slightly self-conscious with him. He never wore a hat; his graying hair was long behind his big bald brow, and his trousers, which he never seemed to press, flapped about his heels. The flat depressed her too: two large rooms on the ground floor, a dirty toilet without a bolt in the hallway, and a communal bathroom three floors up. It had the tidy and joyless look of bachelor quarters anywhere. But it was pleasant to sit in the dusk by the large window and watch the lights come on like stars in the great pink mass of a city square, and tell him about all the young men who had courted her from the age of sixteen on. Denis was a good listener, and everything she told him moved him to some comment. When she talked of Jimmy, he repeated his advice with even more conviction. This time it struck her as positively funny, because he had his arm about her waist. Jimmy wouldn't exactly approve of this oily old clerk as an advocate.

"You see, Una," he said in his earnest paternal way, "it's no good telling me what you think of Jimmy now. You're just at a dead end with him. You'll think differently when you're married, because you'll change and he'll change as well."

"As much as all that?" she cried in mock alarm.

"Pretty much," he replied gravely. "And it won't be all for the better, of course. It may even be for the worse."

"And all after one night?" she went on in the same *gamine* tone.

"Not after one night, Una," he replied reproachfully. "Maybe not till a good many nights—and days. You're making too much of the night altogether."

"Denis, am I an old maid?"

"No, dear," he went on, refusing to be interrupted. "The way I see it, girls like you with plenty of life, if you're not married by the time you're thirty, you start exaggerating because your mind's gone off in one direction and your body in another. You talk far too much about sex. That's because you should be enjoying it instead. And that's why I think Jimmy and you quarrel as you do. You have to get your mind and body working together, the way they did when you were a kid."

He was a very unusual man, she decided; he talked in a solemn, silky, almost clerical tone, with a touch of mysticism, yet here he was at the same time making love to her, and the inconsistency gave it all a sort of fairy-tale quality.

When she reached home, Joan talked severely to her. She and her husband were very fond of Denis and were now convinced that Una was leading him on, amusing herself with him. Here she was, running away from a most desirable young man to whom she should have been married years before, and running round with a married man who was lonely, disappointed, and poor and had to work in a small job in a government office to provide the alimony he had to pay because of a previous indiscretion. Someone was going to be hurt, and it wasn't she.

Una had a good deal of conscientiousness as well as natural good sense, and instead of quarrelling with Joan she thanked her and promised to behave better. The more she thought of it, the more she saw Joan was right, and that she had only been flirting with Denis, quite regardless of the consequences to him. She was also rather flattered at the idea that it was she and not Denis who was doing the flirting.

Next evening, she gave the same sales-talk to Denis with a slight change of emphasis. With great frankness she pointed out his irresponsibility and lack of regard for the future of his children. He listened to her quietly with bowed head until she mentioned the children, and then he flashed her a quick, angry look and said: "Let the kids out of it, Una, please." She was so satisfied with her own maturity of judgment that she rang up Jimmy and told him gaily that she had had a proposition from a married man with two children.

"Some people have all the luck," he replied darkly.

"Why?" she asked in surprise. "What's wrong with the flappers?"

"Not biting this weather," he said.

Next morning she woke with a slight feeling of discomfort. When she thought about it she realized that it was caused by Denis's look when she spoke to him of his children. Something about the look suggested that he must think her not only a coquette but a hypocrite as well. She rang him up to invite him for a walk. Now that she had the situation in hand, she saw no reason why they should not be friends and regretted the words that might have caused him pain.

At midnight she found herself in bed with him, lying in a most extraordinary position, which made her giggle to herself, and realized that Joan's warning had not been superfluous. What a dozen men with ten times his attraction had failed to do, he had managed without the slightest difficulty. At one he was fast asleep and snoring in the little single bed under the window. She rose, dressed, and looked for a long time at the innocent round red face with the mouth slightly open and said aloud in a scandalized tone: "His mistress." Then she looked at herself in the mirror and frowned. She tiptoed out of the room, closed the front door quietly behind her, and was startled by the echo of her own footsteps from the other side of the square, like those of the secondary personality who had taken her place and was now returning furtively from her midnight adultery. "Adultery," she added in the same hushed voice. She felt very solemn and wanted the quiet of her own room, where she could meditate on the strangeness of her own conduct without being disturbed by his snores or the touch of his body. She was alarmed and disillusioned: alarmed that she had deliberately behaved in such an irrational and shocking way, and disillusioned because it had produced no effect on her. If this was what was supposed to change people's characters, they must be considerably more susceptible than she was.

When she woke, it was with a full sense of the possible consequences and she flew into a panic. She decided that she would marry Jimmy at once. She had now reached a stage where she could not trust herself without being married. She rang him up to tell him she was returning next day. He sounded relieved and she felt relieved herself, as though she were escaping from a great danger. She went into town and spent a lot of money on a really beautiful pullover for him. This and the crowds in the sunlight in Stephen's Green reassured her and covered up the memory of those stealthy echoing footsteps in the dark and silent square.

They reassured her so much that at last she could see no point in rushing home. After all, it was a new experience, something that people generally agreed was essential to the character, and the least she

could do was to give it a chance. She returned to Denis's to cook dinner for him that evening. This, too, was an experience that she wanted
to have, just to see what marriage to him would have been like. He
seemed touched by the sight of her, making a muck of his clean
kitchen. "Eh, girl," he said fondly, "you look a different woman in that
apron. You look quite beautiful." She felt it. She was much happier
this way than without her clothes. Denis was not a good lover as
Jimmy was; he never made her feel exalted as Jimmy did; but he did
make her feel comfortable, as though they had been married for years.
And what impressed her most was that she had no more sense of guilt
than if they had been married. It struck her that in a girl of such strict
principles, a girl who never coddled herself but set off to early Mass,
winter and summer, this was most remarkable and must mean something, if only she knew what.

Instead of going home in a hurry, she spent an extra week in Dublin,
visiting museums and galleries and going on excursions with Denis.
She ceased to be embarrassed by his baldness and his baggy trousers.
She realized that, wherever they went, there was always about him an
air of quiet distinction which marked him out. Poor but intelligent, he
knew every object of interest within twenty miles of the city. It was a
revelation to see it in his company.

At the station, when she threw her arms about his neck, the Sheehys
exchanged glances of alarm. They had known something was happening, but not this. She kept her tears for the train. Then, after it had
passed Maryboro, and Dublin was well behind, she cheered herself
with the thought of her return, and was her old gay self when her father met her.

It was pleasant and restful to slip back into the familiar routine of
evenings with Jimmy, the walks out the Lee Road and the visits to the
pictures, but even the pullover did not entirely wipe out her feelings of
guilt, so she tried to make it up to him in other ways. She felt unusually mature and motherly, and capable at last of coping with his
moods. For the first time, thanks to Denis, she realized how many of
their quarrels had been caused by her own unsettled state, and resolved that they must not fall back into the same pattern. She even
made discoveries about Jimmy. He wasn't an easy man to understand
because he didn't understand himself. He was touchy about orthodoxy
because he wasn't happy with it himself. There was a critical side of
Jimmy which he never gave rein to. So when he had what he considered a trying day and needed sympathy, she let him put his head on
her lap and stroked his hair while he moaned about his intolerable existence. When he frowned at one of her hasty conclusions, she withdrew it immediately. It was really quite easy, though she had never

realized it until Denis made it plain to her; a mere matter of technique that never really impinged upon her own freedom of judgment, and she wondered at the crises she had needlessly provoked because of such trifles. Jimmy noticed the change in her and said suspiciously that her holiday seemed to have done her good.

"I suppose it's really that fellow, O'Brien," he growled, "with the—how many is it?—five children."

"Some day I'm afraid I'll have to confess everything, love," she replied with a mocking grin, and hugged herself at the thought of how little poor Jimmy knew. As she walked through the main streets, exchanging gossip with her friends, she seemed to hear echoing footsteps in the silent square, romantic now and far away, and thought what her friends would say if only they knew. Una MacDermott! You're not serious. Her poor father would drop dead.

Then one night she and Jimmy had a thundering row. It began quite innocently, in an argument about a current political scandal, something about a distillery. Political scandals always seemed to involve a distillery or two. Jimmy would not admit that there was any scandal at all, and finally, in a rage, Una stamped out, swearing that she would never speak to him again; that he didn't know what manliness was. By the time she reached home it had dawned on her that the old pattern had reasserted itself exactly as before. And this time it definitely wasn't only her unsettled state. Jimmy was unsettled too, and it was only too plain that he took the wrong side and stuck to it because in life he had taken the wrong side and was unable to detach himself from it. But it wasn't to be supposed that he would find a feminine equivalent of Denis or even listen to her if he did.

"Steady up, girl!" she told herself. "Somebody in this establishment has to have a sense of responsibility."

Before she went to bed she rang up Jimmy and proposed going to Glengarriff for the weekend. It was a favorite haunt of theirs. She was syrupy, as though she had forgotten all about their quarrel, and Jimmy was sour as though he had no intention of allowing her to forget, but he said in a weary tone that if she really wanted to go so badly, he didn't mind. When Jimmy's orthodoxy was challenged he seemed to revert to the age of twelve.

However, the trip down put him in better humor, as it always did, and when they walked along the village street and watched the moon rising over Cab Du, he was in high spirits. While the ripples broke the moon's reflection in the water till it looked like a great tree of leaves, they lingered over the wall, chatting to the boatmen of the first arrivals among the summer visitors.

When he said good-night to her in her room, she pulled his head down to hers and asked in a low voice: "Aren't you going to stay with me, Jimmy?" He grew very red. "Are you sure you want me to?" he replied. For answer, she turned her back on him and pulled her frock over her head. He still stood there, embarrassed and silent, till she embraced him. She felt in control of the situation again. All the nonsense between them was over. She would soon force him to admit the connection between his smugness and his celibacy. And as a lover there was no comparison between him and Denis. There never had been. Jimmy wasn't only a lover; he was a sweetheart whom she had known for years, whose ways she understood and whose honesty she trusted. She felt a pleasure with him she had never felt with Denis, and when they lay quietly, listening to the ripples on the beach and watching the moonlight streak about the blind, she patted his leg and explained in whispers what imbeciles they had been and how close they had gone to wrecking their relationship. Jimmy agreed drowsily.

Next morning he got up and dressed before the maids were about, and Una sat cross-legged on the bed, watching him in admiration. He raised the blind, and she noticed his unusual gravity as he stared over the bay.

"What's the day going to be like?" she asked brightly.

"I wasn't looking," he replied in a faraway voice without looking round. "I was thinking that perhaps we'd better get married as soon as we can. Don't you think so?"

The proposal did not upset her so much as the funereal tone in which it was spoken.

"Oh," she replied blithely but with a sinking heart, "do you think so?"

He leaned his shoulder against the window frame, and the morning light caught his handsome, big-boned, gloomy face and brought out the deep vertical lines between his eyes.

"We don't have to rush into it," he said. "Your people wouldn't like it. Neither would mine."

"I dare say not," she said doubtfully, and then gazed anxiously at him. "You're not disappointed, are you?"

He turned a penetrating look on her. "Aren't you?"

"Me?" she cried, between astonishment and laughter. "Good Lord, no! I think it's marvellous."

"Perhaps disappointment is the wrong word," he said in the same faraway voice, and nodded over his shoulder towards the door. "But we don't want much more of this."

"You mean it's—furtive?"

"Oh, and wrong," he said wearily.

"Wrong?"

By way of reply, he shrugged his shoulders with the broken-down air he wore after a bad day at the office. Translated, it meant: "If you can't see that!"

"Well, it's better than fighting, isn't it?" she asked wistfully. "We know one another long enough, anyway."

"That only makes it worse," he said coldly. "Having stuck it so long, we should have been able to stick it a bit longer. After all, we're not just out for a good time."

He sounded as though he were explaining the policy of his paper. At any other time his tone would have set her at his throat, but now she winced. It was true enough. Their squabbles and misunderstandings had been merely part of the normal behavior of two grown people who contemplated a lifetime of each other's society and were sensitive to the trifles that threatened their happiness. There had been nothing wrong with them but her own misinterpretation. She sprang out of bed and threw her arms round him.

"Oh, for Heaven's sake, Jimmy, don't blame yourself for this," she cried in an agony of maternal feeling. "This was all my fault."

"No, it wasn't," he said miserably, turning his head away and dropping his editorial air. "It was mine."

"It wasn't, Jimmy, it wasn't," she said eagerly, shaking her head. "I brought you here with that intention. I know I'm a fool. I know I don't know anything about it. You can't imagine what a bitch I am."

"Oh, you're not," he replied in the same tone, his body as stiff as that of a small boy in a fit of the glooms. "It's just that you're so changed. I don't seem to be able to get at you as I used."

"But that's exactly why I wanted you to make love to me, Jimmy," she cried. "I can't get at you either."

"Yes," he added with a sob of jealous rage. "And it's all that damn fellow in Dublin. He's the one who changed you."

"You're wrong there, Jimmy," she cried earnestly, taking him by the shoulders and making him look her between the eyes. "I swear you're wrong. I'm not in the least changed, and he didn't do anything to me. You do believe me, don't you? You know I wouldn't let him do that?" Then the falsehood touched the chord of hysteria in her and she began to sob, pulling wildly at her hair. "Oh, I'm a fool. I do my best, but I don't know anything. And you're right. It is awful."

"Not awful," he said, weeping. "It's just that it's not the right thing for us."

And again she saw the situation through his eyes—as something beautiful that had been irretrievably spoiled by an hour of boredom and dissatisfaction, and which could never be the same again, because innocence had gone out of it.

When he left her, she threw herself on the bed and wept in earnest. She was finished. She had done her best and everything had been wrong. The morning light brightened her room and revealed to her her own wickedness and folly. She knew that, whatever about her deception of him, Jimmy would never forgive her lies. She could not marry him while any possibility existed of his discovering the truth.

Yet, even while she wept, she seemed to see Denis, his plump face aglow with good-natured laughter, and hear his silky, insinuating voice. So she imagined she could get along without him now, did she? She thought there was nothing left for her to learn? She felt so resentful that she stopped crying, put her fists under her chin, and glared at the wall before her while she argued it out with herself. After all, where had she gone wrong? What lesson was it she had failed to learn properly? Was it her fault or was it Jimmy's?

"Oh, damn!" she said suddenly. She sprang up, dressed in a hurry and rushed downstairs to the telephone. She had some minutes to wait for her call and stamped nervously up and down the hall with her eye on the stairs, afraid that Jimmy might appear. Then the bell rang and a meek, sleepy voice answered her. She could almost see the narrow bed against the wall with the telephone on a table at its head and hear the bells in the square, calling people to Mass, and her heart overflowed. All the time she had thought that she was learning the business of love, but now she knew every man and woman is a trade in himself, and he was the only trade she knew.

The Little Mother

IN MY YOUTH there was a family that lived up Gardiner's Hill in Cork called Twomey. It consisted of father, mother, and three pretty daughters, Joan, Kitty, and May. The father was a small builder, honest, hard-working, unbusinesslike, and greatly esteemed. The mother was a real beauty, tall, attractive, and sentimental, who wept profusely over the wrongs of Ireland, romantic love, and the sufferings of the poor. At least once a day Mick Twomey, coming in and finding a beggar eating his dinner on a chair outside the front door, or warming himself in the kitchen over the fire, denounced her imbecility, but in secret he adored her, and told his daughters that there wasn't a woman in the world like her.

The girls were as wild as they make them; they were spoiled; there was no doubt of that. May, being only thirteen, couldn't be really wild, but there was something about her gentle smile and insinuating air which indicated that this was only a pleasure deferred. Joan, the eldest, had a broad, humorous face, an excitable manner, and a great flow of gab. Kitty, the second girl, was an untidy, emotional sort, who took more after her mother than the others and was her father's pet. Mrs. Twomey couldn't control them. She would fly into a wild rage against one of them, and threaten to tell their father, and then remember an identical occasion in her own girlhood and laugh at her own naughtiness and her dead mother's fury till, the immediate occasion of her emotion forgotten, she went about the house singing sentimental songs like "Can You Recall that Night in June?"

She shamelessly searched their rooms and handbags for love-letters, ostensibly because it was her duty, but really because they reminded her of the letters she had received herself when she was a girl and of the writers, now married, scattered or dead. She was usually so enchanted by them that she never bothered to inquire whether or not the writers were suitable companions for her daughters. She tried to read some of them to her husband, not realizing that all men hated to be reminded of their adolescent follies. "For God's sake, don't be encouraging them in that sort of nonsense!" he snapped. But what was nonsense to him was the breath of life to Mrs. Twomey. She loved it on Sunday evenings when the gas was lit in the little front room, and the oil lamp was placed in the middle of the big round table to give light to the piano, and the girls' friends dropped in for a cup of tea and a singsong. She hung on there till she couldn't decently do so any longer, beaming and asking in stage whispers: "What do you think of Dick Gordon? People say he's not steady, but there's something very manly about him."

Naturally, Dick Gordon, Joan's boy, was the one whose letters she appreciated the most. He was tall and handsome and bony, with a great back to his head, walked with a swagger, talked with verve, and sang "Toreador" and "The Bandolero" in a reckless baritone. The neighbors were quite right in saying he wasn't steady. He took a drink, was known to have knocked about with bad women, drove a motor bicycle, and brought Joan off to Crosshaven on it for weekends. What was worse, he didn't go to Mass or the Sacraments, and seemed to be entirely lacking in any sense of shame about it. But he was also lacking in any desire to force his views on others. He was an engineer, a well-read boy, and explained to Joan that early in life he had come to the conclusion that people were in a conspiracy to prevent him from enjoying himself, and determined to evade it. It wasn't on principle. He had no principles that anybody could see, and was perfectly respectful of everybody else's, so long as they let him alone.

Dick was not only Joan's sweetheart, but the ideal of the other two girls. Kitty didn't have a boy of her own; she always had a number of them, but none of them came up to Dick's standard. He mightn't be steady, but who at that age ever wanted a sweetheart to be steady? "Here, Joan," she would say, producing a love-letter for her sister, "did you ever read such blooming nonsense as Sonny Lawlor writes?" And while she and Joan compared and argued, May hung round wistfully and asked: "Can't I look?"

Then one day death laid its hand on the family. Mrs. Twomey died suddenly, and for weeks the girls' beauty was masked by mourning and tears. Mick was so stunned that he behaved almost as though it were somebody else's loss rather than his own. On the day they buried her, he took Kitty and May by the hand and presented them to Joan with a curious formality.

"You'll have to be a mother to them now, Joan, girl," he said in a low voice. "They have no one else."

THE LITTLE ceremony made an extraordinary impression on Joan. That night, as she knelt by her bed, she made a solemn vow to be everything to her father and sisters that her mother had been. She had no illusions about its being an easy task, and it filled her with a certain mournful pride. It was as though within a few hours her whole nature had changed; as though she no longer had a father and sisters, only a husband and children: as though, in fact, her girlhood had suddenly become very far away.

Father and sisters, too, realized the seriousness of the occasion and at first gave her every help. On Friday night her father counted out the housekeeping money to her in front of the others and said humbly: "That's eighty-five bob, Joan. Ten for pocket money and five for the club. Think you'll be able to manage?" The girls were so awe-stricken that they hardly dared ask her for money, and it was she who had to press it on them.

But that phase didn't last. She discovered a change even in herself. The excitement in her blood when dusk fell on the fields and trees behind the little terrace house and the gas lamp was lit at the street corner was no longer the same. It was always qualified by her new sense of responsibility. When Kitty was out with a boy, Joan realized that it wasn't any longer an adventure she could share with her on her return, but a burden she could share only with her father. Dick was very quiet and anxious to be helpful, but he couldn't understand her anxiety about Kitty. He knew that Kitty was giddy, but he didn't see what a responsibility it imposed on her. She didn't expect anything unreasonable, only that Kitty should be in at proper hours, but Kitty seemed to resent this far more from her than she had resented it from her mother. "Here, what's coming over you?" she asked pertly. "Who do you think you are?" She even said that Joan was getting too big for her boots. There were times when Joan felt old and tired. Children never understood the responsibilities of their parents and guardians. They never realized the way budgets had to be balanced so that the loss of an umbrella or the breaking of a teapot could leave you worried and distraught for days. When she remembered how often she had blamed her own gentle and self-sacrificing mother on that very score, she wept.

To give her strength to get through the day she took to going to Mass every morning. The neighbors, who saw it only from outside, were enormously impressed by the way a flighty girl of eighteen developed into a mature, responsible young woman who saw that meals were cooked, clothes washed and mended, and bills paid on time. But Kitty and May realized that they had lost a sister and caught a tartar. It was true that Joan had always had a touch of Reverend Mother about her; had been serious and bossy and attempted to make up in knowingness for the affection which had been diverted onto her younger sisters. But this had only been swank. In all essential matters she had remained part of the juvenile conspiracy—treating their parents as enemies, raiding their stores, and defeating their intelligence system.

Now that she had deserted to the enemy, she was worse than any parent because she knew all their tricks—the whole secret set-up of schoolbooks, fees, carfares, clothes, and boy friends—and they could do nothing without her knowledge. Now it was their intelligence system that was dislocated. Whenever they wanted something out of the ordinary, they had to tell her why and they had to tell the truth. They did, but they resented it far more than they resented her occasional fits of panic and meanness, because it derogated from their femininity, and in the intervals of scolding and wheedling they lapsed into a mute and sullen conspiracy which she felt was quite unjustified.

All the family learned things from the new situation, but Joan, who was the heart of it, learned the most. She discovered that it was far from being the romantic change of parts which she had first imagined, and not at all a matter of her father and herself on the one hand and "the children," as she liked to call them, on the other. Her father had a secret life of his own, which was not at all easy to penetrate. At first, when she discussed her difficulties with him, she was flattered by the mournful candor with which he responded, giving her chapter and verse for his earnings, and she loyally and vigorously denounced to shopkeepers and neighbors the thoughtlessness of customers who left big accounts outstanding. Besides, no matter how hard up he might be, he always managed to find her a something extra, wherever he got it or whatever he had to sacrifice to obtain it. Sometimes the sacrifice was so patent that she begged him to take it back, but he shook his head mournfully and replied: "No, no, child. You need it more than I do. I can get along."

But in time she began to suspect that the candor was fallacious and the sacrifice imaginary—the accounts varied too much. It was hard to believe, and it hurt her to believe it, but it had to be faced: her father was not truthful. What she was too young to see was that it had to be so; a man's income and expenditure are necessarily up to a point subjective, for you must leave room for optimism and pessimism, and to tie him to mere figures is to deny him a temperament. Joan wanted an objective income because it was she who was blamed when things went short. Kitty even went so far as to call her "a mean bitch," and Joan, to keep from weeping, drew herself up and said with dignity: "I'm afraid you're not old enough to understand Daddy's difficulties, Kit."

But even if she couldn't break down her father's secrets, nothing her sisters did could be kept from her. One day, when she was really worried about making ends meet, she saw Kitty open her handbag and turn over a handful of silver. Her first scared thought was that Kitty might have stolen it.

"Where did you get all that money, Kit?" she asked.

"What money?" Kitty asked with an attempt at brazenness, though she turned pale. "I have no money."

"Don't try to fool me. That money in your bag."

"But 'tis only a couple of pence—look!" Kitty wailed, opening her handbag and taking out a few coppers. Joan had had time to realize that she hadn't stolen it. She hadn't stolen it, but she was going to spend it on the pictures or on buying cigarettes for some young waster she was going out with, while Joan was left to worry.

"Would you like to show me your bag so?" she asked icily.

"Why would I show you my bag?" Kitty asked indignantly.

"You got that money from Father," Joan said.

"I did not get it from Father," shouted Kitty, now thoroughly scared as she saw the source of her independence threatened. "I got it from Aunt Molly, as you're so blooming inquisitive."

Joan didn't even bother to reply. She felt too bitterly about it. Now she understood a certain air of independence that "the children" had worn for months. Their father had been keeping them in funds. In spite of the credit she had earned among the neighbors, in spite of her struggles to keep the house going, he conspired with them as though she were some sort of ogre who denied them the necessities of life. She could see it all exactly as if it were some man who was being unfaithful to her. It never occurred to her to excuse him because he had been equally generous to her during her mother's life, because he had always responded fondly when she came to him, bubbling with her secret crises, because, in fact, he was the sort of man who was at his best only when you went to him in a scrape. Any form of regular commitment was torture to him because it had no emotional overtones, but he loved the little occasions that enabled him to show the real warmth of his heart.

When she challenged him with it, he was horrified. It would never have occurred to him that anyone could possibly put such a cruel construction on his innocent generosity. He had never seen it in that way at all. He didn't have to go to the neighbors to know what sort of job she was making of the home. It was just that he loved them all!

He argued, he pleaded; he even lost his temper and threatened to hand over the housekeeping to Kitty, but Joan was remorseless. He had been unfaithful to her and she was disillusioned; and, like every other deceived wife, she knew that her disillusionment was a weapon which would keep him in order for the rest of his days with her. Never again would he betray her. He wouldn't have the nerve. Kitty might weep on him for a new dress, but he would only mumble apologies about "the troubles of poor Joan," and even when she went beyond the beyonds and tackled him about the amount he spent on drink—a thing her mother would never have dared to do—he was humble and apologetic. He had never behaved so abjectly to his wife, but then, she had spurts of sentiment which he well knew how to take advantage of. All he had to do to get around Mrs. Twomey was to mention some fellow he had met who had spent a holiday in Killarney, where he and she had spent their honeymoon, and within a half an hour Mrs. Twomey was washing up while she sang in a sweet cracked voice "By Killarney's Lakes and Fells." He had no such hold over Joan. Now she had three quivering victims, a thing that might have gone to the head of a less emotional girl than she was.

It horrified her to see how badly they had all been brought up. Until then, when she heard criticism of their wildness, she had only mocked at the neighbors and said that they were jealous. Now that she found herself in the neighbors' camp, she saw how right they had been. No attempt had ever been made to correct herself and her sisters until she had taken things into her own hands. She could not blame her mother for this and found it hard to attach anything so substantial as blame to an unstable character like her father. It must, she thought, be plain, crude original sin. There were even moments when she wondered whether God in His infinite wisdom had not been compelled to remove her mother to bring her to a proper sense of responsibility—a common stage in the development of spiritual pride.

But Dick Gordon was the one who really saw the profound change that was taking place in her. Till her mother died, she had seen no harm in him; neither her parents nor herself had taken his atheism seriously, and her father had even said that every intelligent young fellow went through the same thing; it had given her a feeling of broad-mindedness to listen to his dashing, cynical talk. But now she had only to imagine him saying the same sort of things to Kitty to realize that there are two ways of looking at a man.

It troubled her a lot; she prayed a good deal, and tried to break off with him gently by diminishing the number of occasions when she went out with him, but there was a curious thickness about Dick that made him come back again and again. Finally she had to speak to him seriously about it, but it was with real regret and pity.

"I think, Dick, boy, we've got to give up going with one another," she said with a gentle smile.

"Go on!" Dick said lightly, raising his head and looking at her curiously. "Why do you think that?"

"Well, you see, I have certain responsibilities, and I don't see how we can ever get married."

"I have a few responsibilities myself, and we never expected to be able to get married in a hurry."

"But this is a long job, Dick—years and years."

Dick shrugged his shoulders uncomprehendingly.

"Well, if we have to wait, we have to wait. If you find someone that suits you, you have to put up with the inconveniences."

"But that's the trouble, Dick," she said, realizing that she was not going to escape without open discussion. "I don't think we do suit one another."

He still refused to be shaken. Dick was an engineer, and he tended to treat life very like a delicate machine. If something went wrong, you opened it up and fixed it, and then it worked again.

"How long have you thought that, Joan?"

"For quite a while."

"Since your mother's death?"

"I dare say."

"Well, I know it upset you; that's only to be expected, but it's also only to be expected that you'll get over it."

"I don't think so, Dick. Not so far as that goes. You see, I was young and giddy, and I didn't realize how much certain things meant to me. Religion, for instance. I couldn't marry a man who didn't believe the same things as I do."

Dick shrugged his shoulders. "It hasn't affected you very much up to this."

"No, Dick, but it could."

"Could!" he repeated with light mockery. He was bewildered. He couldn't help feeling that religion had nothing to do with it; that a cog wasn't engaging somewhere or a plug wasn't sparking. He continued to argue. At last he rose with a shrug.

"Oh, well," he said, "if that's how you feel about it."

He was really very fond of Joan and enjoyed knocking about the house, so he was quite incredulous at her dropping him. It was a thing to hurt the feelings of any man, but Dick was worse than hurt, he was bewildered. From his limited, logical, liberal point of view, the thing didn't make sense. Sometimes he even wondered whether there wasn't something in religion after all, and whether he wasn't a freak of nature whom any sensible girl must naturally drop. At other times it seemed to him that Joan was becoming slightly touched, and that it was his duty to speak to her father about it. Either way you took it, it seemed monstrous. He knew the wild side of Joan better than anyone else, and loved it in his own limited way, and he could not understand how it could disappear like that, overnight, leaving nothing behind but a soured, censorious old maid. He talked lightly to Kitty about it.

"It's all pride, Dick," she said violently. "It's all rotten pride and vanity."

He was a creature of habit, and he continued to come to the house; to rag May, who adored him, and chat with Mick Twomey, who liked his manliness. When Joan refused to make it up, he shrugged his shoulders and flirted with Kitty instead. To put the crowning touch on it, Kitty fell head and ears in love with him; she could scarcely believe that the ideal of her early girlhood was now at her feet, and Kitty in love could be observed not only by Joan but by half the road. When she was kept five minutes late for an appointment, she burst into tears and threatened suicide.

Then Joan grew really angry. This was a development she hadn't intended at all, and Kitty was far too young and too spoiled to understand her objections. She chose to think that the breach between Joan and Dick had been caused by Dick's resentment at the change in her, and that her objections to Dick going with herself were merely jealousy. Joan, intensely aware of the purity of her own motives, found it hard to realize what was going on in Kitty's head.

"I suppose it's because you can't have him yourself you don't want anyone else to have him?" blazed Kitty.

"I don't give a button who has him," Joan said flatly. "I just don't want you to have anything to do with him, that's all."

"Ah, we know all about this."

"What on earth do you mean, child?" asked Joan.

"Where do you get your women from?" retorted Kitty. "I'm not such a child as all that. You pretend you don't want him; other people might think 'twas the way he didn't want you."

Joan looked at Kitty in stupefaction. It was only now she was beginning to realize the change in her own character. Six months before, that skinny little brat wouldn't have dared to tell Joan that any man in the world preferred herself to Joan without Joan's showing her pretty soon the mistake she was making. Even then she could feel a certain temptation to take Dick back, just to teach the little fool a good lesson about the nature of men and the facts of life. But it was only for a moment.

"You're welcome to think it, if it gives you any satisfaction," she said coldly.

In spite of it, Kitty continued to defy her, and Dick, with that unshakable self-confidence of his, continued to come to the house and behave exactly as though nothing whatever had happened, beyond the change from herself to Kitty. He even did with Kitty the sort of things he had done with herself, and took her off on the pillion of his motor bicycle to Crosshaven for the weekend without saying a word to her about it. This was really too much for Joan, who had no faith whatever in Kitty's capacity for keeping out of mischief, and she complained to her father.

Now, Mick was a bad man to complain to, because he was full of pity for humanity in general and young fellows of Dick's age in particular. He too thought she was jealous—it was extraordinary, the number of people who got that impression.

"Ah, listen, Joan," he said with an anguished air, "wouldn't you make it up with him, whatever he did to you?"

"Honestly, Daddy," she protested, "he did nothing to me."

"Whatever ye did to one another so."

"But I tell you we did nothing to one another. It's just that I don't think Dick and I are suited to one another. He doesn't go to Mass. I don't think he has a proper sense of responsibility. And Kitty is much too young and too giddy to be mixing round with that Crosshaven crowd. She's bound to drink too much, and Dick will only encourage her. I tell you, unless we put a stop to it, she'll be ruined within a year."

"Ah, God, Joanie," muttered her father with a distraught air, "I was very like Dick at that age. He's only knocking round with Kitty to spite you. It only shows how fond of you he is. Damn it, I nearly married your Aunt Molly after one row I had with your poor mother, God rest her."

In fact, though he did speak to Kitty, he only made matters worse, for he mumbled that he didn't know what was after coming over Joan, but she was mad jealous of anyone who looked crosswise at Dick Gordon—nothing, it seemed, could convince him of the nobility of Joan's motives—and that it would be very unkind of Kitty to go between them. Kitty, who had a violent temper, flew off the handle, told him no one could live in the house since her mother's death; that it was all his fault because he let Joan do what she liked; and swore that if he wasn't careful, she'd leave and get a job in Dublin. She scared him so badly that he withdrew to his bedroom and sulked in protest against both of them.

But Joan wasn't to be beaten so easily. One day she called at the office where Dick Gordon worked. He brought her into the waiting-room, looking quite pleasant and collected, and stood at the fireplace with his hands behind his back.

"Dick," she said sweetly, "I want to ask a favor of you."

"Sure," said Dick with his usual amiability. "Fire ahead."

"It's about Kitty."

He pursed his lips and tossed his head deprecatingly. He knew now that he was in for a scene.

"What about her?"

"Please, Dick, for my sake, will you stop taking her out?"

"Why should I stop taking her out?"

"Because it's upsetting her, and you know you don't really care about her."

Hands still behind his back, he drew himself up on his heels.

"It seems to be upsetting more than her," he said pleasantly.

"It is, if you want to know," she replied quietly. "You're only doing it to spite me."

"You have a very high opinion of yourself, haven't you?" he asked with a laugh.

"You don't have to talk to me like that," she said reproachfully.

"I don't have to talk to you at all, if it comes to that," he retorted indifferently.

She knew that the indifference was only assumed, and that he would have welcomed the chance of a good breakdown like anyone else.

"You know you think a great deal of me, and I think the same of you," she said appealingly. "Why won't you do this for me?"

Joan could be angelic when it suited her, and it suited her then. She didn't leave till he had given his promise, though he gave it grudgingly, feeling that in some way he was being exploited. Even then he insisted on telling Kitty himself. Kitty wept for hours and then packed her bag and announced that she was leaving for Dublin at once. Her father was very upset, but Joan, still indignant at Kitty's defiance, assured him that this was the best way of bringing "the child" to her senses. Left to herself for a while in lodgings, she would soon learn the value of a good home.

THERE was more peace after she left, and to everyone's surprise Joan became friendly with another fellow, a civil servant named Chris Dwyer. Chris was the very opposite of Dick Gordon; a pale, pious, harassed young fellow with an angular, irritable sense of humor and a passion for music. Where Dick swaggered into any group, entirely at his ease, Chris arrived with a bundle of gramophone records under his arm and a politeness and pleasure which he couldn't keep up and which gradually gave place to an air of doubt and distress. Even when he was playing one of his beloved records on the gramophone, he clasped his hands and watched the gramophone feverishly, as though he expected that at any moment it would come out with a wrong note. He lived in Sunday's Well—a classy quarter—was of a good family which had come down in the world, and devoted himself to the care of his mother, a woman of such invincible refinement that she couldn't even understand what had happened to her income. Chris couldn't enlighten her much, for he understood it all so well that to explain anything at all, he had to begin with the history of banking.

Joan confided in Chris her troubles with her sisters, and Chris, after a certain amount of hesitation, admitted that he, too, had serious difficulties with his older brothers, Bob and Jim, neither of whom seemed to have any sense of responsibility. Between family confidences and a love of music, he and Joan seemed made for one another, the only obstacle being that each had so many responsibilities that there did not seem to be the slightest prospect of their ever being able to get married; but even this common element of frustration formed something of a bond, and in their conscientious way, going to concerts and walking up the Lee Fields in the evening, they were profoundly happy in one another's company.

But Joan's troubles with her sisters were very far from being ended. By the time May was seventeen, she was a handful, and a much bigger handful than Kitty. Kitty had a temper and wept on the least provocation, but May was a girl of extraordinary sweetness, with a disposition as clear as her complexion. You could hear Kitty getting into a scrape a mile off, but May merely glided into it like a duck into water. It was her natural element. She was cool, resourceful, and insinuating, and frequently turned the tables on Joan, who was none of these things. For instance, she could appeal to Joan's sense of humor, which was fatal to her dignity. Or she could get her to talk about her own troubles and then advise her as though she and not Joan were the elder. May could be involved in a police-court case and, in some way Joan couldn't understand, it would all be turned into a warning against Chris Dwyer. May had never got over her early hero-worship of Dick Gordon, and everything about Chris annoyed her: his dark suits and white shirts, his clumsy attempts to please her, and the intensity with which he bowed his head and clasped his long, thin hands while listening to a Beethoven quartet. May didn't know much about music, but she felt that it was never worth all that strain.

"Ah, listen, Joan," she would say peremptorily, "take that fellow by the scruff of the neck and drag him up to the priest yourself. You'll never get married at all if you leave it to him."

"But we haven't a chance of getting married anyhow, girl," Joan would say with resignation. "Between his mother and Daddy, it looks as if we have another twenty years to wait."

"But even if Chris buried his mother tomorrow, he'd find an old aunt that had to be looked after," May would say with exasperation. "I'm warning you, Joan—that fellow is a born grandmother. He's not your sort at all."

May was like quicksilver: you had her cornered, and then, before you knew what was happening, she had you cornered. She slipped in and out of the Ten Commandments as if they were ten harmless old aunts, not in the least trying to discredit them—on the contrary, she thought them delightful, in the manner of characters in a Jane Austen novel, and deeply resented anyone's speaking disrespectfully of them—but she never gave them more than the affection and respect due to ancient monuments.

May's principal achievement— no small one for a girl living at home in a small city like Cork— was to become involved with a married man. Timmy MacGovern was a fat, greasy man with a long lock of black hair that fell over his left eye, small merry eyes, a jovial air, and small, unsteady feminine feet that positively refused to support his weight. He rarely went anywhere except by car, and even when he dislodged himself from the car he usually tried out the feet first to see if they were still functioning.

He was the commercial representative of several big firms, and in line for the Dublin management of one, which must have been largely due to his charm, for he was very rarely in his office on the Grand Parade, and when he was, he either sat at his desk as though he were sitting for his portrait, or thudded to and from the window, riffling his hair and interrupting his adoring secretary, till somebody came to bring him out for a drink. Usually this was Tony Dowse, who had some undefined job in the County Council that left him free to go and come as he pleased. He was as big a man as Timmy, with a pasty face and an anxious air, and always adopted a protective attitude to Timmy. He was very fond of Timmy, but regarded him as the last word in fantasy and excitability. While Timmy riffled his hair and knit his black brows in a thunderous frown, Tony flapped his fat hands feebly. "You take things to the fair, MacGovern," he would moan, curling his long, mournful upper lip in distaste. "If 'tisn't women, 'tis ghosts." (Timmy was a strong believer in ghosts and had seen a number of them in his time, but Dowse blamed it all on his excitability and unreasonableness. Dowse had never seen a ghost, and except for one distressing little episode with a girl at the age of sixteen he had never had anything to do with women.) Timmy was a born boon companion, had a small army of admirers, and brought light and laughter to any pub he chose to patronize. Among his other accomplishments, he was an out-and-out Voltairean, a part that was possible for him, as Tony Dowse remarked, only because nobody believed him. "If that was me or you," Tony would say, shaking his head over the injustice of it, "we'd be for the long drop. They think Timmy is only cod-acting."

This was an injustice to Timmy, who had genuine aspirations after a fuller life; aspirations you wouldn't understand until you met his wife, one of the Geraghty girls from Glenareena. "The Grip of the

Geraghtys" was a proverbial saying in that part of the country. Eily MacGovern was a small, thrifty, pious, unimaginative woman whom Timmy was supposed to have married for her money—another example of the way people are misjudged, because he really married her for her voice. But the voice was all the romance there was in Eily. The soul of order, she had given Timmy a small house in the suburbs, with small rooms that were a clutter of small useless tables which Timmy was always falling over, and a son and daughter as neatly matched as the two china dogs on her parlor mantelpiece. Timmy was a conscientious husband and father, but he would often look at his family in their surroundings and shake his head as if he wondered who had been putting spells on him. Eily had nursed him through a dozen different ailments, all mortal. Timmy, an imaginative man, never got any disease that wasn't mortal, and when he had a gastric attack, he took to his bed in a state of icy terror, while Eily, who never ceased to marvel at the ways of imaginative men, said with a stunned air to Tony Dowse: "And they call *us* the weaker sex!"

May, who loved imaginative men, was delighted with Timmy's big frame and robust humor, his songs and stories and bawdy jokes. Then—just like the second figure on the weather-clock that pops out on the approach of rain—out came the second Timmy, a bewildered man with aspirations after a fuller life, and complained of Eily and denounced the pettiness of Cork, and begged May to leave everything and come away with him; even if they had nothing, and no home but the lonesome roads of Ireland.

It was just like Timmy, who couldn't walk half a mile with his poor feet, to talk about the roads, but May thought the way he described them was something beautiful, with castles and fairs and tinkers and asses, just as though he had served his time to them, and at once she saw herself swinging a shawl and dragging a barefoot child behind her while they tramped the boglands in the warm days of June. There was no humbug about May's ambitions. She had a genuine streak of the vagrant in her, and a real liking for the extremes that give a sharp edge to sensation—hunger and thirst and cold and weariness. It had always seemed to her that people attached too much importance to security, and that the happiest souls in the world were the tinkers who built their campfires by the road and stretched old bags across the shafts of their carts by way of tents.

But when Joan heard that Timmy and May had been practicing the simple life in the mountain country outside Macroom, sitting in pubs and talking to tinkers, she thought May must have taken leave of her senses. She searched May's room till she found Timmy's letters, and read them in a state of utter incredulity. She knew from of old that all love-letters were silly, but these were mad. They would go on for a paragraph in a jerky style like a broken-down Ford, and then suddenly soar into passages of inspired rhetoric in which Timmy declared that when he was with May the real world didn't exist any longer for him, and there was nobody and nothing only the two of themselves. They were so queer that she hardly knew what to say to May about them.

"Tell me, May," she asked that evening, "what's going on between Timmy MacGovern and you?"

"How do you mean, going on?" May asked with mock ingenuousness.

"Ah, stop playing the innocent with me," Joan said impatiently. "You know quite well what I mean."

"Nothing's been going on to get in a bake like that about," May said reproachfully.

"I read his letters to you."

"Well, you know all about it, so."

"You should be proud of them," Joan said bitterly.

"They suit me all right."

"They'd probably suit Mrs. MacGovern too. Listen, May, what are you going to do about this thing?"

"We didn't decide that yet," May said with a slight touch of guilt as though she didn't quite know how she had come to let such opportunities slip. "I dare say eventually I'll go and live with him."

"You'll what, May?" Joan asked in a dangerous tone.

"Ah, not here, of course," May added impatiently. "I mean when he gets his transfer to Dublin. He might even have to get a job in London. People in this country are so blooming narrow-minded. They get in a rut by the time they're eighteen, any of them that weren't in one to begin with."

At any moment now Joan felt May would tell her that Ireland didn't exist any longer either, nothing only Timmy and herself.

"Are you in your right mind, May Twomey?" she asked.

"Now, Joan, it's no use your talking that schoolgirl stuff to me," snapped May. "It's not because Chris Dwyer was born in a rut."

"What has Chris Dwyer to do with it?"

"Chris Dwyer has you driven out of your mind," said May hotly. "You're becoming as big an old maid as he is. You ought to be old enough to talk sensibly about things like this. Timmy made a mistake in his marriage, that's all. Lots of men do. He has either to put up with Eily Geraghty for the rest of his life or make a fresh start."

"Well, he's making a still bigger mistake if he thinks he's going to make a fresh start on you," said Joan.

"We'll see about that," said May with a shrug. She was apparently beginning to think that Joan didn't exist either.

First Joan complained to her father. As usual he behaved as though the person who made the complaint was at least equally guilty with the offender. It was the attitude of a man born weak, who hates to have his peace of mind disturbed. "Oh, for Christ's sake!" he said, and shambled in to May. He told May it was a happy day for her poor mother the day she died, and then went on to threaten her as though her mother were still alive and May was breaking her heart. May, who loved him even more than the Ten Commandments, listened to him with respect, but within ten minutes she had him admitting that there were damn few women in the world like her poor mother, God rest her, and that only for what people might say, you wouldn't blame their husbands, whatever they did. He then went off to bed, apparently under the impression that he had restored order in the household.

But Joan had no intention of being satisfied with that sort of moral cowardice. Next afternoon she bearded Timmy in his office. Timmy had his usual look of having dropped in for a chat with his secretary. He was obviously very pleased to see Joan, and smiled with the whole array of his discolored teeth as he led her into the back office. It was a small room with a window opening on a vent. He closed the window carefully and sat down, riffling his hair. On the desk before him was a photograph of May, looking romantic against a mountain. It was most improbable that he left it there permanently; more likely he had taken it out to remind himself that offices weren't real either, but it gave Joan a fresh grievance.

"I think I'd better take charge of this, Timmy," she said, opening her handbag.

"What do you mean, Joan?" Timmy asked, rising with a look of alarm. It was a divided look, for the eyes frowned but the teeth still grinned wistfully beneath them.

"If you can't protect my sister's reputation, I must, Timmy," Joan said briskly. "Now, if you'd give me her letters—"

"Her letters?"

"Yes."

"But I haven't them, Joan."

"Nonsense, Timmy. You know you wouldn't have the nerve to keep them at home."

"I'm sorry you feel like this about it, Joan," he said gravely, twiddling nervously with the spring of his pince-nez.

"I don't see what other way I can feel," she replied frankly.

"I don't think you'd be so severe if you knew the sort of life I have to lead, Joan," he said, his eyes clouding with tears. "I don't want you to think I'm complaining of Eily. I'm not. She was always a good wife, according to her lights, and I'm grateful; but there was never any understanding between us. When I met May, I knew she was the only girl in the world for me. I love that girl, Joan," he added with manly simplicity. "I'd die for her this minute."

"I'm sorry, Timmy," Joan said coldly, "but I can't help your disagreements with Mrs. MacGovern. I didn't come here to discuss them. I came to get my sister's letters, and to warn you that the next time you see her or write to her, I'll go straight to your wife and then to the parish priest."

Joan was bluffing, and she knew it. She was playing it as if she were haggling over a pound of vegetables in the market. Timmy, like the rest of us, was vulnerable, but there were few in a stronger position to resist threats of that sort. If he had stuck to his guns, there was very little Joan could have done which wouldn't have brought more trouble on herself than on him, but, scared by the hysteria in her tone, he didn't realize it. That is the worst of poetic sentiments; they so rarely stand up to a well-played bluff.

"You wouldn't do that to us, Joan?" he asked, growing pale.

Joan strode to the door with an actressy air.

"The child has no other mother," she said with her hand on the handle and the door half-open. "I have to be a mother to her."

This was another bluff, for at that moment Joan's sentiments were very far from being maternal, but it worked. Timmy grabbed her and closed the door again. He was, as Tony Dowse said, an excitable man. He begged her to be reasonable, not to be so uncompromising—nothing would happen beyond an occasional meeting and letter.

"The first time I see another letter of yours with May, I go straight to your wife," she said.

That did it. Timmy shed a few tears, but he produced the bundle of letters, and Joan went down the stairs and along the Grand Parade in the afternoon sunlight, full of triumph and miserable as hell. She had a stocky figure with a permanent roll on it, and she bowed and called greetings to her friends, and at the same time wished she were dead. Like most of the men who came her way, Timmy was a coward. If only he had had the courage to tell her to go to blazes, the story might have had a different ending, for she loved a man of spirit. Having denounced Timmy to his face as a vile seducer, she was now filled with the desire to go back and denounce him as an old molly. She knew if she had been in love with anybody as Timmy was supposed to be in love with May, and written him all those poetic letters about reality not existing for her, she wouldn't have been scared off by the threats of any relative, least of all a girl. "Schoolgirl stuff," indeed! She'd show May which of them was the schoolgirl.

That evening, as they were washing up after supper, May gave her her opportunity. Very gently, as though she were ashamed of the way she had spoken earlier, she asked if there was anything else Joan wished her to do, as she had promised to meet Timmy and some friends at a hotel in town for a drink. She spoke as though Joan were already a confidante and partner.

"I'm afraid you won't be seeing any more of Timmy MacGovern, May," Joan replied in a hesitating tone which was intended to represent regret. And at that moment she did feel rather sorry for "the child."

"Won't I?" May asked with amusement, taking up the challenge.

"I doubt it," Joan said candidly.

"You mean you'd like me to try?" May asked quietly, putting down the dish she had been drying. By this time Kitty would probably have broken it on Joan's head, but May's fantasy was of a kind which could not be easily affected from outside.

"Oh, I'm not trying to stop you, girl," said Joan with a shrug, and went into the sitting room. She came back with her handbag, took out the picture of May, and tossed it on the table with the air of an old card-sharper producing the missing ace. "Don't you think you'd better have that back?" she asked mildly.

May grew a little more serious, but she was not one to be swept off her feet by any sort of histrionics.

"Where did you pinch that?" she asked lightly.

This time it was Joan who had to restrain herself from flinging something at May. Instead, she smiled and took out the bundle of letters.

"And those," she said mockingly.

May picked one up and looked at it casually. Then she glanced at Joan.

"Check," she said. "Now tell us what it's all about."

Then as May swung her legs from a corner of the kitchen table, Joan described her interview with Timmy. She didn't exaggerate her own part in it. She didn't need to with the evidence of Timmy's weakness of character staring them both in the face. By the time she had finished, Joan had talked herself into good humor again. "To tell you the truth, May," she said candidly, "I think you're a hundred times too good for him."

"I'm beginning to think the same myself," said May, and Joan knew that she meant it. If Timmy came crawling to her now, May wouldn't have him. Not after that humiliation. Schoolgirls were queer like that. Joan knew. She had been one herself—an awful long time ago, it seemed.

That was the end. Timmy took to his bed with thrombosis; Eily Geraghty nursed him and marvelled again at men's reputation for endurance; Tony Dowse visited him and found him sitting up with a shawl round his head, weeping and waving his hands.

"It's the old mistake, MacGovern," Tony said, showing his big teeth in a mournful smile. "I knew what was going to happen. It's just like that ghost in Glengarriff. It's all imagination, all imagination."

But May's imagination was playing about a tall and sulky young man who played golf and drove a small sports car. She tried to interest him in a caravan and talked a lot to him about tinkers, but he wasn't even interested. In this world one can't have everything.

JOAN had to confide her troubles to somebody, so, even though she felt it was letting down the family, she told Chris the details of May's affair with Timmy MacGovern. Chris appreciated the gravity of the situation, was disgusted at Timmy, and admired Joan's courage, but he wasn't as scandalized as she had feared. He even admitted that at one time there had nearly been a nasty scandal about his brother Bob. "Bob?" Joan cried in stupefaction. "But I thought Bob was a saint." "That's what we thought too," said Chris, and described the horror of the early morning call from an old policeman with whom he was friendly and who wanted it hushed up, and the scene at the Bridewell, where some of those who were plaster saints by day were bailed out at night. She respected his reserve in not having told her sooner. Apparently every family, even the most respectable, had things to hide. Respectability, far from being a dull and quiet virtue, was like walking a tight-rope.

Indeed, there were few pleasures more satisfying than those of normality. To walk out of an evening from your normal happy home with a normal respectable young man, and realize that the head of his department, though a Sanskrit scholar, lives in a home where the dirt and confusion created by eight children make life intolerable, and that the second assistant, though a man of genius, is also a dipsomaniac, makes you feel that if cleanliness isn't next to godliness, respectability certainly is. Joan was only beginning to realize her luck and to see that Chris was not only good but beautiful.

But she wasn't yet done with family troubles. May showed a disappointing lack of gratitude for the favor that Joan had done her in breaking off her relations with Timmy MacGovern. She wasn't the sort of girl to make herself unhappy by being cold or distant, but Joan had the feeling that there was watchfulness behind that pleasant manner of hers. A week or two before she married the golfer, she passed Joan a letter from Kitty.

"I don't know that this is any business of yours," she said dryly, "but it looks to me as if Daddy should be told."

It certainly looked as if somebody should be told, for Kitty announced in the calmest way in the world she was having a baby by a student called Rahilly. He was apparently a young fellow of very fine character, but with no job and entirely dependent on his parents. Joan read the letter and saw ruin staring her in the face. She realized that if Kitty had a baby, it was doubtful if Chris could marry her, and Kitty's chance of ever getting married would be nil. That was one of the drawbacks of respectability—the odds were so high.

"I suppose you're going to tell Jimmie all about this?" she asked.

"Why wouldn't I?" May asked in surprise.

"If you do," said Joan, "don't be surprised if your marriage is broken off in a hurry."

She hoped she might have scared May out of the assumption that her future in-laws would consider Kitty's plight the best of good news. But her father was no better. Weak as usual, he wanted to take all the blame on himself—as much of it as he didn't by implication shoulder off onto her.

"I can't blame the girl, Joan," he said, shaking his head mournfully from side to side. "It was all my fault for letting her go. That would never have happened if she was in her own home. What is she, after all, but a child, and away there among strangers?"

Joan could have told her father pretty shrewdly what Kitty was, but she thought it better not to. His only solution seemed to be to bring Kitty home, let her have her baby there, and face the shame of it as best they could. Joan knew that was no solution. She decided she must talk to Chris about it, and that evening she met him outside his office and they went to a restaurant.

She didn't have to explain anything to him. No sooner had she begun than she saw by his face that he was already foreseeing even more disaster than was apparent to herself.

"Your father should go to Dublin and see this fellow himself," he said with a frown.

"But you know what will happen? They'll go out and have a drink and Father will sympathize with him."

He said nothing to that and talked tangentially for about ten minutes about how difficult things were in the office. Then he asked with something like embarrassment: "Would you like me to go?"

"No, thanks, Chris," she said, shaking her head. "You might be able to deal with this fellow, but you couldn't deal with Kitty. You don't know what a handful she is. If you think someone must go, I'll go myself."

"I wish you hadn't to," he said. "It's going to be very unpleasant."

"Don't I know it?" she said with a sigh.

Next afternoon she set off for Dublin and was met at Kingsbridge Station by a sullen and resentful Kitty. While they crossed the bridge to the bus stop, Kitty asked with no great interest after her father, May, and the neighbors, and Joan answered good-humoredly. But as they passed the Four Courts, Kitty, affecting innocence, asked what had brought her.

"Well, I hope I came up to meet your future husband, Kit," Joan replied quietly.

"Not blooming likely!" said Kitty.

"What on earth do you mean, Kitty?" Joan asked sternly.

"I know what you want, you jealous thing!" Kitty muttered fiercely with the throb of tears in her voice. "You want to interfere between me and Con the way you interfered between me and Dick Gordon and between Timmy MacGovern and May. I know all about it. You're not going to be let."

"I suppose you'll tell me next I shouldn't have interfered between Timmy MacGovern and May," Joan asked sweetly.

"I don't see what the hell business it was of yours," Kitty retorted hotly.

"I'd soon be told what business it was if I had to meet your young man's family with a scandal like that hanging over us," said Joan. "I hope you're not going to tell me that he's married?"

No, he wasn't married, but as it turned out, it was almost as bad. Joan met him that night in a cinema restaurant. He came in with a heap of books under his arm, a thin, dyspeptic, worried-looking lad with spectacles.

"Really, Miss Twomey," he began, "I'm terribly sorry about all this. I really am."

"I'm sure of it," Joan agreed sweetly, "but what we've got to discuss now is what we're going to do about it."

"I know," he said. "I don't think about anything else. I keep racking my brains, but I simply don't seem to be able to think of anything."

"Well, I presume at least that you're going to marry her?"

"You're presuming a lot," Kitty cut in. "It isn't as easy as all that."

"Would you mind telling me what the objections are?"

"Well, it's my parents," he wailed. "It would be an awful shock to them."

"And I suppose you think it hasn't been a shock to my father?" she said sternly.

"Con doesn't mean that at all," Kitty put in hotly.

"Then what does he mean?"

"I mean, Miss Twomey, that I haven't got anything, and if I did marry Kitty we'd have to keep it dark or my parents might throw me out."

"That would be a very peculiar sort of marriage, Mr. Rahilly."

He shrugged his shoulders, looking more crushed than ever, and his eyes wandered all over the restaurant as though in search of counsel.

"I don't think Kitty's father would like that sort of marriage at all," she added firmly.

"Well, I can't say I like it, but I don't see what else we can do."

"And who's to support Kitty until you've finished college and got a job." Con clutched his head and looked at Kitty, but even Kitty didn't seem to be able to help him in this dilemma. Joan could see that he was an intolerably weak character, entirely under the thumb of his parents; that he wasn't even considering seriously the possibility of a secret marriage, and that even this she would not succeed in achieving unless she dealt with him firmly. "I suppose you mean my father can support her while she hides away in furnished lodgings like a criminal, all to spare your parents the shock. Really, I think you're as irresponsible as Kitty, if not worse."

"It's easy for you to talk," Kitty said bitterly. "You don't know his mother."

"Well, she can't eat him, Kitty."

"That remains to be seen, Miss Twomey," he said, and she flashed an angry look at him, but he seemed to be quite serious. "As Kitty says, you don't know her."

"Well, I'm going to get to know her within the next couple of days," said Joan. "I'll leave it to you to prepare her."

He threw up his hands in despair.

"You're not going to get to know her," said Kitty. "This is my business, not yours."

"Very well, Kitty. Then I'll wire for Father, and he can deal with you. As a matter of fact," she added untruthfully, "he'd be here now, only for me."

"Then I can give up all hope of continuing at college," Con said, giving it up as a bad job. "I don't mind. I probably wouldn't have been any good as a doctor anyway. I suppose I can be a clerk, if anyone will take me. As you can see, I'm not the type for a laborer."

Joan thought she had never seen such a weak specimen of an entirely degenerate type. She wasn't at all sure but that it would be better for everybody if she didn't interfere. The following evening she took the bus to the Rahillys' house. It was an old-fashioned terrace house on the strand with a great view of the bay and Howth. The door was opened for her by Mr. Rahilly, a red-faced, boozy man with pleasant manners. Mrs. Rahilly was sitting in the front room by the window. Mr. Rahilly introduced them and then disappeared.

Mrs. Rahilly was a plump, pasty-faced woman with rather syrupy manners. To give herself courage, Joan talked in a loud breezy tone, but it came back to her with a hollow echo. She was in a quandary and knew it. To treat the matter too gravely would imply such a reflection on Kitty that Mrs. Rahilly might make it an excuse for refusing to agree to it at all, while if she treated it too lightly, she might conclude that Joan was of the same kind.

"Well, I'm sure I'm very sorry, Miss Twomey," the older woman said effusively. "But I don't see there's anything I can do about it. I had to pinch and scrape to send Con to college, and if it was to save my life, I couldn't do more."

"But surely you'll agree that they must get married," Joan said eagerly.

"Well, indeed, I'm sure I'd be delighted," said Mrs. Rahilly; "that's if your family can support them."

"We have nothing," replied Joan, realizing that she wasn't going to get a shilling.

"Nor more have we," said Mrs. Rahilly as if it was a great joke.

"Then I suppose they must only do what others did before them," Joan said in chagrin. "Kitty can't support a child on her own."

"She might find she has to support a husband and child," said Mrs. Rahilly. "There's no use putting a tooth in it, Miss Twomey, but Con would be no head to her. His father was a weak man—I can say that to you—it was the drink with him; there's no use in denying it. But Con is weaker still. I never thought I'd rear him. It is the digestion with him. He has every delicacy in his own home, but he cannot keep it down. What chance has a boy like that of providing for a wife and child? It's foolishness, Miss Twomey—foolishness!"

Joan was beginning to think that much as she disliked Mrs. Rahilly, they were in agreement about this at least. She was very angry with Kitty and refused to tell her what had happened. "I know what happened all right," Kitty said. "You met your match at last," and this made Joan angrier still. But when Con turned up to Kitty's lodging next day he was resolute for the marriage. Joan had no great faith in his resolution. It was desperation rather than courage. Bad as poverty was, it now had less terrors for him than life with Mother.

When all this was fixed, Joan brought Kitty home to prepare for the wedding. She didn't speak to her all the way down on the train. Her interview with Mrs. Rahilly still rankled. She refused to let her father have anything to say to her either, and except for confidences with May, Kitty was treated as an outcast, an abandoned woman who had brought disgrace to them all. Joan was still very doubtful whether when the moment came, Con Rahilly would have the nerve to defy his mother, and she had to prepare her father and Chris for the worst. She watched every letter which Kitty received, sure that each one must contain the bad news.

This was the beginning of what Kitty called Joan's hypocrisy, though at no time did Joan ever feel in the least hypocritical. It was only that during those difficult months her attitude to Chris changed completely. She became more dependent on him. She asked his advice about everything. She clung to him with a passion that surprised herself. It surprised Chris too, but if he had any qualms about it, he put it down to the strain that she was enduring. Having suffered so much himself, he was prepared to be tolerant of her.

To everybody's astonishment, Con arrived the evening before the wedding. To Joan he seemed a different young man. He had packed his bag and walked out of the house alone. His father had shaken him silently by the hand and slipped him a five-pound note, but his mother had refused to leave her room or admit him to say farewell. The father of a college friend had made a small job for him. He had rented one furnished room in Lower Leeson Street. His friends had treated the whole thing as no better than suicide, and he took them off with great gusto while he cracked ghastly jokes about starvation, which Joan found tasteless. But to her surprise, her father took an instant liking to him. He laughed at Con's grim jokes and took him aside to offer to raise a loan for him. When Con refused, he told Joan that Kitty had picked the best of the bunch.

Joan didn't at all share her father's views, but she didn't try to disillusion him, because his satisfaction seemed to round off her task. Now that her sisters were both married, she felt she had kept the promise made after her mother's death, and proposed to devote the rest of her days to Chris. She proclaimed joyously that they were now getting married too, just as quick as they could. They would live in Dublin because he must have the chance of hearing good music. Every obstacle was brushed aside. Chris's mother would have to live with Bob;

her father would either have to live with May or fend for himself. There was to be no further talk of her responsibilities or of Chris's. To her surprise, her father agreed enthusiastically.

"That's just the way I see it too, Joan," he said emotionally. "There's nothing I'd hate so much as to see you turning into an old maid. You're a great girl, a great girl. I'm glad you're getting a good, steady fellow like Chris. Young Gordon was a nice chap too, but he wasn't your sort, and you're better off with someone like yourself."

Mick might almost be said to have overdone it, but I am afraid the truth is he was almost lightheaded with relief. I suppose you have to have as good a daughter as Joan to realize what a blessing it is when she marries and takes herself off. A man with marriageable daughters never has a house he can call his own. If it was only an old barn, you would prefer to have it to yourself.

So she and Chris bought a little bungalow in the hills behind Dublin; a new house without even a cottage near, and with a wonderful view across the city to the Mourne Mountains and over the bay to Howth, and indulged themselves in the solitude they both longed for. They rarely visited or had visitors, and Joan's letters described their solitary evenings, watching the lights come on in the city beneath and listening to the Beethoven quartets right through on the gramophone.

It sounded idyllic, but Kitty and Con got a different impression one evening when they were cycling through Rathfarnham and dropped in unexpectedly. Con was something of a surprise to everybody except Mick Twomey. Though so modest that he scarcely dared express an opinion of his own, he had developed into an extraordinarily acute businessman. Joan was sure he was doing it out of spite, though whether against her or his mother she wasn't sure. At any rate, he and Kitty now had a small house of their own and were talking of buying a car. He stood at the window and generously admired the view while Joan, in her vivacious way, enthused about the calm of the bungalow and the voices of the birds in the early morning. Kitty said nothing. She thought Joan's bungalow was the last word in inconvenience: an emotional girl with no side, she was very fond of the noise of buses, and thought there was an awful lot of nonsense talked about birds. Suddenly she heard a sound that made her start.

"What's that?" she said incredulously. "A baby?"

Joan smiled, looking rather uncomfortable, and Chris rose with an anguished air.

"I'll see to him, Joan," he volunteered.

He went out and the crying ceased. For several minutes the others stared at one another. Then, in turn, they all grew red. At last Joan grinned insinuatingly.

"We have to keep it dark on Chris's account," she explained apologetically, as though it were all Chris's doing and he had given birth to the baby himself. "Of course, it could be used against him in the civil service."

"That's right," Con said with complete gravity. "You can't be too careful. There's an awful lot of hypocrisy in this country."

"Are you telling us there's hypocrisy?" Kitty asked bitterly as she rose.

"You might as well stay and have something to eat as you're at it," Joan said with more warmth than she had previously shown. "It's a relief that you know about it, because now you can come whenever you like."

"Quartets are not enough," said Con.

"Ah, you'd be dead for want of someone to talk to," said Joan.

"We'd better be going back to our own brat," Kitty said, just managing to keep her temper. "He's probably bawling the house down by now."

All the way downhill she pedalled madly, keeping well ahead of her husband. "God Almighty!" she said bitterly when he caught up on her, "the rest of us can have babies but she can only have quartets. Did you hear her—herself and her birds? That one was crooked from the cradle."

Con only thought it a great joke. May was the same when Kitty wrote and told her. "What name did she call him?" she replied. "Is it Gordon or Dick?" Kitty, who knew that the child could be no one but Chris's, found it a puzzling question.

A Sense of Responsibility

MICK and Jack Cantillon lived up our road when I was a young fellow. They were very much alike in general appearance, small, stout, and good-natured, but there the resemblance stopped. Mick was a thundering blackguard, while Jack was a slow, quiet, conscientious chap.

Naturally, Mrs. Cantillon—a tall, mournful, pious woman with the remains of considerable good looks—adored Mick and despised Jack. She liked men to be manly; she liked the way Mick, after drinking the housekeeping money or being arrested for being drunk and disorderly, approached her with his arms out and said mockingly, "Mother, forgive your erring son." Even when Jack had a drop taken, he didn't regard himself as being in error, and was out to work the next morning, head or no head; he seemed to have no religious feelings at all, wouldn't be bothered going to a mission or retreat, and expected the poor woman to keep accounts. Accounts were things Mrs. Cantillon couldn't keep.

Jack was a great friend of another young man called Farren, and the two of them went everywhere together, though they were as much unlike as lads could be. Farren was tall and handsome, with a clear, delicate, tubercular complexion. He was quick-witted and light-hearted. Having been brought up in a household of women, sent to work in an office full of women, he seemed at times to be half a woman himself. He certainly seemed happier with women than with most men. Meeting some well-to-do educated young lady from Sunday's Well who swallowed all her words in the best Sunday's Well manner, he called her "sweetheart," and when she'd got over the shock of that, coaxed her into telling him how changed her boy friend seemed to be since he'd come back from Paris. Farren was just like another girl with her; so understanding, sympathetic, and light in touch that it didn't strike her till later that this was the only thing feminine about him, and by that time it was usually too late. As a result women were always trying to get him over the phone, and the things he said about them were shocking. Not that he meant them to be, but there was something almost treasonable about the way he talked so intimately of them, and some men didn't like it because it so resembled eavesdropping.

Apart from Farren, Jack's great friends were the Dwyers, a large, loud-voiced family. The father was a small building contractor, known to his wife as "poor Dwyer," whose huffy shyness had never permitted him to get anywhere in life. His wife had ten times his brains and he lectured her as if she were an idiot, and she put up with it as if she were. She was a big, buxom, bonny woman, very devout and very caustic. They had three boys and three girls, and Jack went drinking and bowl-playing with the boys and dancing with the girls until the latter held a council about him and decided, as he was completely incapable of making up his own mind, that they had better do it for him. It was decided that he should marry Susie, the middle girl. Annie, the youngest, whom he was supposed to favor, was compensated with a blue frock.

If Jack noticed anything peculiar about the way Susie was thrust on him, he didn't say much. He never said much anyway. Soon after, the Dwyers had plenty of opportunity for observing how close Jack could be when it suited him.

Mick, you see, had married a girl called Madge Hunt, a good-natured, stupid, sentimental woman who adored him. She was shocked at the harshness of his employers, who actually expected him to be at work six days out of every week, and at the intolerable behavior of people he owed money to, who expected him to pay it back, whether he had it or not. A couple of years of marriage to Mick improved her sense of reality enormously. She became hard as nails, cold and knowing. Then Mick was killed, not too gloriously, in a motoring accident, and Madge had to go out and work as a charwoman.

Jack was very upset by Mick's death. He took to calling regularly on Madge and her little boy. The Dwyers at first saw nothing wrong with this; a decent grief is a very respectable thing, and the Dwyers were nothing if not respectable. But Jack's concern bordered on insincerity. And it didn't stop there. The eldest of the Dwyer girls, Babs, who heard everything, heard from the Mrs. MacDunphy who employed Madge that Jack had made her give up the daily work and was supplying the equivalent of her wages out of his own pocket. According to Mrs. MacDunphy, this was to go on till her son left school. What Mrs. MacDunphy had said was "There's a good brother-in-law for you!" What Babs said was "How well I wouldn't find some old fool to keep me!" But what her mother said was "That's very queer behavior in a man who's walking out with Susie." It was the first glimpse she'd caught of that side of Jack's character, and she didn't like it.

She wanted Susie to have it out with him, but Susie flew in a panic and said she'd be afraid. Mrs. Dwyer wasn't afraid. Anyone who employed one of the Dwyer family could rely on her to see that the goods came up to scratch, and she wasn't the sort to tolerate a slight on her daughter.

"I hear you're looking after Madge Hunt while the little fellow is at school, Jack," she said pleasantly one evening when she managed to get Jack alone.

Jack looked embarrassed. He didn't like his charities to be known.

"There isn't much I can do for her," he said apologetically. "But it isn't good for the little fellow to have to be left with strangers every day."

" 'Tis hard," she agreed. "I dare say it won't make it too easy for you to settle down yourself," she added.

"I dare say not," agreed Jack.

"Isn't it a long time to ask Susie to wait, Jack?" she asked reproachfully.

"It's longer than I like to wait myself, Mrs. D.," he said, knocking out his pipe. "I have some hopes I might get a rise, but I can't be certain. Of course, if Susie got a better chance, I wouldn't stand in her way."

"I think we'd better leave it at that, Jack," she replied with the least trace of pompousness. Whatever else Mrs. Dwyer might be, she was not pompous, but she had the mortifying feeling that she was being bested by an amateur without a trump in his hand. Madge Hunt, who wasn't even intelligent, could get round Jack and she couldn't.

"I'd have nothing more to do with that fellow, Susie," she told her daughter unemotionally. "He hasn't enough manliness to make anyone a good husband. The Cantillons all take after their mother."

But Susie wasn't like that at all. She was gentle and a nagger; alarmed at the idea that Jack did not appreciate her, she was more concerned with making him change his mind than maintaining her dignity.

So she began in the most flagrant way to throw herself at Pat Farren's head. She didn't really like Pat; she could not like any man with a reputation of his sort, and he knew more than Susie approved of about her little weaknesses. It's all very well, a man dancing attendance on you, but not when he shows that he knows what's going on in your mind. Susie couldn't have a grievance without Pat's seeing it first. At the same time she wanted Jack to see that others besides himself could appreciate her.

Another man would have withdrawn from a situation of such profound delicacy, but Pat lacked all niceness of feeling. He thought it the funniest thing ever. He was delighted with Susie's conviction that nobody knew what she was doing, and was passionately inquisitive to know how far she'd go with it. It was just the sort of situation that appealed to him because it showed up a woman's character like a searchlight. If Susie had known, she would have died of mortification, but he even discussed it with Jack. When the three of them were together he acted it for all he was worth.

"Are you coming home with me, Susie?" he would say, throwing his arms about her. "I can't live another day without you."

"I can't, sure," Susie would cry, half-pleased, half-terrified by his manner.

"Is it that fellow you're afraid of?" he would say, pointing at Jack. "He'd kill me!"

"That fellow? He doesn't care a snap of his fingers about you. I'm the one that really loves you."

"Go on out of that, ye pair of whoors!" Jack would cry with tears of laughter in his eyes.

In Crosshaven, where the Dwyers had a cottage for the summer and where Pat spent most of his time, the flirtation continued, and Susie even began to enjoy it. But it seemed to have no effect on Jack. She began to wonder whether her mother mightn't be right, and if Jack was a man at all.

Coming on to Christmas, Pat fell ill and had to be operated on. Susie had never seen Jack so upset. He spent every afternoon at the hospital. She discovered from Pat's mother that he had offered to guarantee a loan to get his friend to Switzerland. But it was too late for that. Pat died the week after Christmas. Jack took to visiting the Farrens as he had visited Madge Hunt, and busied himself with tidying up Pat's small business interests. But it was far worse than the business of Mick's death. He kept a picture of Pat on his mantelpiece, and sometimes when Susie called she found him glancing at it and realized that she was interrupting some sort of colloquy between him and the picture. As time went on and she saw that it had become a sort of fixation with him, she became more concerned. It was morbid; she felt it was her duty to put a stop to it, but she could not get him to listen to ordinary reasonable criticism of Pat. Either he looked pained and changed the subject or he told her gently that she didn't understand. The latter charge really riled Susie. After all, which of them had been made love to by Pat?

"You're very foolish," she said in a distant tone. "You let people influence you too much. Now, I'd never let anyone influence me like that, not even a man. Pat was amusing enough, but you never realized how shallow he was."

"Now, Susie, don't let's argue," he said with a slight pained smile. "Pat had a very fine brain."

"Ah, he was very insincere, Jack," Susie said with a frown and a shake of the head.

"Pat was sincere enough in his own way. It wasn't your way or my way. We all have different ways of being sincere."

"Ah, for goodness' sake," she exclaimed with a superior air. "Pat was all right as long as he was with you, but he let you down the moment your back was turned. My goodness, didn't I know him?"

"You didn't, Susie. Pat made fun of us, as he made fun of everybody, but he'd never do anything to harm a friend. He didn't even know what it was."

Then Susie realized that she must make the sacrifice of her life. Nothing else would ever shake Jack out of his absorption in his dead friend.

"That's all you know," she said in a low voice, her lip trembling at the thought of her own nobility.

"I know as much as anyone."

"I suppose so, you know that Pat and myself were—living together?" she asked with a long underhung look while she tried to keep her voice level.

"You were what?" Jack exclaimed testily.

Susie broke down.

"Oh, it's all very well for you to criticize," she sobbed, "but it's your own fault for keeping me dragging on like this from year to year. How soft you have it! Any other girl would do the same."

"Not making you a saucy answer, Sue," Jack said irritably, "I don't give a damn what you do, but I'm not going to have you going round telling lies about a man who can't defend himself."

"Lies?" she cried indignantly.

"What the hell else is it?"

"It is not lies," she cried, really furious with him this time. "The impudence of you! I suppose you think no one could do a thing like that to you. Well, Pat Farren did, and I can hardly blame him. You're not natural. My mother said it. You don't even know the temptations people have."

"And as I said before, I don't give a damn," Jack said, almost wagging his finger at her as though she were nothing but a schoolgirl kicking up a scene at a funeral. "But it could cause great pain to Pat's people to have stories like that going round about him. So don't do it again, like a good girl."

Susie realized with stupefaction that whether he believed her or not, he would still continue to think it more important not to cause pain to Farren's parents than to consider her warnings. What made it worse was that she could not tell them at home what the quarrel was about. They would never realize the magnitude of the sacrifice she had made to bring Jack round to a sense of reality. Either they would believe her and regard her as a monster, or they wouldn't and regard her as a fool. She went home in a state approaching hysterics and said that Jack was a most appalling man, a most unnatural man. Her mother said quietly: "Well, girl, you can't say you weren't warned," which was about the most useless thing she could have said, for the more Susie was warned against Jack, the more interesting he became to her. It was inquisitiveness more than anything else. When a girl ceases to be inquisitive about a man, she is finished with him.

It was five years before he was in a position to marry her, and by that time Susie's spirit was broken. He had become a habit with her. It was no use pretending that Mrs. Dwyer was pleased; she had sized the man up, once for all, but as Susie seemed so set on him, she supposed she must only do her best to put up with him. By this time Jack was chief clerk in the carrier's where he worked, and they were fairly comfortable. They bought a nice house on a terrace only a stone's throw from the Dwyers', and produced two children, a girl and a boy. It seemed as if everything was running smooth for them at last. Almost too smooth for Susie's comfort. She had never really got over the way Jack had slighted her great sacrifice. According to her mood, she had two entirely different versions of her relations with Pat. The first and general one was that it had been entirely innocent—which it had; the second was that it had been nothing of the sort—which was equally true, according to the way you viewed it. When she was in good humor—which was most of the time—there had been nothing between Pat and herself except what she called "old nonsense"; when she was out of sorts, she had had a dark past, forced on her entirely by Jack, and had made a magnificent gesture in confessing it to him, only to have it dismissed as childishness. And when she felt like this, and had repeated it in Confession as a sin of her past life which she particularly regretted, and remembered her own nobility, grief and fury rose in her till she made Jack a thorough, good, old-fashioned scene in which she wept and screamed and called him an old molly. Jack, with his feet on the mantelpiece and a book or paper in his hands, would look up at her with concern from time to time over his spectacles and make some reasonable masculine protest, which only started her off again. Finally it would get too much for him. He would dash down his paper, say "F— you!" in a choking voice, and go out to get drunk. The first time he did this, Susie was thrilled, but she soon discovered that Jack's emotional vocabulary was limited to one word, which he used only under extreme provocation, and once he had done this, he had nothing more to say for himself.

THEN, at the height of their married happiness, the worst happened. Mrs. Cantillon, having managed to exhaust her small means and entangle herself in a labyrinth of tiny debts, none of which could be explained at less than novel length, was threatened with eviction. Jack was profoundly worried. He went to Madge Hunt for advice. Madge was the only woman whose judgment he really trusted.

"Well, it seems to me you'll just have to be a bit of a bastard for once in your life, Jack," she said.

"Would I have to take lessons for that?" he asked gently.

"The first lesson is that you ought to put your mother in a home," she said coldly.

He shook his head.

"That's what I mean," she said with a shrug. "If you weren't the sort who couldn't be sensible, I wouldn't be sitting here on my bottom advising you to be sensible. You know she'll make a wreck of your house."

"I fancy she'll try," he agreed with a sombre nod.

"Don't kid yourself, Jack, she will. The only thing you can do is ask her to come here. There's a room here, and she's welcome to it on your account. But my bet is she'll go to the workhouse first."

Then Madge saw him go off despondent, and thought in her cynical way that he was probably the one man in the world she could have been happy with.

But she had seen through Mrs. Cantillon, for those, more or less, were the words Mrs. Cantillon used. First she looked at Jack with a timid smile as if wondering if he was in earnest. Then she explained in her simple, homely way that Madge had killed poor Mick before his time; that though at the time she had lied herself black in the face for the child's sake, everyone knew poor Mick had committed suicide, and that, though as a Christian she had long forgiven and forgotten all that, the daily contact with her son's murderess would be more than a sensitive woman like herself could bear. Mrs. Cantillon, for all her silliness, was a woman of infinite perception. She saw that in the matter of mischief-making, Madge Hunt was a woman you'd get nowhere with; a hard, cynical woman who would see through an old lady's tricks before she even began them, while Susie, as well as being a much better cook, would be clay in her hands.

Mrs. Dwyer, a woman of small silliness and excellent perception, saw the situation in the same light. She warned Susie that Mrs. Cantillon would drive her out of her home by hook or by crook. She went further. Seeing Susie's complete lack of gumption, she spoke to Jack herself about it. This time there was no pleasantness. The gloves were off so far as she was concerned.

"I don't think you realize the danger of in-laws in your house, Jack," she said severely.

"I think I do, Mrs. D.," said Jack with a sigh.

"I don't think so, Jack," she said, her voice growing hard, "or you wouldn't offer your mother a home with Susie and the children. I've seen more of that sort of thing than you have, and I never yet saw it come to any good. People may mean no harm, but they make mischief just the same."

"Mrs. Dwyer," Jack said almost appealingly, "even my mother's worst enemy wouldn't accuse her of meaning no harm," and for a moment Mrs. Dwyer's eyes twinkled. She knew Mrs. Cantillon too.

"That's all the more reason she shouldn't share a house with Susie, Jack," she said remorselessly. "When you married Susie, you took on certain responsibilities to her. Young people have to have their disagreements, and they have to have them in some sort of privacy. I never interfered, good or bad, between Susie and you because I know what it leads to. Marriage is a secret between two people. 'Tis at an end when outsiders join in."

"If you think I'd be likely to side with anyone in the world against Susie!" Jack exclaimed, almost with a groan.

"You mightn't be able to help it, Jack. 'Tis all very well talking, but your mother is your mother."

"If that day came, I could always cut my throat," said Jack with something like passion. "But old people have to live, Mrs. Dwyer."

"They have, Jack," she said almost with resignation, "but they haven't the same claims as young people, and there's no good denying it. For everybody's sake, your mother would be better in a home. I have to think of Susie."

"And I have to think of Susie and my mother," said Jack with an embarrassed smile.

"I think you may have to choose between them, Jack," Mrs. Dwyer said quietly.

"There are certain things you have no choice about, Mrs. Dwyer," he said gloomily, and again she realized with irritation that this intolerably weak man, this sucker who was allowing himself to be imposed on by his mischievous and selfish mother, had some source of strength that made him immune from being imposed upon by a woman of character like herself.

"Well, don't blame me if you wreck your home, Jack," she said with finality.

From that on, she refused to visit Jack's house again, and though the children came regularly to see her, and Jack himself came every Sunday morning after Mass and she received him warmly, the old relationship was at an end. She had too much pride to let herself be flouted.

It must be admitted that she had miscalculated Mrs. Cantillon's style though not her content. Mrs. Cantillon made hell of the home all right, but not in the straightforward way a woman of Mrs. Dwyer's character expected. She made no attempt to make Susie's life impossible. She contented herself with making Jack's impossible. The imbecility of women like Mrs. Cantillon has an aspect that is never far removed from genius. She knew Jack's weaknesses in a way Susie had never known them. She remembered with sentimental attachment childish humiliations he had suffered. She knew that though a married man and a father, he had always remained temperamentally a bit of a bachelor, remote from the stresses of courtship and marriage. Perhaps it is only bachelors who can have a sense of responsibility. He had lived all his life in one small corner of Cork, nodding and smiling to his neighbors without ever knowing more about them than was necessary for congratulation or sympathy. He had managed to head Susie off intimacies, but it would have taken a tank to head off his mother. To her, the great joy in life was knowing everybody's business.

She knew that after his day's work he liked to change ceremonially into old trousers and read or play with the children, so she began to jolly him into taking Susie out. On the surface it was the height of good nature, and Susie, who found long-extinguished flutterings revive in her, took it at its face value and seconded her mother-in-law.

"Ah, what other use is there for an old woman like me," asked Mrs. Cantillon with a mournful smile, "except to let ye free to enjoy yeerselves?"

The extraordinary thing was that as the home grew more wretched, Susie came to depend more and more on her mother-in-law. She even had arguments with her mother about it. Mrs. Dwyer believed that Jack was weak, but nothing would persuade her but that his mother was bad to the heart. Susie argued with her. She said it wasn't Mrs. Cantillon at all; Mrs. Cantillon wasn't bad when you came to know her; it was Jack. She came to see that in all the disagreements between them, it was Jack with his monstrous selfishness who had been at fault. It seemed he had always been that way, even as a boy—hard-natured. She listened eagerly to Mrs. Cantillon's tales of Mick, who had none of Jack's faults, and though her own memory told her differently, she allowed herself to be persuaded that, even admitting everything, Mick was the better man. "Ah, poor Mick," Mrs. Cantillon said with the tears in her eyes, "in spite of his little faults, you couldn't begrudge him anything." If Madge Hunt had decided she had married the wrong brother, Susie was now well on the way to believing the same. Even Jack's one dirty word had ceased to cover the situation. He stayed out in the evenings, boozing.

* * *

ONE DAY Susie came in to find the children crying and Mrs. Cantillon sprawled at the foot of the stairs unconscious. For two days she hung on while Jack waited at the hospital. Mrs. Dwyer came to look after the children, and it was clear when they met that the old quarrel was over. In fact, it had been over for a long time, for it impressed her that Mrs. Cantillon had succeeded in moving Susie but not him. At the funeral he pretended no great grief, and Susie, who automatically broke down at all funerals, received the sympathy of a number of women who believed her to be the daughter of the deceased. This made her furious, and she said that Jack would show no more nature for her than he had for his mother.

Mrs. Dwyer had troubles of her own to think of at the time. Jim, the last of the boys, had married, and she was on her own. This, according to herself, was the day she had always been waiting for, and she plunged into a life of dissipation, going to the pictures, playing cards, and refusing to mind her grandchildren. "Wisha, aren't I right?" she asked Jack. "Aren't I fussing round them long enough? 'Tis time I had a bit of enjoyment out of life." Then she developed arthritis. Susie came to nurse her, and after that it became clear to the family that their mother's short-lived period of independence was over. She could not be left in the house alone. She would have to go and live with one of the boys—a bitter humiliation for a strong-minded woman.

Tim, an easy-going fellow, would have had her willingly, but easy-going fellows get easy-going wives, and it wasn't likely that Mrs. Dwyer, who boasted that she had never seen the day when a properly cooked dinner was not served in her house, would long put up with Nora and her perpetual round of frying.

Ned's wife had six children, and there would be no room for her unless they took a bigger house. Jim, being just married, had only the minimum of furniture, and it would take a considerable capital expenditure to set him up. It wasn't that they didn't love their mother or wouldn't have died for her if occasion arose, but none of them wanted to be the sucker when a little hesitation might mean a considerable easing of the sacrifice asked of them.

Susie, who had a heart for everyone's troubles, understood it perfectly and wept for all of them equally, but her sister, Babs, told them they were a bloody pack of wasters and went upstairs to tell their mother the same. "How often did I say it to you?" she demanded. "You ruined that gang. One of us could get nothing in this house, and that's all the thanks you get for it."

Babs was a forthright girl who could always be relied upon to make things as difficult as possible for everyone else. Her mother only listened to her splutterings with sly amusement.

"The Lord lighten their burdens!" she said dryly. "As if I'd be under an obligation to any of them!"

"Well, what are you going to do, woman?" asked Babs.

"Don't bother your head about what I'm going to do," said her mother with a wave of her hand. "I'm going up to the Little Sisters where I can be properly looked after. I had all that arranged six months ago. Do you think, after all my years, I'm going into another woman's house to play second fiddle to her? I am not."

The whole family realized when this was reported to them that it was precisely what they'd always imagined their mother would do, and, much as they regretted it, they were almost relieved. The only person who was not was Jack. When Susie told him he stretched his legs to the fire, pulled on his pipe, and looked grave.

"That will kill her, Susie," he said at last.

"Do you think so really, Jack?" she asked wonderingly.

"I'm sure of it."

"But anyway it's not as bad as having to live with an in-law."

"Why?" he asked. "Do you think she's going to escape other women by going into a home?"

"I suppose not," said Susie, beginning to be troubled again herself. "But what can you do with her? You know what she's like when she has her mind made up."

"I wonder if she has her mind made up," he said doubtfully.

The following evening he went for a long walk, up Montenotte and back by Mayfield. On his way home he called at the Dwyers'. Babs was there, and her mother instantly ordered her out to make tea for him. Marriage made no difference to the Dwyer girls. Inside her door they instantly reverted to a dependent position. Mrs. Dwyer never had had any regard for the principle of women's rights. "If they'll give me enough money, they can have their rights," she had said, and only voted to humor her husband. " 'Tis alike to me which of them gets in," was her view.

"I hear you're going up to the Little Sisters?" said Jack as they sat over the fire together.

"Arrah, of course I am, child," she replied lightly. "You know what I always thought of in-laws."

"I do," he replied with a grin.

"And can't you imagine me turned loose on them? Not, between ourselves, Jack Cantillon, that I'm not a better woman than any of them."

"No one said you weren't."

"God knows," she went on with resignation, "I don't know what sort of women are they turning out. They're good for nothing only raising their elbows and resting their backsides. That wife of Tim's—I don't know is she ever right. If I was a man and a woman offered me sausages for my dinner, I'd take the frying-pan to her. I declare to God I would."

"You wouldn't come to Susie and me?" he asked, dropping his voice. "You'd be no trouble. The room is there since the mother died."

"Was Susie talking about it?" she asked sharply.

"She was not," Jack replied with vigor, answering two questions; one which had been implied but not asked, the other not even implied. The implied question was "Are you encouraging Susie to patronize me?" "Of course, Susie must have the last word," he added, answering the question which existed only in his own mind.

"Wisha, Jack, boy," she said, dropping her defenses, "I'm easy where I go. I had my day, and I must only be satisfied. At the same time, mind you, I like to be asked. I suppose we all have our bit of vanity."

"You're well entitled to it," he said with a laugh. "Will you come?"

"I will not come, Jack, thanks all the same. Ye had enough of in-laws to last ye the rest of yeer lives—not criticizing your poor mother, God rest her, whatever I might have said when she was alive. 'Tis only when you come to it yourself that you realize. Besides," she added with sudden candor, "I wouldn't give it to say to the boys."

"I thought of that," Jack agreed with a nod. "I don't think they'd mind if you let me put it up to them first. I think I might get round them. You see, we are a bit better off than they are, and I don't think they'd stand in the way of making you more comfortable."

She looked at him closely to see if he was smiling, and realized that there was no intentional irony behind his remarks. She gave a sudden shrug.

"To tell you the God's truth, Jack," she said, "I'd hate to be in an institution. I'd nearly sooner put up with Tim's wife. I could never get on with nuns, God forgive me. Half the time I don't think they're natural. Mind, Jack, I'll be no acquisition to you. I'll do my best but I won't promise you anything. Old people get very selfish. You have no idea. You'd be waiting here for a cup of tea, and if half Cork died, you wouldn't care till you got it. And isn't it only natural?" she asked, cocking an argumentative eyebrow. "What else have we to look forward to?"

Of course, it had to be done tactfully, and even then created a few scenes and some protests, but somehow, from the moment it was mentioned, it seemed the family had always known it would happen that way. Their mother would be impossible in an institution unless she were made matron at once. Jack was steady; he was fairly well-to-do; he was the born burden-carrier, and in the matter of money would be much easier to deal with than any member of the family.

Curiously, as things turned out, Mrs. Dwyer proved a real acquisition, at least to Jack. The thought that she hadn't to go into a home seemed to give her a new lease of life, and almost up to her death she was livelier than Susie. The first evening Jack came home from work, she had his old trousers warming on a chair at the fire and made him change there instead of in the bedroom. "Wisha, at my age, as if I couldn't look at a man with his trousers off! Do you want me to go out?" "I don't." "Wisha, why would you?" Mrs. Dwyer looked after him as if he were a child, trying to judge what he really wanted—never an easy thing with a man so bottled-up. She was so pleased not to be treated as an imbecile the way "poor Dwyer" treated her that she even tried to develop an interest in politics to please him. When Susie started her first big row with him, her mother said sharply: "Susie, what way is that to talk to Jack?" and Susie broke down and went upstairs to weep. When Jack made to follow her, Mrs. Dwyer said firmly: "Stop where you are, Jack. You only make her worse."

She went upstairs to deal with Susie herself. She knew Jack didn't like it; she knew he hated anybody's interfering between himself and Susie, but she also knew how women should be treated, which he never would.

"The trouble with you is that you don't know a good man when you see one," she told Susie dryly. "I only wish to God I had a husband like him—not criticizing poor Dwyer."

"God is good," sniffed Susie. "I mightn't last long between the pair of ye."

But Susie had enough respect for her mother to realize that she was right, and even after Mrs. Dwyer's death she no longer looked elsewhere for a model of what men should be. On her deathbed Mrs. Dwyer asked to be buried with Jack and Susie. She didn't ask it with any particular emotion, and even at that Jack was surprised, for she was a woman who loathed sentiment, disliked anyone who professed to ideals above money and security, and had always pretended complete indifference to where they slung her when her time was up, but he promised just the same.

He also broke his promise, but she would hardly have held that against him, because she knew how he hated to inflict unnecessary pain. All he had to remember her by was the undertaker's bill, which he kept and looked at from time to time. It puzzled him that he who had always hated his own mother should care so much for her. He didn't think it right that anyone else should share in the funeral expenses, and, fortunately, no member of the family wanted to contest the privilege with him.

Counsel for Oedipus

To sit in court and watch a case between wife and husband is like seeing a performance of *Oedipus*. You know that no matter what happens the man hasn't a chance. A colt will consider it a matter of conscience to pass a filly, and a court of law is the same. Even the man's own counsel will be ashamed of him and envy counsel for the wife, who, whatever she did or didn't do, has the ear of the court. As for judges—every single one that I've known had a mother fixation.

But the worst thing of all is that even the man is divided against himself. Now, take the day when Mickie Joe Dougherty was defending a big country man called Lynam, whose wife was suing him for legal separation and accusing him of cruelty and adultery. The adultery was admitted, and all that was needed to prove the cruelty was to put Tom Lynam in the box. He was a big, good-looking man with a stiff, morose manner; one of those men who are deceptively quiet and good-humored for months on end and then lay you out with a stick for a casual remark about politics.

His wife was a trim, mousy little female about half his height and a quarter his weight, with an anxious face and a gentle, bedraggled air. She cocked her little head while she listened to her counsel's questions, as though they were uttered in a foreign language, and replied to them in something of the same way, raising her colorless little voice and illustrating her answers with pathetic, half-completed gestures. It reminded you of fourth-form French. All the same, it gave impressiveness to the picture she drew of her husband, drunk and violent, smashing everything in the kitchen on her. You could see O'Meara, the judge, adored her. "Come over here where we can hear you, ma'am," he said, pointing to a seat on the bench beside him, and he leaned one elbow on the bench, crossed his legs, and studied her. Poor O'Meara was a bad case; he had blood pressure as well as a mother fixation. Once or twice, as she gave her evidence, she glanced sadly and pityingly at her husband, who stared back at her with a gloomy hatred that was awe-inspiring. Most men, hearing how they have beaten and strangled their wives, even if they never laid a finger on them, don't know where to look—the poor devils are wondering what everyone thinks of them—but here was a man who watched his wife as if he was wondering why the blazes he hadn't taken a hatchet and finished the job as he was at it.

"And what did he say then?" asked Kenefick, her counsel.

"He called me—do I have to say that?" she asked with a wistful girlish look at O'Meara.

"Oh, not at all, not at all, ma'am," he said hastily. "Write it down," and pushed pencil and paper towards her. She wrote as she talked, slowly and carefully, raising her eyes sightlessly as she thought of all the cruel things her husband had said to her. Then she passed the paper apologetically to the judge, who glanced at it and passed it down to counsel. Tom Lynam, his face black with fury, leaned forward and whispered something to his solicitor, Matt Quill, but Matt only shook his head. If Matt had had his way, he'd have settled the case out of court.

"Did he say anything else?" asked Kenefick.

"Only if I didn't get out of the house in five minutes, sir, that he'd do to me what the Jews did to Jesus."

"What the Jews did to who?" O'Meara asked incredulously.

"Jesus, my lord," she replied, bowing her head reverently at the Holy Name. "Our Blessed Lord, you know. Crucify me, he meant."

"Huh!" snorted O'Meara with his blood pressure going up several degrees.

"Tell my lord what happened then," prompted Kenefick.

"So then I told him I could not go out at that hour of night, and the state of feebleness I was in," Mrs. Lynam continued with growing animation, "and he dragged me off the sofa and twisted my wrist behind my back." She illustrated "wrist" and "back" with another feeble gesture which she didn't complete.

"And did he know the state you were in?"

"Sure, how could he not know it?" cried Mrs. Lynam with her little hands outspread. "I wasn't able to get up from the sofa the whole day. That was what he had against me, of course. He wouldn't believe I was sick. Shamming he said I was."

"And what did he do?"

"Oh, he kicked me."

"Where was this?"

Her hand went to her back again, and she blushed. "Oh, in the—"

"No, no, no. I don't mean that. Where did this occur? What direction did he kick you in?"

"Oh, out the front door, sir," she replied hastily. "I fell on the path. Tommy—that's our little boy—knelt alongside me and began to cry, and my husband told him if he didn't get to bed, he'd do the same to him."

"He'd do the same to Tommy. How old is the child?"

"Five, sir, the fourteenth of February."

"And your husband made no effort to see were you injured in the fall?"

"Oh, indeed he didn't, sir," she replied with a smile like a rainbow—an optical illusion between two downpours. "Only to give me another kick off the path and into the flower-bed."

"And didn't you, at any time, make some appeal to him to cease this cruel treatment?" demanded Kenefick, stepping up his voice to indignation.

"Oh, indeed, I did, sir," she replied, responding sadly with a shake of her head. Whatever brand of French she spoke, it was clearly going down well, and she was beginning to enjoy it herself. "I asked him did he think I was in a fit state to go crawling across the fields in the dark to a neighbor's house, but he only used a filthy expression and banged the door in my face."

"And those were the marks that you showed next day to Dr. O'Mahony?"

"They were, sir. The same. A week he made me stop in bed with them."

"Tell me, ma'am," the judge interrupted, "this second kick he gave you—the one that sent you off the path into the flower-bed—where were you when he did that?"

"Oh, on the ground, my lord. I was too bad to get up. Half the way across the fields, I was crawling like that, on my hands and knees."

After this it was scarcely necessary to prove her husband's behavior with Nora MacGee, a woman of notorious bad character, for in fact she had had a child by him and his paternity was not denied. He had even visited her and nursed the child himself.

"And did you ask him to give up seeing this woman?"

"Why then, indeed, I did, sir. A dozen times if I did it once."

"And what did he say?"

"He said he wouldn't give up seeing a Lynam child for all the Hanafeys that were ever pupped, sir. The Hanafeys are my family," she added with her rainbow smile.

At this, Kenefick sat down as though he could not bear to prolong the poor woman's agony further, and Mickie Joe rose. Now, it cannot be pretended that, the best day he ever was, Mickie Joe was much of a lawyer or made a good appearance in court. Mickie Joe had begun life as a schoolmaster, but abandoned it, first for politics and then for the law. He really loved the art of oratory, and his soul filled with emotion whenever he spoke of the great orators of old who swayed vast audiences with the power of their voices, but Mickie Joe's own voice was like the whistle of a train, and the only effect he had ever had on an audience was to make them laugh. He had a long, thin, mournful face, and big, blackberry-colored sunken eyes, and he looked at you over his pince-nez as though at any moment he might burst into tears. Everybody loved Mickie Joe, everybody tried to throw business in his way, but nobody ever took him seriously. He had a tendency which was very obvious in the Lynam case to identify himself with his client, a thing no real lawyer will do. A client is a fact, and a true lawyer hates facts. A lawyer is like an actor who can never bother about what sort of play he appears in, but tells himself some little story to cover as many of the incidents as he can be bothered to remember. The only thing he hates is to be reminded—for instance by the author—what the real story is about.

But Mickie Joe got up bursting with indignation, and even O'Meara smiled at the picture of Mickie Joe, who never said a cross word to anybody, identifying himself with this uproarious, drunken farmer. He felt Tom Lynam had been wronged and was bent on proving it. What made it funnier was that he began with a series of questions which nobody understood, which only reflected further Mrs. Lynam's virtue and his client's beastliness, but which he asked with a bitter reserve. Mrs. Lynam wasn't afraid of him. No woman was ever afraid of Mickie Joe. She answered steadily and quietly. Yes, she had been educated in a convent. Yes, she was a great friend of Sister Dominic. And of Father O'Regan, the parish priest. Yes, she had asked their advice before beginning proceedings against her husband. Yes, she was a member of the Women's Sodality and the Children of Mary.

Then Mickie Joe began to expand, and it became clear what his purpose had been. But it also looked as though Mickie Joe had lost his reason. It's bad enough to attack a woman, but to attack her because she's a pious woman is to go looking for trouble.

"And when you were at the Women's Sodality," he asked icily, looking at her between the wig and the pince-nez, "who got your husband's supper?"

"Sometimes he got it himself."

"And the children's supper?"

"Of an odd time."

"And when you were out at Mass, he got his breakfast, I suppose?"

"Unless he wanted to wait till I got in."

"But you always got it for him when you came in?"

"Always, except when I wasn't able."

"And I take it you weren't always able?"

"Well, no," she admitted candidly. "Not always." She still didn't take him seriously.

"You were able to go to Mass," he said, drawling every word, "but you were not able to get your husband's breakfast? Is that what you're telling my lord?"

"Sometimes I went to Mass when I wasn't able, either," she replied with a noble pathos which would have silenced another man but not Mickie Joe.

"You went to Mass when you weren't able," he repeated with a bitter smile, "but you didn't get your husband's breakfast when you weren't able. Is that what you mean?"

"I think I ought to explain that," she said, beginning to get flurried. "I'm not strong. I have a pain in my back. I hurted it years ago in a fall I got. Dr. O'Mahony treated me."

"Mrs. Lynam, do you also suffer from headaches?"

"I do. Bilious," she replied, pointing to her stomach.

"Really, Mr. Dougherty," said O'Meara wearily, "if a headache is an offense we're all bad characters."

Of course, by this time O'Meara was champing at the bit, waiting to get on with his judgment. For a judge with a mother fixation to listen to evidence at all when he wants to rush to the rescue of some poor afflicted female is an ordeal in itself, but it made it worse that all there was between himself and it was a poor fish like Mickie Joe. But for once Mickie Joe did not give way. He looked at the judge reprovingly over his pince-nez and replied in a wail:

"My lord, if the petitioner is presented to the court as something out of a medical museum, I have nothing more to say."

"Oh, go on, Mr. Dougherty, go on!" said O'Meara, but all the same he grew red. He was beginning to notice like the rest of us that Mickie Joe had ceased to be a figure of fun, but no more than ourselves did he realize what was happening. The truth was that there is only one person who can stand up to a man with a mother fixation, and that is a woman-hater. Exactly as O'Meara wanted to get at that big hulk of a man in the court, Mickie Joe wanted to get at that gentle, pious little woman sitting up beside the judge with her hands in her lap. And, in a queer way, his dislike was beginning to affect people's opinion. It wasn't only that you couldn't any longer patronize Mickie Joe. You couldn't any longer see her the way you had seen her first. Whether it was right or wrong, another picture was beginning to emerge of a woman who was both ruthless and designing and who ruled her great brute of a husband by her weakness. This was only one stage of his ruin. In the next she would be living in comfort in a terrace house on his earnings, while he dragged out an impoverished and lonely existence.

Lynam himself began to perk up, and, instead of looking at his wife, looked at the people round him. The court had gradually begun to fill up, the way it does when a case gets interesting. He still scowled, but now he seemed to be challenging the people in court to say if he wasn't justified.

"Did you and your husband do much visiting together, Mrs. Lynam?" Mickie Joe asked gently.

"Well, you can't do much with two children, sir, can you?" she asked with soft reproach.

"That depends, ma'am," he said with a mournful smile. "A lot of people seem to be able to do it."

"I dare say they have servants," she said nervously.

"Strange to say, ma'am, friendships have been known to persist even in the humblest homes," sighed Mickie Joe with a smile like a glacier.

"I'm sure I don't know how they manage it, then."

"There are such things as neighbors, ma'am."

"Well, you can't be always asking the neighbors."

"No," he said bitterly. "You can ask them to put you up after a quarrel with your husband, but you can't ask them to mind your children. And how much attention do the children need? What age is your little girl, ma'am?"

"She's ten."

"And she couldn't look after the little fellow and herself?"

"Well, I can explain that," she said with a nervous glance at the judge. "You see, they don't get on, and you couldn't leave little Tommy with her, on account of that."

"You mean, she would beat him?" Mickie Joe asked sternly.

"Well, not beat him exactly," said Mrs. Lynam, getting more rattled than ever. "But she might be tormenting him."

"Mrs. Lynam," he asked gravely, "is it the way you didn't like to ask the neighbors or the neighbors didn't like to be asked?"

"I don't know why you say that," she said, shaking her head. "The children don't like going to strange houses, and you wouldn't blame them."

"Do you mean that, ma'am, or do you mean they did not like going to houses where they would have to behave themselves? Mrs. Lynam, isn't it true that your children are too spoiled and vicious to be left in the home of any reasonable person?"

"No," she replied shrilly, starting in her seat. "Certainly not. I never heard such a thing."

But Tom Lynam himself looked at his counsel with such an expression of astonishment that it was clear to everyone that intuitively Mickie Joe had stumbled on the truth. He knew it himself too, and for the first time a smile of satisfaction played about his thin, mournful lips.

"Did many of your husband's friends visit you?"

"Some of them did, yes."

"He had a lot of friends at the time he married you, hadn't he?"

"He had. A few."

"And at the time of this break-up, how many of them were still coming to the house?"

The witness's eyes sought out one tall man sitting at the back of the court.

"I'm sure I couldn't say," she replied doubtfully. "There was one of them at any rate."

"The local St. Sebastian, I presume?"

"The local—I beg your pardon; I didn't catch."

"Mrs. Lynam, every married man has at least one friend who sticks to him, even in spite of his wife's attempts to separate them," Mickie Joe said savagely. "What happened his other friends?"

"I'm sure I don't know."

"Mrs. Lynam, why did they stop coming to your house? Was it, for instance, that when they came for a meal, you sent your husband out to do the shopping?"

"Only a couple of times," she said excitedly. "And that is a thing that might happen to anybody. No matter how careful a housekeeper you were, you couldn't remember everything."

"And I dare say that while he was out, you left them there to entertain themselves?" he asked with a wicked smile.

"Only if I was putting the children to bed, sir," she said sanctimoniously.

"And I suppose, too, that when this last remaining friend of your husband—this Last Rose of Summer left blooming alone—came to bring him out, say, to the greyhounds, it sometimes happened that they couldn't go?"

"Well, I explained about my back," she said earnestly.

"You did, ma'am, fully," said Mickie Joe cruelly. "We are now better acquainted with your back than with any other portion of your anatomy. And we may take it that your husband and his friend had to stay at home and mind the children instead of enjoying themselves."

"I'm sure they enjoyed themselves more than I did," she said. "They played cards a lot. They're both very fond of cards."

But Tom Lynam was still staring incredulously at Mickie Joe. The tall man at the back of the court had grown red. He smiled and nodded amiably to the judge, to the counsel, and even to the pressmen. The Last Rose of Summer, a shy, neighborly sort of man, was clearly enjoying the publicity. Lynam leaned forward and whispered something to his solicitor, but Quill only frowned and brushed him off. Quill was beginning to see the power and pathos of the play Mickie Joe was producing and no more than any other man of the theatre had he time to spare for the author's views.

"Tell me, ma'am," Mickie Joe asked, "how long is it since you had relations with your husband?"

"Since I what?" she asked in a baby voice, her head raised expectantly.

"Since you went to bed with him, if you like."

"Oh, I forgot to mention that," she said hastily. "He doesn't sleep with me, of course. He has a bedroom of his own."

"Oh, he has a bedroom of his own, has he?" Mickie Joe asked with a new light in his eye. "We'll come back to that. But that wasn't the question I asked just now. The question I asked was how long it was since you had relations with him."

"Well, with my back," she began, raising her hand illustratively to her hip.

"Never mind your back now, ma'am. It's not your back we're talking about at the moment. How long is it?"

"Oh, I suppose about two years," she replied pertly.

"Or more?"

"It could be."

"No doubt it left no impression on your mind," said Mickie Joe. "But when you asked your husband not to have further relations with Mrs. MacGee, you weren't inviting him to have them with you?"

"He never asked me."

"And when he was at Mrs. MacGee's, nursing his child by her, he was in the only decent sort of home he had," said Mickie Joe with a throb of pathos in his voice that, for once, didn't make anybody laugh. "Would it be true to say that you don't think much of married life, ma'am?"

"Oh, I wouldn't say that," she replied vigorously. "The Church, of course, takes a very high view of it."

"I was referring to you, ma'am, not to the Church. Now, weren't you always baaing and bleating to Sister Dominic about the drawbacks of married life?"

"I went to her for advice," Mrs. Lynam replied anxiously. She was beginning to be doubtful of the impression she was creating, and small wonder.

"On your oath, ma'am," shouted Mickie Joe, "didn't you say to Sister Dominic that you never had a happy day after you left the convent?"

"Did I?" Mrs. Lynam asked nervously with a finger to her chin.

"Didn't you?"

"I don't remember. But I might, when I was upset."

"And to Father O'Regan, when you were trying to set him against your unfortunate, decent husband?"

"I never tried to set anyone against him," she retorted indignantly. "All I asked Father O'Regan was to ask him to be more natural."

"Natural?"

"Reasonable, I mean. Ah, 'tis all very well to be talking, Mr. Dougherty. That may be all right for young people, but 'tis no way for people like us to be behaving."

The tables were turned now with a vengeance. Tom Lynam had ceased to look at anyone now but his wife, and at her he looked with an expression of overpowering gravity. He seemed to be saying: "I told you what would happen and you wouldn't believe me. Now look at the result." He knew as everyone else did that she had failed to prove her case, and that even the policemen at the back of the court who had wives of cast iron were looking reproachfully at the gentle, insinuating little woman who was being revealed as a gray, grim, discontented monster with a mania for power.

When the court adjourned, Mickie Joe's cross-examination wasn't over, but he could easily have closed there, for even O'Meara's mother fixation could find nothing to fix on in the petitioner's case. She was probably the only person in court who didn't realize she had lost, but even she was badly shaken. She grabbed her handbag and waddled quickly down the court, looking neither to right nor to left. As she passed, her husband looked reproachfully at her, but she refused to catch his eye. Suddenly to everyone's astonishment he jumped up and followed her. The lawyers followed too without delay. They were afraid that in their moment of triumph he would snatch the victory from them by finishing the job in the hall. Instead, when they went out he was standing before her, talking in a low, pleading voice. She, with an actressy air, was listening, but half turned away from him as if caught in flight. Finally he approached Quill and Mickie Joe with a frown on his handsome face.

"Nellie and me are settling this between us," he muttered.

"You're what?" Quill asked in consternation. "But damn it, man, you have it won."

"I know that," Lynam replied in an apologetic mutter, "and I'm very grateful, but I wouldn't like her to have to answer any more questions. She thinks I told you all the things you mentioned. You know yourself I didn't."

Mickie Joe was fit to be tied. He stared at his client over his pince-nez.

"You mean you're going back to live with that woman?" he asked coldly.

"I am."

"And you know that within forty-eight hours she'll be making your life a misery again?"

"If she does itself, we'll settle it between us," Tom Lynam retorted in a low voice, though his anger could be heard rumbling beneath, like a volcano.

"You certainly will," Mickie Joe said with icy fury. "You will not get me to assist you. A man tries to help you, but it is only talent thrown away. Go and commit suicide in your own way. I have nothing further to do with you."

"There's a pair of us there," Lynam exploded. "I don't know where you got your information, but you can go back to the people that told you and tell them to mind their own business. I won't let you or anyone talk to my wife that way."

Quill almost had to separate them. Two madder men he had rarely seen. But from the window of the barristers' room he and Mickie Joe saw the Lynams depart together, she small and sprightly, he tall and morose, and realized that never would they see justice done to a man in a court of law. It was like Oedipus. You couldn't say whether it was the Destiny that pursued the man or the man the Destiny; but you could be quite sure that nothing in the world would ever keep the two of them apart.

The Old Faith

IT WAS a great day when, on the occasion of the Pattern at Kilmulpeter, Mass was said in the ruined cathedral and the old Bishop, Dr. Gallogly, preached. It was Father Devine, who was a bit of an antiquarian, who looked up the details of the life of St. Mulpeter for him. There were a lot of these, mostly contradictory and all queer. It seemed that, like most of the saints of that remote period, St. Mulpeter had put to sea on a flagstone and floated ashore in Cornwall. There, the seven harpers of the King had just been put to death through the curses of the Druids and the machinations of the King's bad wife. St. Mulpeter miraculously brought them all back to life, and, through the great mercy of God, they were permitted to sing a song about the Queen's behavior, which resulted in St. Mulpeter's turning her into a pillar-stone and converting the King to the one true faith.

The Bishop had once been Professor of Dogmatic Theology in a seminary; a subject that came quite naturally to him, for he was a man who would have dogmatized in any station of life. He was a tall, powerfully built, handsome old man with a face that was both long and broad, with high cheekbones that gave the lower half of his face an air of unnatural immobility but drew attention to the fine blue, anxious eyes that moved slowly and never far. He was a quiet man who generally spoke in a low voice, but with the emphasizing effect of a pile-driver.

For a dogmatic theologian, he showed great restraint on reading Father Devine's digest of the saint's life. He raised his brows a few times and then read it again with an air of resignation. "I suppose that's what you'd call allegorical, father," he said gravely.

He was a man who rarely showed signs of emotion. He seemed to be quite unaffected by the scene in the ruined cathedral, though it deeply impressed Father Devine, with the crowds of country people kneeling on the wet grass among the tottering crosses and headstones, the wild countryside framed in the mullioned windows, and the big, deeply molded clouds drifting overhead. The Bishop disposed neatly of the patron by saying that though we couldn't all go to sea on flagstones, a feat that required great faith in anyone who attempted it, we could all have the family Rosary at night.

After Mass, Father Devine was showing the Bishop and some of the other clergy round the ruins, pointing out features of archaeological interest, when a couple of men who had been hiding in the remains of a twelfth-century chapel bolted. One of them stood on a low wall, looking down on the little group of priests with a scared expression. At once the Bishop raised his umbrella and pointed it accusingly at him.

"Father Devine," he said in a commanding tone, "see what that fellow has."

"I have nothing, your eminence," wailed the man on the wall.

"You have a bottle behind your back," said the Bishop grimly. "What's in that?"

"Nothing, your eminence, only a drop of water from the Holy Well."

"Give it here to me till I see," ordered the Bishop, and when Father Devine passed him the bottle he removed the cork and sniffed.

"Hah!" he said with great satisfaction. "I'd like to see the Holy Well that came out of. Is it any use my preaching about poteen year in year out when ye never pay any attention to me?"

" 'Tis a cold, windy quarter, your eminence," said the man, "and I have the rheumatics bad."

"I'd sooner have rheumatics than cirrhosis," said the Bishop. "Bring it with you, father," he added to Devine, and stalked on with his umbrella pressed against his spine.

The same night they all had dinner in the palace: Father Whelan, a dim-witted, good-natured old parish priest; his fiery Republican curate, Father Fogarty, who was responsible for the Mass in the ruined cathedral as he was for most other manifestations of life in that wild part, and Canon Lanigan. The Bishop and the Canon never got on, partly because the Canon was an obvious choice for the Bishop's job and he and his supporters were giving it out that the Bishop was getting old and needed a coadjutor, but mainly because he gave himself so many airs. He was tall and thin, with a punchinello chin and a long nose, and let on to be an authority on Church history and on food and wine. That last was enough to damn anyone in the Bishop's eyes, for he maintained almost *ex cathedra* that the best food and wine in the world were to be had on the restaurant car from Holyhead to Euston. The moment Lanigan got on to his favorite topic and mentioned Châteauneuf-du-Pape, the Bishop turned to Father Devine.

"Talking about drink, father," he said with his anxious glare, "what happened the bottle of poteen you took off that fellow?"

"I suppose it's in the hall," said Father Devine. "I need hardly say I wasn't indulging in it."

"You could indulge in worse," said the Bishop with a side-glance at the Canon. "There was many a good man raised on it. Nellie," he added, going so far as to turn his head a few inches, "bring in that bottle of poteen, wherever it is. . . . You can have it with your tea," he added graciously to the Canon. "Or is it coffee you want?"

"Oh, tea, tea," sighed the Canon, offering it up. He had a good notion what the Bishop's coffee was like.

When Nellie brought in the poteen, the Bishop took out the cork and sniffed it again with his worried look.

"I hope 'tis all right," he said in his expressionless voice. "A pity we didn't find out who made it. When they can't get the rye, they make it out of turnips or any old thing."

"You seem to know a lot about it, my lord," said Devine with his waspish air.

"Why wouldn't I?" said the Bishop. "Didn't I make it myself? My poor father—God rest him!—had a still of his own. But I didn't taste it in something like sixty years."

He poured them out a stiff glass each and drank off his own in a gulp, without the least change of expression. Then he looked at the others anxiously to see how they responded. Lanigan made a wry face; as a member of the Food and Wine Society he probably felt it was expected of him. Father Fogarty drank it as if it were altar wine, but he was a nationalist and only did it on principle. Father Devine disgraced himself; spluttered, choked, and then went petulantly off to the bathroom.

Meanwhile the Bishop, who had decided that it wasn't bad, was treating his guests to another round, which they seemed to feel it might be disrespectful to refuse. Father Devine did refuse, and with a crucified air that the Bishop didn't like. The Bishop, who, like all bishops, knew everything and had one of the most venomously gossipy tongues in the diocese, was convinced that he was a model of Christian charity and had spoken seriously to Father Devine about his sharpness.

"Was it on an island you made this stuff?" the Canon asked blandly.

"No," replied the Bishop, who always managed to miss the point of any remark that bordered on subtlety. "A mountain."

"Rather desolate, I fancy," Lanigan said dreamily.

"It had to be if you didn't want the police coming down on top of you," said the Bishop. "They'd have fifty men out at a time, searching the mountains."

"And bagpipes," said the Canon, bursting into an old woman's cackle as he thought of the hilly road from Beaune to Dijon with the vineyards at each side. "It seems to go with bagpipes."

"There were no bagpipes," the Bishop said contemptuously. "As a matter of fact," he continued with quiet satisfaction, "it was very nice up there on a summer's night, with the still in a hollow on top of the mountain, and the men sitting round the edges, talking and telling stories. Very queer stories some of them were," he added with an old man's complacent chuckle.

"Ah," the Canon said deprecatingly, "the people were half-savage in those days."

"They were not," said the Bishop mildly, but from his tone Father Devine knew he was very vexed. "They were more refined altogether."

"Would you say so, my lord?" asked Father Fogarty, who, as a good nationalist, was convinced that the people were rushing to perdition and that the only hope for the nation was to send them all back to whitewashed cabins fifty miles from a town.

"Ah, a nicer class of people every way," put in Father Whelan mournfully. "You wouldn't find the same nature at all in them nowadays."

"They had a lot of queer customs all the same, father," said the Bishop. "They'd always put the first glass behind a rock. Would that have something to do with the fairies?" he asked of Father Devine.

"Well, at any rate," the Canon said warmly, "you can't deny that the people today are more enlightened."

"I deny it in toto," the Bishop retorted promptly. "There's no comparison. The people were more intelligent altogether, better balanced and better spoken. What would you say, Father Whelan?"

"Oh, in every way, my lord," said Father Whelan, taking out his pipe.

"And the superstitions, my lord?" the Canon hissed superciliously. "The ghosts and the fairies and the spells?"

"They might have good reason," said the Bishop with a flash of his blue eyes.

"By Gor, you're right, my lord," Father Fogarty said in a loud voice, and then, realizing the attention he had attracted, he blushed and stopped short.

"There are more things in heaven and earth, Horatio, than are dreamt of in our philosophy," added the Bishop with a complacent smile.

"Omar Khayyám," whispered Father Whelan to Father Fogarty.

"He's a fellow you'd want to read. He said some very good things."

"That's a useful quotation," said the Canon, seeing he was getting the worst of it. "I must remember that the next time I'm preaching against fortune-tellers."

"I wouldn't bother," the Bishop said curtly. "There's no analogy. There was a parish priest in our place one time," he added reflectively. "A man called Muldoon. Father Whelan might remember him."

"Con Muldoon," defined Father Whelan. "I do, well. His nephew, Peter, was on the Chinese Mission."

"He was a well-meaning man, but very coarse, I thought," said the Bishop.

"That was his mother's side of the family," explained Whelan. "His mother was a Dempsey. The Dempseys were a rough lot."

"Was she one of the Dempseys of Clasheen?" said the Bishop eagerly. "I never knew that. Anyway, Muldoon was always preaching against superstition, and he had his knife in one poor old fellow up the Glen called Johnnie Ryan."

"Johnnie the Fairies," said Father Whelan with a nod. "I knew him."

"I knew him well," said the Bishop. "He was their Living Man."

"Their what?" asked Father Devine in astonishment.

"Their Living Man," repeated the Bishop. "They had to take him with them wherever they were going, or they had no power. That was the way I heard it anyway. I remember him well playing the Fairy Music on his whistle."

"You wouldn't remember how it went?" Father Fogarty asked eagerly.

"I was never much good at remembering music," said the Bishop, to the eternal regret of Father Devine, who felt he would cheerfully have given five years of his life to hear the Bishop of Moyle whistle the Fairy Music. "Anyway, I was only a child. Of course, there might be something in that. The mountain over our house, you'd often see queer lights on it that they used to say were a fairy funeral. They had some story of a man from our place that saw one on the mountain one night, and the fairies let down the coffin and ran away. He opened the coffin, and inside it there was a fine-looking girl, and when he bent over her she woke up. They said she was from the Tuam direction; a changeling or something. I never checked the truth of it."

"From Galway, I believe, my lord," said Father Whelan respectfully.

"Was it Galway?" said the Bishop.

"I dare say, if a man had enough poteen in, he could even believe that," said the Canon indignantly.

"Still, Canon," said Father Fogarty, "strange things do happen."

"Why then, indeed, they do," said Father Whelan.

"Was this something that happened yourself, father?" the Bishop asked kindly, seeing the young man straining at the leash.

"It was, my lord," said Fogarty. "When I was a kid going to school. I got fever very bad, and the doctor gave me up. The mother, God rest her, was in a terrible state. Then my aunt came to stay with us. She was a real old country woman. I remember them to this day arguing downstairs in the kitchen, the mother saying we must be resigned to the will of God, and my aunt telling her not to be a fool; that everyone knew there were ways."

"Well! Well! Well!" Father Whelan said, shaking his head.

"Then my aunt came up with the scissors," Father Fogarty continued with suppressed excitement. "First she cut off a bit of the tail of my shirt; then she cut a bit of hair from behind my ear, and the third time a bit of fingernail, and threw them all into the fire, muttering something to herself, like an old witch."

"My! My! My!" exclaimed Father Whelan.

"And you got better?" said the Bishop, with a quelling glance at the Canon.

"I did, my lord," said Father Fogarty. "But that wasn't the strangest part of it." He leaned across the table, scowling, and dropped his eager, boyish voice to a whisper. "I got better, but her two sons, my first cousins, two of the finest-looking lads you ever laid eyes on, died inside a year." Then he sat back, took out a cigar, and scowled again. "Now," he asked, "wasn't that extraordinary? I say, wasn't it extraordinary?"

"Ah, whatever was waiting to get you," Father Whelan said philosophically, emptying his pipe on his plate, "I suppose it had to get something. More or less the same thing happened to an old aunt of mine. The cock used to sleep in the house, on a perch over the door—you know, the old-fashioned way. One night the old woman had occasion to go out, and when she went to the door, the cock crowed three times and then dropped dead at her feet. Whatever was waiting for her, of course," he added with a sigh.

"Well! Well! Well!" said the Canon. "I'm astonished at you, Father Whelan. Absolutely astonished! I can't imagine how you can repeat these old wives' tales."

"I don't see what there is to be astonished about, Canon," said the Bishop. "It wasn't anything worse than what happened to Father Muldoon."

"That was a bad business," muttered Father Whelan, shaking his head.

"What was it, exactly?" asked Father Devine.

"I told you he was always denouncing old Johnnie," said the Bishop. "One day, he went up the Glen to see him; they had words, and he struck the old man. Within a month he got a breaking-out on his knee."

"He lost the leg after," Father Whelan said, stuffing his pipe again.

"I suppose next you'll say it was the fairies' revenge," said the Canon, throwing discretion to the winds. It was too much for him; a man who knew Church history, had lived in France, and knew the best vintages backwards.

"That was what Father Muldoon thought," said the Bishop grimly.

"More fool he," the Canon said hotly.

"That's as may be, Canon," the Bishop went on sternly. "He went to the doctor, but treatment did him no good, so he went back up the valley to ask Johnnie what he ought to do. 'I had nothing to do with that, father,' said Johnnie, 'and the curing of it isn't in my hands.' 'Then who was it?' asks Muldoon. 'The Queen of the Fairies,' said Johnnie, 'and you might as well tell the doctor to take that leg off you while he's at it, for the Queen's wound is the wound that never heals.' No more it did," added the Bishop. "The poor man ended his days on a peg leg."

"He did, he did," muttered Father Whelan mournfully, and there was a long pause. It was clear that the Canon was routed, and soon afterwards they all got up to go. It seemed that Father Fogarty had left his car outside the seminary, and the Bishop, in a benevolent mood, offered to take them across the field by the footpath.

"I'll take them," said Father Devine.

"The little walk will do me good," said the Bishop.

He, the Canon, and Father Fogarty went first. Father Devine followed with Father Whelan, who went sideways down the steps with the skirts of his coat held up.

"As a matter of fact," the Bishop was saying ahead of them, "we're lucky to be able to walk so well. Bad poteen would deprive you of the use of your legs. I used to see them at home, talking quite nicely one minute and dropping off the chairs like bags of meal the next. You'd have to take them home on a door. The head might be quite clear, but the legs would be like gateposts."

"Father Devine," whispered Father Whelan girlishly, stopping in his tracks.

"Yes, what is it?" asked Father Devine gently.

"What his lordship said," whispered Father Whelan guiltily. "That's the way I feel. Like gateposts."

And before the young priest could do anything, he put out one of the gateposts, which didn't seem to alight properly on its base, the other leaned slowly towards it, and he fell in an ungraceful parody of a ballet dancer's final curtsy.

"Oh, my! My! My!" he exclaimed. Even in his liquor he was melancholy and gentle.

The other three turned slowly round. To Father Devine they looked like sleepwalkers.

"Hah!" said the Bishop with quiet satisfaction. "That's the very thing I mean. We'll have to mind ourselves."

And away the three of them went, very slowly, as though they owed no responsibility whatever towards the fallen guest. Paddy, the Bishop's "boy," who was obviously expecting something of the sort, immediately appeared and, with the aid of Father Devine, put the old man on a bench and carried him back to the palace. Then, still carrying the bench between them, they set out after the others. They were just in time to see the collapse of the Canon, but in spite of it the other two went on. Father Fogarty had begun to chuckle hysterically. They could hear him across the field, and it seemed to Father Devine that he was already rehearsing the lovely story he would tell about "the night I got drunk with the Bishop."

Devine and Paddy left the Canon where he had fallen, and where he looked like being safe for a long time to come, and followed the other two. They had gone wildly astray, turning in a semicircle round the field till they were at the foot of the hill before a high fence round the plantation. The Bishop never hesitated, but immediately began to climb the wall.

"I must be gone wrong, father," he said anxiously. "I don't know what happened to me tonight. I can usually do this easy enough. We'll go over the wall and up the wood."

"I can't," shouted Father Fogarty in a paroxysm of chuckles.

"Nonsense, man!" the Bishop said sternly, holding on to a bush and looking down at him from the top of the wall. "Why can't you?"

"The fairies have me," roared Father Fogarty.

"Pull yourself together, father," the Bishop said sternly. "You don't want to be making an exhibition of yourself."

Next moment Father Fogarty was lying flat at the foot of the wall, roaring with laughter. Father Devine shouted to the Bishop, but he slid obstinately down at the other side of the wall. "The ould divil!" Paddy exclaimed admiringly. "That's more than we'll be able to do at his age, father."

A few minutes later they found him flat under a tree in the starlight, quite powerless, but full of wisdom, resignation, and peace. They lifted him on a bench, where he reclined like the effigy on a tomb, his hands crossed meekly on his breast, and carried him back to bed.

"Since that evening," Father Devine used to say in the waspish way the Bishop so much disliked, "I feel there's nothing I don't know about fairies. I also have some idea about the sort of man who wrote the life of St. Mulpeter of Moyle."

Unapproved Route

BETWEEN men and women, as between neighboring states, there are approved roads which visitors must take. Others they take at their peril, no matter how high-minded their intentions may be.

When I lived in England I became friendly with another Irishman named Frankie Daly. Frankie was the sort of man men like. He was scrupulous, but not so as to irritate people who might have scruples of a different kind. Exacting with himself, he was tolerant of others. The good qualities he had—conscientiousness, loyalty, and generosity— were not those he demanded of his friends, and, as a result, they made great efforts to show them where he was concerned. Even Mick Flynn, who lived by borrowing, made a hullabaloo about paying back a pound he owed to Frankie.

Frankie and I were also friendly with two schoolmistresses who had a little cottage in School Lane, and they frequently joined us in the pub for a drink. Rosalind and Kate could have been sisters, they had so little in common. Kate was a born spinster, lean, plain, and mournful, and with the kindest heart in the world. She was very left-wing and tended to blame capitalism for most of her troubles. Rosalind was a good-looking girl with a fat and rather sullen face, who was always up and down with some man, usually—according to Kate, at any rate—of the shadiest kind. Women with a man on their hands usually vote

Tory—they dislike being interrupted—and Rosalind was a Conservative. Cooking being a form of activity associated with love-making, she was also an excellent cook, while Kate, who adored food, not only couldn't cook herself but was driven into hysterics of fastidiousness by the mere sight of cooking fat. She felt about grease as she felt about men, and I sometimes had a suspicion that she identified the two. I often wondered how she could face the liquidation of capitalists and all the blood and mess it would involve.

One day another fellow countryman of Frankie and myself turned up on a temporary job. He was a shambling, good-natured, high-spirited man, given to funny stories and inexplicable fits of morose anger. Lodgings were scarce and hotels expensive, so the girls offered him a room in the cottage. He settled down so well with them that inside a week or so he and Rosalind were lovers. She simply could not be kept away from men.

Kate then devoted herself entirely to the task of hating Jim Hourigan, and being as rude to him as she dared with Rosalind there. Having a lover of Rosalind's in the cottage was like having endless greasy frying-pans to dodge; she couldn't move without seeing a masculine singlet or a pair of socks. Kate derived enormous pleasure from her own griefs, and she told us with gloomy humor that it had been bad enough before, lying awake and wondering what Rosalind was up to. She couldn't kick up a row with Rosalind, who had an unpredictable and violent temper where men were concerned. Kate rationalized this to herself by saying that Rosalind, being a girl of exceptional intelligence, knew they were all wasters but was too proud to admit it. She told us that Rosalind never had had any taste, that all the men she knew had exploited her, that Jim Hourigan was only another of them, and that the only consolation was that she was there herself, ready to pick up the pieces when the inevitable disillusionment came. Frankie and I only laughed at Kate's groans. We didn't know what sort Jim Hourigan was, and we didn't really care much.

When his job ended, he returned to Ireland after making many promises of bringing the girls for a long summer holiday there, and of returning himself at the first opportunity. Kate was very cheerful because she was quite convinced that he didn't mean a word of it—she had the lowest view of his character and motives—and was delighted to have Rosalind and the cottage to herself again. Rosalind, too, was cheerful because, never before having had anything to do with an Irishman, she took all his promises for gospel, had everything ready for her holiday in the summer, and was certain that Hourigan would then ask her to marry him. She wrote him long, animated letters, cleverly recalling our little town and the characters he had met there, and quoting Kate's doleful predictions about the weather, the European situation, and the cost of living.

There was an alarming lack of response to her letters; finally they did produce a wet spark of a picture postcard saying how much Hourigan looked forward to coming back, which might have encouraged a more persevering correspondent but merely infuriated Rosalind. She wasn't accustomed to having her brilliant letters treated with such lack of ceremony and told him so, but this didn't produce even a spark. Kate began to put on weight, though how she did was a miracle, because Rosalind was so upset that she refused to cook, and Kate had not only to eat sausages—which she loathed—but even to clean the disgusting frying-pan herself.

But that wasn't the end of Kate's troubles. Imprudent as usual, Rosalind was having a baby. Now, in the natural way of things, a nice baby without any messy father to get in the way would have been Kate's idea of bliss, but bliss of that sort is not contemplated in English provincial towns. To begin with, Rosalind would lose her job; women teachers cannot have babies without marriage lines; the thing is unknown. Besides, the landlady would be bound to ask them to leave; this was also part of the drill, and even if the landlady had been a considerate woman, which she wasn't, she would still have found it difficult to overlook such conduct. They would have to try and hush things up and put the baby out to nurse.

This was where Rosalind became completely unmanageable. She said she wanted to keep her baby, and she didn't mind who knew. Just the same, she stopped coming to the public-house with the rest of us, and Kate, gloomier than ever, came alone. She was depressed by her failure to make Rosalind see reason. It would only be for a couple of years, and then they could make some arrangement, like pretending to adopt the baby.

"That wouldn't be so very good, Kate," Frankie said when she mentioned it to him.

"Well, what else can she do, Frankie? Go out as a charwoman?"

"Those are questions that answer themselves, Kate," he said stubbornly. "A baby put out to nurse is a question that never answers itself."

Next evening, without saying anything to Kate or me, he called at the cottage and found Rosalind sitting alone over the fire.

"Coming down to the pub, Rosa?" he asked cheerfully.

"No, Frankie, thanks," she said, without looking up.

"Why not? You know it's not the same without you."

She covered her face with her hands. Frankie sat awkwardly with his legs stretched out, sucking his pipe.

"Kate tells me you don't want to part with the child."

"It seems I'm not likely to be asked."

"All the same, I think you're right and Kate is wrong," he said gravely.

"That's easily said, Frankie," she replied. "It isn't so easy for Kate, with her job to mind."

"If that's how you feel about it, wouldn't it be better for you to marry?"

"The man who got me would get a treasure," she said savagely. "Whistled after in the street!"

"That's a matter for him," said Frankie. "Plenty of men would be very glad to marry you. You mustn't let a thing like this make you undervalue yourself."

"Ah, talk sense, Frankie!" she said wearily. "Who'd marry me in the middle of all this scandal?"

"I would, to begin with—if you hadn't anyone you liked better."

"You?" she asked incredulously.

"And consider myself very much honored," Frankie added steadily.

"Are you serious, Frankie?" she asked, almost angrily.

"Of course I'm serious."

"And face all the humiliation of it?"

"There isn't any humiliation," he said flatly. "That's where you're mistaken. There's no humiliation where there hasn't been any offense. The offense is in deceiving others, not in being deceived ourselves."

"Oh, I can't, Frankie, I can't," she said desperately. "I've made a fool of myself over this waster, and I can't let another man shoulder my burdens."

"There's no particular burden either," he said. "You mustn't think I'm asking you only because you're in a fix. I'd have asked you anyway when this thing was all over and you could make up your own mind. I'm only asking now in case it might make the immediate future a bit easier."

"Why didn't you ask me before?"

"Maybe because I felt I hadn't much to offer you," Frankie said with a shy smile.

"My God," she said, rising. "I'd have married you like a shot."

She sat on his knee and hugged him despairingly. He was a clumsy lover. He talked in an apologetic, worried tone about his job, his home, and his family; how much he earned and where they could live. She didn't listen. She thought of what it would mean to her to start life again, free of this nightmare. Then she took him by the shoulders and looked into his eyes with the air of a sleepwalker.

"I'll do it," she said. "God help me, Frankie, I hate it, but I'll do it for the kid's sake. All I can say is that I'll make it up to you. You needn't be afraid of that. I'll make it up to you all right."

Kate, whose low view of life had led her to take a low view of its Creator, almost got converted because of it. She had always liked Frankie, but her experience of people she liked had been that they only got her into fresh trouble, and that it was better, if you could manage it, to have nothing to do with anybody. She wasn't the only one who admired Frankie's behavior. It dawned on others of us that he had done exactly what we would have done ourselves except for what people might think. Actually, as we discovered, "people," meaning the neighbors with one or two exceptions, liked Rosalind and were pleased to see her escape the machine of social ignominy reserved for women with more feeling than calculation in them.

Frankie and Rosalind were married quietly and went to live in a little cottage some miles outside the town, a rather lonely cottage with low beams, high chimneys, and breakneck staircases, but it had a big garden, which Rosalind enjoyed. She kept on her job; she knew the other teachers knew, but now it only amused her. It was wonderful to have Frankie there as a prop. Up to this, all the men she had lived with had taken advantage of her, and she had accepted it in a cynical, good-humored way as part of the price you had to pay for being too fond of them. She believed, as Kate did, that men were like that, but she was lacking in any desire to reform them.

Under Frankie's care she grew round as a tub, stupid, and quite remarkably beautiful, while Kate managed to look as like the anxious father of her unborn child as a girl could look. But the change in Frankie was even more remarkable. He had always kept a youthful freshness, but now he suddenly began to look like a boy of seventeen. It might have been something to do with Rosalind's cooking—Kate, who had begun to feel the lack of it, visited them every day—but he rang her up regularly at the school to see that she was all right, raced for his bus to get home early in the evenings, and took her for her evening walk to the pub. He was full of banter and tricks, and Rosalind looked on with the affectionate calm of a woman watching the man she loves make a fool of himself. And it really was pleasant those summer evenings outside the public-house, watching that late flowering of emotion, the bachelor crust of caution breaking up, the little shoots of sentiment beginning to peer out.

Their happiness was lyrical. It was only at odd times that Rosalind remembered her griefs, and usually it was in the early morning when she was waked by the heaving of the child within her, listened to the birds outside their window, and felt deserted even with Frankie beside her. Not to wake him, she sniffled quietly into her handkerchief, her back turned on him and her body shaken with suppressed sobs. When he woke, she still tried to keep away from him.

"What ails you now didn't ail you before?" he would ask humorously.

"What you've got in me."

"What's that?"

"I told you—a daisy!"

"No, that was what I told you," he said, and slapped her bottom affectionately.

Then she bawled without restraint and beat her stomach.

"Why can't it be yours?" she cried despairingly.

"One thing at a time," said Frankie.

He believed her; that was his mistake. He really thought when he heard her lonely weeping that it was merely the ambiguity of her position that caused it, and not the humiliation of being rejected and hounded into marriage with someone else by a tramp like Hourigan. Frankie was a decent man; he didn't realize that in circumstances like those no woman can ever be happy, even with the best man in the world—even with the man she loves. Love, in fact, has nothing to do with it. To ignore that is to ignore a woman's vanity, the mainspring of her character.

Her time came in the middle of the night, and Frankie returned from the nursing home in the early morning in a stupor of misery and astonishment; misery at the mere possibility that her life might be in danger, astonishment that anyone's life could possibly mean so much to him. He lit the fire, but then found that he couldn't bear the little cottage without her; it, too, seemed in a stupor of misery, wondering when she would come back, put on that housecoat, boil that kettle, and wash those dishes. He wanted to make himself breakfast, but could not bring himself to touch the things that were properly hers and that stood waiting for her with the infinite patience of inanimate things. He swore at himself when he realized that he was identifying his grief with that of a common teakettle. He had some breakfast in a café, and then went off walking through the countryside, merely halting for a drink while he rang up the nursing home. It was evening before everything was over and Rosalind and the child—a son—safe, and then he took a car straight there.

She was still stupefied with drugs when he was admitted, but she clung to him passionately.

"Don't look!" she said fiercely. "Not till the next time."

"I thought he was yours," Frankie said with a grin, and smiled down at the little morsel in the cot. "Cripes!" he added savagely. "Wouldn't you think they could get them out without clawing them?"

"Did you hear the children playing on the doorstep?" she asked happily.

"No," Frankie said in surprise. "What were they playing?"

"*Hamlet,* I think," she said, closing her eyes, and, seeing how her thoughts drifted in and out of the drug, he tiptoed out. In sheer relief he knocked back three whiskeys in quick succession, but failed to get drunk. Then he tried for some of the old gang to sit and drink with, but, by one of those coincidences that always occur at moments like that, we were all out. It was just that he didn't want to go home. When he did get out of the bus and crossed the common towards the cottage, he saw a man's figure step out of the shadow of the trees beside it and knew at once who it was. His heart sank.

"Frankie!" Jim Hourigan said imploringly, "I'd like a word with you."

Frankie halted. He had a sudden feeling of foreboding.

"You'd better come inside," he said in a troubled voice.

He went ahead into the sitting room and switched on the light and the electric fire, which stood in the big open hearth. Then he turned and faced Hourigan, who was standing by the door. The man looked half-distracted, his eyes were wild, his hair was in disorder.

"What is it?" Frankie asked curtly.

"Frankie," Hourigan muttered, "I want a word with Rosalind."

"Rosalind is in hospital."

"I know, I know," Hourigan said, flapping his hands like an old man. "She said she was going there. But I wanted to see you first, to get your permission. It's only to explain to her, Frankie—that's all."

Frankie concealed his surprise at Hourigan's statement that Rosalind had told him anything.

"I don't think she's in a state for seeing anybody, you know," he said in a level tone. "The boy was born only a couple of hours ago."

"Christ!" Hourigan said, beating the table with his fist and shaking his head as though tossing water from his eyes. "That's all that was missing. I came late for the fair as usual. My first child is born and I'm not even there. All right, Frankie, all right," he added in a crushed tone, "I see 'tis no good. But tell her all the same. Tell her I never knew a thing about it till I got her letter. That God might strike me dead this minute if the idea ever crossed my mind!"

Frankie looked at him in surprise. There was no mistaking the man's abject misery.

"What letter was this?" he asked.

"The letter she sent me before she went in," Hourigan hurried on, too distraught to notice the bewilderment in Frankie's voice. "You don't think I'd have treated her like that if I knew? You can think what you like of me, Frankie, and it won't be anything worse than I think of myself, but not that, Frankie, not that! I wouldn't do it to a woman I picked up in the street, and I loved that girl, Frankie. I declare to God I did." He began to wave his arms wildly again, looking round the little sitting room without seeing anything. "It's just that I'm no damn good at writing letters. The least thing puts me off. I'd be saying to myself I'd be there before the letter. I said the same thing to her on a card, Frankie, but then the mother died, and I was in a terrible state—oh, the usual things! I know 'tis no excuse, and I'm not making excuses, but that's the way I am. If I had any idea, I'd have been over to her by the first boat. You must tell her that, Frankie. She must know it herself."

"When did you get this letter?" asked Frankie.

"Oh, only yesterday, Frankie," exclaimed Hourigan, entirely missing the import of Frankie's question. "I swear to God I didn't waste an hour. I'm travelling all night. I couldn't sleep and I couldn't eat. It was all that damn letter. It nearly drove me out of my mind. Did you see it, Frankie?"

"No," said Frankie.

"Well, you'd better. Mind, I don't blame her a bit, but it's not true, it's not true!"

He took the letter from his wallet and passed it to Frankie. Frankie sat down and put on his glasses. Hourigan bent over the back of the armchair, reading it again in a mutter.

"Dear Jim Hourigan," Frankie read silently. "By this time tomorrow I'll be in a hospital, having your child. This will probably be more satisfaction to you than it is to me and my husband. I am sure you will be disappointed to know that I have a husband, but in this life we can't expect everything."

"Now, that's what I mean, Frankie," Hourigan said desperately, jabbing at the lines with his forefinger. "That's not fair and she knows it's not fair. She knows I'm not as mean as that, whatever faults I have."

"I wouldn't worry too much about that," Frankie said heavily, realizing that Hourigan and he were not reading the same letter. It was almost as though they were not concerned with the same woman. This was a woman whom Frankie had never seen. He went on reading.

"If the child takes after you, it might be better for more than Frank and myself that it shouldn't live. My only hope is that it may learn something from my husband. If ever a good man can make up to a child for the disaster of a bad father, your child will have every chance. So far as I can, I'll see that he gets it, and will never know any more of you than he knows now." It was signed in full: "Rosalind Daly."

Hourigan sighed. "You explain to her, Frankie," he said despairingly. "I couldn't."

"I think it would be better if you explained it yourself," Frankie said, folding up the letter and giving it back.

"You think she'll see me?" Hourigan asked doubtfully.

"I think she'd better see you," Frankie said in a dead voice.

"Only for ten minutes, Frankie; you can tell her that. Once I explain to her, I'll go away, and I give you my word that neither of you will ever see me here again."

"I'll talk to her myself in the morning," Frankie said. "You'd better ring me up at the office some time after twelve."

Hourigan shambled away across the common, babbling poetic blessings on Frankie's head and feeling almost elated. How Frankie felt he never said. Perhaps if Hourigan had known how he felt, he might have left that night without seeing Rosalind. He wasn't a bad chap, Jim Hourigan, though not exactly perceptive, even as regards the mother of his child.

But Rosalind had perception enough for them both. When Frankie called next morning, the effect of the drug had worn off, and she knew from the moment he entered that something serious had happened. He was as gentle as ever, but he had withdrawn into himself, the old Frankie of the days before his marriage, hurt but self-sufficient. She grabbed his hands feverishly.

"Is anything wrong at home, Frankie?"

"Nothing," he replied in embarrassment. "Just a visitor, that's all."

"A visitor? Who?"

"I think you know," he said gently.

"What brought that bastard?" she hissed.

"Apparently, a letter from you."

Suddenly she began to weep, the core of her hysteria touched.

"I didn't tell you, because I didn't want to upset you," she sobbed. "I just wanted him to know how I despised him."

"He seems to have got the idea," Frankie said dryly. "Now he wants to see you, to explain."

"Damn his explanations!" she cried hysterically. "I know what you think—that I sent that letter without telling you so as to bring him here. How could I know there was enough manliness in him to make him even do that? Can't you imagine how I felt, Frankie?"

"You know," he said paternally, "I think you'd better have a word with him and make up your mind about exactly what you did feel."

"Oh, Christ!" she said. "I tell you I only meant to hurt him. I never meant to hurt you, and that's all I've succeeded in doing."

"I'd rather you didn't let your feelings run away with you again and hurt yourself and the child," Frankie said in a gentler tone.

"But how can I avoid hurting myself when I'm hurting you?" she asked wildly. "Do you think this is how I intended to pay you back for what you did for me? Very well; if he's there, send him up and I'll tell him. I'll tell him in front of you. I'll tell you both exactly how I feel. Will that satisfy you?"

"He'll call this afternoon," Frankie said firmly. "You'd better see him alone. You'd better let him see the child alone. And remember," he added apologetically, "whatever you decide on I agree to beforehand. I may have behaved selfishly before. I don't want to do it again."

He smiled awkwardly and innocently, still bewildered by the disaster which had overtaken him, and Rosalind held her hands to her temples in a frenzy. She had never realized before how hurt he could be, had probably not even known that she might hurt him.

"I suppose you think I'm going to let you divorce me so that I can go back to Ireland with that waster? I'd sooner throw myself and the child into a pond. Oh, very well, I'll settle it, I'll settle it. Oh, God!" she said between her teeth. "What sort of fool am I?"

And as he went down the stairs, Frankie knew that he was seeing her for the last time as his wife, and that when they met again, she would be merely the mother of Jim Hourigan's child, and realized with a touch of bitterness that there are certain forms of magnanimity which are all very well between men but are misplaced in dealing with women, not because they cannot admire them but because they seem to them irrelevant to their own function in life. When he saw Hourigan again, he knew that the change had already taken place. Though nothing had been decided, Jim Hourigan was almost professionally protective of Frankie's interests and feelings. That was where the iron in Frankie came out. He made it plain that his interests were not in question.

There were plenty—Kate among them—to say that he had behaved absurdly; that with a little more firmness on his part the crisis would never have arisen; that Rosalind was in no condition to make the decision he had forced on her and needed only gentle direction to go on as she had been going; that, in fact, he might have spared her a great deal of unhappiness by refusing to see Jim Hourigan in the first place.

As for unhappiness, nothing I have heard suggests that Rosalind is unhappy with Jim Hourigan. It is a grave mistake to believe that that sort of thing leads to unhappiness. Frankie's conduct certainly does, but is that not because to people like him happiness is merely an incidental, something added which, taken away, leaves them no poorer than before?

The Study of History

THE DISCOVERY of where babies came from filled my life with excitement and interest. Not in the way it's generally supposed to, of course. Oh, no! I never seem to have done anything like a natural child in a standard textbook. I merely discovered the fascination of history. Up to this, I had lived in a country of my own that had no history, and accepted my parents' marriage as an event ordained from the creation; now, when I considered it in this new, scientific way, I began to see it merely as one of the turning-points of history, one of those apparently trivial events that are little more than accidents but have the effect of changing the destiny of humanity. I had not heard of Pascal, but I would have approved his remark about what would have happened if Cleopatra's nose had been a bit longer.

It immediately changed my view of my parents. Up to this, they had been principles, not characters, like a chain of mountains guarding a green horizon. Suddenly a little shaft of light, emerging from behind a cloud, struck them, and the whole mass broke up into peaks, valleys, and foothills; you could even see whitewashed farmhouses and fields where people worked in the evening light, a whole world of interior perspective. Mother's past was the richer subject for study. It was extraordinary the variety of people and settings that woman had had in her background. She had been an orphan, a parlormaid, a companion, a traveller; and had been proposed to by a plasterer's apprentice, a French chef who had taught her to make superb coffee, and a rich and elderly shopkeeper in Sunday's Well. Because I liked to feel myself different, I thought a great deal about the chef and the advantages of being a Frenchman, but the shopkeeper was an even more vivid figure in my imagination because he had married someone else and died soon after—of disappointment, I had no doubt—leaving a large fortune. The fortune was to me what Cleopatra's nose was to Pascal: the ultimate proof that things might have been different.

"How much was Mr. Riordan's fortune, Mummy?" I asked thoughtfully.

"Ah, they said he left eleven thousand," Mother replied doubtfully, "but you couldn't believe everything people say."

That was exactly what I could do. I was not prepared to minimize a fortune that I might so easily have inherited.

"And weren't you ever sorry for poor Mr. Riordan?" I asked severely.

"Ah, why would I be sorry, child?" she asked with a shrug. "Sure, what use would money be where there was no liking?"

That, of course, was not what I meant at all. My heart was full of pity for poor Mr. Riordan who had tried to be my father; but, even on the low level at which Mother discussed it, money would have been of great use to me. I was not so fond of Father as to think he was worth eleven thousand pounds, a hard sum to visualize but more than twenty-seven times greater than the largest salary I had ever heard of—that of a Member of Parliament. One of the discoveries I was making at the time was that Mother was not only rather hard-hearted but very impractical as well.

But Father was the real surprise. He was a brooding, worried man who seemed to have no proper appreciation of me, and was always wanting me to go out and play or go upstairs and read, but the historical approach changed him like a character in a fairy-tale. "Now let's talk about the ladies Daddy nearly married," I would say; and he would stop whatever he was doing and give a great guffaw. "Oh, ho, ho!" he would say, slapping his knee and looking slyly at Mother. "You could write a book about them." Even his face changed at such moments. He would look young and extraordinarily mischievous. Mother, on the other hand, would grow black.

"You could," she would say, looking into the fire. "Daisies!"

" 'The handsomest man that walks Cork!' " Father would quote with a wink at me. "That's what one of them called me."

"Yes," Mother would say, scowling. "May Cadogan!"

"The very girl!" Father would cry in astonishment. "How did I forget her name? A beautiful girl! 'Pon my word, a most remarkable girl! And still is, I hear."

"She should be," Mother would say in disgust. "With six of them!"

"Oh, now, she'd be the one that could look after them! A fine head that girl had."

"She had. I suppose she ties them to a lamp-post while she goes in to drink and gossip."

That was one of the peculiar things about history. Father and Mother both loved to talk about it but in different ways. She would only talk about it when we were together somewhere, in the Park or down the Glen, and even then it was very hard to make her stick to the facts, because her whole face would light up and she would begin to talk about donkey-carriages or concerts in the kitchen, or oil-lamps, and though nowadays I would probably value it for atmosphere, in those days it sometimes drove me mad with impatience. Father, on the other hand, never minded talking about it in front of her, and it made her angry—particularly when he mentioned May Cadogan. He knew this perfectly well and he would wink at me and make me laugh out-right, though I had no idea of why I laughed, and, anyway, my sympathy was all with her.

"But, Daddy," I would say, presuming on his high spirits, "if you liked Miss Cadogan so much why didn't you marry her?"

At this, to my great delight, he would let on to be filled with doubt and distress. He would put his hands in his trouser pockets and stride to the door leading into the hallway.

"That was a delicate matter," he would say, without looking at me. "You see, I had your poor mother to think of."

"I was a great trouble to you," Mother would say, in a blaze.

"Poor May said it to me herself," he would go on as though he had not heard her, "and the tears pouring down her cheeks. 'Mick,' she said, 'that girl with the brown hair will bring me to an untimely grave.'"

"She could talk of hair!" Mother would hiss. "With her carroty mop!"

"Never did I suffer the way I suffered then, between the two of them," Father would say with deep emotion as he returned to his chair by the window.

"Oh, 'tis a pity about ye!" Mother would cry in an exasperated tone and suddenly get up and go into the front room with her book to escape his teasing. Every word that man said she took literally. Father would give a great guffaw of delight, his hands on his knees and his eyes on the ceiling, and wink at me again. I would laugh with him, of course, and then grow wretched because I hated Mother's sitting alone in the front room. I would go in and find her in her wicker chair by the window in the dusk, the book open on her knee, looking out at the

Square. She would always have regained her composure when she spoke to me, but I would have an uncanny feeling of unrest in her and stroke her and talk to her soothingly as if we had changed places and I were the adult and she the child.

But if I was excited by what history meant to them, I was even more excited by what it meant to me. My potentialities were double theirs. Through Mother I might have been a French boy called Laurence Armady or a rich boy from Sunday's Well called Laurence Riordan. Through Father I might, while still remaining a Delaney, have been one of the six children of the mysterious and beautiful Miss Cadogan. I was fascinated by the problem of who I would have been if I hadn't been me, and, even more, by the problem of whether or not I would have known that there was anything wrong with the arrangement. Naturally, I tended to regard Laurence Delaney as the person I was intended to be, and so I could not help wondering whether as Laurence Riordan I would not have been aware of Laurence Delaney as a real gap in my make-up.

I remember that one afternoon after school I walked by myself all the way up to Sunday's Well, which I now regarded as something like a second house. I stood for a while at the garden gate of the house where Mother had been working when she was proposed to by Mr. Riordan, and then went and studied the shop itself. It had clearly seen better days, and the cartons and advertisements in the window were dusty and sagging. It wasn't like one of the big stores in Patrick Street, but at the same time, in size and fittings, it was well above the level of a village shop. I regretted that Mr. Riordan was dead because I would have liked to see him for myself instead of relying on Mother's impressions, which seemed to me to be biased. Since he had, more or less, died of grief on Mother's account, I conceived of him as a really nice man; lent him the countenance and manner of an old gentleman who always spoke to me when he met me on the road; and felt I could have become really attached to him as a father. I could imagine it all: Mother reading in the parlor while she waited for me to come home up Sunday's Well in a school cap and blazer, like the boys from the Grammar School, and with an expensive leather satchel instead of the old cloth schoolbag I carried over my shoulder. I could see myself walking slowly and with a certain distinction, lingering at gateways and looking down at the river; and later I would go out to tea in one of the big houses with long gardens sloping to the water, and maybe row a boat on the river along with a girl in a pink frock. I wondered only whether I would have any awareness of the National School boy with the cloth schoolbag who jammed his head between the bars of a gate and thought of me. It was a queer, lonesome feeling that all but reduced me to tears.

But the place that had the greatest attraction of all for me was the Douglas Road, where Father's friend Miss Cadogan lived, only now she wasn't Miss Cadogan but Mrs. O'Brien. Naturally, nobody called Mrs. O'Brien could be as attractive to the imagination as a French chef or an elderly shopkeeper with eleven thousand pounds, but she had a physical reality that the other pair lacked. As I went regularly to the library at Parnell Bridge, I frequently found myself wandering up the road in the direction of Douglas and always stopped in front of the long row of houses where she lived. There were high steps up to them, and in the evening the sunlight fell brightly on the house-fronts till they looked like a screen. One evening as I watched a gang of boys playing ball in the street outside, curiosity overcame me. I spoke to one of them. Having been always a child of solemn and unnatural politeness, I probably scared the wits out of him.

"I wonder if you could tell me which house Mrs. O'Brien lives in, please?" I asked.

"Hi, Gussie!" he yelled to another boy. "This fellow wants to know where your old one lives."

This was more than I had bargained for. Then a thin, good-looking boy of about my own age detached himself from the group and came up to me with his fists clenched. I was feeling distinctly panicky, but all the same I studied him closely. After all, he was the boy I might have been.

"What do you want to know for?" he asked suspiciously.

Again, this was something I had not anticipated.

"My father was a great friend of your mother," I explained carefully, but, so far as he was concerned, I might as well have been talking a foreign language. It was clear that Gussie O'Brien had no sense of history.

"What's that?" he asked incredulously.

At this point we were interrupted by a woman I had noticed earlier, talking to another over the railing between the two steep gardens. She was small and untidy-looking and occasionally rocked the pram in an absent-minded way as though she only remembered it at intervals.

"What is it, Gussie?" she cried, raising herself on tiptoe to see us better.

"I don't really want to disturb your mother, thank you," I said, in something like hysterics, but Gussie anticipated me, actually pointing me out to her in a manner I had been brought up to regard as rude.

"This fellow wants you," he bawled.

"I don't really," I murmured, feeling that now I was in for it. She skipped down the high flight of steps to the gate with a laughing, puzzled air, her eyes in slits and her right hand arranging her hair at the back. It was not carroty as Mother described it, though it had red lights when the sun caught it.

"What is it, little boy?" she asked coaxingly, bending forward.

"I didn't really want anything, thank you," I said in terror. "It was just that my daddy said you lived up here, and, as I was changing my book at the library, I thought I'd come up and inquire. You can see," I added, showing her the book as proof, "that I've only just been to the library."

"But who is your daddy, little boy?" she asked, her gray eyes still in long, laughing slits. "What's your name?"

"My name is Delaney," I said. "Larry Delaney."

"Not *Mike* Delaney's boy?" she exclaimed wonderingly. "Well, for God's sake! Sure, I should have known it from that big head of yours." She passed her hand down the back of my head and laughed. "If you'd only get your hair cut I wouldn't be long recognizing you. You wouldn't think I'd know the feel of your old fellow's head, would you?" she added roguishly.

"No, Mrs. O'Brien," I replied meekly.

"Why, then indeed I do, and more along with it," she added in the same saucy tone, though the meaning of what she said was not clear to me. "Ah, come in and give us a good look at you! That's my eldest, Gussie, you were talking to," she added, taking my hand. Gussie trailed behind us for a purpose I only recognized later.

"Ma-a-a-a, who's dat fella with you?" yelled a fat little girl who had been playing hopscotch on the pavement.

"That's Larry Delaney," her mother sang over her shoulder. I don't know what it was about that woman but there was something about her high spirits that made her more like a regiment than a woman. You felt that everyone should fall into step behind her. "Mick Delaney's son from Barrackton. I nearly married his old fellow once. Did he ever tell you that, Larry?" she added slyly. She made sudden swift transitions from brilliance to intimacy that I found attractive.

"Yes, Mrs. O'Brien, he did," I replied, trying to sound as roguish as she, and she went off into a delighted laugh, tossing her red head.

"Ah, look at that now! How well the old divil didn't forget me! You can tell him I didn't forget him either. And if I married him, I'd be your mother now. Wouldn't that be a queer old three and fourpence? How would you like me for a mother, Larry?"

"Very much, thank you," I said complacently.

"Ah, go on with you, you would not," she exclaimed, but she was pleased all the same. She struck me as the sort of woman it would be easy enough to please. "Your old fellow always said it: your mother was a *most* superior woman, and you're a *most* superior child. Ah, and I'm not too bad myself either," she added with a laugh and a shrug, wrinkling up her merry little face.

In the kitchen she cut me a slice of bread, smothered it with jam, and gave me a big mug of milk. "Will you have some, Gussie?" she asked in a sharp voice as if she knew only too well what the answer would be. "Aideen," she said to the horrible little girl who had followed us in, "aren't you fat and ugly enough without making a pig of yourself? Murder the Loaf we call her," she added smilingly to me. "You're a polite little boy, Larry, but damn the politeness you'd have if you had to deal with them. Is the book for your mother?"

"Oh, no, Mrs. O'Brien," I replied. "It's my own."

"You mean you can read a big book like that?" she asked incredulously, taking it from my hands and measuring the length of it with a puzzled air.

"Oh, yes, I can."

"I don't believe you," she said mockingly. "Go on and prove it!"

There was nothing I asked better than to prove it. I felt that as a performer I had never got my due, so I stood in the middle of the kitchen, cleared my throat, and began with great feeling to enunciate one of those horribly involved opening paragraphs you found in children's books of the time. "On a fine evening in Spring, as the setting sun was beginning to gild the blue peaks with its lambent rays, a rider, recognizable as a student by certain niceties of attire, was slowly, and perhaps regretfully making his way . . ." It was the sort of opening sentence I loved.

"I declare to God!" Mrs. O'Brien interrupted in astonishment. "And that fellow there is one age with you, and he can't spell house. How well you wouldn't be down at the library, you caubogue, you! ... That's enough now, Larry," she added hastily as I made ready to entertain them further.

"Who wants to read that blooming old stuff?" Gussie said contemptuously.

Later, he took me upstairs to show me his air rifle and model aeroplanes. Every detail of the room is still clear to me: the view into the back garden with its jungle of wild plants where Gussie had pitched his tent (a bad site for a tent as I patiently explained to him, owing to the danger from wild beasts); the three cots still unmade; the scribbles on the walls; and Mrs. O'Brien's voice from the kitchen telling Aideen to see what was wrong with the baby, who was screaming his head off from the pram outside the front door. Gussie, in particular, fascinated me. He was spoiled, clever, casual; good-looking, with his mother's small clean features; gay and calculating. I saw that when I left and his mother gave me a sixpence. Naturally I refused it politely, but she thrust it into my trouser pocket, and Gussie dragged at her skirt, noisily demanding something for himself.

"If you give him a tanner you ought to give me a tanner," he yelled.

"I'll tan you," she said laughingly.

"Well, give up a lop anyway," he begged, and she did give him a penny to take his face off her, as she said herself, and after that he followed me down the street and suggested we should go to the shop and buy sweets. I was simpleminded, but I wasn't an out-and-out fool, and I knew that if I went to a sweet-shop with Gussie I should end up with no sixpence and very few sweets. So I told him I could not buy sweets without Mother's permission, at which he gave me up altogether as a sissy or worse.

It had been an exhausting afternoon but a very instructive one. In the twilight I went back slowly over the bridges, a little regretful for that fast-moving, colorful household, but with a new appreciation for my own home. When I went in the lamp was lit over the fireplace and Father was at his tea.

"What kept you, child?" Mother asked with an anxious air, and suddenly I felt slightly guilty, and I played it as I usually did whenever I was at fault—in a loud, demonstrative, grown-up way. I stood in the middle of the kitchen with my cap in my hand and pointed it first at one, then at the other.

"You wouldn't believe who I met!" I said dramatically.

"Wisha, who, child?" Mother asked.

"Miss Cadogan," I said, placing my cap squarely on a chair, and turning on them both again. "Miss May Cadogan. Mrs. O'Brien as she is now."

"Mrs. O'Brien?" Father exclaimed, putting down his cup. "But where did you meet Mrs. O'Brien?"

"I said you wouldn't believe it. It was near the library. I was talking to some fellows, and what do you think but one of them was Gussie O'Brien, Mrs. O'Brien's son. And he took me home with him, and his mother gave me bread and jam, and she gave me *this*." I produced the sixpence with a real flourish.

"Well, I'm blowed!" Father gasped, and first he looked at me, and then he looked at Mother and burst into a loud guffaw.

"And she said to tell you she remembers you too, and that she sent her love."

"Oh, by the jumping bell of Athlone!" Father crowed and clapped his hands on his knees. I could see he believed the story I had told and was delighted with it, and I could see, too, that Mother did not believe it and that she was not in the least delighted. That, of course, was the trouble with Mother. Though she would do anything to help me with an intellectual problem, she never seemed to understand the need for experiment. She never opened her mouth while Father cross-questioned me, shaking his head in wonder and storing it up to tell the men in the factory. What pleased him most was Mrs. O'Brien's remembering the shape of his head, and later, while Mother was out of the kitchen, I caught him looking in the mirror and stroking the back of his head.

But I knew too that for the first time I had managed to produce in Mother the unrest that Father could produce, and I felt wretched and guilty and didn't know why. This was an aspect of history I only studied later.

That night I was really able to indulge my passion. At last I had the material to work with. I was myself as Gussie O'Brien, standing in the bedroom, looking down at my tent in the garden, and Aideen as my sister, and Mrs. O'Brien as my mother, and, like Pascal, I re-created history. I remembered Mrs. O'Brien's laughter, her scolding, and the way she stroked my head. I knew she was kind—casually kind—and hot-tempered, and recognized that in dealing with her I must some-how be a different sort of person. Being good at reading would never satisfy her. She would almost compel you to be as Gussie was: flatter-ing, impertinent, and exacting. Though I couldn't have expressed it in those terms, she was the sort of woman who would compel you to flirt with her.

Then, when I had had enough, I deliberately soothed myself as I did whenever I had scared myself by pretending that there was a burglar in the house or a wild animal trying to get in the attic window. I just crossed my hands on my chest, looked up at the window, and said to myself: "It is not like that. I am not Gussie O'Brien. I am Larry Delaney, and my mother is Mary Delaney, and we live in Number Eight, Wellington Square. Tomorrow I'll go to school at the Cross, and first there will be prayers, and then arithmetic, and after that composition."

For the first time the charm did not work. I had ceased to be Gussie, all right, but somehow I had not become myself again, not any self that I knew. It was as though my own identity was a sort of sack I had to live in, and I had deliberately worked my way out of it, and now I couldn't get back again because I had grown too big for it. I practiced every trick I knew to reassure myself. I tried to play a counting game; then I prayed, but even the prayer seemed different, as though it didn't belong to me at all. I was away in the middle of empty space, divorced from mother and home and everything permanent and familiar. Suddenly I found myself sobbing. The door opened and Mother came in in her nightdress, shivering, her hair over her face.

"You're not sleeping, child," she said in a wan and complaining voice.

I snivelled, and she put her hand on my forehead.

"You're hot," she said. "What ails you?"

I could not tell her of the nightmare in which I was lost. Instead, I took her hand, and gradually the terror retreated, and I became myself again, shrank into my little skin of identity, and left infinity and all its anguish behind.

"Mummy," I said, "I promise I never wanted anyone but you."

Expectation of Life

WHEN Shiela Hennessey married Jim Gaffney, a man twenty years older than herself, we were all pleased and rather surprised. By that time we were sure she wouldn't marry at all. Her father had been a small builder, and one of the town jokers put it down to a hereditary distaste for contracts.

Besides, she had been keeping company with Matt Sheridan off and on for ten years. Matt, who was a quiet chap, let on to be interested only in the bit of money her father had left her, but he was really very much in love with her, and, to give her her due, she had been as much in love with him as time and other young men permitted. Shiela had to a pronounced extent the feminine weakness for second strings. Suddenly she would scare off the prospect of a long life with a pleasant, quiet man like Matt, and for six months or so would run a tearing line with some young fellow from the College. At first Matt resented this, but later he either grew resigned or developed the only technique for handling it, because he turned it all into a great joke, and called her young man of the moment "the spare wheel."

And she really did get something out of those romances. A fellow called Magennis left her with a sound appreciation of Jane Austen and Bach, while another, Jack Mortimer, who was unhappy at home, taught her to admire Henry James and persuaded her that she had a father fixation. But all of them were pretty unsuitable, and Matt in his quiet determined way knew that if only he could sit tight and give no sign of jealousy, and encourage her to analyze their characters, she would eventually be bound to analyze herself out of love altogether. Until the next time, of course, but he had the hope that one of these days she would tire of her experiments and turn to him for good. At the same time, like the rest of us he realized that she might not marry at all. She was just the type of pious, well-courted, dissatisfied girl who as often as not ends up in a convent, but he was in no hurry and prepared to take a chance.

And no doubt, unless she had done this, she would have married him eventually, only that she fell violently in love with Jim Gaffney. Jim was a man in his early fifties, small and stout and good-natured. He was a widower with a grown son in Dublin, a little business on the Grand Parade, and a queer old house on Fair Hill, and as if these weren't drawbacks enough for anyone, he was a man with no religious beliefs worth mentioning.

According to Shiela's own story, which was as likely as not to be true, it was she who had to do all the courting and she who had to propose. It seemed that Jim had the Gaffney expectation of life worked out over three generations, and according to this he had only eight years to go, so that even when she did propose, he practically refused her.

"And what are you going to do with yourself when the eight years are up?" asked Matt when she broke the news to him.

"I haven't even thought about it, Matt," she said. "All I know is that eight years with Jim would be more to me than a lifetime with anyone else."

"Oh, well," he said with a bitter little smile, "I suppose you and I had better say good-bye."

"But you will stay friends with me, Matt?" she asked anxiously.

"I will not, Shiela," he replied with sudden violence. "The less I see of you from this onwards, the better pleased I'll be."

"You're not really as bitter as that with me?" she said, in distress.

"I don't know whether I am or not," he said flatly. "I just don't want to be mixed up with you after this. To tell you the truth, I don't believe you give a damn for this fellow."

"But I do, Matt. Why do you think I'm marrying him?"

"I think you're marrying him because you're hopelessly spoiled and neurotic, and ready for any silly adventure. What does your mother say to it?"

"Mummy will get used to Jim in time."

"Excuse my saying so, Shiela, but your mother will do nothing of the sort. If your father was alive he'd beat the hell out of you before he let you do it. Is it marry someone of his own age? Talk sense! By the time you're forty he'll be a doddering old man. How can it end in anything but trouble?"

"Matt, I don't care what it ends in. That's my look-out. All I want is for you and Jim to be friends."

It wasn't so much that Shiela wanted them to be friends as that she wanted to preserve her claim on Matt. Women are like that. They hate to let one man go even when they have sworn life-long fidelity to another.

"I have no desire to be friends," said Matt angrily. "I've wasted enough of my life on you as it is."

"I wish you wouldn't say things like that, Matt," she said, beginning to sniff. "I know I'm queer. I suppose I'm not normal. Jack Mortimer always said I had a father fixation, but what can I do about that? I know you think I just strung you along all these years, but you're wrong about that. I cared more for you than I did for all the others, and you know it. And if it wasn't for Jim I'd marry you now sooner than anybody."

"Oh, if it wasn't for Jim," he said mockingly. "If it wasn't Jim it would be somebody else, and I'm tired of it. It's all very well being patient, Shiela, but a man reaches the point where he has to protect himself, even if it hurts him or someone else. I've reached it."

And she knew he had, and that she had no hope of holding on to him. A man who had stuck to her for all those years, and through all her vagaries, was not the sort to be summoned back by a whim. Parting with him was more of a wrench than she had anticipated.

SHE WAS radiantly happy through the brief honeymoon in France. She had always been fascinated and repelled by sex, and on their first night on the boat, Jim, instead of making violent love to her as a younger man might have done, sat on his bunk and made her listen to a long lecture on the subject, which she found more interesting than any love-making; and before they had been married a week, she was making the difficult adjustment for herself, and without shock.

As a companion Jim was excellent, because he was ready to be pleased with everything from urinals to cathedrals; he got as much pleasure out of small things as big ones, and it put her in good humor just to see the way he enjoyed himself. He would sit in the sunlight outside a café, a bulky man with a red face and white hair, enthusing over his pastries and coffee and the spectacle of good-looking well-dressed people going by. When his face clouded, it was only because he had remembered the folly of those who would not be happy when they could.

"And the whoors at home won't even learn how to make a cup of coffee!" he would declare bitterly.

The only times he got mad were when Shiela, tall and tangential, moved too fast for him and he had to shuffle after her on his tender feet, swinging his arms close to his chest like a runner, or when she suddenly changed her mind at a crossing and left him in the middle of the traffic to run forward and back, alarmed and swearing. In his rage he shouted and shook his fist at the taxi-drivers, and they shouted back at him without his even knowing what they said. At times like these he even shouted at Shiela, and she promised in the future to wait for him, but she didn't. She was a born fidget, and when he left her somewhere to go to one of his beloved urinals, she drifted on to the nearest shop-window, and he lost her. Because all the French he knew came from the North Monastery, and French policemen only looked astonished when they heard it, and because he could never remember the name of his hotel, he was plunged in despair once a day.

It was a great relief to him to get back to Fair Hill, put his feet on the mantelpiece, and study in books the places he had been. Shiela, too, came to understand how good a marriage could be, with the inhibitions of a lifetime breaking down and new and more complicated ones taking their place. Their life was exceedingly quiet. Each evening Jim came puffing up the hill from town under a mountain of pullovers, scarves, and coats, saying that the damn height was getting too much for him, and that they'd have to—have to—have to get a house in town. Then he changed into old trousers and slippers, and lovingly poured himself a glass of whiskey, the whiskey carefully measured against the light as it had been any time in twenty years. He knew to a drop the amount of spirits it needed to give him the feeling of a proper drink without slugging himself. Only a man with a steady hand could know how much was good for him. Moderation was the secret.

After supper he put his feet on the mantelpiece and told her the day's news from town. About nine they had a cup of tea, and, if the night was fine, took a short ramble over the hill to get the view of the illuminated city below. As Shiela had learned, by this time Jim was usually at the top of his form, and it had become unsafe for anyone to suggest a house in town. Fair Hill had again become the perfect place of residence. The tension of the day completely gone, he had his bath and pottered about the stiff, ungainly old house in his pajama trousers, scratching himself in elaborate patterns and roaring with laughter at his own jokes.

"Who the hell said I had a father fixation?" Shiela asked indignantly. "I didn't marry my father; I married my baby."

All the same, she knew he wasn't all that simple. Paddy, his son, lived in Dublin, and though Shiela suspected that he was somewhat of a disappointment to Jim, she could never get a really coherent account of him from Jim. It was the same with his first marriage. He scarcely spoke of it, except once in a while to say "Margaret used to think" or "a friend of Margaret's"—bubbles rising to the surface of a pool whose depths she could not see, though she suspected the shadow that covered it. Nor was he much more informative about less intimate matters. If he disliked people, he disliked talking of them, and if he liked them, he only wished to say conventional things in their praise. As a student of Jane Austen and Henry James, Shiela wanted to plumb things to their depths, and sometimes it made her very angry that he would not argue with her. It suggested that he did not take her seriously.

"What is it about Kitty O'Malley that makes her get in with all those extraordinary men?" she would ask. "Is it a reaction against her mother?"

"Begor, I don't know, girl," he would say, staring at her over his reading glasses, as though he were a simpleminded man to whom such difficult problems never occurred.

"And I suppose you never bothered to ask yourself," she would retort angrily. "You prefer to know people superficially."

"Ah, well, I'm a superficial sort of chap," he would reply with a benign smile, but she had the furious feeling that he was only laughing at her. Because once, when she did set out deliberately to madden him by sneering at his conventionality, he lost his temper and snapped: "Superficially is a damn good way to know people." And this, as she realized, wasn't what he meant either. She suspected that, whereas her plumbing of the depths meant that she was continually changing planes in her relations with people, moving rapidly from aloofness to intimacy and back, enthusing and suspecting, he considered only the characteristics that could be handled consistently on one plane. And though his approach was by its nature inaccurate, she had to admit that it worked, because in the plumbing business you never really knew where you were with anyone.

They had other causes of disagreement, though at first these were comic rather than alarming. Religion was one; it was something of an obsession with Shiela, but on the only occasion when she got him to Mass, he sighed, as he did when she took him to the pictures, and said mournfully as they left the church: "Those fellows haven't changed in thirty years." He seemed to think that religion should be subject to the general improvement in conditions of living. When she pressed him about what he thought improvements would be, it turned out that he thought churches should be used for lectures and concerts. She did not lose hope of converting him, even on his death-bed, though she realized that it would have to be effected entirely by the power of prayer, since precept and example were equally lost on him.

Besides this there was the subject of his health. In spite of his girth and weight, she felt sure he wasn't strong. It seemed to her that the climb from the city each evening was becoming too much for him. He puffed too much, and in the mornings he had an uproarious cough, which he turned into a performance. She nagged him to give up the pipe and the whiskey or to see a doctor, but he would do neither. She surprised him by bringing the doctor to him during one of his bronchial attacks, and the doctor backed her up by advising him to give up smoking and drinking and to take things easily. Jim laughed as if this were a good joke, and went on behaving in precisely the same way. "Moderation is the secret," he said as he measured his whiskey against the light. "The steady hand." She was beginning to realize that he was a man of singular obstinacy, and to doubt whether, if he went on in this way, she would have him even for the eight years that the Gaffney expectation of life promised him.

Besides, he was untidy and casual about money, and this was one of the things about which Shiela was meticulous.

"It's not that I want anything for myself," she explained with conscious virtue. "It's just that I'd like to know where I stand if anything happens to you. I'll guarantee Paddy won't be long finding out."

"Oh, begor, you mightn't be far wrong," he said with a great guffaw.

Yet he did nothing about it. Beyond the fact that he hated to be in debt, he did not seem to care what happened to his money, and it lay there in the bank, doing no good to anyone. He had not made a will, and when she tried to get him to do so, he only passed it off with a joke.

Still refusing to be beaten, she invited his solicitor to supper, but, whatever understanding the two men had reached, they suddenly started to giggle hysterically when she broached the matter, and everything she said after that only threw them into fresh roars of laughter. Jim actually had tears in his eyes, and he was not a man who laughed inordinately on other occasions.

It was the same about insurance. Once more, it was not so much that she wanted provision for herself, but to a girl who always carried an identification card in her handbag in case of accidents it seemed the height of imprudence to have no insurance at all, even to pay for the funeral. Besides—and this was a matter that worried her somewhat—the Gaffney grave was full, and it was necessary to buy a new plot for herself and Jim. He made no protest at the identification card she had slipped in his wallet, instructing the finder of the body to communicate at once with herself, though she knew he produced this regularly in the shop for the entertainment of his friends, but he would have nothing to say to insurance. He was opposed to it, because money was continuously decreasing in value and insurance was merely paying good money for bad. He told her of a tombstone he had seen in a West Cork cemetery with an inscription that ran: "Here Lie the Remains of Elizabeth Martin who." "Poor Elizabeth Martin Who!" he guffawed. "To make sure she had the right sort of tombstone, she had it made herself, and the whoors who came after her couldn't make head or tail of the inscription. See what insurance does for you. . . . Anyway, you little bitch," he growled good-humoredly, "what the hell do you always want to be burying me for? Suppose I bury you for a change?"

"At any rate, if you do, you'll find my affairs in order," Shiela replied proudly.

SHE HAD sent postcards to Matt from France, hoping he might make things up, but when they returned to Cork she found that he had taken a job in the Midlands, and later it was reported that he was walking out with a shopkeeper's daughter who had a substantial fortune. A year later she heard of his engagement and wrote to congratulate him. He replied promptly and without rancor to say that the report was premature, and that he was returning to a new job in Cork. Things had apparently not gone too well between himself and the shopkeeper's daughter.

Shiela was overjoyed when at last he called on them in Fair Hill, the same old Matt, slow and staid, modest and intelligent and full of quiet irony. Obviously he was glad to be back in Cork, bad as it was. The Midlands were too tame, even for him.

Then Shiela had her great idea. Kitty O'Malley was the old friend of Jim's whose chequered career Shiela had tried to analyze. She was a gentle girl with an extraordinary ability for getting herself entangled with unsuitable men. There had already been a married man, who had not liked to let her know he was married for fear of hurting her feelings, a mental patient, and a pathological liar, who had got himself engaged to two other girls because he just could not stop inventing personalities for himself. As a result, Kitty had a slightly bewildered air, because she felt (as Shiela did) that there must be something in her which attracted such people, though she couldn't imagine what it was.

Shiela saw it all quite clearly, problem and solution, on the very first evening Matt called.

"Do you know that I have the perfect wife for you?" she said.

"Is that so?" asked Matt with amusement. "Who's she?"

"A girl called O'Malley, a friend of Jim's. She's a grand girl, isn't she, Jim?"

"Grand girl," agreed Jim.

"But can she support me in the style I'm accustomed to?" asked Matt who persisted in his pretense of being mercenary.

"Not like your shopkeeper's daughter, I'm afraid."

"And you think she'd have me?"

"Oh, certain, if only you'll let me handle her. If she's left to herself, she'll choose an alcoholic or something. She's shy, and shy girls never get to be courted by anything less dynamic than a mental case. She'll never go out of her way to catch you, so you'd better leave all that to me."

Shiela had great fun, organizing meetings of her two sedate friends, but to her great surprise Jim rapidly grew bored and angry with the whole thing. After Matt and Kitty had been three times to Fair Hill and he had been twice to supper with them, he struck. This time Shiela had arranged that they were all to go to the pictures together, and Jim lost his temper with her. Like all good-natured men, when he was angry he became immoderate and unjust.

"Go with them yourself!" he shouted. "What the hell do you want mixing yourself up in it at all for? If they can't do their own courting, let them live single."

She was downcast, and went to the bedroom to weep. Soon after, he tiptoed into the room and took her hand, talking about everything except the subject on her mind. After ten minutes he rose and peered out of the low window at the view of the city he had loved from boyhood. "What the hell do they want building houses here for and then not giving you a decent view?" he asked in chagrin. All the same, she knew he knew she was jealous. It was all very well arranging a match between Matt and Kitty, but she hated the thought of their going out together and talking of her the way she talked of them. If only Jim had been her own age, she would not have cared much what they said of her, but he was by comparison an old man and might die any day, leaving her alone and without her spare wheel. She could even anticipate how it would happen. She was very good at anticipating things, and she had noticed how in the middle of the night Jim's face smoothed out into that of a handsome boy, and she knew that this was the face he would wear when he was dead. He would lie like that in this very room, with a rosary bead he could no longer resent between his transparent fingers, and Matt, in that gentle firm way of his, would take charge of everything for her. He would take her in his arms to comfort her, and each would know it had come too late. So, though she did wish him to have Kitty if he could not have her, she did not want them to be too much together in her absence and hoped they might not be too precipitate. Anything might happen Jim; they were both young—only thirty or so—and it would not hurt them to wait.

When they did marry six months later, neither Matt nor Kitty knew the generosity that had inspired her, or the pain it had caused her. She suspected that Jim knew, though he said no more about it than he did about all the other things that touched him closely.

Yet he made it worse for her by his terrible inability to tidy up his affairs. All that winter he was ill, and dragged himself to the shop and back, and for three weeks he lay in bed, choking—as usual, with a pipe that gave him horrible spasms of coughing. It was not only that he had a weak chest; he had a weak heart as well, and one day the bronchitis would put too much tension on the overstrained heart. But instead of looking after himself or making a will or insuring himself, or doing any of the things one would expect a sickly old man with a young wife to do, he spent his time in bed, wrapped in woollies and shawls, poring over house-plans. He had occupied his father's unmanageable house on Fair Hill for twenty years without ever wishing to change it, but now he seemed to have got a new lease of life. He wanted to get rid of the basement and have one of the back rooms turned into a modern kitchen, with the dining room opening off it.

Shiela was alarmed at the thought of such an outlay on a house she had no intention of occupying after his death. It was inconvenient enough to live in with him, but impossibly lonely for a woman living alone, and she knew that no other man, unless he had Jim's awkward tastes, would even consider living there. Besides, she could not imagine herself living on in any house that reminded her of her loss. That, too, she could anticipate—his favorite view, his chair, his pipe rack, emptied of his presence—and knew she could never bear it.

"But you said yourself it was hell working in that kitchen," he protested. "And it's awful to have to eat there. It gives you the creeps if you have to go down there after dark."

"But the money, Jim, the money!" she protested irritably.

"We have the money, girl," he said. "That's what you keep on saying yourself. It's lying there in the bank, doing no good to anybody."

"We might be glad of it one of these days," said Shiela. "And if we
had to sell the house, we'd never get back what we spent. It's too inconvenient."

"Who the hell said I wanted it back?" he snorted. "I want a place I
can have some comfort in. Anyway, why would we sell it?"

This was something she did not like to say, though he knew what
was on her mind, for after a moment he gave a wicked little grin and
raised a warning forefinger at her.

"We'll make the one job of it," he whispered. "We'll build the
kitchen and buy the grave at the same time."

"It's no joking matter, Jim."

He only threw back his head and roared in his childish way.

"And we'll buy the bloody tombstone and have it inscribed. 'Sacred
to the Memory of James Gaffney, beloved husband of Shiela Gaffney
Who.' I declare to my God, we'll have people writing books on the
Whos. The first family in Cork to take out insurance."

She tried to get him to compromise on an upstairs kitchen of an
inexpensive kind, a shed with a gas oven in it, but he wouldn't even
listen to her advice.

"Now, mind what I'm telling you, girl," he said, lecturing her as he
had done on the first night of their marriage, "there's some maggot of
meanness in all Irish people. They could halve their work and double
their pleasure, but they'd sooner have it in the bank. Christ, they'd put
themselves in a safe deposit if only they'd keep. Every winter of their
lives shivering with the cold; running out to the haggard the wickedest
night God sent; dying in hundreds and leaving the food for the flies in
summer—all sooner than put the money into the one business that
ever gives you a certain return: living! Look at that bloody city down
there, full of perishing old misers!"

"But, Jim," she cried in dismay, "you're not thinking of putting in
heating?"

"And why the hell wouldn't I put in heating? Who keeps on complaining about the cold?"

"And a fridge?"

"Why not, I say? You're the one that likes ice-cream."

"Ah, Jim, don't go on like that! You know we haven't enough money
to pay for the kitchen as it is."

"Then we'll get it. You just decide what you want, and I'll see about
the money."

By the following summer Jim, who was behaving as though he
would never die, was planning to get rid of the old improvised bath-

room downstairs and install a new one of the most expensive kind off their bedroom.

"Jim," she said desperately, "I tell you we cannot afford it."

"Then we'll borrow it," he replied placidly. "We can't afford to get pneumonia in that damned old outhouse either. Look at the walls! They're dripping wet. Anyway, now we have security to borrow on."

But she hated the very thought of getting into debt. It wasn't that she didn't appreciate the fine new kitchen with a corner window that looked over the hill and up the valley of the river, or was not glad of the refrigerator and the heating, and it was certainly not that she wished Jim to die, because she worried herself into a frenzy trying to make sure he looked after himself and took the pills that were supposed to relieve the strain on his heart. No, if only someone could have assured her once for all that Jim would live to be eighty, she could have resigned herself to getting in debt for the sake of the new bathroom. But it was the nagging feeling that he had such a short time to live, and would die leaving everything in a mess of debt and extravagance as it was now, that robbed her of any pleasure she might feel.

She could not help contrasting themselves and the Sheridans. Matt had everything in order. It was true that he did not carry any regular identification card, but this, as she knew, was due more to modesty than irresponsibility. Matt would have felt self-conscious about instructing a totally unknown person as to what to do with his body. But he did have as much insurance as he could afford, and his will was made. Nothing serious was left unprovided for. Shiela could not help feeling that Kitty owed her a lot, and Kitty was inclined to feel the same. For a girl with such a spotty career, it was a joy to be married to someone as normal as Matt.

Not that Shiela found so much to complain of in Jim, apart from the one monstrous fact that he was too set in his ways. She saw that no matter how dearly you loved a man of that age or how good and clever he might be, it was still a mistake, because there was nothing you could do with him, nothing you could even modify. She did not notice that Jim's friends thought he was different, or if she did she never ascribed it to her own influence. A girl who could not get him to do a simple thing like giving up smoking could not realize that she might have changed him in matters of more importance to himself. For we do not change people through the things in them that we would wish to change, but through the things that they themselves wish to change. What she had given Jim, though she did not recognize it, was precisely the thing whose consequences she deplored, the desire to live and be happy.

Then came the tragedy of Kitty's death after the birth of her second child. Matt and the children came to stay with them in Fair Hill until Matt's mother could close up her own home and come to keep house for him. Jim was deeply shocked by the whole business. He had always been exceedingly fond of Kitty, and he went so far as to advise Matt not to make any permanent arrangement with his mother but to marry again as soon as he could. But Matt, as he told Shiela on the side, had no intention of marrying again, and, though he did not say as much, she knew that he would never remarry—at least until she was free herself. And at once she was seized with impatience because everything in life seemed to happen out of sequence, as if a mad projectionist had charge of the film, and young and necessary people like Kitty died while old men like Jim with weak hearts and ailing chests dragged on, drinking and smoking, wheezing and coughing, and defying God and their doctors by planning new homes for themselves.

Sometimes she was even horrified at the thoughts that came into her mind. There were days when she hated Jim, and snapped and mocked at him until she realized that her behavior was becoming monstrous. Then she went to some church and, kneeling in a dark corner, covered her face with her hands and prayed. Even if Jim believed in nothing, she did, and she prayed that she might be enlightened about the cause of her anger and discontent. For, however she tried, she could find in herself no real hostility to Jim. She felt that if she were called upon to do it, she could suffer anything on his behalf. Yet at the same time she was tormented by the spectacle of Matt, patient and uncomplaining, the way he looked and the way he spoke, and his terrible need of her, and had hysterical fits of impatience with Jim, older and rougher but still smiling affectionately at her as if he really understood the torments she was enduring. Perhaps he had some suspicion of them. Once when he came into the bedroom and saw her weeping on the bed, he grabbed her hand and hissed furiously: "Why can't you try to live more in the present?"

It astonished her so much that she ceased weeping and even tried to get him to explain himself. But on matters that concerned himself and her, Jim was rarely lucid or even coherent, and she was left to think the matter out for herself. It was an idea she could not grasp. It was the present she was living in, and it was the present she hated. It was he who lived in the future, a future he would never enjoy. He tried to curb himself because he now realized how upset she became at his plans, but they proved too much for him, and because he thought the front room was too dark and depressing with its one tall window, he had a big picture window put in so that they could enjoy the wonderful view of the city, and a little terrace built outside where they could sit and have their coffee on fine summer evenings. She watched it all listlessly because she knew it was only for a year or two, and meanwhile Matt was eating his heart out in a little house by the river in Tivoli, waiting for Jim to die so that he could realize his life's dream.

Then, to her astonishment, she fell ill and began to suspect that it might be serious. It even became clear to her that she might not be going to live. She was not really afraid of something for which she had prepared herself for years by trying to live in the presence of God, but she was both bewildered and terrified at the way in which it threatened to make a mockery of her life and Matt's. It was the mad projectionist again, and again he seemed to have got the reels mixed up till the story became meaningless. Who was this white-faced brave little woman who cracked jokes with the doctors when they tried to encourage her about the future? Surely, she had no part in the scenario.

She went to hospital in the College Road, and each day Jim came and sat with her, talking about trifles till the nuns drove him away. He had shut up the house on Fair Hill and taken a room near the hospital so as to be close to her. She had never seen a human being so anxious and unhappy, and it diverted her in her own pain to make fun of him. She even flirted with him as she had not done since the days of their courtship, affecting to believe that she had trapped him into accepting her. But when Matt came to see her the very sight of him filled her with nausea. How on earth could she ever have thought of marrying that gentle, devoted, intelligent man! All she now wanted health for was to return to Fair Hill and all the little improvements that Jim had effected for their happiness. She could be so contented, sitting on the terrace or behind the picture window looking down at the city with its spires and towers and bridges that sent up to them such a strange, dissociated medley of sound. But as the days went by she realized with her clear penetrating intelligence that this was a happiness she had rejected, and which now she would never be permitted to know. All that her experience could teach her was its value.

"Jim," she said the day before she died, as she laid her hand in his, "I'd like you to know that there never was anybody only you."

"Why?" he asked, trying to keep the anguish out of his face. "Did you think I believed it?"

"I gave you cause enough," she said regretfully. "I could never make up my mind, only once, and then I couldn't stick by it. I want you to promise me if I don't come back that you'll marry again. You're the sort who can't be happy without someone to plan for."

"Won't you ever give up living in the future?" he asked with a reproachful smile, and then raised her hand and kissed it.

It was their last conversation. He did not marry again, even for her sake, though in public at least he did not give the impression of a man broken down by grief. On the contrary, he remained cheerful and thriving for the rest of his days. Matt, who was made of different stuff, did not easily forgive him his callousness.

The Ugly Duckling

MICK COURTNEY had known Nan Ryan from the time he was four-teen or fifteen. She was the sister of his best friend, and youngest of a family of four in which she was the only girl. He came to be almost as fond of her as her father and brothers were; she had practically lost her mother's regard by inheriting her father's looks. Her ugliness indeed was quite endearing. She had a stocky, sturdy figure and masculine features all crammed into a feminine container till it bulged. None of her features was really bad, and her big, brown, twinkling eyes were delightful, but they made a group that was almost comic.

Her brothers liked her spirit; they let her play with them while any of them were of an age for play, and, though she suffered from night panics and Dinny broke the maternal rule by letting her into his bed, they never told. He, poor kid, would be wakened in the middle of the night by Nan's pulling and shaking. "Dinny, Dinny," she would hiss fiercely, "I have 'em again!" "What are they this time?" Dinny would ask drowsily. "Li-i-ons!" she would reply in a bloodcurdling tone, and then lie for half an hour in his arms, contracting her toes and kicking spasmodically while he patted and soothed her.

She grew up a tomboy, fierce, tough, and tearless, fighting in Dinny's gang, which contested the old quarry on the road with the hill-tribes from the slum area above it; and this was how Mick was to remember her best—an ugly, stocky little Amazon, leaping from rock to rock, hurling stones in an awkward but effective way, and screaming deadly insults at the enemy and encouragement to her own side.

He could not have said when she gave up fighting, but between twelve and fourteen she became the pious one in a family not remarkable for piety, always out at Mass or diving into church on her way from school to light candles and make novenas. Afterwards it struck Mick that it might have been an alternative to getting in Dinny's bed, for she still suffered from night fears, only now when they came on she grabbed her rosary beads instead.

It amused him to discover that she had developed something of a crush on himself. Mick had lost his faith, which in Cork is rather similar to a girl's loss of her virtue and starts the same sort of flutterings among the quiet ones of the opposite sex. Nan would be waiting for him at the door in the evening, and when she saw him would begin to jump down the steps one by one with her feet together, her hands stiff at her sides, and her pigtail tossing.

"How are the novenas coming on, Nan?" he would ask with amusement.

"Fine!" she would reply in a shrill, expressionless voice. "You're on your way."

"I'll come quietly."

"You think you won't, but I know better. I'm a fierce pray-er."

Another stiff jump took her past him.

"Why don't you do it for the blacks, Nan?"

"I'm doing it for them, too, sure."

But though her brothers could ease the pangs of childhood for her, adolescence threw her on the mercy of life. Her mother, a roly-poly of a woman who went round a great deal with folded arms, thus increasing the impression of curves and rolls, was still a beauty, and did her best to disguise Nan's ugliness, a process that mystified her husband, who could see nothing wrong with the child except her shaky mathematics.

"I'm no blooming beauty," Nan would cry, with an imitation of a schoolboy's toughness, whenever her mother tried to get her out of the rough tweeds and dirty pullovers she fancied into something more feminine.

"The dear knows you're not," her mother would say, folding her arms with an expression of resignation. "I don't suppose you want to advertise it, though."

"Why wouldn't I advertise it?" Nan would cry, squaring up to her. "I don't want any of your dirty old men."

"You needn't worry, child. They'll let you well alone."

"Let them!" Nan would say, scowling. "I don't care. I want to be a nun."

All the same, it made her self-conscious about friendships with girls of her own age, even pious ones like herself. They, too, would have boys around, and the boys wanted nothing to do with Nan. Though she carefully avoided all occasion for a slight, even a hint of one was enough to make her brooding and resentful, and then she seemed to become hideous and shapeless and furtive. She slunk round the house with her shoulders up about her ears, her red-brown hair hanging loose, and a cigarette glued loosely to her lower lip. Suddenly and inexplicably she would drop some nice girl she had been friendly with for years, and never even speak of her again. It gave her the reputation of being cold and insincere, but as Dinny in his shrewd, old-mannish way observed to Mick, she made her real friends among older women and even sick people—"all seventy or paralyzed," as he put it. Yet even with these she tended to be jealous and exacting.

Dinny didn't like this, and his mother thought it was awful, but Nan paid no attention to their views. She had become exceedingly obstinate in a way that did not suit either her age or her sex, and it made her seem curiously angular, almost masculine, as though it were the psychological aspect of her ugliness. She had no apparent shyness and stalked in and out of a room, swinging her arms like a boy. Her conversation changed, too, and took on the tone of an older woman's. It was not dull—she was far too brainy to be dull—but it was too much on one key—"crabbed" to use a local word—and it did not make the sharp distinctions young people's conversation makes between passion and boredom. Dinny and Mick could be very bored indeed in one another's company, but suddenly some topic would set flame to their minds, and they would walk the streets by the hour with their coats buttoned up, arguing.

Her father was disappointed when she refused to go to college. When she did go to work, it was in a dress shop, a curious occupation for a girl whose only notions of dress were a trousers and jersey.

THEN one night something happened that electrified Mick. It was more like a transformation scene in a pantomime than anything in his experience. Later, of course, he realized that it had not happened like that at all. It was just that, as usual with those one has known too well, he had ceased to observe Nan, had taken her too much for granted, and the change in her had come about gradually and imperceptibly till it forced itself on his attention in the form of a shock.

Dinny was upstairs, and Mick and she were arguing. Though without formal education, Mick was a well-read man, and he had no patience with Nan's literary tastes, which were those of her aged and invalid acquaintances—popular novels and biographies. As usual, he made fun of her and, as usual, she grew angry. "You're so damn superior, Mick Courtney," she said with a scowl and went to search for the book they had discussed in the big mahogany bookcase, which was one of the handsome pieces of furniture her mother took pride in. Laughing, Mick got up and stood beside her, putting his arm round her shoulder as he would have done at any other time. She misunderstood the gesture, for she leaned back on his shoulder and offered herself to be kissed. At that moment only did he realize that she had turned into a girl of startling beauty. He did not kiss her. Instead, he dropped his arm and looked at her incredulously. She gave him a malicious grin and went on with her search.

For the rest of the evening he could not take his eyes from her. Now he could easily analyze the change for himself. He remembered that she had been ill with some type of fever and had come out of it white and thin. Then she had seemed to shoot up, and now he saw that during her illness her face had lengthened, and one by one each of those awkward lumps of feature had dropped into place and proportion till they formed a perfect structure that neither age nor illness could any longer quite destroy. It was not in the least like her mother's type of beauty, which was round and soft and eminently pattable. It was like a translation of her father's masculinity, tight and strained and almost harsh, and she had deliberately emphasized it by the way she pulled her hair back in a tight knot, exposing the rather big ears. Already it had begun to effect her gait, for she no longer charged about a room swinging her arms like a sergeant-major. At the same time she had not yet learned to move gracefully, and she seemed to drift rather than walk, and came in and went out in profile as though afraid to face a visitor or turn her back on him. And he wondered again at the power of habit that causes us to live with people historically, with faults or virtues that have long disappeared to every eye but our own.

For twelve months Mick had been going steadily with a nice girl from Sunday's Well, and in due course he would have married her. Mick was that sort, a creature of habit who controlled circumstances by simplifying them down to a routine—the same restaurant, the same table, the same waitress, and the same dish. It enabled him to go on with his own thoughts. But whenever anything did happen to disturb this routine it was like a convulsion of Nature for him; even his favorite restaurant became a burden, and he did not know what to do with his evenings and weekends. The transformation of Nan into a beauty had a similar effect on him. Gradually he dropped the nice girl from Sunday's Well without a word of explanation or apology and went more and more to the Ryans', where he had a feeling of not being particularly welcome to anyone but Dinny and—sometimes at least—Nan herself. She had plenty of admirers without him. The change was there all right. Mr. Ryan, a tall, bald, noisy man with an apelike countenance of striking good-nature, enjoyed it as proof that sensible men were not put off by a girl's mathematics—he, poor man, had noticed no change whatever in his daughter. Mrs. Ryan had no such pleasure. Naturally, she had always cared more for her sons, but they had not brought home with them attractive young men who were compelled to flirt with her, and now Nan took an almost perverse delight in keeping the young men and her mother apart. Beauty had brought out what ugliness had failed to do—a deep resentment of her mother that at times went too far for Mick's taste. Occasionally he saw it in a reversion to a heavy, stolid, almost stupid air that harked back to her childhood, sometimes in a sparkle of wit that had malice in it. She made up for this by what Mick thought of as an undue consideration for her father. Whenever he came into the room, bellowing and cheerful, her face lit up.

She had ceased to wear the rough masculine tweeds she had always preferred, and to Mick's eye it was not a change for the better. She had developed a passion for good clothes without an understanding of them, and used powder and lipstick in the lavish tasteless manner of a girl of twelve.

But if he disapproved of her taste in dress, he hated her taste in men. What left Dinny bored made Mick mad. He and Nan argued about this in the same way they argued about books. "Smoothies," he called her admirers to her face. There was Joe Lyons, the solicitor, a suave, dark-haired young man with mysterious slitlike eyes, who combined a knowledge of wines with an intellectual Catholicism, and Matt Healy, a little leprechaun of a butter merchant, who had a boat and rattled on cheerfully about whiskey and "dames." The pair of them could argue for a full half-hour about a particular make of car or a Dublin hotel without, so far as Mick could see, ever uttering one word of sense, and obviously Lyons despised Healy as a chatter-box and Healy despised Lyons as a fake, while both of them despised Mick. They thought he was a character, and whenever he tried to discuss religion or politics with them they listened with an amusement that made him furious.

"I stick to Mick against the day the Revolution comes," said Healy with his leprechaun's laugh.

"No," Lyons said, putting his arm patronizingly about Mick, "Mick will have nothing to do with revolutions."

"Don't be too sure," said Healy, his face lit up with merriment. "Mick is a sans-culotte. Isn't that the word, Mick?"

"I repeat no," said Lyons with his grave smile. "I know Mick. Mick is a wise man. Mind," he added solemnly, raising his finger, "I didn't say an intelligent man. I said a wise one. There's a difference."

Mick could not help being angry. When they talked that way to Dinny, he only blinked politely and drifted upstairs to his book or his gramophone, but Mick stayed and grew mad. He was hard-working, but unambitious; too intelligent to value the things commonplace people valued, but too thin-skinned to ignore their scorn at his failure to do so.

Nan herself had no objection to being courted by Mick. She was still under the influence of her childish infatuation, and it satisfied her vanity to be able to indulge it. She was an excellent companion, active and intelligent, and would go off for long walks with him over the hills through the fields to the river. They would end up in a public-house in Glanmire or Little Island, though she soon stopped him trying to be extravagant in the manner of Healy and Lyons. "I'm a whiskey-drinker, Mick," she would say with a laugh. "You're not a whiskey-buyer." She could talk for an hour over a glass of beer, but when Mick tried to give their conversation a sentimental turn she countered with a bluff practicality that shocked him.

"Marry you?" she exclaimed with a laugh. "Who died and left you the fortune?"

"Why, do I have to have a fortune?" he asked quietly, though he was stung by her good-natured contempt.

"Well, it would be a help if you're thinking of getting married," she replied with a laugh. "As long as I remember my family, we never seem to have been worried by anything else."

"Of course, if you married Joe Lyons, you wouldn't have to worry," he said with a hint of a sneer.

"From my point of view, that would be a very good reason," she said.

"A classy car and St. Thomas Aquinas," Mick went on, feeling like a small boy, but unable to stop himself. "What more could a girl ask?"

"You resent people having cars, don't you?" she asked, leaning her elbows on the table and giving him a nasty look. "Don't you think it might help if you went and got one for yourself?"

The wordly, middle-aged tone, particularly when linked with the Ryan go-getting, could be exceedingly destructive. There was something else that troubled him, too, though he was not sure why. He had always liked to pose a little as a man of the world, but Nan could sometimes shock him badly. There seemed to be depths of sensuality in her that were out of character. He could not believe that she really intended it, but she could sometimes inflame him with some sudden violence or coarseness as no ordinary girl could do.

Then one evening when they were out together, walking in the Lee Fields, he noticed a change in her. She and another girl had been spending a few days in Glengarriff with Healy and Lyons. She did not want to talk of it, and he had the feeling that something about it had disappointed her. She was different—brooding, affectionate, and intense. She pulled off her shoes and stockings and sat with her feet in the river, her hands joined between her knees, while she gazed at the woods on the other side of the river.

"You think too much of Matt and Joe," she said, splashing her feet. "Why can't you feel sorry for them?"

"Feel sorry for them?" he repeated, so astonished that he burst into a laugh.

She turned her head and her brown eyes rested on him with a strange innocence. "If you weren't such an old agnostic, I'd say pray for them."

"For what?" he asked, still laughing. "Bigger dividends?"

"The dividends aren't much use to them," she said. "They're both bored. That's why they like me—I don't bore them. They don't know what to make of me. . . . Mind," she added, laughing in her enthusiastic way, "I love money, Mick Courtney. I love expensive clothes and flashy dinners and wines I can't pronounce the name of, but they don't take me in. A girl who was brought up as I was needs more than that to take her in."

"What is it you need?" asked Mick.

"Why don't you go and do something?" she asked with sudden gravity.

"What?" he replied with a shrug.

"What?" she asked, waving her hands. "What do I care? I don't even know what you like. I don't mind if you make a mess of it. It's not failure I'm afraid of. It's just getting stuck in the mud, not caring for anything. Look at Daddy! You may not think so, but I know he's a brilliant man, and he's stuck. Now he hopes the boys will find out whatever secret there is and do all the things he couldn't do. That doesn't appeal to me."

"Yes," Mick agreed thoughtfully, lighting a cigarette and answering himself rather than her. "I know what you mean. I dare say I'm not ambitious. I've never felt the need for being ambitious. But I fancy I could be ambitious for someone else. I'd have to get out of Cork though. Probably to Dublin. There's nothing here in my line."

"Dublin would do me fine," she said with satisfaction. "Mother and I would get on much better at that distance."

He said nothing for a few moments, and Nan went on splashing gaily with her feet.

"Is that a bargain then?" he asked.

"Oh, yes," she said, turning her big soft eyes on him. "That's a bargain. Don't you know I was always mad about you?"

Their engagement made a big change in Mick. He was, as I have said, a creature of habit, a man who lived by associations. He really knew the city in a way that few of us knew it, its interesting corners and queer characters, and the idea of having to exchange it for a place of no associations at all was more of a shock to him than it would have been to any of us; but though at certain times it left him with a lost feeling, at others it restored to him a boyish excitement and gaiety, as though the trip he was preparing for was some dangerous voyage from which he might not return, and when he lit up like that he became more attractive, reckless, and innocent. Nan had always been attracted by him; now she really admired and loved him.

All the same, she did not discontinue her outings with her other beaux. In particular, she remained friendly with Lyons, who was really fond of her and believed that she wasn't serious about marrying Mick. He was, as she said, a genuinely kind man, and was shocked at the thought that so beautiful a girl should even consider cooking and washing clothes on a clerk's income. He went to her father about it, and explained patiently to him that it would mean social extinction for Nan, and he would even have gone to Mick himself but that Nan forbade it. "But he can't do it, Nan," he protested earnestly. "Mick is a decent man. He can't do that to you." "He can't, like hell," said Nan, chuckling and putting her head on Lyons's chest. "He'd send me out on the streets to keep himself in fags."

These minor infidelities did not in the least worry Mick, who was almost devoid of jealousy. He was merely amused by her occasional lies and evasions, and even more by the fits of conscience that followed them.

"Mick," she asked between anger and laughter, "why do I tell you all these lies? I'm not naturally untruthful, am I? I didn't go to Confession on Saturday night. I went out with Joe Lyons instead. He still believes I'm going to marry him, and I would, too, if only he had a brain in his head. Mick, why can't you be attractive like that?"

But if Mick didn't resent it, Mrs. Ryan resented it on his behalf, though she resented his complaisance even more. She was sufficiently feminine to know she might have done the same herself, and to feel that if she had, she would need correction. No man is ever as anti-feminist as a really feminine woman.

No, it was Nan's father who exasperated Mick, and he was sensible enough to realize that he was being exasperated without proper cause. When Joe Lyons lamented Nan's decision to Tom Ryan as though it were no better than suicide, the old man was thunder-struck. He had never mixed in society himself, which might be the reason that he had never got anywhere in life.

"You really think it would come to that, Joe?" he asked, scowling.

"But consider it yourself, Mr. Ryan," pleaded Joe, raising that warning finger of his. "Who is going to receive them? They can always come to my house, but I'm not everybody. Do you think they'll be invited to the Healys'? I say, the moment they marry, Matt will drop them, and I won't blame him. It's a game, admitted, but you have to play it. Even I have to play it, and my only interest is in philosophy."

By the end of the evening, Tom Ryan had managed to persuade himself that Mick was almost a ne'er-do-well and certainly an adventurer. The propect of the Dublin job did not satisfy him in the least. He wanted to know what Mick proposed to do then. Rest on his oars? There were examinations he could take which would insure his chances of promotion. Tom would arrange it all and coach him himself.

At first Mick was amused and patient; then he became sarcastic, a great weakness of his whenever he was forced on the defensive. Tom Ryan, who was as incapable as a child of understanding sarcasm, rubbed his bald head angrily and left the room in a flurry. If Mick had only hit him over the head, as his wife did whenever he got on her nerves, Tom would have understood that he was only relieving his feelings and liked him the better for it. But sarcasm was to him a sort of silence, a denial of attention that hurt him bitterly.

"I wish you wouldn't speak to Daddy like that," Nan said one night when her father had been buzzing about Mick with syllabuses he had refused even to look at.

"I wish Daddy would stop arranging my life for me," Mick said wearily.

"He only means it in kindness."

"I didn't think he meant it any other way," Mick said stiffly. "But I wish he'd get it into his head that I'm marrying you, not him."

"I wouldn't be too sure of that either, Mick," she said angrily.

"Really, Nan!" he said reproachfully. "Do you want me to be pushed round by your old man?"

"It's not only that," she said, rising and crossing the room to the fireplace. He noticed that when she lost her temper, she suddenly seemed to lose command of her beauty. She scowled, bowed her head, and walked with a heavy guardsman's tread. "It's just as well we've had this out because I'd have had to tell you anyway. I've thought about it enough, God knows. I can't possibly marry you."

Her tone was all that was necessary to bring Mick back to his own tolerant, reasonable self.

"Why not?" he asked gently.

"Because I'm scared, if you want to know." And just then, looking down at him, she seemed scared.

"Of marriage?"

"Of marriage as well." He noticed the reservation.

"Of me, so?"

"Oh, of marriage and you and myself," she said explosively. "Myself most of all."

"Afraid you may kick over the traces?" he asked with affectionate mockery.

"You think I wouldn't?" she hissed with clenched fists, her eyes narrowing and her face looking old and grim. "You don't understand me at all, Mick Courtney," she added with a sort of boyish braggadocio that made her seem again like the little tomboy he had known. "You don't even know the sort of things I'm capable of. You're wrong for me. I always knew you were."

Mick treated the scene lightly, as though it were merely another of their disagreements, but when he left the house he was both hurt and troubled. Clearly there was a side of her character that he did not understand, and he was a man who liked to understand things, if only so that he could forget about them and go on with his own thoughts. Even on the familiar hill-street, with the gas lamp poised against the night sky, he seemed to be walking a road without associations. He knew Nan was unhappy and felt it had nothing to do with the subject of their quarrel. It was unhappiness that had driven her into his arms in the first place, and now it was as though she were being driven out again by the same wind. He had assumed rather too complacently that she had turned to him in the first place because she had seen through Healy and Lyons, but now he felt that her unhappiness had nothing to do with them either. She was desperate about herself rather than them. It struck him that she might easily have been tempted too far by Lyons's good looks and kindness. She was the sort of passionate girl who could very easily be lured into an indiscretion, and who would then react from it in loathing and self-disgust. The very thought that this might be the cause moved him to a passion of protective tenderness, and before he went to bed he wrote and posted an affectionate letter, apologizing for his rudeness to her father and promising to consider her feelings more in the future.

In reply, he got a brief note, delivered at his house while he was at work. She did not refer at all to his letter, and told him that she was marrying Lyons. It was a dry note and, for him, full of suppressed malice. He left his own house and met Dinny on the way up to call for him. From Dinny's gloomy air Mick saw that he knew all about it. They went for one of their usual country walks, and only when they were sitting in a country pub over their beer did Mick speak of the breach.

Dinny was worried and his worry made him rude, and through the rudeness Mick seemed to hear the voices of the Ryans discussing him. They hadn't really thought much of him as a husband for Nan, but had been prepared to put up with him on her account. At the same time there was no question in their minds but that she didn't really care for Lyons and was marrying him only in some mood of desperation induced by Mick. Obviously, it was all Mick's fault.

"I can't really imagine what I did," Mick said reasonably. "Your father started bossing me, and I was rude to him. I know that, and I told Nan I was sorry."

"Oh, the old man bosses us all, and we're all rude," said Dinny. "It's not that."

"Then it's nothing to do with me," Mick said doggedly.

"Maybe not," replied Dinny without conviction. "But, whatever it is, the harm is done. You know how obstinate Nan is when she takes an idea into her head."

"And you don't think I should see her and ask her?"

"I wouldn't," said Dinny, looking at Mick directly for the first time. "I don't think Nan will marry you, old man, and I'm not at all sure but that it might be the best thing for you. You know I'm fond of her, but she's a curious girl. I think you'll only hurt yourself worse than you're hurt already."

Mick realized that Dinny, for whatever reasons, was advising him to quit, and for once he was in a position to do so. With the usual irony of events, the job in Dublin he had been seeking only on her account had been offered to him, and he would have to leave at the end of the month.

This, which had seemed an enormous break with his past, now turned out to be the very best solace for his troubled mind. Though he missed old friends and familiar places more than most people, he had the sensitiveness of his type to any sort of novelty, and soon ended by wondering how he could ever have stuck Cork for so long. Within twelve months he had met a nice girl called Eilish and married her. And though Cork people might be parochial, Eilish believed that anything that didn't happen between Glasnevin and Terenure had not happened at all. When he talked to her of Cork, her eyes simply glazed over.

So entirely did Cork scenes and characters fade from his memory that it came as a shock to him to meet Dinny one fine day in Grafton Street. Dinny was on his way to his first job in England, and Mick at once invited him home. But before they left town they celebrated their reunion in Mick's favorite pub off Grafton Street. Then he could ask the question that had sprung to his mind when he caught sight of Dinny's face.

"How's Nan?"

"Oh, didn't you hear about her?" Dinny asked with his usual air of mild surprise. "Nan's gone into a convent, you know."

"Nan?" repeated Mick. "Into a convent?"

"Yes," said Dinny. "Of course, she used to talk of it when she was a kid, but we never paid much attention. It came as a surprise to us. I fancy it surprised the convent even more," he added dryly.

"For God's sake!" exclaimed Mick. "And the fellow she was engaged to? Lyons."

"Oh, she dropped him inside a couple of months," said Dinny with distaste. "I never thought she was serious about him anyway. The fellow is a damned idiot."

Mick went on with his drink, suddenly feeling embarrassed and strained. A few minutes later he asked, with the pretense of a smile:

"You don't think if I'd hung on she might have changed her mind?"

"I dare say she might," Dinny replied sagaciously. "I'm not so sure it would have been the best thing for you, though," he added kindly. "The truth is I don't think Nan is the marrying kind."

"I dare say not," said Mick, but he did not believe it for an instant. He was quite sure that Nan was the marrying kind, and that nothing except the deep unhappiness that had first united and then divided them had kept her from marrying. But what that unhappiness was about he still had no idea, and he saw that Dinny knew even less than he did.

Their meeting had brought it all back, and at intervals during the next few years it returned again to his mind, disturbing him. It was not that he was unhappy in his own married life—a man would have to have something gravely wrong with him to be unhappy with a girl like Eilish—but sometimes in the morning when he kissed her at the gate and went swinging down the ugly modern avenue towards the sea, he would think of the river or the hills of Cork and of the girl who had seemed to have none of his pleasure in simple things, whose decisions seemed all to have been dictated by some inner torment.

THEN, long after, he found himself alone in Cork, tidying up things after the death of his father, his last relative there, and was suddenly plunged back into the world of his childhood and youth, wandering like a ghost from street to street, from pub to pub, from old friend to old friend, resurrecting other ghosts in a mood that was half anguish, half delight. He walked out Blackpool and up Goulding's Glen only to find that the big mill-pond had all dried up, and sat on the edge remembering winter days when he was a child and the pond was full of skaters, and summer nights when it was full of stars. His absorption in the familiar made him peculiarly susceptible to the poetry of change. He visited the Ryans and found Mrs. Ryan almost as good-looking and pattable as ever, though she moaned sentimentally about the departure of her boys, her disappointment with Nan, and her husband's growing crankiness.

When she saw him to the door she folded her arms and leaned against the jamb.

"Wisha, Mick, wouldn't you go and see her?" she asked reproachfully.

"Nan?" said Mick. "You don't think she'd mind?"

"Why would she mind, boy?" Mrs. Ryan said with a shrug. "Sure the girl must be dead for someone to talk to! Mick, boy, I was never one for criticizing religion, but, God forgive me, that's not a natural life at all. I wouldn't stand it for a week. All those old hags!"

Mick, imagining the effect of Mrs. Ryan on any well-organized convent, decided that God would probably not hold it too much against her, but he made up his mind to visit Nan. The convent was on one of the steep hills outside the city, with a wide view of the valley from its front lawn. He was expecting a change, but her appearance in the ugly convent parlor startled him. The frame of white linen and black veil gave her strongly marked features the unnatural relief of a fifteenth-century German portrait. And the twinkle of the big brown eyes convinced him of an idea that had been forming slowly in his mind through the years.

"Isn't it terrible I can't kiss you, Mick?" she said with a chuckle. "I suppose I could, really, but our old chaplain is a terror. He thinks I'm the New Nun. He's been hearing about her all his life, but I'm the first he's run across. Come into the garden where we can talk," she added with an awed glance at the holy pictures on the walls. "This place would give you the creeps. I'm at them the whole time to get rid of that Sacred Heart. It's Bavarian, of course. They love it."

Chattering on, she rustled ahead of him on to the lawn with her head bowed. He knew from the little flutter in her voice and manner that she was as pleased to see him as he was to see her. She led him to a garden seat behind a hedge that hid them from the convent, and then grabbed in her enthusiastic way at his hand.

"Now, tell me all about you," she said. "I heard you were married to a very nice girl. One of the sisters went to school with her. She says she's a saint. Has she converted you yet?"

"Do I look as if she had?" he asked with a pale smile.

"No," she replied with a chuckle. "I'd know that agnostic look of yours anywhere. But you needn't think you'll escape me all the same."

"You're a fierce pray-er," he quoted, and she burst into a delighted laugh.

"It's true," she said. "I am. I'm a terror for holding on."

"Really?" he asked mockingly. "A girl that let two men slip in— what was it? a month?"

"Ah, that was different," she said with sudden gravity. "Then there were other things at stake. I suppose God came first." Then she looked at him slyly out of the corner of her eye. "Or do you think I'm only talking nonsense?"

"What else is it?" he asked.

"I'm not, really," she said. "Though I sometimes wonder myself how it all happened," she added with a rueful shrug. "And it's not that I'm not happy here. You know that?"

"Yes," he said quietly. "I've suspected that for quite a while."

"My," she said with a laugh, "you *have* changed!"

He had not needed her to say that she was happy, nor did he need her to tell him why. He knew that the idea that had been forming in his mind for the last year or two was the true one, and that what had happened to her was not something unique and inexplicable. It was something that happened to others in different ways. Because of some inadequacy in themselves—poverty or physical weakness in men, poverty or ugliness in women—those with the gift of creation built for themselves a rich interior world; and when the inadequacy disappeared and the real world was spread before them with all its wealth and beauty, they could not give their whole heart to it. Uncertain of their choice, they wavered between goals—were lonely in crowds, dissatisfied amid noise and laughter, unhappy even with those they loved best.

The interior world called them back, and for some it was a case of having to return there or die.

He tried to explain this to her, feeling his own lack of persuasiveness, and at the same time aware that she was watching him keenly and with amusement, almost as though she did not take him seriously. Perhaps she didn't, for which of us can feel, let alone describe, another's interior world? They sat there for close on an hour, listening to the convent bells calling one sister or another, and Mick refused to stay for tea. He knew convent tea parties, and had no wish to spoil the impression that their meeting had left on him.

"Pray for me," he said with a smile as they shook hands.

"Do you think I ever stopped?" she replied with a mocking laugh, and he strode quickly down the shady steps to the lodge-gate in a strange mood of rejoicing, realizing that, however the city might change, that old love affair went on unbroken in a world where disgust or despair would never touch it, and would continue to do so till both of them were dead.

Fish for Friday

NED MACCARTHY, the teacher in a village called Abbeyduff, was wakened one morning by his sister-in-law. She was standing over him with a cynical smile and saying in a harsh voice:

"Wake up! 'Tis started."

"What's started, Sue?" Ned asked wildly, jumping up in bed with an anguished air.

"Why?" she asked dryly. "Are you after forgetting already? You'd better dress and go for the doctor."

"Oh, the doctor!" sighed Ned, remembering all at once why he was sleeping alone in the little back room and why that unpleasant female who so obviously disapproved of him was in the house.

He dressed in a hurry, said a few words of encouragement to his wife, talked to the children while swallowing a cup of tea, and got out the old car. He was a sturdy man in his early forties with fair hair and pale gray eyes, nervous and excitable. He had plenty to be excitable about—the house, for instance. It was a fine house, an old shooting lodge, set back at a distance of two fields from the road, with a lawn in front leading to the river and steep gardens climbing the wooded hills behind. It was, in fact, an ideal house, the sort he had always dreamed of, where Kitty could keep a few hens and he could dig the garden and get in a bit of shooting. But scarcely had he settled in when he realized it had all been a mistake. A couple of rooms in town would have been better. The loneliness of the long evenings when dusk had settled on the valley was something he had never even imagined.

He had lamented it to Kitty, who had suggested the old car, but even this had its drawbacks because the car demanded as much attention as a baby. When Ned was alone in it he chatted to it encouragingly; when it stopped because he had forgotten to fill the tank he kicked it viciously, as if it were a wicked dog, and the villagers swore that he had actually been seen stoning it. This, coupled with the fact that he sometimes talked to himself when he hadn't the car to talk to, had given rise to the legend that he had a slate loose.

He drove down the lane and across the little footbridge to the main road, and then stopped before the public-house at the corner, which his friend Tom Hurley owned.

"Anything you want in town, Tom?" he shouted from the car.

"What's that, Ned?" replied a voice from within, and Tom himself, a small, round, russet-faced man, came out with his wrinkled grin.

"I have to go into town. I wondered, was there anything you wanted?"

"No, no, Ned, thanks, I don't think so," replied Tom in his nervous way, all the words trying to come out together. "All we wanted was fish for the dinner, and the Jordans are bringing that."

"That stuff!" exclaimed Ned, making a face. "I'd sooner 'twas them than me."

"Och, isn't it the devil, Ned?" Tom spluttered with a similar expression of disgust. "The damn smell hangs round the shop all day. But what the hell else can you do on a Friday? You going for a spin?"

"No," replied Ned with a sigh. "It's Kitty. I have to call the doctor."

"Oh, I see," said Tom, beginning to beam. His expression exaggerated almost to caricature whatever emotion his interlocutor might be expected to feel. "Ah, please God, it'll go off all right. Come in and have a drink."

"No, thanks, Tom," Ned said with resignation. "I'd better not."

"Ah, hell to your soul, you will," fussed Tom. "It won't take you two minutes. Hard enough it was for me to keep you off it the time the first fellow arrived."

"That's right, Tom," Ned said in surprise as he left the car and followed Tom into the pub. "I'd forgotten about that. Who was it was here?"

"Ah, God!" moaned Tom, "you had half the countryside in here. Jack Martin and Owen Hennessey, and that publican friend of yours from town—Cronin, ay, Cronin. There was a dozen of ye here. The milkman found ye next morning, littering the floor, and ye never even locked the doors after ye! Ye could have had my license endorsed on me."

"Do you know, Tom," Ned said with a complacent smile, "I'd forgotten about that completely. My memory isn't what it was. I suppose we're getting old."

"Ah, well," Tom said philosophically, pouring out a large drink for Ned and a small one for himself, " 'tis never the same after the first. Isn't it astonishing, Ned, the first," he added in his eager way, bending over the counter, "what it does to you? God, you feel as if you were beginning life again. And by the time the second comes, you're beginning to wonder will the damn thing ever stop. . . . God forgive me for talking," he whispered, beckoning over his shoulder with a boyish smile. "Herself wouldn't like to hear me."

" 'Tis true just the same, Tom," Ned said broodingly, relieved at understanding a certain gloom he had felt during the preceding weeks. "It's not the same. And that itself is only an illusion. Like when you fall in love, and think you're getting the one woman in the world, while all the time it's just one of Nature's little tricks for making you believe you're enjoying yourself when you're only putting yourself wherever she wants you."

"Ah, well," said Tom with his infectious laugh, "they say it all comes back when you're a grandfather."

"Who the hell wants to be a grandfather?" asked Ned with a sniff, already feeling sorry for himself with his home upset, that unpleasant female in the house, and more money to be found.

He drove off, but his mood had darkened. It was a beautiful bit of road between his house and the town, with the river below him on the left, and the hills at either side with the first wash of green on them like an unfinished sketch, and, walking or driving, it was usually a delight to him because of the thought of civilization at the other end. It was only a little seaside town, but it had shops and pubs and villas with electric light, and a water supply that did not fold up in May, and there were all sorts of interesting people to be met there, from summer visitors to Government inspectors with the latest news from Dublin. But now his heart didn't rise. He realized that the rapture of being a father does not repeat itself, and it gave him no pleasure to think of being a grandfather. He was decrepit enough as he was.

At the same time he was haunted by some memory of days when he was not decrepit, but careless and gay. He had been a Volunteer and roamed the hills for months with a column, wondering where he would spend the night. Then it had all seemed uncomfortable and dangerous enough, and, maybe like the illusion of regeneration at finding himself a father, it had been merely an illusion of freedom, but, even so, he felt he had known it and now knew it no more. It was linked in his mind with high hills and wide vistas, but now his life seemed to have descended into a valley like that he was driving along, with the river growing deeper and the hills higher as they neared the sea. He had descended into it by the quiet path of duty: a steady man, a sucker for responsibilities—treasurer of the Hurling Club, treasurer of the Republican Party, secretary for three other organizations. Bad! Bad! He shook his head reprovingly as he looked at the trees, the river, and the birds who darted from the hedges as he approached, and communed with the car.

"You've nothing to complain of, old girl," he said encouragingly. "It's all Nature. It gives you an illusion of freedom, but all the time it's bending you to its own purposes as if you were only cows or trees."

Being nervous, he didn't like to drive through a town. He did it when he had to, but it made him flustered and fidgety so that he missed seeing whoever was on the streets, and the principal thing about a town was meeting people. He usually parked his car outside Cronin's pub on the way in, and then walked the rest of the way. Larry Cronin was an old comrade of revolutionary days who had married into the pub.

He parked the car and went to tell Larry. This was quite unnecessary as Larry knew every car for miles around and was well aware of Ned's little weakness, but it was a habit, and Ned was a man of more habits than he realized himself.

"I'm just leaving the old bus for half an hour, Larry," he called through the door in a plaintive tone that conveyed regret for the inconvenience he was causing Larry and grief for the burden being put on himself.

"Come in, man, come in!" cried Larry, a tall, engaging man with a handsome face and a wide smile that was quite sincere if Larry liked you and damnably hypocritical if he didn't. His mouth was like a show-case with the array of false teeth in it. "What the hell has you out at this hour of morning?"

"Oh, Nature, Nature," said Ned with a laugh, digging his hands in his trouser pockets.

"How do you mean, Nature?" asked Larry, who did not understand the allusive ways of intellectuals but appreciated them none the less.

"Kitty, I mean," Ned said. "I'm going to get the doctor. I told you she was expecting again."

"Ah, the blessings of God on you!" Larry cried jovially. "Is this the third or the fourth? Christ, you lose count, don't you? You might as well have a drop as you're here. For the nerves, I mean. 'Tis hard on the nerves. That was a hell of a night we had the time the boy was born."

"Wasn't it?" said Ned, beaming at being reminded of something that seemed to have become a legend. "I was just talking to Tom Hurley about it."

"Ah, what the hell does Hurley know about it?" asked Larry, filling him out a drink in his lordly way. "The bloody man went to bed at two. That fellow is too cautious to be good. But Martin gave a great account of himself. Do you remember? The whole first act of *Tosca*, orchestra and all. Tell me, you didn't see Jack since he was home?"

"Jack?" Ned exclaimed in surprise, looking up from his drink. (He felt easier in his mind now, being on the doctor's doorstep.) "Was Jack away?"

"Arrah, Christ, he was," said Larry, throwing his whole weight on the counter. "In Paris, would you believe it? He's on the batter again, of course. Wait till you hear him on Paris! 'Tis only the mercy of God if the parish priest doesn't get to hear of it. Martin would want to mind himself."

"That's where you're wrong, Larry," Ned said with sudden bitterness, not so much against Jack Martin as against Life itself. "Martin doesn't have to mind himself. The parish priest will mind him. If an inspector comes snooping round while Martin is on it, Father Clery will be taking him out to look at antiquities."

"Ah, 'tis the God's truth for you," Larry said in mournful disapproval. "But you or I couldn't do it. Christ, man, we'd get slaughtered alive. 'Tisn't worried you are about Kitty?" he asked in a gentler tone.

"Ah, no, Larry," said Ned. "It's not that. It's just that at times like this a man feels himself of no importance. You know what I mean? A messenger boy would do as well. We're all dragged down to the same level."

"And damn queer we'd be if we weren't," said Larry with his good-natured smile. "Unless, that is, you'd want to have the bloody baby yourself."

"Ah, it's not only that, Larry," Ned said irritably. "It's not that at all. But a man can't help thinking."

"Why, then indeed, that's true for you," said Larry, who, as a result of his own experience in the pub, had developed a gloomy and philosophic view of human existence. After all, a man can't be looking at schizophrenia for ten hours a day without feeling that Life isn't simple. "And 'tis at times like this you notice it—men coming and going, like the leaves on the trees. Isn't it true for me?"

But that wasn't what Ned was thinking about at all. He was thinking of his lost youth and what had happened in it to turn him from a firebrand into a father.

"No, Larry, that's not what I mean," he said, drawing figures on the counter with the bottom of his glass. "It's just that you can't help wondering what's after happening you. There were so many things you wanted to do that you didn't do, and you wonder if you'd done them would it be different. And here you are, forty-odd, and your life is over and nothing to show for it! It's as if when you married some good went out of you."

"Small loss, as the fool said when he lost Mass," retorted Larry, who had found himself a comfortable berth in the pub and lost his thirst for adventure.

"That's the bait, of course," Ned said with a grim smile. "That's where Nature gets us every time."

"Arrah, what the hell is wrong with Nature?" asked Larry. "When your first was born you were walking mad around the town, looking for people to celebrate it with. Now you sound as though you were looking for condolences. Christ, man, isn't it a great thing to have someone to share your troubles and give a slap in the ass to, even if she does let the crockery fly once in a while? What the hell about an old bit of china?"

"That's all very well, Larry," Ned said, scowling, "if—*if*, mind—that's all it costs."

"And what the hell else does it cost?" asked Larry. "Twenty-one meals a week and a couple of pounds of tea on the side. Sure, 'tis for nothing!"

"But *is* that all?" Ned asked fiercely. "What about the days on the column?"

"Ah, that was different, Ned," Larry said with a sigh while his eyes took on a faraway look. "But, sure, everything was different then. I don't know what the hell is after coming over the country at all."

"The same thing that's come over you and me," said Ned. "Middle age. But we had our good times, even apart from that."

"Oh, begod, we had, we had," Larry admitted wistfully.

"We could hop in a car and not come home for a fortnight if the fancy took us."

"We could, man, we could," said Larry, showing a great mouthful of teeth. "Like the time we went to the Junction Races and came back by Donegal. Ah, Christ, Ned, youth is a great thing. Isn't it true for me?"

"But it wasn't only youth," cried Ned. "We had freedom, man. Now our lives are run for us by women the way they were when we were kids. This is Friday, and and what do I find? Hurley waiting for someone to bring home the fish. You're waiting for the fish. I'll go home to a nice plate of fish. One few words in front of an altar, and it's fish for Friday the rest of our lives."

"Still, Ned, there's nothing nicer than a good bit of fish," Larry said dreamily. "If 'tis well done, mind you. *If* 'tis well done. And 'tisn't often you get it well done. I grant you that. God, I had some fried plaice in Kilkenny last week that had me turned inside out. I declare to God, if I stopped that car once I stopped it six times, and by the time I got home I was shaking like an aspen."

"And yet I can remember you in Tramore, letting on to be a Protestant just to get bacon and eggs," Ned said accusingly.

"Oh, that's the God's truth," Larry said with a wondering grin. "I was a devil for meat, God forgive me. It used to make me mad, seeing the Protestants lowering it. And the waitress, Ned—do you remember the waitress that wouldn't believe I was a Protestant till I said the Our Father the wrong way for her? She said I had too open a face for a Protestant. How well she'd know a thing like that about the Our Father, Ned?"

"A woman would know anything she had to know to make a man eat fish," Ned said, rising with gloomy dignity. "And you may be reconciled to it, Larry, but I'm not. I'll eat it because I'm damned with a sense of duty, and I don't want to get Kitty into trouble with the neighbors, but with God's help I'll see one more revolution before I die if I have to swing for it."

"Ah, well," sighed Larry, "youth is a great thing, sure enough. . . . Coming, Hanna, coming!" he replied as a woman's voice yelled from the bedroom above them. He gave Ned a smug wink to suggest that he enjoyed it, but Ned knew that that scared little rabbit of a wife of his would be wanting to know what all the talk was about his being a Protestant, and would then go to Confession and tell the priest that her husband had said heretical prayers and ask him was it a reserved sin and should Larry go to the Bishop. It was no life, no life, Ned thought as he sauntered down the hill past the church. And it was a great mistake taking a drink whenever he felt badly about the country, because it always made the country seem worse.

Suddenly someone clapped him on the shoulder. It was Jack Martin, the vocational-school teacher, a small, plump, nervous man, with a baby complexion, a neat graying mustache, and big blue innocent eyes. Ned's grim face lit up. Of all his friends, Martin was the one he warmed to most. He was a talented man and a good baritone. His wife had died a few years before and left him with two children, but he had never married again and had been a devoted, if overanxious, father. Yet always two or three times a year, particularly approaching his wife's anniversary, he went on a tearing drunk that left some legend behind. There was the time he had tried to teach Italian music to the tramp who played the penny whistle in the street, and the time his house-keeper had hidden his trousers and he had shinned down the drainpipe and appeared in the middle of town in pajamas, bowing in the politest way possible to the ladies who passed.

"MacCarthy, you scoundrel!" he said delightedly in his shrill nasal voice, "you were hoping to give me the slip. Come in here one minute till I tell you something. God, you'll die!"

"If you'll just wait there ten minutes, Jack, I'll be along to you," Ned said eagerly. "There's just one job, one little job I have to do, and then I'll be able to give you my full attention."

"Yes, but you'll have one drink before you go," Martin said cantankerously. "You're not a messenger boy yet. One drink and I'll release you on your own recognizances to appear when required. You'll never guess where I was, Ned. I woke up there—as true as God!"

Ned, deciding good-humoredly that five minutes' explanation in the bar was easier than ten minutes' argument in the street, allowed himself to be steered to a table by the door. It was quite clear that Martin was "on it." He was full of clockwork vitality, rushing to the counter for fresh drinks, fumbling for money, trying to carry glasses without spilling, and talking, talking, all the time. Ned beamed at him. Drunk or sober, he liked the man.

"Ned," Martin burst out ecstatically, "I'll give you three guesses where I was."

"Let me see," said Ned in mock meditation. "I suppose 'twould never be Paris?" and then laughed outright at Martin's injured air.

"You can't do anything in this town," Martin said bitterly. "I suppose next you'll be telling me about the women I met there."

"No," said Ned gravely, "it's Father Clery who'll be telling you about them—from the pulpit."

"To hell with Clery!" snapped Martin. "No, Ned, this is se-e-e-rious. It only came to me in the past week. You and I are wasting our bloody time in this bloody country."

"Yes, Jack," said Ned, settling himself in his seat with sudden gravity, "but what else can you do with Time?"

"Ah, this isn't philosophy, man," Martin said testily. "This is—is se-e-e-rious, I tell you."

"I know how serious it is, all right," Ned said complacently, "because I was only saying it to Larry Cronin ten minutes ago. Where the hell is our youth gone?"

"But that's only a waste of time, too, man," Martin said impatiently. "You couldn't call that youth. Drinking bad porter in pubs after closing time and listening to somebody singing 'The Rose of Tralee.' That's not life, man."

"No," said Ned, nodding, "but what is life?"

"How the hell would I know?" asked Martin. "I suppose you have to go out and look for it the way I did. You're not going to find the bloody thing here. You have to go south, where they have sunlight and wine and good cookery and women with a bit of go in them."

"And don't you think it would be the same thing there?" Ned asked relentlessly while Martin raised his eyes to the ceiling and moaned.

"Oh, God, dust and ashes! Dust and ashes! Don't we get enough of that every Sunday from Clery? And Clery knows no more about it than we do."

Now, Ned was very fond of Martin, and admired the vitality with which in his forties he still pursued a fancy, but all the same he could not let him get away with the simpleminded notion that life was merely a matter of topography.

"That is a way life has," he pronounced oracularly. "You think you're seeing it, and it turns out it was somewhere else at the time. It's like women—the girl you lose is the one that could have made you happy. I suppose there are people in the south wishing they could be in some wild place like this—I admit it's not likely, but I suppose it could happen. No, Jack, we might as well resign ourselves to the fact that, wherever the hell life was, it wasn't where we were looking for it."

"For God's sake, man!" Martin exclaimed irritably. "You talk like a man of ninety-five."

"I'm forty-two," Ned said with quiet emphasis, "and I have no illusions left. You still have a few. Mind," he went on with genuine warmth, "I admire you for it. You were never a fighting man like Cronin or myself, but you put up a better fight than either of us. But Nature has her claws in you as well. You're light and airy now, but what way will you be this time next week? And even now," he added threateningly, "even at this minute, you're only that way because you've escaped from the guilt for a little while. You've got down the drainpipe and you're walking the town in your night clothes, but sooner or later they'll bring you back and make you put your trousers on."

"But it isn't guilt, Ned," Martin interrupted. "It's my stomach. I can't keep it up."

"It isn't only your stomach, Jack," Ned said triumphantly, having at last steered himself into the open sea of argument. "It's not your stomach that makes you avoid me in the Main Street."

"Avoid you?" Martin echoed, growing red. "When did I avoid you?"

"You did avoid me, Jack," said Ned with a radiant smile of forgiveness. "I saw you, and, what's more, you said it to Cronin. Mind," he added generously, "I'm not blaming you. It's not your fault. It's the guilt. You're pursued by guilt the way I'm pursued by a sense of duty, and they'll bring the pair of us to our graves. I can even tell you the way you'll die. You'll be up and down to the chapel ten times a day for fear once wasn't enough, with your head bowed for fear you'd catch a friend's eye and be led astray, beating your breast, lighting candles, and counting indulgences, and every time you see a priest your face will light up as if he was a pretty girl, and you'll raise your hat and say 'Yes, father,' and 'No, father,' and 'Father, whatever you please.' And it won't be your fault. That's the real tragedy of life, Jack—we reap what we sow."

"I don't know what the hell is after coming over you," Martin said in bewilderment. "You—you're being positively personal, MacCarthy. I never tried to avoid anybody. I resent that statement. And the priests know well enough the sort I am. I never tried to conceal it."

"I know, Jack, I know," Ned said gently, swept away by the flood of his own melancholy rhetoric, "and I never accused you of it. I'm not being personal, because it's not a personal matter. It's Nature working through you. It works through me as well, only it gets me in a different way. I turn every damn thing into a duty, and in the end I'm fit for nothing. And I know the way I'll die too. I'll disintegrate into a husband, a father, a schoolmaster, a local librarian, and fifteen different sort of committee officials, and none of them with justification enough to remain alive—unless I die on a barricade."

"What barricade?" asked Martin, who found all this hard to follow.

"Any barricade," said Ned wildly. "I don't care what 'tis for so long as 'tis a fight. I don't want to be a messenger boy. I'm not even a good one. Here I am, arguing with you in a pub instead of doing what I was sent to do. Whatever the hell that was," he added with a hearty laugh as he realized that for the moment—only for the moment, of course—he had forgotten what it was. "Well, that beats everything," he said with a grin. "But you see what I mean. What duty does for you. I'm after forgetting what I came for."

"Ah, that's only because it wasn't important," said Martin, who was anxious to talk of Paris.

"That's where you're wrong again, Jack," said Ned, really beginning to enjoy the situation. "Maybe, 'twas of no importance to us but it was probably of great importance to Nature. It's we that aren't important. What was the damn thing? My memory has gone to hell. One moment. I have to close my eyes and empty my mind. That's the only way I have of beating it."

He closed his eyes and lay back limply in his seat, though even through his self-induced trance he smiled lightly at the absurdity of it all.

"No good," he said, starting out of it briskly. "It's an extraordinary thing, the way it disappears as if the ground opened and swallowed it. And there's nothing you can do. 'Twill come back of its own accord, and there won't be rhyme nor reason to that either. I was reading an article about a German doctor who says you forget because it's too unpleasant to think about."

"It's not a haircut?" Martin asked helpfully, but Ned, a tidy man, just shook his head.

"Or clothes?" Martin went on. "Clothes are another great thing with them."

"No," Ned said frowning. "I'm sure 'twas nothing for myself."

"Or for the kids? Shoes or the like?"

"Something flashed across my mind just then," murmured Ned.

"If it's not that it must be groceries."

"I don't see how it could," Ned said argumentatively. "Williams delivers them every week, and they're always the same."

"In that case," Martin said flatly, "it's bound to be something to eat. They're always forgetting things—bread or butter or milk."

"I suppose so," Ned said in bewilderment, "but I'm damned if I know what. Jim!" he called to the barman. "If you were sent on a message today, what would you say 'twould be?"

"Fish, Mr. Mac," the barman replied promptly. "Every Friday."

"Fish!" repeated Martin exultantly. "The very thing!"

"Fish?" repeated Ned, feeling that some familiar chord had been struck. "I suppose it could be. I know I offered to bring it to Tom Hurley, and I was having a bit of an argument with Larry Cronin about it. I remember he said he rather liked it."

"Like it?" cried Martin. "I can't stand the damn stuff, but the housekeeper has to have it for the kids."

"Ah, 'tis fish, all right, Mr. Mac," the barman said knowingly. "In an hour's time you wouldn't be able to forget it with the smell around the town."

"Well, obviously," Ned said, resigning himself to it, "it has something to do with fish. It may not be exactly fish, but it's something like it."

"Whether it is or not, she'll take it as kindly meant," said Martin comfortingly. "Like flowers. Women in this country seem to think they're alike."

"It's extraordinary," said Ned as they went out. "We have minds we have less control of than we have of our cars. Wouldn't you think with all their modern science they'd find some way of curing a memory like that?"

Two hours later the two friends, more loquacious than ever, drove up to Ned's house for lunch. "Mustn't forget the fish," Ned said as he reached back in the car for it. At that moment he heard the wail of a newborn infant and went very white.

"What the hell is that, Ned?" Martin asked in alarm.

"That, Martin," said Ned, "is the fish, I'm afraid."

"I won't disturb you, now, Ned," Martin said hastily, getting out of the car. "I'll get a snack from Tom Hurley."

"Courage, man!" said Ned frowningly. "Here you are and here you'll stop. But why fish, Martin? That's what I can't understand. Why did I think it was fish?"

A Set of Variations on
a Borrowed Theme

KATE MAHONEY was sixty when her husband died and, like many another widow, she had to face the loss of her little home.

Her two daughters, Nora and Molly, were married, and even if either of them had been in a position to offer her a home, she would have hesitated over it. As she said in her patient, long-suffering way to her old crony Hanna Dinan, they shouted too much. Hanna raised her head in mock surprise and exclaimed, "You don't say so, ma'am!" Kate looked at her reproachfully for a moment and then murmured with almost sensual bliss, "Oh, you cheeky thing." The truth was, as Hanna implied, that Kate shouted enough for a regimental sergeant-major, and the girls, both gentle and timid, had learned early in life that the only way of making themselves heard was to shout back. Kate didn't mind that; in fact, she rather enjoyed it. Nor did she shout all the time. She had another tone, which was low-pitched and monotonous, and in which she tended to break off a sentence as though she had forgotten what she was saying. But low-pitched or loud, her talk was monumental, like headstones. Her hands and legs were knotted with rheumatics, and she had a battered, inexpressive country woman's face, like a butcher's block, in which the only good feature was the eyes, which looked astonishingly girlish and merry. Maybe it would be only later that you would remember the hands—which were rarely still—fastening or unfastening a button on her blouse.

Her cottage was in a lane outside Cork. There was high rocky ground behind it that could never be built on, and though as a result it got little or no sunlight and another row of cottages between her and the roadway shut off the view, it was quiet and free of traffic. She wanted to die there, in the bed her husband had died in, but with the rheumatics she couldn't go out and do a day's work, as other widows did. It was this that made her think of taking in a foster child. It was a terrible comedown—more particularly for her, a respectable woman who had brought up two honest transactions of her own, but at her age what else could she do? So she took her problem to Miss Hegarty, the nurse.

Miss Hegarty was a fine-looking woman of good family, but so distracted with having to deal with the endless goings on of male and female that there were times she didn't seem right in the head. "Ahadie!" she would cry gaily to a woman in labor. "Fun enough you got out of starting it. Laugh now, why don't you?"

But Kate found her a good friend. She advised Kate against taking foster children from the local authorities, because they paid so badly that it was no better than slavery. The thing to do was to take the child of a girl of good family who could afford to maintain it.

"Ah, where would I meet a girl like that?" Kate asked humbly, and Miss Hegarty gave a loud, bitter laugh and stood up to lean against the mantelpiece with her arms folded.

" 'Tis easy seen you don't know much about it, Mrs. Mahoney," she said. "What chance, indeed, and the whole country crawling with them!"

"Oh, my!" said Kate.

"But I warn you, ma'am, that you can't rely on any of them," said Miss Hegarty. "They're so mad for men they'll go anywhere for them. And for all you know, a girl like that would be off next month to London and you might never hear of her again. The stick, ma'am, the stick is what the whole lot of them want."

Kate, however, decided to take the risk; there was something that appealed to her in the idea of a child of good family, and Miss Hegarty knew the very girl. She was the manageress of a store in Waterford, who had got entangled with a scoundrel whose name nobody even knew, but indeed he couldn't be much good to leave her that way. When Kate told her daughters, Nora, the flighty one, didn't seem to mind, but Molly, who was more sensitive, wept and begged her mother to come and live with them instead. "Oh yes, what a thing I'd do," said Kate, whose mind was made up. From Nora, who now had children of her own, she borrowed back the old family perambulator, and one spring morning it appeared again outside the door in the lane, with a baby boy asleep in it. "My first!" Kate shouted jocosely when any of the neighbors commented on it, and then she went on to explain, in the monotonous voice she used for solemn occasions, that this was no ordinary baby such as you'd get from the workhouse, without knowing who it was or where it came from, but the child of a beautiful educated girl from one of the best families in Waterford. She went on to tell how the poor child had been taken advantage of, and the neighbors tch-tch'd and agreed that it was a sad, sad story and didn't believe a word of it. The young married women didn't even pretend to believe in Kate's rigmarole. They muttered fiercely among themselves that you couldn't let decent children grow up alongside the likes of that, and that the priest or the landlord should put a stop to it. But they didn't say it too loud, for however embarrassed Kate might be by her situation she was a very obstinate old woman, and she had a dirty tongue when she was roused.

So Jimmy Mahoney was allowed to grow up in the lane along with the honest transactions, and turned into a fat, good-looking, moody boy, who seemed to see nothing peculiar in his mother's being a cranky old woman with a scolding tongue. On the contrary, he seemed to depend on her more than the other kids did on their mothers, and sometimes when she left him with Hanna Dinan and went off to see one of her daughters, he sat and sulked on the doorstep till she got home. One day when Hanna's back was turned, he went after Kate, right across the city to Molly's house on the Douglas Road. Kate, talking to Molly, glanced up and saw him glaring at her from the doorway and started, thinking that something must have happened to him and this was his ghost. "Oh, you pest!" she shouted when she saw that it wasn't. Then she gave him a grin. "I suppose it was the way you couldn't get on without me?"

Molly, a beautiful, haggard woman, gave him a smile of Christian charity and said quietly, "Come in, Jimmy." It was a thing she would not have wished for a pound, for it would have to be explained to her neighbors, and she felt it degraded them all. But after that, whatever she or Nora might think, Kate had to bring Jimmy with her by the hand. It didn't look right—their old mother in her black hat and coat hobbling up to the door with a child younger than their own by the hand.

Even then Jimmy wasn't satisfied. He wanted a brother or sister as well—preferably a brother. He had a great weakness for babies and was mad jealous of other boys who had babies to look after. "Every bloomin' fella in the road have a brudder or sister except me," he said to Kate. But she told him roughly that they couldn't afford it.

All the same, he got his wish. One evening Miss Hegarty came to her and asked if she would take in the child of a well-to-do girl in Bantry. The mother was engaged to marry a rich Englishman, but at the last moment she had thrown herself into a wild affair with a married man who had courted her when she was only seventeen. "Oh, my, my, the things that go on," sighed Kate.

"Mrs. Mahoney," Miss Hegarty cried, "don't talk to me about it! If you knew the half of it, it would make you lose your faith in religion."

Then and there Kate accepted. Later she felt she had been hasty. She needed the money, but not as badly as all that. When Nora came to see her and Kate told her what she had done, there was a terrible scene.

"Ah, Mammy, you're making a holy show of us!" Nora cried.

"*I'm* making a show of ye?" Kate pointed at her bosom with the mock-innocent air that had so often maddened her daughters. "I do my business, and I don't cost ye a penny. Is that what ye call making a show of ye?"

"Ah, you'd think we were something out of a circus instead of an old respectable family," Nora said. "That I can hardly face the neighbors when I come up the lane! Ahadie, 'tis well my poor daddy can't see what you're making of his house! He's the one that would deal with you. A woman of sixty-five! I suppose you think you're going to live forever."

"God is good," Kate muttered stiffly. "I might have a couple of years in me yet."

"You might," Nora said ironically. "And I suppose you imagine that if anything happens you, Molly and I will carry on the good work."

"Ye mightn't be asked," said Kate. "Their people have plenty—more than you'll ever be able to say." This was a dirty thrust at Nora, whose poor husband was not bright. "And how sure you are of yourself! My goodness, that we'd never do anything if we were to be always thinking of what might happen us. And what about my rent? Are you going to pay it?"

"Ah, 'tisn't the rent with you at all," Nora said. "Nor it never was. You only do it because you like it."

"I like it? An old woman like me that's crippled with the rheumatics? Oh, my, that 'tis in a home I ought to be if I had my rights. In a home!"

"Ah, I'd like to see the home that would keep you," Nora replied contemptuously. "Don't be making any more excuses. You love it, woman. And you care more about that little bastard than you ever did about Molly or me."

"How dare you?" Kate cried, rising with as much dignity as the rheumatics permitted. "What way is that to speak to your own mother? And to talk about a poor innocent child in my house like that, you dirty, jealous thing! Yes, jealous," she added in a wondering whisper as though the truth had only dawned on her in that moment. "Oh, my! Ye that had everything!"

THE SCENE upset her, but not because of the row with Nora; the Mahoneys always quarrelled like that, at the top of their lungs, as though they all suffered from congenital deafness, and they got the same pleasure out of it that a baby gets out of hammering a tin can. What really mortified her was that she had given herself away in front of Nora, whose intelligence she had no respect for. It was true that she had taken Jimmy in for perfectly good mercenary reasons; and it was very wrong of Nora to impute sentimental considerations to her—a determined, managing woman, who had lived that long with no thanks to anybody. But all the same, Nora wasn't altogether wrong. Motherhood was the only trade Kate knew, and though her rheumatics were bad and her sight wasn't what it used to be and she had to get Jimmy to thread her needles for her, she felt the older she got the better she practiced it. It was even true to say that she enjoyed Jimmy more than she had enjoyed her own children, but this was natural enough, because she hadn't the same anxieties about him. If you had pressed her hard enough, she would have said that if there was a better boy on the road she didn't know him. And was there anything wrong with that? You could say what you liked, but there was something in good blood.

She might have got angry if you had accused her of being an old dreamer who was really attracted by the romance and mystery of Jimmy's birth—something she had missed in her own sober and industrious life—but that was what she and Hanna enjoyed speculating about over a little glass when Jimmy was in bed. And later, when she had covered him for the night and lay awake in the next room saying her rosary, she would often forget her prayers and imagine how she would feel if one stormy night—one of those nights when the whole harbor seemed to move in on the town and try to push it down—there came a knock to the door and she saw Jimmy's father standing outside in the lane, tall and handsome, with a small black mustache and the tears in his eyes. "Mr. Mulvany," she would say to the teacher (she was always making up ideal names and occupations for Jimmy's father), "your son wants nothing from you." Or, if she was in a generous mood, "Senator MacDunphy, come in. Jimmy was beginning to think you'd never come."

Nora was right. Stupid or not, Nora had seen through her. She was an old fool. And when Miss Hegarty had dangled the extra money in front of her, it wasn't the money that appealed to her so much as the girl who had been ready to throw away her chances with the rich Englishman for the sake of one wild fling with an old sweetheart. "An old fool," Kate said to herself. She didn't feel repentant, though.

But dreamers are forever running into degrading practical realities, and there was one thing about her extraordinary family that Kate could do nothing about. Before she even laid eyes on him, the second boy was also christened James, and, so that Jimmy shouldn't be too upset and that she herself should do nothing against the law, she called him James—an unnatural name for any child, as she well knew. James was a baby with a big head, a gaping mouth, and a sickly countenance, and even from the first day he seemed to realize that he was in the world only on sufferance, and resigned himself to it. But Jimmy could see nothing wrong with him. He explored the neighborhood to study all the other babies, and told Kate that James was brighter than the whole lot of them. He adopted a possessive attitude, and wheeled the perambulator up and down the main road so that people could see for themselves the sort James was. When he came back, he reported with great satisfaction that three people, two men and a woman, had stopped him to admire his baby brother.

* * *

A COUPLE of times a year, Jimmy's real mother, whom he knew as Aunt Nance, came to stay with the friends in Cork who had arranged with Miss Hegarty for his being boarded out, and then Jimmy visited there and played with the two children, Rory and Mary. They were altogether too polite for Jimmy, but he liked his Aunt Nance a lot. She was tall and plump and good-looking, with a swarthy complexion and dark, dark hair. She talked in a crisp, nervous, almost common way, and was always forgetting herself and saying dirty words, like "Cripes!" and "Damn!," that only men were supposed to know. Kate liked him to go there, and when he got home, she asked him all sorts of questions about his visit, like how many rooms there were in the house, what he ate, what sort of furniture there was and the size of the garden—things that never interested Jimmy in the least.

When James began to grow up, he too asked questions. He wanted to know what school Rory and Mary went to, what they learned there, and whether or not Mary played the piano. These too were questions that did not interest Jimmy, but it dawned on him that James was lonely when he was left behind and wanted to see the Martins' place for himself. This seemed an excellent idea to Jimmy, because James was a steady quiet kid who would get on much better with Rory and Mary than he did, but when he suggested it Kate only said James was too young and Aunt Nance said she'd see.

It ended by his suspecting that there was something fishy about James. There always had been something unusual about him—as though he weren't a member of the family at all. He didn't like rough games and he preferred little girls to little boys. Jimmy didn't know how you did become a member of the family, but from what he could see your mother had either to go to the hospital or lie up in the house, and he couldn't remember that Kate had done either. James had just been there one morning when he woke. The more he thought of it, the surer he became that James was adopted. He didn't know what "adopted" meant, except that kids it happened to lived with people who weren't really related to them, and he found the idea of this very stimulating.

One evening, when Kate was complaining of her rheumatics, he asked her if she hadn't gone to hospital with it.

"Oye, why would I go to hospital?" she asked sourly. "I was never in one in my life and I hope I'll never have to go there."

James was sitting by the window, scribbling, and Jimmy didn't say anything more. But later, when James was in bed, he asked her casually, "You're not James's mother, are you, Mammy?"

He was surprised at the way she turned on him. "What's that you say?"

"Nothing, only that you're not James's mother."

"Who told you that?" she asked angrily.

"Nobody told me," he said, becoming defensive, "but you never went to hospital, like Mrs. Casey. You told me yourself."

"Don't let the child hear you saying things like that, you caffler!" she hissed.

"I never told him anything," he said sullenly. "But it's true, isn't it? That's the reason you get the money."

"Mind your own business!" she retorted.

Still, she was frightened. "Oh, my! The cunning of him!" she said next day to her old crony. "The way he cross-examined me—that poor Jack Mahoney never did the like! And what am I to say to him? Who will I get to advise me?"

Hanna, who had an answer for everything, was all for telling Jimmy the whole truth at once, but what did Hanna know about it and she an old maid? The other neighbors were inclined to think it was a judgment on Kate for her foolishness. And all the while, Jimmy's behavior got worse. At the best of times it wasn't very good. Though sometimes he was in high spirits and entertained herself and James telling funny stories, more often he was low-spirited and lay on his bed sulking over a comic. After that, he would go out with other boys and return with a guilty air she could spot from the end of the lane, and she would know he had been up to mischief and broken a window or stolen from a shop. At times like that, she was never free of anxiety for him, because apart from the fact that she had a holy terror of the law, she knew his naughtiness threatened the sufferance the neighbors extended to him on her account, and that they would be only too ready to say that it was all you could expect of a boy like that.

Finally, she decided to take Hanna Dinan's advice. But when James was asleep and she and Jimmy were sitting together in the darkness over the fire, she lost courage. She had no notion of how he would take it, and if he took it badly, she'd get the blame. She told him, instead, about James and his mother. She told him how some people, like herself, were lucky, because their fancy never strayed from the one person, while others, like James's mother, had the misfortune to love someone they couldn't marry. She was pleased by Jimmy's silent attention. She thought she had impressed him. But his first words startled her. "All the same, Mammy," he said, "James should be with his own mother."

She was astonished at the maturity in his tone. This was no longer any of the Jimmys she had known, but one who spoke with the sort of authority poor Jack had exercised on the rare occasions when he had called his family to order.

"Ah, how could he be with her?"

"Then she ought to tell him who he is and why she can't have him."

"Is it to be upsetting the child?" she asked complainingly.

"If she doesn't upset him, somebody else will," he said with his brooding, old-mannish air.

"They will, they will, God help us!" she sighed. "People are bad enough for anything. But the poor child may as well be happy while he can."

But it wasn't of James that she was thinking. James might get by, a colorless, studious, well-behaved boy who never gave offense to anybody, but one day Jimmy would beat up another boy or steal from a shop, and some woman would spite him by using the word Kate now dreaded—the word she had so often used lightly herself when she had no one to protect from it. Again she was tempted to tell him the whole truth, and again she was too afraid.

Meanwhile, for a short time at least, she had given Jimmy a purpose in life. Jimmy was always like that, either up or down, either full of purpose or shiftless and despondent. Now he took James over personally. He said it was bad for James to be so much alone, and took him along with him when he went down the Glen with the bigger boys. James didn't like being with the bigger boys. He liked to go at his own slow pace, gaping at everything, and he didn't in the least mind being left alone, but he was flattered by Jimmy's attention. When he came home he repeated his adventures to Kate in the manner of a policeman making a report. "Jimmy showed me a blackbird's nest. You can't touch a bird's nest, because the bird would know and leave the little eggs to die. I think it is wrong to rob a bird's nest, don't you, Mammy?" James collected bits of information, right and wrong, apparently thinking that they would all come in handy someday, and to each he managed to attach a useful moral lesson. No wonder he made Jimmy laugh.

But Jimmy still continued to worry about James's future. He waited till Aunt Nance came to Cork, and when he got her to himself he poured it all out to her in his enthusiastic way. He had managed to persuade himself that Kate didn't understand the seriousness of the situation but that Aunt Nance would. Before he had even finished, Aunt Nance gave him a queer look and cut him off. "You're too young to understand these things, Jimmy," she said.

"But don't *you* think he should be with his mother?" he asked indignantly.

"I don't know a thing about it, and if I did I wouldn't be able to do anything."

Jimmy left her in one of his mutinous, incoherent fits of rage. Instead of taking the bus, he walked, and when he reached the river he stood on the bank in the darkness throwing stones. It was late when he got home, but Kate was waiting up for him. He tossed his cap on the chair and went upstairs.

"What kept you?" she asked after him.

"Nothing."

"Don't you want a cup of tea?"

"I don't."

"He knows about it," Kate muttered to herself. "She must have told him. Now what'll I do?"

After a time she went upstairs to bed, but she heard him from the little attic room next door, where he and James slept, tossing and muttering to himself. She lit the candle and went in. He sat up in bed and looked at her with mad eyes.

"Go away!" he said. "You're not my mother."

"Oye!" she whimpered, sleepy and scared. "You and your goings on."

"You're not, you're not, you're not," he muttered. "I'm like James, only you wouldn't tell me. You tell me nothing but lies."

"Whisht, whisht, and don't wake the child!" she whispered impatiently. "You ought to be ashamed, a big boy like you. Come into the other room."

He stumbled out ahead of her, and she sat on the edge of her bed and put her arm round him. He was shivering. She no longer felt capable of handling him. She was old and tired and bothered in her head.

"What made you think of that, child?"

"Aunt Nance," he said with a sob.

"What did she tell you?"

"She wouldn't tell me anything, only I saw she was afraid."

"What was she afraid of?"

"I asked her to get James's mother to bring him home and she got frightened."

"Oh, oh, oh, you poor misfortunate child!" she said with a wail. "And you only did it for the best."

"I want to know who my mother is," he cried despairingly. "Is it Aunt Kitty or Aunt Nance?"

"Look, child, lie down here and you can sleep with Mammy."

"How can I sleep?" he asked frantically. "I only want to know who my mother is, and ye all tell me lies." Then, turning suddenly into a baby again, he put his head in her lap and bawled. She put her hand under his nightshirt and patted his fat bottom.

"Oh, you poor putog, you're perished," she sighed. Then she raised him onto the bed and pulled the covers about his shoulders.

"Will I get you a cup of tea?" she asked in a loud voice, and as he shook his head she muttered, "I will, I will."

She threw an old coat round her and went downstairs to the kitchen, where the oil lamp was turned low. There was still red ash in the grate, and she blew on it and boiled the kettle. Then her troubles seemed to get the better of her, and she spoke to herself in a loud, angry, complaining tone. " 'Twas the price of me for having anything to do with them—me that was never used to anything but decent people." When she heard herself she was ashamed. And then she shrugged, and whined, "I'm too old." As she climbed awkwardly back up the stairs with the two big mugs of tea, she heard him still sobbing, and stopped, turning her eyes to the ceiling. "God direct me!" she said aloud.

She sat on the edge of the bed and shook him. "Drink this!" she said roughly.

"I don't want it," said Jimmy. "I want to know who my mother is."

"Drink it, you dirty little caffler!" she said angrily. "Drink it or I won't tell you at all."

He raised himself in the big bed and she held the mug to his lips, though he could not keep himself from shivering and the tea spilled over his shirt and the bedclothes. "My good sheet," she muttered, and then took up her own cup and looked away into a corner of the room as if to avoid his eyes. "She is your mother, your Aunt Nance," she said in a harsh, expressionless voice, "and a good mother she is, and a good woman as well, and it will be a bad day for you when you talk against her or let anyone else do it. She had the misfortune to meet a man that was beneath her. She was innocent. He took advantage of her. She wasn't the first and she won't be the last."

He said nothing for a while, then he asked in a low voice, "And who was my daddy?"

"How would I know who he was? Whoever he was, he wasn't much."

"When I find out I'm going to kill him."

"Indeed you'll do nothing of the sort," she said sharply. "Whatever he did, he is your father and you wouldn't be here without him. He's there inside you, and the thing you will slight in yourself will be the rock you will perish on."

"And why did Aunt Nance like him if he was what you said?"

"Because she had no sense," said Kate. "What sense have any young girl? 'Tis unknown what they expect. If they had more sense they would be said by their fathers and mothers, that know what life is like, but they won't be said nor led by anyone. And the better they are the more they expect. That was all that was wrong with your mother, child. She was too innocent and too hopeful."

The dawn came in the window, and still she rambled on, half dead with sleep. Later, when she reported it to Hanna, she said that it was nothing but lies from beginning to end, and what other way could it be when she hadn't a notion how a girl like that would feel, but at the time it did not seem to be lies. It seemed rather as though she were reporting a complete truth that was known only to herself and God. And in a queer way it steadied Jimmy and brought out the little man in him.

"Mammy, does this mean that there's something wrong with James and me?" he asked at last, and she knew that this was the question that preoccupied him above all others.

"Indeed, it means nothing of the sort," she cried, and for the first time it seemed to herself that she was answering in her own person. "It is nothing. Only bad, jealous people would say the likes of that. Oh, you'll meet them, never fear," she said, joining her hands, "the scum of the earth with their marriage lines and their baptismal lines, looking down on their betters. But mark what I say, child, don't let any of them try and persuade you that you're not as good as them. And better! A thousand times better."

Strange notions from a respectable old woman who had never even believed in love!

WHAT it all meant was brought home to her when Jimmy was fourteen and James between eight and nine. Jimmy's mother married a commercial traveller from Dublin who accepted Jimmy as a normal event that might happen to any decent girl, and he had persuaded her they should have Jimmy to live with them. It came as a great shock to Kate, though why it should have done so she couldn't say, because for years it was she who had argued with Hanna Dinan that the time had come for Jimmy to get a proper education and mix with what she called his equals. Now she realized that she was as jealous and possessive as if she were his real mother. She had never slighted Jimmy's mother, or allowed anyone else to do so, but she did it now. "She neglected him when it suited her, and now when it suits her she wants him back," she said to Hanna, and when Hanna replied that Kate wasn't being fair, she snapped, "Let them that have it be fair. Them that haven't are entitled to their say."

Besides, Jimmy provoked her. He had no power of concealing his emotions, and she could see that he had thoughts only for the marvellous new world that was opening up before him. He returned in high spirits from an evening with his mother and his new stepfather, and told Kate and James all about his stepfather's car, and his house outside Rathfarnham, at the foot of the Dublin Mountains. He told Kate blithely that he would always come back for the holidays, and comforted James by saying that his turn would come next. When Kate burst out suddenly, "Yourself is all you think about—no thought for me or the child," he got frantic and shouted, "All right, I won't go if you don't want me to!"

"Who said I didn't want you to go?" she shouted. "How could I keep you and me with nothing? Go to the well-heeled ones! Go to the ones that can look after you!"

By the time he left, she had regained control of herself, and she and James went with him to the station. They were stopped several times by old neighbors, who congratulated Jimmy. At the station he broke down, but she suspected that his grief wouldn't last long. And she had the impression that James felt the parting more deeply, though he was a child who didn't show much what he felt. He seemed to have come into the world expecting this sort of thing.

And yet, curiously, next day, when she woke and remembered Jimmy was gone, she had a feeling of relief. She realized that she wasn't the one to look after him. He was too big and noisy and exacting; he needed a man to keep him in his place. And besides, now that she had become old and stiff and half blind, the housekeeping was more of a trial. She would decide to give the boys a treat, and go to town to get the stewing beef, and suddenly realize when she got back to the kitchen that she didn't remember how to make stew. Then she would close her eyes and pray that God would direct her how to make stew as she made it when she was a young married woman—"delicious" poor Jack used to say it was. James was an easier proposition altogether, a boy who would live forever on tea and sweet cakes, so long as he got the penny exercise books for his writings and drawings.

The loss of Jimmy showed her how precarious was her hold on James, and in the evenings, when they were alone, she sat with him before the kitchen fire and let him hold forth to her on what he was going to be when he grew up. It seemed, according to himself, he was going to be a statue, and sometimes Kate suspected that the child wouldn't notice much difference, because he was a bit that way already. Jimmy had been a great boy to raise a laugh, particularly against himself, and James seemed to think it was his duty to do the same, but if she was to be killed for it she couldn't laugh at James's jokes. And yet she knew that James was gentler, steadier, and more considerate. When you asked him to do anything you had to explain to him why, but you never had to explain it twice. "Jimmy have the fire, but James have the character" was how she put it to Hanna.

And yet she fretted over Jimmy as she wouldn't have fretted over

James. From Dublin he had sent her one postcard, that was all, and he hadn't replied to either of the letters James wrote to him. "As true as God, that fellow is in trouble," she said.

"It's not that, Mammy," said James, "it's just that he doesn't like writing."

"Who wants him to write? All I want is to know how he is. If he was dying that vagabond wouldn't tell me!"

It was a queer way for a woman to feel who had been congratulating herself on having got rid of him.

Then, one morning, she heard a hammering at the front door and knew that the thing she had been dreading had happened. Without even asking who it was, she stumbled down the stairs in the darkness. When she opened the door and saw Jimmy, she threw her arms about his neck. "Oh, child, child!" she whimpered. "Sure, I thought you'd never come home! How did you get here?"

"I came on the bike," he said with a swagger.

"You did, you did, you divil you, you did," she muttered, seeing the bicycle against the wall. And then, her voice rising to a squeal of anguish. "Are them your good trousers?"

"Who is it, Mammy?" James shouted from upstairs.

"Come down yourself," she said, and went to lay the fire. James came down the stairs sedately in his nightshirt. Jimmy went up to him with a grin, and it startled her to see how big and solid he looked beside the frail, spectacled boy.

"Hallo, James," Jimmy said, shaking hands. "I suppose you're sorry I'm back?"

"No, Jimmy," James said in a small voice, "I'm glad you're back. The house isn't the same without you."

"Put on your topcoat, you little divil!" cried Kate. "How often have I to be telling you not to go round like that? That fellow," she said to Jimmy, "he have the heart scalded in me. I'd want ten eyes and hands, picking things up after him. . . . Go on, you little gligeen!"

It was a joyous reunion in the little kitchen when the sun was just beginning to pick out the high ground behind the house. Kate marvelled how she had managed to listen to James all that time and the way Jimmy could tell a story. Whatever James told you, the point of it always seemed to be how clever he was. Jimmy's stories always showed him up as a fool, and somehow it never crossed your mind that he was a fool at all. And yet there was something about him this morning that didn't seem right.

"Never mind about that!" Kate cried at last. "Tell us what your mother said."

"How do you mean?" asked Jimmy, turning red.

"What did she say when you told her you were coming back?"

"She didn't say anything," Jimmy replied with a brassy air. "She doesn't mind what I do."

"She doesn't, I hear," Kate retorted mockingly. "I suppose 'twas jealous you were?"

"What would I be jealous of?" Jimmy asked defiantly.

"Your stepfather, who else?" she said, screwing up her eyes in mockery at him. "You wanted all the attention. And now she'll be blaming it all on me. She'll be saying I have you spoiled. And she'll be right. I have you ruined, you little caffler! Ruined!" she repeated meditatively as she went and opened the back door. The whole hill behind was reflecting the morning light in a great rosy glow. "Oh, my!" she said as though to herself. "There's a beautiful morning, glory be to God!"

Just then she heard the unfamiliar sound of a car in the lane, and it stopped outside the front door. She knew then what it was that had seemed wrong in Jimmy's story, and turned on him. "You ran away from home," she said. "Is that the police?"

Jimmy didn't seem to be listening to her. "If that's my stepfather, I'm not going back with him," he said.

Kate went to the front door and saw a good-looking young man with large ears and the pink-and-white complexion she called "delicate." She knew at once it was Jimmy's stepfather.

"Mrs. Mahoney?" he asked.

"Come in, sir, come in," she said obsequiously, and now she was no longer the proud, possessive mother whose boy had come back to her but the old hireling who had been caught with property that wasn't hers.

The young man strode into the kitchen with a confident air and stopped dead when he saw Jimmy.

"Now, what made me think of coming here first?" he shouted good-humoredly. "Mrs. Mahoney, I have the makings of a first-class detective, only I never got a chance."

When Jimmy said nothing, he tossed his head and went on in the same tone. "Want a lift, Jimmy?"

Jimmy glared at him. "I'm not going back with you, Uncle Tim," he said.

"Oh, begod, that's exactly what you *are* going to do, Jimmy," his stepfather said. "If you think I'm going to spend the rest of my days chasing you round Ireland, you're wrong." He dropped into a chair and rubbed his hands, as though to restore the circulation. "Mrs. Mahoney," he asked, "what do we have them for?"

Kate liked his way of including her in the conversation. She knew, too, he was only talking like that to make things easier for Jimmy.

"I don't want to go back, Uncle Tim," Jimmy said furiously. "I want to stop here."

"Listen to that, Mrs. Mahoney," his stepfather said, cocking his head at Kate. "Insulting Dublin to a Dublin man! And in Cork, of all places!"

"I'm not saying anything against Dublin!" Jimmy cried, and again he was a child and defenseless against the dialectic of adults. "I want to stay here."

Kate immediately came to his defense. "Wisha, 'tis only the way he got a bit homesick, sir. He thought he'd like to come back for a couple of days."

"I don't want to come back for a couple of days!" Jimmy shouted. "This is my home. I told Aunt Nance so."

"And wasn't that a very hard thing to say to your mother, Jimmy?" his stepfather asked. He said it gently, and Kate knew he liked the boy.

"It's true," Jimmy said. "I knew I wasn't wanted."

"You really think that, Jimmy?" his stepfather asked reproachfully, and Jimmy burst into wild tears.

"I didn't say *you* didn't want me. I know you did want me, and I wanted you. But my mammy didn't want me."

"Jimmy!"

"She didn't, she didn't."

"What made you think she didn't?"

"She thought I was too like my father."

"She said you were too like your father?" his stepfather asked incredulously.

"She didn't have to say it," sobbed Jimmy. "I knew it, every time she looked at me when I done something wrong. I reminded her of him, and she doesn't want to think of him. She only wants to think of you. And it's not my fault if I'm like my father, but if she didn't want me to be that way she should have took me sooner. She shouldn't have left it so late, Uncle Tim."

His stepfather said nothing for a moment and then rose in a jerky movement and walked to the back door. "You might be right there, son," he said with a shrug. "But you're not going the right way about it, either."

"All right, Uncle Tim," Jimmy cried. "What is the right way? I'll do whatever you tell me."

"Talk it over properly with your mother, and then come back here after the holidays," his stepfather said. "You see, old man, you don't seem to realize what it cost your mother to bring you to live with her at all. Now, you don't want her explaining why you ran away after a couple of weeks, do you?"

"He's right, Jimmy boy, he's right," Kate pleaded. "You could never go back there again, with all the old talk there'd be."

"Oh, all right, all right," Jimmy said despairingly, and went to get his cap.

"Sit down, the pair of ye, till I make a cup of tea!" cried Kate. But Jimmy shook his head.

"I'd sooner go now," he said.

And it was real despair, as she well knew, not sham. Of course, he showed off a bit, the way he always did, and didn't kiss her when he was getting into the car. And when James in his gentle way said, "You'll be back soon," Jimmy only drew a deep breath and looked up at the sky.

But she knew he really meant it, and that day she had great boasting over it among the neighbors. "A boy of fourteen, ma'am, that was never away from home all the days of his life, coming back like that, on an old bicycle, without food or sleep. Oh, my! Where would you find the likes of him?"

The neighbors, too, were impressed. "Well, Jimmy," they said, when he came back at the end of the holidays, to go to school. "You couldn't do without us, I see."

There was only one change in the relationship between Kate, James, and Jimmy. The day after his return, Jimmy said, "I'm not going to call you Mammy any more."

"Oye, and what are you going to call me?" she asked with sour humor.

"I'm going to call you Granny," he said. "The other sounds too silly."

After a few weeks James said "Granny," too. Though she didn't complain, she resented it. Stumbling about the house, talking to herself, she would suddenly say, "Glad enough they were of someone to call Mammy."

AFTER Jimmy had been back for a year or so, Kate's health began to break up. She had to go to hospital, and Nora and Molly offered to take one of the boys each. But neither Jimmy nor James would agree to this. They didn't want to leave the house and they didn't want to be separated, so they stayed on, and each week one of the girls came to clear up after them. They reported to Kate that the mess was frightful. But it wasn't this that really worried her, it was the wild streak in Jimmy.

In the evenings, instead of doing his lessons like James, he was tramping the city with wild young fellows. He had no sense of the value of money, and when he wanted it thought nothing of stealing from herself or James.

She came home before she should have, but even then she was too late to prevent mischief. While she was away, Jimmy had left school and got himself a job in a packing store.

"Oh, you blackguard, you!" she said. "I knew well you'd be up to something when my back was turned. But to school you go tomorrow, my fine gentleman, if I have to drag you there myself."

"I can't go back to school," Jimmy said indignantly. "They could have the law on me if I didn't give a month's notice." He knew she was very timid of policemen, lawyers, and officials and even at her age was in great dread of being dragged off to jail for some crime she didn't even know she had committed.

"Who's the manager?" she said. "I'll see him myself."

"You can't," said Jimmy. "He's on holidays."

"Oh, you liar," she muttered. "The truth isn't in you. Who is it?"

"Anyway, I have to have a job," said Jimmy. "If anything happened you while you were in hospital, who was going to look after James?"

She was taken aback, because that was something that had been all the time on her own mind. She knew her James, and knew that if she died and he was sent to live with some foster mother who didn't understand him, he would break his heart. In every way he was steadier than Jimmy, and yet he was far more defenseless. If you took Jimmy's home away from him, he would fight, steal, or run away, but James would only lie down and die. Still, though she was impressed by Jimmy's manliness, she wasn't taken in by it. She knew that in an emotional fit he was capable of these big gestures, but he could never live up to them, and in no time he would be thinking how he could turn them to his own advantage.

" 'Tisn't James at all with you," she said. " 'Tis more money you want for yourself. Did you tell your mother first?"

"I'm working till after six every night!" he cried, confounded by her injustice. "What time have I to write to my mother?"

"Plenty of time you have to write to her when 'tis something you want," she said. "Sit down and write to her now, you scamp! I'm not going to be taking the blame for your blackguarding."

Jimmy, with a martyred air, sat at the table and agonized over a note to his mother. "How do you spell 'employment'?" he asked James.

"Listen to him!" Kate said, invoking Heaven. "He wants to give up school and he don't know how to spell a simple word."

"All right, spell it you, so," he said.

"In my time, for poor people, the education was not going," she replied with great dignity. "Poor people hadn't the chances they have now, and what chances they had, they respected, not like the ones that are going today. Go on with your letter, you thing!"

AGAIN his Uncle Tim came and argued with him. He explained patiently that without an education Jimmy would get nowhere. Unless he finished his schooling, he couldn't go to the University. Jimmy, who couldn't stand gentleness in an argument, broke down and said he didn't want to go to the University, he only wanted to be independent. Kate didn't understand what Jimmy's stepfather meant, but she felt that it was probably only the old conflict in a new form: Jimmy's stepfather wanted him to be one of his own class, and Jimmy didn't. Leaving school at that age was what a working-class boy would do. Except for the occasional brilliant boy who was kept on at the monks' expense, there was no education beyond sixth book.

His stepfather seemed to realize it, too, for he gave in with a suddenness that surprised her. "Oh, all right," he said. "But you'd better let me try and find you something better than the job you have. And for God's sake go to night school and learn office work."

When he left, Jimmy accompanied him to the car, and they had a conversation that made Kate suspicious.

"What were you talking to your stepfather about?" she asked.

"Nothing," said Jimmy. "Only asking him who my father was."

"And did he tell you?"

"He said he didn't know."

"How inquisitive we're getting!" said Kate.

"He said I was entitled to know," Jimmy said defensively. "He told me to ask Nance the next time I go up to them." She noticed that sometimes he said "Mother" and sometimes "Nance," and both sounded awkward.

When next he came back from a holiday in Dublin he had discovered what he wished to know. As he described the scene with his mother, Kate was again overcome by a feeling of the strangeness of it all. At first his mother had refused point-blank to tell him anything. She had been quite cool and friendly about it, and explained that she had been only a girl when it all happened and when she had been deserted had cut Jimmy's father out of her life. She hadn't spoken his name since and never proposed to speak it. When Jimmy persisted, arguing and pleading with her, she had grown furious. "Christ, boy," she said, "it's my life as well as yours!" Then she had wept and said she never wanted him in the house again. At this moment, her husband had walked into the room, looking like murder, Jimmy said, and snapped, "All right, Jimmy. Beat it!" He had closed the door after Jimmy, and Jimmy heard the pair of them arguing from the kitchen. Finally, his stepfather had come out and shouted, "Your mother wants to see you, Jimmy," and rushed upstairs. When Jimmy went into the living room, she was standing by the fireplace, pale and dry-eyed. "Your father's name is Tom Creedon," she said coolly. "He had a business in Tramore, but he's left it for years. The last I heard of him he was in London. If you want any more information, you'll have to ask one of his friends. A man called Michael Taylor in Dungarvan is your best chance." And then she, too, had gone out and followed her husband upstairs, and Jimmy had sat by the fire and sobbed to himself till it was nearly out and the whole house was silent. He felt he had outraged two people who cared for him for the sake of someone who had never inquired whether he was alive or dead.

When he had finished his story, Kate felt the same. "And what use is it to you, now you know it?" she asked maliciously.

"I had to know it," Jimmy said with easy self-confidence. "Now I can go and see him."

"You can what?" she asked wearily.

"I can go and see him. Why wouldn't I?"

"Why wouldn't you, indeed, and all the attention he paid to you," she said sourly. "You're never right."

There were times when she almost thought he wasn't right in the head. For months on end he never seemed to think at all of his parentage, and then he would begin to daydream till he worked himself up into a fever of emotion. In a fit like that she never knew what he might do. He was capable of anything—of anything, that is, except writing a letter. One weekend he set off on his bicycle for County Waterford and came back with his father's address. After that it was only a question of getting a friend on the cross-Channel boat to fix him a passage for nothing.

All the time he was away Kate fretted, and, being Jimmy, he didn't even send her as much as a picture postcard. She had the vague hope that he wouldn't be able to locate his father. She thought of it all as if it were something she'd read in a newspaper—how in a terrible fit of anger Jimmy struck and killed his father and then turned himself in to the police. She could even see his picture in the paper with handcuffs on his wrists. "Ah," Hanna Dinan said, "God is good!" But this didn't comfort Kate at all.

And then, one autumn morning after James had left for school, Jimmy walked in. He had had no breakfast, and she fumbled blindly about the little kitchen getting it ready for him, and cursing old age that made it seem such a labor. But all the same, her heart was light. She knew now that she had only been deceiving herself, pretending to think that Jimmy and his father might disagree, when all she dreaded was that they would agree too well.

"Well," she said fondly, leaning on the kitchen table and grinning into his face. "Now you seen him, how do you like him?"

"Oh, he's all right," Jimmy said casually—too casually, for her taste. "He's drinking himself to death, that's all." And instantly she was ashamed of her own pettiness, and tears came into her eyes.

"Wisha, child, child, why do you be upsetting yourself about them?" she cried. "They're not worth it. There's no one worth it."

She sat in the kitchen with him while he unburdened himself about it all. It was just as when he had described to her how he had asked his mother for his father's name, as though he were saving up every detail—the walk across England, the people who had given him lifts, the truck driver who had given him a dinner and five bob after Jimmy confided in him, till the moment he knocked at the door of the shabby lodging house near Victoria Station and an unshaven man with sad red eyes looked out and asked timidly, "Yes, boy, what is it?" As though nobody ever called on him now with anything but bad news.

"And what did you say?" Kate asked.

"I said, 'Don't you know me?' and he said, 'You have the advantage of me.' So I said, 'I'm your son.' "

"Oh, my!" exclaimed Kate, profoundly impressed, though she had resolved to hate everything she heard about Jimmy's father. "And what did he say to that?"

"He didn't say anything. He only started to cry."

" 'Twas a bit late in the day for him," said Kate. "And what did he say about your mother?"

"Only that she didn't miss much when she missed him."

"That was one true word he said, anyway," said Kate.

"He paid for it," said Jimmy.

"He deserved it all," said Kate.

"You wouldn't say that if you saw him now," said Jimmy, and he went on to describe the squalid back room where he had stayed for a week with his father, sleeping in the same dirty bed, going out with him to the pub. And yet through Jimmy's disillusionment Kate felt a touch of pride in the way he described the sudden outbursts of extravagant humor that lit up his father's maudlin self-pity. He described everything, down to the last evening, when his father had brought him to Paddington Station, forced him to take the last five shillings he had in the world, tearfully kissed him, and begged him to come again.

She knew from Jimmy's tone that it was unlikely that he would go again. His father was only another ghost that he had laid.

WHEN he was eighteen, Jimmy took up with a girl of his own, and at first Kate paid no attention, but when it went on for more than six months and Jimmy took the girl out every Friday night, she began to grow nervous. Steady courting of one girl was something she had never thought him capable of. When she learned who the girl was, she understood. Tessie Flynn was an orphan who had been brought up by a staid old couple on the road as their own daughter. They had brought her up so well that every other young fellow on the road was in dread to go near her, and when the old couple discovered that she was actually walking out with Jimmy they didn't talk to her for days. She wasn't allowed to bring Jimmy to the house, and Kate, for the sake of her own self-respect, was forced to invite her instead.

Not that this made her like Tessie any the more. She dreaded Friday evenings, when Jimmy would come in from work, and shave, and strip to wash under the tap in the back yard, and then change into his best blue suit and put cream on his hair.

"You won't be late tonight?" she would ask.

"Why wouldn't I be late?" Jimmy would ask cheerfully.

"You know I can't sleep while you do be out."

It was true. Any other night of the week she could sleep comfortably at her proper time, but when she knew he was out with "that vagabond," as she called poor Tessie, she would lie awake worrying and saying her rosary. Even James reproved her. One Friday evening, he closed his book carefully, raised his big glasses on his forehead, and said, "Granny, you worry too much about Jimmy and his girl friend. Jimmy is much steadier than you think."

But James didn't realize, as she did, that even in his choice of a girl Jimmy was only reliving the pattern of his own life. To anyone else he might seem the most ordinary of young fellows, but she could watch the fever mount in him, and always she was taken aback at the form it took. Once, he lit out on his bicycle to a little town eighty miles away, where his father's brother had a grocery shop. Another time, with the help of his sailor friend, he crossed again to Fishguard and cycled through southern England to the little seaside town in Dorset where he had been born. And she knew that whatever she might say he would go on like that to the end of his days, pursued by the dream of a normal life that he might have lived and of a normal family in which he might have grown up.

James observed it, too, but with a deep disapproval. He thought Jimmy cheapened himself.

"Ah, that's only because you can get away from them, boy," Jimmy said with his toughest air. "Boy, if my family was living in England, *I* wouldn't worry about them, either."

"Well, your father *is* living in England, and you went to see him," said James. "I daresay I'll see my family, too, one day, but I don't want to see them now, thank you."

"If you have any sense you'll have nothing to do with them," said Jimmy. "They'll only look down on you."

"I don't think so," said James. "At the moment they might, but if they meet me when I'm a professor at the University, or a senior civil servant, they'll behave differently. You see, Jimmy," he went on in the tone he would use when he was a professor at the University, "people like that pay far too much attention to public opinion, and they won't neglect anyone who can be useful to them."

Kate felt that there was a sad wisdom in what James said. While Jimmy, who had something of his father's weakness and charm, might prove a liability to those who didn't understand him, James would work and save, and only when he was established and independent would he satisfy his curiosity about those who had abandoned him. And, though she mightn't live to see it, James would make quite certain that nobody patronized him. She would have given a great deal to see how James dealt with his family.

But she knew that she wouldn't see it. She fell ill again, and this time Molly came to the house to nurse her, while Nora, who looked after Molly's children, came in the evenings, and sometimes one of the husbands. Molly made an immediate change in the house. She was swift and efficient; she fed the boys and made conversation with callers, leaning against the doorpost with folded arms as though she had no thought in the world but of them, though occasionally she would slip away into the front room and weep savagely to herself for a few minutes before returning to her tasks.

The priest came, and Molly invited him into the front room and chatted with him about the affairs of the parish. After he had left, Kate asked to see Jimmy and James. They went up the stairs quietly and stood at either side of the bed. Her eyes were closed and her hands outstretched on the bed. Jimmy took one, and after a moment James took the other. James was never a boy for a deathbed.

"Don't upset yeerselves too much over me," she said. "I know ye'll miss me, but ye have nothing to regret. Ye were the two best boys a mother ever reared, and I'm proud of ye." She thought hard for a moment and then added something that shocked them all. "And yeer father is proud of ye, I'm sure."

Molly, who was standing with Nora behind James, leaned forward and said urgently, "Mammy, 'tisn't who you think. 'Tis Jimmy and James."

Kate opened her eyes for a moment and looked straight at her, and her eyes were no colder than the words she spoke. "Excuse me, child, I know perfectly well who I have." Her eyes closed again, and she breathed noisily for what seemed a long, long time, as though she were vainly trying to recollect herself. "Don't either of ye do anything yeer father would be ashamed of. He was a good man, and a kind man, and a clean-living man, and he never robbed anyone of a ha'penny. . . . Jimmy," she added in a voice of unexpected strength, "look after your little brother for me."

"I will, Mammy," Jimmy said through his tears.

Something in that sudden reversion to the language of childhood made Molly break down. She left the room and took refuge in the parlor downstairs. Nora, realizing that something had upset her sister, followed and shouted at her as all the Mahoneys had always shouted at one another. "Wisha, Molly, will you have a bit of sense? Sure you know poor Mammy's mind was wandering."

"It was *not* wandering, Nora," Molly said hysterically. "She knew perfectly well what she was saying, and Jimmy knew it, too. They were her real children all the time, and we were only outsiders. Oh, Nora, Nora, how could she do *that* to us?"

That night, when Kate was quiet at last in her brown shroud, with her hands clutching the rosary beads on her breast, and the neighbors were coming from all parts into the little front room to say a prayer for her, people in every little house around were asking the same question that Molly had been asking herself, though they asked it with a touch of envy. How could a woman who was already old take the things the world had thrown away and out of them fashion a new family, dearer to her than the old and finer than any she had known? Hanna Dinan had the last word. Having sat there for an hour, she took a last look at her old crony on the bed, then pulled her coat about her and said casually, "Wisha, wasn't she a great little woman! She had them all against her and she bested them. They had everything, and she had nothing, and she bested them all in the end."

The American Wife

ELSIE COLLEARY, who was on a visit to her cousins in Cork, was a mystery even to them. Her father, Jack Colleary's brother, had emigrated when he was a kid and done well for himself; he had made his money in the liquor business, and left it to go into wholesale produce when Elsie was growing up, because he didn't think it was the right background for a girl. He had given her the best of educations, and all he had got out of it was to have Elsie telling him that Irishmen were more manly, and that even Irish-Americans let their wives boss them too much. What she meant was that *he* let her mother boss him, and she had learned from other Irish people that this was not the custom at home. Maybe Mike Colleary, like a lot of other Americans, did give the impression of yielding too much to his wife, but that was because she thought she knew more about things than he did, and he was too soft-hearted to disillusion her. No doubt the Americans, experienced in nostalgia, took Elsie's glorification of Irishmen good-humoredly, but it did not go down too well in Cork, where the men stood in perpetual contemplation of the dangers of marriage, like cranes standing on one leg at the edge of the windy water.

She stood out at the Collearys' quiet little parties, with her high waist and wide skirts, taking the men out to sit on the stairs while she argued with them about religion and politics. Women having occasion to go upstairs thought this very forward, but some of the men found it a pleasant relief. Besides, like all Americans, she was probably a millionaire, and the most unworldly of men can get a kick out of flirting with a real millionaire.

The man she finally fell in love with did not sit on the stairs with her at all, though, like her, he was interested in religion and politics. This was a chap called Tom Barry. Tom was thirty-five, tall and thin and good-looking, and he lived with his mother and two good-looking sisters in a tiny house near the Barrack, and he couldn't even go for a walk in the evening without the three of them lining up in the hallway to present him with his hat, his gloves, and his clean handkerchief. He had a small job in the courthouse, and was not without ambition; he had engaged in several small business enterprises with his friend Jerry Coakley, but all they had ever got out of these was some good stories. Jerry was forty, and *he* had an old mother who insisted on putting his socks on for him.

Elsie's cousins warned her against setting her cap at Tom, but this only seemed to make her worse. "I guess I'll have to seduce him," she replied airily, and her cousins, who had never known a well-bred Catholic girl to talk like that, were shocked. She shocked them even more before she was done. She called at his house when she knew he wasn't there and deluded his innocent mother and sisters into believing that she didn't have designs on him; she badgered Tom to death at the office, gave him presents, and even hired a car to take him for drives.

They weren't the only ones who were shocked. Tom was shocked himself when she asked him point-blank how much he earned. However, he put that down to unworldliness and told her.

"But that's not even a street cleaner's wages at home," she said indignantly.

"I'm sure, Elsie," he said sadly. "But then, of course, money isn't everything."

"No, and Ireland isn't everything," she replied. It was peculiar, but from their first evening together she had never ceased talking about America to him—the summer heat, and the crickets chattering, and the leaves alive with fireflies. During her discussions on the stairs, she had apparently discovered a great many things wrong with Ireland, and Tom, with a sort of mournful pleasure, kept adding to them.

"Oh, I know, I know," he said regretfully.

"Then if you know, why don't you do something about it?"

"Ah, well, I suppose it's habit, Elsie," he said, as though he weren't quite sure. "I suppose I'm too old to learn new tricks."

But Elsie doubted if it was really habit, and it perplexed her that a man so clever and conscientious could at the same time be so lacking in initiative. She explained it finally to herself in terms of an attachment to his mother that was neither natural nor healthy. Elsie was a girl who loved explanations.

On their third outing she had proposed to him, and he was so astonished that he burst out laughing, and continued to laugh whenever he thought of it again. Elsie herself couldn't see anything to laugh at in it. Having been proposed to by men who were younger and better-looking and better off than he was, she felt she had been conferring an honor on him. But he was a curious man, for when she repeated the proposal, he said, with a cold fury that hurt her, "Sometimes I wish you'd think before you talk, Elsie. You know what I earn, and you know it isn't enough to keep a family on. Besides, in case you haven't noticed it, I have a mother and two sisters to support."

"You could earn enough to support them in America," she protested.

"And I told you already that I had no intention of going to America."

"I have some money of my own," she said. "It's not much, but it would mean I'd be no burden to you."

"Listen, Elsie," he said, "a man who can't support a wife and children has no business marrying at all. I have no business marrying anyway. I'm not a very cheerful man, and I have a rotten temper."

Elsie went home in tears, and told her astonished uncle that all Irishmen were pansies, and, as he had no notion what pansies were, he shook his head and admitted that it was a terrible country. Then she wrote to Tom and told him that what he needed was not a wife but a psychiatrist. The writing of this gave her great satisfaction, but next morning she realized that her mother would only say she had been silly. Her mother believed that men needed careful handling. The day after, she waited for Tom outside the courthouse, and when he came out she summoned him with two angry blasts on the horn. A rainy sunset was flooding the Western Road with yellow light that made her look old and grim.

"Well," she said bitterly, "I'd hoped I'd never see your miserable face again."

But that extraordinary man only smiled gently and rested his elbows on the window of the car.

"I'm delighted you came," he said. "I was all last night trying to write to you, but I'm not very good at it."

"Oh, so you got my letter?"

"I did, and I'm ashamed to have upset you so much. All I wanted to say was that if you're serious—I mean really serious—about this, I'd be honored."

At first she thought he was mocking her. Then she realized that he wasn't, and she was in such an evil humor that she was tempted to tell him she had changed her mind. Then common sense told her the man would be fool enough to believe her, and after that his pride wouldn't let him propose to her again. It was the price you had to pay for dealing with men who had such a high notion of their own dignity.

"I suppose it depends on whether you love me or not," she replied. "It's a little matter you forgot to mention."

He raised himself from the car window, and in the evening light she saw a look of positive pain on his lean, sad, gentle face. "Ah, I do, but—" he was beginning when she cut him off and told him to get in the car. Whatever he was about to say, she didn't want to hear it.

THEY settled down in a modern bungalow outside the town, on the edge of the harbor. Elsie's mother, who flew over for the wedding, said dryly that she hoped Elsie would be able to make up to Tom for the loss of his mother's services. In fact, it wasn't long before the Barrys were saying she wasn't, and making remarks about her cooking and her lack of tidiness. But if Tom noticed there was anything wrong, which is improbable, he didn't mention it. Whatever his faults as a sweetheart, he made a good husband. It may have been the affection of a sensitive man for someone he saw as frightened, fluttering, and insecure. It could have been the longing of a frustrated one for someone that seemed to him remote, romantic, and mysterious. But whatever it was, Tom, who had always been God Almighty to his mother and sisters, was extraordinarily patient and understanding with Elsie, and she needed it, because she was often homesick and scared.

Jerry Coakley was a great comfort to her in these fits, for Jerry had a warmth of manner that Tom lacked. He was an insignificant-looking man with a ravaged dyspeptic face and a tubercular complexion, a thin, bitter mouth with bad teeth, and long lank hair; but he was so sympathetic and insinuating that at times he even gave you the impression that he was changing his shape to suit your mood. Elsie had the feeling that the sense of failure had eaten deeper into him than into Tom.

At once she started to arrange a match between him and Tom's elder sister, Annie, in spite of Tom's warnings that Jerry would never marry till his mother died. When she realized that Tom was right, she said it was probably as well, because Annie wouldn't put his socks on him. Later she admitted that this was unfair, and that it would probably be a great relief to poor Jerry to be allowed to put on his socks himself. Between Tom and him there was one of those passionate relationships that spring up in small towns where society narrows itself down to a handful of erratic and explosive friendships. There were always people who weren't talking to other people, and friends had all to be dragged into the disagreement, no matter how trifling it might be, and often it happened that the principals had already become fast friends again when *their* friends were still ignoring one another in the street. But Jerry and Tom refused to disagree. Jerry would drop in for a bottle of stout, and Tom and he would denounce the country, while Elsie wondered why they could never find anything more interesting to talk about than stupid priests and crooked politicians.

Elsie's causes were of a different kind. The charwoman, Mrs. Dorgan, had six children and a husband who didn't earn enough to keep them. Elsie concealed from Tom how much she really paid Mrs. Dorgan, but she couldn't conceal that Mrs. Dorgan wore her clothes, or that she took the Dorgan family to the seaside in the summer. When Jerry suggested to Tom that the Dorgans might be doing too well out of Elsie, Tom replied, "Even if they were, Jerry, I wouldn't interfere. If 'tis people's nature to be generous, you must let them be generous."

For Tom's causes she had less patience. "Oh, why don't you people do something about it, instead of talking?" she cried.

"What could you do, Elsie?" asked Jerry.

"At least you could show them up," said Elsie.

"Why, Elsie?" he asked with his mournful smile. "Were you thinking of starting a paper?"

"Then, if you can't do anything about it, shut up!" she said. "You and Tom seem to get some queer masochistic pleasure out of these people."

"Begor, Elsie, you might have something there," Jerry said, nodding ruefully.

"Oh, we adore them," Tom said mockingly.

"You do," she said. "I've seen you. You sit here night after night denouncing them, and then when one of them gets sick you're round to the house to see if there's anything you can do for him, and when he dies you start a collection for his wife and family. You make me sick." Then she stamped out to the kitchen.

Jerry hunched his shoulders and exploded in splutters and giggles. He reached out a big paw for a bottle of stout, with the air of someone snaring a rabbit.

"I declare to God, Tom, she has us taped," he said.

"She has you taped anyway," said Tom.

"How's that?"

"She thinks you need an American wife as well."

"Well, now, she mightn't be too far out in that, either," said Jerry with a crooked grin. "I often thought it would take something like that."

"She thinks you have *problems*," said Tom with a snort. Elsie's favorite word gave him the creeps.

"She wouldn't be referring to the mother, by any chance?"

FOR a whole year Elsie had fits of depression because she thought she wasn't going to have a baby, and she saw several doctors, whose advice she repeated in mixed company, to the great embarrassment of everybody except Jerry. After that, for the best part of another year, she had fits of depression because she was going to have a baby, and she informed everybody about that as well, including the occasion of its conception and the probable date of its arrival, and again they were all embarrassed only Jerry. Having reached the age of eighteen before learning that there was any real difference between the sexes, Jerry found all her talk fascinating, and also he realized that Elsie saw nothing immodest in it. It was just that she had an experimental interest in her body and mind. When she gave him bourbon he studied its taste, but when he gave her Irish she studied its effect—it was as simple as that. Jerry, too, liked explanations, but he liked them for their own sake, and not with the intention of doing anything with them. At the same time, Elsie was scared by what she thought was a lack of curiosity on the part of the Cork doctors, and when her mother learned this she began to press Elsie to have the baby in America, where she would feel secure.

"You don't think I should go back, Tom?" she asked guiltily. "Daddy says he'll pay my fare."

It came as a shock to Tom, though the idea had crossed his mind that something of the kind might happen. "If that's the way you feel about it, I suppose you'd better, Elsie," he replied.

"But you wouldn't come with me."

"How can I come with you? You know I can't just walk out of the office for a couple of months."

"But you could get a job at home."

"And I told you a dozen times I don't want a job in America," he said angrily. Then, seeing the way it upset her, he changed his tone. "Look, if you stay here, feeling the way you do, you'll work yourself into a real illness. Anyway, sometime you'll have to go back on a visit, and this is as good an occasion as any."

"But how can I, without you?" she asked. "You'd only neglect yourself."

"I would not neglect myself."

"Would you stay at your mother's?"

"I would not stay at my mother's. This is my house, and I'm going to stop here."

Tom worried less about the effect Elsie's leaving would have on him than about what his family would say, particularly Annie, who never lost the chance of a crack at Elsie. "You let that girl walk on you, Tom Barry," she said. "One of these days she'll walk too hard." Then, of course, Tom walked on *her*, in the way that only a devoted brother can, but that was no relief to the feeling that something had come between Elsie and him and that he could do nothing about it. When he was driving Elsie to the liner, he knew that she felt the same, for she didn't break down until they came to a long gray bridge over an inlet of water, guarded by a lonely gray stone tower. She had once pointed it out to him as the first thing she had seen that represented Ireland to her, and now he had the feeling that this was how she saw him—a battered old tower by a river mouth that was no longer of any importance to anyone but the sea gulls.

SHE WAS away longer than she or anyone else had expected. First there was the wedding of an old school friend; then her mother's birthday; then the baby got ill. It was clear that she was enjoying herself immensely, but she wrote long and frequent letters, sent snapshots of herself and the baby, and—most important of all—had named the baby for Jerry Coakley. Clearly Elsie hadn't forgotten them. The Dorgan kids appeared on the road in clothes that had obviously been made in America, and whenever Tom met them he stopped to speak to them and give them the pennies he thought Elsie would have given them.

Occasionally Tom went to his mother's for supper, but otherwise he looked after himself. Nothing could persuade him that he was not a natural housekeeper, or that whatever his sisters could do he could not do just as well himself. Sometimes Jerry came and the two men took off their coats and tried to prepare a meal out of one of Elsie's cookbooks. "Steady, squad!" Tom would murmur as he wiped his hands before taking another peep at the book. "You never know when this might come in handy." But whether it was the result of Tom's supervision or Jerry's helplessness, the meal usually ended in a big burnup, or a tasteless mess from which some essential ingredient seemed to be missing, and they laughed over it as they consoled themselves with bread and cheese and stout. "Elsie is right," Jerry would say, shaking his head regretfully. "We have problems, boy! We have problems!"

Elsie returned at last with trunks full of new clothes, a box of up-to-date kitchen stuff, and a new gaiety and energy. Every ten minutes Tom would make an excuse to tiptoe upstairs and take another look at his son. Then the Barrys arrived, and Elsie gave immediate offense by quoting Gesell and Spock. But Mrs. Barry didn't seem to mind as much as her daughters. By some extraordinary process of association, she had discovered a great similarity between Elsie and herself in the fact that she had married from the south side of the city into the north and had never got used to it. This delighted Elsie, who went about proclaiming that her mother-in-law and herself were both displaced persons.

The next year was a very happy one, and less trying on Elsie, because she had another woman to talk to, even if most of the time she didn't understand what her mother-in-law was telling her, and had the suspicion that her mother-in-law didn't understand her either. But then she got pregnant for the second time, and became restless and dissatisfied once more, though now it wasn't only with hospitals and doctors but with schools and schoolteachers as well. Tom and Jerry had impressed on her that the children were being turned into idiots, learning through the medium of a language they didn't understand— indeed, according to Tom, it was a language that nobody understood. What chance would the children have?

"Ah, I suppose the same chance as the rest of us, Elsie," said Jerry in his sly, mournful way.

"But you and Tom don't want chances, Jerry," she replied earnestly. "Neither of you has any ambition."

"Ah, you should look on the bright side of things. Maybe with God's help they won't have any ambition either."

But this time it had gone beyond a joke. For days on end, Tom was in a rage with her, and when he was angry he seemed to withdraw into himself like a snail into a shell.

Unable to get to him, Elsie grew hysterical. "It's all your damned obstinacy," she sobbed. "You don't do anything in this rotten hole, but you're too conceited to get out of it. Your family treat you as if you were God, and then you behave to me as if you were God! God! God!" she screamed, and each time she punched him viciously with her fist, till suddenly the humor of their situation struck him and he went off into laughter.

After that, he could only make his peace with her and make excuses for her leaving him again, but he knew that the excuses wouldn't impress his sisters. One evening when he went to see them, Annie caught him, as she usually did, when he was going out the front door, and he stood looking sidewise down the avenue.

"Are you letting Elsie go off to America again, Tom?" she asked.

"I don't know," Tom said, pulling his long nose with an air of affected indifference. "I can't very well stop her, can I?"

"Damn soon she'd be stopped if she hadn't the money," said Annie. "And you're going to let her take young Jerry?"

"Ah, how could I look after Jerry? Talk sense, can't you!"

"And I suppose we couldn't look after him either? We're not sufficiently well read."

"Ah, the child should be with his own mother, Annie," Tom said impatiently.

"And where should his mother be? Ah, Tom Barry," she added bitterly, "I told you what that one was, and she's not done with you yet. Are you sure she's going to bring him back?"

Then Tom exploded on her in his cold, savage way. "If you want to know, I am not," he said, and strode down the avenue with his head slightly bowed.

Something about the cut of him as he passed under a street lamp almost broke Annie's heart. "The curse of God on that bitch!" she said when she returned to her mother in the kitchen.

"Is it Elsie?" her mother cried angrily. "How dare you talk of her like that!"

"He's letting her go to America again," said Annie.

"He's a good boy, and he's right to consider her feelings," said her mother anxiously. "I often thought myself I'd go back to the south side and not be ending my days in this misfortunate hole."

The months after Elsie's second departure were bitter ones for Tom. A house from which a woman is gone is bad enough, but one from which a child is gone is a deadhouse. Tom would wake in the middle of the night thinking he heard Jerry crying, and be half out of bed before he realized that Jerry was thousands of miles away. He did not continue his experiments with cooking and housekeeping. He ate at his mother's, spent most of his time at the Coakleys, and drank far too much. Like all inward-looking men he had a heavy hand on the bottle. Meanwhile Elsie wavered and procrastinated worse than before, setting dates, canceling her passage, sometimes changing her mind within twenty-four hours. In his despondency Tom resigned himself to the idea that she wouldn't return at all, or at least persuaded himself that he had.

"Oh, she'll come back all right," Jerry said with a worried air. "The question is, will she stay back. . . . You don't mind me talking about it?" he asked.

"Indeed no. Why would I?"

"You know, Tom, I'd say ye had family enough to last ye another few years."

Tom didn't look up for a few moments, and when he did he smiled faintly. "You think it's that?"

"I'm not saying she knows it," Jerry added hastily. "There's nothing calculating about her, and she's crazy about you."

"I thought it was something that went with having the baby," Tom said thoughtfully. "Some sort of homing instinct."

"I wouldn't say so," said Jerry. "Not altogether. I think she feels that eventually she'll get you through the kids."

"She won't," Tom said bitterly.

"I know, sure, I know. But Elsie can't get used to the—the irremediable." The last word was so unlike Jerry that Tom felt he must have looked it up in a dictionary, and the absurdity of this made him feel very close to his old crony. "Tell me, Tom," Jerry added gently, "wouldn't you do it? I know it wouldn't be easy, but wouldn't you try it, even for a while, for Elsie's sake? 'Twould mean a hell of a lot to her."

"I'm too old, Jerry," Tom said so deliberately that Jerry knew it had been in his mind as well.

"Oh, I know, I know," Jerry repeated. "Even ten years ago I might have done it myself. It's like jail. The time comes when you're happier in than out. And that's not the worst of it," he added bitterly. "The worst is when you pretend you like it."

It was a strange evening that neither of them ever forgot, sitting in that little house to which Elsie's absence seemed a rebuke, and listening to the wind from the harbor that touched the foot of the garden. They knew they belonged to a country whose youth was always escaping from it, out beyond that harbor, and that was middle-aged in all its attitudes and institutions. Of those that remained, a little handful lived with defeat and learned fortitude and humor and sweetness, and these were the things that Elsie, with her generous idealism, loved in them. But she couldn't pay the price. She wanted them where she belonged herself, among the victors.

A few weeks later, Elsie was back; the house was full of life again, and that evening seemed only a bad dream. It was almost impossible to keep Jerry Og, as they called the elder child, away from Tom. He was still only a baby, and a spoiled one at that, but when Tom took him to the village Jerry Og thrust out his chest and took strides that were too big for him like any small boy with a father he admired. Each day, he lay in wait for the postman and then took the post away to sort it for himself. He sorted it by the pictures on the stamps, and Elsie noted gleefully that he reserved all the pretty pictures for his father.

Nobody had remembered Jerry's good advice, even Jerry himself, and eighteen months later Elsie was pregnant again. Again their lives took the same pattern of unrest. But this time Elsie was even more distressed than Tom.

"I'm a curse to you," she said. "There's something wrong with me. I can't be natural."

"Oh, you're natural enough," Tom replied bitterly. "You married the wrong man, that's all."

"I didn't, I didn't!" she protested despairingly. "You can say anything else but that. If I believed that, I'd have nothing left, because I never cared for anyone but you. And in spite of what you think, I'm coming back," she went on, in tears. "I'm coming back if it kills me. God, I hate this country; I hate every God damn thing about it; I hate what it's done to you and Jerry. But I'm not going to let you go."

"You have no choice," Tom said patiently. "Jerry Og will have to go to school, and you can't be bringing him hither and over, even if you could afford it."

"Then, if that's what you feel, why don't you keep him?" she cried. "You know perfectly well you could stop me taking him with me if you wanted to. You wouldn't even have to bring me into court. I'll give him to you now. Isn't that proof enough that I'm coming back?"

"No, Elsie, it is not," Tom replied, measuring every word. "And I'm not going to bring you into court either. I'm not going to take hostages to make sure my wife comes back to me."

And though Elsie continued to delude herself with the belief that she would return, she knew Tom was right. It would all appear different when she got home. The first return to Ireland had been hard, the second had seemed impossible. Yet, even in the black hours when she really considered the situation, she felt she could never resign herself to something that had been determined before she was born, and she deceived herself with the hope that Tom would change his mind and follow her. He must follow her. Even if he was prepared to abandon her, he would never abandon Jerry Og.

And this, as Big Jerry could have told her, was where she made her biggest mistake, because if Tom had done it at all it would have been for her. But Big Jerry had decided that the whole thing had gone beyond his power to help. He recognized the irremediable, all right, sometimes perhaps even before it became irremediable. But that, as he would have said himself, is where the ferryboat had left him.

Thanks to Elsie, the eldest of the Dorgans now has a job in Boston and in the course of years the rest of them will probably go there as well. Tom continues to live in his little bungalow beside the harbor. Annie is keeping house for him, which suits her fine, because Big Jerry's old mother continued to put his socks on for him a few years too long, and now Annie has only her brother to worship. To all appearances they are happy enough, as happiness goes in Cork. Jerry still calls, and the two men discuss the terrible state of the country. But in Tom's bedroom there are pictures of Elsie and the children, the third of whom he knows only through photographs, and apart from that, nothing has changed since Elsie left five years ago. It is a strange room, for one glance is enough to show that the man who sleeps there is still in love, and that everything that matters to him in the world is reflected there. And one day, if he comes by the dollars, he will probably go out and visit them all, but it is here he will return and here, no doubt, he will die.

The Impossible Marriage

IT WASN'T till he was nearly thirty that Jim Grahame realized the trick that life had played on him. Up to that time he had lived very much like any other young man, with no great notion that he was being imposed upon. His father had died ten years before. Jim, an accountant in a provision store, had continued to accept his father's responsibilities, and his mother, a lively, sweet-natured little woman, had kept house for him in the way that only mothers can. They lived on in the house into which she had married; a big, roomy, awkward house on the edge of the country where the rent they paid was barely enough to keep the building in repair. Jim had never been very shy with girls, but none of them he had met seemed to him to be half the woman his mother was, and, unknown to himself, he was turning into a typical comfortable old bachelor who might or might not at the age of forty-five decide to establish a family of his own. His mother spoiled him, of course, and, in the way of only children, he had a troubled conscience because of the way he took advantage of it. But spoiling is a burden that the majority of men can carry a great deal of without undue hardship.

Then, by the seaside in Crosshaven, one Sunday, he went for a walk with a girl called Eileen Clery who lived in the same quarter of Cork as himself, though he had never noticed her before. She wasn't the sort of girl who thrusts herself on people's attention, though she was good-looking enough, with a thin face that lit up beautifully when she smiled, and pale hair with gold lights in it. He tried to flirt with her, and was surprised and a little offended by her quick, almost violent, withdrawal. He had not mistaken her for a flighty type, but neither had he expected to meet an untouchable.

The curious thing was that she seemed to like him, and even arranged to meet him again. This time they sat in a nook on the cliffs, and Jim became more pressing. To his astonishment, she began to cry. He was exasperated, but he pretended a solicitude he did not altogether feel, and when she saw him apparently distressed, she sat up and smiled, though her tears still continued to flow freely. "It's not that I wouldn't like it, Jim," she said, drying her eyes and blowing her nose into a ridiculous little scrap of a handkerchief, "only I don't like thinking about it."

"Why on earth not, Eileen?" he asked with some amusement.

"Well, you see, I'm an only child, and I have my mother to look after," she said, still sniffing.

"And I'm an only child, and I have a mother to look after," Jim replied triumphantly, and then laughed outright at the absurdity of the coincidence. "We're a pair," he added with a rueful chuckle.

"Yes, aren't we?" Eileen said, laughing and sobbing at once, and then she rested her head on his chest, and made no further difficulties about his love-making.

Now, all books on the subject describe attraction in similar terms; tanned chests and voluptuous contours which really have very little to do with the matter. But what they rarely mention, the most powerful of all, is human loneliness. This is something that women face earlier than men, and Eileen had already faced it. Jim, though he had not faced it in the same way, was perceptive enough to see it reaching out before him, and up there on the cliffs overlooking Cork Harbour, watching a score of little sailing-boats headed for Currabinny, they realized that they were in love, and all the more in love because their position was so obviously hopeless.

After that, they met regularly every week in Cork, to walk, or go to the pictures when it rained. They did it in the way of only children, taking precautions that became something of a joke to those who knew them. One evening, a girl crossing the New Bridge saw Jim Grahame standing there, and when she came to the second bridge was amused to see Eileen. "Excuse my interfering, Miss Clery," she said, "but if it's Mr. Grahame you're waiting for, he's waiting for you at the other bridge." Eileen didn't know where to look; she blushed, she laughed, and finally joined her hands and said, "Oh, thank you, thank you," and ran like the wind.

It was like them to meet that way, miles from home, because they were pursued by the sense of guilt. They felt more pity for their mothers than for themselves and did their best to hide their dreadful secret out of some instinctive understanding of the fear of loneliness and old age that besets women whose families have grown and whose husbands are dead. Perhaps they even understood it too well, and apprehended more of it than was really there.

Mrs. Grahame, whose intelligence service was better than Mrs. Clery's, was the first to speak of the matter to them.

"I hear you're great friends with a girl called Clery from the Cross," she said one evening in a tone of modest complaint. Jim was shaving by the back door. He started and turned to her with a look of amusement, but she was absorbed in her knitting, as always when she did not wish to look him in the face.

"Go on!" he said. "Who told you that?"

"Why wouldn't I hear it when the whole road knows it?" she replied, avoiding his question. She liked her little mysteries. "Wouldn't you bring her up some night?"

"You wouldn't mind?"

"Why would I mind, child? Little enough company we see."

This was another of her favorite myths; that she never saw or spoke to anyone, though Jim could do little or nothing that she didn't hear about sooner or later.

One evening he brought Eileen home for tea, and though she was nervous and giggly, he could see that his mother took to her at once. Mrs. Grahame worshipped her son, but she had always wished for a daughter, someone she could talk to as she could not talk to a man. Later in the evening, Eileen, realizing that she really was welcome, began to relax, and she and his mother exchanged the sort of gossip they both loved.

"Ah, Dinny Murphy was a bad head to her," his mother would say darkly, referring to some object of charity in the neighborhood.

"No, no, no, Mrs. Grahame," Eileen would say hastily, in her eagerness laying her hand on Mrs. Grahame's arm. "Poor Dinny wasn't the worst."

"Look at that now!" Mrs. Grahame would cry, putting down her knitting to fix Eileen with eyes that were bleak with tragedy. "And the things they said about him! Eileen, haven't people *bad* tongues?"

"No, he wasn't, he wasn't," Eileen would repeat, shaking her head. "He took a drop, of course, but which of them doesn't, would you tell me?"

And Jim, who said nothing, smiled as he noticed how the voice of Eileen, young, eager, and intelligent, blended with his mother's in a perfect harmony of gossip. Mrs. Grahame did not let her go without hinting delicately at her lost and lonely condition that made it impossible for her to know the truth about anything, and made her promise to come again. She became accustomed to Eileen's visits, and was quite hurt if a week went by without one. She even said with great resignation that of course she was no company for a lively young girl like that.

Then it was Mrs. Clery's turn. She might hear of Eileen's visits to the Grahames, and be upset, but, on the other hand, she might be equally upset by an unexpected visit. So Eileen had to prepare her by telling her first how Jim was situated with regard to his own mother so that she wouldn't think he came to the house with any designs on Eileen. All they had to live on was Eileen's earnings and a few shillings' pension which her mother drew.

They lived in a tiny cottage in a terrace off the road, with a parlor, a kitchen that they used as a living room, and two attic bedrooms upstairs. Mrs. Clery was a shrewd old lady with a battered humorous face. She suffered from a variety of ailments, and, being slightly deaf, complained of them at great length in a loud, hectoring tone. She would put a firm hand on her interlocutor's knee while she talked, to make sure he didn't escape, and then stare blankly at the fireplace in concentration.

"So then, Jim, I had this second pain I was telling you about, and I had Doctor O'Mahoney to the house, and he said—what did doctor O'Mahoney say about the second pain, Eileen?"

"He said you were an old humbug," bawled Eileen

"Dr. O'Mahoney?" her mother said in wonderment. "He did not. Ah, you divil you!"

At home, Eileen talked nervously, at the top of her voice, interrupting, contradicting, and bantering her mother till the old woman's face wrinkled up with glee and she blinked at Jim and groaned: "Didn't I say she was a divil, Jim? Did you ever hear a girl talk to her mother that way? I'll engage you don't talk like that to your own poor mother."

"His mother isn't always grousing," Eileen yelled blithely from the back yard.

"Grousing? Who's grousing?" asked Mrs. Clery, her eyes half-closing with pleasure, like a cat's when you stroke it. "Oh, my, I live in terror of her. Jim, boy, you never heard such a tongue! And the lies she tells! Me grousing!"

ALL THE SAME it was pleasant for Jim and Eileen to have a place to turn to on a wet night when they didn't want to go to the pictures.

Mostly, they went to Jim's. Mrs. Grahame was more jealous than Eileen's mother. Even a hint of slight on the part of either of them would reduce her to mutinous tears, but if they sat with her for half an hour, she would get up and tiptoe gently out of the room as though she thought they were asleep. Her jealousy was only the measure of her generosity.

"Wisha, Jim," she said roguishly one evening, putting down her knitting, "wouldn't you and Eileen make a match of it?"

"A match?" Jim repeated mockingly, looking up from his book. "I suppose you want to get rid of me?"

His mother could usually be diverted from any subject by teasing because she took everything literally even if she rarely took it far.

"Indeed, what a thing I'd do!" she said in a huff and went on with her knitting, full of childish rage at his reception of her generous proposal. But, of course, it didn't last. Ten minutes later, having forgotten her huff, she added, this time as though speaking to herself: "Why, then, you wouldn't find many like her."

"And where would we live?" he asked with gentle irony.

"My goodness, haven't ye the house?" she said, looking at him severely over her glasses. "You don't think I'd stop to be in your way?"

"Oh, so you'd go to the workhouse and let Mrs. Clery come here?"

"Wisha, aren't things very peculiar?" she said vaguely, and he knew that she was brooding on the coincidence by which he and Eileen had been drawn together. His mother and he were both familiar with the situation in its simple form, common as it is in Ireland, and could have listed a score of families where a young man or woman walked out for years before he or she was in a position to marry, too often only to find themselves too old or tired for it.

"We're not thinking in that direction at all, Mrs. Grahame, thank you all the same," he said, giving her a sweet smile. "It's got to be a double murder or nothing at all."

HE KNEW that in spite of her jealousy, Mrs. Grahame resented this fate for them, but Mrs. Clery jovially pretended that they should be grateful for their good fortune.

"Ye don't know how well off ye are," she said. "Ye're young and healthy; a lot ye have to complain of. The way they rush into marriage you'd think they were robbing a bank. Soon enough they get tired of it, and then, oh my! Nothing is bad enough for them to say about one another."

"So you don't approve of marriage, Mammy?" Eileen would ask demurely.

"Who said I don't approve of marriage?" her mother asked suspiciously, certain that the "divils" were trapping her again. "What matter whether you approve of it or not? That doesn't make it any better. Let ye be young while ye can, Jim," she counseled, laying a rocky hand on Jim's knee. "Ye'll be married long enough."

But, of course, Eileen and himself did not share her views. On their evening walks they usually passed through one of the new developments, glanced into half-built houses with the enthusiasm of the children who played cowboys and Indians in them; chatted with young husbands digging in little patches of garden that were mainly builders' rubble, and let themselves be invited in for cups of tea by young couples in all the pride and joy of recent possession. They saw nothing of the ugliness of it. They saw only the newness of everything as though it were life itself renewed; the way the evening sunlight brought up the freshness of the paint, the whiteness of the curtains, the tender green of the new grass. Later in the evening Eileen would say, shaking her head: "I didn't think the curtains were right in the big corner windows, Jim, did you?" and Jim would know she had furnished the house in her own mind.

THAT YEAR Jim suggested that he and Eileen should take their holidays together. This didn't suit Mrs. Clery at all. She was sure it would give Eileen a bad name. Mrs. Clery was all for their being young while they could, but only as long as they were being young under her eye. Jim knew it wasn't Eileen's good name that her mother worried about at all, but the possibility that their holiday might start something she could not control. He had his way; they went to a seaside place north of Dublin, and walked and swam and sun-bathed to their hearts' content for a fortnight, going into the city when it rained.

On their way home, looking out at the Galtee Mountains from the window of their carriage, he said: "Next time we go on holidays like that, we should be married. It's not the same thing."

"No, Jim, it isn't," she agreed. "But what can we do?"

"What's to stop us getting married?" he asked with a smile.

"Now?" she asked in alarm. "But what would we do with our mothers?"

"What we do with them now," he said with a shrug.

"You mean get married and go on the way we're going?"

"Why not? Of course, it's not what we want, but it's better than nothing."

"But suppose—well, Jim, you know yourself there might be children."

"I should hope so," he replied. "We can cross that bridge when we come to it. But anyhow, there's no particular reason we should have kids yet."

"But Jim," she asked timidly, "wouldn't people talk?"

"Do you think they don't talk now?"

Jim was like that, and what Jim thought his mother would think, regardless of public opinion. She, of course, had seen nothing wrong with their going on holidays together, and Eileen, who had felt rather doubtful of it herself, now knew that she was right. She felt he was probably right now too, but she wasn't sure.

The more she thought of it, the more she felt he was, though her reasons were of a different kind. Jim didn't want to wait; he didn't want to grow old and sour in expectation of the day when they could get married; he wanted something, however little it might be, of the pleasure of marriage while they were still young enough to enjoy it. Eileen thought of it in a more mystical way, as a sort of betrothal which would bind them to one another, whatever life might have in store for them. She knew it was too much to hope that she and Jim would both be set free at the same time; one would be bound to be free long before the other, and then the real temptation would begin.

But she knew that even this she would not get without a fight with her mother. Mrs. Clery was conventional to the heart, and besides she knew what happened in marriage. Eileen was very sweet and gentle now, but Eileen as wife or mother would be an altogether different proposition and one an old lady might be unable to handle at all.

"What a thing you'd do!" Mrs. Clery gasped with one hand on her hip. "What sort of marriage would that be? Him living there and you living here! You'd have the whole town laughing at you."

"I don't really see what they'd have to laugh at, Mammy," Eileen said earnestly. "Any more than they have now."

"Go off with him!" her mother said brokenly. "Go on off with him! I'd sooner go to the workhouse than be disgraced by ye."

"But, Mammy," persisted Eileen, laughing in spite of herself, "we won't do anything to disgrace you, and you won't have to go to the workhouse or anywhere else."

MRS. GRAHAME was upset too, but it was her pride that was hurt. What the neighbors would say did not worry her at all, but it seemed to her that it was her dependence on Jim that forced him into this caricature of a marriage. If by getting out of his way she could have made it easier for him, she would cheerfully have gone into the workhouse.

But when Jim explained that even if he agreed to her doing so, it would change nothing regarding Eileen and her mother, she saw that he was right. When next Eileen called, Mrs. Grahame embraced her and muttered: "Ye poor children! Ye poor, distracted children!"

"You don't think we're doing wrong, Mrs. Grahame?" Eileen asked, beginning to be tearful herself.

"Sure, how could you be doing wrong, child?" Mrs. Grahame exclaimed angrily. "Why would ye care what anybody thinks? People who never sacrificed a thing in their lives!"

Then Mrs. Clery threw a fit of the sulks, would not speak to Jim when he called, and finally refused to attend what she called "the mock wedding." Mrs. Clery had little experience of that sort of thing but she did know when she had been tricked, and she had been tricked by Jim. He had come to the house as a friend and stolen her only daughter from under her eyes. As for all this talk of putting her first, she didn't believe a word of it. A man who would do what he had done would think nothing of putting arsenic in her cup of tea.

BEFORE she left for the church that morning, Eileen went into her mother and asked gently: "Mammy, won't you even wish me luck?" But all her mother said was "Go away, you bold thing!"

"I'll be back tomorrow night in time to get your supper, Mammy," Eileen said meekly.

"You needn't come back at all," said her mother.

Eileen was very upset, but Mrs. Grahame only scoffed at it when they said good-bye outside the church.

"Ah, she'll get over it, child," she said. "Old people are all lick alike. I'm the same myself, if the truth was known. I'll see her on the way home and give her a bit of my mind."

"And, Mrs. Grahame, if you wouldn't mind making her an egg flip, she'd be easier to talk to," Eileen said earnestly. "She's very fond of egg flips, and she likes a lot of whiskey in them."

"I'll give her an egg flip," said Mrs. Grahame, suddenly lighthearted because her own savage jealousy melted in the thought of comforting another old woman in her tantrums. She had a job on her hands, even with the egg flip.

"Don't talk to me, ma'am!" cried Mrs. Clery. "Young people today are all the same; all selfish, all for pleasure."

"How can you say it, Mrs. Clery?" Mrs. Grahame asked indignantly. "There isn't a better daughter in Ireland. I'd be the last to criticize Jim, but I only wish I had one like her."

"And when the children start coming?" asked Mrs. Clery, looking at her as if she were out of her mind.

"You reared one yourself."

" 'Tisn't alike, ma'am," said Mrs. Clery and refused to be comforted. She was intelligent enough to realize that the presence of another baby in the house might rob her of some of the attention to which she felt entitled, and might even result in her being totally deprived of her privileges. Young people today were so selfish!

AFTER their one-day honeymoon, Jim and Eileen obediently returned to their duties as though they had never been married at all. Yet Eileen, when you met her on the road, was exceedingly lighthearted and lightheaded, sporting her ring like any young bride. She needed all the joy her new position gave her because her mother had been shrewd enough in her summing up of what the neighbors' attitude would be. The marriage had become a matter of scandalous jokes, and remained so as long as it lasted. Even from intimate friends, Eileen got little jabs that reminded her of her anomalous wifehood. It wasn't that the neighbors were uncharitable, but their feelings about marriage, like their feelings about death, had a certain fierceness that was obvious even in their dislike of second marriages. This marriage that seemed to end at the church door was a mockery of all they believed in, so they took their revenge as people will whose dearest beliefs have been slighted.

Jim affected not to notice the scandal: he had his mother's curious imperviousness to public opinion, and he dropped in on Eileen as though nothing in particular could be said against him. Eileen dropped in rather more frequently on him and his mother, and Jim and she went off for a fortnight in the summer to Kerry or Connemara. It took Mrs. Clery a full year to get used to it, and all that time she watched Eileen closely, expecting her each week to show signs of pregnancy. Perhaps it was fortunate that there were none. Heaven alone knows what she might have done.

Then Mrs. Grahame fell ill, and Jim nursed her by day while Eileen took over from him at night. She was dying, and in the intervals of consciousness, she molded Eileen's hands with her own and said: "I always wanted a daughter, and I had my wish. I had my wish. Ye'll be happy now that ye have the house to yerselves. You'll look after Jim for me?"

"I'll look after him for you," Eileen said, and on the night when his mother died, she let him sleep on.

"I thought I'd better not wake you, Jim," she said when she roused him next morning. "You were so tired and Mammy went so peacefully. . . . That's the way she'd have wished it, Jim," she added gravely when she saw his look of surprise.

"I dare say you're right, Eileen," he agreed.

BUT their troubles were far from being at an end. When they proposed to shift into Jim's house, Mrs. Clery raised more of a hullabaloo than she had raised over the marriage.

"Is it up among strangers?" she cried aghast.

"Strangers half a mile away, Mammy?" Eileen exclaimed, still unable to conceal a laugh at her mother's extraordinary reception of every new proposal.

"Half a mile?" her mother echoed dully. " 'Tis a mile."

"And you think your old friends would desert you?" asked Eileen.

"I wouldn't ask them," her mother replied with dignity. "I couldn't sleep in a place where I wouldn't hear the sound of the trams. Jim's mother died in her own house. Oh, my, isn't it a queer thing he wouldn't let me die in mine!"

And once more Jim and Eileen had to resign themselves to frustration. They could offer no adequate substitute for the soothing squeak of the trams climbing Summerhill from the city, and as Eileen saw, it would be folly for them to give up Jim's excellent house, which they would need later on, and come to share her own tiny cottage with a cranky mother-in-law.

Instead, they played at being married. On a couple of evenings each week, Eileen would give her mother supper early, and then come to Jim's house and have supper ready for him when he got in from the shop. When she heard his key in the lock, she ran to the front door to meet him in her white housecoat, and he would let on to be suitably astonished at seeing her. As they went in, she would point silently to the big fire she had lit in the living room, and they would have supper together and read or talk till he saw her home coming on to midnight. Yet, even with the extra work, it gave them both a deep pleasure to make the big bed that Eileen never slept in except as a visitor, to wash up together, or best of all, to entertain some friends, just as though Eileen did not, like Cinderella, have to fly back at midnight to her old part as daughter and nurse. Someday, they felt, the house would really be theirs, and she would open the door in the morning to milkman and breadman.

But this was not how things happened. Instead, Jim fell seriously ill, and rather than consent to the conflict which he knew this would set up in Eileen's mind between her duty to him and her duty to her mother, he chose to go to hospital. Two years after his mother's death, he died there.

SOMETHING seemed to happen to Eileen at this point that made even her mother afraid. There was no argument between them as to what she should do. She shut up her own cottage, and her mother joined her in Jim's house, where she received his relatives. The body had been taken to the church, and when Jim's family came, Eileen had lunch ready for them, and chatted as she served, as though the trouble had been theirs rather than hers. It was a cold lunch, and she was full of apologies. At the graveside while they wept, she showed no sign of tears. When the grave had been covered over Jim and his mother, she stood there silently, her head bowed, and Jim's aunt, an enormous woman, came up and took her two hands.

"You're a great little girl," she whispered huskily. " 'Twon't be forgotten for you."

"But, Auntie," Eileen replied, "that's the way Jim would have liked it. It makes me feel close to him, and it won't be too long till we're together again. Once Mammy goes, there'll be nothing to keep me."

There was something about her words and her dry-eyed air and her still youthful face, that the other woman found disconcerting.

"Ah, nonsense, child!" she said lightly. "We all feel that way. You'll be happy yet, and you'll deserve it. One of these days you'll have a houseful of your own."

"Oh, no, Auntie," Eileen replied with a sweet smile that was curiously knowledgeable and even condescending, as though Jim's aunt were too much of a child to understand. "You know yourself I could never find another husband like Jim. People can't be as happy as that a second time, you know. That would be too much to ask."

And relatives and even neighbors began to realize that Eileen was only telling the truth; that in spite of everything she had been intensely happy, happy in some way they could not understand, and that what had seemed to them a mockery of marriage had indeed been one so complete and satisfying that beside it, even by their standards, a woman might think everything else in the world a mere shadow.

The Cheat

THE ONLY THING that distinguished Dick Gordon from the other young men of my time in Cork was his attitude to religion. As an engineer he seemed to feel that he could not afford to believe in anything but the second law of thermodynamics: according to him, this contained everything a man required to know.

For years he courted a girl called Joan Twomey, and everyone expected he would marry her and settle down as most men of his kind do. Usually, they are of a serious disposition and settle down more easily than the rest of humanity. You often see them in their later years, carrying round the collecting bag at twelve-o'clock Mass, and wonder what has happened to all their wild dreams of free thought and social justice. Marriage is the great leveller.

But Joan's mother died, and she had to do the housekeeping for a father and two younger sisters, so she became serious too, and there was no more reckless behavior in the little seaside house they rented in summer. She was afraid of marrying a man who did not believe in anything and would probably bring up his children the same way. She was wrong in this, because Dick was much too tolerant a man to deprive his worst enemy of the pleasure of believing in eternal damnation, much less his wife, but Joan's seriousness had developed to the dimensions of spiritual pride and she gave him up as she might have given up some pleasure for Lent.

Dick was mystified and hurt: it was the first shock to his feeling of the basic reasonableness of life; but he did not allow it to change him. After all, his brother Tom was an ex-cleric and he had been worked on by experts. Some time later he met a girl called Barbara Hough who was a teacher in a Protestant school and started to walk out with her. On the surface Barbara was much more his style. She was good-looking and urbane, vaguely atheistic and left-wing in her views, and she thought that all Irish people, Catholic and Protestant, were quite insane on the subject of religion. All the same, for a young fellow of good

Catholic family to take up with a Protestant at all was a challenge, and Barbara, who was a high-spirited girl, enjoyed it and made the most of it. His friends were amused and his family alarmed. Of course, Dick could get a dispensation if Barbara signed the paper guaranteeing that their children would be brought up as Catholics, but would Barbara, who was a rector's daughter, agree to it? Characteristically, when his brother Tom asked him this, Dick only smiled and said, "Funny, isn't it? I never asked her." He would probably have been quite safe in doing so, for though Barbara herself did not recognize it, she had all the loneliness of one brought up in a minority religion, always feeling that she was missing something, and much of Dick's appeal for her was that he was a Prince Charming who had broken the magic circle in which she felt she would be trapped until the day she died. But Dick did not ask her. Instead he proposed a quiet register-office marriage in London, and she was so moved by his consideration for her that she did not even anticipate what the consequences might be.

You see, it was part of Dick's simplicity of mind that he could not realize that there were certain perfectly simple things you couldn't do without involving yourself in more trouble than they were worth, or if he did see it, he underrated its importance. A few of his old friends stood by him, but even they had to admit that there was an impossible streak in him. When Barbara was having a baby the family deputed his brother Tom to warn him of what he was doing. Tom was tall, good-looking, dreamy, and morbidly sensitive. He did not want to approach Dick at all, but seeing that he was the nearest thing to a priest in the family, he felt that it might be his duty.

"You know what people are going to think, Dick," he said with a stammer.

"The same as they think now, I suppose, " Dick replied with his gentle smile.

"This is different, Dick."

"How, Tom?"

"This concerns a third party, you see," said Tom, too embarrassed even to mention such things as babies to his brother.

"And a fourth and fifth, I hope," Dick said cheerfully. "It's a natural result of marriage, you know. And children do take after their parents, for the first few years anyway."

"Not in this country, they don't," Tom said ruefully. "I suppose there are historical reasons for it," he added, being a great student of history.

"There are historical reasons for everything in this country, Tom," said Dick with a jolly laugh. "But because some old fool believes in the fairies for good historical reasons is no excuse for bringing up my kids the same way."

"Ah, well, it's not as foolish as all that, Dick," said Tom, looking more miserable than ever. "It's poetic, or fanciful, or whatever you like, but it's what we were brought up to believe, and our fathers and grandfathers before us."

"And the monks told us that Ireland was such a holy country that we'd have the end of the world eight years before anywhere else. . . . I'm not sure what the advantage was supposed to be. . . . I don't suppose you still believe that?"

"Why would I?" asked Tom. "It's not an article of faith."

"It was an article of faith to you and me, and I wouldn't have liked to be the fellow that disbelieved it," said Dick with a sniff. "Anyway, it's no worse than the rest of the nonsense we listen to. That sort of thing is looked on as childishness everywhere else today, and it'll be looked on as childishness here, too, in your lifetime and mine. In fifteen years' time people will only laugh at it."

That was Dick all out, entirely reasonable and tolerant, and yet as big a misfit as if he had two heads. How could any responsible superior recommend a man as pig-headed as that for promotion? The sensible thing for Dick would have been to emigrate and start all over again in England or America where apparitions were not so highly regarded, but there was a dogged, cynical streak in him that derived a sort of morose pleasure from seeing some devotee of apparitions promoted over his head and making a mess of some perfectly simple job.

He had a number of friends who sympathized with his views and who met at his little house in the College Road on Sundays to discuss the latest piece of jobbery in the University. They grew mad about it, but Dick's attitude of amused tolerance rarely varied. At most he sighed: it was as though he saw things that they could not see. One old schoolteacher called Murphy used to grow furious with him over this. He was a gloomy-looking, handsome man who was at the same time very pious and very anticlerical. Passion made him break out in angles, as when he called his old friends "Mister."

"Mister Gordon," he shouted one night, "you're out of your mind. A hundred years from now the descendants of those hobblers will still be seeing apparitions behind every bush."

"They won't, Ned," Dick said with a smile. He was particularly fond of Murphy and enjoyed seeing him in a rage.

"What'll stop them, Mister Gordon?"

"Facts, Ned!"

"Facts!"

"Facts impose their own logic, Ned. They're imposing it now, at this very minute, here and everywhere, even though we may not see it. It's only an elaboration of skills. Skills here are still too rudimentary. But women are beginning to do men's work, and they'll have to think men's thoughts. You can't control that, you know. The world you're talking about is finished. In ten or fifteen years' time it'll be a joke. Simple facts will destroy it."

THAT was all very well. Dick might have a good eye for what was going on in the outside world, but he had no eye at all for what was going on in his own very house. One evening, after they had been married for ten years, Dick was at home and Barbara out with their son, Tom, when there was a knock at the door. Outside was a young priest; a tall, thin, good-looking young man with a devil-may-care eye.

"Can I come in?" he asked, as though he had no doubt whatever of his welcome.

"Oh, come in, come in!" said Dick with a thin smile. He hated those embarrassing occasions when people with more self-confidence than manners enquired how his soul was doing. He was a friendly man and did not like to appear rude or ungrateful.

"Mrs. G. out?" the priest asked cheerfully.

"Yes, gone into town for some messages," Dick said resignedly. "She won't be long."

"Ah, it gives us the chance of a little chat," said the priest, pulling at the legs of his trousers.

"Look, father, I don't want a little chat, as you call it," Dick said appealingly. "This town is full of people who want little chats with me, and they can't understand that I don't appreciate them. I gave up religion when I was eighteen, and I have no intention in the world of going back to it."

"Did I ask you to go back to it?" the priest asked with an air of consternation. "I wasn't expecting to see you at all, man! I came here to talk to your wife. You are Mrs. Gordon's husband, aren't you?"

"Yes," Dick replied, somewhat surprised by the priest's tone.

"Well, she's been receiving instruction. Didn't you know that?"

Dick was a hard man to catch off balance, and when he replied he did not even sound surprised.

"Instruction? No. I didn't."

"Crumbs, I'm after saying the wrong thing again!" the priest said angrily. "I shouldn't be left out without a male nurse. Look, I'm terribly sorry. I'll come back another time."

"Oh, as you're here, you may as well stay," Dick said amiably. It was partly pride, partly pity. He could see that the priest was genuinely distressed.

"Another time! Another time!"

"Who will I say called?" Dick asked as he saw him to the door.

"The name is Hogan. Mr. Gordon, I wouldn't have wished it for a hundred pounds."

"It was hardly your fault," Dick said with a friendly smile.

But as he closed the door the smile faded and he found himself cold and shaking. He poured himself a drink but it only made him feel sick. Nothing that could have happened to him would have been quite so bad as this. He had been betrayed shamelessly and treacherously and he could already see himself as the laughing stock of the city. A man's loneliness is his strength and only a wife can really destroy him because only she can understand his loneliness.

He heard her key in the lock and wished he had left before her return. He liked to be master of himself and now he feared he had no control over what he did or said.

"Dick!" she called in her clear ringing voice and opened the living-room door. "Is something wrong?" she asked as he did not turn round. "One moment, Tom!" she said to the child in the hall. "Run upstairs and take your things off. I'll call you when tea is ready. Don't argue now, sweetheart. Mummy is busy." She closed the door behind her and approached him. "I suppose Father Hogan called," she added in her weary well-bred voice. "Was that it? You should know I intended to tell you. I wanted to make up my own mind first." Still he did not reply and she burst out into a wail. "Oh, Dick, I've tried to tell you so often and I didn't have the courage."

She knew the moment he looked at her that she had fooled herself; persuaded herself that he was dull and tolerant and gentle and that nothing she did to him would affect their relationship. It is the weak spot in the cheat, man and woman.

"You hadn't the courage," he repeated dully. "But you had the courage to make a fool of me before your clerical friends."

"I didn't, Dick," she said hotly. "But you know yourself it's something I can't discuss with you. It's a subject you can't be reasonable about."

The word "reasonable" stung him.

"Is that what you call being reasonable?" he asked bitterly. "I should have been reasonable and made you conform before I married you. I should have been reasonable and brought Tom up as my family wanted him brought up. Every day of my life I had to accept humiliation on your account when I could have been reasonable about it all. And then you don't even have the courage to discuss with me what you're going to do or what the consequences will be for Tom. You prefer to bring him up believing that his father is damned! There's reasonableness for you!"

"But I'd discuss it with you now, Dick, if only you'd listen to me patiently." She began to wring her hands. "It's not my fault if I can't live without believing in something."

"In Heaven," he said cynically.

"In Heaven, if you like. Anyway, in something for you and me and Tom. I was brought up to believe in it, and I threw it away because I didn't value it, and now I need it—maybe because I haven't anything else. If only you wouldn't tell me it's all just nonsense!"

"Why should I tell you anything?" he asked. "You have better advisers now."

In fact, he never did discuss it with her. He even allowed Tom to go to Mass with her and attend the local monks' school without protest. The older Tom was Barbara's biggest surprise. She knew that in arguments with Dick he had taken her side, but when they discussed it together he seemed to judge her far more severely than Dick. It was curious, because the diffidence, the slight stammer, the charming smile did not change.

"Of course, Barbara, as a Catholic I am naturally pleased, for your sake and the kid's, but as Dick's brother I can't help feeling that it's unfortunate."

"But don't you think it may help Dick to see things a bit differently in the course of time?"

"No, Barbara, I don't," he said with a gentle, almost pitying smile.

"But, Tom, I don't see that it should make any more difference than it does between you and Dick."

"Marriage is different, Barbara," he said, and she didn't even see anything peculiar about being told of marriage by a man who had almost been given up by his own family as unmarriageable. "People don't know it, but they marry for protection as much as anything else, and sometimes they have to be protected at the cost of other people's principles."

"And you think Dick needs protection?" she asked wonderingly.

"I think Dick needs a great deal of protection, Barbara," he said with an accusing look.

There was a good deal of talk in the city, much of it ill-natured, though on the whole it did Dick less harm than good. He had ceased to be an active force for evil and become a mere figure of fun, as vulnerable to ridicule as any University intriguer. It had even become safe to promote him.

But it was old Ned Murphy who said the thing that stuck. He and two of Dick's other friends were drinking in a public-house one night, and the others—Cashman and Enright, who was a bit of a smart aleck—were making good-humored fun of Dick. Murphy alone did not laugh at all. He scowled and rubbed his forehead with his fist till it grew inflamed.

"It's like your wife having an affair with another man," he said sourly, and because he was unmarried, Cashman and Enright laughed louder. Still there was something uncomfortably apt about the analogy; both were married men and there had been a small scandal about Enright's wife, who had had an affair with a commercial traveller. They knew there was always another man, a shadowy figure, not real as they were, and they dreaded his presence in the background.

"Still, you'd think he'd have given her some cause," said Cashman.

"He gave her plenty of cause," said Murphy.

"But they always got on well together."

"They got on all right," Murphy admitted. "But she must have had a terrible life with him. She's a religious girl."

"Lots of religious girls marry men like that, though," said Enright, as though he were following the conversation, which he wasn't.

"Not men like Dick Gordon," Murphy said broodingly. "He's an optimist, and optimism is the plague of a religious mind. Dick has no notion how intolerable life can be. A man like that doesn't even believe in evil."

DICK'S optimism was tested severely enough a few years later. He was ill, and word was going round that he would never be well again.

This put half Cork in a flutter, because everyone who had ever had a conversation with him seemed to feel a personal responsibility for seeing that he was converted, and those who might see him were warmly advised of what they should do and say. His boss put a car at the disposal of his friends so that they could rush a priest to his bedside at any hour of the day or night. "Vultures are a breed of bird that has always fascinated me, though I thought they were supposed to be extinct," said Ned Murphy.

Barbara was exasperated by all the hysteria, more particularly because it put her in such a false position, and her replies became shorter. "I'm afraid it is a matter I never discuss with my husband," she said. "There are certain things that are too personal even for a wife." Even that did not put people off the subject. They said that converts were never really like their own people.

One rainy evening Dick was alone in the house, trying to read, when a strange priest called. He was tall and fat and very grave.

"Mr. Gordon?" he said.

"Yes," said Dick.

"Can I come in for a moment?"

"Oh, certainly. Sit down."

"You don't know who I am, Mr. Gordon," the priest said jovially as he took a chair. "I know quite a lot about you, though. I'm the parish priest, Father Ryan."

Dick nodded.

"Mr. Gordon, I want to talk to you about your soul," he said with a change of tone.

Dick smiled and lit a cigarette. He had been through it all so often.

"Surely, among your congregation you could find plenty of others," he suggested mildly.

"Not many in such danger, shall we say," the priest replied with a smile. Something about the smile shook Dick. It seemed to radiate a sort of cold malice which was new to him.

"Considering that we've only just met, you seem to know a lot about the state of my soul," Dick said with the same weary sarcasm.

"Mr. Gordon," the priest said, raising his hand, "I wasn't speaking only of your spiritual danger. Mr. Gordon, you're a very sick man."

Dick rose and opened the door for him.

"Father Ryan, you're concerning yourself with things that have nothing to do with you," he said icily. "Now, do you mind getting out of my house?"

"Your arrogance won't last long, Mr. Gordon," the priest said. "You're dying of cancer."

"You heard me," Dick said menacingly.

"You have less than three months to live."

"All the more reason I shouldn't be persecuted by busybodies like you," Dick said with sudden anger. "Now get out before I throw you out."

He scarcely raised his voice, but anger was so rare with him that it had a sinister quality that overawed the priest.

"You'll regret this," he said.

"Probably," Dick said between his teeth. "I'll regret that I didn't treat you as you deserve."

Afterward he went back to his book, but he was even more incapable of reading or of understanding what he read. Something about the priest's tone had upset him. He was himself almost devoid of malice and had shrugged off the opposition to himself as mere foolishness, but this was something more and worse than foolishness. This was foolishness going bad, foolishness turning into naked evil. And Dick, as Ned Murphy had said, did not really believe in evil.

When Barbara came in he was still sitting in darkness before the fire, brooding.

"Hello, dear," she said with false brightness. "All alone?"

"Except for a clerical gentleman who just called," he said with an air of amusement.

"Oh, dear!" she said in distress. "Who was it?"

"His name is Ryan. A rather unusual character."

"What did he want?"

"Oh, just to tell me I had cancer and had less than three months to live," Dick said bitterly.

"Oh, God, no, Dick! He didn't say that?" she cried, and began to weep.

He looked at her in surprise and concern and then got up.

"Oh, don't worry about that, Babs!" he said with a shrug. "It's only their stock in trade, you know. You should have heard the pleasure with which he said it! Where would they be without their skeleton to brandish?"

It was only the sort of thing he had said to her in the early days of their marriage and had not said since her conversion. She did not know whether he really meant it or said it just to comfort her. After their years of married life he was still gentle and considerate. His brother Tom was little help to her.

"I'll only have to try and be at the house more," he said gloomily. "This thing could happen again."

"But can't we complain to the Bishop about it?" she said angrily.

"I'm afraid that wouldn't do much good, Barbara. The Bishop would be more likely to take Father Ryan's side. By the way, have you confidence in that doctor of yours?"

"Dr. Cullen? Oh, I suppose he did what he could."

"I don't mean that," Tom said patiently. "Are you sure he didn't go to Father Ryan himself?"

"Oh, God, Tom!" she said. "What sort of people are they?"

"Much like people anywhere else, I suppose," he said despondently.

After this, she dreaded leaving Dick alone. She knew now the hysteria that surrounded them and knew that those who indulged in it were ruthless in a way that Dick would never understand.

One day she was upstairs chatting with him when the doorbell rang.

She answered it and saw Father Hogan outside. He was now parish priest in a village ten miles outside the town, and they saw less of him. He was one of the few friends she had whom Dick seemed to like.

"Come in here, please, father," she said, and led him into the little front room. She closed the door and spoke in a low voice. "Father, I can't have Dick persecuted now."

"Persecuted?" he asked in surprise. "Who's persecuting him?"

"You know what he believes," she said. "I daresay he's wrong, and if you catch him in a moment of weakness he may say he's wrong, but it will be his weakness, not him."

"What the hell are you talking about?" he asked angrily. "Are you out of your mind? I rang him up when I heard he was sick, and he asked me to call for a drink. I'm not going to do anything to him—except maybe give him conditional absolution when it's all over, and that won't be on his account. There are people in this town who'd try to refuse him Christian burial. You don't know it, but you wouldn't like it. No more would his family."

"You had nothing to do with the man who told him he was dying?"

"Why?" he asked quietly. "Did someone do that?"

"The parish priest did it."

"And am I to be held responsible for every fool and lout who happens to wear a soutane?" he asked bitterly. "He asked me in for a drink, Barbara, and I'm going to have it with him, whatever you may think. . . ." Then with one of his quick changes of mood he asked, "Did it upset him?"

"Fortunately, he didn't believe it."

"Didn't believe it, or pretended not to believe it?" he asked shrewdly and then threw the question away. "Ah, how would you know? I won't disturb him, Barbara," he added gently. "I wish I was as sure of my own salvation as I am of his."

"So do I—now," she said, and he knew as though he were inside her that she was regretting the weakness of years before and wishing that she could go into the dark with her husband as they had both imagined it when they were young and in love. It was the only way that would have meant anything to Dick now. But he was a good priest and he could not afford to brood on what it all meant. He still had a duty to the living as well as to the friend who was about to die.

The Weeping Children

JOE SAUNDERS and his wife, Brigid, had been married a year when they had their first baby—a little girl they called Nance, after Brigid's mother. Brigid was Irish, and Joe had always had a feeling that there must be some Irish blood in himself. She was a Catholic, and, though Joe was an unbeliever, he liked it in her, and encouraged her to put up holy pictures and statues all over the house. He even went to Mass with her occasionally, but she said he put her off her prayers with his air of devotion, which made him laugh. She often made him laugh, and he liked it, because he had a natural gravity that turned easily to melancholy and even tears. She had good breeding as well, and he liked that too, though she sometimes upset him by the way she unconsciously patronized his mother and sisters. They were common, and he knew they were common, but he didn't like it to be rubbed in. Brigid had kept her girlish gaiety and her delight in flirting shamelessly with any man who fancied her. It amused Joe, because for all her charm, he knew the wild, chaste, innocent streak in her, and realized that the smart operators would get absolutely nowhere with her.

After Nance's birth Joe felt that life had done him proud. There were times when he saw everything with a sort of double vision, as though he were not only doing whatever he was doing—like pushing the pram round the estate, or creeping into the back room at night to see that the baby was covered—but watching himself do it, as though he were someone in a film or a book, and the conjunction of the two visions gave the thing itself an intense stereoscopic quality. He was sure that this must be what people meant when they talked of happiness.

But he realized that it was different for Brigid. Though at times she could forget herself and play with the baby like a girl with a doll, she was often gloomy, tearful, and irritable. This was not like her. Joe's great friend, Jerry Cross, called it something like postpartum psychosis, and though Joe had no great faith in the long names Jerry liked to give things, he accepted his advice and took Brigid for a week to Brighton. It did her good but only for a short while. Joe—a sensitive man—sometimes thought he knew exactly how she felt—a wild girl with a vivacious temperament, who loved outings and parties, trapped by a morsel of humanity who took everything and gave nothing.

Joe was attentive to the point of officiousness, seeing that she went to the cinema and visited friends. But even to old friends she had changed, and had taken a positive dislike to Jerry Cross. Though Jerry was great at giving women little presents, he didn't seem to like them much, and now Brigid chose to interpret this as dislike of herself. With a sort of schoolgirl pertness that drove Joe to despair she mocked Cross about his overheated bachelor flat, his expensive gramophone and collection of records, and his liqueur cabinet that always seemed to contain some new exotic drink that Jerry would press on his visitors, rubbing his hands and saying in his anxious way, "It's not bad, is it? I mean, it really is not bad. You think that, too, Joe." Twice, to protect Cross, Joe had to reprove her, and though he did it gently, it cut him to the heart to have to do it at all.

"Why can't you be nicer to Jerry?" he asked as they were going home one night. "He hasn't so many friends."

"He has no friends at all, if you ask me," Brigid said coldly. "He's too bloody selfish to afford them."

"Selfish?" Joe exclaimed, stopping dead. "A man who put a check for two hundred quid on my mantelpiece while I was out of the room!"

"We know all that," Brigid said contemptuously. "Damn well he knew you wouldn't take it."

"He knew more than I did," Joe said, resuming his walk. "Anyway, it wasn't the money that mattered at the time. It was his confidence in me. It gave me confidence in myself. I tell you, Brigid, there are things between men that you'll never understand, not till the day you die."

But argument had no effect on Brigid except perhaps to give her fresh grounds for spite. One evening at Joe's house, Cross was boasting innocently of some shady deal he had refused to be connected with, and Brigid, with mock admiration, drew him skillfully out. It was one of Cross's little weaknesses that he liked to think himself a really shrewd businessman—"a bloody dreamer" was how an uncle had described him to Joe.

"You always play it safe, Jerry, don't you?" she asked at last.

"What's that, Brigid?" Cross asked eagerly, too pleased with himself to be aware of her malice.

"Brigid!" Joe said warningly.

"Anyone who had anything to do with you would want to watch out," she said.

Cross got up and clutched the lapels of his coat as though he were about to make a speech. It suddenly struck Joe that he was a little man who lived in expectation of having to make speeches—unpleasant ones, in his own defense.

"I assure you, Brigid, that nobody who had anything to do with me ever had to watch out, as you put it," he said overloudly, speaking as it were to a faraway audience. "I do play it safe, though. You're right there, I do. And I'll play it safer for the future by not calling here, as I have been doing."

Then he made for the door, and Joe, holding his coat for him, realized that he was shivering violently. Joe opened the door, put his arm round Cross's shoulder, and walked slowly to the gate with him. Cross walked close to him, so as not to break the embrace, and yet Joe knew he did not feel it in a homosexual way. The estate road went uphill to the bus stop on the tree-shaded suburban road, and the two men walked together like sweethearts till they reached it. Then Joe took Cross's hand in his own two.

"Try not to think of it, Jerry," he said in a low voice. "She doesn't even know what she's saying. The girl is sick in her mind."

"She is, Joe, she is, she is," Cross said with pathetic eagerness. "I thought it from the first, but now I'm sure. I'm sorry I was so sharp with her."

"You weren't, Jerry; not so sharp as I'd have been."

It was only when he had waved good-bye to Cross from the pavement that Joe gave way to tears. He walked slowly up and down the road till the fit had passed. As he entered the house, Brigid was waiting for him in the sitting room, sitting exactly as when he had left.

"Come in, Joe," she said quietly. "We have to talk."

"I'm sorry, Brigid, but I don't want to talk," he said, feeling sure that if he did he would break down again.

"I want to talk," she said in a flat tone. "It may be the last chance we'll get. I'll have to clear out."

"What's that?" he asked incredulously.

"I have to clear out," she said again, and he knew that she meant it.

It was at moments like these that all the wise passivity in Joe came on top. In his time he had been humiliated, hurt so that the pain had never left him, but he knew you had to give in to it, let the pain wash over you, if you didn't want it to destroy you.

"Why do you think you have to clear out, dear?" he asked mildly, taking a chair inside the door and joining his hands before him.

"Because I don't want to destroy your life the way I destroyed my own," she said.

"Well, I should have something to say to that," he said. "So should the baby, of course. Unless you're proposing to take her with you."

"I'm not," she said with artificial casualness. "I dare say your mother can look after her."

"I dare say she could," he said calmly. "But it's not my idea of what a child needs."

"At least your mother won't insult your friends," Brigid said bitterly. He knew then that she had no illusions about her behavior to Cross, and his heart softened.

"You mean more to me than any of my friends, dear," he said. "Even Jerry—and Heaven knows, he means quite a lot. But why do you have to do things like that? They hurt you as much as they hurt other people. What is it, Brigid? Why don't you trust me? Is it another man?"

For a moment Joe thought she really was going to strike him. Then the humor of it seemed to dawn on her, and she gave a weak grin.

"You have a very poor opinion of yourself, haven't you?" she asked pertly. "Even that jenny-ass Cross wouldn't think of a silly thing like that. I never looked at the side of the road a man walked at since I married you."

There was no mistaking the absolute truthfulness of that, and again he felt the sense of relief, and with it the old tenderness and admiration.

"Naturally, that's what I hoped, dear," he said. "And damn it all, nothing else matters."

"Not even the ones I met before I met you?" she asked mockingly, and her tone struck him cold again.

"I see," he said. "You mean there was someone else?"

"Naturally," she said angrily. And then, as though reading his thoughts, she reverted to her tone of exasperated amusement. "Now, I suppose you think I'm breaking my heart over him? I am, like hell! I hope to God I never lay eyes on him again. I wish I could say the same thing about his child."

"His child?" Joe repeated stupidly. Now he felt that the world really was collapsing about him. "You mean you had a child already?"

"What do you think brought me over to London in the first place?" she asked reasonably.

"I don't know," Joe said with simple dignity. "I just thought you might have been telling me the truth when you said you came over for a job. I suppose you're right to think I'm a bit simpleminded."

"I never thought you were simpleminded," she retorted with the fury of a hellcat. "I thought you were too good to be true, if you want to know what I thought."

"And you have this child where? With your people?"

"No, outside Cork," she said shortly. "I suppose I wanted her as far away as possible. And, as I'm about it, there's another thing. I pinched some of the housekeeping money to support her. After I left the job I had nothing of my own."

"You could scarcely have left the child to starve," he said lightly. "That doesn't count beside the other things."

"What other things?"

"All the lies you've told me," he said bitterly. "I didn't deserve that from you. Look, Brigid, it's no use pretending I'm not hurt—not by what you've just told me. That was your business. But you might have told me before you married me."

"So that you needn't have married me?" she asked bitterly.

"I mean nothing of the sort," said Joe. "I don't know what I should have done, but I don't think it would have come between you and me. You were unfair to me and unfair to the child. You might have trusted me as I trusted you."

"As if the two things were alike!" she retorted. "I told you I thought you were too good to be true. You weren't, but to get to know you that way I had to marry you first, and to marry you I had to tell you lies. At least, that's how it seemed to me. And a hell of a lot of good it did me!"

Joe sighed.

"Anyway, we have to think what we're to do about this child, and that's something we can't decide tonight."

"There's only one thing to do, Joe," she said. "I'll have to go back to London and get a job." She said it manfully enough, but he knew she didn't mean it. She was begging him to find some way out for her.

"We don't have to break up this house," he said with determination. "Damn it, it's our own. We can still bring her to live with us."

"But I don't want her to live with us," she said angrily. "Can't you understand? It was all a miserable bloody mistake, and I don't want to have to live with it for the rest of my life. And I don't want you to have to live with it either. It's just that I feel such a bitch, having everything in the world I want while she has nothing."

"I see that," Joe said gently. "I see it's not an easy question. We'll have to think of something, that's all."

He thought a lot about it that night, though less of what they were to do with Brigid's child than of the disaster that had overtaken his beautiful world. Again he could see himself acting, doing whatever he felt he had to do, but beyond that he could see it all as though it were happening to someone in a book or a movie. He could almost hear his own voice as if it were in the third person. " 'We'll have to think of something, that's all,' he said." And he supposed that this must be what people meant when they talked of grief.

Yet when Brigid waked him, bringing him a cup of tea in bed, it seemed to have taken nothing out of her. Unburdening herself of her secret seemed to have restored all her native liveliness, in fact.

When he got home that evening, he was astonished to see Cross waiting for him in the front room, and he knew from Cross's manner that Brigid had made her peace with him. At any other time this would have made him happy, but now it merely seemed an irrelevance. As he saw Cross off, Cross said urgently, "You won't think me interfering, Joe, but Brigid came to the office and told me about your little trouble. I guessed there was something upsetting her. I only wanted to say how sorry I am." Joe was amused at Cross's delicacy, and touched that Brigid, for all her fierce pride, had humiliated herself so abjectly before him, but this didn't seem to matter either.

"I know, Jerry, I know," he said squeezing Cross's arm, but Cross was full of the subject.

"It's going to be terrible, however you arrange things," he said, "and I only want you to know that I'll be delighted to do anything. Delighted! Because I have a great admiration for Brigid, Joe. You know that." Joe realized that by ways that could have been no great pleasure to her, Brigid had at last managed to pierce Cross's defenses. Being Cross, he was doing more than interceding for her. He was hiding the check on the mantelpiece.

After supper Joe said to Brigid:

"I've been thinking this thing over, dear, and I see only one way out. We have to bring the child here."

"I've been thinking it over too, and I don't see the necessity for that at all," she said hastily. "Cross thinks the same. To tell you the truth, I think 'twould be impossible for everybody."

Joe could see exactly what she was thinking about. Now that the burden of secrecy had been lifted, she had fled to the opposite extreme of self-confidence. Only a wild outburst of self-confidence could have given her the courage to go to Cross at all. But with self-confidence she had regained all her old devious personality, and was plotting like mad to retrieve as much as possible from the wreck and avoid humiliating herself before the neighbors and before Joe's decent, common, working-class family.

"Not impossible," he said. "Difficult, I grant you. We've made a good many friends on the estate, and it's not going to make our position here any better. But others have had to do the same and worse."

"It's easier for a man than for a woman," Brigid said ruefully.

"It's harder for a woman because she does more to make the position she finds herself in," said Joe sternly. "It's not easy for anybody. All the same, it doesn't count compared with a child's life."

"And there's your mother to be considered," she said.

"Exactly. There's Mother, and there's Barbara and Coralie, and we know what they'll think and say. They'll make you pay, Brigid, and I'll suffer for it. But that's not the worst. The worst is that we may get the kid too late for her to be able to fit in. Still, bad as that is, it will be easier now than it would be in ten or fifteen years' time."

"I don't know, Joe," Brigid said earnestly. "I cracked up on you before because I was trying to handle it on my own. I won't crack up on you again, and I think there are a lot of things I can do without making ourselves miserable into the bargain."

"Such as?"

"Well, it was really Jerry who suggested it—getting her over here to a decent home where we can keep an eye on her, taking her on holidays with Nance, and seeing that she goes to a good school when she's old enough."

"And I suppose Jerry offered to help?"

"He did," she admitted. "He's damn decent."

"He is decent," said Joe. "All the same, he's wrong. Dead wrong." Like many gentle souls, Joe had a streak of iron in him, and when he made up his mind about something he could be very obstinate. "Jerry is a bachelor. He doesn't even know what he's talking about. You can cut off a man or woman as a loss, and feel that maybe they'll keep afloat, but you can't do that to a child. A child is too helpless. And this time, it isn't only you who have to live with the consequences. I have to live with them as well, and if anything happened to that child, I'd be a murderer as well. I've got my faults, Brigid, but I'm not a murderer."

A FORTNIGHT later they were flying in from the sea over Dublin, and Joe knew that Brigid was losing her nerve. Every moment seemed to leave her more panic-stricken. When they travelled into the city on the tall, bumpy, swaying bus, she kept silent, but in the hotel room she broke down.

"Look, Joe, I can't face it," she said.

"Now, Brigid, you've done things a great deal more difficult than this," he said comfortingly.

"I haven't, Joe," she said. "You don't understand, I tell you. I can't go down to Cork tomorrow and meet people I used to know, and start inventing excuses for coming back."

"You don't have to invent excuses," he said patiently. "You're just here with your husband on a holiday—what's wrong with that?"

"And with a two-year-old baby in my arms?" she said bitterly. "I tell you, Joe, I don't give a damn what happens the child. I'm not going down."

She frightened Joe. It was as though behind this façade of a capital with its Georgian squares and flashy hotels and expensive restaurants there was a jungle of secrecy and panic. But he did not want Brigid to see how he felt about it.

"Very well, dear," he said patiently. "I'll go. I dare say your family can direct me."

"I suppose they could," she said doubtfully. "But if you have any consideration for them, you'll keep as far away from them as you can."

He knew it was unsafe to argue with her. She was close to hysteria or he would have said it was rather peculiar to have a foreigner searching in unfamiliar country for a child of his family who had already been neglected for two years.

"Very well, dear," he said. "If you say so, I shall."

The trip on the train to Cork was pleasant, and his only regret was that Brigid wasn't there to share it with him and point out the places of interest: it seemed like the waste of a good excursion. The city itself seemed pleasant enough too, and he had a good view of the river and quays from his bedroom window. Downstairs, he talked to the hotel manager, who was big-boned, deep-voiced, and amiable and threw himself into the business of getting Joe to his destination as though he had no other aim in life. "Throw" seemed the word that suited him, for he literally heaved himself across the desk, looking at a map and studying a timetable, bellowed softly to members of the staff who might help, and even called in casual passers-by. This scared Joe, who did not want his business made public too soon. It would be time enough for explanations when he returned to the hotel with a baby—a difficult moment enough, as even he realized.

But the last ten miles of his journey seemed the most difficult of all.

"It's all right, Mr. Coleman," said Joe. "I'll hire a car."

The hotel manager glanced at the clock in the hall and said in his deep voice:

"You won't hire any car. I'll take an hour off after dinner and drive you."

"That's very kind of you," whispered Joe, "but it might be better if I did take a car. You see, it's rather a delicate matter."

"Oh, sorry, I didn't mean to be inquisitive," Coleman said with a touch of resentment.

"Don't be silly!" Joe said with a laugh. "You're not being inquisitive. I haven't anything to hide, and anyhow I'd have had to tell you sooner or later. Sit down for a moment and let me explain."

The two men sat in a corner of the lounge and Joe explained. The hotel manager listened with a vague smile.

"So far as I'm concerned, I can keep my mouth shut," he said. "But don't be surprised if a lot of the staff know who you are already. If they don't know tonight they'll know tomorrow. They'll also know who your wife is. This may seem a big city to you, but it's not big enough for those who have to live in it. Mind," he added with a smile, "I wouldn't let that disturb me too much either. Will I get a cot into your room?"

"Not tonight," said Joe. "I've tried to sort this thing out. It isn't easy for a man, you know, but I don't think it would be fair to the kid to bring her back tonight, particularly with no woman around. Even if Brigid was here it would be a shock. No, I thought I'd go to this house first, and let the kid get to know me before I bring her back."

"Tomorrow I have the whole morning clear," said Coleman.

"No, I didn't mean it that way either," said Joe. "I can afford to hire a car. Damn it, having come all this way, I can't be stopped by the hire of a car."

"No reason you should unless you want to," Coleman said gruffly. "I think you're wise not to bring her back tonight, though. I'll see you in the lounge after dinner. I'd stick to the roast beef, if I were you."

After dinner the two men set off in Coleman's old car. After a few minutes Coleman spoke.

"This isn't an aspect of life you get much advice on when you go into the hotel business," he said in his good-humored way. "But, if you'll excuse my being personal, Mr. Saunders, you seem to me a rather unusual sort of man."

"Do I?" Joe asked in genuine surprise. "I should have said in my circumstances most men would have felt the same."

"Felt the same, I've no doubt," said Coleman. "I'm not so sure they'd have acted the same, though. Naturally, the first thing I did when you told me your story was to ask myself what I'd have done in your place."

"Yes?" Joe said eagerly.

"And I decided—don't think me impertinent now!—that I'd think twice about it."

"Don't worry, old man," Joe said with a loud laugh. "I did. I thought three times about it, as a matter of fact."

But those few words seemed to have cleared the air between them.

They had passed the city boundaries and were driving along a river-bank with a tree-lined walk at the other side of the water. The main road led along a smaller river wooded to its bank. Finally they reached a little village with a church and public-house where they went off on a byroad up the hill. They came out of it above the river and harbor, stopped to inquire their way, and drove slowly for some miles along a deserted upland road. It was darkening, and Coleman drove more carefully. There was a cottage on their right and two small children with bare feet were playing in the roadway outside. He stopped the car suddenly.

"I have a feeling this is it," he said, and bellowed to the children: "Is this Mrs. Ryan's?"

"What's that, sir?" asked a little boy.

"Mrs. Ryan's, I said."

" 'Tis, sir."

"And is this Marie?" Coleman asked, pointing to the little girl who accompanied him.

"No, sir, 'tis Martha," said the child.

"Then where is Marie?" Coleman asked, and suddenly a tall, rough-looking woman with rosy cheeks appeared by the white gatepost. Afterward Joe thought he would never forget that first impression of her with the white gatepost and dark fuchsia bushes, cut out against the sky.

"Is this the gentleman from England I have?" she called. "Marie is inside, gentlemen. Won't ye come in?"

Joe got out first and held out his hand.

"I'm Joe Saunders, Brigid Healy's husband," he said. "And this is Mr. Coleman, the hotel manager from Cork. He was kind enough to give me a lift."

"I was after giving up expecting ye," she said, showing her big teeth in a smile. "Come in, let ye! I'm afraid the house is in a mess, but 'tis only the children."

"You don't have to apologize, Mrs. Ryan," Joe said. "I come of a large family myself."

But even Joe's large London family had not prepared him for the little cottage, even if the shadows inside gave little opportunity for deciding whether or not it was in a mess. An open door into the bedroom suggested a big bed that had not been made, and the walls of the kitchen were bare but for a grocer's calendar inside the door. Sitting round the open fire were three other children whose faces he could scarcely see, but it was clear that the bare-legged two-year-old who toasted her feet before it was Brigid's child. Suddenly he wondered what he was doing there.

"This is Miss Healy's little girl, gentlemen," said Mrs. Ryan. "She's the spit of her mother, but ye can't see. I'll light the lamp. I suppose ye'd like a cup of tea after yeer journey?"

"No, thanks, Mrs. Ryan," said Joe. "We've only just had dinner. Besides, we won't stay long. We thought we'd come back tomorrow morning for Marie, just to give you time to get her ready. . . . Hello, Marie," he said, taking the child's hand. "I bet you don't know who I am."

"Hullo, Marie," Coleman said with casual amiability and took her hand as well. She looked up at them without expression and Joe suddenly recognized her resemblance to Brigid. That gave him a turn too.

"Run out and play with Martha and Michael," Mrs. Ryan shouted to the other boy in the room. "And bring Kitty along with you." Silently the two children got up and went out, closing the half-door behind them. It was not as though they were frightened but as though they saw no reason for disobeying, and for some reason this struck Joe as even worse. He felt that a natural child should be curious. Mrs. Ryan lit the lamp, squinting up at it.

"Wisha, sit down, let ye," she said, pulling up two chairs and wiping the seats vaguely with her apron. "And how is Miss Healy? You'll have to forgive me. I forget her married name."

"Saunders," said Joe, sitting down and opening the little case he had brought with him. "She's fine, Mrs. Ryan. She probably told you we have a little girl of our own now. She wasn't well or she'd have been here herself. I don't want to rush you. These are a few clothes I brought, and perhaps you can tell me if they'll fit."

He passed the frock, overcoat, and hat to her and she held them to the light with a vague smile. Then she peered at the shoes.

"Wisha, aren't they lovely?" she said. "Aren't you the lucky girl, Marie? Ye're sure ye won't have the tea? 'Twouldn't take me a minute to boil the kettle."

"Certain, thanks," said Joe, who only wanted to get out of the house quick. He crossed to the half-door, and again he caught an image he felt he would never forget of the lamplight on the hedge and whitewashed gatepost where four children were crowded together, talking in whispers. "Better come in now," he said with a laugh. "I bet you heard every word we said. Are they all yours, Mrs. Ryan?"

"Ah, no, sir," she replied almost reproachfully. "We had no children of our own. 'Tis on account of my husband's death I had to take them."

The four children came in and stood fidgeting by the dresser, two little boys and two little girls, apparently well fed if not well dressed or clean, but somehow lacking all the spontaneity of other children. Joe took out a fistful of coins and distributed them. The children took the money meekly, without gratitude.

"Well, Marie," he asked, stooping over the child on the stool, "how do you think you're going to like me for a daddy?"

"She's strange," Mrs. Ryan said apologetically. "Most of the time she have plenty to say for herself."

"I'll bet she has," said Joe. "And in a couple of days she'll be giving me cheek as well. Won't you, old lady?"

They sat and talked for a few minutes longer. Then Joe said good-night, kissed Marie, and patted the other children on the head. It was already dark on the road, and he was glad of the headlights that made the green banks seem theatrical but concealed his face.

"Well, I don't know how you feel, but I'm ready for a drink," said Coleman. "A large one, at that."

"What I should like is to buy a few toys for the other kids," said Joe.

"Too late for that, I'm afraid," said Coleman. "The shops are shut until Monday. You might be able to pick up a few cheap toys in a sweetshop, and a couple of bags of sweets. If you mean they won't have the money long I'm inclined to agree with you."

As they entered the hotel the tall night porter looked up from his evening paper and said, "Night, sir. Night, Mr. Saunders," and already Joe knew that his business was being discussed. The waiter who brought them their drinks in the lounge seemed to know as well, but Joe had the idea that he approved. He might have been a father himself. He might even have known Brigid and Marie's father. The pair of them might have sat drinking in this very lounge like any of the couples who sat there now. It was only the other side of the picture that he had been looking at that evening in a lonesome cottage on the hills. He felt very depressed.

Next morning he was more cheerful. He woke to the sound of bells. He had never heard so many bells, or else they sounded louder in the hollow of the city. A pious people all right, he thought. On their way out of town he saw the well-dressed crowds on their way to Mass. In the first village they came to there was a large group outside the church and a smaller one outside the public-house.

The four elder children were waiting for them in the roadway, and as they approached, two of these rushed in to give warning. They had all been washed and two of them even wore boots. When they went into the cottage Marie was sitting stiffly on a low chair by the door, as though she had been glued there to keep her from soiling her new dress, and she looked up at them blankly and pointed to her shoes. "Look! Shoes!" she said shrilly, and Joe, stooping to admire them, saw that they were too big.

"We'll get you properly fitted tomorrow, old lady," he said.

He distributed the few presents he had managed to buy, shook hands with Mrs. Ryan, and carried Marie to the car. The other children followed, and he shook hands with each in turn, and then laid his hand gently on each one's head. Over the low wooden gate he could see the tall figure of Mrs. Ryan, holding the doorpost and gazing up and down the deserted road.

As the car started he turned to wave to the little group of children. They stood in the roadway, their presents clutched in their hands, and he saw that they were all weeping quietly. It seemed to him that they were not weeping as real children weep, with abandonment and delight, but hopelessly, as old people weep whom the world has passed by. He was the world and he had passed them by. He knew now why he had not dared to kiss any of them. If he had kissed them he could not have left them there. His first thought was to prevent Marie's seeing them, but he realized that he needn't have worried. She was leaning forward, enchanted, trying to touch her beautiful new shoes. Coleman drove with his eyes fixed on the winding roadway over the hills, and his fat sulky face was expressionless.

"I wonder if you saw what I did?" Joe said at last to break the silence, and Coleman stared at him despairingly.

"I'm in dread I'll never forget it," he said.

An Out-and-Out Free Gift

WHEN Jimmy began to get out of hand, his father was both disturbed and bewildered. Anybody else, yes, but not Jimmy! They had always been so close! Closer, indeed, than Ned ever realized, for the perfectly correct picture he had drawn of himself as a thoughtful, considerate father who treated his son as though he were a younger brother could have been considerably expanded by his wife. Indeed, to realize how close they had been you needed to hear Celia on it, because only she knew how much of the small boy there still was in her husband.

Who, for instance, would have thought that the head of a successful business had such a passion for sugar? Yet during the war, when sugar was rationed in Ireland, Celia, who was a bit of a Jansenist, had felt herself bound to give up sugar and divide her ration between Ned and Jimmy, then quite a small boy. And, even at that, Ned continued to suffer. He did admire her self-denial, but he couldn't help feeling that so grandiose a gesture deserved a better object than Jimmy. It was a matter of scientific fact that sugar was bad for Jimmy's teeth, and anything that went wrong with Jimmy's teeth was going to cost his father money. Ned felt it unfair that in the middle of a war, with his salary frozen, Celia should inflict additional burdens on him.

Most of the time he managed to keep his dignity, though he could rarely sit down to a meal without an angry glance at Jimmy's sugar bowl. To make things harder for him, Jimmy rationed himself so that toward the end of the week he still had some sugar left, while Ned had none. As a philosopher, Ned wondered that he should resent this so deeply, but resent it he did. A couple of times, he deliberately stole a spoonful while Celia's back was turned, and the absurdity of this put him in such a frivolous frame of mind for the rest of the evening that she eventually said resignedly, "I suppose you've been at the child's sugar again? Really, Ned, you are hopeless!" On other occasions, Ned summoned up all his paternal authority and with a polite "You don't mind, old man?" took a spoonful from under Jimmy's nose. But that took nerve, and a delicate appreciation of the precise moment when Jimmy could be relied on not to cry.

Towards the end of the war, it became a matter of brute economic strength. If Jimmy wanted a bicycle lamp, he could earn it or pay up in good sugar. As Ned said, quoting from a business manual he had studied in his own youth, "There is no such thing in business as an out-and-out free gift." Jimmy made good use of the lesson. "Bicycle lamp, old man?" Ned would ask casually, poising his spoon over Jimmy's sugar bowl. "Bicycle lamp *and* three-speed gear," Jimmy would reply firmly. "For a couple of spoons of sugar?" his father would cry in mock indignation. "Are you mad, boy?" They both enjoyed the game.

They could scarcely have been other than friends. There was so much of the small boy in Ned that he was sensitive to the least thing affecting Jimmy, and Jimmy would consult him about things that most small boys keep to themselves. When he was in trouble, Ned never dismissed it lightly, no matter how unimportant it seemed. He asked a great many questions and frequently reserved his decisions. He had chosen Jimmy's school himself; it was a good one for Cork, and sometimes, without informing Jimmy, he went off to the school himself and had a chat with one of the teachers. Nearly always he managed to arrange things without embarrassment or pain, and Jimmy took it for granted that his decisions were usually right. It is a wise father who can persuade his son of anything of the sort.

But now, at sixteen, Jimmy was completely out of control, and his mother had handed him over to the secular arm, and the secular arm, for all its weight, made no impression on his sullen indifference. The first sign of the change in him was the disintegration of his normally perfect manners; now he seemed to have no deference towards or consideration for anyone. Ned caught him out in one or two minor falsehoods and quoted to him a remark of his own father's that "a lie humiliates the man who tells it, but it humiliates the one it's told to even more." What puzzled Ned was that, at the same time, the outbreak was linked in some ways to qualities he had always liked in the boy. Jimmy was strong, and showed his strength in protecting things younger and weaker than himself. The cat regarded him as a personal enemy because he hurled himself on her the moment he saw her with a bird. At one time, there had been a notice on his door that read, "Wounded Bird. Please Keep Out." At school, his juniors worshipped him because he would stand up for them against bullies, and though Ned, in a fatherly way, advised him not to get mixed up in other people's quarrels, he was secretly flattered. He felt Jimmy was taking after him.

But the same thing that attracted Jimmy to younger and weaker boys seemed now to attract him to wasters. Outside of school, he never associated with lads he might have to look up to but only with those his father felt a normal boy should despise. All this was summed up in his friendship with a youngster called Hogan, who was a strange mixture of spoiling and neglect, a boy who had never been young and would never be old. He openly smoked a pipe, and let on to be an authority on brands of tobacco. Ned winced when Hogan addressed him as a contemporary and tried to discuss business with him. He replied with heavy irony—something he did only when he was at a complete loss. What went on in Hogan's house when Jimmy went there he could only guess at. He suspected that the parents went out and stayed out, leaving the boys to their own devices.

At first, Ned treated Jimmy's insubordination as he had treated other outbreaks, by talking to him as an equal. He even offered him a cigarette—Jimmy had stolen money to buy cigarettes. He told him how people grew up through admiration of others' virtues, rather than through tolerance of their weaknesses. He talked to him about sex, which he suspected was at the bottom of Jimmy's trouble, and Jimmy listened politely and said he understood. Whether he did or not, Ned decided that if Hogan talked sex to Jimmy, it was a very different kind of sex.

Finally, he forbade Hogan the house and warned Jimmy against going to Hogan's. He made no great matter of it, contenting himself with describing the scrapes he had got into himself at Jimmy's age, and Jimmy smiled, apparently pleased with this unfamiliar picture of his grave and rather stately father, but he continued to steal and lie, to get bad marks and remain out late at night. Ned was fairly satisfied that he went to Hogan's, and sat there smoking, playing cards, and talking filth. He bawled Jimmy out and called him a dirty little thief and liar, and Jimmy raised his brows and looked away with a pained air, as though asking himself how long he must endure such ill breeding. At this, Ned gave him a cuff on the ear that brought a look of hatred into Jimmy's face and caused Celia not to talk to Ned for two days. But even she gave in at last.

"Last night was the third time he's been out late this week," she said one afternoon in her apparently unemotional way. "You'll really have to do something drastic with him."

These were hard words from a soft woman, but though Ned felt sorry for her, he felt even sorrier for himself. He hated himself in the part of a sergeant-major, and he blamed her for having let things go so far.

"Any notion where he has been?" he asked stiffly.

"Oh, you can't get a word out of him," she said with a shrug. "Judging by his tone, I'd say Hogan's. I don't know what attraction that fellow has for him."

"Very well," Ned said portentously. "I'll deal with him. But, mind, I'll deal with him in my own way."

"Oh, I won't interfere," she said wearily. "I know when I'm licked."

"I can promise you Master Jimmy will know it, too," Ned added grimly.

At supper he said in an even tone, "Young man, for the future you're going to be home every night at ten o'clock. This is the last time I'm going to speak to you about it."

Jimmy, apparently under the impression that his father was talking to himself, reached for a slice of bread. Then Ned let fly with a shout that made Celia jump and paralyzed the boy's hand, still clutching the bread.

"Did you hear me?"

"What's that?" gasped Jimmy.

"I said you were to be in at ten o'clock."

"Oh, all right, all right," said Jimmy, with a look that said he did not think any reasonable person would require him to share the house any longer with one so uncivilized. Though this look was intended to madden Ned, it failed to do so, because he knew that, for all her sentimentality and high liberal principles, Celia was a woman of her word and would not interfere whenever he decided to knock that particular look off Master Jimmy's face. He knew, too, that the time was not far off; that Jimmy had not the faintest intention of obeying, and that he would be able to deal with it.

"Because I warn you, the first night you're late again I'm going to skin you alive," he added. He was trying it out, of course. He knew that Celia hated expressions of fatherly affection like "skin you alive," "tan you within an inch of your life," and "knock your head off," which, to her, were relics of a barbarous age. To his great satisfaction, she neither shuddered nor frowned. Her principles were liberal, but they were principles.

TWO NIGHTS after, Jimmy was late again. Celia, while pretending to read, was watching the clock despairingly. "Of course, he may have been delayed," she said smoothly, but there was no conviction in her tone. It was nearly eleven when they heard Jimmy's key in the door.

"I think perhaps I'd better go to bed," she said.

"It might be as well," he replied pityingly. "Send that fellow in on your way."

He heard her in the hallway, talking with Jimmy in a level, friendly voice, not allowing her consternation to appear, and he smiled. He liked that touch of the Roman matron in her. Then there was a knock, and Jimmy came in. He was a big lad for sixteen but he still had traces of baby fat about the rosy cheeks he occasionally scraped with Ned's razor, to Ned's annoyance. Now Ned would cheerfully have given him a whole shaving kit if it would have avoided the necessity for dealing with him firmly.

"You wanted to talk to me, Dad?" he asked, as though he could just spare a moment.

"Yes, Jimmy, I did. Shut that door."

Jimmy gave a resigned shrug at his father's mania for privacy but did as he was told, and stood against the door, his hands joined and his chin in the air.

"When did I say you were to be in?" Ned said, looking at the clock. "When?"

"Yes. When? At what time, if you find it so hard to understand."

"Oh, ten," Jimmy replied wearily.

"Ten? And what time do you make that?"

"Oh, I didn't know it was so late!" Jimmy exclaimed with an astonished look at the clock. "I'm sorry. I didn't notice the time."

"Really?" Ned said ironically. "Enjoyed yourself that much?"

"Not too bad," Jimmy replied vaguely. He was always uncomfortable with his father's irony.

"Company good?"

"Oh, all right," Jimmy replied with another shrug.

"Where was this?"

"At a house."

"Poor people?" his father asked in mock surprise.

"What?" exclaimed Jimmy.

"Poor people who couldn't afford a clock?"

Jimmy's indignation overflowed in stammering protest. "I never said they hadn't a clock. None of the other fellows had to be in by ten. I didn't like saying I had to be. I didn't want them to think I was a blooming . . ." The protest expired in a heavy sigh, and Ned's heart contracted with pity and shame.

"Juvenile delinquent," he added patiently. "I know. Neither your mother nor I want you to make a show of yourself. But you didn't answer my question. Where was this party? And don't tell me any lies, because I'm going to find out."

Jimmy grew red and angry. "Why would I tell you lies?"

"For the same reason you've told so many already—whatever that may be. You see, Jimmy, the trouble with people who tell lies is that you have to check everything they say. Not on your account but on theirs; otherwise, you may be unfair to them. People soon get tired of being fair, though. Now, where were you? At Hogan's?"

"You said I wasn't to go to Hogan's."

"You see, you're still not answering my questions. Were you at Hogan's?"

"No," Jimmy replied in a whisper.

"Word of honor?"

"Word of honor." But the tone was not the tone of honor but of shame.

"Where were you, then?"

"Ryans'."

The name was unfamiliar to Ned, and he wondered if Jimmy had not just invented it to frustrate any attempt at checking on his statements. He was quite prepared to hear that Jimmy didn't know where the house was. It was as bad as that.

"Ryans'," he repeated evenly. "Do I know them?"

"You might. I don't know."

"Where do they live?"

"Gardiner's Hill."

"Whereabouts?"

"Near the top. Where the road comes up from Dillon's Cross, four doors down. It has a tree in the garden." It came so pat that Ned felt sure there was such a house. He felt sure of nothing else.

"And you spent the evening there? I'm warning you for your own good. Because I'm going to find out." There was a rasp in his voice.

"I told you I did."

"I know," Ned said between his teeth. "Now you're going to come along with me and prove it."

He rose and in silence took his hat from the hall stand and went out. Jimmy followed him silently, a pace behind. It was a moonlit night, and as they turned up the steep hill, the trees overhung a high wall on one side of the street. On the other side, there were steep gardens filled with shadows.

"Where did you say this house was?"

"At the top," Jimmy replied sullenly.

The hill stopped, the road became level, and at either side were little new suburban houses, with tiny front gardens. Near the corner, Ned saw one with a tree in front of it and stopped. There was still light in the front room. The family kept late hours for Cork. Suddenly he felt absurdly sorry for the boy.

"You don't want to change your mind?" he asked gently. "You're sure this is where you were?"

"I told you so," Jimmy replied almost in exasperation.

"Very well," Ned said savagely. "You needn't come in."

"All right," Jimmy said, and braced himself against the concrete gatepost, looking over the moonlit roofs at the clear sky. In the moonlight he looked very pale; his hands were drawn back from his sides, his lips drawn back from his teeth, and for some reason his white anguished face made Ned think of a crucifixion.

Anger had taken the place of pity in him. He felt the boy was being unjust toward him. He wouldn't have minded the injustice if he'd ever been unjust to Jimmy, but two minutes before he had again shown his fairness and given Jimmy another chance. Besides, he didn't want to make a fool of himself.

He walked up the little path to the door, whose colored-glass panels glowed in light that seemed to leak from the sitting-room door. When he rang, a pretty girl of fifteen or sixteen came out and screwed up her eyes at him.

"I hope you'll excuse my calling at this unnatural hour," Ned said in a bantering tone. "It's only a question I want to ask. Do you think I could talk to your father or your mother for a moment?"

"You can, to be sure," the girl replied in a flutter of curiosity. "Come in, can't you? We're all in the front room."

Ned, nerving himself for an ordeal, went in. It was a tiny front room with a fire burning in a tiled fireplace. There was a mahogany table at which a boy of twelve seemed to be doing his lessons. Round the fire sat an older girl, a small woman, and a tubby little man with a graying mustache. Ned smiled, and his tone became even more jocular.

"I hope you'll forgive my making a nuisance of myself," he said. "My name is Callanan. I live at St. Luke's. I wonder if you've ever met my son Jimmy?"

"Jimmy?" the mother echoed, her hand to her cheek. "I don't know that I did."

"I know him," said the girl who had let him in, in a voice that squeaked with pride.

"Fine!" Ned said. "At least, you know what I'm talking about. I wonder if you saw him this evening?"

"Jimmy?" the girl replied, taking fright. "No. Sure, I hardly know him only to salute him. Why? Is anything wrong?"

"Nothing serious, at any rate," said Ned with a comforting smile. "It's just that he said he spent the evening here with you. I daresay that's an excuse for being somewhere he shouldn't have been."

"Well, well, well!" Mrs. Ryan said anxiously, joining her hands. "Imagine saying he was here! Wisha, Mr. Callanan, aren't they a caution?"

"A caution against what, though?" Ned asked cheerfully. "That's what I'd like to know. I'm only sorry he wasn't telling the truth. I'm afraid he wasn't in such charming company. Good-night, everybody, and thank you."

"Good-night, Mr. Callanan," said Mrs. Ryan, laying a hand gently on his sleeve. "And don't be too hard on him! Sure, we were wild ourselves once."

"Once?" he exclaimed with a laugh. "I hope we still are. We're not dead yet, Mrs. Ryan."

The same girl showed him out. She had recovered from her fright and looked as though she would almost have liked him to stay.

"Good-night, Mr. Callanan," she called blithely from the door, and when he turned, she was silhouetted against the lighted doorway, bent halfway over, and waving. He waved back, touched by this glimpse of an interior not so unlike his own but seen from outside, in all its innocence. It was a shock to emerge on the roadway and see Jimmy still standing where he had left him, though he no longer looked crucified. Instead, with his head down and his hands by his sides, he looked terribly weary. They walked in silence for a few minutes, till they saw the valley of the city and the lamps cascading down the hillsides and breaking below into a foaming lake of light.

"Well," Ned said gloomily, "the Ryans seem to be under the impression that you weren't there tonight."

"I know," Jimmy replied, as though this were all that might be expected from him.

Something in his tone startled Ned. It no longer seemed to breathe defiance. Instead, it hinted at something very like despair. But why? he thought in exasperation. Why the blazes did he tell me all those lies? Why didn't he tell me even outside the door? Damn it, I gave him every chance.

"Don't you think this is a nice place to live, Dad?" asked Jimmy.

"Is it?" Ned asked sternly.

"Ah, well, the air is better," said Jimmy with a sigh. They said no more till they reached home.

"Now, go to bed," Ned said in the hallway. "I'll consider what to do with you tomorrow."

Which, as he well knew, was bluff, because he had already decided to do nothing to Jimmy. Somehow he felt that, whatever the boy had done to himself, punishment would be merely an anticlimax, and perhaps a relief. Punishment, he thought, might be exactly what Jimmy would have welcomed at that moment. He went into the sitting room and poured himself a drink, feeling that if anyone deserved it, he did. He had a curious impression of having been involved in some sort of struggle and escaped some danger to which he could not even give a name.

When he went upstairs, Celia was in bed with a book, and looked up at him with a wide-eyed stare. She proved to be no help to him. "Jimmy usen't to be like that," she said wistfully, and he knew she had been lying there regretting the little boy who had come to her with all his troubles.

"But why, why, why, in God's name, did he tell me all those lies?" Ned asked angrily.

"Oh, why do people ever tell lies?" she asked with a shrug.

"Because they hope they won't be found out," Ned replied. "Don't you see that's what's so queer about it?"

She didn't, and for hours Ned lay awake, turning it over and over in his mind. It was easy enough to see it as the story of a common falsehood persisted in through some mood of bravado, and each time he thought of it that way he grew angry again. Then, all at once, he would remember the face of Jimmy against the pillar in the moonlight, as though he were being crucified, and give a frustrated sigh.

"Go to sleep!" Celia said once, giving him a vicious nudge.

"I can't, damn it, I can't," he said, and began all over again.

Why had the kid chosen Ryans' as an excuse? Was that merely to put him further astray, or did it really represent some dream of happiness and fulfillment? The latter explanation he rejected as too simple and sentimental, yet he knew quite well that Ryans' house *had* meant something to the boy, even if it was only an alternative to whatever house he had been in and the company he had met there. Ned could remember himself at that age, and how, when he had abandoned himself to something or somebody, an alternative image would appear. The image that had flashed up in Jimmy's mind, the image that was not one of Hogan's house, was Ryans'. But it needed more than that to explain his own feeling of danger. It was as though Jimmy had deliberately challenged him, if he were the man he appeared to be, to struggle with the demon of fantasy in him and destroy it. It was as though not he but Jimmy had been forcing the pace. At the same time, he realized that this was something he would never know. All he ever would know was that somewhere behind it all were despair and loneliness and terror, under the magic of an autumn night. And yet there were sentimental fools who told you that they would wish to be young again.

NEXT MORNING at breakfast, he was cold and aloof, more from embarrassment than hostility. Jimmy, on the other hand, seemed to be in the highest spirits, helping Celia with the breakfast things, saying "Excuse me, Daddy," as he changed Ned's plate. He pushed the sugar bowl towards Ned and said with a grin, "Daddy likes sugar."

Ned just restrained himself from flinging the bowl at him. "As a matter of fact, I do," he said coldly.

He had done the same sort of thing too often himself. He knew that, with the threat of punishment over his head, Jimmy was scared, as well he might be. It is one thing to be defiant at eleven o'clock at night, another thing altogether to be defiant at eight in the morning.

All day, at intervals, he found himself brooding over it. At lunch he talked to his chief clerk about it, but MacIntyre couldn't advise him. "God, Ned," he said impatiently, "every kid is different. There's no laying down rules. My one told the nuns that her mother was a religious maniac and kicked the statue of the Blessed Virgin around the floor. For God's sake, Ned, imagine Kate kicking a statue around the floor!"

"Difficult, isn't it?" replied Ned with a grin, though to himself he thought complacently that that sort of fantasy was what he would expect from Kate's daughter. Parents so rarely sympathize with one another.

That evening, when he came in, Celia said coolly, "I don't know what you said to Jimmy, but it seems to have worked."

Relief came over Ned like a cold shower. He longed to be able to say something calm like "Oh, good!" or "Glad I could help" or "Any time I can advise you again, just let me know." But he was too honest. He shook his head, still the schoolboy that Celia had loved such a long time ago, and his forehead wrinkled up.

"That's the awful part of it," he said. "I said nothing at all to him. For the first time in my life I didn't know what to say. What the hell could I say?"

"Oh, no doubt you said something and didn't notice it," Celia said confidently. "There's no such thing in business as an out-and-out free gift."

The Corkerys

MAY MACMAHON was a good-looking girl, the only child of Jack MacMahon, the accountant, and his wife, Margaret. They lived in Cork, on Summerhill, the steep street that led from the flat of the city to the heights of Montenotte. She had always lived the life of a girl of good family, with piano lessons, dancing class, and crushes on her school friends' brothers. Only occasionally did she wonder what it was all about, and then she invariably forgot to ask her father, who would certainly know. Her father knew everything, or almost everything. He was a tall, shy, good-looking man who seemed to have been expecting martyrdom from his earliest years and drinking Irish whiskey to endure it. May's mother was small and pretty and very opinionated, though her opinions varied, and anyway did not last long. Her father's opinions never varied, and lasted forever.

When May became friendly with the Corkery family, it turned out that he had always had strong opinions about them as well. Mr. Corkery, a mild, inarticulate solicitor, whom May remembered going for lonely walks for the good of his health, had died and left his family with very limited means, but his widow had good connections and managed to provide an education (mostly free) for all six children. Of the boys, the eldest, Tim, was now a Dominican, and Joe, who came next in line, was also going in for the priesthood. The Church was in the family's blood, because Mrs. Corkery's brother was the Dean and her sister was Mother Superior of the convent of an enclosed order outside the city. Mrs. Corkery's nickname among the children was "Reverend Mother," and they accused her of imitating her sister, but Mrs. Corkery only sniffed and said if everybody became priests and nuns there would soon be no Church left. Mrs. Corkery seemed to believe quite seriously that the needs of the Church were the only possible excuse for sex.

From knowing the Corkerys May began to realize at last what life was about. It was no longer necessary to ask her father. Anyway he wouldn't know. He and her mother were nice but commonplace. Everything they said and did was dull and predictable, and even when they went to Mass on Sunday they did so only because everyone else did it. The Corkerys were rarely dull and never predictable. Though their whole life seemed to center on the Church, they were not in the least pietistic. The Dean fought with Mrs. Corkery; Father Tim fought with Joe; the sisters fought with their brothers, who, they said, were getting all the attention, and fought one another when their brothers were not available. Tessie, the eldest girl, known as "The Limb of the Devil," or just "The Limb," was keeping company with a young stockbroker who told her a lot of dirty stories, which she repeated with great gusto to her brothers, particularly to Father Tim. This, however, was for family reasons, because they all agreed that Tim was inclined to put on airs.

And then The Limb astonished everybody by entering the convent where her aunt was Mother Superior. May attended the reception in the little convent chapel, which struck her to the heart by its combination of poverty and gentility. She felt that the ceremony might have been tolerable in a great cathedral with a choir and thundering organ, but not in that converted drawing room, where the nuns knelt along the side walls and squeaked like mourners. The Limb was laid out on the altar and first covered with roses as though she were dead; then an old nun clipped her long black hair with a shears. It fell and lay at her head as though it too had died. May drew a quick breath and glanced at Joe, who was kneeling beside her. Though he had his hand over his face, she knew from the way his shoulders moved that he was crying. Then she cried too.

For a full week the ceremony gave her the horrors every time she remembered it, and she felt she should have nothing more to do with such an extraordinary family. All the same, a week with her parents was enough to make her realize the attraction of the Corkerys even more than before.

"Did it scare you, May?" Rosie, the second girl, asked with a wicked grin. "Cripes, it put the fear of God into me. I'm not having any of that *de profundis* stuff; I'm joining a decent missionary order." This was the first May had heard of Rosie's vocation. Inside a year, she, too, was in a convent, but in Rome, and "having a gas time," as she casually reported home.

They really were an extraordinary family, and the Dean was as queer as any of them. The Sunday following the ceremony May was at dinner there, and he put his hand firmly on her shoulder as though he were about to yank off her dress, and gave her a crooked smile that would have convinced any reasonable observer that he was a sex maniac, and yet May knew that almost every waking moment his thoughts were concentrated on outwitting the Bishop, who seemed to be the greatest enemy of the Church since Nero. The Bishop was a Dominican, and the Dean felt that a monk's place was in the cloister.

"The man is a bully!" he said, with an astonishment and grief that would have moved any audience but his own family.

"Oh, now, Mick!" said Mrs. Corkery placidly. She was accustomed to hearing the Bishop denounced.

"I'm sorry, Josephine," the Dean said with a formal regret that rang equally untrue. "The man is a bully. An infernal bully, what's more. I'm not criticizing you or the order, Tim," he said, looking at his nephew over his spectacles, "but monks simply have no place in ecclesiastical affairs. Let them stick to their prayers is what I say."

"And a queer way the world would be only for them," Joe said. Joe was going for the secular priesthood himself, but he didn't like to see his overwhelming uncle get away with too much.

"Their influence on Church history has been disastrous!" the Dean bellowed, reaching for his cigarette case. "Always, or almost always, disastrous. That man thinks he knows everything."

"Maybe he does," said Joe.

"Maybe," said the Dean, like an old bull who cannot ignore a dart from any quarter. "But as well as that, he interferes in everything, and always publicly, always with the greatest possible amount of scandal. 'I don't like the model of that church'; 'Take away that statue'; 'That painting is irreverent.' Begob, Joe, I don't think even you know as much as that. I declare to God. Josephine, I believe if anyone suggested it to him that man would start inspecting the cut of the schoolgirls' panties." And when everyone roared with laughter, the Dean raised his head sternly and said, "I mean it."

Peter, the youngest boy, never got involved in these family arguments about the Bishop, the orders, or the future of the Church. He was the odd man out. He was apprenticed in his father's old firm and would grow up to be owner or partner. In every Irish family there is a boy like Peter whose task it is to take on the family responsibilities. It was merely an accident that he was the youngest. What counted was that he was his mother's favorite. Even before he had a mind to make up, he knew it was not for him to become too involved, because someone would have to look after his mother in her old age. He might marry, but it would have to be a wife who suited her. He was the ugliest of the children, though with a monkey ugliness that was almost as attractive as Father Tim's film-star looks and Joe's ascetic masculine fire. He was slow, watchful, and good-humored, with high cheekbones that grew tiny bushes of hair, and he had a lazy malice that could often be as effective as the uproarious indignation of his brothers and sisters.

May, who saw the part he had been cast for, wondered whether she couldn't woo Mrs. Corkery as well as another girl.

AFTER Rosie there was Joe, who was ordained the following year, and then Sheela did what seemed—in that family, at least—the conventional thing and went into the same convent as Tessie.

It was an extraordinary family, and May was never quite able to understand the fascination it had for her. Partly, of course—and this she felt rather than understood—it was the attraction of the large family for the only child, the sheer relief of never having to wonder what you were going to play next. But beside this there was an attraction rather like that of a large theatrical family—the feeling that everything was related to a larger imaginative world. In a sense, the Corkerys always seemed to be playing.

She knew that her own being in love with Peter was part of her love affair with the family as a whole, the longing to be connected with them, and the teasing she got about Peter from his brothers and sisters suggested that they, too, recognized it and were willing to accept her as one of themselves. But she also saw that her chance of ever marrying Peter was extremely slight, because Peter was not attracted by her. When he could have been out walking with her he was out walking with his friend Mick MacDonald, and when the pair of them came in while she was in the house, Peter behaved to her as though she were nothing more than a welcome stranger. He was always polite, always deferential—unlike Tim and Joe, who treated her as though she were an extra sister, to be slapped on the bottom or pushed out of the way as the mood struck them.

May was a serious girl; she had read books on modern psychology, and she knew that the very quality that made Peter settle for a life in the world made him unsuitable as a husband. It was strange how right the books were about that. He was dominated by his mother, and he could flirt with her as he never flirted with May. Clearly, no other woman would ever entirely replace his mother in his heart. In fact (May was too serious a girl not to give things their proper names), Peter was the very type of the homosexual—the latent homosexual, as she learned to call it.

Other boys *wanted* to go out with her, and she resented Peter's unfailing courtesy, though in more philosophic spells she realized that he probably couldn't help it, and that when he showed his almost boyish hero worship of Mick MacDonald before her it was not his fault but Nature's. All the same, she thought it very uncalled-for on the part of Nature, because it left her no particular interest in a world in which the only eligible young man was a queer. After a year or two of this, her thoughts turned more and more to the quiet convent where the Corkery girls contentedly carried on their simple lives of meditation and prayer. Once or twice she dropped a dark hint that she was thinking of becoming a nun herself, but each time it led to a scene with her father.

"You're a fool, girl!" he said harshly, getting up to pour himself an extra drink. May knew he didn't altogether resent being provoked, because it made him feel entitled to drink more.

"Now, Jack, you must not say things like that," her mother said anxiously.

"Of course I have to say it. Look at her! At her age! And she doesn't even have a boy!"

"But if there isn't a boy who interests her!"

"There are plenty of boys who'd interest her if only she behaved like a natural girl," he said gloomily. "What do you think a boy wants to do with a girl? Say the Rosary? She hasn't behaved naturally ever since she got friendly with that family—what's their name?"

"Corkery," Mrs. MacMahon said, having failed to perceive that not remembering the Corkerys' name was the one way the poor man had of getting back at them.

"Whatever their name is, they've turned her into an idiot. That's no great surprise. They never had any brains to distribute, themselves."

"But still, Jack, you will admit they've got on very well."

"They've got on very well!" he echoed scornfully. "In the Church! Except that young fellow, the solicitor's clerk, and I suppose he hadn't brains enough even for the Church. They should have put him in the friars."

"But after all, their uncle is the Dean."

"Wonderful Dean, too," grumbled Jack MacMahon. "He drove me out of twelve-o'clock Mass, so as not to listen to his drivel. He can hardly speak decent English, not to mind preaching a sermon. 'A bunch of baloney!' " he quoted angrily. "If we had a proper bishop, instead of the one we have, he'd make that fellow speak correctly in the pulpit at least."

"But it's only so that his congregation will understand him, Jack."

"Oh, his congregation understands him only too well. Himself and his tall hat and his puffed-up airs! Common, that's what he is, and that's what all the family are, on both sides. If your daughter wants to be a nun, you and the Corkerys can arrange it between you. But not one penny of my money goes into their pockets, believe me!"

May was sorry to upset him, but for herself she did not mind his loathing of the whole Corkery family. She knew that it was only because he was fond of her and dreaded being left without her in his old age. He had spoiled her so long as she was not of an age to answer him back, and she guessed he was looking forward to spoiling his grandchildren even worse because he would not live long enough to hear them answer him back. But this, she realized, was what the Corkerys had done for her—made all that side of life seem unimportant.

She had a long talk with Mother Agatha, Mrs. Corkery's sister, about her vocation, which confirmed her in her resolution. Mother Agatha was very unlike her sister, who was loud-voiced and humorous. The Mother Superior was pale, thin, cool, and with the slightest trace of an ironic wit that might have passed unnoticed by a stupider girl. But May noticed it, and realized that she was being observed very closely indeed.

She and her mother did the shopping for the trousseau, but the bills and parcels were kept carefully out of her father's sight. Drunk or sober, he refused to discuss the matter at all. "It would only upset him just now, poor man," her mother said philosophically. He was drinking heavily, and when he was in liquor he quarreled a lot with her mother about little things. With May he avoided quarrels, or even arguments, and it struck her that he was training himself for a life in which he would no longer have her to quarrel with. On the day of the reception he did not drink at all, which pleased her, and was icily polite to everybody, but when, later, she appeared behind the parlor grille, all in white, and the sun caught her, she saw his face in the darkness of the parlor, with all the life drained out of it, and suddenly he turned and left without a word. It was only then that a real feeling of guilt sprang up in her at the thought of the miserable old age that awaited him—a man like him, who loved young creatures who could not answer him back, and who would explain to them unweariedly about the sun and moon and geography and figures. She had answered him back in a way that left him with nothing to look forward to.

ALL THE SAME, there was something very comforting about the life of an enclosed order. It had been organized a long, long time before, by people who knew more about the intrusions of the outside world than May did. The panics that had seized her about her ability to sustain the life diminished and finally ceased. The round of duties, services, and mortifications was exactly what she had needed, and little by little she felt the last traces of worldliness slip from her—even the very human worry about the old age of her father and mother. The convent was poor, and not altogether from choice. Everything in the house was mean and clean and cheerful, and May grew to love the old drawing room that had been turned into a chapel, where she knelt, in her own place, through the black winter mornings when at home she would still be tucked up comfortably in bed. She liked the rough feeling of her clothes and the cold of the floor through her sandals, though mostly she liked the proximity of Tessie and Sheela.

There were times when, reading the lives of the saints, she wished she had lived in more heroic times, and she secretly invented minor mortifications for herself to make sure she could endure them. It was not until she had been in the convent for close on a year that she noticed that the minor mortifications were liable to be followed by major depressions. Though she was a clever woman, she did not try to analyze this. She merely lay awake at night and realized that the nuns she lived with—even Tessie and Sheela—were not the stuff of saints and martyrs but ordinary women who behaved in religion very much as they would have behaved in marriage, and who followed the rule in the spirit in which her father went to Mass on Sundays. There was nothing whatever to be said against them, and any man who had got one of them for a wife would probably have considered himself fortunate, but all the same, there was something about them that was not quite grown-up. It was very peculiar and caused her great concern. The things that had really frightened her about the order when she was in the world—the loneliness, the austerity, the ruthless discipline—now seemed to her meaningless and harmless. After that she saw with horror that the great days of the Church were over, and that they were merely a lot of perfectly commonplace women play-acting austerity and meditation.

"But my dear child," Mother Agatha said when May wept out her story to her, "of course we're only children. Of course we're only play-acting. How else does a child learn obedience and discipline?"

And when May talked to her about what the order had been in earlier days, that vague, ironic note crept into Mother Superior's voice, as though she had heard it all many times before. "I know, sister," she said, with a nod. "Believe me, I do know that the order was stricter in earlier times. But you must remember that it was not founded in a semi-arctic climate like ours, so there was less chance of the sisters' dying of double pneumonia. I have talked to half the plumbers in town, but it seems that central heating is not understood here. . . . Everything is relative. I'm sure we suffer just as much in our very comfortable sandals as the early sisters suffered in their bare feet, and probably at times rather more, but at any rate we are not here for the sole purpose of suffering mortification, whatever pleasures it may hold for us."

Every word Mother Agatha said made perfect sense to May while she was saying it, and May knew she was being ungrateful and hysterical, but when the interview was over and the sound of her sobs had died away, she was left with the impression that Mother Agatha was only another commonplace woman, with a cool manner and a sarcastic tongue, who was also acting the part of a nun. She was alone in a world of bad actors and actresses, and the Catholicism she had known and believed in was dead.

A few weeks later she was taken to a private nursing home. "Just for a short rest, sister," as Mother Agatha said. "It's a very pleasant place, and you will find a lot of other religious there who need a rest as well."

THERE FOLLOWED an endless but timeless phase of weeping and confusion, when all May's ordinary life was broken up and strange men burst into her room and examined her and asked questions she did not understand and replied to questions of hers in a way that showed they had not understood them either. Nobody seemed to realize that she was the last Catholic in the world; nobody understood her tears about it. Above all, nobody seemed to be able to hear the gramophone record that played continuously in her head, and that stopped only when they gave her an injection.

Then, one spring day, she went into the garden for a walk and a young nurse saw her back to her room. Far ahead of them, at the other end of a long, white corridor, she saw an old man with his back to her, and remembered that she had seen his face many times before and had perceived, without paying attention to, his long, gloomy, ironic face. She knew she must have remembered him, because now she could see nothing but his back, and suddenly the words "Who is that queer old man?" broke through the sound of the gramophone record, surprising her as much as they seemed to surprise the young nurse.

"Oh, him!" the nurse said, with a smile. "Don't you know him? He's here for years."

"But why, nurse?"

"Oh, he doesn't think he's a priest, and he is one really, that's the trouble."

"But how extraordinary!"

"Isn't it?" the nurse said, biting her lower lip in a smile. "Cripes, you'd think 'twas something you wouldn't forget. He's nice, really, though," she added gravely, as though she felt she had been criticizing him.

When they reached May's room, the young nurse grinned again, in a guilty way, and May noticed that she was extravagantly pretty, with small, gleaming front teeth.

"*You're* getting all right, anyway," she said.

"Oh, really?" May said vaguely, because she knew she was not getting all right. "Why do you think that, nurse?"

"Oh, you get to spot things," the nurse said with a shrug, and left May uncomforted, because she didn't know if she really did get well how she could face the convent and the other nuns again. All of them, she felt, would be laughing at her. Instead of worrying about the nuns, she went into a mournful daydream about the old priest who did not think he was a priest, and next day, when her father called, she said intensely, "Daddy, there's a priest in here who doesn't believe he's a priest—isn't that extraordinary?" She did not hear the tone of her own voice or know how reasonable it sounded, and so she was surprised when her father looked away and started fumbling mechanically in his jacket pocket for a cigarette.

"Well, you don't have to think you're a nun either," he said, with an unsteady voice. "Your mother has your own room ready for you when you come home."

"Oh, but Daddy, I have to go back to the convent."

"Oh, no you don't. No more convents for you, young lady! That's fixed up already with Mother Superior. It was all a mistake from the beginning. You're coming straight home to your mother and me."

Then May knew she was really going to get well, and she wanted to go home with him at once, not to go back up the stairs behind the big iron door where there was always an attendant on duty. She knew that going back home meant defeat, humiliation, and despair, but she no longer cared even about that. She just wanted to take up her life again at the point where it had gone wrong, when she had first met the Corkerys.

HER FATHER brought her home and acted as though he had rescued her from a dragon's den. Each evening, when he came home from work, he sat with her, sipping at his drink and talking quietly and comfortably. She felt he was making great efforts to assure that she felt protected and relaxed. Most of the time she did, but there were spells when she wanted her mother to put her back in the nursing home.

"Oh, I couldn't do that," her mother said characteristically. "It would upset your poor father too much."

But she did discuss it with the doctor—a young man, thin and rather unhealthy-looking, who looked as though he, too, was living on his nerves—and he argued with May about it.

"But what am I to do, doctor, when I feel like this?" she asked plaintively.

"Go out and get jarred," he said briskly.

"Get what, doctor?" she asked feebly.

"Jarred," he repeated without embarrassment. "Stoned. Polluted. Drunk. I don't mean alone, of course. You need a young fellow along with you."

"Oh, not that again, doctor!" she said, and for some reason her voice came out exactly like Mother Agatha's—which was not how she intended it to sound.

"And some sort of a job," he went on remorselessly. "There isn't a damn thing wrong with you except that you think you're a failure. You're not, of course, but as a result of thinking you are you've scratched the surface of your mind all over, and when you sit here like this, looking out at the rain, you keep rubbing it so that it doesn't heal. Booze, love-making, and hard work—they keep your hands away from the sore surface, and then it heals of its own accord."

She did her best, but it didn't seem to heal as easily as all that. Her father got her a job in the office of a friend, and she listened, in fascination, to the chatter of the other secretaries. She even went out in the evening with a couple of them and listened to their common little love stories. She knew if she had to wait until she talked like that about fellows in order to be well, her case was hopeless. Instead, she got drunk and told them how she had been for years in love with a homosexual, and, as she told it, the story became so hopeless and dreadful that she sobbed over it herself. After that she went home and wept for hours, because she knew that she had been telling lies, and betrayed the only people in the world whom she had really cared for.

Her father made a point of never referring at all to the Corkerys, the convent, or the nursing home. She knew that for him this represented a real triumph of character, because he loathed the Corkerys more than ever for what he believed they had done to her. But even he could not very well ignore the latest development in the saga. It seemed that Mrs. Corkery herself had decided to become a nun. She announced placidly to everyone that she had done her duty by her family, who were now all comfortably settled, and that she felt free to do what she had always wanted to do anyhow. She discussed it with the Dean, who practically excommunicated her on the spot. He said the family would never live down the scandal, and Mrs. Corkery told him it wasn't the scandal that worried him at all but the loss of the one house where he could get a decent meal. If he had a spark of manliness, she said, he would get rid of his housekeeper, who couldn't cook, was a miserable sloven, and ordered him about as if he were a schoolboy. The Dean said she would have to get permission in writing from every one of her children, and Mrs. Corkery replied calmly that there was no difficulty whatever about that.

May's father didn't really want to crow, but he could not resist pointing out that he had always said the Corkerys had a slate loose.

"I don't see anything very queer about it," May said stubbornly.

"A woman with six children entering a convent at her age!" her father said, not even troubling to grow angry with her. "Even the Dean realizes it's mad."

"It *is* a little bit extreme, all right," her mother said, with a frown, but May knew she was thinking of her.

May had the feeling that Mrs. Corkery would make a very good nun if for no other reason than to put her brother and Mother Agatha in their place. And of course, there were other reasons. As a girl she had wanted to be a nun, but for family reasons it was impossible, so she had become a good wife and mother, instead. Now, after thirty years of pinching and scraping, her family had grown away from her and she could return to her early dream. There was nothing unbalanced about that, May thought bitterly. *She* was the one who had proved unbalanced.

For a while it plunged her back into gloomy moods, and they were made worse by the scraps of gossip that people passed on to her, not knowing how they hurt. Mrs. Corkery had collected her six letters of freedom and taken them herself to the Bishop, who had immediately given in. "Spite!" the Dean pronounced gloomily. "Nothing but spite—all because I don't support his mad dream of turning a modern city into a medieval monastery."

On the day of Mrs. Corkery's reception, May did not leave the house at all. It rained, and she sat by the sitting-room window, looking across the city to where the hills were almost invisible. She was living Mrs. Corkery's day through—the last day in the human world of an old woman who had assumed the burden she herself had been too weak to accept. She could see it all as though she were back in that mean, bright little chapel, with the old woman lying out on the altar, covered with roses like a corpse, and an old nun shearing off her thin gray locks. It was all so intolerably vivid that May kept bursting into sudden fits of tears and whimpering like a child.

ONE EVENING a few weeks later, she came out of the office in the rain and saw Peter Corkery at the other side of the street. She obeyed her first instinct and bowed her head so as not to look at him. Her heart sank as he crossed the road to accost her.

"Aren't you a great stranger, May?" he asked, with his cheerful grin.

"We're very busy in the office these days, Peter," she replied, with false brightness.

"It was only the other night Joe was talking about you. You know Joe is up in the seminary now?"

"No. What's he doing?"

"Teaching. He finds it a great relief after the mountains. And, of course, you know about the mother." This was it!

"I heard about it. I suppose ye're all delighted?"

"*I* wasn't very delighted," he said, and his lips twisted in pain. " 'Twas the most awful day I ever spent. When they cut off her hair—"

"You don't have to remind me."

"I disgraced myself, May. I had to run out of the chapel. And here I had two nuns after me, trying to steer me to the lavatory. Why do nuns always think a man is looking for a lavatory?"

"I wouldn't know. I wasn't a very good one."

"There are different opinions about that," he said gently, but he only hurt her more.

"And I suppose you'll be next?"

"How next?"

"I was sure you had a vocation, too."

"I don't know," he said thoughtfully. "I never really asked myself. I suppose, in a way, it depends on you."

"And what have I to say to it?" she asked in a ladylike tone, though her heart suddenly began to pant.

"Only whether you're going to marry me or not. Now I have the house to myself and only Mrs. Maher looking after me. You remember Mrs. Maher?"

"And you think I'd make a cheap substitute for Mrs. Maher, I suppose?" she asked, and suddenly all the pent-up anger and frustration of years seemed to explode inside her. She realized that it was entirely because of him that she had become a nun, because of him she had been locked up in a nursing home and lived the life of an emotional cripple. "Don't you think that's an extraordinary sort of proposal—if it's intended to be a proposal."

"Why the hell should I be any good at proposing? How many girls do you think I've proposed to?"

"Not many, since they didn't teach you better manners. And it would never occur to yourself to say you loved me. Do you?" she almost shouted. "Do you love me?"

"Sure, of course I do," he said, almost in astonishment. "I wouldn't be asking you to marry me otherwise. But all the same—"

"All the same, all the same, you have reservations!" And suddenly language that would have appalled her to hear a few months before broke from her, before she burst into uncontrollable tears and went running homeward through the rain. "God damn you to Hell, Peter Corkery! I wasted my life on you, and now in the heel of the hunt all you can say to me is 'All the same.' You'd better go back to your damn pansy pals, and say it to them."

She was hysterical by the time she reached Summerhill. Her father's behavior was completely characteristic. He was the born martyr and this was only another of the ordeals for which he had been preparing himself all his life. He got up and poured himself a drink.

"Well, there is one thing I'd better tell you now, daughter," he said quietly but firmly. "That man will never enter this house in my lifetime."

"Oh, nonsense, Jack MacMahon!" his wife said in a rage, and she went and poured herself a drink, a thing she did under her husband's eye only when she was prepared to fling it at him. "You haven't a scrap of sense. Don't you see now that the boy's mother only entered the convent because she knew he'd never feel free while she was in the world?"

"Oh, Mother!" May cried, startled out of her hysterics.

"Well, am I right?" her mother said, drawing herself up.

"Oh, you're right, you're right," May said, beginning to sob again. "Only I was such a fool it never occurred to me. Of course, she was doing it for me."

"And for her son," said her mother. "And if he's anything like his mother, I'll be very proud to claim him for a son-in-law."

She looked at her husband, but saw that she had made her effect and could now enjoy her drink in peace. "Of course, in some ways it's going to be very embarrassing," she went on peaceably. "We can't very well say 'Mr. Peter Corkery, son of Sister Rosina of the Little Flower' or whatever the dear lady's name is. In fact, it's very difficult to see how we're going to get it into the press at all. However, as I always say, if the worst comes to the worst, there's a lot to be said for a quiet wedding. . . . I do hope you were nice to him, May?" she asked.

It was only then that May remembered that she hadn't been in the least nice and, in fact, had used language that would have horrified her mother. Not that it would make much difference. She and Peter had travelled so far together, and by such extraordinary ways.

A Story by Maupassant

PEOPLE who have not grown up in a provincial town won't know what I mean when I say what Terry Coughlan meant to me. People who have won't need to know.

As kids we lived a few doors from each other on the same terrace, and his sister, Tess, was a friend of my sister, Nan. There was a time when I was rather keen on Tess myself. She was a small plump gay little thing, with rosy cheeks like apples, and she played the piano very well. In those days I sang a bit, though I hadn't much of a voice. When I sang Mozart, Beethoven, or even Wagner Terry would listen with brooding approval. When I sang commonplace stuff Terry would make a face and walk out. He was a good-looking lad with a big brow and curly black hair, a long, pale face, and a pair of intense dark eyes. He was always well-spoken and smart in his appearance. There was nothing sloppy about him.

When he could not learn something by night he got up at five in the morning to do it, and whatever he took up, he mastered. Even as a boy he was always looking forward to the day when he'd have money enough to travel, and he taught himself French and German in the time it took me to find out I could not learn Irish. He was cross with me for wanting to learn it; according to him it had "no cultural significance," but he was crosser still with me because I couldn't learn it. "The first thing you should learn to do is to work," he would say gloomily. "What's going to become of you if you don't?" He had read somewhere that when Keats was depressed, he had a wash and brushup. Keats was his God. Poetry was never much in my line, except Shelley, and Terry didn't think much of him.

We argued about it on our evening walks. Maybe you don't remember the sort of arguments you had when you were young. Lots of people prefer not to remember, but I like thinking of them. A man is never more himself than when he talks nonsense about God, eternity, prostitution, and the necessity for having mistresses. I argued with Terry that the day of poetry was over, and that the big boys of modern literature were the fiction writers—the ones we'd heard of in Cork at that time, I mean—the Russians and Maupassant.

"The Russians are all right," he said to me once. "Maupassant you can forget."

"But why, Terry?" I asked.

"Because whatever you say about the Russians, they're noble," he said. "Noble" was a great word of his at the time: Shakespeare was "noble," Turgenev was "noble," Beethoven was "noble." "They are a religious people, like the Greeks, or the English of Shakespeare's time. But Maupassant is slick and coarse and commonplace. Are his stories literature?"

"Ah, to hell with literature!" I said. "It's life."

"Life in this country?"

"Life in his own country, then."

"But how do you know?" Terry asked, stopping and staring at me. "Humanity is the same here as anywhere else. If he's not true of the life we know, he's not true of any sort of life."

Then he got the job in the monks' school and I got the job in Carmody's and we began to drift apart. There was no quarrel. It was just that I liked company and Terry didn't. I got in with a wild group— Marshall and Redmond and Donnelan, the solicitor—and we sat up until morning, drinking and settling the future of humanity. Terry came with us once but he didn't talk, and when Donnelan began to hold forth on Shaw and the Life Force I could see his face getting dark. You know Donnelan's line—"But what I mean—what I want to say— Jasus, will somebody let me talk? I have something important to say." We all knew that Donnelan was a bit of a joke, and when I said good-night to Terry in the hall he turned on me with an angry look.

"Do those friends of yours do anything but talk?" he asked.

"Never mind, Terry," I said. "The Revolution is coming."

"Not if they have anything to say to it," Terry said and walked away from me. I stood there for a while feeling sorry for myself, as you do when you know that the end of a friendship is in sight. It didn't make me happier when I went back to the room and Donnelan looked at me as if he didn't believe his eyes.

"Magner," he asked, "am I dreaming or was there someone with you?"

Suddenly, for no particular reason, I lost my temper.

"Yes, Donnelan," I said. "But somebody I wouldn't expect you to recognize."

That, I suppose, was the last flash of the old love, and after that it was bogged down in argument. Donnelan said that Terry lacked flexibility—flexibility!

Occasionally I met Tess with her little shopping basket and her round rosy cheeks, and she would say reproachfully, "Ah, Ted, aren't you becoming a great stranger? What did we do to you at all?" And a couple of times I dropped around to sing a song and borrow a book, and Terry told me about his work as a teacher. He was a bit of a disillusioned with his job, and you wouldn't wonder. Some of the monks kept a mackintosh and muffler handy so that they could drop out to the pictures after dark with some doll. And then there was a thundering row when Terry discovered that a couple of his brightest boys were being sent up for public examinations under the names of notorious ignoramuses, so as to bolster up the record. When Brother Dunphy, the headmaster, argued with Terry that it was only a simple act of charity, Terry replied sourly that it seemed to him more like a criminal offense. After that he got the reputation of being impossible and was not consulted when Patrick Dempsey, the boy he really liked, was put up for examination as Mike MacNamara, the county councillor's son—Mike the Moke, as Terry called him.

Now, Donnelan is a gasbag, and speaking charitably, a bit of a fool, but there were certain things he learned in his Barrack Street slum. One night he said to me, "Ted, does that fellow Coughlan drink?"

"Drink?" I said, laughing outright at him. "Himself and a sparrow would have about the same consumption of liquor." Nothing ever embarrassed Donnelan, who had the hide of a rhinoceros.

"Well, you might be right," he said reasonably, "but, begor, I never saw a sparrow that couldn't hold it."

I thought myself that Donnelan was dreaming, but next time I met Tess I sounded her. "How's that brother of yours keeping?" I asked.

"Ah, fine, Ted, why?" she asked, as though she was really surprised.

"Oh, nothing," I said. "Somebody was telling me that he wasn't looking well."

"Ah, he's that way this long time, Ted," she replied, "and 'tis nothing only the want of sleep. He studies too hard at night, and then he goes wandering all over the country, trying to work off the excitement. Sure, I'm always at him!"

That satisfied me. I knew Tess couldn't tell a lie. But then, one moonlight night about six months later, three or four of us were standing outside the hotel—the night porter had kicked us out in the middle of an argument, and we were finishing it there. Two was striking from Shandon when I saw Terry coming up the pavement towards us. I never knew whether he recognized me or not, but all at once he crossed the street, and even I could see that the man was drunk.

"Tell me," said Donnelan, peering across at him, "is that a sparrow I see at this hour of night?" All at once he spun round on his heels, splitting his sides with laughing. "Magner's sparrow!" he said. "Magner's sparrow!" I hope in comparing Donnelan with a rhinoceros I haven't done injustice to either party.

I saw then what was happening. Terry was drinking all right, but he was drinking unknown to his mother and sister. You might almost say he was drinking unknown to himself. Other people could be drunkards but not he. So he sat at home reading, or pretending to read, until late at night, and then slunk off to some low pub on the quays where he hoped people wouldn't recognize him, and came home only when he knew his family was in bed.

For a long time I debated with myself about whether I shouldn't talk to him. If I made up my mind to do it once, I did it twenty times. But when I ran into him in town, striding slowly along, and saw the dark, handsome face with the slightly ironic smile, I lost courage. His mind was as keen as ever—it may even have been a shade too keen. He was becoming slightly irritable and arrogant. The manners were as careful and the voice was as pleasant as ever—a little too much so. The way he raised his hat high in the air to some woman who passed and whipped the big handkerchief from his breast pocket reminded me of an old actor going down in the world. The farther down he went the worse the acting got. He wouldn't join me for a drink; no, he had this job that simply must be finished tonight. How could I say to him, "Terry, for God's sake, give up trying to pretend you have work to do. I know you're an impostor and you're drinking yourself to death." You couldn't talk like that to a man of his kind. People like him are all of a piece; they have to stand or fall by something inside themselves.

He was forty when his mother died, and by that time it looked as though he'd have Tess on his hands for life as well. I went back to the house with him after the funeral. He was cruelly broken up. I discovered that he had spent his first few weeks abroad that summer and he was full of it. He had stayed in Paris and visited the cathedrals round, and they had made a deep impression on him. He had never seen real architecture before. I had a vague hope that it might have jolted him out of the rut he had been getting into, but I was wrong. It was worse he was getting.

Then, a couple of years later, I was at home one evening, finishing up some work, when a knock came to the door. I opened it myself and saw old Pa Hourigan, the policeman, outside. Pa had a schoolgirl complexion and a white mustache, china-blue eyes, and a sour elderly mouth, like a baby who has learned the facts of life too soon. It surprised me because we never did more than pass the time of day.

"May I speak to you for a moment, Mr. Magner?" he asked modestly. " 'Tis on a rather private matter."

"You can be sure, sergeant," I said, joking him. "I'm not a bit afraid. 'Tis years since I played ball on the public street. Have a drink."

"I never touch it, going on night duty," he said, coming into the front room. "I hope you will pardon my calling, but you know I am not a man to interfere in anyone else's private affairs."

By this time he had me puzzled and a bit anxious. I knew him for an exceptionally retiring man, and he was clearly upset.

"Ah, of course you're not," I said. "No one would accuse you of it. Sit down and tell me what the trouble is."

"Aren't you a friend of Mr. Coughlan, the teacher?" he asked.

"I am," I said.

"Mr. Magner," he said, exploding on me, "can you do nothing with the man?"

I looked at him for a moment and had a premonition of disaster.

"Is it as bad as that?" I asked.

"It cannot go on, Mr. Magner," he said, shaking his head. "It cannot go on. I saved him before. Not because he was anything to me, because I hardly knew the man. Not even because of his poor decent sister, though I pity her with my whole heart and soul. It was for the respect I have for education. And you know that, Mr. Magner," he added earnestly, meaning (which was true enough) that I owed it to him that I had never paid a fine for drinking during prohibited hours.

"We all know it, sergeant," I said. "And I assure you, we appreciate it."

"No one knows, Mr. Magner," he went on, "what sacrifices Mrs. Hourigan and myself made to put that boy of ours through college, and I would not give it to say to him that an educated man could sink so low. But there are others at the barracks who don't think the way I do. I name no names, Mr. Magner, but there are those who would be glad to see an educated man humiliated."

"What is it, sergeant?" I asked. "Drink?"

"Mr. Magner," he said indignantly, "when did I ever interfere with an educated man for drinking? I know when a man has a lot on his mind he cannot always do without stimulants."

"You don't mean drugs?" I asked. The idea had crossed my mind once or twice.

"No, Mr. Magner, I do not," he said, quivering with indignation. "I mean those low, loose, abandoned women that I would have whipped and transported."

If he had told me that Terry had turned into a common thief I couldn't have been more astonished and horrified. Horrified is the word.

"You don't mind my saying that I find that very hard to believe, sergeant?" I asked.

"Mr. Magner," he said with great dignity, "in my calling a man does not use words lightly."

"I know Terry Coughlan since we were boys together, and I never as much as heard an unseemly word from him," I said.

"Then all I can say, Mr. Magner, is that I'm glad, very glad, that you've never seen him as I have, in a condition I would not compare to the beasts." There were real tears in the old man's eyes. "I spoke to him myself about it. At four o'clock this morning I separated him from two of those vile creatures that I knew well were robbing him. I pleaded with him as if he was my own brother. 'Mr. Coughlan,' I said, 'what will your soul do at the Judgment?' And Mr. Magner, in decent society I would not repeat the disgusting reply he made me."

"Corruptio optimi pessima," I said to myself.

"That is Latin, Mr. Magner," the old policeman said with real pleasure.

"And it means 'Lilies that fester smell far worse than weeds,' sergeant," I said. "I don't know if I can do anything. I suppose I'll have to try. If he goes on like this he'll destroy himself, body and soul."

"Do what you can for his soul, Mr. Magner," whispered the old man, making for the door. "As for his body, I wouldn't like to answer." At the door he turned with a mad stare in his blue eyes. "I would not like to answer," he repeated, shaking his gray pate again.

It gave me a nasty turn. Pa Hourigan was happy. He had done his duty, but mine still remained to be done. I sat for an hour, thinking about it, and the more I thought, the more hopeless it seemed. Then I put on my hat and went out.

Terry lived at that time in a nice little house on College Road; a little red-brick villa with a bow window. He answered the door himself, a slow, brooding, black-haired man with a long pale face. He didn't let on to be either surprised or pleased.

"Come in," he said with a crooked smile. "You're a great stranger, aren't you?"

"You're a bit of a stranger yourself, Terry," I said jokingly. Then Tess came out, drying her hands in her apron. Her little cheeks were as rosy as ever but the gloss was gone. I had the feeling that now there was nothing much she didn't know about her brother. Even the nervous smile suggested that she knew what I had come for—of course, old Hourigan must have brought him home.

"Ah, Ted, 'tis a cure for sore eyes to see you," she said. "You'll have a cup? You will, to be sure."

"You'll have a drink," Terry said.

"Do you know, I think I will, Terry," I said, seeing a nice natural opening for the sort of talk I had in mind.

"Ah, you may as well have both," said Tess, and a few minutes later she brought in the tea and cake. It was like old times until she left us, and then it wasn't. Terry poured out the whiskey for me and the tea for himself, though his hand was shaking so badly that he could scarcely lift his cup. It was not all pretense; he didn't want to give me an opening, that was all. There was a fine print over his head—I think it was a Constable of Salisbury Cathedral. He talked about the monastery school, the usual clever, bitter contemptuous stuff about monks, inspectors and pupils. The whole thing was too carefully staged, the lifting of the cup and the wiping of the mustache, but it hypnotized me. There was something there you couldn't do violence to. I finished my drink and got up to go.

"What hurry is on you?" he asked irritably.

I mumbled something about its getting late.

"Nonsense!" he said. "You're not a boy any longer."

Was he just showing off his strength of will or hoping to put off the evil hour when he would go slinking down the quays again?

"Ah, they'll be expecting me," I said, and then, as I used to do when we were younger, I turned to the bookcase. "I see you have a lot of Maupassant at last," I said.

"I bought them last time I was in Paris," he said, standing beside me and looking at the books as though he were seeing them for the first time.

"A deathbed repentance?" I asked lightly, but he ignored me.

"I met another great admirer of his there," he said sourly. "A lady you should meet some time."

"I'd love to if I ever get there," I said.

"Her address is the Rue de Grenelle," he said, and then with a wild burst of mockery, "the left-hand pavement."

At last his guard was down, and it was Maupassant's name that had done it. And still I couldn't say anything. An angry flush mounted his pale dark face and made it sinister in its violence.

"I suppose you didn't know I indulged in that hideous vice?" he snarled.

"I heard something," I said. "I'm sorry, Terry."

The angry flush died out of his face and the old brooding look came back.

"A funny thing about those books," he said. "This woman I was speaking about, I thought she was bringing me to a hotel. I suppose I was a bit muddled with drink, but after dark, one of these places is much like another. 'This isn't a hotel,' I said when we got upstairs. 'No,' she said, 'it's my room.' "

As he told it, I could see that he was living it all over again, something he could tell nobody but myself.

"There was a screen in the corner. I suppose it's the result of reading too much romantic fiction, but I thought there might be somebody hidden behind it. There was. You'd never guess what?"

"No."

"A baby," he said, his eyes boring through me. "A child of maybe eighteen months. I wouldn't know. While I was looking, she changed him. He didn't wake."

"What was it?" I asked, searching for the message that he obviously thought the incident contained. "A dodge?"

"No," he said almost grudgingly. "A country girl in trouble, trying to support her child, that's all. We went to bed and she fell asleep. I couldn't. It's many years now since I've been able to sleep like that. So I put on the light and began to read one of these books that I carried round in my pocket. The light woke her and she wanted to see what I had. 'Oh, Maupassant,' she said. 'He's a great writer.' 'Is he?' I said. I thought she might be repeating something she'd picked up from one of her customers. She wasn't. She began to talk about *Boule de Suif.* It reminded me of the arguments we used to have in our young days." Suddenly he gave me a curious boyish smile. "You remember, when we used to walk up the river together."

"Oh, I remember," I said with a sigh.

"We were terrible young idiots, the pair of us," he said sadly. "Then she began to talk about *The Tellier Household.* I said it had poetry. 'Oh, if it's poetry you want, you don't go to Maupassant. You go to Vigny, you go to Musset, and Maupassant is life, and life isn't poetry. It's only when you see what life can do to you that you realize what a great writer Maupassant is.' . . . Wasn't that an extraordinary thing to happen?" he asked fiercely, and again the angry color mounted his cheeks.

"Extraordinary," I said, wondering if Terry himself knew how extraordinary it was. But it was exactly as if he were reading the thoughts as they crossed my mind.

"A prostitute from some French village; a drunken old waster from an Irish provincial town, lying awake in the dawn in Paris, discussing Maupassant. And the baby, of course. Maupassant would have made a lot of the baby."

"I declare to God, I think if I'd been in your shoes, I'd have brought them back with me," I said. I knew when I said it that I was talking nonsense, but it was a sort of release for all the bitterness inside me.

"What?" he asked, mocking me. "A prostitute and her baby? My dear Mr. Magner, you're becoming positively romantic in your old age."

"A man like you should have a wife and children," I said.

"Ah, but that's a different story," he said malevolently. "Maupassant would never have ended a story like that."

And he looked at me almost triumphantly with those mad, dark eyes. I knew how Maupassant would have ended that story all right. Maupassant, as the girl said, was life, and life was pretty nearly through with Terry Coughlan.

A Great Man

ONCE when I was visiting a famous London hospital, I met the matron, Miss Fitzgerald, a small, good-looking woman of fifty. She was Irish, and we discussed acquaintances in common until I mentioned Dermot O'Malley, and then I realized that somehow or other I had said the wrong thing. The matron frowned and went away. A few minutes later she returned, smiling, and asked me to lunch in a way that, for some reason, reminded me of a girl asking a young fellow for the first time to her home. "You know, Dr. O'Malley was a great friend of my father," she said abruptly and then frowned again.

"Begor, I was," said O'Malley when I reported this to him later. "And I'll tell you a story about it, what's more." O'Malley is tall and gentle, and has a wife who is a pain in the neck, though he treats her with a consideration that I can only describe as angelic. "It was when I was a young doctor in Dublin, and my old professor, Dwyer, advised me to apply for a job in the hospital in Dooras. Now, you never heard of Dooras, but we all knew about it then, because that was in the days of Margaret's father, old Jim Fitzgerald, and he was known, all right.

"I met him a couple of nights later in a hotel in Kildare Street. He had come up to Dublin to attend a meeting of doctors. He was a man with piercing eyes and a long, hard face—more the face of a soldier than a doctor. The funny thing was his voice, which was rather high and piping and didn't seem to go at all with his manner.

" 'Dooras is no place for a young man who likes entertainment,' he said.

" 'Ah, I'm a country boy myself,' said I, 'so that wouldn't worry me. And of course, I know the hospital has a great reputation.'

" 'So I understand,' he said grimly. 'You see, O'Malley, I don't believe in all this centralization that's going on. I know it's all for the sake of equipment, and equipment is a good thing, too, but it's taking medicine away from where it belongs. One of these days, when their centralization breaks down, they'll find they haven't hospitals, doctors, or anything else.'

"By the time I'd left him, I'd as good as accepted the job, and it wasn't the job that interested me so much as the man. It could be that, my own father having been a bit of a waster, I'm attracted to men of strong character, and Fitzgerald was a fanatic. I liked that about him.

"Now, Dwyer had warned me that I'd find Dooras queer, and Dwyer knew the Dublin hospitals weren't up to much, but Dooras was dotty. It was an old hospital for infectious diseases that must have dated from about the time of the Famine, and Fitzgerald had got a small local committee to take it over. The first couple of days in it gave me the horrors, and it was weeks before I even began to see what Fitzgerald meant by it all. Then I did begin to see that in spite of all the drawbacks, it worked in a way bigger hospitals didn't work, and it was happy in a way that bigger hospitals are never happy. Everybody knew everybody else, and everybody was madly curious about everybody else, and if anybody ever gave a party, it wasn't something devised by the staff to entertain the patients; it was more likely to be the patients entertaining the staff.

"Partly this was because Margaret Fitzgerald, the woman you met in London, was the head nurse. I don't know what she's like now, and from all I can hear, she's a bit of a Tartar, but in those days she was a pretty little thing with an air of being more efficient than anybody ever was. Whenever you spoke to Margaret, she practically sprang to attention and clicked her heels, and if you were misguided enough to ask her for anything she hadn't handy, she gave you a demonstration of greyhound racing. And, of course, as you can see from the job she has now, she was a damn great nurse.

"But mainly the place worked because of Fitzgerald and his colleagues, the local doctors. Apart from him, none of them struck me as very brilliant, though he himself had a real respect for an old doctor called Pat Duane, a small, round, red-faced man with an old-fashioned choker collar and a wonderful soupy bedside manner. Pat looked as though some kind soul had let him to mature in a sherry cask till all the crude alcohol was drawn out of him. But they were all conscientious; they all listened to advice, even from me—and God knows I hadn't much to offer—and they all deferred in the most extraordinary way to Fitzgerald. Dwyer had described him to me as a remarkable man, and I was beginning to understand the full force of that, because I knew Irish small towns the way only a country boy knows them, and if those men weren't at one another's throats, fighting for every five-bob fee that could be picked up, it was due to his influence. I asked a doctor called MacCarthy about it one night and he invited me in for a drink. MacCarthy was a tall old poseur with a terrible passion for local history.

" 'Has it occurred to you that Fitzgerald may have given us back our self-respect, young man?' he asked in his pompous way.

" 'Our what?' I asked in genuine surprise. In those days it hadn't occurred to me that a man could at the same time be a show-box and be lacking in self-respect.

" 'Oh, come, O'Malley, come!' he said, sounding like the last Duke of Dooras. 'As a medical man you are more observant than you pretend. I presume you have met Dr. Duane?'

" 'I have. Yes,' said I.

" 'And it didn't occur to you that Dr. Duane was ever a victim of alcohol?' he went on portentously. 'You understand, of course, that I am not criticizing him. It isn't easy for the professional man in Ireland to maintain his standards of behavior. Fitzgerald has a considerable respect for Dr. Duane's judgment—quite justified, I may add, quite justified. But at any rate, in a very short time Pat eased off on the drink, and even began to read the medical journals again. Now Fitzgerald has him in the hollow of his hand. We all like to feel we are of some use to humanity—even the poor general practitioner. . . . But you saw it all for yourself, of course. You are merely trying to pump a poor country doctor.'

"Fitzgerald was not pretentious. He liked me to drop in on him when I had an hour to spare, and I went to his house every week for dinner. He lived in an old, uncomfortable family house a couple of miles out on the bay. Normally, he was cold, concentrated, and irritable, but when he had a few drinks in he got melancholy, and this for some reason caused him to be indiscreet and say dirty things about his committee and even about the other doctors. 'The most interesting thing about MacCarthy,' he said to me once, 'is that he's the seventh son of a seventh son, and so he can diagnose a case without seeing the patient at all. It leaves him a lot of spare time for local history.' I suspected he made the same sort of dirty remarks about me, and that secretly the man had no faith in anyone but himself. I told him so, and I think he enjoyed it. Like all shy men he liked to be insulted in a broad masculine way, and one night when I called him a flaming egotist, he grunted like an old dog when you tickle him and said, 'Drink makes you very offensive, O'Malley. Have some more!'

"It wasn't so much that he was an egotist (though he was) as that he had a pernickety sense of responsibility, and whenever he hadn't a case to worry over, he could always find some equivalent of a fatal disease in the hospital—a porter who was too cheeky or a nurse who made too free with the men patients—and he took it all personally and on a very high level of suffering. He would sulk and snap at Margaret for days over some trifle that didn't matter to anyone, and finally reduce her to tears. At the same time, I suppose it was part of the atmosphere of seriousness he had created about the makeshift hospital, and it kept us all on our toes. Medicine was his life, and his gossip was shop. Duane or MacCarthy or some other local doctor would drop in of an evening to discuss a case—which by some process I never was able to fathom had become Fitzgerald's case—and over the drinks he would grow gloomier and gloomier about our ignorance till at last, without a word to any of us, he got up and telephoned some Dublin specialist he knew. It was part of the man's shyness that he only did it when he was partly drunk and could pretend that instead of asking a favor he was conferring one. Several times I watched that scene with amusement. It was all carefully calculated, because if he hadn't had enough to drink he lacked the brass and became apologetic, whereas if he had had one drink too much he could not describe what it was about the case that really worried him. Not that he rated a specialist's knowledge any higher than ours, but it seemed the best he could do, and if that didn't satisfy him, he ordered the specialist down, even when it meant footing the bill himself. It was only then I began to realize the respect that Dublin specialists had for him, because Dwyer, who was a terrified little man and hated to leave home for fear of what might happen him in out-of-the-way places like Cork and Belfast, would only give out a gentle moan about coming to Dooras. No wonder Duane and MacCarthy swore by him, even if for so much of the time they, like myself, thought him a nuisance.

"Margaret was a second edition of himself, though in her the sense of responsibility conflicted with everything feminine in her till it became a joke. She was small. She was pretty, with one of those miniature faces that seem to have been reduced until every coarse line has been refined in them. She moved at twice the normal speed and was forever fussing and bossing and wheedling, till one of the nurses would lose her temper and say, 'Ah, Margaret, will you for God's sake give us time to breathe!' That sort of impertinence would make Margaret scowl, shrug, and go off somewhere else, but her sulks never lasted, as her father's did. The feminine side of her wouldn't sustain them.

"I remember one night when all hell broke loose in the wards, as it usually does in any hospital once a month. Half a dozen patients decided to die all together, and I was called out of bed. Margaret and the other nurse on night duty, Joan Henderson, had brewed themselves a pot of tea in the kitchen, and they were scurrying round with a mug or a bit of seedcake in their hands. I was giving an injection to one of my patients, who should have been ready for discharge. In the next bed was a dying old mountainy man who had nothing in particular wrong with him except old age and a broken heart. I suddenly looked up from what I was doing and saw he had come out of coma and was staring at Margaret, who was standing at the other side of the bed from me, nibbling the bit of cake over which she had been interrupted. She started when she saw him staring at the cake, because she knew what her father would say if ever he heard that she was eating in the wards. Then she gave a broad grin and said in a country accent, 'Johnny, would 'oo like a bit of seedcake?' and held it to his lips. He hesitated and then began to nibble, too, and then his tongue came out and licked round his mouth, and somehow I knew he was saved. 'Tay, Johnny,' she said mockingly. 'Thot's what 'oo wants now, isn't it?' And that morning as I went through the wards, my own patient was dead but old Johnny was sitting up, ready for another ten years of the world's hardship. That's nursing.

"Margaret lived in such a pitch of nervous energy that every few weeks she fell ill. 'I keep telling that damn girl to take it easy,' her father would say with a scowl at me, but any time there was the least indication that Margaret was taking it easy, he started to air his sufferings with the anguish of an elephant. She was a girl with a real sense of service, and at one time had tried to join a nursing order in Africa, but dropped it because of his hatred for all nursing orders. In itself this was funny, because Margaret was a liberal Catholic who, like St. Teresa, was 'for the Moors, and martyrdom' but never worried her head about human weaknesses and made no more of an illegitimate baby than if she had them herself every Wednesday, while he was an old-fashioned Catholic and full of obscure prejudices. At the same time, he felt that the religious orders were leaving Ireland without nurses—not that he thought so much of nurses!

" 'And I suppose nuns can't be nurses?' Margaret would ask with a contemptuous shrug.

" 'How can they?' he would say, in his shrillest voice. 'The business of religion is with the soul, not the body. My business is with the body. When I'm done with it, the nuns can have it—or anyone else, for that matter.'

" 'And why not the soul and the body?' Margaret would ask in her pertest tone.

" 'Because you can't serve two masters, girl.'

" 'Pooh!' Margaret would say with another shrug. 'You can't serve one Siamese twin, either.'

"As often as I went to dinner in that house, there was hardly a meal without an argument. Sometimes it was about no more than the amount of whiskey he drank. Margaret hated drink, and watched every drop he poured in his glass, so that often, just to spite her, he went on to knock himself out. I used to think that she might have known her father was a man who couldn't resist a challenge. She was as censorious as he was, but she had a pertness and awkwardness that a man rarely has, and suddenly, out of the blue, would come some piece of impertinence that plunged him into gloom and made her cringe away to her bedroom, ready for tears. He and I would go into the big front room, overlooking Dooras Bay, and without a glance at the view he would splash enormous tasheens of whiskey into our glasses, just to indicate how little he cared for her, and say in a shrill, complaining voice, 'I ruined that girl, O'Malley. I know I did. If her mother was alive, she wouldn't talk to me that way.'

"Generally, they gave the impression of two people who hated one another with a passionate intensity, but I knew well that he was crazy about her. He always brought her back something from his trips to Dublin or Cork and once when I was with him, he casually wasted my whole afternoon looking for something nice for her. It never occurred to him that I might have anything else to do. But he could also be thoughtful; for once when for a full week he had been so intolerable that I could scarcely bring myself to answer him he grinned and said, 'I know exactly what you think of me, O'Malley. You think I'm an old slave driver.'

" 'Not exactly,' I said, giving him tit for tat. 'Just an old whoor!'

"At this, he gave a great gaffaw and handed me a silver cigarette case, which I knew he must have bought for me in town the previous day, and added sneeringly, 'Now, don't you be going round saying your work is quite unappreciated.'

" 'Did I really say that?' I asked, still keeping my end up, even though there was something familiar about the sentiment.

" 'Or if you do, say it over the loudspeaker. Remember, O'Malley, I hear *everything*.' And the worst of it was, he did!

"Then, one night, when my year's engagement was nearly ended, I went to his house for dinner. That night there was no quarrelling, and he and I sat on in the front room, drinking and admiring the view. I should have known there was something wrong, because for once he didn't talk shop. He talked about almost everything else, and all the time he was knocking back whiskey in a way I knew I could never keep pace with. When it grew dark, he said with an air of surprise, 'O'Malley, I'm a bit tight. I think we'd better go for a stroll and clear our heads.'

"We strolled up the avenue of rhododendrons to the gate and turned left up the hill. It was a wild, rocky bit of country, stopped dead by the roadway and then cascading merrily down the little fields to the bay. There was still a coppery light in the sky, and the reflection of a bonfire on one of the islands, like a pendulum, in the water. The road fell again, between demesne walls and ruined gateways where the last of the old gentry lived, and I was touched—partly, I suppose, by all the whiskey, but partly by the place itself.

" 'I'll regret this place when I leave it,' I said.

" 'Oh, no, you won't,' he snapped back at me. 'This is no place for young people.'

" 'I fancy it might be a very pleasant memory if you were in the East End of London,' said I.

" 'It might,' said Fitzgerald, 'if you were quite sure you wouldn't have to go back to it. That's what worries me about Margaret.'

"I had never noticed him worrying very much about Margaret—or anyone else, for that matter—so I took it as merely a matter of form.

" 'Margaret seems to do very well in it,' I said.

" 'It's no place for Margaret,' he said sharply. 'People need friends of their own age and ideas old men like myself can't supply. It's largely my fault for letting her come back here at all. I made this place too much of my life, and that's all right for a man, but it's not good enough for a high-spirited girl like that.'

" 'But doesn't Margaret have friends here?' I asked, trying to comfort him.

" 'She has friends enough, but not of her own age,' he said. 'She's too mature for the girls here that are her own age. Not that I ever cared much for her friends from Dublin,' he added shortly. 'They struck me as a lot of show-boxes. I don't like those intellectual Catholics, talking to me about St. Thomas Aquinas. I never read St. Thomas Aquinas, and from all I can hear I haven't missed much. But young people have to make their own mistakes. All the men around here seem to want is some good-natured cow who'll agree to everything they say, and because she argues with them they think she's pert and knowing. Well, she *is* pert, and she *is* knowing—I realize that as well as anybody. But there's more than that to her. They'd have said the same about me, only I proved to them that I knew what I was doing.'

"Suddenly I began to realize what he was saying, and I was frightened out of my wits. I said to myself that it was impossible, that a man like Fitzgerald could never mean a thing like that, but at the same time I felt he did mean it, and that it had been in his mind from the first night he met me. I muttered something about her having more chances in Dublin.

" 'That's the trouble,' he said. 'She didn't know what she was letting herself in for when she came back here, and no more did I. Now she won't leave, because I'd be here on my own, and I know I wouldn't like it, but still I have my work to do, and for a man that's enough. I like pitting my wits against parish priests and county councillors and nuns. Besides, when you reach my age you realize that you could have worse, and they'll let me have my own way for the time I have left me. But I haven't so long to live, and when I die, they'll have some champion footballer running the place, and Margaret will be taking orders from the nuns. She thinks now that she won't mind, but she won't do it for long. I know the girl. She ought to marry, and then she'd have to go wherever her husband took her.'

" 'But you don't really think the hospital will go to pieces like that?' I asked, pretending to be deeply concerned but really only trying to head Fitzgerald off the subject he seemed to have on his mind. 'I mean, don't you think Duane and MacCarthy will hold it together?'

" 'How can they?' he asked querulously. 'It's not their life, the way it's been mine. I don't mean they won't do their best, but the place will go to pieces just the same. It's a queer feeling, Dermot, when you come to the end of your time and realize that nothing in the world outlasts the man that made it.'

"That sentence was almost snapped at me, out of the side of his mouth, and yet it sounded like a cry of pain—maybe because he'd used my Christian name for the first time. He was not a man to use Christian names. I didn't know what to say.

" 'Of course, I should have had a son to pass on my responsibilities to,' he added wonderingly. 'I'm not any good with girls. I dare say that was why I liked you, the first time we met—because I might have had a son like you.'

"Then I couldn't bear it any longer, and it broke from me. 'And it wasn't all on one side!'

" 'I guessed that. In certain ways we're not so unlike. And that's what I really wanted to say to you before you go. If ever you and Margaret got to care for one another, it would mean a lot to me. She won't have much, but she'll never be a burden on anybody, and if ever she marries, she'll make a good wife.'

"It was the most embarrassing moment of my life—and mind, it wasn't embarrassing just because I was being asked to marry a nice girl I'd never given a thought to. I'm a country boy, and I knew all about 'made' matches by the time I was seventeen, and I never had anything but contempt for the snobs that pretend to despise them. Damn good matches the most of them are, and a thousand times better than the sort you see nowadays that seem to be made up out of novelettes or moving pictures! Still and all, it's different when it comes to your own turn. I suppose it's only at a moment like that you realize you're just as silly as any little servant girl. But it wasn't only that. It was because I was being proposed to by a great man, a fellow I'd looked up to in a way I never looked up to my own father, and I couldn't do the little thing he wanted me to do. I muttered some nonsense about never having been able to think about marriage—as if there ever was a young fellow that hadn't thought about it every night in his life!—and he saw how upset I was and squeezed my arm.

" 'What did I tell you?' he said. 'I knew I was drunk, and if she ever gets to hear what I said to you, she'll cut me in little bits.'

"And that tone of his broke my heart. I don't even know if you'll understand what I mean, but all I felt was grief to think a great man who'd brought life to a place where life never was before would have to ask a favor of me, and me not to be able to grant it. Because all the time I wanted to be cool and suave and say of course I'd marry his daughter, just to show the way I felt about himself, and I was too much of a coward to do it. In one way, it seemed so impossible, and in another it seemed such a small thing.

"Of course, we never resumed the conversation, but that didn't make it any easier, because it wasn't only between myself and him; it was between me and Margaret. The moment I had time to think of it, I knew Fitzgerald was too much a gentleman to have said anything to me without first making sure that she'd have me.

"Well, you know the rest yourself. When he died, things happened exactly the way he'd prophesied; a local footballer got his job, and the nuns took over the nursing, and there isn't a Dublin doctor under fifty that could even tell you where Dooras is. Fitzgerald was right. Nothing in the world outlasts a man. Margaret, of course, has a great reputation, and I'm told on the best authority that there isn't a doctor in St. Dorothy's she hasn't put the fear of God into so I suppose it's just as well that she never got the opportunity to put it into me. Or don't you agree?"

I didn't, of course, as O'Malley well knew. Anyway, he could hardly have done much worse for himself. And I had met Margaret, and I had seen her autocratic airs, but they hadn't disturbed me much. She was just doing it on temperament, rather than technique—a very Irish way, and probably not so unlike her father's. I knew I didn't have to tell O'Malley that. He was a gentleman himself, and his only reason for telling me the story was that already, with the wisdom that comes of age, he had begun to wonder whether he had not missed something in missing Margaret Fitzgerald. I knew that he had.

Androcles and the Army

"POLITICS and religion!" Healy said when Cloone announced that he was joining the army. "Even a lion tamer you can't trust not to get patriotic on you. The next thing will be the clown wanting to join the Trappists." He argued, he pleaded, he threatened proceedings for breach of contract, but Cloone retorted with arguments about the state of the country. Threatened by the Germans, threatened by the English, threatened even by the Americans, she needed all her children. Healy's long red nose, that ascended and descended like a helicopter, shuddered and began to mount at the very mention of Ireland.

"Look, Cloone," he said, reasonably, "there's nothing wrong with the bloody country. It's the show I'm thinking of. 'Twill only be the mercy of God if we can keep going at all. And if you leave us there isn't another man in Ireland can do the job, and with a war on, I'm not going to be able to get one in."

"Ah, damn it, I know, I know," Cloone replied in anguish. "I'm not against the show, and I care more for my lions than I do for the show, but if I have to choose between my lions and my country, I have to choose my country. It's as hard on me as it is on you, but war is always like that. Look at the sugar!"

Till the last moment Healy continued to plead. He knew that not only would it be impossible to get another lion tamer, but even if he did, the man would not be as good as Cloone. Healy knew an artist when he saw one and Cloone was an artist. What others could do by fear, he could do by a simple dropping of his voice. Healy couldn't hear the magic in that sudden change of pitch, but he could see the result, for an angry lion would suddenly uncoil his tightened springs of muscle and lie down to be stroked like a cat. Cloone would play with it like a cat, his blue eyes soft with emotion, and mutter as though to himself, "God, Ned, isn't he beautiful?"

"Beautiful my ass!" Healy would think as his red nose began to ascend, but he would keep it to himself.

Anyone seeing Cloone with animals would be bound to think at once of St. Francis of Assisi, but Healy knew that that was all the saint there was in Cloone. He had a devil of a temper, and brooded for months on imaginary insults and injuries. He would begin to mutter about a half a crown that he swore had been unjustly stopped from his pay six months before till Healy, in despair, raised his eyes and hands to Heaven. "Listen, Cloone," he would say. "I told you fifty times that there was nothing stopped. If you don't believe me, I'll give you the bloody half-crown to take your puss off me." Then spasms of injured pride would run through Cloone like electric shocks, and he would cry: "It's not the money, Ned! It's not the money! It's the principle." But Healy, who had been in the show business from the time he was five, knew that when artists talked about principle, it was never anything but temperament, and it took a man like him who hated animals but loved human beings to put up with it at all. Cloone knew that too, and knew that Healy had some sort of hold over him. "Cloone tames lions but I tame Cloone," Healy had boasted one night in a pub, and Cloone had agreed with an exasperated giggle. He would do things for Healy he would do for no one else, but even Healy couldn't persuade him to stay on for the emergency. And it wasn't just because the show was only a ghost of itself, stripped by restrictions and regulations. It was pure, unqualified, bloodthirsty patriotism, a thing Healy simply could not understand in a mature man. "If," he added darkly, "you can ever say an artist is mature."

IT WAS a wrench for Cloone, because he really loved the few animals that had been left him; he loved Healy, and he loved the wandering life of the circus and the crowds of the small towns and fair greens. He went away with a breaking heart to be shut up in a Nissen hut, dressed in uniform, stood to attention, stood at ease, presented, formed twos with, formed fours with, as if he himself were only a mangy old circus lion, jumping to a cruel tamer's whip. Besides, he was an awkward, excitable man who could never remember his left from his right, and shouldered arms when he should have presented them, and he had to listen to tongue-lashings from a sergeant and not tell the sergeant what he could do with himself. It often reduced him to mutinous tears, and he lay on his cot at night exhausted, thinking of himself as a caged old animal, its spirit broken, dreaming of the jungle. Then he shed more tears because he felt he had never understood wild animals till his own turn came. All the same his desperate sincerity won through. They had to make a corporal of him, and, in the way of other great artists, he was prouder of his two miserable stripes than of all his other gifts. Drinking in a pub with another man, he couldn't help glancing at his sleeve with a smirk of delight.

Then one day he opened a local paper and saw that Doyle's World-Famous Circus was visiting Asragh one evening the following week. Filled with excitement, he went off to ask for a pass. Of course, everyone in the battalion knew his trade, and he had no difficulty in getting the pass. The trouble was that everyone from the officers down wanted a pass as well. They all felt that they had a personal interest in the circus. On the afternoon of the show two lorryloads of troops left the camp for town. In the Main Street they scattered to the public-houses to wait for the circus, but Cloone hurried off joyously to the Fair Green, where Healy was waiting for him. In his temperamental way he threw his arms about Healy and sobbed with pleasure till Healy, in embarrassment, grabbed him by the shoulders and mockingly inspected his uniform, with the green gloves tucked neatly in the shoulder strap and the natty little cane.

"Give it up, John," he said with a grin. "They'll never make a soldier out of you."

"How well they gave me the stripes!" Cloone said defensively, and followed Healy to his caravan.

"Stripes never made a soldier yet," said Healy. "A raw recruit is all you'll ever be." He took down a bottle and poured half a tumbler of neat whiskey for Cloone and another for himself. "And why? Because that's not where you belong at all, John. You belong round here with the rest of the crowd."

"Ah, God, Ned, I know, I know," said Cloone, wriggling miserably on the edge of the bed. "I wake up in the night and think about it. But the Germans have it all planned out. They caught a parachutist with the plans. You have to face it, Ned."

"I do not have to face it," retorted Healy, his delicate nose vibrating at the very thought of it. "You'll never see a shot fired in this country, man. Sure, who the hell would want it? And anyone that did would be welcome to it as far as I'm concerned. I have enough of it."

"I'll give you my word, the moment it's over, I'll belt it back here," said Cloone. "Sometimes I think it'll never be over. Tell me, who have you on the lions?"

"Who do you think?" Healy asked gloomily. "Darcy—the strong man." The last words he added not by way of information but as a sneer, for Healy, who had a wretched stomach, had seen the strong man screaming his head off with a toothache, and it had left a terrible impression on him.

"Ah, God, Ned," Cloone moaned, shaking his head, "sure Darcy could never handle a lion. Darcy is too rough."

"Darcy is too frightened," Healy added sternly. "Drink that and we'll finish the bottle."

"Is he any good with them?" asked Cloone.

"Ah, he's all right," Healy replied with a frown—he was a fair man. "They don't like him, that's the only thing."

"But how could they, Ned?" Cloone asked feverishly. "Lions could never get on with a strong man. Lions are sensitive, like women. What possessed you to give them to Darcy?"

"Who else could I give them to?" Healy asked angrily. "Damn grateful I was to him for taking them off my hands."

It was like old times for Cloone, sitting in the twilight with his friend, and the old hands dropping in to ask how he was. He told them all about the importance of the army and the danger to the country, and they listened politely but with utter incredulity. It was at times like this that you could see Cloone wasn't really one of them.

When Healy went to take the gate, Cloone with a foolish smile nodded in the direction of the big cage and said, "I'll slip round and have a look at Jumbo and Bess." They might have been two old sweethearts, the way he talked of them, thought Healy.

"Oh, plenty of time, John," he said with a toss of his head. "They won't be on for half an hour yet."

THE MAIN satisfaction of the evening from Healy's point of view was the number of soldiers who came, officers and all. Healy could not help liking a bit of style, and style was something that was disappearing from the Irish countryside. He was only sorry for the miserable show he had for them, and the two lions that were all he had left him. And then their turn came, and Darcy stood ready, a huge and handsome man with a self-conscious air as though he did not even see the audience.

"Ladies and Gentlemen," the ringmaster explained, "owing to emergency restrictions, Doyle's collection of wild animals—the greatest in the world—has been considerably reduced. But the two lions you are going to see aren't just ordinary animals. No, ladies and gentlemen, these two terrible lions are among the most savage ever captured alive. In the capture of these two lions—especially for Doyle's Circus—no less than eight famous big-game hunters lost their lives, as well as an untold number of simple natives."

Then the big cage was rolled on; Darcy smartly whipped the curtains back; there was a moment of incredulous silence, and then a laugh that grew into a roar. For, inside the cage with his cap off and his tunic open, was Cloone, sprawled on the ground against the bars, embracing Jumbo with one arm and Bess with the other. The two lions had a meditative air, as if they were posing for a photograph. At the tumult in the audience they raised their heads suspiciously, and fresh screams broke out, because Jumbo was seen to be holding Cloone's green gloves in his jaws while Bess sedately held his cane. There was an atmosphere of intense domesticity about the scene that made one feel that instead of a cage there should be a comfortable living room with a good fire burning.

"Mind the lions or the soldier will ate 'em!" roared someone from the back row, and this brought fresh shrieks. As a turn it was superior to anything that had yet been seen, but to the circus hands it seemed like disaster.

"Oh, my God!" muttered the ringmaster. "This is awful! This is terrible entirely! How could a thing like that happen, Darcy?"

"That's Cloone," said Darcy with a puzzled frown.

"Sure I know damn well 'tis Cloone," said the ringmaster severely. "But how the hell did he get in there, and how are we going to get him out? Come out now, John," he called appealingly. "Come on out and let the show go on!"

"In a minute now, in a minute," replied Cloone with a knowing smile. "We'll give ye yeer show when we're ready."

"Ah, come on now, come on!" snapped the ringmaster. "We'll be the laughingstock of Ireland. Darcy, you go in and get him out!"

"Is it me?" Darcy asked indignantly. "How the hell can I go in with him there? They'd ate you, man. Where's my hot bar?"

Two policemen who had been sitting near the front approached with their uniform caps in their hands to indicate that this was merely friendly curiosity on their part and that nothing had yet occurred that required their official attention.

"Now, lads, what's this disturbance about?" asked the sergeant in a friendly boom. "Come out of that cage now like a good man, and don't be obstructing the traffic."

Then Cloone began to giggle feebly as the humor of it struck him.

"Ye can't get me," he said coyly.

"What's that you said?" asked the sergeant.

"You're afraid," said Cloone.

"Who's afraid?" asked the sergeant.

"You are," replied Cloone with an explosion of laughter. "There's nothing to be afraid of. We're all friends here."

The sergeant looked at him for a moment and then put on his cap. It had something of the effect of a judge's donning of the black cap in a murder trial. The younger policeman with a shy air put on his own.

"Someone will have to get him," the sergeant announced in an entirely different tone, the one that went with the cap.

"All right, all right," Darcy said irritably. "Wait till I get my hot bar." He grabbed it with a determined air and opened the door of the cage. The two lions rose and growled at him.

"Put down that bar!" Cloone said in an outraged voice as he staggered to his feet. "Put it down, I say!"

"Get out of my way, God blast you!" snarled Darcy. "Haven't I trouble enough without you?"

All in a moment the atmosphere of domesticity had vanished. It was clear that Darcy hated the lions and Cloone, and Cloone and the lions hated Darcy. For a few moments the lions eyed the strong man hungrily and growled; then they slunk slowly back to the end of the cage where a separate compartment was opened. Darcy, white in the face, slammed the door behind them, and then the ringmaster and the policemen, followed by Healy, entered the main cage.

"Come on, John," Healy said, taking Cloone by the arm. "Come on now."

"That's no way to treat my animals," Cloone said, pointing at Darcy.

"John," Healy said in a low voice, "remember the uniform!" A remark, as he said afterward, that he'd have to answer for on the Last Day, because he cared as much about the uniform as he did about the state of the country. But he was a man tamer as Cloone was a lion tamer. Each of them made his own sort of soothing, nonsensical noise.

"All right," muttered Cloone, heading off in the direction of the lions. "Let me say good-bye to them and I won't trouble ye again."

"Don't let that man open that cage door again or I won't be responsible!" Darcy shouted in a frenzy.

"I'll be responsible, Darcy," Healy said shortly. "Go on, John, and do whatever you want to do, but do it quick—and for God's sake don't let them out on us! Come on outside, boys, and we'll shut the gate."

And there they had to stand outside the cage, powerlessly, watching the performance within. Cloone opened the gate of the inner cage and stood there for a moment, overcome with emotion. The lions seemed to be overcome as well. After a moment Jumbo sadly raised his big head and joined Cloone. Cloone bent and kissed him on the snout. As he did so Bess came up to him and licked his hand. He kissed her as well. Then, before he closed the door behind him, he drew himself up and gave them a military salute. The soldiers in the audience were delighted with this. "Company, present arms!" yelled one of them. As Healy said, "There was never the like of it seen as show business. If you could have put it on as an act, you'd be turning them away."

But for Cloone, it was anything but show business. As he came out of the big cage he strode up to Darcy.

"You big, bloody bully!" he said. "You had to take a red-hot bar to frighten those poor innocent creatures! Like every other bully, you're a coward."

He gave Darcy a punch, and the strong man was so astonished that he went down flat on the grass. There were fresh roars from the audience; the soliders were getting restive. Darcy rose with a dazed expression as the two policemen seized Cloone from behind. To give them their due, they were less afraid of what Cloone would do to Darcy than of what Darcy would do to Cloone. He was one of those sad powerful men whose tragedy is that they can't have a little disagreement in a pub without running the risk of manslaughter. Cloone pulled himself away, leaving his tunic in the policemen's hands, and dashed for the side of the tent. He disappeared under it with two guards close behind, and a score of soldiers after the guards, to see that their comrade got fair play. As they were pulling off their belts while they ran, two officers got up as well and ran through the main entrance after them to protect the guards. It was all very confusing, and the show was as good as over for the night.

THEY RAN Cloone to earth at last in the kitchen of a cottage down a lane from which there was no escape. By this time he had had the opportunity of considering his behavior, and all the fight had gone out of him. He apologized to the woman of the house for the fright he had given her, and she moaned over him like a Greek chorus, blaming it all on the bad whiskey. He apologized to the guards for the trouble he had given them and begged them to go back to the circus while he surrendered himself at the barrack. He apologized all over again to the two young lieutenants who appeared soon after; by this time he was trembling like an aspen leaf.

"It's my lions!" he said in a broken voice. "I'd never shame the uniform only for them."

At his court-martial he appeared on a charge of "conduct prejudicial to good order and discipline, in that he, Corporal John Cloone, on the eighteenth day of September, of the current year, had allowed himself to be seen in a public place with his tunic in disorder and minus certain articles of equipment: viz. one pair of gloves and one walking stick (regulation)." The charge of assault was dropped at the instance of the president, who suggested to the prosecution that there might have been provocation. The prosecutor agreed that, considering the prisoner's occupation in civil life, this might be so. But armies are alike the whole world over, and, whatever their disregard for civilian rights, they all have the same old-maidish preoccupation with their own dignity, and Cloone was lucky to get off with nothing worse than the loss of his stripes. Healy asked him what better he could expect from soldiers, people who tried to turn decent artists into people like themselves. As if anybody had ever succeeded in turning a soldier into anything that was the least use to God or man!

But Healy, as Cloone knew, was lacking in idealism.

Public Opinion

NOW I KNOW what you're thinking. You're thinking how nice 'twould be to live in a little town. You could have a king's life in a house like this, with a fine garden and a car so that you could slip up to town whenever you felt in need of company. Living in Dublin, next door to the mail boat and writing things for the American papers, you imagine you could live here and write whatever you liked about MacDunphy of the County Council. Mind, I'm not saying you couldn't say a hell of a lot about him! I said a few things myself from time to time. All I mean is that you wouldn't say it for long. This town broke better men. It broke me and, believe me, I'm no chicken.

When I came here first, ten years ago, I felt exactly the way you do, the way everybody does. At that time, and the same is nearly true today, there wasn't a professional man in this town with a housekeeper under sixty, for fear of what people might say about them. In fact, you might still notice that there isn't one of them who is what you might call "happily" married. They went at it in too much of a hurry.

Oh, of course, I wasn't going to make that mistake! When I went to choose a housekeeper I chose a girl called Bridie Casey, a handsome little girl of seventeen from a village up the coast. At the same time I took my precautions. I drove out there one day when she was at home, and I had a look at the cottage and a talk with her mother and a cup of tea, and after that I didn't need anyone to recommend her. I knew that anything Bridie fell short in her mother would not be long in correcting. After that, there was only one inquiry I wanted to make.

"Have you a boy, Bridie?" said I.

"No, doctor, I have not," said she with an innocent air that didn't take me in a bit. As a doctor you soon get used to innocent airs.

"Well, you'd better hurry up and get one," said I, "or I'm not going to keep you."

With that she laughed as if she thought I was only joking. I was not joking at all. A housekeeper or maid without a fellow of her own is as bad as a hen with an egg.

"It's no laughing matter," I said. "And when you do get a fellow, if you haven't one already, you can tell him I said he could make free with my beer, but if ever I catch you diluting my whiskey I'll sack you on the spot."

Mind, I made no mistake in Bridie or her mother either. She mightn't be any good in the Shelbourne Hotel, but what that girl could cook she cooked well and anything she cleaned looked as if it was clean. What's more, she could size a patient up better than I could myself. Make no mistake about it, as housekeepers or maids Irish girls are usually not worth a damn, but a girl from a good Irish home can turn her hand to anything. Of course, she was so good-looking that people who came to the house used to pass remarks about us, but that was only jealousy. They hadn't the nerve to employ a good-looking girl themselves for fear of what people would say. But I knew that as long as a girl had a man of her own to look after she'd be no bother to me.

No, what broke up my happy home was something different entirely. You mightn't understand it, but in a place like this 'tis the devil entirely to get ready money out of them. They'll give you anything else in the world only money. Here, everything is what they call "friendship." I suppose the shops give them the habit because a regular customer is always supposed to be in debt and if ever the debt is paid off it's war to the knife. Of course they think a solicitor or a doctor should live the same way, and instead of money what you get is presents: poultry, butter, eggs, and meat that a large family could not eat, let alone a single man. Friendship is all very well, but between you and me it's a poor thing for a man to be relying on at the beginning of his career.

I had one patient in particular called Willie Joe Corcoran of Clashanaddig—I buried him last year, poor man, and my mind is easier already—and Willie Joe seemed to think I was always on the verge of starvation. One Sunday I got in from twelve-o'clock Mass and went to the whiskey cupboard to get myself a drink when I noticed the most extraordinary smell. Doctors are sensitive to smells, of course— we have to be—and I couldn't rest easy till I located that one. I searched the room and I searched the hall and I even poked my head upstairs into the bedrooms before I tried the kitchen. Knowing Bridie, I never even associated the smell with her. When I went in, there she was in a clean white uniform, cooking the dinner, and she looked round at me.

"What the hell is that smell, Bridie?" said I.

She folded her arms and leaned against the wall, as good-looking a little girl as you'd find in five counties.

"I told you before," says she in her thin, high voice, " 'tis that side of beef Willie Joe Corcoran left on Thursday. It have the whole house ruined on me."

"But didn't I tell you to throw that out?" I said.

"You did," says she as if I was the most unreasonable man in the world, "but you didn't tell me where I was going to throw it."

"What's wrong with the ash can?" said I.

"What's wrong with the ash can?" says she. "There's nothing wrong with it, only the ashmen won't be here till Tuesday."

"Then for God's sake, girl, can't you throw it over the wall into the field?"

"Into the field," says she, pitching her voice up an octave till she sounded like a sparrow in decline. "And what would people say?"

"Begor, I don't know, Bridie," I said, humoring her. "What do *you* think they'd say?"

"They're bad enough to say anything," says she.

I declare to God I had to look at her to see was she serious. There she was, a girl of seventeen with the face of a nun, suggesting things that I could barely imagine.

"Why, Bridie?" I said, treating it as a joke. "You don't think they'd say I was bringing corpses home from the hospital to cut up?"

"They said worse," she said in a squeak, and I saw that she took a very poor view of my powers of imagination. Because you write books, you think you know a few things, but you should listen to the conversation of pious girls in this town.

"About me, Bridie?" said I in astonishment.

"About you and others," said she. And then, by cripes, I lost my temper with her.

"And is it any wonder they would," said I, "with bloody fools like you paying attention to them?"

I have a very wicked temper when I'm roused and for the time being it scared her more than what people might say of her.

"I'll get Kenefick's boy in the morning and let him take it away," said she. "Will I give him a shilling?"

"Put it in the poor box," said I in a rage. "I'll be going out to Dr. MacMahon's for supper and I'll take it away myself. Any damage that's going to be done to anyone's character can be done to mine. It should be able to stand it. And let me tell you, Bridie Casey, if I was the sort to mind what anyone said about me, you wouldn't be where you are this minute."

I was very vicious to her, but of course I was mad. After all, I had to take my drink and eat my dinner with that smell round the house, and Bridie in a panic, hopping about me like a hen with hydrophobia. When I went out to the pantry to get the side of beef, she gave a yelp as if I'd trodden on her foot. "Mother of God!" says she. "Your new suit!" "Never mind my new suit," said I, and I wrapped the beef in a couple of newspapers and heaved it into the back of the car. I declare, it wasn't wishing to me. I had all the windows open, but even then the smell was high, and I went through town like a coursing match with the people on the footpaths lifting their heads like beagles to sniff after me.

I wouldn't have minded that so much only that Sunday is the one day I have. In those days before I was married I nearly always drove out to Jerry MacMahon's for supper and a game of cards. I knew poor Jerry looked forward to it because the wife was very severe with him in the matter of liquor.

I stopped the car on top of the cliffs to throw out the meat, and just as I was looking for a clear drop I saw a long galoot of a country man coming up the road towards me. He had a long, melancholy sort of face and mad eyes. Whatever it was about his appearance I didn't want him to see what I was up to. You might think it funny in a professional man but that is the way I am.

"Nice evening," says he.

"Grand evening, thank God," says I, and not to give him an excuse for being too curious I said: "That's a powerful view."

"Well," says he sourly, just giving it a glance, "the view is all right but 'tis no good to the people that has to live in it. There is no earning in that view," says he, and then he cocked his head and began to size me up, and I knew I'd made a great mistake, opening my mouth to him at all. "I suppose now you'd be an artist?" says he.

You might notice about me that I'm very sensitive to inquisitiveness. It is a thing I cannot stand. Even to sign my name to a telegram is a thing I never like to do, and I hate a direct question.

"How did you guess?" said I.

"And I suppose," said he, turning to inspect the view again, "if you painted that, you'd find people to buy it?"

"That's what I was hoping," said I.

So he turned to the scenery again, and this time he gave it a studied appraisal as if it was a cow at a fair.

"I dare say for a large view like that you'd nearly get five pounds?" said he.

"You would and more," said I.

"Ten?" said he with his eyes beginning to pop.

"More," said I.

"That beats all," he said, shaking his head in resignation. "Sure, the whole thing isn't worth that. No wonder the country is the way it is. Good luck!"

"Good luck," said I, and I watched him disappear among the rocks over the road. I waited, and then I saw him peering out at me from behind a rock like some wild mountain animal, and I knew if I stayed there till nightfall I wouldn't shake him off. He was beside himself at the thought of a picture that would be worth as much as a cow, and he probably thought if he stayed long enough he might learn the knack and paint the equivalent of a whole herd of them. The man's mind didn't rise above cows. And, whatever the devil ailed me, I could not give him the satisfaction of seeing what I was really up to. You might think it shortsighted of me, but that is the sort I am.

I got into the car and away with me down to Barney Phelan's pub on the edge of the bay. Barney's pub is the best in this part of the world and Barney himself is a bit of a character; a tall excitable man with wild blue eyes and a holy terror to gossip. He kept filling my glass as fast as I could lower it, and three or four times it was on the tip of my tongue to tell him what I was doing; but I knew he'd make a story out of it for the boys that night and sooner or later it would get back to Willie Joe Corcoran. Bad as Willie Joe was, I would not like to hurt his feelings. That is another great weakness of mine. I never like hurting people's feelings.

Of course that was a mistake, for when I walked out of the pub, the first thing I saw was the cliff dweller and two other yokels peering in at the parcel in the back of my car. At that I really began to feel like murder. I cannot stand that sort of unmannerly inquisitiveness.

"Well," I said, giving the cliff dweller a shoulder out of my way, "I hope ye saw something good."

At that moment Barney came out, drying his hands in his apron and showing his two front teeth like a weasel.

"Are them fellows at your car, doctor?" says he.

"Oho!" said the cliff dweller to his two friends. "So a docthor is what he is now!"

"And what the hell else did you think he was, you fool?" asked Barney.

"A painter is what he was when last we heard of him," said the lunatic.

"And I suppose he was looking for a little job painting the huts ye have up in Beensheen?" asked Barney with a sneer.

"The huts may be humble but the men are true," said the lunatic solemnly.

"Blast you, man," said Barney, squaring up to him, "are you saying I don't know the doctor since he was in short trousers?"

"No man knows the soul of another," said the cliff dweller, shaking his head again.

"For God's sake, Barney, don't be bothering yourself with that misfortunate clown," said I. " 'Tis my own fault for bringing the likes of him into the world. Of all the useless occupations, that and breaking stones are the worst."

"I would not be talking against breaking stones," said the cliff dweller sourly. "It might not be long till certain people here would be doing the same."

At that I let a holy oath out of me and drove off in the direction of Jerry MacMahon's. When I glanced in the driving mirror I saw Barney standing in the middle of the road with the three yokels around him, waving their hands. It struck me that in spite of my precautions Barney would have a story for the boys that night, and it would not be about Willie Joe. It would be about me. It also struck me that I was behaving in a very uncalled-for way. If I'd been a real murderer trying to get rid of a real corpse I could hardly have behaved more suspiciously. And why? Because I did not want people discussing my business. I don't know what it is about Irish people that makes them afraid of having their business discussed. It is not that it is any worse than other people's business, only we behave as if it was.

I stopped the car at a nice convenient spot by the edge of the bay miles from anywhere. I could have got rid of the beef then and there but something seemed to have broken in me. I walked up and down that road slowly, looking to right and left to make sure no one was watching. Even then I was perfectly safe, but I saw a farmer crossing a field a mile away up the hill and decided to wait till he was out of sight. That was where the ferryboat left me, because, of course, the moment he glanced over his shoulder and saw a strange man with a car stopped on the road he stopped himself with his head cocked like an old setter.

Mind, I'm not blaming him! I blame nobody but myself. Up to that day I had never felt a stime of sympathy with my neurotic patients, giving themselves diseases they hadn't got, but there was I, a doctor, giving myself a disease I hadn't got and with no excuse whatever.

By this time the smell was so bad I knew I wouldn't get it out of the upholstery for days. And there was Jerry MacMahon up in Cahirnamona, waiting for me with a bottle of whiskey his wife wouldn't let him touch till I got there, and I couldn't go for fear of the way he'd laugh at me. I looked again and saw that the man who'd been crossing the field had changed his mind. Instead he'd come down to the gate and was leaning over it, lighting his pipe while he admired the view of the bay and the mountains.

That was the last straw. I knew now that even if I got rid of the beef my Sunday would still be ruined. I got in the car and drove straight home. Then I went to the whiskey cupboard and poured myself a drink that seemed to be reasonably proportionate to the extent of my suffering. Just as I sat down to it Bridie walked in without knocking. This is one fault I should have told you about—all the time she was with me I never trained her to knock. I declare to God when I saw her standing in the doorway I jumped. I'd always been very careful of myself and jumping was a new thing to me.

"Did I tell you to knock before you came into a room?" I shouted.

"I forgot," she said, letting on not to notice the state I was in. "You didn't go to Dr. MacMahon's so?"

"I did not," I said.

"And did you throw away the beef?"

"I didn't," I said. Then as I saw her waiting for an explanation I added: "There were too many people around."

"Look at that now!" she said complacently. "I suppose we'll have to bury it in the garden after dark?"

"I suppose so," I said, not realizing how I had handed myself over to the woman, body and bones, holus-bolus.

That evening I took a spade and dug a deep hole in the back garden and Bridie heaved in the side of beef. The remarkable thing is that the whole time we were doing it we talked in whispers and glanced up at the backs of the other houses in the road to see if we were being watched. But the weight off my mind when it was over! I even felt benevolent to Bridie. Then I went over to Jim Donoghue, the dentist's, and told him the whole story over a couple of drinks. We were splitting our sides over it.

When I say we were splitting our sides I do not mean that this is a funny story. It was very far from being funny for me before it was over. You wouldn't believe the scandal there was about Bridie and myself after that. You'd wonder how people could imagine such things, let alone repeat them. That day changed my whole life. . . . Oh, laugh! Laugh! I was laughing out the other side of my mouth before it was through. Up to that I'd never given a rap what anyone thought of me, but from that day forth I was afraid of my own shadow. With all the talk there was about us I even had to get rid of Bridie and, of course, inside of twelve months I was married like the rest of them. . . . By the way, when I mentioned unhappy marriages I wasn't speaking of my own. Mrs. Ryan and myself get on quite well. I only mentioned it to show what might be in store for yourself if ever you were foolish enough to come and live here. A town like this can bend iron. And if you doubt my word, that's only because you don't know what they are saying about you.

Achilles' Heel

IN ONE THING only is the Catholic Church more vulnerable than any human institution, and that is in the type of woman who preys on celibates—particularly the priest's housekeeper. The priest's housekeeper is one of the supreme examples of natural selection, because it has been practically proved that when for any reason she is transferred to a male who is not celibate, she pines away and dies. To say that she is sexless is to say both too much and too little, for, like the Church itself, she accepts chastity for a higher end—in her case, the subjection of some unfortunate man to a degree unparalleled in marriage. Wives, of course, have a similar ambition, but their purposes are mysteriously deflected by love-making, jealousy of other women, and children, and it is well known that many Irish wives go into hysterics of rage at the thought of the power vested in priests' housekeepers. *Their* victims, being celibate, have no children, and are automatically sealed off from other women, who might encourage them to greater independence.

But the most powerful among these are the housekeepers of bishops. Nellie Conneely, the Bishop of Moyle's housekeeper, had been with him since he was a canon, and even in those days he had been referred to by his parishioners as "Nellie and the Canon." "Nellie and the Canon" didn't approve of all-night dances, so all-night dances were stopped. Half the population depended for patronage on "Nellie and the Canon," and presents were encouraged—food for the Canon and something a little less perishable for Nellie. The townspeople had no doubt as to which was the more important partner. She had even appeared on the altar steps on one occasion and announced that there would be no eight-o'clock Mass because she was keeping the Canon in bed. She was a comparatively young woman for such a responsible position, and even at the time I speak of she was a well-preserved little body, with a fussy, humble, sugary air that concealed a cold intelligence. Her great rival was Canon Lanigan, who was the favorite in the succession of the diocese. In private he sniggered over her and called her La Maintenon, but when he visited the Bishop he was as sugary as herself and paid her flowery compliments on her cooking and even on her detestable bottled coffee. But Nellie, though she giggled and gushed in response, wasn't in the least taken in; she knew Lanigan preferred old French mishmash to her own candid cooking, and she warned the Bishop not to trust him. "God forgive me," she said sadly, "I don't know how it is I can't warm to Canon Lanigan. There is something about him that is not quite sincere. I know, of course, that I'm only a foolish old woman, and you don't have to mind me."

But the Bishop had to mind her and he did. The poor man had one great fear, which was that he was fading away for lack of proper nourishment. He knew what the old-fashioned clerics were like, with their classical scholarship and their enormous appetites, and, comparing his own accomplishments and theirs, he couldn't see for the life of him how he was ever going to reach ninety. After eating a whole chicken for his dinner, he would sit in his study for hours, wondering what the connection was between serious scholarship and proper meals, till Nellie thrust her head in the door.

"You're all right?" she would ask coyly.

"I'm not, Nellie," he would reply with a worried air. "I'm feeling a bit low tonight."

" 'Tis that chicken!" she would cry, making a dramatic entrance. "I knew it. I said it to Tim Murphy. There wasn't a pick on it."

"I was wondering about that myself," he would say, fixing her with his anxious blue eyes. "Murphy's chickens don't seem to be the same at all."

"What you want is a nice grilled chop," she would say authoritatively.

"I don't know," he would mutter, measuring his idea of a chop against his idea of night starvation. "There's a lot of eating in a chop."

"Well, you could have cutlets," she would say with a shrug, implying that she didn't think much of cutlets for a bad case like his own.

"Cutlets make a nice snack," he agreed.

"Ah, they do, but they're too dry," she would cry, waving them away in disgust. "What you want is a good plate of nice curly rashers, with lots of fat on them. 'Twas my own fault. I knew there was nothing in that chicken. I should have served them with the chicken, but I declare to you my wits are wandering. I'm getting too old. . . . And a couple of chips. Sure, 'twill be the making of you."

ONE DAY, Nellie came in terrible trouble to the Bishop. She had just been visited by one of the local customs officers, Tim Leary. The Bishop's diocese was on the border between Northern and Southern Ireland, and since there was never a time when something that was plentiful on one side wasn't scarce on the other, there was constant smuggling in both directions. The South sent butter, eggs, ham, and whiskey to the North, and the North sent back petrol, tea, and sugar—all without benefit of duty. The customs officials of the two countries worked together in their efforts to prevent it. Nellie seemed to have the greatest difficulty in explaining to the Bishop what Tim Leary wanted of her. You'd have thought she was not bright in the head.

"You said it yourself," she said ingenuously. "This diocese was ever notorious for backbiting, but why do they pick on me? I suppose they want to have their own housekeeper, someone that would do their whispering for them. It is something I never would do, not even for your sake, and I will not do it for them, even if they do say you're too old."

"Who says I'm too old?" the Bishop asked mildly, but his blue eyes had an angry light in them. He knew the people who would say such things, and there were plenty of them.

"Don't, don't ask me to carry stories!" she begged, almost in frenzy. "I won't do it, even to save my life. Let Canon Lanigan and the rest of them say what they like about me."

"Never mind Canon Lanigan," the Bishop said shortly. "What did Leary say about you?"

"But what could he say about me? What have he against me only old *doorsha-dawrsha* he picked up in the low public-houses of the town? Oh, 'tisn't that at all, my lord, but the questions he asked me. They put the heart across me. 'Who was the chief smuggler?'—wasn't that a nice thing for him to ask me?"

"He thought you knew the chief smuggler?" the Bishop asked incredulously.

"He thought I *was* the chief smuggler," she replied with her hand to her heart. "He didn't say it, but I could read it in that mean little mind of his. Whiskey, petrol, tea, and things, my lord, that I declare to you and to my Maker, if I was to go before Him at this minute of time, I never even knew the names of."

"He must be mad," the Bishop said with a worried air. "Which Learys is he belonged to? The ones from Clooneavullen?" The Bishop had a notion that most of the mysteries of human conduct could be solved by reference to heredity. He said he had never yet met a good man who came from a bad family.

"Aha!" Nellie cried triumphantly. "Didn't I say it myself? That his own father couldn't read or write, and the joke of the countryside for his foolish talk!"

"Never mind his father," the Bishop said sternly. "He had an uncle in the lunatic asylum. All that family were touched. Tell him to come up here to me tomorrow, and I'll give him a bit of my mind."

"You will to be sure, my lord," she said complacently as she rose. Then at the door she stopped. "But why would you talk to a little whippersnapper like that—a man like you, that has the ear of the government? I suppose someone put him up to it."

The Bishop meditated on that for a moment. He saw Nellie's point about the impropriety of people's going over his head, and recognized that it might be the work of an enemy. Like Nellie, he knew the secrets of power and understood that the most important is never to deal directly with people you look down on.

"Give me my pen!" he said at last in a voice that made Nellie's heart flutter again. When some parish priest had been seen drunk in a public place, the Bishop would say in the same dry voice to his secretary, "Give me my pen till I suspend Father Tom," or when some gang of wild young curates had started a card club in some remote village, "Give me my pen till I scatter them!" It was the voice of ultimate authority, of the Church Militant personified in her own dear, simple man.

IN SPITE of strenuous detective work, Nellie never did get to see the Bishop's letter to his friend in the government, Seumas Butcher, the Irish Minister of Revenue, but, on the other hand, neither did the

Bishop ever get to see the Minister's reply. It was one of the features of Nellie's concern for him that she did not like him to know of anything that would upset his health, and she merely removed such letters from the hall. But even she had never seen a letter so likely to upset the Bishop as that from the Minister:

Dear Dr. Gallogly:

It was a real pleasure to hear from you again. Mrs. Butcher was only saying a week ago that it was ages since you paid us a visit. I have had careful inquiries made about the matter you mention, and I am very sorry indeed to inform you that the statements of the local Revenue Officer appear to be fully substantiated. Your housekeeper, Miss Ellen Conneely, is the owner of licensed premises at the other side of the Border which have long been known as the headquarters of a considerable smuggling organization, whose base on this side appears to be the Episcopal Palace. You will realize that the Revenue Officers have no desire to take any steps that could be an embarrassment to you, but you will also appreciate that this traffic involves a considerable loss of revenue for both our country and the North of Ireland, and might in the event of other gangs operating in the neighborhood being tried and convicted, result in serious charges. I should be deeply grateful for your lordship's kind assistance in putting an early end to it.

> Mise le meas,
> *Seumas O. Butcher*
> *Aire*

Nellie fully understood, when she had read this, the tone with which the Bishop said "Give me my pen," as a father might say "Give me my stick." There were certain matters that could only be dealt with by a pen like a razor, and that evening she sat in her own room and wrote:

Dear Sir:

His Lordship, the Most Reverend Dr. Gallogly, Bishop of Moyle, has handed me your letter of the 3rd inst. and asked me to reply to it on his behalf. He says it is a tissue of lies and that he does not want to be bothered anymore with it. I suppose his lordship would not know what is going on in his own house? Or is it a rogue and robber you think he is? I do not know how you can have the face to say such things to a bishop. All those lies were started by Tim Leary, and as his lordship says, what better could you expect of a man whose uncle died in the Moyle Asylum, a wet and dirty case? The public-house you talk about is only another of the lies. It does not belong to me at all but to my poor brother who, after long years of suffering for Ireland in English prisons, is now an incurable invalid with varicose veins and six children. How would the likes of him be a smuggler? Tim Leary will be thrown out if he calls here again. It is all lies. Did Tim Leary suffer for Ireland? Has Tim Leary six children? What has happened our Christian principles and what do we pay taxes for? We were better off when we had the English.

Yours sincerely,
Ellen Conneely

There was something about this letter that gave Nellie a real thrill of pride and satisfaction. Like all women of her kind, she had always had the secret desire to speak out boldly with the whole authority of the Church behind her, and now she had done it.

She had also illustrated to perfection the Achilles' heel of Catholicism, because, though Dr. Gallogly would probably have had a heart attack if he had known the contents of her letter, no layman could be quite sure of this, and the Minister and his staff were left with a vague impression that, somehow or other, the Bishop of Moyle was now the ringleader of a smuggling gang. Being all of them good Catholics, they took the charitable view that the Bishop was no longer responsible for his actions and had taken to smuggling the way some old men take to other peculiar pursuits, but all the same it was a nasty situation. Whatever happened, you could not raid the palace for contraband. The very thought of what the newspapers would say about this made the Minister sick. The *Irish Times* would report it in full, with a smug suggestion that Protestant bishops never did things like that; the *Irish Independent* would assert that instructions for the raid had come direct from Moscow through the local Communist cell; while the *Irish Press* would say, without fear of contradiction, that it was another British plot against the good name of Irishmen.

"Jesus, Joe!" the Minister said, with a moan, to his secretary. "Forget it! Forget it, if you can!"

BUT the local customs officers could not forget it. Nellie didn't allow them. Scared by Tim Leary and the Minister's letter, she worked openly and feverishly to get rid of all the contraband in her possession, and the professional pride of the customs officers was mortified. Then, one day, a man was caught trying to cross the border into the North with a keg of whiskey under the seat of his car, and he swore by God and the Twelve Apostles that he had no notion how it had got there.

But Tim Leary, who knew the man's friendship with Nellie, knew damn well how it had got there, and went to Paddy Clancy's liquor store in Moyle, from which it had originally come. Paddy, a crushed and quivering poor man, had to admit that the keg had been sold to the Bishop.

"Get me the Bishop's account, Paddy," Tim said stiffly, and poor Paddy produced the ledger. It was an ugly moment, because Paddy was a man who made a point of never interfering with any man's business but he knew of old that the Bishop's liquor account was most peculiar. Tim Leary studied it in stupefaction.

"Honor of God!" he said angrily. "Are you trying to tell me that the Bishop drinks all that?"

"Bishops have a lot of entertaining to do, Tim," Paddy said meekly.

"Bishops don't have to have a bloody bonded store to entertain in!" shouted Tim.

"Well, Tim, 'tis a delicate matter," Paddy said, sweating with anxiety. "If a man is to have customers in this country, he cannot afford to ask questions."

"Well, begod, I'm going to ask a few questions," cried Tim, "and I'm going to do it this very morning, what's more. Give me that ledger!"

Then, with the ledger under his arm, he went straight up to the palace. Nellie tried to head him off. First she said the Bishop was out; then she said the Bishop was ill; finally she said that the Bishop had given orders that Tim was not to be admitted.

"You try to stop me, Nellie, and I'll damn soon show you whether I'm going to be admitted or not," said Tim, pushing past her, and at that moment the study door opened and the Bishop came out. It was no coincidence, and at that moment Nellie knew she was lost, for along with the appetite of a child the Bishop had the curiosity of a child, and a beggar's voice at the door would be sufficient for him to get up and leave the door of his study ajar so that he could listen in comfort to the conversation.

"That will do, Nellie," he said, and then came up to Tim with a menacing air—a handsome old man of six foot two, with a baby complexion and fierce blue eyes.

"What do you want?" he asked sternly, but on his own ground Tim could be as infallible as any bishop.

"I'm investigating the smuggling that's going on in this locality, and I want to ask you a few questions, my lord," he replied grimly.

"So I heard," said the Bishop. "I told the Minister already I couldn't see why you had to do your investigating in my house."

"I'm a public servant, my lord," Tim said, his voice rising, "and I'm entitled to make my investigations wherever I have to."

"You're a very independent young man," the Bishop said dryly but without rancor. "Tell me, are you John Leary's son from Clooneavullen?"

"I'm nothing of the sort. Who said I was John Leary's son? My father was from Manister."

"For God's sake!" the Bishop said softly. "You're not Jim Leary's boy, by any chance?"

"I am, then," said Tim with a shrug.

"Come on in," the Bishop said, holding out his hand to Tim, while his eyes searched away into the distance beyond the front door. "Your father was headmaster there when I was a canon. I must have seen you when you were a little fellow. Come in, anyway. No son of Jim Leary's is going to leave this house without a drink."

"But I'm on duty, my lord," said Tim, following him in.

"Aren't we all?" the Bishop asked mildly as he went to the sideboard. "I'm as much a bishop now as I'll ever be." With shaky hands he produced two glasses and a bottle of whiskey. He gave one tiny glass to Tim and took another himself. It was obviously a duty rather than a pleasure. The Bishop did not go in for drinking, because it seemed to ruin his appetite and that was bad enough already.

"Now, tell me what all this is about," he said comfortably.

Tim was beginning to realize that he really liked the man—an old weakness of his, which, combined with his violent temper, made him a bad investigator. He sometimes thought the bad temper and the good nature were only two aspects of the same thing.

"A man was caught trying to cross the border a few days ago with a keg of your whiskey in his car," he said firmly as he could.

"A keg of my whiskey?" the Bishop repeated with real interest and apparent enjoyment. "But what would I be doing with a keg of whiskey?"

"That's what I came to ask you," replied Tim. "You seem to have bought enough of them in the past year."

"I never bought a keg of whiskey in my whole life, boy," said the Bishop with amusement. "Sure, if I take a drop of punch before I go to bed, that's all the whiskey I ever see. It's bad for a man of my age," he added earnestly. "I haven't the constitution."

"If you'll take one look at your account in Clancy's ledger, you'll see you're supposed to have an iron constitution," said Tim, and as he opened the book, there was a knock and Nellie came in modestly with a bundle of receipted bills in her hand. "Or maybe this is the one with the iron constitution," Tim added fiercely. He still had not forgotten his unmannerly reception.

"You need say no more," she said briskly. "I admit it, whatever little harm I did to anyone. 'Twas only to keep my unfortunate angashore of a brother out of the workhouse. Between drinking and politics, he was never much head to his poor wife, God rest her. Not one penny did I ever make out of it, and not one penny of his lordship's money ever went astray. I'll go if I have to, but I will not leave this house without a character."

"I'll give you the character," Tim said savagely. "And furthermore I'll see you have a place to go. You can do all the smuggling you like there—if you're able."

"That will do!" the Bishop said sternly. "Go away, Nellie!" he added over his shoulder, in the tone he used when he asked for his pen to suspend Father Tom.

Nellie looked at him for a moment in stupefaction and then burst into a howl of grief and went out, sobbing to herself about "the fifteen good years of my life that I wasted on him and there's his gratitude." The Bishop waited imperturbably till her sobs had subsided in the kitchen before he spoke again.

"How many people know about this?"

"Begod, my lord, by this time I think you might say 'twas common property," said Tim with a laugh.

The Bishop did not laugh. "I was afraid of that," he said. "What do they think of it?"

"Well, of course, they all have a great regard for you," Tim replied, in some embarrassment.

"I'm sure of that," the Bishop said without a hint of irony. "They have so much regard for me that they don't care if I turn my house into a smuggler's den. They didn't suggest what I might be doing with the Cathedral?"

Tim saw that the Bishop was more cut up than he affected to be.

"Ah, I wouldn't worry about that," he said anxiously.

"I'm not worrying. What will they do to Nellie?"

"Oh, she'll get the jail," said Tim. "As well as a bloody big fine that'll be worse to her."

"A fine? What sort of a fine?"

"That will be calculated on the value of the contraband," said Tim. "But if you ask me quietly, 'twill run well into the thousands."

"Into the thousands?" the Bishop asked in alarm. "But where would either of us get that sort of money, boy?"

"You may be damn full sure she has it," Tim said grimly.

"Nellie?"

"Aye, and more along with it," said Tim.

"For God's sake!" the Bishop exclaimed softly. He had put away his glass, and his long, fine fingers were intertwined. Then he gave a little snort that might have passed for laughter. "And me thinking she was an old fool! Which of us was the fool, I wonder. After this, they'll be saying I'm not able to look after myself. They'll be putting in a co-adjutor over me, as sure as you're there!"

"They wouldn't do that?" Tim asked in astonishment. It had never occurred to him before that there might be anybody who could inter-fere with a bishop.

"Oh, indeed they would," the Bishop said, almost with enjoyment. "And I wouldn't mind that itself if only they'd leave me my house-keeper. The jail won't take much out of her, but 'twill kill me. At my age I'm not going to be able to find another woman to look after me the way she does. Unless they'd let me go to jail along with her."

Tim was an emotional young man, and he could hardly contemplate the personal problems that the Bishop set up in that casual way of his.

"There's nobody in this place would do anything to upset you," he said, growing red. "I'm sure they'll be well satisfied if she paid the fine, without sending her to jail. The only thing is, from my point of view, could you control her?"

"I could do nothing of the kind," the Bishop replied in his blank way. "If I was to give you my oath to control her for the future, would you believe me? You would not. I couldn't control her. You might be able to do it."

"I'd damn soon do it if I had a free hand," Tim said loyally.

"I'd give you all the hand you want," the Bishop said placidly. "I'd give you quarters here if you wanted them. You see, 'tis more in my interest than yours to stop the scandal, before they have me married to her." From the dryness of his tone, the Bishop, an unemotional man, seemed to be suffering. "I wouldn't forget it for you," he added anx-iously. "Anyway, I'll have a talk to Butcher, and see if he can't do something for you. Not that that poor fool knows what he's doing, most of the time."

THAT AFTERNOON, the Bishop sat on by his window and watched as a lorry drove up before his palace and Tim Leary loaded it with com-modities the Bishop had thought long gone from the world—chests of tea, bags of sugar, boxes of butter. There seemed to be no end to them. He felt crushed and humbled. Like all bishops, he was addicted to power, but he saw now that a bishop's power, like a bishop's knowledge, was little better than a shadow. He was just a lonely old man who was dependent on women, exactly as when they had changed his napkin and he had crowed and kicked his heels. There was no escape.

Mercifully, Nellie herself didn't put in an appearance as the premises were gone through. That evening, when she opened the door and said meekly, "Dinner is served, my lord," the Bishop went in to a royal spread—the juiciest of roast beef, with roast potatoes and tender young peas drowned in butter. The Bishop ate stolidly through it, reading the book in front of his plate and never addressing a word to her. He was too bitter. He went to his study and took down the history of the diocese, which had so often consoled him in earlier griefs, but that night there was no consolation in it. It seemed that none of the men who had held the see before him was of the sort to be dominated by an old housekeeper, except for an eighteenth-century bishop who, in order to inherit a legacy, had become a Protestant. The door opened, and Nellie looked shyly in.

"What way are you feeling now?" she whispered.

"Let me alone," he said in a dry voice, without looking at her. "My heart is broken!"

" 'Tisn't your heart at all," she said shamefastly. " 'Tis that beef. 'Twasn't hung long enough, that's all. There isn't a butcher in this town will be bothered to hang beef. Would I get you a couple of scrambled eggs?"

"Go away, I said."

"You're right, my lord. There's nothing in eggs. Would I fry you a couple of rashers?"

"I don't want anything, woman!" he said, almost shouting at her.

"The dear knows, the rashers aren't worth it," she admitted with a heavy sigh. "Nothing only old bones, and the hair still sprouting on them. What you want is a nice little juicy bit of Limerick ham with a couple of mashed potatoes and milk sauce with parsley. That'll make a new man of you."

"All right, all right," he said angrily. "But go away and let me alone."

His mouth was already watering, but he knew that there was no ham in Limerick or out of it that could lift his sorrow; that whenever a woman says something will make a new man of you, all she means is that, like the rest of her crooked devices, it will make an old man of you before your time.

The Wreath

WHEN FATHER FOGARTY read of the death of his friend Father Devine in a Dublin nursing home, he was stunned. He was a man who did not understand the irremediable.

He took out an old seminary group, put it on the mantelpiece, and spent the evening looking at it. Devine's clever, pale, shrunken face stood out from all the others, not very different from what it had been in his later years except for the absence of pince-nez. He and Fogarty had been boys together in a provincial town where Devine's father was a schoolmaster and Fogarty's mother kept a shop. Even then everybody had known that Devine was marked by nature for the priesthood. He was clever, docile, and beautifully mannered. Fogarty's vocation had come later and was a surprise.

They had been friends over the years, affectionate when together, critical and sarcastic when apart, and had seen nothing of one another for close on a year. Devine had been unlucky. As long as the old Bishop lived he had been fairly well sheltered, but Lanigan, the new one, disliked him. It was partly his own fault; because he could not keep his mouth shut; because he was witty and waspish and said whatever came into his head about his colleagues who had nothing like his gifts. Fogarty remembered the things Devine had said about himself. He affected to believe that Fogarty was a man of many personalities, and asked with mock humility which of them he was now dealing with—Nero, Napoleon, or St. Francis of Assisi.

It all came back, the occasional jaunts together, the plans for holidays abroad which never came to anything; and now the warm and genuine love for Devine which was natural to him welled up, and realizing that never again in this world would he be able to express it, he began to weep. He was as simple as a child in his emotions. He forgot lightly, remembered suddenly and with exaggerated intensity, and blamed himself cruelly and unjustly for his own shortcomings. He would have been astonished to learn that, for all the intrusions of Nero and Napoleon, his understanding had continued to develop through the years, when that of clever men had dried up, and that he was a better and wiser priest at forty than he had been twenty years before.

Because there was no one else to whom he could communicate his sense of loss, he rang up Jackson, a curate who had been Devine's other friend. He did not really like Jackson, who was worldly, cynical, and a bit of a careerist, and had always wondered what it was that Devine saw in him.

"Isn't that terrible news about Devine?" he said, barely keeping the tears out of his voice.

"Yes," drawled Jackson in his usual cautious, fishy tone, as though even on such a subject he were afraid of committing himself. "I suppose it's a happy release for the poor devil."

This was the sort of talk which maddened Fogarty. It sounded as if Jackson were talking of an old family pet who had been sent to the vet's.

"I dare say," he said gruffly. "I was thinking of going to town and coming back with the funeral. You wouldn't come?"

"I don't see how I could, Jerry," Jackson replied in a tone of concern. "It's only a week since I was up last."

"Ah, well, I'll go myself," said Fogarty. "I suppose you don't know what happened him?"

"Oh, you know he was always anemic. He ought to have looked after himself, but he didn't get much chance with that old brute of a parish priest of his. He was fainting all over the shop. The last time, he fainted at Mass."

"You were in touch with him, then?" Fogarty asked in surprise.

"I just saw him for a while last week. He couldn't talk much, of course."

And again the feeling of his own inadequacy descended on Fogarty. He realized that Jackson, who seemed to have as much feeling as a mowing machine, had kept in touch with Devine and gone out of his way to see him at the end, while he, the warm-hearted, devoted, generous friend, had let him slip from sight into eternity and was now wallowing in the sense of his own loss.

"God, I feel thoroughly ashamed of myself, Jim," he said with a new humility. "I never even knew he was sick."

"I'll see about getting off for the funeral," Jackson said. "I think I might manage it."

THAT EVENING, the two priests set off in Fogarty's car for the city. Jackson brought Fogarty to a very pleasant restaurant for dinner. He was a tall, thin man with a prim, watchful, clerical air, who knew his way round. He spent at least ten minutes over the menu and the wine list, and the headwaiter danced attendance on him as headwaiters do only when there is a big tip in view or they have to deal with an expert.

"I'm having steak," Fogarty said to cut it short.

"Father Fogarty is having steak, Paddy," said Jackson, looking at the headwaiter over his spectacles. "Make it rare. And stout, I suppose?"

"I'll spare you the stout," said Fogarty. "Red wine."

"Mind, Paddy," said Jackson warningly. "Father Fogarty said *red* wine. You're in Ireland now, remember."

Next morning, they went to the mortuary chapel, where the coffin was resting on trestles before the altar. Beside it, to Fogarty's surprise, was a large wreath of red roses. When they rose from their knees, Devine's uncle Ned had come in with his son. Ned was a broad-faced, dark-haired, nervous man, with the anemic complexion of the family.

"I'm sorry for your trouble, Ned," Father Fogarty said.

"I know that, father," said Ned.

"I don't know if you know Father Jackson. He was a great friend of Father Willie's."

"I heard him speak of him," said Ned. "He talked a lot about both of you. Ye were his great friends. Poor Father Willie!" he added with a sigh. "He had few enough of them."

Just then the parish priest entered and spoke to Ned Devine. He was a tall man with a stern, unlined, wooden face. He stood for a few moments by the coffin, then studied the breastplate and the wreath, looking closely at the tag of the wreath. It was only then that he beckoned the two younger priests aside.

"Tell me," he asked in a professional tone, "what are we going to do about this?"

"About what?" Fogarty asked in surprise.

"This wreath," said Father Martin, giving him a candid glare.

"What's wrong with it?"

" 'Tis against the rubrics."

"For Heaven's sake!" Fogarty said impatiently. "What have the rubrics to do with it?"

"The rubrics have a lot to do with it," Martin said sternly. "And, apart from that, 'tis a bad custom."

"You mean Masses bring in more money?" Fogarty asked with amused insolence.

"I do not mean Masses bring in more money," said Martin, who seemed to reply to every remark verbatim, like a solicitor's letter. "I mean that flowers are a pagan survival." He looked at the two young priests with the same innocent, anxious, wooden air. "And here am I, week in, week out, preaching against flowers, and a blooming big wreath of them in my own church. And on a priest's coffin too, mind you! What am I going to say about that?"

"Who asked you to say anything?" asked Fogarty. "The man wasn't from your diocese."

"Oh, now, that's all very well," said Martin. "And that's not the whole story, and you know it."

"You mean, the wreath is from a woman?" broke in Jackson.

"I do mean the wreath is from a woman."

"A woman?" Fogarty exclaimed in astonishment. "Does it say so?"

"It does not say so. But 'tis red roses."

"And does that mean it's from a woman?"

"What else could it mean?"

"It could mean it's from somebody who didn't study the language of flowers the way you seem to have done," said Fogarty.

"Oh, well," Jackson intervened again with a shrug, "we know nothing about it. You'll have to decide about it yourself. It's nothing to do with us."

"I don't like doing anything when I wasn't acquainted with the man," said Martin, but he made no further attempt to interfere, and one of the undertaker's men took the wreath and placed it on the hearse. Fogarty controlled himself with difficulty. As he banged open the door of the car and started the engine, his face was very flushed. He drove with his head bowed and his brows jutting down like rocks above his eyes. As they cleared the Main Street he burst out.

"That's the sort of thing that makes me ashamed of myself! 'Flowers are a pagan survival.' And they take it from him, Jim! They listen to that sort of stuff instead of telling him to shut his ignorant gob."

"Oh, well," Jackson said in his nonchalant, tolerant way, "he was right, of course."

"Right?"

"I mean, on the appearance of the thing. After all, he didn't know Devine."

"All the more reason why he shouldn't have interfered. Do you realize that he'd have thrown out that wreath only for us being there? And for what? His own dirty, mean, suspicious mind!"

"Ah, I wouldn't say that. I wouldn't have let that wreath go on the coffin."

"You wouldn't? Why not?"

"It was from a woman all right."

Jackson lit his pipe and looked over his spectacles at Fogarty.

"Yes, one of Devine's old maids."

"Ever heard of an old maid sending a wreath of red roses?"

"To tell you the God's truth," Fogarty confessed with boyish candor, "it would never have struck me that there was anything wrong with it."

"It would have struck the old maid, though."

Fogarty missed a turning and reversed with a muttered curse.

"You're not serious, Jim?" he said after a few moments.

"Oh, I'm not saying there was anything wrong in it," Jackson replied with a shrug. "Women get ideas like that. You must have noticed that sort of thing yourself."

"These things can happen in very innocent ways," Fogarty said with ingenuous solemnity. Then he began to scowl again, and a blush spread over his handsome craggy face that was neither anger nor shame. Like all those who live greatly in their imaginations, he was always astonished and shocked at the suggestion that reached him from the outside world: he could live with his fantasies only by assuming that they were nothing more. The country began to grow wilder under the broken spring light; the valley of the river dropped away with a ruined abbey on its bank, and a pine-clad hill rose on their right, the first breath of the mountains. "I can't believe it," he said angrily, shaking his head.

"You don't have to believe it," Jackson said, nursing his pipe. "I'd nearly be glad if Martin's suspicions were right. If ever a man needed somebody to care for him, Devine did."

"But not Devine, Jim," Fogarty said obstinately. "You could believe a thing like that if it was me. I could nearly believe it if it was you. But I knew Devine since we were kids, and he wouldn't be capable of it."

"I never knew him like that," Jackson admitted mildly. "In fact, I scarcely knew him at all, really. But I'd have said he was as capable of it as we are. He was a good deal lonelier than we'll ever be."

"God, don't I know it!" Fogarty ground out in self-reproach. "If it was drinking, I could understand it."

"Devine was too fastidious."

"But that's what I say."

"There's a big difference," said Jackson. "A very intelligent woman, for instance, might have appealed to him. You can imagine how he'd appeal to her. After all, you know, what he meant to us; the most civilized chap we could meet. Just fancy what a man like that would mean to some woman in a country town: maybe a woman married to some lout of a shopkeeper or a gentleman farmer."

"He didn't tell you about her?" Fogarty asked incredulously, because Jackson spoke with such plausibility that it impressed him as true.

"Oh, no, no, I'm only guessing," Jackson said hastily, and then he blushed too.

FOGARTY remained silent, aware that Jackson had confessed something about himself, but he could not get the incredible idea of Devine out of his mind. As the country grew wilder and furze bushes and ruined keeps took the place of pastures and old abbeys, he found his eyes attracted more and more to the wreath that swayed lightly with the swaying of the hearse and seemed to concentrate all the light. It seemed an image of the essential mystery of a priest's life.

What, after all, did he know of Devine? Only what his own temperament suggested, and mostly—when he wasn't being St. Francis of Assisi, in Devine's phrase—he had seen himself as the worldly one of the pair, the practical, coarse-grained man who cut corners, and Devine as the saint, racked by his own fastidiousness and asceticism that exploded in his bitter little jests. Now his mind boggled at the agony which could have driven a man like Devine to seek companionship in such a way; yet the measure of his incredulity was that of the conviction which he would soon feel, the new level on which his thought must move.

"God!" he burst out. "Don't we lead lonely lives. We probably knew Devine better than anyone else in the world, and there's that damn thing in front of us, and neither of us has a notion what it means."

"Which might be just as well for our own comfort," Jackson said.

"If you're right, I'll take my oath it did very little for Devine's," Fogarty said grimly.

"Oh, I don't know," Jackson said. "Isn't that the one thing we all really want from life?"

"Would you say so?" Fogarty asked in astonishment. He had always thought of Jackson as a cold fish, a go-getter, and suddenly found himself wondering about that too; wondering what it was in him that had appealed so much to Devine. He had the feeling that Jackson, who was, as he modestly recognized, by far the subtler man, was probing him, and for the same reason. Each of them was looking in the other for the quality which had attracted Devine, and which having made him their friend might make them friends also. "I couldn't do it though, Jim," he said somberly. "I went as close to it as I'm ever likely to do. It was the wife of one of the chaps that was with me in the seminary. She seemed to be all the things I ever wanted a woman to be. Then, when I saw what her marriage to the other fellow was like, I realized that she hated him like poison. It might have been me she hated that way. It's only when you see what marriages are like, as we do, that you know how lucky we are in escaping them."

"Lucky?" Jackson repeated with light irony. "Do you really think we're lucky? Have you ever known a seminary that wasn't full of men who thought themselves lucky? They might be drinking themselves to death, but they never once doubted their luck. Clerical sour grapes. . . . Anyway, you're rather underrating yourself if you think she'd have hated you."

"You think I might have made her a good husband?" Fogarty asked, flushing with pleasure, for this was what he had always thought himself when he permitted his imagination to rest on Una Whitton.

"Probably. You'd have made a good father at any rate."

"God knows you might be right," said Fogarty. "It's easier to do without a woman than it is to do without kids. My mother was the same. She was wrapped up in us; she always wanted us to be better than anyone else, and when we did badly at school or got into trouble it nearly broke her heart. She said it was the Fogarty blood breaking out in us—the Fogartys were all horse dealers." His handsome, happy face clouded again with the old feelings of remorse and guilt, unjustified, like most of his self-reproach. "I'm afraid she died under the impression that I was a Fogarty after all."

"If the Fogartys are any relation to the Martins, I'd say it was most unlikely," said Jackson.

"I never really knew till she was dead how much she meant to me," Fogarty said broodingly. "I insisted on performing the burial service myself, though Hennessey warned me not to. My God, the way we gallop through it till it comes home to ourselves! I broke down and bawled like a kid and Hennessey got up and finished it."

Jackson shook his head uncomprehendingly. "You feel these things more than I do. I'm a cold fish."

It struck Fogarty that, though this was precisely what he had always believed, he would now believe it no longer. "That settled me," he said. "Up to that, I used to be a bit flighty, but afterwards, I knew I could never care for another woman as I cared for her."

"Nonsense!" Jackson said lightly. "That's the best proof you could offer a woman that you'd care for her as much. Love is just one thing, not a half dozen. If I had my eye on a woman, I'd take good care to choose one who cared that way for her father. You're the sort who'd go to hell for a woman if ever you let yourself go. I couldn't go to hell for anybody. The nearest I ever got to it was with one woman in a town I was in. I didn't realize the state she was getting herself into till I found her outside my door at two o'clock one morning. She wanted me to take her away! You can imagine what happened to her afterwards."

"She went off with someone else?"

"No. Drink. And it was nothing but loneliness. After that, I decided that people of my sort have no business with love."

AT THE WORD "love" Fogarty felt his heart contract. It was partly the wreath, brilliant in the sunlight, that had drawn him out of his habitual reserve and linked him with a man of even greater reserve, partly the excitement of returning to the little town where he had grown up. He hated it; he avoided it; it seemed to be the complete expression of all the narrowness and meanness that he tried to banish from his own thoughts; but at the same time, it contained all the violence and longing that had driven him out of it, and when once he drew near it a tumult of emotions rose in him that half strangled him.

"There it is!" he said triumphantly, pointing to a valley where a tapering Franciscan tower rose from a clutter of low Georgian houses and thatched cabins. "They'll be waiting for us at the bridge. That's the way they'll be waiting for me when my turn comes."

"They" were the priests and townspeople who had come out to escort the hearse to the cemetery. Ned Devine steered people to their places. Four men shouldered the coffin over the high-arched bridge past the ruined castle and up the hilly Main Street. Shutters were up on the shop fronts, blinds were drawn, everything was at a standstill except here and there where a curtain was lifted and an old woman, too feeble to make the journey, peered out.

A laneway led off the hilly road, and they came to the abbey; a tower and a few walls with tombstones thickly sown in choir and nave. The hearse was already drawn up and people gathered in a semi-circle about it. Ned Devine came hastily up to the car where the two priests were donning their surplices.

"Whisht, Father Jerry," he muttered in a strained, excited voice. "People are talking about that wreath. I wonder would you know who sent it?"

"I know nothing at all about it, Ned," Fogarty replied roughly, and suddenly felt his heart begin to pant violently.

"Come here a minute, Sheela," Ned called, and a tall, pale girl in black, with the stain of tears on her long, bony face, left the little group of mourners and joined them. "You know Father Jerry. This is Father Jackson, Father Willie's other friend. They don't know anything about it."

"Then I'd let them take it back," she said doggedly.

"What would you say, father?" Ned asked, appealing to Fogarty.

Fogarty suddenly felt his courage desert him. In arguing with Martin, he had felt himself dealing with an equal, but now the intense passions and prejudices of the little town seemed to rise up and oppose him, and he felt himself again an adolescent, rebellious but frightened.

"I can only tell you what I told Father Martin," he blustered.

"Did Father Martin talk about it too?" Ned asked sharply.

"He did."

"There!" Sheela said vindictively. "What did I tell you?"

"Well, the pair of you may be cleverer than I am," Fogarty said. "I can only say what I said before: I'd never have noticed anything wrong with it."

"It was no proper thing to send to a priest's funeral," she hissed with prim fury. "Whoever sent it was no friend of my brother."

"You wouldn't agree with that, father?" Ned asked anxiously.

"But I tell you, Uncle Ned, if that wreath goes into the graveyard we'll be the laughingstock of the town," she said furiously.

"Whisht, girl, whisht, and let Father Jerry talk!" he snapped angrily.

"Well, Ned, it seems to me to be entirely a matter for yourselves," Fogarty replied. "I can only tell you what I think." He was really scared now; he realized that he was in danger of behaving imprudently in public, and that sooner or later the story would get back to the Bishop and it would be suggested that he knew more than he pretended.

"If you'll excuse my interrupting, father," Jackson said suavely, giving him a warning glance over his spectacles, "I know it isn't my place to speak—"

"But that's the very thing we want, father," Ned said passionately. "If you say 'tis all right, that's enough for me."

"Oh, well, Mr. Devine, that would be too great a responsibility for me to take," Jackson said with a cautious smile, though his pale face had grown flushed. "You know this town. I don't. I only know what it would mean in my own place. I've told Father Fogarty already that I agree with Miss Devine. I think it was wrong to send it. But," and his mild voice suddenly grew menacing, and he shrugged his shoulders and spread out his hands with a contemptuous look, "if you were to send that wreath back from the graveyard, you'd make yourself something far worse than a laughingstock. You'd throw mud on a dead man's name that would never be forgotten for you, the longest day you lived.... Things may be different here, of course," he added superciliously.

Ned Devine suddenly came to his senses. He clicked his fingers impatiently.

"Of course, of course, of course," he snarled. "That's something we should have thought of ourselves. 'Twould be giving tongues to the stones."

And he took the wreath and carried it behind the coffin to the graveside. That was sufficient to dissipate the growing hysteria which Fogarty felt about him. He touched Jackson's hand lightly.

"Good man, Jim!" he said in a voice that was full of love and tears.

Side by side they stood at the head of the open grave where the other surpliced priests had gathered. Their voices rose in the psalms for the dead. But Fogarty's brooding, curious eyes swept the crowd of faces he had known since childhood, now caricatured by age and pain, and each time they came to rest on the wreath which stood to one side of the grave. Each time it came over him in a flood of emotion that what he and Jackson had saved was something more than a sentimental token. It was the thing which formerly had linked them to Devine and which now linked them with one another; the feeling of their own integrity as men beside their integrity as priests; the thing which gave significance and beauty to their sacrifice.

The Teacher's Mass

FATHER FOGARTY, the curate in Crislough, used to say in his cynical way that his greatest affliction was having to serve the teacher's Mass every morning. He referred, of course, to his own Mass, the curate's Mass, which was said early so that Father Fogarty could say Mass later in Costello. Nobody ever attended it, except occasionally in summer, when there were visitors at the hotel. The schoolteacher, old Considine, served as acolyte. He had been serving the early Mass long before Fogarty came, and the curate thought he would also probably be doing it long after he had left. Every morning, you saw him coming up the village street, a pedantically attired old man with a hollow face and a big mustache that was turning gray. Everything about him was abstract and angular, even to his voice, which was harsh and without modulation, and sometimes when he and Fogarty came out of the sacristy with Considine leading, carrying the book, his pace was so slow that Fogarty wondered what effect it would have if he gave him one good kick in the behind. It was exactly as Fogarty said—as though *he* were serving Considine's Mass, and the effect of it was to turn Fogarty into a more unruly acolyte than ever he had been in the days when he himself was serving the convent Mass.

Whatever was the cause, Considine always roused a bit of the devil in Fogarty, and he knew that Considine had no great affection for him, either. The old man had been headmaster of the Crislough school until his retirement, and all his life he had kept himself apart from the country people, like a parish priest or a policeman. He was not without learning; he had a quite respectable knowledge of local history, and a very good one of the ecclesiastical history of the Early Middle Ages in its local applications, but it was all book learning, and, like his wing collar, utterly unrelated to the life about him. He had all the childish vanity of the man of dissociated scholarship, wrote occasional scurrilous letters to the local paper to correct some error in etymology, and expected everyone on that account to treat him as an oracle. As a schoolmaster he had sneered cruelly at the barefoot urchins he taught, describing them as "illiterate peasants" who believed in the fairies and in spells, and when, twenty years later, some of them came back from Boston or Brooklyn and showed off before the neighbors, with their big American hats and high-powered cars, he still sneered at them. According to him, they went away illiterate and came home illiterate.

"I see young Carmody is home again," he would say to the curate after Mass.

"Is that so?"

"And he has a car like a house," Considine would add, with bitter amusement. "A car with a grin on it. 'Twould do fine to cart home his mother's turf."

"The blessings of God on him," the curate would say cheerfully. "I wish I had a decent car instead of the old yoke I have."

"I dare say it was the fairies," the old teacher would snarl, with an ugly smile that made his hollow, high-cheeked face look like a skull. "It wasn't anything he ever learned here."

"Maybe we're not giving the fairies their due, Mr. Considine," said the curate, with the private conviction that it would be easier to learn from them than from the schoolmaster.

The old man's scornful remarks irritated Fogarty because he liked the wild, barefooted, inarticulate brats from the mountainy farms, and felt that if they showed off a bit when they returned from America with a few dollars in their pockets, they were well entitled to do so. Whoever was entitled to the credit, it was nothing and nobody at home. The truth was he had periods of terrible gloom when he felt he had mistaken his vocation. Or, rather, the vocation was all right, but the conditions under which he exercised it were all wrong, and those conditions, for him, were well represented by the factitious scholarship of old Considine. It was all in the air. Religion sometimes seemed no more to him than his own dotty old housekeeper, who, whatever he said, invested herself with the authority of a bishop and decided who was to see him and about what, and settled matters on her own whenever she got half a chance. Things were so bad with her that whenever the country people wanted to see him, they bribed one of the acolytes to go and ask him to come himself to their cottages. The law was represented by Sergeant Twomey, who raided the mountain pubs half an hour after closing time, in response to the orders of some lunatic superintendent at the other side of the county, while as for culture, there was the library van every couple of months, from which Considine, who acted as librarian, selected a hundred books, mainly for his own amusement. He was partial to books dealing with voyages in the Congo or Tibet ("Tibet is a very interessting country, father"). The books that were for general circulation he censored to make sure there were no bad words like "navel" in them that might corrupt the ignorant "peasantry." And then he came to Fogarty and told him he had been reading a very "interessting" book about birdwatching in the South Seas, or something like that.

Fogarty's own temptation was toward action and energy, just as his depression was often no more than the expression of his frustration. He was an energetic and emotional man who in other circumstances would probably have become a successful businessman. Women were less of a temptation to him than the thought of an active instinctual life. All he wanted in the way of a holiday was to get rid of his collar and take a gun or rod or stand behind the bar of a country hotel. He ran the local hurling team for what it was worth, which wasn't much, and strayed down the shore with the boatmen or up the hills with the poachers and poteen-makers, who all trusted him and never tried to conceal any of their harmless misdemeanors from him. Once, for instance, in the late evening, he came unexpectedly on a party of scared poteen-makers on top of a mountain and sat down on the edge of the hollow where they were operating their still. "Never mind me, lads!" he said, lighting a pipe. "I'm not here at all." "Sure we know damn well you're not here, father," one old man said, and chuckled. "But how the hell can we offer a drink to a bloody ghost?"

These were his own people, the people he loved and admired, and it was principally the feeling that he could do little or nothing for them that plunged him into those suicidal fits of gloom in which he took to the bottle. When he heard of a dance being held in a farmhouse without the permission of the priest or the police, he said, "The blessings of God on them," and when a girl went and got herself with child by one of the islanders, he said, "More power to her elbow!"—though he had to say these things discreetly, for fear they should get back. But the spirit of them got back, and the acolytes would whisper, "Father, would you ever go out to Dan Mike's when you have the time?" or young men and girls would lie in wait for his car on a country road and signal timidly to him, because the country people knew that from him they would either get a regular blasting in a language they understood or the loan of a few pounds to send a girl to hospital in England so that the neighbors wouldn't know.

Fogarty knew that in the teacher's eyes this was another black mark against him, for old Considine could not understand how any educated man could make so little of the cloth as to sit drinking with "illiterate peasants" instead of talking to a fine, well-informed man like himself about the situation in the Far East or the relationship of the Irish dioceses to the old kingdoms of the Early Middle Ages.

Then one evening Fogarty was summoned to the teacher's house on a sick call. It only struck him when he saw it there at the end of the village—a newish, red-brick box of a house, with pebble dash on the front and a steep stairway up from the front door—that it was like the teacher himself. Maisie, the teacher's unmarried daughter, was a small, plump woman with a face that must once have been attractive, for it was still all in curves, with hair about it like Mona Lisa's, though now she had lost all her freshness, and her skin was red and hard and full of wrinkles. She had a sad smile, and Fogarty could not resist a pang of pity for her because he realized that she was probably another victim of Considine's dislike of "illiterates." How could an "illiterate" boy come to a house like that, or how could the teacher's daughter go out walking with him?

She had got the old man to bed, and he lay there with the engaged look of a human being at grips with his destiny. From his narrow window there was a pleasant view of the sea road and a solitary tree by the water's edge. Beyond the bay was the mountain, with a cap on it—the sign of bad weather. Fogarty gave him the last Sacraments, and he confessed and received Communion with a devotion that touched Fogarty in spite of himself. He stayed on with the daughter until the doctor arrived, in case any special medicines were needed. They sat in the tiny box of a front room with a bay window and a high mahogany bookcase that filled one whole wall. She wanted to stay and make polite conversation for the priest, though all the time she was consumed with anxiety. When the doctor left, Fogarty left with him, and pressed Maisie's hand and told her to call on him for anything, at any time.

Dr. Mulloy was more offhand. He was a tall, handsome young man of about Fogarty's own age. Outside, standing beside his car, he said to Fogarty, "Ah, he might last a couple of years if he minded himself. They don't, of course. You know the way it is. A wonder that daughter of his never married."

"How could she?" Fogarty asked in a low voice, turning to glance again at the ill-designed, pretentious little suburban house. "He'd think her too grand for any of the boys round this place."

"Why then, indeed, if he pops off on her, she won't be too grand at all," said the doctor. "A wonder an educated man like that wouldn't have more sense. Sure, he can't have anything to leave her?"

"No more than myself, I daresay," said Fogarty, who saw that the doctor only wanted to find out how much they could pay; and he went off to summon one of the boy acolytes to take Considine's place at Mass next morning.

BUT the next morning when Fogarty reached the sacristy, instead of the boy he had spoken to, old Considine was waiting, with everything neatly arranged in his usual pedantic manner, and a wan old man's smile on his hollow face.

"Mr. Considine!" Fogarty exclaimed indignantly. "What's the meaning of this?"

"Ah, I'm fine this morning, father," said the old man, with a sort of fictitious, drunken excitement. "I woke up as fresh as a daisy." Then he smiled malevolently and added, "Jimmy Leary thought he was after doing me out of a job, but Dr. Mulloy was too smart for him."

"But you know yourself what Dr. Mulloy said," Fogarty protested indignantly. "I talked to him myself about it. He said you could live for years, but any exertion might make you go off any time."

"And how can man die better?" retorted the teacher, with the triumphant air he wore whenever he managed to produce an apt quotation. "You remember Macaulay, I suppose," he added doubtfully, and then his face took on a morose look. " 'Tisn't that at all," he said. "But 'tis the only thing I have to look forward to. The day wouldn't be the same to me if I had to miss Mass."

Fogarty knew that he was up against an old man's stubbornness and love of habitual things, and that he was wasting his breath advising Considine himself. Instead, he talked to the parish priest, a holy and muddleheaded old man named Whelan. Whelan shook his head mournfully over the situation, but then he was a man who shook his head over everything. He had apparently decided many years ago that any form of action was hateful, and he took to his bed if people became too pressing.

"He's very obstinate, old John, but at the same time, you wouldn't like to cross him," Whelan said.

"If you don't do something about it, you might as well put back the Costello Mass another half an hour," Fogarty said. He was forever trying to induce Whelan to make up his mind. "He's getting slower every day. One of these days he'll drop dead on me at the altar."

"Oh, I'll mention it to him," the parish priest said regretfully. "But I don't know would it be wise to take too strong a line. You have to humor them when they're as old as that. I daresay we'll be the same ourselves, father."

Fogarty knew he was wasting his breath on Whelan as well. Whelan would no doubt be as good as his word, and talk about the weather to Considine for an hour, and then end by dropping a hint, which might be entirely lost, that the old teacher shouldn't exert himself too much, and that would be all.

A MONTH later, the old teacher had another attack, but this time Fogarty only heard of it from his mad housekeeper, who knew everything that went on in the village.

"But why didn't he send for me?" he asked sharply.

"Ah, I suppose he wasn't bad enough," replied the housekeeper. "Mrs. MacCarthy said he got over it with pills and a sup of whiskey. They say whiskey is the best thing."

"You're sure he didn't send for me?" Fogarty asked. There were times when he half expected the woman, in the exercise of her authority, to refuse the Last Rites to people she didn't approve of.

"Sure, of course he didn't. It was probably nothing."

All the same, Fogarty was not easy in his mind. He knew what it meant to old people to have the priest with them at the end, and he suspected that if Considine made light of his attack, it could only be because he was afraid Fogarty would take it as final proof that he was not fit to serve Mass. He felt vaguely guilty about it. He strode down the village street, saluting the fishermen who were sitting on the sea wall in the dusk. The teacher's cottage was dark when he reached it. The cobbler, a lively little man who lived next door, was standing outside.

"I hear the old master was sick again, Tom," said the curate.

"Begor, he was, father," said the cobbler. "I hear Maisie found him crawling to the fire on his hands and knees. Terrible cold they get when they're like that. He's a sturdy old divil, though. You needn't be afraid you'll lose your altar boy for a long time yet."

"I hope not, Tom," said Fogarty, who knew that the cobbler, a knowledgeable man in his own way, thought there was something funny about the old schoolmaster's serving Mass. "And I hope we're all as good when our own time comes."

He went home, too thoughtful to chat with the fishermen. The cobbler's words had given him a sudden glimpse of old Considine's sufferings, and he was filled with the compassion that almost revolted him at times for sick bodies and suffering minds. He was an emotional man, and he knew it was partly the cause of his own savage gloom, but he could not restrain it.

Next morning, when he went to the sacristy, there was the old teacher, with his fawning smile, the smile of a guilty small boy who has done it again and this time knows he will not escape without punishment.

"You weren't too good last night, John," the curate said, using Considine's Christian name for the first time.

"No, Father Jeremiah," Considine replied, pronouncing the priest's name slowly and pedantically. "I was a bit poorly in the early evening. But those pills of Dr. Mulloy's are a wonder."

"And isn't it a hard thing to say you never sent for me?" Fogarty went on.

Considine blushed furiously, and this time he looked really guilty and scared.

"But I wasn't that bad, father," he protested with senile intensity, his hands beginning to shake and his eyes to sparkle. "I wasn't as frightened yesterday as I was the first time. It's the first time it frightens you. You feel sure you'll never last it out. But after that you get to expect it."

"Will you promise me never to do a thing like that again?" the curate asked earnestly. "Will you give me your word that you'll send for me, any hour of the day or night?"

"Very well, father," Considine replied sullenly. " 'Tis very good of you. I'll give you my word I'll send for you."

And they both recognized the further, unspoken part of the compact between them. Considine would send for Fogarty, but nothing Fogarty saw or heard was to permit him again to try to deprive the old teacher of his office. Not that he any longer wished to do so. Now that he recognized the passion of will in the old man, Fogarty's profound humanity only made him anxious to second it and enable Considine to do what clearly he wished to do—die in harness. Fogarty had also begun to recognize that it was not mere obstinacy that got the old man out of his bed each morning and brought him shivering and sighing and shuffling up the village street. There was obstinacy there, and plenty of it, but there was something else, which the curate valued more; something he felt the lack of in himself. It wasn't easy to put a name on it. Faith was one name, but it was no more than a name and was used to cover too many excesses of devotion that the young priest found distasteful. This was something else, something that made him ashamed of his own human weakness and encouraged him to fight the depression, which seemed at times as if it would overwhelm him. It was more like the miracle of the Mass itself, metaphor become reality. Now when he thought of his own joke about serving the teacher's Mass, it didn't seem quite so much like a joke.

ONE MORNING in April, Fogarty noticed as he entered the sacristy that the old man was looking very ill. As he helped Fogarty, his hands shook piteously. Even his harsh voice had a quaver in it, and his lips were pale. Fogarty looked at him and wondered if he shouldn't say something, but decided against it. He went in, preceded by Considine, and noticed that though the teacher tried to hold himself erect, his walk was little more than a shuffle. He went up to the altar, but found it almost impossible to concentrate on what he was doing. He heard the laboring steps behind him, and as the old man started to raise the heavy book onto the altar, Fogarty paused for a moment and looked under his brows. Considine's face was now white as a sheet, and as he raised the book he sighed. Fogarty wanted to cry out, "For God's sake, man, lie down!" He wanted to hold Considine's head on his knee and whisper into his ear. Yet he realized that to the strange old man behind him this would be no kindness. The only kindness he could do him was to crush down his own weak warmheartedness and continue the sacrifice. Never had he seemed farther away from the reality of the Mass. He heard the laboring steps, the panting breath, behind him, and it seemed as if they had lasted some timeless time before he heard another heavy sigh as Considine managed to kneel.

At last, Fogarty found himself waiting for a response that did not come. He looked round quickly. The old man had fallen silently forward onto the altar steps. His arm was twisted beneath him and his head was turned sideways. His jaw had fallen, and his eyes were sightless.

"John!" Fogarty called, in a voice that rang through the church. "Can you hear me? John!"

There was no reply, and the curate placed him on his back, with one of the altar cushions beneath his head. Fogarty felt under the surplice for his buttons and unloosed them. He felt for the heart. It had stopped; there was no trace of breathing. Through the big window at the west end he saw the churchyard trees and the sea beyond them, bright in the morning light. The whole church seemed terribly still, so that the mere ticking of the clock filled it with its triumphant mocking of the machine of flesh and blood that had fallen silent.

Fogarty went quickly to the sacristy and returned with the sacred oils to anoint the teacher. He knew he had only to cross the road for help, to have the old man's body removed and get an acolyte to finish the Mass, but he wanted no help. He felt strangely lightheaded. Instead, when he had done, he returned to the altar and resumed the Mass where he had left off, murmuring the responses to himself. As he did so, he realized that he was acutely aware of every detail, of every sound, he had no feeling that he was lacking in concentration. When he turned to face the body of the church and said "Dominus vobiscum," he saw as if for the first time the prostrate form with its fallen jaw and weary eyes, under the light that came in from the sea through the trees in their first leaf, and murmured "Et cum spiritu tuo" for the man whose spirit had flown. Then, when he had said the prayers after Mass beside the body, he took his biretta, donned it, and walked by the body, carrying his chalice, and feeling as he walked that some figure was walking before him, slowly, saying good-bye. In his excited mind echoed the rubric: "Then, having adored and thanked God for everything, he goes away."

The Martyr

THERE'S your martyr! Commandant Myles Hartnett, killed by Free State Troops in Asragh Barrack, November 18, 1922. "For the glory of God and the honor of Ireland." Every year they lay a wreath there.

It was really my fault that he was killed. I was in charge of the barrack. A young fellow called Morrissey captured him, and, as he was carrying a gun at the time, that meant one thing only. I didn't like

Morrissey; he was one of those conceited young fellows who go through life with a grievance against everybody, and he had a particular grievance against me because I tried to keep some sort of discipline in the infernal place.

I was alone in the office, wondering what all the row was about, when Morrissey, Daly, and a few others pushed him in. I could see they'd knocked him about pretty badly already. He was a tall, powerful man with fair hair, blue, short-sighted eyes (they had smashed his glasses), and that air of a born athlete that I, for one, always like in a man. Even then, he looked as though he could still have made smithereens of them but for the guns.

"And who have we here?" I asked.

"This is the fellow that organized the Duncartan ambush," said Morrissey triumphantly. Now the Duncartan ambush was a bad slip-up on my part. Believing the information I had got, I had just walked my men right into it. In the scrap I had lost the only friend I had in the barrack, MacDunphy.

"Oh, is that so?" I asked. "You're the chap we're indebted to for our welcome there? How nice!"

"I am not," he said contemptuously.

"You are," shouted Morrissey, clenching his fists. "You were the man who used the Lewis gun that killed MacDunphy. You needn't try to get out of it."

"I'm not trying to get out of it," said Hartnett in the same scornful tone. "I'm only telling you you don't know what you're talking about."

"Shut up, you—liar!" shouted Morrissey, and drove his fist into Hartnett's mouth.

Hartnett took out his handkerchief, wiped off the blood, and looked at me. Then he smiled. I knew what the smile meant and he knew I knew.

"Have you quite finished with the prisoner, Captain Morrissey?" I asked.

"But don't you know this was the fellow that killed Harry Mac-Dunphy?" he shouted.

"No," I said, "and as things are shaping I'm hardly likely to find out."

He muttered an obscenity, turned on his heel, and went out, banging the door.

"Were you in the Duncartan ambush?" I asked.

"Ah, not at all," said Hartnett. "I was over in Derreen the day it happened. Not that it makes any difference."

"Not the least," I said. "All right, Jimmie," I said to Daly, a young lieutenant. "Take him downstairs. And tell the sentry that Captain Morrissey isn't to go into his cell without my permission."

IT WAS the same at the court-martial. He was quiet, self-possessed, and almost contemptuous of the men who were supposed to be trying him. He denied nothing and stood on his right as an officer and prisoner of war. He had the education which they lacked (I discovered he was a spoiled priest), and succeeded in making them look like the fools they were. Not that that made the least difference either. The verdict and sentence were a foregone conclusion; so was the sanction unless he had friends in Headquarters.

Then one night about a week later I was working alone in the office when a sentry came in. He was a little Dubliner, one of my own men and one I could trust.

"Mick," he whispered conspiratorially (he always called me "Mick" when we were alone), "that Hartnett fellow would like to talk to you."

"What does he want to talk to me for at this hour?" I asked irritably.

"He said he wanted to speak to yourself," said the sentry. "Morrissey and Daly are out, boozing. I think you ought to have a word with him."

I knew that Hartnett had managed to get round my sentry and that I wouldn't get any peace till I saw him.

"Oh, all right," I said. "Don't bring him up here. I'll come down and see him later."

"Good man!" said the sentry. "I'll leave on the light in his cell."

I finished up and then went down to the cells with my own keys. It wasn't very pleasant at that hour. The cell was small; the high barred window had no glass in it; the only furniture was a mattress and a couple of blankets. Hartnett was standing up in his shirtsleeves and socks. He had got a spare pair of spectacles. He tried to smile, but it didn't come off.

"I'm sorry for disturbing you at this hour," he said in a low voice so as not to be heard in the neighboring cells.

"Well?" I asked. "What is it?"

"Tell me, by the way," he said, cocking his head, "aren't you a friend of Phil Condon's?"

"Very much by the way," I replied. "Was it to talk about Phil Condon that you brought me here?"

"There are times you'd be glad to talk about anything," he said with a touch of bitterness. Then, after a moment, "I thought any friend of

Phil's would be a decent man. That's more than you could say for most of your officers."

"What is it?" I asked.

"I suppose I'm going to be shot?" he asked, throwing back his head and looking at me through the big glasses.

"I'm afraid so," I said without much emotion.

"When, do you know?"

"I don't know. If the sentence is confirmed by tomorrow, probably the following morning. Unless you have friends in Headquarters."

"That gang!" he said scornfully. "I haven't, only all the enemies I have." He put his hands in his trouser pockets and took a couple of short steps up the cell beside the mattress. Then he looked at me over the glasses and dropped his voice still farther. "You could stop that, couldn't you?"

I was a bit taken aback by this direct appeal. It wasn't what I had expected.

"I dare say I could," I said lightly, "but I'm not going to."

"Not on any account?" he asked, still looking at me over the glasses, his eyebrows slightly raised.

"Not on any account."

He waited. Then he took two steps towards me and stood, looking at me.

"Not even if I made it worth your while?"

Again I was taken aback. I felt the first time I saw him that we understood one another, and now I was irritated at his low opinion of me. I tried to smile.

"Are you trying to bribe me?" I asked.

"Were you ever in my position?" he asked, cocking his head again.

"No."

"Would you blame me if I was?"

"I'm not short of money, thanks," I said. "If you want anything else you can ask the sentry."

"Ah, you know what I mean all right," he said, nodding. "You know well enough 'tisn't money I'm talking of."

"What the hell is it then?" I asked angrily.

"Something that fellow, Morrissey, said upstairs, about the Duncartan ambush," he said, nodding in the direction of the door. "This MacDunphy—was he a great friend of yours?"

"He was," I said. "Can you bring him back to life?"

"Do you know who the chap was that shot him?"

"I have a fairly good idea."

"The man who had the Lewis gun that day?" he said scornfully, raising his voice so that I was certain he could be heard. "You have not."

"All right," I said. "I haven't."

"You'd like to know who he was, wouldn't you?"

"Why?" I asked mockingly. "Are you thinking of turning informer?"

I was sorry the moment I'd said it. It wasn't fair from a man at liberty to one with only his wits between him and the firing squad. His big face grew as red as if I'd slapped it.

"All right," he muttered, "I was asking for that. But you see the way I am! The man is no particular friend of mine, and it's his life or mine."

"That's what you're assuming," I said.

"And aren't I right?" he asked, pushing his big face into mine with a sort of hypnotic look in his eyes.

The trouble was, he was. That's the curse of civil war. No matter what high notions you start with, it always degenerates into a series of personal quarrels, family against family, individual against individual, until at last you hardly mind what side they're on.

"Very well," I said. "You are. Who was it?"

"Micky Morgan—Monkey Morgan from Dirrane."

"And what was Monkey Morgan from Dirrane doing in Duncartan?"

"Ah, he shouldn't have been there at all, man," he said, tapping me on the elbow, and for a moment it was just one officer speaking to another. " 'Tisn't his area. But fellows like that, nobody can control them."

"And where does Monkey Morgan hang out?" I asked.

"Mostly in Mick Tom Ogue's in Beensheen; Mick is a sort of cousin of his mother's."

"This isn't another invitation like the one in Duncartan?" I asked.

"What sort of fool do you take me for?" he asked contemptuously.

"I don't know," I said. "I was just wondering.... All right, hang on!"

Then I went out and ordered up two lorries and twenty men. I made sure the sentry was out of the way before I went back to the cell. I had a cap and greatcoat with me.

"Put these on," I said, and Hartnett did.

"They're a good fit," he said, thrusting his hands into the pockets.

"Yes," I said. "They belonged to MacDunphy."

Then we went out to the waiting lorries. Hartnett avoided the headlights; apart from that there was nothing to show that he wasn't just another officer from Dublin on a tour of inspection.

"All right, colonel," I said in a loud voice to him. "Step in!"

He sat in front between me and the driver. It was a dark night with brilliant stars. We went up through the hills by roads we both knew well, though he knew them far better than I. Once he made me cross an open field to avoid the delay at a blown-up bridge. At last we stopped at the foot of a lane, and the men got out quietly. He pointed out to me where to post sentries so that the house was completely covered, and then he and I led the way up the lane. When we reached the door of the farmhouse he stood on one side and let me do the knocking. We didn't knock long because the door began to give under the rifle butts, and it was hastily opened for us by an old man in his shirt.

"Ye can't do anything to me," he shouted. "I have varicose veins."

We caught Morgan in the bedroom, pulling on his socks. He made a dive for his Peter the Painter, but two of our men got him on the floor before he could use it. He was a slight man with a long, hard, fighting face. We waited while he dressed. Then he pulled himself erect and went out with his chin in the air. He didn't notice the tall man standing by the door with his chin in his chest. I wondered what Hartnett's feelings were just at that moment.

I wondered more a few days later when I glanced out of the office window and saw the prisoners exercising within the barbed wire. Hartnett and Morgan were walking side by side. I stood leaning for a long time on the window, thinking how curious it was.

IT WAS next day or perhaps the day after that that Morrissey slouched into my office in his usual uninhibited manner with a cigarette hanging from one corner of his mouth. He stood with his back to the fire, his hands folded behind him.

"Did you hear anything about this escape?" he asked.

"No," I said without interest. "Has there been one?"

"There's going to be. It's all arranged with the fellows outside. One of our contacts brought in the news."

"And who's planned it?" I asked. "Hartnett?"

"I don't know. I suppose it is. Listen," he added in a squeaky voice, knocking his ashes behind him into the fire, "when is that fellow going to be bumped?"

I was exasperated almost beyond endurance by the fellow's tone. It was both ill-bred and childish. He was like a schoolboy expecting a prize. Hartnett was his prize.

"I'm not sure that he is going to be—bumped," I said. (In fact, I knew perfectly well that he wasn't, but I was taking care that Morrissey didn't know. Nobody must know if Hartnett's life was to be saved from his own men.)

"Well, all I can say is, it's a damn shame," said Morrissey. "Any idea what's behind it?"

"Some people have friends in high places," I said oracularly.

"Looks like it," Morrissey said impudently, and I knew he meant me.

"You might remember," I said, "that there was a time when people like Hartnett were considered quite useful. . . . All right. I'll speak to him myself. Send him up, will you, please?"

Hartnett was led up a few moments later by the sentry. He looked rather more like himself, confident and at the same time watchful.

"Tell me," I asked, "what's all this about an escape?"

"An escape?" he asked wonderingly. "What escape? 'Tis news to me."

"Oh, is it?" I asked. "Are you quite sure you're not the ringleader?"

He looked at me doubtfully for a moment and then his lip began to curl.

"You're not by any chance looking for an excuse to break your bargain?" he asked almost contemptuously.

"No," I said without taking offense, "I don't have to look for excuses. Your friend, Morrissey, has just been in to know why you haven't been executed. Several others would like to know the same thing. They're not going to be told if I can manage it. So there isn't going to be any escape. Do you understand?"

He thought for a moment, sighed, and nodded.

"I understand," he said hopelessly. "You're right, of course."

He was going out when I stopped him. I couldn't let him go like that. Afterward I was glad I didn't.

"Don't think I'm criticizing you," I said. "It's just that there are certain actions we can't hedge about, that's all."

He nodded again and went out.

TWO DAYS later Morgan was executed. I was wakened by the noises outside and then I lay awake listening for the bangs. "That's for you, MacDunphy," I said, but it gave me no satisfaction. I wondered if Hartnett was awake listening to them, too. Two men regretting a bargain. When I got up there was the usual air of gloom and hysteria in the barrack. Morrissey was on the drink from early morning. Shutters had been put up in the town, and I sent round a lorry of men to take them down again. Then I went off to Moorlough for a conference.

While I was there a telephone message came through from Daly to say that two of our men had been shot in the street. I realized the danger at once.

"All right, Jimmie," I said, trying to make my voice sound natural. "Hold everything till I come back."

I didn't even wait to clear up things after the conference but got the driver to go hell for leather through the dusk. It was the darkness I was afraid of, and darkness had fallen when we reached the barrack gate.

"Everything all right, sergeant?" I asked at the guardroom.

"Everything all right, sir," he said. "You heard that two of our fellows were shot."

"Yes, I heard that. Nothing else?"

"Only one of the prisoners shot, trying to escape."

"I see," I said. "Hartnett, I suppose?"

"That's right, sir," he said in confusion. "Did they tell you?"

"I was expecting something of the sort," I said. "And Captain Morrissey shot him. Where is the body, sergeant?"

He began to stammer. The damn fools had even been trying to keep the truth from me! I found the body lying in a shed in the yard, abandoned on the straw. I picked it out with my torch. The head had fallen sideways as though he were trying to sleep. He had been shot through the back.

As I was coming in, Morrissey came up to me; he was recovering from his drinking bout and a bit frightened.

"Oh, about that fellow, Hartnett," he began to stammer.

"I know," I said. "You murdered him. Good-night."

Afterward he came up and started hammering on my door, demanding an explanation, but I only told him to go to hell. I felt sick of it all. That's what I mean about civil war. Sooner or later it turns into a set of personal relationships. Hartnett and I were like that; accomplices, if you care to put it that way.

Requiem

FATHER FOGARTY, the curate in Crislough, was sitting by the fire one evening when the housekeeper showed in a frail little woman of sixty or sixty-five. She had a long face, with big eyes that looked as though they had wept a great deal, and her smile lit up only the lower half of her face. Father Fogarty was a young man with a warm welcome for the suffering and the old. A man with emotions cut too big for the scale of his existence, he was forever floundering in enthusiasms and disillusionments, wranglings and reconciliations; but he had a heart like a house, and almost before the door closed behind her, he was squeezing the old woman's hand in his own two fat ones.

"You're in trouble," he said in a low voice.

"Wisha, aren't we all, father?" she replied.

"I'm sorry, I'm sorry," he said. "Is it something I can do for you?"

"Only to say Mass for Timmy, father."

"I'll do that, to be sure," he said comfortingly. "You're cold. Sit down a minute and warm yourself." Then he laid a big paw on her shoulder and added in a conspiratorial whisper, "Do you take anything? A drop of sherry, maybe?"

"Ah, don't be putting yourself out, father."

"I'm not putting myself out at all. Or maybe you'd sooner a sup of whiskey. I have some damn good whiskey."

"Wisha, no, father, I wouldn't, thanks. The whiskey goes to my head."

"It goes to my own," he replied cheerfully. "But the sherry is good, too." He didn't really know whether it was or not, because he rarely drank, but, being a hospitable man, he liked to give his visitors the best. He poured a glass of sherry for her and a small one for himself, and lit one of his favorite cheroots.

The old woman spread her transparent hands to the blaze and sipped at her wine. "Oh, isn't the heat lovely?" she exclaimed with girlish delight, showing her old gums. "And the sherry is lovely, too,

father. Now, I know you're surprised to see me, but I know all about
you. They told me to come to you if I was in trouble. And there aren't
many priests like that, father. I was never one to criticize, but I have to
say it."

"Ah," he said jovially, throwing himself back in his big leather chair
and pulling on his cheroot, "we're like everybody else, ma'am. A
mixed lot."

"I dare say you're right," she said, "but they told me I could talk to
you."

"Everyone talks to me," he said without boastfulness. It was true.
There was something about him that invited more confidences than a
normal man could respect, and Father Fogarty knew he was often indiscreet. "It's not your husband?" he added doubtfully.

"Ah, no, father," she replied with a wistful smile. "Poor Jim is dead
on me these fifteen years. Not, indeed, that I don't miss him just the
same," she added thoughtfully. "Sometimes I find myself thinking of
him, and he could be in the room with me. No, it's Timmy."

"The son?"

"No, father. Though he was like a son to me. I never had any of my
own. He was Jim's. One of the last things Jim did was to ask me to look
after him, and indeed, I did my best. I did my best."

"I'm sure you did, ma'am," said Father Fogarty, scowling behind
his cheroot. He was a man who took death hard, for himself and for
others. A stepchild was not the same thing, of course, but he supposed
you could get just as attached to one of those. That was the trouble;
you could get attached to anything if only you permitted yourself to
do so, and he himself was one who had never known how to keep back.
"I know how hard it is," he went on, chewing at his cheroot till his left
eyebrow descended and seemed to join in the process, and he resembled nothing so much as a film gangster plotting the murder of an innocent victim. "And there's little anyone can say that will console you.
All I know from my own experience is that the more loss we feel the
more grateful we should be for whatever it was we had to lose. It
means we had something worth grieving for. The ones I'm sorry for
are the ones that go through life not even knowing what grief is. And
you'd be surprised the number of them you'd meet."

"I dare say in one way they're lucky," she said broodingly, looking
into the fire.

"They are not lucky, ma'am, and don't you believe it," he said
gruffly. "They miss all the things that make life worth while, without
even knowing it. I had a woman in here the other night," he added,
pointing his cheroot at the chair she sat in, "sitting where you're sit-

ting now, and she told me when her husband gave the last breath she went on her knees by the bed and thanked God for taking him."

"God help us," the old woman said, clasping her hands. "I hope no one does the same thing over herself someday."

"Thanked God for taking him," Fogarty repeated with his troubled boyish frown. "What sort of mind can a woman like that have?"

"Oh, she's hard, she's hard," agreed the old woman, still looking into the fire.

"Hard as that hearthstone," he said dramatically. "My God, a man she'd lived with the best part of her life, whatever his faults might have been! Wouldn't you think at least she'd have some remorse for the things she'd done to him in all those years?"

"Oh, indeed, 'tis true," she said. "I often blamed myself over poor Jim. Sometimes I think if only I might have been a bit easier on him, he might be here yet."

"Most of us have to go through that sooner or later," he said, feeling that perhaps he had gone too far and reopened old wounds. His own old wounds were never far from breaking open, because often a light or careless word would bring back the memory of his mother and of his diabolical adolescent temperament. "We have to be careful of that, too," he added. "Because it's not the guilty ones who go on brooding but the others—the people who're only partly guilty, or maybe not guilty at all. That can happen, too. I had a man here last week talking about his wife's death, and nothing I could say would persuade him but that he'd wronged her. And I knew for a fact that he was a husband in a million—a saint. It's something we can't afford to indulge. It turns into a sort of cowardice before life. We have to learn to accept our own limitations as human beings—our selfishness and vanity and bad temper."

He spoke with passion, the passion of a man teaching a lesson he has never been able to learn himself. Something in his tone made the old woman look at him, and her face softened into a sweet, toothless old smile.

"Haven't you great wisdom for such a young man!" she exclaimed admiringly.

"Great," he agreed with a jolly laugh. "I'm the biggest idiot of them all."

But she shrugged this off. "Ah, what else were the saints?"

"Look here, ma'am," he said, rising and standing over her with mock gravity. "Don't you be going round talking about me as a saint or you'll be having me sent to a punishment parish. The poor Bishop has trouble enough on his hands without having to deal with saints. I'll say eight-o'clock Mass on Sunday for your boy. Will that do you?"

"My boy?" she said in surprise. "But Timmy wasn't my son, father. Sure, I said I had no children."

"No. I took it he was your stepson."

"Is it Jim's?" she exclaimed with a laugh of genuine amusement at his mistake. "Ah, sure, Jim wasn't married before, father. Don't you see, that's why I had to come to you?"

"I see," he said, though he didn't, and anyhow he felt it was none of his business. The woman, after all, hadn't come to make her confession. "What was his surname so?"

"Ah, father," she said, still laughing but in a bewildered way, "I'm so distracted that I can't explain myself properly. You have it all mixed up. Sure, I thought I explained it."

"You didn't explain it, ma'am," he said, repressing his curiosity. "And anyway it's nothing to me who Timmy was. That's a matter between you and your confessor."

"My what?" she cried indignantly. "Ah, father, you have me distracted completely now. This has nothing to do with confession. Oh, my, what's that Timmy was? If I could only think!"

"Take your time, ma'am," he said, but he wondered what was coming next.

"A poodle!" she exclaimed. "Now I have it."

"A what?"

"A poodle—a French poodle is what they called him," she said, delighted to remember the proper term. And then her big eyes began to fill with tears. "Oh, father, I don't know how I'm going to get on without him. He was everything to me. The house isn't the same without him."

"You don't mean you're asking me to say Mass for your *dog?*"

"Oh, I'm not asking you to do it for nothing," she added with dignity, opening her handbag.

"Are you a Catholic at all, ma'am?" he asked sternly, fixing her with a glowering look that only seemed to amuse her. She tossed her head with a sudden saucy, girlish air.

"Wisha, what else would I be?" she asked gently, and he felt that there was nothing much he could say in reply.

"And do you know what the sacrifice of the Mass is?" he went on.

"Well, as I go every morning of my life, father, I should have some idea," she replied, and again he had the feeling that she was laughing at him.

"And don't you know that you're asking me to commit sacrilege? Do you even know what sacrilege is?"

"Ah, what sacrilege?" she exclaimed lightly, shrugging it off. She took three five-pound notes from her old handbag. He knew she intended the money as an offering; he knew it was probably all she had in the world, and he found himself torn between blind rage and admiration.

"Here," he said. "Let me get you another drink. And put that blooming money back in your bag or you'll be losing it."

BUT the very sound of his voice told him that he was losing conviction. The terrible little old woman with her one idea exercised a sort of fascination over him that almost frightened him. He was afraid that if he wasn't careful he would soon find himself agreeing to do what she wanted. He poured her a drink, threw himself back again in his armchair, and at once gave way to his indignation.

"I cannot stand this damn sentimentality!" he shouted, hitting the arm of his chair with his clenched fist. "Every day of my life I have to see good Christians go without food and fire, clothes and medicine, while the rich people taunt them with the sight of their pampered pets. I tell you I can't stand it!"

"Why, then, I'm sure you're right, father. But I'm not rich, and no poor person was ever sent away from my door with nothing, as long as I had it."

"I'm sure of that, ma'am," he said humbly, ashamed of his outburst. "I'm sure you're a better Christian than I am, but there are different needs and different duties, and we must not confuse them. There are animal needs and human needs, and human needs and spiritual needs. Your dog has no need of the Mass."

"He was very fond of Mass. Every morning he came with me and lay down outside the chapel door."

"And *why* did you leave him outside the chapel door?" asked Fogarty.

"Why?"

"Yes, why? Wasn't it that you made a distinction between an animal and a spiritual need?"

"It was nothing of the kind," she said hotly. "It was the parish priest that asked me, because some old fools complained. Hah, but I often sneaked him in when they weren't looking, and let me tell you, father, none of those old craw-thumpers behaved as devotionally as my Timmy. Up with the Gospel and down at the Elevation, without my saying a word to him. And don't tell me that Our Blessed Lord wasn't as pleased with Timmy as with them."

"I'm not telling you anything of the sort," he said, touched and amused. "All I am telling you is that now that your dog is dead, prayers can make no difference to him. Your dog couldn't incur guilt. Your prayers may make a difference to your husband because, like the rest of us, he did incur guilt in this life and may have to atone for it in the next."

"Ah, it's easy seen you didn't know Jim, father. Poor Jim was innocent as a child. He never did anything wrong only taking the little sup of whiskey when I wouldn't be looking. I know he got a bit cranky when he had a drop in and I wouldn't give him any more, but sure that's a thing you wouldn't give a second thought to.... No, father," she added thoughtfully, looking into the fire again, "I don't mind admitting that the first day or two after he died I wasn't easy in my mind at all. I didn't know what little thing he might have said or done on the side, unknown to me, or what little taste of punishment they might give him. I couldn't rest, thinking of him burning down there in Purgatory, with people he didn't know at all. A shy man, like that, and a man—I won't belie him—that would scream the house down if he as much as got a splinter in his nail. But then I realized that nobody in his right mind could be doing anything to him. Oh, no, father, that's not why I get Masses said for Jim."

"Then why do you get them said for him?" Fogarty asked, though he knew the answer. His own big heart answered for him when his reason didn't.

"Sure, what other way have I of letting him know I'm thinking about him?" she asked with a childlike smile. "He's always in my mind, morning, noon, and night. And now Timmy is the same."

"And when I tell you that it makes no difference to Timmy—that Timmy can't know he's in your mind?"

"Ah, well, father, these things are great mysteries," she replied comfortably, "and we don't know all about them yet. Oh, I know there's a difference, and I'm not asking for anything impossible. Only one small Mass, so that he'll know. But when I talk to people about it, you'd think I was mad from the way they go on. They tell me he has no soul, because he never committed sin. How does anybody know he didn't commit sin? A little child doesn't commit sin and he has a soul. No, father," she went on with iron determination, "I know I'm old and I have no one to advise me, and my head isn't as good as it was, but thank God I still have my wits about me. Believe me, father, a dog is no different from a child. When I was feeling low coming on to Jim's anniversary, Timmy would know it. He'd know it as if he could read what I was thinking, and he'd come and put his head on my lap to show how sorry he was. And when he was sick himself, he'd get into my bed and curl up beside me, begging me with his eyes to make him better. Yes, indeed, and when he was dying I felt the same way about him as I felt about poor Jim—just the way you described it, thinking of all the times I was hard on him when he didn't deserve it at all. That is the hardest part of it, father, when you have to try and forgive yourself."

"I'm sure you have very little to forgive yourself for, ma'am," Fogarty said with a smile. "And God knows, if it was anything I could do for you I'd do it, but this is something that, as a priest, I can't do."

"And there's no one else I could go to? You don't think if I went to the Bishop myself he'd let you do it?"

"I'm quite certain he wouldn't, ma'am."

"Ah," she said bitterly as she raised herself heavily from her chair, "if I was younger and smarter with my pen I'd write to the Pope about it myself." She turned to the door, and Fogarty sprang to open it for her, but the courtesy was lost on her. She looked at him with deep mournful eyes that seemed to contain all the loneliness in the world. "And it's wrong, father, wrong," she said in a firm voice. "I'm as good a Catholic as the next, but I'd say it to the Pope himself this minute if he walked into this room. They *have* souls, and people are only deluding themselves about it. Anything that can love has a soul. Show me that bad woman that thanked God her husband was dead and I'll show you someone that maybe hasn't a soul, but don't tell me that my Timmy hadn't one. And I know as I'm standing here that somewhere or other I'll see him again."

"I hope you do, ma'am," he said, his big voice suddenly growing gentle and timorous. "And whenever you say a prayer for him, don't forget to add one for me."

"I will not indeed, father," she said quietly. "I know you're a good man, and I'll remember you with the others that were good to me, and one of these days, with God's help, we'll all be together again."

An Act of Charity

THE PARISH PRIEST, Father Maginnis, did not like the second curate, Father Galvin, and Father Fogarty could see why. It was the dislike of the professional for the amateur, no matter how talented, and nobody could have said that Father Galvin had much in the way of talent. Maginnis was a professional to his fingertips. He drove the right car, knew the right people, and could suit his conversation to any company, even that of women. He even varied his accent to make people feel at home. With Deasy, the owner of the garage, he talked about "the caw," but to Lavin, the garage hand, he said "the cyarr," smiling benignly at the homeliness of his touch.

Galvin was thin, pale, irritable, and intense. When he should have kept a straight face he made some stupid joke that stopped the conversation dead; and when he laughed in the proper place at someone else's joke, it was with a slight air of vexation, as though he found it hard to put up with people who made him laugh at all. He worried himself over little embarrassments and what people would think of them, till Fogarty asked bluntly, "What the hell difference does it make what they think?" Then Galvin looked away sadly and said, "I suppose you're right." But Fogarty didn't mind his visits so much except when he had asked other curates in for a drink and a game of cards. Then he took a glass of sherry or something equally harmless and twiddled it awkwardly for half an hour as though it were some sort of patent device for keeping his hands occupied. When one of the curates made a harmless dirty joke, Galvin pretended to be looking at a picture so that he didn't have to comment. Fogarty, who loved giving people nicknames, called him Father Mother's Boy. He called Maginnis the Old Pro, but when that nickname got back, as everything a priest says gets back, it did Fogarty no harm at all. Maginnis was glad he had a curate with so much sense.

He sometimes asked Fogarty to Sunday dinner, but he soon gave up on asking Galvin, and again Fogarty sympathized with him. Maginnis was a professional, even to his dinners. He basted his meat with one sort of wine and his chickens with another, and he liked a guest who could tell the difference. He also liked him to drink two large whiskeys before dinner and to make sensible remarks about the wine; and when he had exhausted the secrets of his kitchen he sat back, smoked his cigar, and told funny stories. They were very good stories, mostly about priests.

"Did I ever tell you the one about Canon Murphy, father?" he would bellow, his fat face beaming. "Ah, that's damn good. Canon Murphy went on a pilgrimage to Rome, and when he came back he preached a sermon on it. 'So I had a special audience with His Holiness, dearly beloved brethren, and he asked me, "Canon Murphy, where are you now?" "I'm in Dromod, Your Holiness," said I. "What sort of a parish is it, Canon Murphy?" says he. "Ah, 'tis a nice, snug little parish, Your Holiness," says I. "Are they a good class of people?" says he. "Well, they're not bad, Your Holiness," said I. "Are they good-living people?" says he. "Well, they're as good as the next, Your Holiness," says I. "Except when they'd have a drop taken." "Tell me, Canon Murphy," says he, "do they pay their dues?" And like that, I was nearly struck dumb. "There you have me, Your Holiness!" says I. "There you have me!" ' "

At heart Fogarty thought Maginnis was a bit of a sham and that most of his stories were fabrications; but he never made the mistake of underestimating him, and he enjoyed the feeling Maginnis gave him of belonging to a group, and that of the best kind—well balanced, humane, and necessary.

At meals in the curates' house, Galvin had a tendency to chatter brightly and aimlessly that irritated Fogarty. He was full of scraps of undigested knowledge, picked up from newspapers and magazines, about new plays and books that he would never either see or read. Fogarty was a moody young man who preferred either to keep silent or engage in long emotional discussions about local scandals that grew murkier and more romantic the more he described them. About such things he was hopelessly indiscreet. "And that fellow notoriously killed his own father," he said once, and Galvin looked at him in distress. "You mean he really killed him?" he asked—as though Fogarty did not really mean everything at the moment he was saying it—and then, to make things worse, added, "It's not something I'd care to repeat—not without evidence, I mean."

"The Romans used eunuchs for civil servants, but we're more enlightened," Fogarty said once to Maginnis. "We prefer the natural ones." Maginnis gave a hearty laugh; it was the sort of remark he liked to repeat. And when Galvin returned after lunching austerely with some maiden ladies and offered half-baked suggestions, Maginnis crushed him, and Fogarty watched with malicious amusement. He knew it was turning into persecution, but he wasn't quite sure which of the two men suffered more.

WHEN he heard the explosion in the middle of the night, he waited for some further noise to interpret it, and then rose and put on the light. The housekeeper was standing outside her bedroom door in a raincoat, her hands joined. She was a widow woman with a history of tragedy behind her, and Fogarty did not like her; for some reason he felt she had the evil eye, and he always addressed her in his most commanding tone.

"What was that, Mary?" he asked.

"I don't know, father," she said in a whisper. "It sounded as if it was in Father Galvin's room."

Fogarty listened again. There was no sound from Galvin's room, and he knocked and pushed in the door. He closed the door again immediately.

"Get Dr. Carmody quick!" he said brusquely.

"What is it, father?" she asked. "An accident?"

"Yes, a bad one. And when you're finished, run out and ask Father Maginnis to come in."

"Oh, that old gun!" she moaned softly. "I dreaded it. I'll ring Dr. Carmody." She went hastily down the stairs.

Fogarty followed her and went into the living room to pick up the sacred oils from the cupboard where they were kept. "I don't know, doctor," he heard Mary moaning. "Father Fogarty said it was an accident." He returned upstairs and lifted the gun from the bed before anointing the dead man. He had just concluded when the door opened and he saw the parish priest come in, wearing a blue flowered dressing gown.

Maginnis went over to the bed and stared down at the figure on it. Then he looked at Fogarty over his glasses, his face almost expressionless. "I was afraid of something like this," he said knowingly. "I knew he was a bit unstable."

"You don't think it could be an accident?" Fogarty asked, though he knew the question sounded ridiculous.

"No," Maginnis said, giving him a downward look through the spectacles. "Do you?"

"But how could he bring himself to do a thing like that?" Fogarty asked incredulously.

"Oh, who knows?" said Maginnis, almost impatiently. "With weak characters it's hard to tell. He doesn't seem to have left any message."

"Not that I can see."

"I'm sorry 'twas Carmody you sent for."

"But he was Galvin's doctor."

"I know, I know, but all the same he's young and a bit immature. I'd have preferred an older man. Make no mistake about it, father, we have a problem on our hands," he added with sudden resolution. "A very serious problem."

Fogarty did not need to have the problem spelled out for him. The worst thing a priest could do was to commit suicide, since it seemed to deny everything that gave his vocation meaning—Divine Providence and Mercy, forgiveness, Heaven, Hell. That one of God's anointed could come to such a state of despair was something the Church could not admit. It would give too much scandal. It was simply an unacceptable act.

"That's his car now, I fancy," Maginnis said.

Carmody came quickly up the stairs with his bag in his hand and his pink pajamas showing under his tweed jacket. He was a tall, spectacled young man with a long, humorous clown's face, and in ordinary life adopted a manner that went with his face, but Fogarty knew he was both competent and conscientious. He had worked for some years in an English hospital and developed a bluntness of speech that Fogarty found refreshing.

"Christ!" he said as he took in the scene. Then he went over and looked closely at the body. "Poor Peter!" he added. Then he took the shotgun from the bedside table where Fogarty had put it and examined it. "I should have kept a closer eye on him," he said with chagrin. "There isn't much I can do for him now."

"On the contrary, doctor," Maginnis said. "There was never a time when you could do more for him." Then he gave Fogarty a meaningful glance. "I wonder if you'd mind getting Jack Fitzgerald for me, father? Talk to himself, and I needn't warn you to be careful what you say."

"Oh, I'll be careful," Fogarty said with gloomy determination. There was something in his nature that always responded to the touch of melodrama, and he knew Maginnis wanted to talk to Carmody alone. He telephoned to Fitzgerald, the undertaker, and then went back upstairs to dress. It was clear he wasn't going to get any more sleep that night.

He heard himself called and returned to Galvin's room. This time he really felt the full shock of it: the big bald parish priest in his dressing gown and the gaunt young doctor with his pajama top open under the jacket. He could see the two men had been arguing.

"Perhaps you'd talk to Dr. Carmody, father?" Maginnis suggested benignly.

"There's nothing to talk about, Father Fogarty," Carmody said, adopting the formal title he ignored when they were among friends. "I can't sign a certificate saying this was a natural death. You know I can't. It's too unprofessional."

"Professional or not, Dr. Carmody, someone will have to do it," Maginnis said. "I am the priest of this parish. In a manner of speaking I'm a professional man too, you know. And this unfortunate occurrence is something that doesn't concern only me and you. It has consequences that affect the whole parish."

"Your profession doesn't require you to sign your name to a lie, father," Carmody said angrily. "That's what you want me to do."

"Oh, I wouldn't call that a lie, Dr. Carmody," Maginnis said with dignity. "In considering the nature of a lie we have to take account of its good and bad effects. I can see no possible good effect that might result from a scandal about the death of this poor boy. Not one! In fact, I can see unlimited harm."

"So can I," Fogarty burst out. His voice sounded too loud, too confident, even to his own ears.

"I see," Carmody said sarcastically. "And you think we should keep on denouncing the Swedes and Danes for their suicide statistics, just because they don't fake them the way we do. Ah, for God's sake, man, I'd never be able to respect myself again."

Fogarty saw that Maginnis was right. In some ways Carmody was too immature. "That's all very well, Jim, but Christian charity comes before statistics," he said appealingly. "Forget about the damn statistics, can't you? Father Galvin wasn't only a statistic. He was a human being—somebody we both knew. And what about his family?"

"What about his mother?" Maginnis asked with real pathos. "I gather you have a mother yourself, Dr. Carmody?"

"And you expect me to meet Mrs. Galvin tomorrow and tell her her son was a suicide and can't be buried in consecrated ground?" Fogarty went on emotionally. "Would you like us to do that to your mother if it was your case?"

"A doctor has unpleasant things to do as well, Jerry," said Carmody.

"To tell a mother that her child is dying?" Fogarty asked. "A priest has to do that too, remember. Not to tell her that her child is damned."

But the very word that Fogarty knew had impressed Carmody made the parish priest uncomfortable. "Fortunately, father, that is in better hands than yours or mine," he said curtly. And at once his manner changed. It was as though he was a little bit tired of them both. "Dr.

Carmody," he said, "I think I hear Mr. Fitzgerald. You'd better make up your mind quick. If you're not prepared to sign the death certificate, I'll soon find another doctor who will. That is my simple duty, and I'm going to do it. But as an elderly man who knows a little more about this town than you or Father Fogarty here, I'd advise you not to compel me to bring in another doctor. If word got round that I was forced to do such a thing, it might have very serious effects on your career."

There was no mistaking the threat, and there was something almost admirable about the way it was made. At the same time, it roused the sleeping rebel in Fogarty. Bluff, he thought angrily. Damn bluff! If Carmody walked out on them at that moment, there was very little the parish priest or anyone else could do to him. Of course, any of the other doctors would sign the certificate, but it wouldn't do them any good either. When people really felt the need for a doctor, they didn't necessarily want the doctor the parish priest approved of. But as he looked at Carmody's sullen, resentful face, he realized that Carmody didn't know his own strength in the way that Maginnis knew his. After all, what had he behind him but a few years in a London hospital, while behind Maginnis was that whole vast, historic organization that he was rightly so proud of.

"I can't sign a certificate that death was due to natural causes," Carmody said stubbornly. "Accident, maybe—I don't know. I wasn't here. I'll agree to accident."

"Accident?" Maginnis said contemptuously, and this time he did not even trouble to use Carmody's title. It was as though he were stripping him of any little dignity he had. "Young man, accidents with shotguns do not happen to priests at three o'clock in the morning. Try to talk sense!"

And just as Fogarty realized that the doctor had allowed himself to be crushed, they heard Mary let Fitzgerald in. He came briskly up the stairs. He was a small, spare man, built like a jockey. The parish priest nodded in the direction of the bed and Fitzgerald's brows went up mechanically. He was a man who said little, but he had a face and figure too expressive for his character. It was as though all the opinions he suppressed in life found relief in violent physical movements.

"Naturally, we don't want it talked about, Mr. Fitzgerald," said Maginnis. "Do you think you could handle it yourself?"

The undertaker's eyes popped again, and he glanced swiftly from Maginnis to Carmody and then to Fogarty. He was a great man for efficiency, though; if you had asked him to supply the corpse as well as the coffin, he might have responded automatically, "Male or female?"

"Dr. Carmody will give the certificate, of course?" he asked shrewdly. He hadn't missed much of what was going on.

"It seems I don't have much choice," Carmody replied bitterly.

"Oh, purely as an act of charity, of course," Fitz said hastily. "We all have to do this sort of thing from time to time. The poor relatives have enough to worry them without inquests and things like that. What was the age, Father Maginnis, do you know?" he added, taking out a notebook. A clever little man, thought Fogarty. He had put it all at once upon a normal, businesslike footing.

"Twenty-eight," said Maginnis.

"God help us!" Fitz said perfunctorily, and made a note. After that he took out a rule.

"I'd better get ready and go to see the Bishop myself," Maginnis said. "We'll need his permission, of course, but I haven't much doubt about that. I know he had the reputation for being on the strict side, but I always found him very considerate. I'll send Nora over to help your housekeeper, father. In the meantime, maybe you'd be good enough to get in touch with the family."

"I'll see to that, father," Fogarty said. He and Carmody followed Maginnis downstairs. He said good-bye and left, and Fogarty's manner changed abruptly. "Come in and have a drink, Jim," he said.

"I'd rather not, Jerry," Carmody said gloomily.

"Come on! Come on! You need one, man! I need one myself and I can't have it." He shut the door of the living room behind him. "Great God, Jim, who could have suspected it?"

"I suppose I should have," said Carmody. "I got hints enough if only I might have understood them."

"But you couldn't, Jim," Fogarty said excitedly, taking the whiskey from the big cupboard. "Nobody could. Do you think I ever expected it, and I lived closer to him than you did."

The front door opened and they heard the slippers of Nora, Maginnis's housekeeper, in the hall. There was a low mumble of talk outside the door, and then the clank of a bucket as the woman went up the stairs. Fitzgerald was coming down at the same time, and Fogarty opened the door a little.

"Well, Jack?"

"Well, father. I'll do the best I can."

"You wouldn't join us for a—?"

"No, father. I'll have my hands full for the next couple of hours."

"Good-night, Jack. And I'm sorry for the disturbance."

"Ah, 'twas none of your doing. Good-night, father."

The doctor finished his whiskey in a gulp, and his long, battered face had a bitter smile. "And so this is how it's done!" he said.

"This is how it's done, Jim, and believe me, it's the best way for everybody in the long run," Fogarty replied with real gravity.

But, looking at Carmody's face, he knew the doctor did not believe it, and he wondered then if he really believed it himself.

When the doctor had gone, Fogarty got on the telephone to a provincial town fifty miles away. The exchange was closed down, so he had to give his message to the police. In ten minutes or so a guard would set out along the sleeping streets to the house where the Galvins lived. That was one responsibility he was glad to evade.

While he was speaking, he heard the parish priest's car set off and knew he was on his way to the Bishop's palace. Then he shaved, and, about eight, Fitzgerald drove up with the coffin in his van. Silently they carried it between them up the stairs. The body was lying decently composed with a simple bandage about the head. Between them they lifted it into the coffin. Fitzgerald looked questioningly at Fogarty and went on his knees. As he said the brief prayer, Fogarty found his voice unsteady and his eyes full of tears. Fitzgerald gave him a pitying look and then rose and dusted his knees.

"All the same there'll be talk, father," he said.

"Maybe not as much as there should be, Jack," Fogarty said moodily.

"We'll take him to the chapel, of course?" Fitzgerald went on.

"Everything in order, Jack. Father Maginnis is gone to see the Bishop."

"He couldn't trust the telephone, of course," Fitzgerald said, stroking his unshaven chin. "No fear the Bishop will interfere, though. Father Maginnis is a smart man. You saw him?"

"I saw him."

"No nerves, no hysterics. I saw other people in the same situation. 'Oh, Mr. Fitzgerald, what am I going to do?' His mind on essential things the whole time. He's an object lesson to us all, father."

"You're right, Jack, he is," Fogarty said despondently.

Suddenly the undertaker's hand shot out and caught him by the upper arm. "Forget about it, boy! Forget about it! What else can you do? Why the hell should you break your heart over it?"

FOGARTY still had to meet the family. Later that morning, they drove up to the curates' house. The mother was an actressy type and wept a good deal. She wanted somebody to give her a last message, which Fogarty couldn't think up. The sister, a pretty, intense girl, wept a little too, but quietly, with her back turned, while the brother, a young man with a great resemblance to Galvin, said little. Mother and brother accepted without protest the ruling that the coffin was not to be opened, but the sister looked at Fogarty and asked, "You don't think I could see him? Alone? I wouldn't be afraid." When he said the doctor had forbidden it, she turned her back again, and he had an impression that there was a closer link between her and Galvin than between the others and him.

That evening, they brought the body to lie before the altar of the church, and Maginnis received it and said the prayers. The church was crowded, and Fogarty knew with a strange mixture of rejoicing and mortification that the worst was over. Maginnis's master stroke was the new curate, Rowlands, who had arrived within a couple of hours after his own return. He was a tall, thin, ascetic-looking young man, slow-moving and slow-speaking, and Fogarty knew that all eyes were on him.

Everything went with perfect propriety at the Requiem Mass next morning, and after the funeral Fogarty attended the lunch given by Maginnis to the visiting clergy. He almost laughed out loud when he heard Maginnis ask in a low voice, "Father Healy, did I ever tell you the story of Canon Murphy and the Pope?" All that would follow would be the mourning card with the picture of Galvin and the Gothic lettering that said "Ecce Sacerdos Magnus." There was no danger of a scandal any longer. Carmody would not talk. Fitzgerald would not talk either. None of the five people involved would. Father Galvin might have spared himself the trouble.

As they returned from the church together, Fogarty tried to talk to the new curate about what had happened, but he soon realized that the whole significance of it had escaped Rowlands, and that Rowlands thought he was only overdramatizing it all. Anybody would think he was overdramatizing it, except Carmody. After his supper he would go to the doctor's house, and they would talk about it. Only Carmody would really understand what it was they had done between them. No one else would.

What lonely lives we live, he thought unhappily.

The Mass Island

WHEN FATHER JACKSON drove up to the curates' house, it was already drawing on to dusk, the early dusk of late December. The curates' house was a red-brick building on a terrace at one side of the ugly church in Asragh. Father Hamilton seemed to have been waiting for him and opened the front door himself, looking white and strained. He was a tall young man with a long, melancholy face that you would have taken for weak till you noticed the cut of the jaw.

"Oh, come in, Jim," he said with his mournful smile. " 'Tisn't much of a welcome we have for you, God knows. I suppose you'd like to see poor Jerry before the undertaker comes."

"I might as well," Father Jackson replied briskly. There was nothing melancholy about Jackson, but he affected an air of surprise and shock. " 'Twas very sudden, wasn't it?"

"Well, it was and it wasn't, Jim," Father Hamilton said, closing the front door behind him. "He was going downhill since he got the first heart attack, and he wouldn't look after himself. Sure, you know yourself what he was like."

Jackson knew. Father Fogarty and himself had been friends of a sort, for years. An impractical man, excitable and vehement, Fogarty could have lived for twenty years with his ailment, but instead of that, he allowed himself to become depressed and indifferent. If he couldn't live as he had always lived, he would prefer not to live at all.

They went upstairs and into the bedroom where he was. The character was still plain on the stern, dead face, though, drained of vitality, it had the look of a studio portrait. That bone structure was something you'd have picked out of a thousand faces as Irish, with its odd impression of bluntness and asymmetry, its jutting brows and craggy chin, and the snub nose that looked as though it had probably been broken twenty years before in a public-house row.

When they came downstairs again, Father Hamilton produced half a bottle of whiskey.

"Not for me, thanks," Jackson said hastily. "Unless you have a drop of sherry there?"

"Well, there is some Burgundy," Father Hamilton said. "I don't know is it any good, though."

" 'Twill do me fine," Jackson replied cheerfully, reflecting that Ireland was the country where nobody knew whether Burgundy was good or not. "You're coming with us tomorrow, I suppose?"

"Well, the way it is, Jim," Father Hamilton replied, "I'm afraid neither of us is going. You see, they're burying poor Jerry here."

"They're what?" Jackson asked incredulously.

"Now, I didn't know for sure when I rang you, Jim, but that's what the brother decided, and that's what Father Hanafey decided as well."

"But he told you he wanted to be buried on the Mass Island, didn't he?"

"He told everybody, Jim," Father Hamilton replied with growing excitement and emotion. "That was the sort he was. If he told one, he told five hundred. Only a half an hour ago I had a girl on the telephone from the Island, asking when they could expect us. You see, the old parish priest of the place let Jerry mark out the grave for himself, and they want to know should they open it. But now the old parish priest is dead as well, and, of course, Jerry left nothing in writing."

"Didn't he leave a will, even?" Jackson asked in surprise.

"Well, he did and he didn't, Jim," Father Hamilton said, looking as if he were on the point of tears. "Actually, he did make a will about five or six years ago, and he gave it to Clancy, the other curate, but Clancy went off on the Foreign Mission and God alone knows where he is now. After that, Jerry never bothered his head about it. I mean, you have to admit the man had nothing to leave. Every damn thing he had he gave away—even the old car, after he got the first attack. If there was any loose cash around, I suppose the brother has that."

Jackson sipped his Burgundy, which was even more Australian than he had feared, and wondered at his own irritation. He had been irritated enough before that, with the prospect of two days' motoring in the middle of winter, and a night in a godforsaken pub in the mountains, a hundred and fifty miles away at the other side of Ireland. There, in one of the lakes, was an island where in Cromwell's time, before the causeway and the little oratory were built, Mass was said in secret, and it was here that Father Fogarty had wanted to be buried. It struck Jackson as sheer sentimentality; it wasn't even as if it was Fogarty's native place. Jackson had once allowed Fogarty to lure him there, and had hated every moment of it. It wasn't only the discomfort of the public-house, where meals erupted at any hour of the day or night as the spirit took the proprietor, or the rain that kept them confined to the cold dining-and-sitting room that looked out on the gloomy mountainside, with its couple of whitewashed cabins on the shore of the lake. It was the overintimacy of it all, and this was the thing that Father Fogarty apparently loved. He liked to stand in his shirtsleeves behind the bar, taking turns with the proprietor, who was one of his many friends, serving big pints of porter to rough mountainy men, or to sit in their cottages, shaking in all his fat whenever they told broad stories or sang risky folk songs. "God, Jim, isn't it grand?" he would say in his deep voice, and Jackson would look at him over his spectacles with what Fogarty called his "jesuitical look," and say, "Well, I suppose it all depends on what you really like, Jerry." He wasn't even certain that the locals cared for Father Fogarty's intimacy; on the contrary, he had a strong impression that they much preferred their own reserved old parish priest, whom they never saw except twice a year, when he came up the valley to collect his dues. That had made Jackson twice as stiff. And yet now when he found out that the plans that had meant so much inconvenience to him had fallen through, he was as disappointed as though they had been his own.

"Oh, well," he said with a shrug that was intended to conceal his perturbation, "I suppose it doesn't make much difference where they chuck us when our time comes."

"The point is, it mattered to Jerry, Jim," Father Hamilton said with his curious shy obstinacy. "God knows, it's not anything that will ever worry me, but it haunted him, and somehow, you know, I don't feel it's right to flout a dead man's wishes."

"Oh, I know, I know," Jackson said lightly. "I suppose I'd better talk to old Hanafey about it. Knowing I'm a friend of the Bishop's, he might pay more attention to me."

"He might, Jim," Father Hamilton replied sadly, looking away over Jackson's head. "As you say, knowing you're a friend of the Bishop's, he might. But I wouldn't depend too much on it. I talked to him till I was black in the face, and all I got out of him was the law and the rubrics. It's the brother Hanafey is afraid of. You'll see him this evening, and, between ourselves, he's a tough customer. Of course, himself and Jerry never had much to say to one another, and he'd be the last man in the world that Jerry would talk to about his funeral, so now he doesn't want the expense and inconvenience. You wouldn't blame him, of course. I'd probably be the same myself. By the way," Father Hamilton added, lowering his voice, "before he does come, I'd like you to take a look round Jerry's room and see is there any little memento you'd care to have—a photo or a book or anything."

They went into Father Fogarty's sitting room, and Jackson looked at it with a new interest. He knew of old the rather handsome library—Fogarty had been a man of many enthusiasms, though none of long duration—the picture of the Virgin and Child in Irish country costume over the mantelpiece, which some of his colleagues had thought irreverent, and the couple of fine old prints. There was a newer picture that Jackson had not seen—a charcoal drawing of the Crucifixion from a fifteenth-century Irish tomb, which was brutal but impressive.

"Good Lord!" Jackson exclaimed with a sudden feeling of loss. "He really had taste, hadn't he?"

"He had, Jim," Father Hamilton said, sticking his long nose into the picture. "This goes to a young couple called Keneally, outside the town, that he was fond of. I think they were very kind to him. Since he had the attack, he was pretty lonely, I'd say."

"Oh, aren't we all, attack or no attack," Jackson said almost irritably.

FATHER HANAFEY, the parish priest of Asragh, was a round, red, cherubic-looking old man with a bald head and big round glasses. His house was on the same terrace as the curates'. He, too, insisted on producing the whiskey Jackson so heartily detested, when the two priests came in to consult him, but Jackson had decided that this time diplomacy required he should show proper appreciation of the dreadful stuff. He felt sure he was going to be very sick next day. He affected great astonishment at the quality of Father Hanafey's whiskey, and first the old parish priest grew shy, like a schoolgirl whose good looks are being praised, then he looked self-satisfied, and finally he became almost emotional. It was a great pleasure, he said, to meet a young priest with a proper understanding of whiskey. Priests no longer seemed to have the same taste, and as far as most of them were concerned, they might as well be drinking poteen. It was only when it was seven years old that Irish began to be interesting, and that was when you had to catch it and store it in sherry casks to draw off what remained of crude alcohol in it, and give it that beautiful roundness that Father Jackson had spotted. But it shouldn't be kept too long, for somewhere along the line the spirit of a whiskey was broken. At ten, or maybe twelve, years old it was just right. But people were losing their palates. He solemnly assured the two priests that of every dozen clerics who came to his house not more than one would realize what he was drinking. Poor Hamilton grew red and began to stutter, but the parish priest's reproofs were not directed at him.

"It isn't you I'm talking about, Father Hamilton, but elderly priests, parish priests, and even canons, that you would think would know better, and I give you my word, I put the two whiskeys side by side in front of them, the shop stuff and my own, and they could not tell the difference."

But though the priest was mollified by Father Jackson's maturity of judgment, he was not prepared to interfere in the arrangements for the funeral of his curate. "It is the wish of the next of kin, father," he said stubbornly, "and that is something I have no control over. Now that you tell me the same thing as Father Hamilton, I accept it that this was Father Fogarty's wish, and a man's wishes regarding his own interment are always to be respected. I assure you, if I had even one line in Father Fogarty's writing to go on, I would wait for no man's advice. I would take the responsibility on myself. Something on paper, father, is all I want."

"On the other hand, father," Jackson said mildly, drawing on his pipe, "if Father Fogarty was the sort to leave written instructions, he'd hardly be the sort to leave such unusual ones. I mean, after all, it isn't even the family burying ground, is it?"

"Well, now, that is true, father," replied the parish priest, and it was clear that he had been deeply impressed by this rather doubtful logic. "You have a very good point there, and it is one I did not think of myself, and I have given the matter a great deal of thought. You might mention it to his brother. Father Fogarty, God rest him, was *not* a usual type of man. I think you might even go so far as to say that he was a rather *unusual* type of man, and not orderly, as you say—not by any means orderly. I would certainly mention that to the brother and see what he says."

BUT the brother was not at all impressed by Father Jackson's argument when he turned up at the church in Asragh that evening. He was a good-looking man with a weak and pleasant face and a cold shrewdness in his eyes that had been lacking in his brother's.

"But why, father?" he asked, turning to Father Hanafey. "I'm a busy man, and I'm being asked to leave my business for a couple of days in the middle of winter, and for what? That is all I ask. What use is it?"

"It is only out of respect for the wishes of the deceased, Mr. Fogarty," said Father Hanafey, who clearly was a little bit afraid of him.

"And where did he express those wishes?" the brother asked. "I'm his only living relative, and it is queer he would not mention a thing like that to me."

"He mentioned it to Father Jackson and Father Hamilton."

"But when, father?" Mr. Fogarty asked. "You knew Father Jerry, and he was always expressing wishes about something. He was an excitable sort of man, God rest him, and the thing he'd say today might not be the thing he'd say tomorrow. After all, after close on forty years, I think I have the right to say I knew him," he added with a triumphant air that left the two young priests without a leg to stand on.

OVER bacon and eggs in the curates' house, Father Hamilton was very despondent. "Well, I suppose we did what we could, Jim," he said.

"I'm not too sure of that," Jackson said with his "jesuitical air," looking at Father Hamilton sidewise over his spectacles. "I'm wondering if we couldn't do something with that family you say he intended the drawing for."

"The Keneallys," said Father Hamilton in a worried voice. "Actually, I saw the wife in the church this evening. You might have noticed her crying."

"Don't you think we should see if they have anything in writing?"

"Well, if they have, it would be about the picture," said Father Hamilton. "How I know about it is she came to me at the time to ask if I couldn't do something for him. Poor man, he was crying himself that day, according to what she told me."

"Oh dear!" Jackson said politely, but his mind was elsewhere. "I'm not really interested in knowing what would be in a letter like that. It's none of my business. But I would like to make sure that they haven't something in writing. What did Hanafey call it—'something on paper'?"

"I daresay we should inquire, anyway," said Father Hamilton, and after supper they drove out to the Keneallys', a typical small red-brick villa with a decent garden in front. The family also was eating bacon and eggs, and Jackson shuddered when they asked him to join them. Keneally himself, a tall, gaunt, cadaverous man, poured out more whiskey for them, and again Jackson felt he must make a formal attempt to drink it. At the same time, he thought he saw what attraction the house had for Father Fogarty. Keneally was tough and with no suggestion of lay servility towards the priesthood, and his wife was beautiful and scatterbrained, and talked to herself, the cat, and the children simultaneously. "Rosaleen!" she cried determinedly. "Out! Out I say! I told you if you didn't stop meowing you'd have to go out. . . . Angela Keneally, the stick! . . . You do not want to go to the bathroom, Angela. It's only five minutes since you were there before. I will not let Father Hamilton come up to you at all unless you go to bed at once."

In the children's bedroom, Jackson gave a finger to a stolid-looking infant, who instantly stuffed it into his mouth and began to chew it, apparently under the impression that he would be bound to reach sugar at last.

Later, they sat over their drinks in the sitting room, only interrupted by Angela Keneally, in a fever of curiosity, dropping in every five minutes to ask for a biscuit or a glass of water.

"You see, Father Fogarty left no will," Jackson explained to Keneally. "Consequently, he'll be buried here tomorrow unless something turns up. I suppose he told you where he wanted to be buried?"

"On the Island? Twenty times, if he told us once. I thought he took it too far. Didn't you, father?"

"And me not to be able to go!" Mrs. Keneally said, beginning to cry. "Isn't it awful, father?"

"He didn't leave anything in writing with you?" He saw in Keneally's eyes that the letter was really only about the picture, and raised a warning hand. "Mind, if he did, I don't want to know what's in it! In fact, it would be highly improper for anyone to be told before the parish priest and the next of kin were consulted. All I do want to know is whether"—he waited a moment to see that Keneally was following him—"he did leave any written instructions, of any kind, with you."

Mrs. Keneally, drying her tears, suddenly broke into rapid speech. "Sure, that was the day poor Father Jerry was so down in himself because we were his friends and he had nothing to leave us, and—"

"Shut up, woman!" her husband shouted with a glare at her, and then Jackson saw him purse his lips in quiet amusement. He was a man after Jackson's heart. "As you say, father, we have a letter from him."

"Addressed to anybody in particular?"

"Yes, to the parish priest, to be delivered after his death."

"Did he use those words?" Jackson asked, touched in spite of himself.

"Those very words."

"God help us!" said Father Hamilton.

"But you had not time to deliver it?"

"I only heard of Father Fogarty's death when I got in. Esther was at the church, of course."

"And you're a bit tired, so you wouldn't want to walk all the way over to the presbytery with it. I take it that, in the normal way, you'd post it."

"But the post would be gone," Keneally said with a secret smile. "So that Father Hanafey wouldn't get it until maybe the day after tomorrow. That's what you were afraid of, father, isn't it?"

"I see we understand one another, Mr. Keneally," Jackson said politely.

"You wouldn't, of course, wish to say anything that wasn't strictly true," said Keneally, who was clearly enjoying himself enormously, though his wife had not the faintest idea of what was afoot. "So perhaps it would be better if the letter was posted now, and not after you leave the house."

"Fine!" said Jackson, and Keneally nodded and went out. When he returned, a few minutes later, the priests rose to go.

"I'll see you at the Mass tomorrow," Keneally said. "Good luck, now."

Jackson felt they'd probably need it. But when Father Hanafey met them in the hall, with the wet snow falling outside, and they explained about the letter, his mood had clearly changed. Jackson's logic might have worked some sort of spell on him, or perhaps it was just that he felt they were three clergymen opposed to a layman.

"It was very unforeseen of Mr. Keneally not to have brought that letter to me at once," he grumbled, "but I must say I was expecting something of the sort. It would have been very peculiar if Father Fogarty had left no instructions at all for me, and I see that we can't just sit round and wait to find out what they were, since the burial is tomorrow. Under the circumstances, father, I think we'd be justified in arranging for the funeral according to Father Fogarty's known wishes."

"Thanks be to God," Father Hamilton murmured as he and Father Jackson returned to the curates' house. "I never thought we'd get away with that."

"We haven't got away with it yet," said Jackson. "And even if we do get away with it, the real trouble will be later."

All the arrangements had still to be made. When Mr. Fogarty was informed, he slammed down the receiver without comment. Then a phone call had to be made to a police station twelve miles from the Island, and the police sergeant promised to send a man out on a bicycle to have the grave opened. Then the local parish priest and several old friends had to be informed, and a notice inserted in the nearest daily. As Jackson said wearily, romantic men always left their more worldly friends to carry out their romantic intentions.

THE SCENE at the curates' house next morning after Mass scared even Jackson. While the hearse and the funeral car waited in front of the door, Mr. Fogarty sat, white with anger, and let the priests talk. To Jackson's surprise, Father Hanafey put up a stern fight for Father Fogarty's wishes.

"You have to realize, Mr. Fogarty, that to a priest like your brother the Mass is a very solemn thing indeed, and a place where the poor people had to fly in the Penal Days to hear Mass would be one of particular sanctity."

"Father Hanafey," said Mr. Fogarty in a cold, even tone, "I am a simple businessman, and I have no time for sentiment."

"I would not go so far as to call the veneration for sanctified ground mere sentiment, Mr. Fogarty," the old priest said severely. "At any rate, it is now clear that Father Fogarty left instructions to be delivered to me after his death, and if those instructions are what we think them, I would have a serious responsibility for not having paid attention to them."

"I do not think that letter is anything of the kind, Father Hanafey," said Mr. Fogarty. "That's a matter I'm going to inquire into when I get back, and if it turns out to be a hoax, I am going to take it further."

"Oh, Mr. Fogarty, I'm sure it's not a hoax," said the parish priest, with a shocked air, but Mr. Fogarty was not convinced.

"For everybody's sake, we'll hope not," he said grimly.

The funeral procession set off. Mr. Fogarty sat in the front of the car by the driver, sulking. Jackson and Hamilton sat behind and opened their breviaries. When they stopped at a hotel for lunch, Mr. Fogarty said he was not hungry, and stayed outside in the cold. And when he did get hungry and came into the dining room, the priests drifted into the lounge to wait for him. They both realized that he might prove a dangerous enemy.

Then, as they drove on in the dusk, they saw the mountain country ahead of them in a cold, watery light, a light that seemed to fall dead from the ragged edge of a cloud. The towns and villages they passed through were dirtier and more derelict. They drew up at a crossroads, behind the hearse, and heard someone talking to the driver of the hearse. Then a car fell into line behind them. "Someone joining us," Father Hamilton said, but Mr. Fogarty, lost in his own dream of martyrdom, did not reply. Half a dozen times within the next twenty minutes, the same thing happened, though sometimes the cars were waiting in lanes and byroads with their lights on, and each time Jackson saw a heavily coated figure standing in the roadway shouting to the hearse driver: "Is it Father Fogarty ye have there?" At last they came to a village where the local parish priest's car was waiting outside the church, with a little group about it. Their headlights caught a public-house, isolated at the other side of the street, glaring with whitewash, while about it was the vague space of a distant mountainside.

Suddenly Mr. Fogarty spoke. "He seems to have been fairly well known," he said with something approaching politeness.

The road went on, with a noisy stream at the right-hand side of it falling from group to group of rocks. They left it for a byroad, which bent to the right, heading toward the stream, and then began to mount, broken by ledges of naked rock, over which hearse and cars seemed to heave themselves like animals. On the left-hand side of the road was a little whitewashed cottage, all lit up, with a big turf fire burning in the open hearth and an oil lamp with an orange glow on the wall above it. There was a man standing by the door, and as they approached he began to pick his way over the rocks towards them, carrying a lantern. Only then did Jackson notice the other lanterns and flashlights, coming down the mountain or crossing the stream, and realize that they represented people, young men and girls and an occasional sturdy old man, all moving in the direction of the Mass Island. Suddenly it hit him, almost like a blow. He told himself not to be a fool, that this was no more than the desire for novelty one should expect to find in out-of-the-way places, mixed perhaps with vanity. It was all that, of course, and he knew it, but he knew, too, it was something more. He had thought when he was here with Fogarty that those people had not respected Fogarty as they respected him and the local parish priest, but he knew that for him, or even for their own parish priest, they would never turn out in midwinter, across the treacherous mountain bogs and wicked rocks. He and the parish priest would never earn more from the people of the mountains than respect; what they gave to the fat, unclerical young man who had served them with pints in the bar and egged them on to tell their old stories and bullied and ragged and even fought them was something infinitely greater.

The funeral procession stopped in a lane that ran along the edge of a lake. The surface of the lake was rough, and they could hear the splash of the water upon the stones. The two priests got out of the car and began to vest themselves, and then Mr. Fogarty got out, too. He was very nervous and hesitant.

"It's very inconvenient, and all the rest of it," he said, "but I don't want you gentlemen to think that I didn't know you were acting from the best motives."

"That's very kind of you, Mr. Fogarty," Jackson said. "Maybe we made mistakes as well."

"Thank you, Father Jackson," Mr. Fogarty said, and held out his hand. The two priests shook hands with him and he went off, raising his hat.

"Well, that's one trouble over," Father Hamilton said wryly as an old man plunged through the mud towards the car.

"Lights is what we're looking for!" he shouted. "Let ye turn her sidewise and throw the headlights on the causeway the way we'll see what we're doing."

Their driver swore, but he reversed and turned the front of the car till it almost faced the lake. Then he turned on his headlights. Somewhere farther up the road the parish priest's car did the same. One by one, the ranked headlights blazed up, and at every moment the scene before them grew more vivid—the gateway and the stile, and beyond it the causeway that ran toward the little brown stone oratory with its mock Romanesque doorway. As the lights strengthened and steadied, the whole island became like a vast piece of theater scenery cut out against the gloomy wall of the mountain with the tiny whitewashed cottages at its base. Far above, caught in a stray flash of moonlight, Jackson saw the snow on its summit. "I'll be after you," he said to Father Hamilton, and watched him, a little perturbed and looking behind him, join the parish priest by the gate. Jackson resented being seen by them because he was weeping, and he was a man who despised tears—his own and others'. It was like a miracle, and Father Jackson didn't really believe in miracles. Standing back by the fence to let the last of the mourners pass, he saw the coffin, like gold in the brilliant light, and heard the steadying voices of the four huge mountainy men who carried it. He saw it sway above the heads, shawled and bare, glittering between the little stunted holly bushes and hazels.

There Is a Lone House

THE WOMAN stood at the foot of the lane, her right hand resting on the gate, her left fumbling at the neck of her blouse. Her face was lined, particularly about mouth and forehead; it was a face that rarely smiled, but was soft for all that, and plump and warm. She was quite gray.

From a distance, this made her seem old; close at hand it had precisely the opposite effect, and tended to emphasize sharply what youthfulness still lingered in her, so that one thought of her as having suffered terribly at some time in the past.

The man came down the road, whistling a reel, the crisp, sprinkled notes of which were like the dripping of water in a cistern. She could hear his footsteps from a long way off, keeping irregular time to the elfin music, and drew aside a whitehorn bush by the gateway to watch him from cover. Apparently satisfied by her inspection, she kicked away the stone that held the gate in place, and, as he drew level with her, stepped out into the roadway. When he saw her he stopped, bringing down his ash plant with a twirl, but she did not look up.

"Morrow, ma'am," he cried jovially.

Then she did look up, and a helpless blush that completely and utterly belied the apparent calculation of her previous behavior flowed over her features, giving them a sudden, startling freshness. "Good morrow and good luck," she answered in a low voice.

"Is it far to Ballysheery, ma'am?"

" 'Tis seven miles."

"Seven Irish, ma'am?"

"Seven English."

"That's better."

She drew her tongue across her lips to moisten them. The man was young. He was decently dressed, but flaunted a rough, devil-may-care expression. He wore no hat, and his dark hair was all a tangle. You were struck by the length of his face, darkened by hot June suns; the high-boned nose jutting out rather too far, the irregular, discolored teeth, the thick cracked lips, the blue eyes so far apart under his narrow, bony forehead that they seemed to sink back into the temples. A craggy face with high cheekbones, all hills and hollows, it was rendered extraordinarily mobile by the unexpected shadows that caught it here and there as the pale eyes drew it restlessly about. She judged him to be about twenty-six or seven.

"You seemed to be belting it out fine enough."

"How's that, ma'am?"

"I heard you whistling."

"That's to encourage the feet, ma'am. . . . You'll pardon my asking, is there any place around a man would get a cup of tea, ma'am?"

"There's no one would grudge you that, surely."

Another would have detected the almost girlish timidity of the answer, but not he. He appeared both puzzled and disappointed.

"I'll go a bit farther so," he said stiffly.

"What hurry is on you?"

" 'Tis my feet gets cramped."

"If you come with me you can rest them a while."

"God increase you, ma'am," he replied.

They went up the boreen together. The house was on top of a hill, and behind it rose the mountainside, studded with rocks. There were trees about it, and in front a long garden with a hedge of fuchsia, at one side of which ran a stream. There were four or five apple trees, and beside the kitchen garden were a few flower-beds with a profusion of tall snapdragon, yellow, red and white.

She put on the kettle and turned the wheel of the bellows. The kitchen filled with blue turf smoke, and the man sat beside the door, almost invisible behind a brilliant column of dust motes, whirling spirally in the evening sunlight. But his hands lay on his knees in a pool of light, great brown hands with knuckles like polished stones. Fascinated, she watched them, and as she laid the table she almost touched them for sheer pleasure. His wild eyes, blue as the turf smoke, took in everything about the kitchen with its deal table, chairs and dresser, all scrubbed white; its delft arranged with a sort of pedantic neatness that suggests the old maid.

"This is a fine, fancy place, ma'am," he said.

" 'Tis a quiet place."

" 'Tis so. The men are all away?"

"There are no men."

"Oh!"

"Only a boy that does turns for me."

"Oh!"

That was all he said before he turned to his meal. He was half-starved, she decided, as she watched him wolf the warm, crumbling bread. He saw her gray eyes fixed on him and laughed brightly.

"I has a great stroke, ma'am."

"You have, God bless you. I might have boiled you another egg."

When tea was over he sighed, stretching himself in his chair, and lit his pipe.

"Would you mind if I took off my boots, ma'am?" he asked shyly.

"Why would I? Take them off and welcome."

"My feet is crucified."

She bent and took up the boot he removed.

"No wonder. Your boots are in need of mending."

He laughed at her expressive politeness.

"Mending, ma'am? Did you say mending? They're long past praying for."

"They are, that's true. I wonder. . . . There's an old pair inside these years and years. They'd be better than the ones you have if they'd fit you."

She brought them in, good substantial boots but stiff, and a trifle large for him. Not that he was in a state to mind.

"God, but they're grand, ma'am, they're grand! One little patch now, and they'd be as good as new. Better than new, for they're a better boot than I could ever buy in a shop. Wait now! Wait!" With boyish excitement he foraged in his pockets, and from the lining of his coat produced a piece of leather. He held it up with the air of a professional conjurer. "Watch me now. Are you watching?" The leather fitted over the slight hole and he gave a whoop of joy. She found him last and hammer; he provided tacks from a paper bag in a vest pocket, and set to mending the damage with something like a tradesman's neatness.

"Is that your trade?" she asked curiously.

"One of my trades, ma'am. Cobbler, carpenter, plumber, gardener, thatcher, painter, poet; everything under the sun and moon, and nothing for long. But a cobbler is what I do be most times."

He walked the kitchen in his new boots with all a child's inconsequent pleasure. There was something childlike about him, she decided, and she liked it. He peered at the battered alarm clock on the smoky heights of the mantelpiece and sighed.

"I'd like to stop here always," he said wistfully, "but I suppose I'd better be going."

"What hurry is on you?"

"Seven miles, ma'am. Two hours. Maybe more. And I have to be in the old doss early if I want to get a place to sleep."

But he sat down once more and put a match to his pipe.

"Not, mind you, ma'am, that there's many could put me out of a warm corner if I'd a mind to stay in it. No indeed, but unless I had a drop in me I'd never fight for a place. Never. I'm apt to be cross when I'm drunk, but I never hit a man sober yet only once. That was a foxy tinker out of the Ranties, and the Ranties are notorious cross men, ma'am. You see, there was a little blind man, ma'am, trying to sleep, and this Ranty I'm talking about, whenever he saw the blind man dozing, he'd give his beard a tug. So I got that mad I rose up, and without saying as much as by your leave, I hit him such a terrible blow under the chin the blood hopped out on me in the dark. Yes, ma'am, hopped clean out on me. That was a frightful hard blow." He looked at her for approval and awe, and saw her, womanlike, draw up her shoulders and shiver. His dramatic sense was satisfied.

It was quite dark when he rose to go. The moon was rising over the hills to the left, far away, and the little stream beside the house sounded very loud in the stillness.

"If there was e'er an old barn or an outhouse," he said as if to himself.

"There's a bed inside," she answered. He looked round at her in surprise.

"Ah, I wouldn't ask to stop within," he exclaimed.

Suddenly her whole manner changed. All the brightness, if brightness it could be called, seemed to drop away from her, leaving her listless, cold and melancholy.

"Oh, please yourself," she said shortly, as if banishing him from her thoughts. But still he did not go. Instead, he sat down again, and they faced one another across the fireplace, not speaking, for he too had lost his chatter. The kitchen was in darkness except for the dwindling glow of the turf inside its cocoon of gray dust, and the wan nightlight above the half-door. Then he laughed, rubbing his palms between his knees.

"And still you know, I'd ask nothing better," he added shyly.

"What's that?"

"I'd ask nothing better than to stop."

"Go or stop as you like."

"You see," he went on, ignoring her gathering surprise, "I'm an honest fellow. I am, on my oath, though maybe you wouldn't think it, with the rough talk I have, and the life I lead. You could leave me alone with a bag of sovereigns, not counting them, and I'd keep them safe for you. And I'm just the same other ways. I'm not a bit forward. They say a dumb priest loses his benefit, and I'm just like that. I'm apt to lose me benefit for want of a bit of daring."

Then (and this time it was he who was surprised) she laughed, more with relief, he thought, than at anything he had said. She rose and closed the door, lit the lamp and hung up the heavy kettle. He leaned back in his chair with a fresh sigh of pleasure, stretching out his feet to the fire, and in that gesture she caught something of his nostalgia. He settled down gratefully to one of those unexpected benefits which are the bait with which life leads us onward.

When she rose next morning, she was surprised to find him about before her, the fire lit, and the kettle boiling. She saw how much he needed a shave, and filled out a pan of water for him. Then when he began to scrub his face with the soap, she produced a razor, strop and brush. He was enchanted with these, and praised the razor with true lyric fire.

"You can have it," she said. "Have them all if they're any use to you."

"By God, aren't they though," he exclaimed reverently.

After breakfast he lit his pipe and sat back, enjoying to the full the last moments which politeness would impose upon hospitality.

"I suppose you're anxious to be on your road?" she asked awkwardly. Immediately he reddened.

"I suppose I'm better to," he replied. He rose and looked out. It was a gray morning and still. The green stretched no farther than the hedge; beyond that lay a silver mist, flushed here and there with rose. "Though 'tis no anxiety is on me—no anxiety at all," he added with a touch of bitterness.

"Don't take me up wrong," she said hastily. "I'm not trying to hunt you. Stop and have your dinner. You'll be welcome."

"I chopped a bit of kindling for you," he replied, looking shyly at her from under lowered lids. "If there was something else I could be doing, I'd be glad enough to stop, mind you."

There was. Plenty else to be doing. For instance, there was an out-house that needed whitewashing, and blithely enough he set about his task, whistling. She came and watched him; went, and came again, standing silently beside him, a strange stiff figure in the bright sunlight, but he had no feeling of supervision. Because he had not finished when dinner was ready he stayed to tea, and even then displayed no hurry to be gone. He sang her some of his poems. There was one about Mallow Races, another about a girl he had been in love with as a boy, "the most beautiful girl that was ever seen in Kerry since the first day," so he naively told her. It began:

> I praise no princesses or queens or great ladies
>   Or figures historical noted for style,
> Or beauties of Asia or Mesopotamia,
>   But sweet Annie Bradie, the rose of Dunmoyle.

A sort of confidence had established itself between them. The evening passed quickly in talk and singing—in whistling too, for he was a good whistler, and sometimes performed for dancing: to judge by his own statements he was a great favorite at wakes and weddings and she could understand that.

It was quite dark when they stopped the conversation. Again he made as if to go, and again in her shy, cold way she offered him the chance of staying. He stayed.

FOR DAYS afterward there seemed to be some spell upon them both. A week passed in excuses and delays, each morning finding him about long before she appeared with some new suggestion, the garden to be weeded, potatoes to be dug, the kitchen to be whitewashed. Neither suggested anything but as it were from hour to hour, yet it did not occur to the man that for her as for him their companionship might be an unexpected benefit.

He did her messages to the village whenever Dan, the "boy," a sullen, rather stupid, one-eyed old man, was absent, and though she gave no sign that she did not like this, he was always surprised afresh by the faint excitement with which she greeted his return; had it been anyone else one might have called her excitement gaiety, but gay was hardly a word one could apply to her, and the emotion quickly died and gave place to a sullen apathy.

She knew the end must come soon, and it did. One evening he returned from an errand, and told her someone had died in the village. He was slightly shocked by her indifference. She would not go with him to the wake, but she bade himself go if he pleased. He did please. She could see there was an itch for company on him; he was made that way. As he polished his boots he confessed to her that among his other vocations he had tried being a Trappist monk, but stuck it only for a few months. It wasn't bad in summer, but it was the divil and all in winter, and the monks told him there were certain souls like himself the Lord called only for six months of the year (the irony of this completely escaped him).

He promised to be back before midnight, and went off very gay. By this time he had formed his own opinion of the woman. It was not for nothing she lived there alone, not for nothing a visitor never crossed the threshold. He knew she did not go to Mass, yet on Sunday when he came back unexpectedly for his stick, he had seen her, in the bedroom, saying her Rosary. Something was wrong, but he could not guess what.

Her mood was anything but gay and the evening seemed to respond to it. It was very silent after the long drought; she could hear the thrush's beak go tip-tap among the stones like a fairy's hammer. It was making for rain. To the northwest the wind had piled up massive archways of purple cloud like a ruined cloister, and through them one's eyes passed on to vistas of feathery cloudlets, violet and gold, packed thick upon one another. A cold wind had sprung up: the trees creaked, and the birds flew by, their wings blown up in a gesture of horror. She stood for a long while looking at the sky, until it faded, chilled by the cold wind. There was something mournful and sinister about it all.

It was quite dark when she went in. She sat over the fire and waited.

At half past eleven she put down the kettle and brewed herself tea. She told herself she was not expecting him, but still she waited. At half past twelve she stood at the door and listened for footsteps. The wind had risen, and her mind filled slowly with its childish sobbing and with the harsh gushing of the stream beside the house. Then it began to rain. To herself she gave him until one. At one she relented and gave him another half-hour, and it was two before she quenched the light and went to bed. She had lost him, she decided.

She started when an hour or more later she heard his footsteps up the path. She needed no one to tell her he was alone and drunk: often before she had waited for the footsteps of a drunken old man. But instead of rushing to the door as she would have done long ago, she waited.

He began to moan drowsily to himself. She heard a thud followed by gusty sighing; she knew he had fallen. Everything was quiet for a while. Then there came a bang at the door which echoed through the house like a revolver shot, and something fell on the flagstones outside. Another bang and again silence. She felt no fear, only a coldness in her bowels.

Then the gravel scraped as he staggered to his feet. She glanced at the window. She could see his head outlined against it, his hands against its frame. Suddenly the voice rose in a wail that chilled her blood.

"What will the soul do at the judgment? Ah, what will the soul do? I will say to ye, 'Depart from me into everlasting fire that was prepared for the divil and his angels. Depart from me, depart!' "

It was like a scream of pain, but immediately upon it came a low chuckle of malice. The woman's fists clenched beneath the clothes. "Never again," she said to herself aloud, "never again!"

"Do you see me, do you?" he shouted. "Do you see me?"

"I see you," she whispered to herself.

"For ye, for ye, I reddened the fire," went on the man, dropping back into his whine, "for ye, for ye, I dug the pit. The black bitch on the hill, let ye torment her for me, ye divils. Forever, forever! Gather round, ye divils, gather round, and let me see ye roast the black bitch that killed a man. . . . Do you hear me, do you?"

"I hear you," she whispered.

"Listen to me!"

> "When the old man was sleeping
> She rose up from her bed,
> And crept into his lone bedroom

> And cruelly struck him dead;
> 'Twas with a hammer she done the deed,
> May God it her repay,
> And then she . . . then she . . .'

"How does it go? I have it.

> And then she lifted up the body
> And hid it in the hay."

Suddenly a stone came crashing through the window and a cold blast followed it. "Never again," she cried, hammering the bedframe with her fists, "dear God, never again." She heard the footsteps stumbling away. She knew he was running. It was like a child's malice and terror.

She rose and stuffed the window with a rag. Day was breaking. When she went back to bed she was chilled and shaken. Despairing of rest, she rose again, lit a candle and blew up the fire.

But even then some unfamiliar feeling was stirring at her heart. She felt she was losing control of herself and was being moved about like a chessman. Sighing, she slipped her feet into heavy shoes, threw an old coat about her shoulders, and went to the door. As she crossed the threshold she stumbled over something. It was a boot; another was lying some little distance away. Something seemed to harden within her. She placed the boots inside the door and closed it. But again came the faint thrill at her heart, so light it might have been a fluttering of untried wings and yet so powerful it shook her from head to foot, so that almost before she had closed the door she opened it again and went out, puzzled and trembling, into a cold noiseless rain. She called the man in an extraordinarily gentle voice as though she were afraid of being heard; then she made the circle of the farmhouse, a candle sheltered in the palm of her hand.

He was lying in the outhouse he had been whitewashing. She stood and looked down at him for a moment, her face set in a grim mask of disgust. Then she laid down the candle and lifted him, and at that moment an onlooker would have been conscious of her great physical strength. Half lifting, half guiding him, she steered the man to the door. On the doorstep he stood and said something to her, and immediately, with all her strength, she struck him across the mouth. He staggered and swore at her, but she caught him again and pushed him across the threshold. Then she went back for the candle, undressed him and put him to bed.

It was bright morning when she had done.

That day he lay on in bed, and came into the kitchen about two o'clock looking sheepish and sullen. He was wearing his own ragged boots.

"I'm going now," he said stiffly.

"Please yourself," she answered coolly. "Maybe you'd be better."

He seemed to expect something more, and because she said nothing he felt himself being put subtly in the wrong. This was not so surprising, because even she was impressed by her own nonchalance that seemed to have come suddenly to her from nowhere.

"Well?" he asked, and his look seemed to say, "Women are the divil and all!" One could read him like a book.

"Well?"

"Have you nothing to say for yourself?"

"Have you nothing to say for yourself?" she retorted. "I had enough of your blackguarding last night. You won't stop another hour in this house unless you behave yourself, mark me well, you won't."

He grew very red.

"That's strange," he answered sulkily.

"What's strange?"

"The likes of you saying that to me."

"Take it or leave it. And if you don't like it, there's the door."

Still he lingered. She knew now she had him at her mercy, and the nonchalance dropped from her.

"Aren't you a queer woman?" he commented, lighting his pipe. "One'd think you wouldn't have the face to talk like that to an honest man. Have you no shame?"

"Listen to who's talking of shame," she answered bitterly. "A pity you didn't see yourself last night, lying in your dirt like an old cow. And you call yourself a man. How ready you were with your stones!"

"It was the shock," he said sullenly.

"It was no shock. It was drink."

"It was the shock I tell you. I was left an orphan with no one to tell me the badness of the world."

"I was left an orphan too. And I don't go round crying about the badness of the world."

"Oh, Christ, don't remind me what you were. 'Tis only myself, the poor fool, wouldn't know, and all the old chat I had about the man I drew blood from, as if I was a terrible fellow entirely. I might have known to see a handsome woman living lonely that she wouldn't be that way only no man in Ireland would look at the side of the road she walked on."

He did not see how the simple flattery of his last words went through her, quickening her with pleasure; he noticed only the savage retort she gave him, for the sense of his own guilt was growing stronger in him at every moment. Her silence was in part the cause of that; her explanation would have been his triumph. That at least was how he had imagined it. He had not been prepared for this silence which drew him like a magnet. He could not decide to go, yet his fear of her would not allow him to remain. The day passed like that. When twilight came she looked across at him and asked:

"Are you going or stopping?"

"I'm stopping, if you please," he answered meekly.

"Well, I'm going to bed. One sleepless night is enough for me."

And she went, leaving him alone in the kitchen. Had she delayed until darkness fell, he would have found it impossible to remain, but there was no suspicion of this in her mind. She understood only that people might hate her; that they might fear her never entered her thoughts.

An hour or so later she looked for the candle and remembered that she had left it in his room. She rose and knocked at his door. There was no answer. She knocked again. Then she pushed in the door and called him. She was alarmed. The bed was empty. She laid her hand to the candle (it was lying still where she had left it, on the dresser beside the door) but as she did so she heard his voice, husky and terrified.

"Keep away from me! Keep away from me, I tell you!"

She could discern his figure now. He was standing in a corner, his little white shirt half-way up his thighs, his hand grasping something, she did not see what. It was some little while before the explanation dawned on her, and with it came a sudden feeling of desolation within her.

"What ails you?" she asked gently. "I was only looking for the candle."

"Don't come near me!" he cried.

She lit the candle, and as he saw her there, her face as he had never seen it before, stricken with pain, his fear died away. A moment later she was gone, and the back door slammed behind her. It was only then he realized what his insane fear had brought him to, and the obsession of his own guilt returned with a terrible clarity. He walked up and down the little room in desperation.

Half an hour later he went to her room. The candle was burning on a chair beside the bed. She lifted herself on the pillow and looked at him with strangely clear eyes.

"What is it?" she asked.

"I'm sorry," he answered. "I shouldn't be here at all. I'm sorry. I'm queer. I'll go in the morning and I won't trouble you anymore."

"Never mind," she said, and held out her hand to him. He came closer and took it timidly. "You wouldn't know."

"God pity me," he said. "I was distracted. You know I was distracted. You were so good to me, and that's the way I paid you out. But I was going out of my mind. I couldn't sleep."

"Sure you couldn't." She drew him down to her until his head was resting on the pillow, and made him lie beside her.

"I couldn't, I couldn't," he said into her ear. "I wint raving mad. And I thought whin you came into the room—"

"I know, I know."

"I did, whatever came over me."

"I know." He realized that she was shivering all over.

She drew back the clothes from him. He was eager to explain, to tell her about himself, his youth, the death of his father and mother, his poverty, his religious difficulties, his poetry. What was wrong with him was, he was wild; could stick to no trade, could never keep away from drink.

"You were wild yourself," he said.

"Fifteen years ago. I'm tame now in earnest."

"Tell me about it," he said eagerly, "talk to me, can't you? Tell me he was bad. Tell me he was a cruel old uncle to you. Tell me he beat you. He used to lock you up for days, usedn't he, to keep you away from boys? He must have been bad or you'd never had done what you did, and you only a girl."

But still she said nothing. Bright day was in the room when he fell asleep, and for a long while she lay, her elbow on the pillow, her hand covering her left breast, while she looked at him. His mouth was wide open, his irregular teeth showed in a faint smile. Their shyness had created a sort of enchantment about them, and she watched over his sleep with something like ecstasy, ecstasy which disappeared when he woke, to find her the same hard quiet woman he knew.

AFTER THAT she ceased making his bed in the small room, and he slept with her. Not that it made any difference to their relations. Between them after those few hours of understanding persisted a fierce, unbroken shyness, the shyness of lonely souls. If it rasped the nerves of either, there was no open sign of it, unless a curiously irritable tenderness revealed anything of their thoughts. She was forever finding things done for her; there was no longer any question of his going, and he worked from morning until late night with an energy and intelligence that surprised her. But she knew he felt the lack of company, and one evening she went out to him as he worked in the garden.

"Why don't you go down to the village now?" she asked.

"Ah, what would I be doing there?" But it was clear that it had been on his mind at that very moment.

"You might drop in for a drink and a chat."

"I might do that," he agreed.

"And why don't you?"

"Me? I'd be ashamed."

"Ashamed? Ashamed of what? There's no one will say anything to you. And if they do, what are you, after all, but a working man?"

It was clear that this excuse had not occurred to him, but it would also have been clear to anyone else that she would have thought poorly of such as gave it credit. So he got his coat and went.

It was late when he came in, and she saw he had drunk more than his share. His face was flushed and he laughed too easily. For two days past a bottle of whiskey had been standing on the dresser (what a change for her!) but if he had noticed it he had made no sign. Now he went directly to it and poured himself out a glass.

"You found it," she said with a hint of bitterness.

"What's that?"

"You found it, I say."

"Of course I did. Have a drop yourself."

"No."

"Do. Just a drop."

"I don't want it."

He crossed to her, stood behind her chair for a moment; then he bent over and kissed her. She had been expecting it, but on the instant she revolted.

"Don't do that again," she said appealingly, wiping her mouth.

"You don't mind me, do you?" he sniggered, still standing behind her.

"I do. I mind it when you're drunk."

"Well, here's health."

"Don't drink any more of that."

"Here's health."

"Good health."

"Take a drop yourself, do."

"No, I tell you," she answered angrily.

"By God, you must."

He threw one arm about her neck and deliberately spilt the whiskey between her breasts. She sprang up and threw him away from her. Whatever had been in her mind was now forgotten in her loathing.

"Bad luck to you!" she cried savagely.

"I'm sorry," he said quickly. "I didn't mean it." Already he was growing afraid.

"You didn't mean it," she retorted mockingly. "Who thought you to do it then? Was it Jimmie Dick? What sort of woman do you think I am, you fool? You sit all night in a public-house talking of me, and when you come back you try to make me out as loose and dirty as your talk."

"Who said I was talking of you?"

"I say it."

"Then you're wrong."

"I'm not wrong. Don't I know you, you poor sheep? You sat there, letting them make you out a great fellow, because they thought you were like themselves and thought I was a bitch, and you never as much as opened your mouth to give them the lie. You sat there and gaped and bragged. That's what you are."

"That's not true."

"And then you come strutting back, stuffed with drink, and think I'll let you make love to me, so that you can have something to talk about in the public-house."

Her eyes were bright with tears of rage. She had forgotten that something like this was what she knew would happen when she made him go to the village, so little of our imagination can we bear to see made real. He sank into a chair, and put his head between his hands in sulky dignity. She lit the candle and went off to bed.

She fell asleep and woke to hear him stirring in the kitchen. She rose and flung open the door. He was still sitting where she had seen him last.

"Aren't you going to bed at all tonight?" she asked.

"I'm sorry if I disturbed you," he replied. The drunkenness had gone, and he did look both sorry and miserable. "I'll go now."

"You'd better. Do you see the time?"

"Are you still cross? I'm sorry, God knows I am."

"Never mind."

" 'Twas all true."

"What was true?" She had already forgotten.

"What you said. They were talking about you, and I listened."

"Oh, that."

"Only you were too hard on me."

"Maybe I was."

She took a step forward. He wondered if she had understood what he was saying at all.

"I was fond of you all right."

"Yes," she said.

"You know I was."

"Yes."

She was like a woman in a dream. She had the same empty feeling within her, the same sense of being pushed about like a chessman, as on the first night when she carried him in. He put his arm about her and kissed her. She shivered and clung to him, life suddenly beginning to stir within her.

ONE DAY, some weeks later, he told her he was going back home on a visit; there were cousins he wished to see; something or other; she was not surprised. She had seen the restlessness on him for some time past and had no particular belief in the cousins. She set about preparing a parcel of food for him, and in this little attention there was something womanly that touched him.

"I'll be back soon," he said, and meant it. He could be moved easily enough in this fashion, and she saw through him. It was dull being the lover of a woman like herself; he would be best married to a lively girl of eighteen or so, a girl he could go visiting with and take pride in.

"You're always welcome," she said. "The house is your own."

As he went down the boreen he was saying to himself "She'll be lost! She'll be lost!" but he would have spared his pity if he had seen how she took it.

Her mood shifted from busy to idle. At one hour she was working in the garden, singing, at another she sat in the sun, motionless and silent for a long, long time. As weeks went by and the year drifted into a rainy autumn, an astonishing change took place in her, slowly, almost imperceptibly. It seemed a physical rather than a spiritual change. Line by line her features divested themselves of strain, and her body seemed to fall into easier, more graceful curves. It would not be untrue to say she scarcely thought of the man, unless it was with some slight relief to find herself alone again. Her thoughts were all contracted within herself.

ONE AUTUMN evening he came back. For days she had been expecting him; quite suddenly she had realized that he would return, that everything was not over between them, and very placidly accepted the fact.

He seemed to have grown older and maturer in his short absence; one felt it less in his words than in his manner. There was decision in it. She saw that he was rapidly growing into a deferred manhood, and was secretly proud of the change. He had a great fund of stories about his wanderings (never a word of the mythical cousins); and while she prepared his supper, she listened to him, smiling faintly, almost as if she were not listening at all. He was as hungry now as the first evening she met him, but everything was easier between them; he was glad to be there and she to have him.

"Are you pleased I came?" he asked.

"You know I'm pleased."

"Were you thinking I wouldn't come?"

"At first I thought you wouldn't. You hadn't it in your mind to come back. But afterward I knew you would."

"A man would want to mind what he thinks about a woman like you," he grumbled good-humoredly. "Are you a witch?"

"How would I be a witch?" Her smile was attractive.

"Are you?" he gripped her playfully by the arm.

"I am not and well you know it."

"I have me strong doubts of you. Maybe you'll say now you know what happened? Will you? Did you ever hear of a man dreaming three times of a crock of gold? Well, that's what happened me. I dreamt three times of you. What sign is that?"

"A sign you were drinking too much."

" 'Tis not. I know what sign it is."

He drew his chair up beside her own, and put his arm about her. Then he drew her face round to his and kissed her. At that moment she could feel very clearly the change in him. His hand crept about her neck and down her breast, releasing the warm smell of her body.

"That's enough love-making," she said. She rose quickly and shook off his arm. A strange happy smile like a newly open flower lingered where he had kissed her. "I'm tired. Your bed is made in there."

"My bed?"

She nodded.

"You're only joking me. You are, you divil, you're only joking."

His arms out, he followed her, laughing like a lad of sixteen. He caught at her, but she forced him off again. His face altered suddenly, became sullen and spiteful.

"What is it?"

"Nothing."

" 'Tis a change for you."

" 'Tis."

"And for why?"

"For no why. Isn't it enough for you to know it?"

"Is it because I wint away?"

"Maybe."

"Is it?"

"I don't know whether 'tis or no."

"And didn't I come back as I said I would?"

"You did. When it suited you."

"The divil is in ye all," he said crossly.

Later he returned to the attack; he was quieter and more persuasive; there was more of the man in him, but she seemed armed at every point. He experienced an acute sense of frustration. He had felt growing in him this new, lusty manhood, and returned with the intention of dominating her, only to find she too had grown, and still outstripped him. He lay awake for a long time, thinking it out, but when he rose next morning the barrier between them seemed to have disappeared. As ever she was dutiful, unobtrusive; by day at any rate she was all he would have her to be. Even when he kissed her she responded; of his hold on her he had no doubt, but he seemed incapable of taking advantage of it.

That night when he went to bed he began to think again of it, and rage grew in him until it banished all hope of sleep. He rose and went into her room.

"How long is this going to last?" he asked thickly.

"What?"

"This. How long more are you going to keep me out?"

"Maybe always," she said softly, as if conjuring up the prospect.

"Always?"

"Maybe."

"Always? And what in hell do you mean by it? You lure me into it, and then throw me away like an old boot."

"Did I lure you into it?"

"You did. Oh, you fooled me right enough at the time, but I've been thinking about it since. 'Twas no chance brought you on the road the first day I passed."

"Maybe I did," she admitted. She was stirred again by the quickness of his growth. "If I did you had nothing to complain of."

"Haven't I now?"

"Now is different."

"Why? Because I wint away?"

"Because you didn't think me good enough for you."

"That's a lie. You said that before, and you know 'tis a lie."

"Then show it."

He sat on the bed and put his face close to hers.

"You mean, to marry you?"

"Yes."

"You know I can't."

"What hinders you?"

"For a start, I have no money. Neither have you."

"There's money enough."

"Where would it come from?"

"Never you mind where 'twould come from. 'Tis there."

He looked at her hard.

"You planned it well," he said at last. "They said he was a miser. . . . Oh, Christ, I can't marry you!"

"The divil send you better meat than mutton," she retorted coarsely.

He sat on the edge of the bed, his big hand caressing her cheek and bare shoulder.

"Why don't you tell the truth?" she asked. "You have no respect for me."

"Why do you keep on saying that?"

"Because 'tis true." In a different voice she added: "Nor I hadn't for myself till you went away. Take me now or leave me. . . . Stop that, you fool!"

"Listen to me—"

"Stop that then! I'm tame now, but I'm not tame enough for that."

Even in the darkness she could feel that she had awakened his old dread of her; she put her arms about his head, drew him down to her, and whispered in his ear.

"Now do you understand?" she said.

A FEW DAYS later he got out the cart and harnessed the pony. They drove into the town three miles away. As they passed through the village people came to their doors to look after them. They left the cart a little outside the town, and, following country practice, separated to meet again on the priest's doorstep. The priest was at home, and he listened incredulously to the man's story.

"You know I'll have to write to your parish priest first," he said severely.

"I know," said the man. "You'll find and see he have nothing against me."

The priest was shaken.

"And this woman has told you everything?"

"She told me nothing. But I know."

"About her uncle?"

"About her uncle," repeated the man.

"And you're satisfied to marry her, knowing that?"

"I'm satisfied."

"It's all very strange," said the priest wearily. "You know," he added to the woman, "Almighty God has been very merciful to you. I hope you are conscious of all He in His infinite mercy has done for you, who deserve it so little."

"I am. From this out I'll go to Mass regularly."

"I hope," he repeated emphatically, "you are fully conscious of it. If I thought there was any lightness in you, if I thought for an instant that you wouldn't make a good wife to this man, my conscience wouldn't allow me to marry you. Do you understand that?"

"Never fear," she said, without lifting her eyes. "I'll make him a good wife. And he knows it."

The man nodded. "I know it," he said.

The priest was impressed by the solemn way in which she spoke. She was aware that the strength which had upheld her till now was passing from her to the young man at her side; the future would be his.

From the priest's they went to the doctor's. He saw her slip on a ring before they entered. He sat in the room while the doctor examined her. When she had dressed again her eyes were shining. The strength was passing from her, and she was not sorry to see it pass. She laid a sovereign on the table.

"Oho," exclaimed the doctor, "how did you come by this?" The man started and the woman smiled.

"I earned it hard," she answered.

The doctor took the coin to the window and examined it.

"By Jove," he said, "it's not often I see one of these."

"Maybe you'll see more of them," she said with a gay laugh. He looked at her from under his eyes and laughed too; her brightness had a strange other-world attraction.

"Maybe I will," he replied. "In a few months' time, eh? Sorry I can't give you change in your own coin. Ah, well! Good luck, anyway. And call me in as often as you please."

The Story Teller

AFRIC and Nance went up the mountain, two little girls in shapeless, colorless smocks of coarse frieze. With them went the lamb. Afric had found it on the mountain, and it insisted on accompanying her everywhere. It was an idiotic, astonished animal which stopped dead and bucked and scampered entirely without reason.

It was drawing on to dusk. Shadow was creeping up the mountain. First light faded from the sea, then from the rocks, then from the roadway and the fields. Soon it would dwindle from the bog; everything there would fill with rich color and the long channels of dark bogwater would burn like mirrors between the purple walls of turf. Behind each of the channels was ranged a file of turf stacks, black sods heaped to dry and looking like great pine cones.

"And the priest came," continued Nance, pursuing a litany.

"And what did he say?"

"He said—he said Grandfather would die tonight."

"You said 'twas the doctor said that."

"The priest said it, too."

"Hike, you divil!" yelled Afric. The lamb had walked straight up to the edge of a bog pool, bent down in innocent rapture and then tossed itself high into the air and off sideways like a crow.

"And Mom said you were to stop talking about the boat."

"What boat?"

"The boat you said would come for Grandfather. Mom said there was no boat."

"There is a boat. Grandfather said it. And lights."

"Mom said there's no lights either."

"Mom doesn't know. Grandfather knows better."

"Mom said Grandfather didn't mean it."

"Ha!" said Afric scornfully.

" 'Tis true."

"And I suppose he didn't mean about Shaun O'Mullarkey and the

Sprid either. Or about Con of the fairies and the Demon Hurler. Or about the Gillygooley. Or the Gawley Cullawney and his mother."

"Mom said," continued Nance in the tone of one reciting a lesson, "that 'twould be better for Grandfather now if he hadn't so much old stories and paid heed to his prayers when he had the chance."

"Grandfather always said his prayers. Grandfather knew more prayers than Mom."

"Mom said he told barbarous stories."

"But if they were true?"

"Mom says they weren't true, that they were all lies, and that God punishes people for telling lies and that's why Grandfather is afraid to die. He's afraid of what God will do to him for telling lies."

"Ha!" sniffed Afric again, but with less confidence. The mountain did not inspire confidence. The shadow, quickening its mighty motion, rose before them among the naked rocks. Two tiny stars came out, vibrating in the green sky. A pair of horses, heads down before them, suddenly took fright and rushed away with a great snorting, their manes tossing and loose stones flying from their hooves. To the right, a cliff, a pale veil dropped sheer to the edge of a dark lake, and from its foot the land went down in terraces of gray stone to the sea's edge, a ghost-pale city without lights or sound.

It was queer, Afric thought, the way Grandfather had stopped telling them stories all at once, the way he seemed to fix his eyes on the wall. Even when she had asked him about the boat he had only muttered, "Whisht, child, whisht!" But all the same Afric knew that Mom must be wrong. Grandfather had meant it all. There must be some other reason for his silence.

"Maybe death will come like a travelling man, like it came to some," she said thoughtfully. "A man with long, long legs and a bandage over his eyes. Maybe that's why Grandfather would be afraid—a big man the size of a mountain. I'd be afraid of him myself, I'm thinking."

It was almost dark when they reached the mountain top. There was a cold wind there, the grasses swayed and whistled, and their bare feet squelched calf-deep in the quaggy ground with its almost invisible hollows. Plunging on, they lost sight of the sea. The other side of the mountain came into view. A chain of lakes with edges like the edges of countries on the maps in school shone out of all the savage darkness, and beyond them, very far away, another inlet of the sea.

They almost failed to see the fire. It was in a deep natural hollow. It burned under a curiously shaped metal drum. On top of the drum was another metal container, narrow below and broad above like a bucket, and a jointed pipe led from this into a barrel with a tap on it. Under the tap was a mug covered by a strip of muslin. Four children were solemnly seated on the edge of the pit looking down on this queer contraption, their bare legs dangling in the firelight, their faces and heads in shadow. They were not speaking but looking with fascinated, solemn eyes at the still. Afric's father was standing before it, his hands in his trouser pockets. He was a tall, handsome man, big-shouldered, broad-chested, with a wide gray kindly face and gray eyes, but now he seemed melancholy and withdrawn.

"What way is your grandfather?" he asked.

"Mom said to tell you there was no change," said Nance.

Nance and Afric sat within the hollow out of the wind so that the heads and shoulders of the other children rose up on every side against the starlit sky like idols grouped in a circle. The lamb seemed to take the greatest interest in the whole proceedings, sniffed at the turf, the tub, the barrel, backed away from them, staggered to the mouth of the hollow and scampered back as though horribly shocked by something, licked the legs of the little girls and gazed with blank eyes into the fire. Its antics caused a sudden diversion among the four other children; they laughed without restraint. Then, as though they had grown self-conscious, they fell silent. Two wiped their noses in the sleeves of their little frieze jackets. Then they rose and went off silently down the mountain. After a few moments the other two did exactly the same thing. It was growing dark.

Then their Uncle Padraic came, and, standing against the sky, leaned on a turf-cutting spade. You nearly always saw Padraic leaning on something; a wall, a turf-rick, the pillar of a gate—there always seemed to be something for Padraic to lean on. Whatever it was, his whole body fell lifelessly about it. He stood like that now against the sky, his hands resting in a crossed position on the handle, his chin resting on his hands. He was a tall, gaunt, gentle man, wearing a frieze vest without sleeves over a knitted gansey and very much patched frieze trousers. He didn't say anything, but seemed to breathe out an atmosphere of tranquility. It looked as if he could go on leaning forever without opening his mouth.

"Himself is the same way," said their father.

Padraic spat sideways and rested his chin again upon his crossed hands.

"He is."

They fell silent again. Their father dipped a mug in the barrel of ale and passed it up to his brother-in-law. Padraic drank and carefully emptied the mug onto the ground before returning it.

"One of ye better go for more turf," said their father.

"I will," said Afric. "Keep a hold on the lamb, Nance."

She took the bag and began to run down the mountain. It was a high hollow starry night full of strange shadows. From behind her she heard Nance's cry of distress, and a few moments later something warm and white and woolly came between her flying feet and nearly threw her. She flung herself head foremost on the soft turf, rolling round and round downhill, while the lamb rolled idiotically on top of her, its warm nose seeking her face. There was a smell of earth and grass which made her drunk. She boxed the lamb's ears, caught it by the budding horns, pushed, shoved, wrestled and rolled with it.

"Ah, lambeen, lambeen, lambeen! You foolish lambeen! I'm going for turf and the fairies will catch you, the fairies will catch you! Look, lambeen, they're searching for you with little lanterns!"

She filled her bag with turf. The bog was now wild and dark. The channels of bogwater were shining with inky brightness; as though the bog were all a-tremble they shook, but with a suave oily motion that barely broke the reflected starlight. Below, very far below, were a few lights along the shore.

She recognized her own house on the little spit of land that pushed out into the bay. There was light only in the west window in the room where her grandfather was lying. She could imagine all the others in the kitchen in the firelight; her mother and the baby, her mother's two sisters, old Brigid, their mother, sucking her pipe, and Padraic's children. They would be talking in low voices, and then her mother or old Brigid would go into the west room to the old man who would tell no more stories, and they would talk to him of the will of God, but still his face, pale as the little beard about his chin, would be bitter because he did not wish to die. Not wish to die and he eighty and more! And up on the mountain were she and her father, making poteen which would be drunk at the old man's wake, because he was a famous and popular man and people would come from twenty miles around on ponies and in traps to pray for his soul.

Maybe he was dying now! But Afric felt sure if he was dying there would be some sign, as there always was in the stories he told: along the road a huge man, dressed in rags, a bandage about his eyes and his hands outstretched, feeling his way to their house: all the air filled with strange lights while the spirits waited: a shining boat making its way across the dark water without a sail. Surely there would be signs like that! She looked about her furtively, suddenly trembling and all atune for the wonder. But there was nothing. Not a sound. In sudden panic she repulsed the lamb and began to run, her bag of dry sods knocking her shoulders.

It was all placid and homely up there. Padraic was sitting on an upturned tub, smoking. It was so silent you could hear the noise of the stream nearby, loud in the darkness. Her father came up from it, carrying a bucket.

"He had a long day," he said, as though continuing a conversation.

"He had a long day," agreed Padraic, not looking up. He spat and sucked his pipe again.

"He was a good man," said Afric's father.

"He was. He was a good father to you."

"He was so. 'Tis a pity he couldn't be more resigned."

" 'Twas what they were saying."

"He said a queer thing last night."

"Did he now?"

"He says a man sees the world when he comes into it and goes out of it: the rest is only foolishness—that's what he said."

" 'Tis a deep saying."

" 'Tis deep."

"But there's meaning in it," Padraic went on.

"I dare say."

"There is. He was always a deep man, a patient, long-thinking man."

Afric was astonished. She never remembered her uncle to have spoken as much.

"Do you remember," he continued, "on the boat? He never liked one of us to do a thing in a hurry. 'Mother was drowned a year ago,' he'd say, 'and she'd have been round the lake since then.' That's what he'd always say."

"He would so."

" 'Tis a pity he didn't do more with himself—a clever man."

" 'Tis. But he wouldn't stop in America."

"He wouldn't sure."

"There was nothing he cared about only the stories."

"No, then. And he was a wonder with them."

"He was. You wouldn't miss a day in a bog or a night in the boat with him. Often he'd keep you that way you wouldn't know you were hungry." Afric's father spat. It was not often he made such admissions. "And there were times we were hungry."

"You never took after him, Con."

"No, then. 'Twasn't in me, I suppose. But 'twasn't in our generation. I'd get great pleasure listening to him, but I could never tell a story myself."

"The place won't be the same without him," said Padraic, rising.

"Ye'd better go home with yeer uncle," said her father.

"I'll stop with you, Father," said Afric.

He thought for a moment.

"Do so," he said.

She knew then he was lonely.

When Padraic and Nance had gone, everything seemed lonelier than before, but she didn't mind because her father was with her. He wrapped his coat about her. The lamb snuggled up beside her. And now she let the mountain come alive with all its stories and its magic. Because she knew it was up here the spirits lived and planned their descents on the little cottages; at night you could often see them from the bay, moving across the mountain with their little lanterns. Sometimes the lights would be close together and you would know it was a fairy funeral. A man from the place, making poteen in the mountains at night, had come across just such a funeral, and the spirits had laid the coffin at his feet. He had opened it, and inside was a beautiful girl with long yellow hair. As he looked at her she had opened her eyes and he had brought her home with him. She had told him she was a girl from Tuam, and when inquiries were made it was found that a girl from Tuam had been buried that same day; but she wouldn't go back to her own people and remained always with the man who had saved her and married him.

Afric could see her father moving about in the smoky light, his legs seeming immense. Sometimes she saw his face when he bent to the fire. Then he sat on the upturned tub with his head between his hands. She went to sleep at last.

When she woke again the helmet of shadow had tilted. It was cold. The high hollow drum of the sky had half filled with low drifting vapors. Someone—she did not know who—was speaking to her father. Then he caught her in his arms, and the jolting and slithering of his feet in the long slopes wakened her completely. He stumbled on blindly as though he did not know she was in his arms. Even when she looked at him he did not seem to be aware of her.

There was a little crowd kneeling even at the door of the west room. The kitchen was in darkness only for the firelight, and this and the flickering of candles made the west room unusually bright and gay. The people kneeling there rose and made way for her father. He put her gently down on a stool by the fire and went in, taking off his hat. The low murmur of prayer went on again. Afric tiptoed to the room door. Yes, the west room was very bright. Her grandfather's great bearded head was lying, very pale and wasted, over the bowed heads under the light of two candles. Her father was kneeling awkwardly by the bedside, covering his face with his hands. Her grandmother, old Brigid, suddenly began to keen and sway from side to side.

Afric went out. She looked up and down the lane. She was looking with a sort of fascinated terror for the big man with the bandage over his eyes. There was no sign of him. The lane was quiet only for the whispering of the bushes and a blackbird's first bewildered, drowsy fluting. There were no lights, no voices. Frightened as she was, she ran down the lane to the little cove where her father's boat was drawn up among the slimy rocks and seaweed. Over it was a grassy knoll. She ran there and threw herself on her face and hands lest anyone should spy her and take fright. The light was breaking over the water. But no boat came shining to her out of the brightness. The blackbird, having tried his voice, threw it out in a sudden burst of song, and the lesser birds joined in with twitters and chuckles. In the little cove there was a ducking of water among the dried weeds, a vague pushing to and fro. She rose, her smock wet, and looked down into the cove. There was no farewell, no clatter of silver oars or rowlocks as magic took her childhood away. Nothing, nothing at all. With a strange choking in her throat she went slowly back to the house. She thought that maybe she knew now why her grandfather had been so sad.

Last Post

BILL CANTILLON and the sergeant-major went together to Sully's wake. It was a lovely summer's evening, and a gang of kids were playing at the end of the lane, but the little front room was dark only for the far corner where poor Sully was laid out in his brown habit, with the rosary beads twisted between his fingers. Jerry Foley was there already with Sully's sister and Mrs. Dunn. He opened a couple of bottles of stout, while the other two said a prayer, and then they all lit their pipes and sat around the table.

"Yes," said Bill, with another glance at the corpse, " 'twasn't today nor yesterday, Miss Sullivan. We were friends when I knew him first in the Depot, forty-three years ago."

"Forty-three years!" exclaimed the sergeant-major. "My, my!"

"Forty-three years," Bill repeated complacently. "October '98; I remember it well. That was when he joined."

"He was a bit wild as a boy, sir," Miss Sullivan said apologetically, "but, God help us, that was all! There was no harm in him."

"If it comes to that, ma'am," said the sergeant-major, "we were all wild."

"Ah, yes," said Bill, "but wildness like that—there's no harm in it. We were young, and high-spirited; we wanted to see a bit of the world; that was all. Life in a town like this, with people that know you, 'tis too quiet for boys of mettle."

" 'Tis," the sergeant-major agreed, " 'tis a bit slow."

" 'Twas the excitement," Bill said, with a nod to the company, "that's what we fancied."

"Oh, and God help us, ye got it," Sully's sister said quietly, rocking herself to and fro. "Oh, my, and never to know till you heard his knock at the door; it might be two or three in the morning, and to see him standing outside with his kitbags and his rifle, after travelling for days."

"Oh," said Jerry, "the kids playing outside there now will never see some of the things we saw!"

"And weren't we right?" exclaimed Bill. "Weren't we wiser in the heel of the hunt? Now, thanks be to God, after all our rambles, we're back among our own. We have our little pensions; they may not be much, but they keep us independent. We can stroll out of a fine summer's morning and sit in the park and talk about old times. And we know what we're talking about. We saw strange countries and strange people. We're not like some of the young fellows you meet now, small or bitter or narrow."

"Ah," said Jerry, mournfully, "we weren't a bad class at all. We had great spirit."

"And have still," said the sergeant-major.

"We have," said Jerry, "but we're dying, and there's no one to take our place. Sully is the fourth this year. We're going fast; and one of these days the time will come for one of us; we'll be laid out the way poor Sully is laid out; the neighbors will sit round us and somebody will say: 'That's the last of them gone now: the last of the old Munster Fusiliers. There isn't one left alive of the old Dirty Coats' that great regiment that carried the name of Ireland to the ends of the earth.' "

"And left their bones there, Jerry," said the sergeant-major.

"Oh, God help us, they did, they did," said Mrs. Dunn, and she burst into tears. The men looked uncomfortable.

"I'm very sorry, ma'am," said the sergeant-major. "Very sorry, indeed. I had no idea."

" 'Twas her son, sir," Sully's sister said in a quiet, little voice.

"My little boy, sir," sobbed Mrs. Dunn. "Hardly more than a child. He was wild, too, sir, like you said, but there was no harm in him. Mr. Sullivan knew him. He was well liked in regiment, he said."

"We'll go out to the kitchen now and let the men have their little drink in peace," said Miss Sullivan.

"I'm sorry, gentlemen," Mrs. Dunn said from the door. "Ye'll excuse me, it comes over me whenever I think of old times. But, oh, Mr. Cantillon, wasn't it queer, wasn't it queer, with all the men that knew him and liked him, that he could go like that on me without tale nor tidings?"

"Who did you say that was, Bill?" whispered the sergeant-major.

"Mrs. Dunn," replied Bill. "You must have seen her before. Every old Munster that dies, she's at his wake."

"Dunn?" said the sergeant, with a puzzled frown. "Dunn? What happened him? Killed?"

"No, missing."

"Dunn? I have no recollection of the name."

"Hourigan was the name," Bill said softly. "Dunn was his stepfather. That was why the boy ran away from home."

"And that's why she has it on her mind," said Jerry. "Every wake of every old Munster, she's at it, hoping she'll get news of him. For years after the war, as long as people were turning up anywhere over the world, she was still expecting he'd turn up. If you ask me, she's still expecting it."

"Ah, how could she?" said Bill.

"I don't think the poor soul is right in her mind," said Jerry softly. "A woman like that is never right unless she can have her cry out. I think she still imagines that one night when she's sitting by the fire she'll hear his step coming up the lane and see him walk in the door to her: a man of—how old would he be now? He was only sixteen when he ran away."

"Oh, God help us! God help us!" said the sergeant-major. "He was young to die!"

And in the darkness they heard a man's step come up the lane, and a moment later a devil's rat-tat at the door. Mrs. Dunn ran to open it.

"Broke!" exclaimed Bill with a grin.

The new arrival stumped in the hall and stood in the doorway with his cap pulled over one eye; a six-footer slumped about a crutch, and under the peak of the cap a long gray haggard face, a bedraggled gray mustache and mad, staring blue eyes. His real name was Shinnick. In France he had lost his leg and whatever bit of sense the Lord had given him to begin with. People said he was queer because he had spent so long at the front without leave. No sooner was he due for it than something occurred; he was detained for looting, leaving his post or beating up an N.C.O. They said he had earned the D.C.M. several times over and lost it again by his own foolishness—a most unfortunate man. Now he had a bed in the workhouse. He got a shilling or two for looking after the corpses. Once a month he came out and drew his pension, and after a day or two stumped back to the workhouse again—without a fluke! A most unfortunate man!

The three old soldiers looked at one another and winked. Broke was notorious for the touch. He could fly like a bird, crutch and all; head and neck strained forward like an old hen; he hadn't a spark of shame, and thought nothing of chasing a man the length of the Western Road on nothing more substantial than the smell of a pint.

"So ye're all there?" he snarled, with a grin of wolfish good humor.

"We're all here, Joe," Jerry said good-naturedly.

"I suppose 'twas the porter brought ye?" Broke said with a leer.

"Whisht, now, whisht," said Bill. "Remember the dead!"

"Ah, God, Sully, is this the way I find you?" said Broke in a wail as he drew down his crutch and manoeuvred himself onto his one good knee by the bed. "Ah, Sully, Sully, wasn't it queer to God to take a good man like you instead of some old cripple like myself and was never no use to anybody?" He was sobbing and clawing the bedclothes with his face buried in them. Then he grabbed the dead man's hands and began kissing them passionately. "Do you hear me, Sully boy, wherever you are tonight? Tell them who you left behind you! Tell them I'm tired of the world! I'm like the Wandering Jew, and I'm sick of pulling and hauling. Do you hear me, I say? I made corpses and I buried corpses, and I'm handling corpses every day of the week; the smell of them is on me, Sully, and 'tis time my own turn came."

"Here, Joe, here," said Jerry, tapping him on the shoulder, "sit in my chair and drink this."

" 'Twasn't for that I came," Broke said passionately, staring from the glass of stout to Jerry and back again.

"Sure, we know that well, old soldier," said Jerry.

"But 'tis welcome all the same," said Broke, swinging himself to his full height and staring down at Jerry with his queer piercing eyes. " 'Tis my one bit of consolation. I have the pension drunk already, Jerry. As sure as God I have! Jerry, could I—? My old campaigner!"

"Ah, to be sure you could," said Jerry.

"Wan tanner, Jerry!" hissed Broke feverishly. "That's all I ask."

"There's two of them for you," said Jerry.

"May God in Heaven bless you, my boy," said Broke as the tears began to pour from his eyes. "I'm an affliction; an old sponger, a good-for-nothing. 'Twill be a relief to ye all when I go. . . . Cantillon," he snarled with an astonishing change of tone, "put something to that like a decent man!"

"I suppose this is for the publicans?" said Bill with a scowl.

"And what do you think 'tis for, hah?" jeered Broke. "A bed in a hospital?" With a toothless smile he whipped off his old cap and waved it before the sergeant-major's face. "Make up the couple of bob for me, sir," he said. " 'Tis for the couple of drinks, I'm telling you no lies."

Then he sat in Jerry's chair, a high-backed armchair with low arm-rests, and took a deep swig of his stout. He was restless; he glared at them all by turns; the face, like the body, lank and drawn with pain.

"Is he having a band?" he asked suddenly.

"Ah, where would he get a band, man?" snapped Bill.

"And isn't he damn well entitled to it?" said Broke.

"Begor, you couldn't get one now if you were a general," said the sergeant-major.

"And why couldn't ye?" cried Broke. "What's stopping ye? The man should have his due. Give him what he's entitled to, his gun-carriage and his couple of volleys. . . . Company!" he shouted. "Re-verse arms! Slow . . . march! Strike up there, drum major!"

It was very queer. He raised his crutch and gave three thumps on the floor. Then, very softly with an inane toothless smile, he began to hum the Funeral March, swaying his hand gently from side to side. The old soldiers bent their heads reverently and Bill began to beat time with the toe of his boot.

"That's a grand tune, that Chopin," the sergeant-major said.

"I heard it one time played over a young fellow in the Sherwood Foresters," Bill said. " 'Twas in Aldershot, and I never forgot it."

"Ah," said Jerry, "for a dead march there's nothing like the pipes. You should hear the Kilties play 'The Flowers of the Forest.' There's a sort of a—"

"There is," said the sergeant-major. "A sort of a wail."

And in the dark room, by the light of the flickering candles, they began to talk of all the soldiers' funerals they had attended, in Africa, in India and at home, and the mothers began to shout from the door-steps, "Kittyaaa! Juliaaa!" and the children's voices died away, and there was no longer any sound but some latecomer's boots echoing off the pavements, and all the time Broke hummed away to himself, swinging his crutch like a drum major. His voice grew noisier and more raucous.

"Mind yourself or you'll do some damage with that crutch," said the sergeant-major.

"The bloody man is drunk," Bill said savagely.

"He isn't drunk, Bill," Jerry said quietly. "Watch his face!"

They stared at him. Suddenly, in the middle of a bar, he stopped dead, laid down the crutch and began to stare over the back of his chair. His face had a curious strained look. With his tongue and teeth he produced a drubbing sound—dddddrr! The old soldiers looked at one another. They heard another sound that seemed to come from very far back in Broke's throat, travel up the roof of his mouth and then expand into a wail and sudden thump—wheeeee-bump! And at the same moment Broke raised his two arms over his head and crouched down in the chair, gasping and staring wildly about him.

"Aha, Jackie," he said in a high-pitched, unnatural voice, "that's the postman's knock, Jackie. That's for us, boy. And that old sod of a ser-geant knew 'twas coming and that's where he left us to the last."

His right hand reached down and picked up the crutch. He raised himself and raised the crutch till it was resting on the back of the chair, and they noticed how his thumb and forefinger worked as though it were a rifle. Sully's sister and Mrs. Dunn stood in the doorway and gazed at him in astonishment. Jerry raised his hand for silence.

"I'm on my last couple of rounds, Jackie," Broke hissed. "Are you all right, little boy? You're not hurt, are you Jackie? Don't be a bit frightened, little boy. This is nothing to some of the things I seen. I'll get you out of this, never fear. They can't kill me, Jackie. I'm like the Wandering Jew, boy. I have a charmed life."

He continued to make those strange noises—wheeeee-bump, wheeeee-bump, and each time he would crouch, following the sound with his mad eyes, his arm raised above his head.

"That's close enough now, Jackie," he said, panting. "They have us taped this time all right. Another five minutes now! I don't mind, Jackie. Curse of God on the care I care! There's no one in the world will bother much about me only yourself. Jackie, if ever you get back to the coal quay, tell them the way I looked after you. Tell them the way old Joe Shinnick minded you when you had no one else on your side."

"Oh, oh, oh!" Mrs. Dunn said, but Jerry glared at her, and she clasped her hands.

"I looked after you, Jackie, didn't I? Didn't I, boy? As if you were my own. And so you were, Jackie. The first day I saw you and that tinker Lowry at you I nearly went mad. I put that cur's teeth down his throat for him anyway. . . ." Broke rocked his head. His voice suddenly dropped. "What's that, Jackie? The guns are stopped! The guns are stopped, boy! Pass us a couple of clips there, quick! Quick, do you hear? We're in for it now. There's something moving over there, beyond the wire. Do you see it? . . . Christ," he snarled between his teeth, "I'll give you something to take home with you." He raised the crutch, lightning-swift, and then his voice dropped to a moan. "Oh, God, Jackie, they're coming! Millions of them! Millions of them! And there's the moon, the way it is now over Shandon, and the old women going to early Mass." Again his voice changed; now it was the voice of the old soldier, curt and commanding. "Keep your head now, boy. Don't fire till I tell you. Where are you? I can't see in here. Shake hands, kid. God knows, if I could get you out of it, I would. Shake hands, can't you. What ails you? Jackie!"

His voice suddenly rang out in a cry. Sully's sister went on her knees by the door and began to give out the Rosary. Mrs. Dunn was talking to herself. "Oh, Jackie!" she was saying over and over, "Jackie, Jackie, Jackie!" Broke was leaning over the edge of the chair as though holding up a deadweight, pressing it close to his side and staring down at it incredulously. Somehow they all said afterwards they could see it quite plainly; the shell-battered dugout with the dawn breaking and the moon paling in the sky, and Broke with the dead boy's head against his side.

"So long, Jackie," he said in a whisper. "So long, kid. I won't be long after you."

Then he seemed to take something from the dead boy's body and throw it over his own shoulder. Bill nodded to the sergeant and the sergeant nodded back. They both knew it was an ammunition belt. Then Broke seemed to lay down the weight in his arms and swung himself up against the back of the chair, raising the crutch as if it were a rifle, but he no longer seemed to bother about cover. As his hands worked an imaginary bolt his whole face was distorted; the mouth drawn sideways in a grin, and he cursed and snarled over it like a madman. Something about it made the other men uncomfortable.

"That's enough, Jerry," the sergeant-major said uneasily. "Wake him up, now, for the love of God!"

"No," said Jerry, though his face was very pale. "It might bring some ease to his poor mind."

"I'm afraid nothing will ever do that now," said the sergeant-major. "Quick, Jerry," he shouted, jumping from his chair, "mind him!"

It was over before Jerry could do anything. Suddenly Broke sprang up on his good leg; his crutch fell to the floor, and he spun clean into the middle of the room before he crashed on his face and hands. Jerry drew a deep breath. There was nothing else to be heard but the gabble of Sully's sister, "Pray for us sinners, now and at the hour of our death." Broke lay there quite motionless for close on a minute. He might have been dead. Then he raised his head from between his hands, and with a tremendous effort tried to lift himself slowly on hands and knees. He crashed down again, sideways. A look of astonishment came into the mad, blue eyes that was always painful to watch. His hand crept slowly down his body and clutched at his leg—the leg that wasn't there.

Then he seemed to come to himself; he swung himself nimbly up from the floor and back into his chair. "Give the man his due," he said in a perfectly normal voice. "An old soldier; his gun-carriage and his couple of volleys." But as he spoke he covered his face with his hands, and a long sigh broke through his whole body and seemed to shake him to the very heart. It was as though he had fallen asleep, but his breath came in great noisy waves that shook him as they passed over him.

"Jackie," said Mrs. Dunn in a whisper. "My boy, my little boy!"

And from far away, over Barrackton Hill, crystal-clear and pure in the clear summer night, they heard the bugler sounding the last post.

The Cornet Player Who Betrayed Ireland

AT THIS HOUR of my life I don't profess to remember what we inhabitants of Blarney Lane were patriotic about: all I remember is that we were very patriotic, that our main principles were something called "Conciliation and Consent," and that our great national leader, William O'Brien, once referred to us as "The Old Guard." Myself and other kids of the Old Guard used to parade the street with tin cans and toy trumpets, singing "We'll hang Johnnie Redmond on a sour apple tree." (John Redmond, I need hardly say, was the leader of the other side.)

Unfortunately, our neighborhood was bounded to the south by a long ugly street leading uphill to the cathedral, and the lanes off it were infested with the most wretched specimens of humanity who took the Redmondite side for whatever could be got from it in the way of drink. My personal view at the time was that the Redmondite faction was maintained by a conspiracy of publicans and brewers. It always saddened me, coming through this street on my way from school, and seeing the poor misguided children, barefoot and in rags, parading with tin cans and toy trumpets and singing "We'll hang William O'Brien on a sour apple tree." It left me with very little hope for Ireland.

Of course, my father was a strong supporter of "Conciliation and Consent." The parish priest who had come to solicit his vote for Redmond had told him he would go straight to Hell, but my father had replied quite respectfully that if Mr. O'Brien was an agent of the devil, as Father Murphy said, he would go gladly.

I admired my father as a rock of principle. As well as being a house-painter (a regrettable trade which left him for six months "under the ivy," as we called it), he was a musician. He had been a bandsman in the British Army, played the cornet extremely well, and had been a member of the Irishtown Brass and Reed Band from its foundation. At home we had two big pictures of the band after each of its most famous contests, in Belfast and Dublin. It was after the Dublin contest when Irishtown emerged as the premier brass band that there occurred an unrecorded episode in operatic history. In those days the best band in the city was always invited to perform in the Soldiers' Chorus scene in Gounod's *Faust*. Of course, they were encored to the echo, and then, ignoring conductor and everything else, they burst into a selection from Moore's Irish Melodies. I am glad my father didn't live to see the day of pipers' bands. Even fife and drum bands he looked on as primitive.

As he had great hopes of turning me into a musician too he frequently brought me with him to practices and promenades. Irishtown was a very poor quarter of the city, a channel of mean houses between breweries and builders' yards with the terraced hillsides high above it on either side, and nothing but the white Restoration spire of Shandon breaking the skyline. You came to a little footbridge over the narrow stream; on one side of it was a red-brick chapel, and when we arrived there were usually some of the bandsmen sitting on the bridge, spitting back over their shoulders into the stream. The bandroom was over an undertaker's shop at the other side of the street. It was a long, dark, barnlike erection overlooking the bridge and decorated with group photos of the band. At this hour of a Sunday morning it was always full of groans, squeaks and bumps.

Then at last came the moment I loved so much. Out in the sunlight, with the bridge filled with staring pedestrians, the band formed up. Dickie Ryan, the bandmaster's son, and myself took our places at either side of the big drummer, Joe Shinkwin. Joe peered over his big drum to right and left to see if all were in place and ready; he raised his right arm and gave the drum three solemn flakes: then, after the third thump the whole narrow channel of the street filled with a roaring torrent of drums and brass, the mere physical impact of which hit me in the belly. Screaming girls in shawls tore along the pavements calling out to the bandsmen, but nothing shook the soldierly solemnity of the men with their eyes almost crossed on the music before them. I've heard Toscanini conduct Beethoven, but compared with Irishtown playing "Marching Through Georgia" on a Sunday morning it was only like Mozart in a girls' school. The mean little houses, quivering with the shock, gave it back to us: the terraced hillsides that shut out the sky gave it back to us; the interested faces of passers-by in their Sunday clothes from the pavements were like mirrors reflecting the glory of the music. When the band stopped and again you could hear the gapped sound of feet, and people running and chattering, it was like a parachute jump into commonplace.

Sometimes we boarded the paddle-steamer and set up our music stands in some little field by the sea, which all day echoed of Moore's Melodies, Rossini, and Gilbert and Sullivan: sometimes we took a train into the country to play at some sports meeting. Whatever it was, I loved it, though I never got a dinner: I was fed on lemonade, biscuits and sweets, and, as my father spent most of the intervals in the pub, I was sometimes half mad with boredom.

One summer day we were playing at a fête in the grounds of Blarney Castle, and, as usual, the band departed to the pub and Dickie Ryan and myself were left behind, ostensibly to take care of the instruments. A certain hanger-on of the band, one John P., who to my knowledge was never called anything else, was lying on the grass, chewing a straw and shading his eyes from the light with the back of his hand. Dickie and I took a side drum each and began to march about with them. All at once Dickie began to sing to his own accompaniment, "We'll hang William O'Brien on a sour apple tree." I was so astonished that I stopped drumming and listened to him. For a moment or two I thought he must be mocking the poor uneducated children of the lanes round Shandon Street. Then I suddenly realized that he meant it. Without hesitation I began to rattle my side drum even louder and shouted "We'll hang Johnnie Redmond on a sour apple tree." John P. at once started up and gave me an angry glare. "Stop that now, little boy!" he said threateningly. It was quite plain that he meant me, not Dickie Ryan.

I was completely flabbergasted. It was bad enough hearing the bandmaster's son singing a traitorous song, but then to be told to shut up by a fellow who wasn't even a bandsman; merely a hanger-on who looked after the music stands and carried the big drum in return for free drinks! I realized that I was among enemies. I quietly put aside the drum and went to find my father. I knew that he could have no idea what was going on behind his back in the band.

I found him at the back of the pub, sitting on a barrel and holding forth to a couple of young bandsmen.

"Now, 'Brian Boru's March,' " he was saying with one finger raised, "that's a beautiful march. I heard the Irish Guards do that on Salisbury Plain, and they had the English fellows' eyes popping out. 'Paddy,' one of them says to me (they all call you Paddy), 'wot's the name of the shouting march?' But somehow we don't get the same fire into it at all. Now, listen, and I'll show you how that should go!"

"Dadda," I said in a whisper, pulling him by the sleeve, "do you know what Dickie Ryan was singing?"

"Hold on a minute now," he said, beaming at me affectionately. "I just want to illustrate a little point."

"But, Dadda," I went on determinedly, "he was singing 'We'll hang William O'Brien from a sour apple tree.' "

"Hah, hah, hah," laughed my father, and it struck me that he hadn't fully appreciated the implications of what I had said.

"Frank," he added, "get a bottle of lemonade for the little fellow."

"But, Dadda," I said despairingly, "when I sang 'We'll hang Johnnie Redmond,' John P. told me to shut up."

"Now, now," said my father with sudden testiness, "that's not a nice song to be singing."

This was a stunning blow. The anthem of "Conciliation and Consent"—not a nice song to be singing!

"But, Dadda," I wailed, "aren't we *for* William O'Brien?"

"Yes, yes, yes," he replied, as if I were goading him, "but everyone to his own opinion. Now drink your lemonade and run out and play like a good boy."

I drank my lemonade all right, but I went out not to play but to brood. There was but one fit place for that. I went to the shell of the castle; climbed the stair to the tower and leaning over the battlements watching the landscape like bunting all round me I thought of the heroes who had stood here, defying the might of England. Everyone to his own opinion! What would they have thought of a statement like that? It was the first time that I realized the awful strain of weakness and the lack of strong principle in my father, and understood that the old bandroom by the bridge was in the heart of enemy country and that all round me were enemies of Ireland like Dickie Ryan and John P.

It wasn't until months after that I realized how many there were. It was Sunday morning, but when we reached the bandroom there was no one on the bridge. Upstairs the room was almost full. A big man wearing a bowler hat and a flower in his buttonhole was standing before the fireplace. He had a red face with weak, red-rimmed eyes and a dark mustache. My father, who seemed as surprised as I was, slipped quietly into a seat behind the door and lifted me on to his knee.

"Well, boys," the big man said in a deep husky voice, "I suppose ye have a good notion what I'm here for. Ye know that next Saturday night Mr. Redmond is arriving in the city, and I have the honor of being Chairman of the Reception Committee."

"Well, Alderman Doyle," said the bandmaster doubtfully, "you know the way we feel about Mr. Redmond, most of us anyway."

"I do, Tim, I do," said the alderman evenly as it gradually dawned on me that the man I was listening to was the Arch-Traitor, locally known as Scabby Doyle, the builder whose vile orations my father always read aloud to my mother with chagrined comments on Doyle's past history. "But feeling isn't enough, Tim. Fair Lane Band will be there of course. Watergrasshill will be there. The Butler Exchange will be there. What will the backers of this band, the gentlemen who helped it through so many difficult days, say if we don't put in an appearance?"

"Well, ye see, Alderman," said Ryan nervously, "we have our own little difficulties."

"I know that, Tim," said Doyle. "We all have our difficulties in troubled times like these, but we have to face them like men in the interests of the country. What difficulties have you?"

"Well, that's hard to describe, Alderman," said the bandmaster.

"No, Tim," said my father quietly, raising and putting me down from his knee, " 'tis easy enough to describe. I'm the difficulty, and I know it."

"Now, Mick," protested the bandmaster, "there's nothing personal about it. We're all old friends in this band."

"We are, Tim," agreed my father. "And before ever it was heard of, you and me gave this bandroom its first coat of paint. But every man is entitled to his principles, and I don't want to stand in your light."

"You see how it is, Mr. Doyle," said the bandmaster appealingly. "We had others in the band that were of Mick Twomey's persuasion, but they left us to join O'Brienite bands. Mick didn't, nor we didn't want him to leave us."

"Nor don't," said a mournful voice, and I turned and saw a tall, gaunt, spectacled young man sitting on the window sill.

"I had three men," said my father earnestly, holding up three fingers in illustration of the fact, "three men up at the hours on different occasions to get me to join other bands. I'm not boasting. Tim Ryan knows who they were."

"I do, I do," said the bandmaster.

"And I wouldn't," said my father passionately. "I'm not boasting, but you can't deny it: there isn't another band in Ireland to touch ours."

"Nor a cornet player in Ireland to touch Mick Twomey," chimed in the gaunt young man, rising to his feet. "And I'm not saying that to coddle or cock him up."

"You're not, you're not," said the bandmaster. "No one can deny he's a musician."

"And listen here to me, boys," said the gaunt young man, with a wild wave of his arm, "don't leave us be led astray by anyone. What were we before we had the old band? Nobody. We were no better than the poor devils that sit on that bridge outside all day, spitting into the river. Whatever we do, leave us be all agreed. What backers had we when we started, only what we could collect ourselves outside the chapel gates on Sunday, and hard enough to get permission for that itself? I'm as good a party man as anyone here, but what I say is, music is above politice. . . . Alderman Doyle," he begged, "tell Mr. Redmond whatever he'll do not to break up our little band on us."

"Jim Ralegh," said the alderman, with his red-rimmed eyes growing moist, "I'd sooner put my hand in the fire than injure this band. I know what ye are, a band of brothers. . . . Mick," he boomed at my father, "will you desert it in its hour of trial?"

"Ah," said my father testily, "is it the way you want me to play against William O'Brien?"

"Play against William O'Brien," echoed the alderman. "No one is asking you to play *against* anyone. As Jim Ralegh here says, music is above politice. What we're asking you to do is to play for something for the band, for the sake of unity. You know what'll happen if the backers withdraw? Can't you pocket your pride and make this sacrifice in the interest of the band?"

My father stood for a few moments, hesitating. I prayed for once he might see the true light; that he might show this group of misguided men the faith that was in him. Instead he nodded curtly, said "Very well, I'll play," and sat down again. The rascally aldlerman said a few humbugging words in his praise which didn't take me in. I don't think they even took my father in, for all the way home he never addressed a word to me. I saw then that his conscience was at him. He knew that by supporting the band in the unprincipled step it was taking he was showing himself a traitor to Ireland and our great leader, William O'Brien.

Afterwards, whenever Irishtown played at Redmondite demonstrations, my father accompanied them, but the moment the speeches began he retreated to the edge of the crowd, rather like a pious Catholic compelled to attend a heretical religious service, and stood against the wall with his hands in his pockets, passing slighting and witty comments on the speakers to any O'Brienites he might meet. But he had lost all dignity in my eyes. Even his gibes at Scabby Doyle seemed to me false, and I longed to say to him, "If that's what you believe, why don't you show it?" Even the seaside lost its attraction when at any moment the beautiful daughter of a decent O'Brienite family might point to me and say: "There is the son of the cornet player who betrayed Ireland."

Then one Sunday we went to play at some idolatrous function in a seaside town called Bantry. While the meeting was on my father and the rest of the band retired to the pub and I with them. Even by my presence in the Square I wasn't prepared to countenance the proceedings. I was looking idly out of the window when I suddenly heard a roar of cheering and people began to scatter in all directions. I was mystified until someone outside started to shout, "Come on, boys! The O'Brienites are trying to break up the meeting." The bandsmen rushed for the door. I would have done the same but my father looked hastily over his shoulder and warned me to stay where I was. He was talking to a young clarinet player of serious appearance.

"Now," he went on, raising his voice to drown the uproar outside. "Teddy the Lamb was the finest clarinet player in the whole British Army."

There was a fresh storm of cheering, and wild with excitement I saw the patriots begin to drive a deep wedge of whirling sticks through the heart of the enemy, cutting them into two fighting camps.

"Excuse me, Mick," said the clarinet player, going white, "I'll go and see what's up."

"Now, whatever is up," my father said appealingly, "you can't do anything about it."

"I'm not going to have it said I stopped behind while my friends were fighting for their lives," said the young fellow hotly.

"There's no one fighting for their lives at all," said my father irascibly, grabbing him by the arm. "You have something else to think about. Man alive, you're a musician, not a bloody infantryman."

"I'd sooner be that than a bloody turncoat, anyway," said the young fellow, dragging himself off and making for the door.

"Thanks, Phil," my father called after him in a voice of a man who had to speak before he has collected his wits. "I well deserved that from you. I well deserved that from all of ye." He took out his pipe and put it back into his pocket again. Then he joined me at the window and for a few moments he looked unseeingly at the milling crowd outside. "Come on," he said shortly.

Though the couples were wrestling in the very gutters no one accosted us on our way up the street; otherwise I feel murder might have been committed. We went to the house of some cousins and had tea, and when we reached the railway station my father led me to a compartment near the engine; not the carriage reserved for the band. Though we had ten minutes to wait it wasn't until just before the whistle went that Tim Ryan, the bandmaster, spotted us through the window.

"Mick!" he shouted in astonishment. "Where the hell were you? I had men out all over the town looking for you! Is it anything wrong?"

"Nothing, Tim," replied my father, leaning out of the window to him. "I wanted to be alone, that's all."

"But we'll see you at the other end?" bawled Tim as the train began to move.

"I don't know will you," replied my father grimly. "I think ye saw too much of me."

When the band formed up outside the station we stood on the pavement and watched them. He had a tight hold of my hand. First Tim Ryan and then Jim Ralegh came rushing over to him. With an intensity of hatred I watched those enemies of Ireland again bait their traps for my father, but now I knew they would bait them in vain.

"No, no, Tim," said my father, shaking his head, "I went too far before for the sake of the band, and I paid dear for it. None of my family was ever called a turncoat before today, Tim."

"Ah, it is a young fool like that?" bawled Jim Ralegh with tears in his wild eyes. "What need a man like you care about him?"

"A man have his pride, Jim," said my father gloomily.

"He have," cried Ralegh despairingly, "and a fat lot any of us has to be proud of. The band was all we ever had, and if that goes the whole thing goes. For the love of the Almighty God, Mick Twomey, come back with us to the bandroom anyway."

"No, no, no," shouted my father angrily. "I tell you after today I'm finished with music."

"Music is finished with us you mean," bawled Jim. "The curse of God on the day we ever heard of Redmond or O'Brien! We were happy men before it.... All right, lads," he cried, turning away with a wild and whirling motion of his arm. "Mick Twomey is done with us. Ye can go on without him."

And again I heard the three solemn thumps on the big drum, and again the street was flooded with a roaring torrent of music, and though it no longer played for me, my heart rose to it and the tears came from my eyes. Still holding my hand, my father followed on the pavement. They were playing "Brian Boru's March," his old favorite. We followed them through the ill-lit town and as they turned down the side street to the bridge, my father stood on the curb and looked after them as though he wished to impress every detail on his memory. It was only when the music stopped and the silence returned to the narrow channel of the street that we resumed our lonely way homeward.

Ghosts

FOR twenty-odd years we've always had Oorawn Sullivans for servants; why I don't know, unless it was the only hope of getting something off the bill. The Sullivans' bill went back long before my time. When one of them got married we took her younger sister, and when she died of consumption we took Kitty. The first week we had Kitty I found her with all the tea things down the lavatory basin, pulling the chain. She told me townspeople had great conveniences.

Then one Thursday last summer, Mary, the eldest girl, came in to do her bit of shopping. I always had a smack for Mary for the way she reared her family. I heard her whispering something across the counter to Nan about a bottle of whiskey and cocked my ears.

Oorawn is the Irish for a spring, but it isn't only water that flows there. All the poteen they drink in our part of the country rises in Oorawn. When they have a wedding or a wake they come in for a bottle or two of the legal stuff and take care that plenty see them with it. A couple of days after they bring it back under cover and get credit for it. They call it "the holy medal."

"What do ye want the medal for, Mary?" said I, taking a rise out of her. "Is it one of the girls getting married on you?"

"Wisha, the Lord love you, Mr. Clancy!" says she. " 'Tisn't that at all, only a cousin that's coming home from America on Friday. He mightn't be able to drink the other stuff."

"Which cousin is that, Mary?" said Nan. "I never knew you had cousins in America."

"Wisha, Mrs. Clancy, love," said Mary, " 'tis a cousin called Jer that we hardly knew we had ourselves," and off she went into the usual rigmarole about her grandfather's brother that married a woman of the Lacys from Drumacre; not one of the Red Lacys mind you, but cousins of theirs. I could just about follow her; she might have been talking double Dutch for all Nan understood.

"And how is he going to get up to Oorawn?" she asked.

"Oye, he can probably get a lift," said Mary, "or he might get the bus as far as Trabawn Cross."

"And walk all the way up the valley with his bags!" said Nan. "Ah, Tim will meet him at the station and drive him up."

Nan is the kindest soul in the world with my time and car. Still, I suppose she could hardly do less, and Kitty with us. So next evening I left her in charge of the shop and drove up to the station. There was the usual small handful on the train, but the devil an American boy could I see. When they cleared there was only a family of four left by the luggage wagon; father, mother, daughter and son, to judge by appearances.

"Is it anyone you were expecting, Tim?" said Hurley, the station-master.

"Only a Yankee cousin of the Oorawns that's coming home," said I.

" 'Twouldn't be one of them?" said Hurley, pointing to the family.

"I wouldn't say so," said I, "but I suppose I'd better make sure."

I went up to the elder man, a fine, tall, handsome-looking fellow about the one age with myself.

"Your name wouldn't be Sullivan, by any chance?" said I.

"That's right," he said, reaching out his hand to me. "Are you one of my Oorawn cousins?"

"No," said I, trusting in God to give me words in the predicament I was in, "only a friend with a car. Mick Hurley and myself will take out the bags for ye."

And while we carried out the bags, I was thinking harder than ever I thought in my life. The American family wasn't my class at all. And as for Oorawn, you might as well drop them on a raft in mid-Atlantic. This was a case for Nan, and damn good right she had to handle it, seeing 'twas she that brought it on us with her interfering in other people's business.

"I'll have to call at the shop first," I said as I got in. "Anyway, I dare say after that journey ye wouldn't say no to a cup of tea."

The one thing about being to a good school is that, like Nan, you can make a fist of anything, even Americans. I took her place in the shop and she went upstairs with them. She came down about ten minutes after, looking a bit dazed.

"Do you know who they are?" said she, frightened and at the same time delighted. "Sullivan Shoes."

"I never heard of Sullivan or his shoes," said I, "but I wish he was in mine this minute."

"Go up and talk to them while I get the tea," said she. "I told them 'twas Kitty's day off. They're on their way to Paris. We'll have to stop them going to Oorawn."

I saw Kitty coming down the stairs as I was going up, and she was like a ghost. She must have caught a glimpse of her American cousins and was thinking about the cabin and the pint of whiskey. With the main responsibility now off my shoulders I didn't mind. They were a nice family; the father was quiet, the mother was bright; Bob, the young fellow, was writing a book on something—he took after the mother, but Rose, the girl, was a real beauty. Every damned thing you told her, she took seriously. She wanted to know had we any fairies! I told her we had no fairies since the poteen was put down but the ghosts were something shocking.

"You mean you have ghosts in this house?" she said.

"Dozens of them," said I, seeing that we were lacking in a lot of the conveniences a girl like that would be accustomed to and we might as well take credit for what she couldn't see. "The mother, God rest her, knew some of them so well that she used to quarrel with them like Christians."

"Didn't I tell you what Grandfather used to say about the ghosts on the farm at home?" said her father, taking a rise out of her too.

I nearly laughed when he talked about "the farm" but I thought it was better to leave that to Nan. All the same I was glad when she came in with the tea. I took a cup and went down to mind the shop, and by the time I came back she was after persuading them to stop at the Grand Hotel. I ran the bags over, and then we set out for Oorawn. The car was pretty full with Rose sitting on Bob's knee. Their father sat in front with me where he could see a bit of the country. On a fine evening the sea road is grand. The sea was like a lake, and the mountains at the other side had a red light on them like plums.

"Is there only this road from Oorawn to Cove?" he asked me.

"There's only this road from Oorawn to Hell," said I. "Why?"

"I was thinking," said he, "this must be the road my grandfather travelled on his way to America. He used to describe himself sitting on their little tin trunk at the back of an open cart. My grandmother was having her first baby, and she was frightened. He sang for her the whole way to keep her courage up."

"There was many a homesick tear shed along this road," I said, because, damn it, the man touched me the way he spoke.

"Count the ruined cottages, and you'll see your grandmother wasn't alone."

Then the road turned off up the valley and over the moors, a bad place to be on a winter's day. When we reached the Sullivans what did we see only Bridgie, rising up like an apparition from behind a bush with her skirts held up behind, and away she flew like the wind to the house. I was wishing then I hadn't Nan with me. It was bad enough, a lonely cottage in the hills that was expecting one American laboring boy from Butte, getting a blooming family of millionaires or near it. Signs on it, that was the last we saw of Bridgie.

I will say for Mary Sullivan that she made a great effort not to look as put out as she was. I smelt when I went in that she had just been baking for him.

"Wisha, and are you Jer?" she cried, wiping her hands in her apron before she'd touch him. "Law, I'm hearing about you always. And your family and all! Ye must be dying for a cup of tea!"

"We've just had tea, Mary," said Nan, being tactful. "I don't want to put your cousins out, but Tim and myself have an appointment in town."

"Why then, indeed," said I, planting my ass on a chair near the fire, "the appointment can wait, because out of this house I don't stir till Mary Sullivan gives me tea. Have you griddle cake, Mary?"

"I have, aru," said she. "Do you like griddle cake?"

Nan gave me a look like poultice, but the woman didn't know what she was talking about. If the Sullivans' cousins had left that cabin without a meal, the disgrace of it would have driven Mary to her grave.

"I hope we're not putting you out too much, Mrs. Clancy," said Sullivan, "but I'd like it too. It isn't every day a man comes back to his grandfather's house."

"Your grandfather's house?" cried Mary. "Ah, my darling, this isn't your grandfather's. Your grandfather's is about three fields away. 'Tis only an old ruin now."

"Whatever it is," he said, "I'd like to see it."

"Will I show it to you?" she said, at her wits' ends to please him.

"After we have the tea, girl, after we have the tea," said I. "What a hurry you're in to get rid of us!"

"Hurry?" she said, laughing. "The divil a hurry then, only the state we're in. Mrs. Sullivan," she said, holding out her two hands to the American woman, "we're a holy show."

"Ah, Mary," said I, "if you took my advice five years ago and bought a vacuum cleaner, you needn't be afraid to hide your face today."

"Do you hear him?" cried Mary. "A vacuum! Lord save us! You'll have to drink your tea out of a mug."

"Have you ne'er a basin?" said I.

"Why?" said she. "Would you prefer a basin? Or is it making fun of me you are?"

The two younger girls were standing in front of Rose with their fingers in their mouths, looking at her as if she were a shop window.

"That's right," I said. "Have a good look at your cousin, and stick to the books and maybe ye'd be like her some day."

"Wisha, how in God's name would they, Mr. Clancy?" said Mary, really upset at last. "And don't be putting foolish notions into the children's heads. . . . Your daughter is a picture, Jer," she said with the tears of delight standing in her eyes, and then she took Rose's two hands and held them. "You are, treasure," she said. "I could be looking at you all day and not get tired."

"Why then, indeed, Miss Sullivan," I said to Mary, "as we're getting so polite with our misters and misses, you're not too bad-looking yourself."

"Och, go away, you ould divil, you," said she, giving me a push. Nan was mortified. She felt she'd never get a day's good of Kitty after that push.

"There never was a Sullivan yet without good looks, Mary," said Sullivan, "and you have your share."

"Wisha, God forgive you, Jer Sullivan!" she said, blushing up, but I could see the way the spirits rose in her.

We had the tea, and the griddle cake, and the boiled eggs and then we had the whiskey—the first bottle of proper whiskey opened in Oorawn for generations, as I told them—and then Sullivan got up.

"Now, Mary," he said, "if you'll forgive me, I'd like to see the old place before it gets too dark."

I noticed he brought his glass. He went on ahead with Mary; his wife and daughter with Nan, Bob with me, and the kids bringing up the rear, too bewitched to talk. Mary was apologizing for the dirt of the fields.

The sun was going down when we reached the ruin of the little cabin. It was all overgrown, and a big hawthorn growing on the hearth. Sullivan's face was a study.

"Grandfather used to say that the first Sullivan to come back should lay a wreath on the grave of the landlord that evicted us," he said in a quiet voice.

"A wreath, is it?" cried Mary, not understanding his form of fun. "I know what sort of wreath I'd lay on it."

"Now," he said gently, a little embarrassed by us all, "I'd like to stay here a few minutes by myself, if you won't think it rude of me."

"Don't stay too long," said his wife. "It's turned quite chilly."

We left him behind us, and made our way back over the fields.

"He's a very gentlemanly sort of man," said Mary Sullivan to me. "Oh, law, wasn't it awful the way ye caught Bridgie?"

I saw the girl thought it was the same thing that was detaining her cousin, but I didn't try to enlighten her. I knew what he wanted with in the old ruin by himself. He was hoping for ghosts; ghosts of his grandfather's people that might be hanging round the old cabin so that they could see him there and know he had brought no disgrace on the name. I was touched by it the way I was touched by what he said about his grandfather. There was something genuine about the man that I couldn't help liking. I had an idea that the Sullivans would have no reason to regret his coming.

"Well," I said, when he came back with his empty glass (I was afraid that someone would start asking him questions and he wouldn't like it), "we may as well be making tracks."

As we were driving back down the hill I was pointing out the various landmarks to him. Behind us, Nan was explaining to his wife that Oorawn was exceptional and that all the "peasants" weren't as backward as the Sullivans. Some of them had fine cottages with beautiful gardens. You could see the Americans were a bit disappointed because there wasn't a garden.

Then as we reached the coast road Nan tapped me on the shoulder and said: "We'll call at Hopkins' as we are passing, Tim."

"We will not," I said.

"We must, Tim," she said, getting as sweet as honey to cover up my bad temper. "Mrs. Hopkins promised me a few slips."

As long as Nan is in the shop she never yet has learned anything about country people. How the blazes would she and she calling them "peasants"? I knew well the game she was up to. She wanted to show the Sullivans that we had good society, and herself and myself were the hub of it. But I had thought even she would know who the Hopkins were and why we couldn't bring the Sullivans there. She didn't. She nagged and nagged till I lost my temper.

"Very well," I said, "go to Hopkins and be damned to you!"

And I turned in by the gate with the urns on top of the pillars. The major was out under the portico with his dirty old cap over his eyes, and his face lit up when he saw me. The major's wife won't let him take a drink unless 'tis with visitors, and he knew I could lower it for him.

"Just in time for a little drink, Clancy," he said. "And is that your charming wife?"

"These are some American friends called Sullivan," said I, "that want to see your house, and I came with them to make sure you didn't try to sell them anything."

"You talk about selling things!" he said, delighted with me. "You damned old ruffian! In the good old days I'd have been on the magistrate's bench and seen you up in the county gaol. Don't believe a word this old rascal says to you, Mrs. Sullivan," he says, pawing the American woman's hand.

It seemed supper was late, and Mrs. Hopkins asked us to have it with them. It went against my grain, but I knew it was what Nan wanted. The major's wife was one of the Fays of Frankfort. In her young days it used to be naval officers, but since the daughter grew up she went in more for social welfare. The Americans were delighted with the big staircase and the plaster panel in the first landing with a big picture in the middle of it. Then Bella came down after changing, a big, tall, broody-looking girl. You never saw anyone light up like that American boy did. We had our supper in the front room overlooking the bay, and then were delighted again with the fireplace and the paneling, and then Bella took Bob and Rose off to see the house. They came back in great excitement, and their mother and father had to be shown it.

"You don't want to see the Bossi mantelpiece, Clancy?" says the major, going off into a roar as he filled my glass.

"If 'tis one of those fireplaces you can't put your boots on, I don't," said I.

"Or the historic plaster ceiling in the saloon, Clancy?" he says. "I'm sure you'd love the historic plaster ceiling. Wonderful for shooting at the champagne corks. Pop!"

"Don't forget to show them your ghost!" said I. "Was it some priest ye hanged or someone ye put out of his house?"

"Look at him!" said the major. "You can see the sort of chap he is, sitting there drinking my whiskey and hating me."

Nan gave me a look meaning that she didn't know where her wits were when she married me, but I was past caring. The younger ones went out to the garden, and after a while the others joined them. Nan was collecting her slips. The major was taking advantage of me beyond my capacity. I knew what he'd say after when his wife studied the decanter. That 'twas my doing.

They all came back for a drink and Sullivan was talking to Mrs. Hopkins about the backwardness of "the peasants" and she was telling him about her club for peasant reform. He mentioned the subject of bathrooms, and I could see he had Bridgie on his mind. The major couldn't get it out of his head that I was trying to sell something to the Americans and using his house as a blind. He kept looking at me and roaring. And, God forgive me, there was I roaring too, calculating how many gallons of petrol it would take to send his historic old house blazing to Heaven. I was excited and when I have a few drinks in I'm very wicked.

By the time we left, the Sullivans were arranging to take Bella out on their way back through London. I tore back the road with the rocks rising up at me like theatre scenery, thinking of the couple that travelled the same road on their tin trunk so long ago. Sullivan had the same thought in his mind.

"That was a delightful end to a remarkable day," he said.

"It was," I said. "Almost as remarkable as the day."

"You probably can't appreciate what it meant to me," he said.

"You might be surprised," I said.

"All my life," he said, "I wanted to stand in the spot where the old couple set off on their journey, and now I feel something inside me satisfied."

"And you laid a wreath on the grave of the man who evicted them as well," said I. "Don't forget that."

The funny thing was, it was his wife that knew what I meant.

"What's that?" she said, leaning forward to me. "You mean the Hopkins were the landlords who evicted them?"

"They were," said I. "And cruel bad landlords, too."

I knew 'twas wicked of me, but the man had roused something in me. What right had any of them to look down on the Sullivans? They were country people as I was, and it was people like them that had gone crying down every road in Ireland to the sea. But they were delighted, delighted! Mrs. Sullivan and Nan and Bob and Rose, they couldn't get over the coincidence of it. You'd think 'twas an entertainment I put on for their benefit. But Sullivan wasn't delighted, and well I knew he wouldn't be. The rest were nice, but they were outside it. They could go looking for ghosts, but he had ghosts there inside himself and I knew in my heart that till the day he died he would never get over the feeling that his money had put him astray and he had turned his back on them.